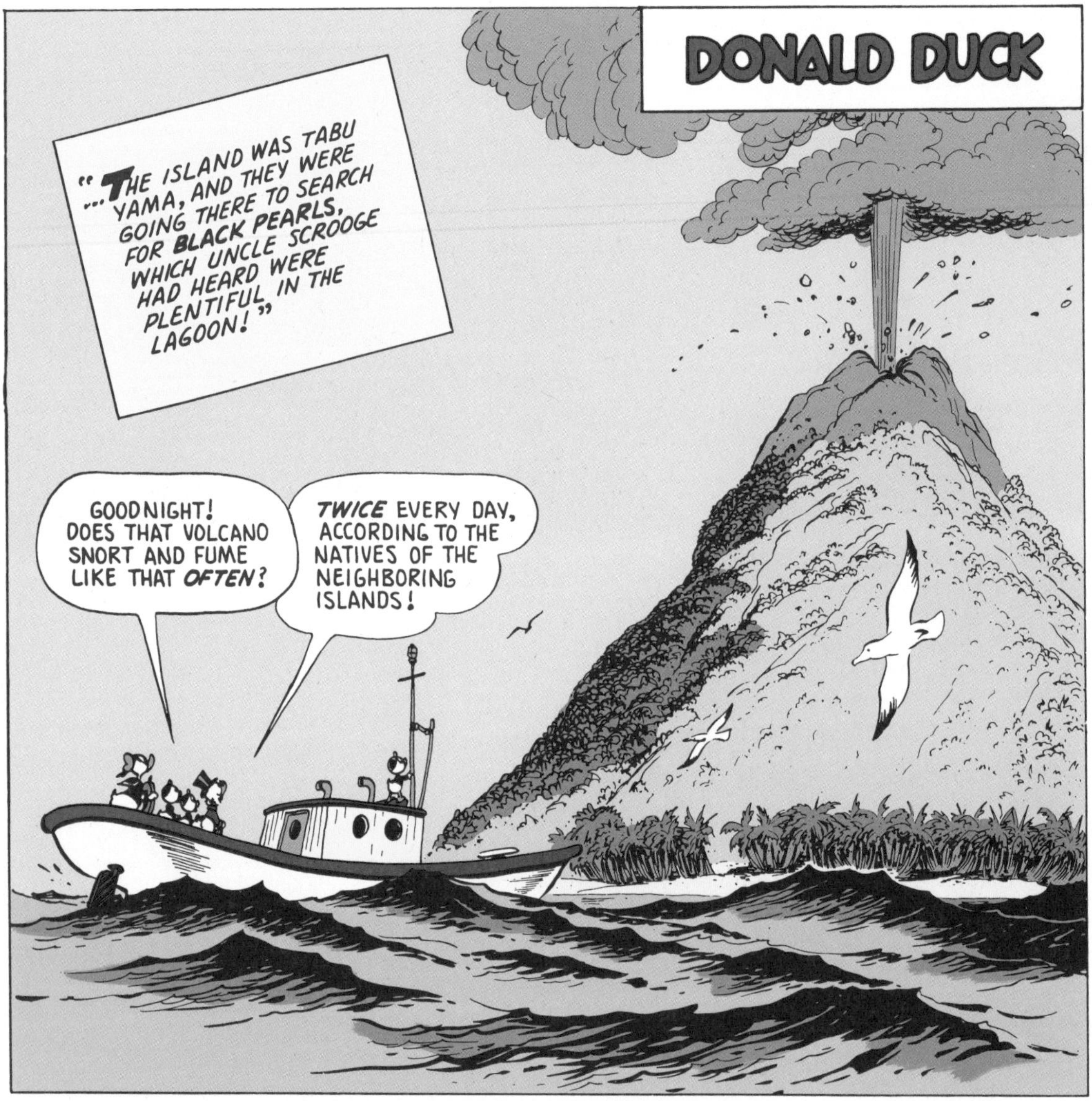
DONALD DUCK
"...THE ISLAND WAS TABU YAMA, AND THEY WERE GOING THERE TO SEARCH FOR BLACK PEARLS, WHICH UNCLE SCROOGE HAD HEARD WERE PLENTIFUL, IN THE LAGOON!"
GOODNIGHT! DOES THAT VOLCANO SNORT AND FUME LIKE THAT *OFTEN*?
TWICE EVERY DAY, ACCORDING TO THE NATIVES OF THE NEIGHBORING ISLANDS!

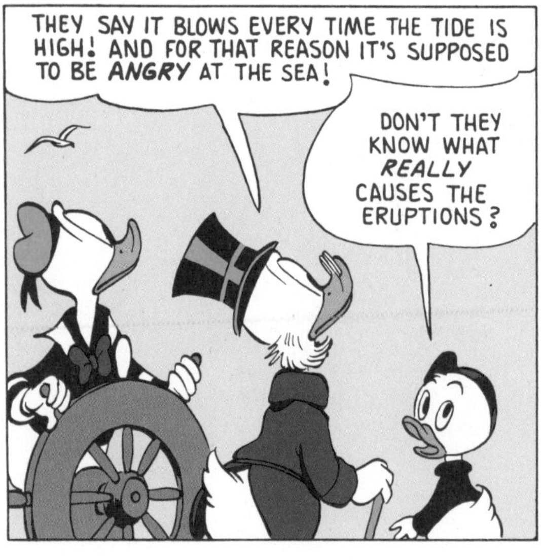
THEY SAY IT BLOWS EVERY TIME THE TIDE IS HIGH! AND FOR THAT REASON IT'S SUPPOSED TO BE **ANGRY** AT THE SEA!
DON'T THEY KNOW WHAT *REALLY* CAUSES THE ERUPTIONS?

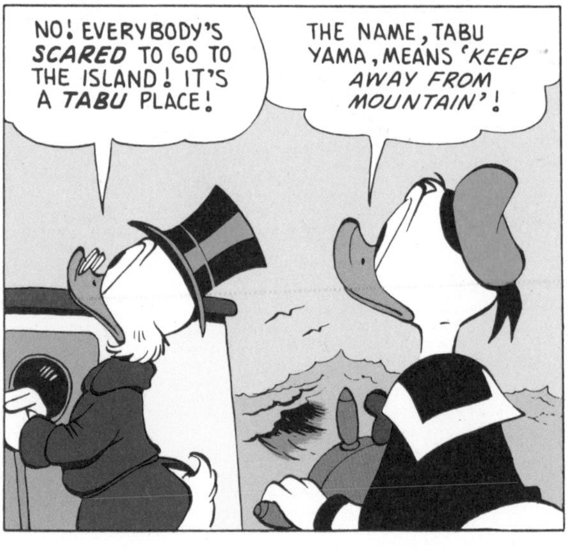
NO! EVERYBODY'S *SCARED* TO GO TO THE ISLAND! IT'S A *TABU* PLACE!
THE NAME, TABU YAMA, MEANS '*KEEP AWAY FROM MOUNTAIN*'!

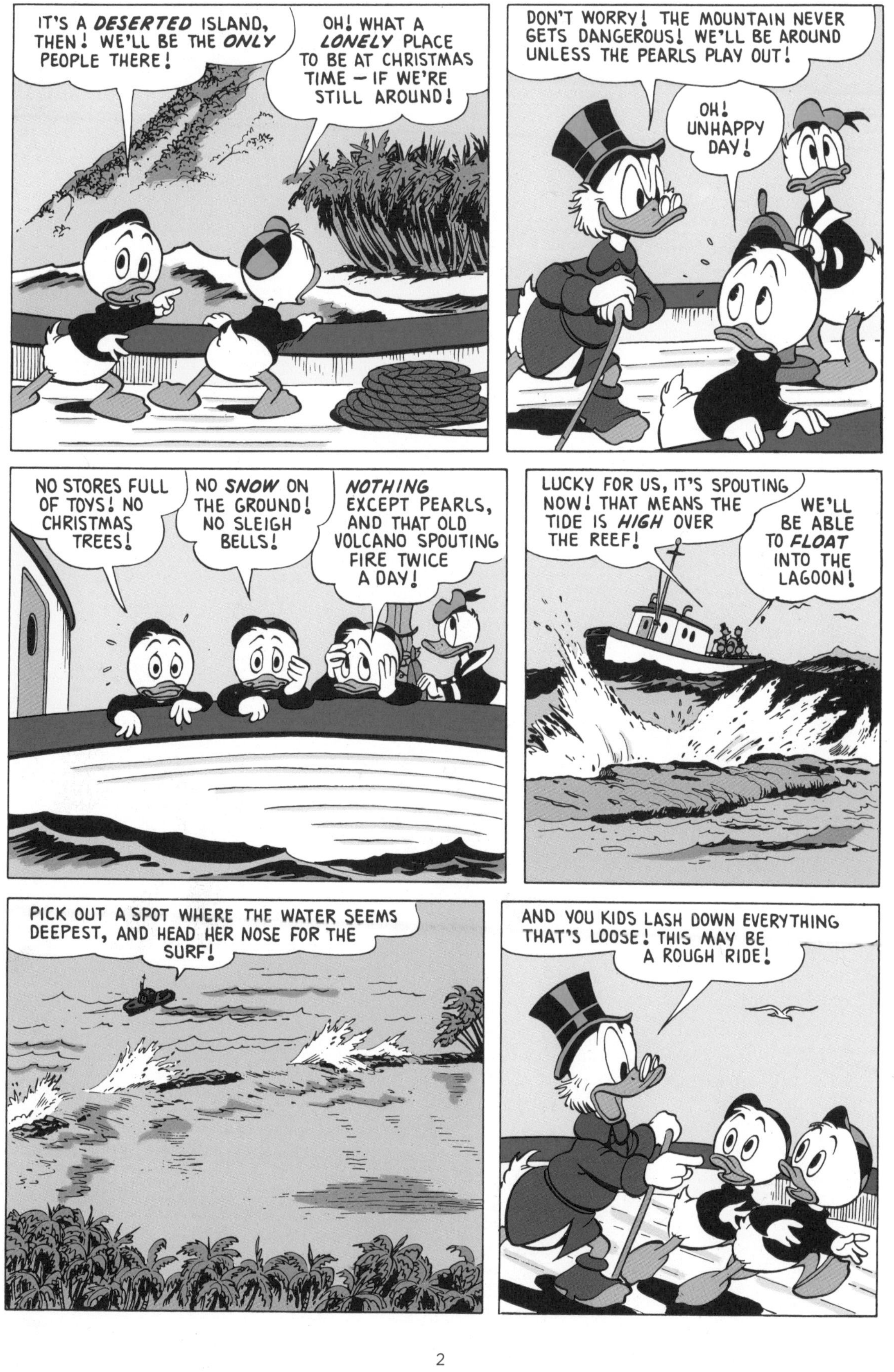
IT'S A DESERTED ISLAND, THEN! WE'LL BE THE ONLY PEOPLE THERE!
OH! WHAT A LONELY PLACE TO BE AT CHRISTMAS TIME — IF WE'RE STILL AROUND!
DON'T WORRY! THE MOUNTAIN NEVER GETS DANGEROUS! WE'LL BE AROUND UNLESS THE PEARLS PLAY OUT!
OH! UNHAPPY DAY!
NO STORES FULL OF TOYS! NO CHRISTMAS TREES!
NO SNOW ON THE GROUND! NO SLEIGH BELLS!
NOTHING EXCEPT PEARLS, AND THAT OLD VOLCANO SPOUTING FIRE TWICE A DAY!
LUCKY FOR US, IT'S SPOUTING NOW! THAT MEANS THE TIDE IS HIGH OVER THE REEF!
WE'LL BE ABLE TO FLOAT INTO THE LAGOON!
PICK OUT A SPOT WHERE THE WATER SEEMS DEEPEST, AND HEAD HER NOSE FOR THE SURF!
AND YOU KIDS LASH DOWN EVERYTHING THAT'S LOOSE! THIS MAY BE A ROUGH RIDE!

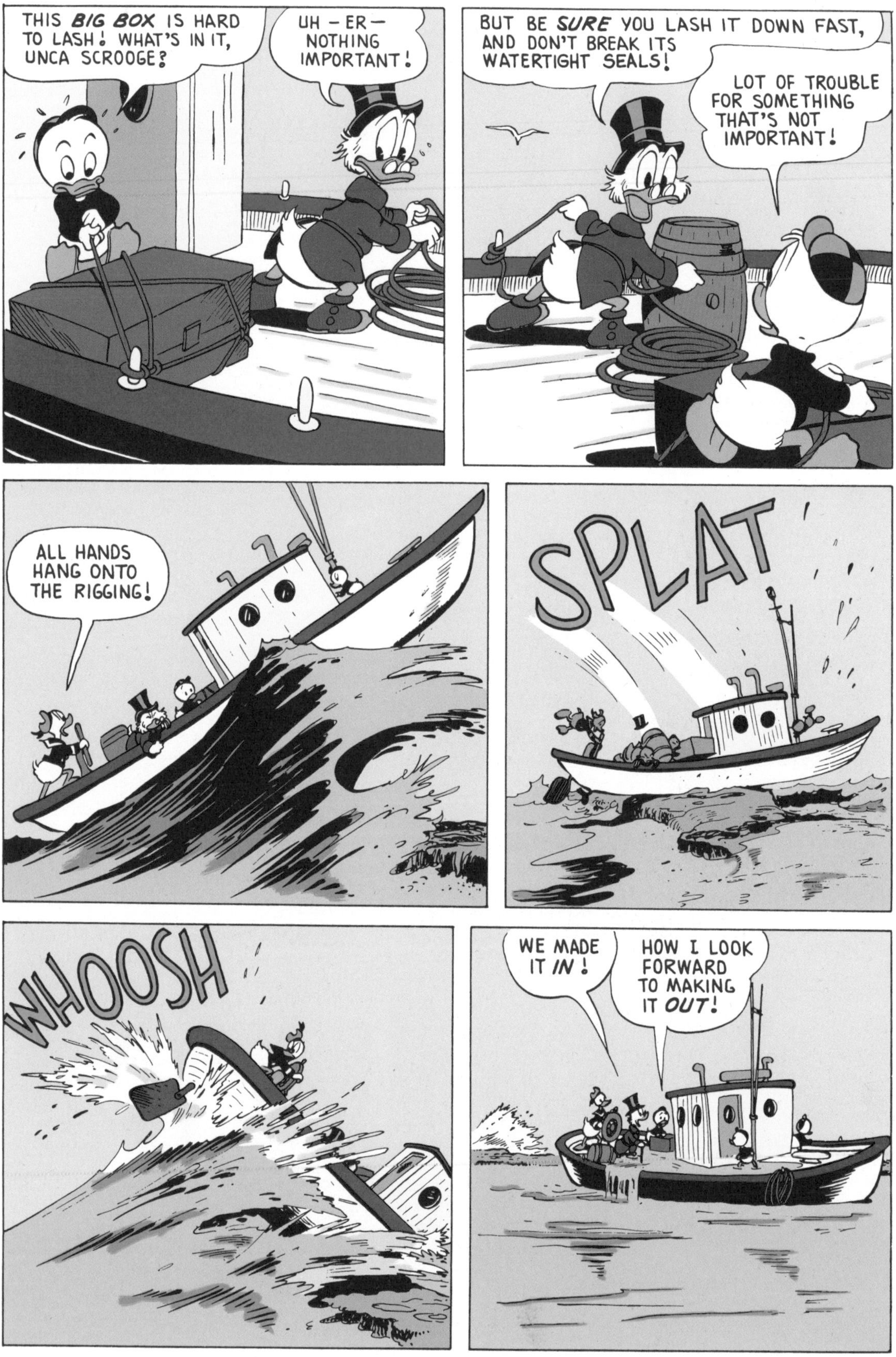

THIS BIG BOX IS HARD TO LASH! WHAT'S IN IT, UNCA SCROOGE?
UH — ER — NOTHING IMPORTANT!
BUT BE SURE YOU LASH IT DOWN FAST, AND DON'T BREAK ITS WATERTIGHT SEALS!
LOT OF TROUBLE FOR SOMETHING THAT'S NOT IMPORTANT!
ALL HANDS HANG ONTO THE RIGGING!
SPLAT
WHOOSH
WE MADE IT IN!
HOW I LOOK FORWARD TO MAKING IT OUT!

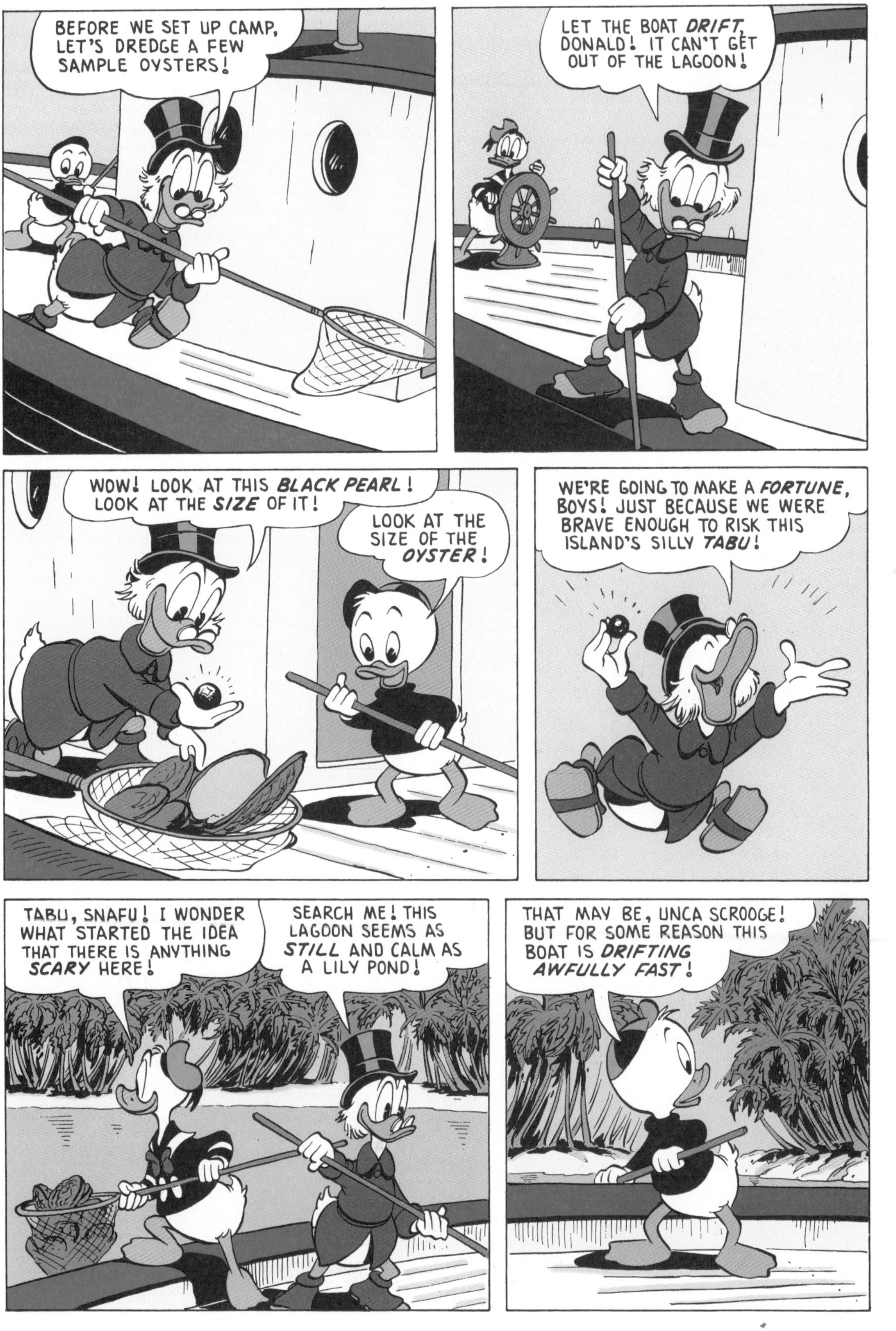
BEFORE WE SET UP CAMP, LET'S DREDGE A FEW SAMPLE OYSTERS!
LET THE BOAT DRIFT, DONALD! IT CAN'T GET OUT OF THE LAGOON!
WOW! LOOK AT THIS BLACK PEARL! LOOK AT THE SIZE OF IT!
LOOK AT THE SIZE OF THE OYSTER!
WE'RE GOING TO MAKE A FORTUNE, BOYS! JUST BECAUSE WE WERE BRAVE ENOUGH TO RISK THIS ISLAND'S SILLY TABU!
TABU, SNAFU! I WONDER WHAT STARTED THE IDEA THAT THERE IS ANYTHING SCARY HERE!
SEARCH ME! THIS LAGOON SEEMS AS STILL AND CALM AS A LILY POND!
THAT MAY BE, UNCA SCROOGE! BUT FOR SOME REASON THIS BOAT IS DRIFTING AWFULLY FAST!

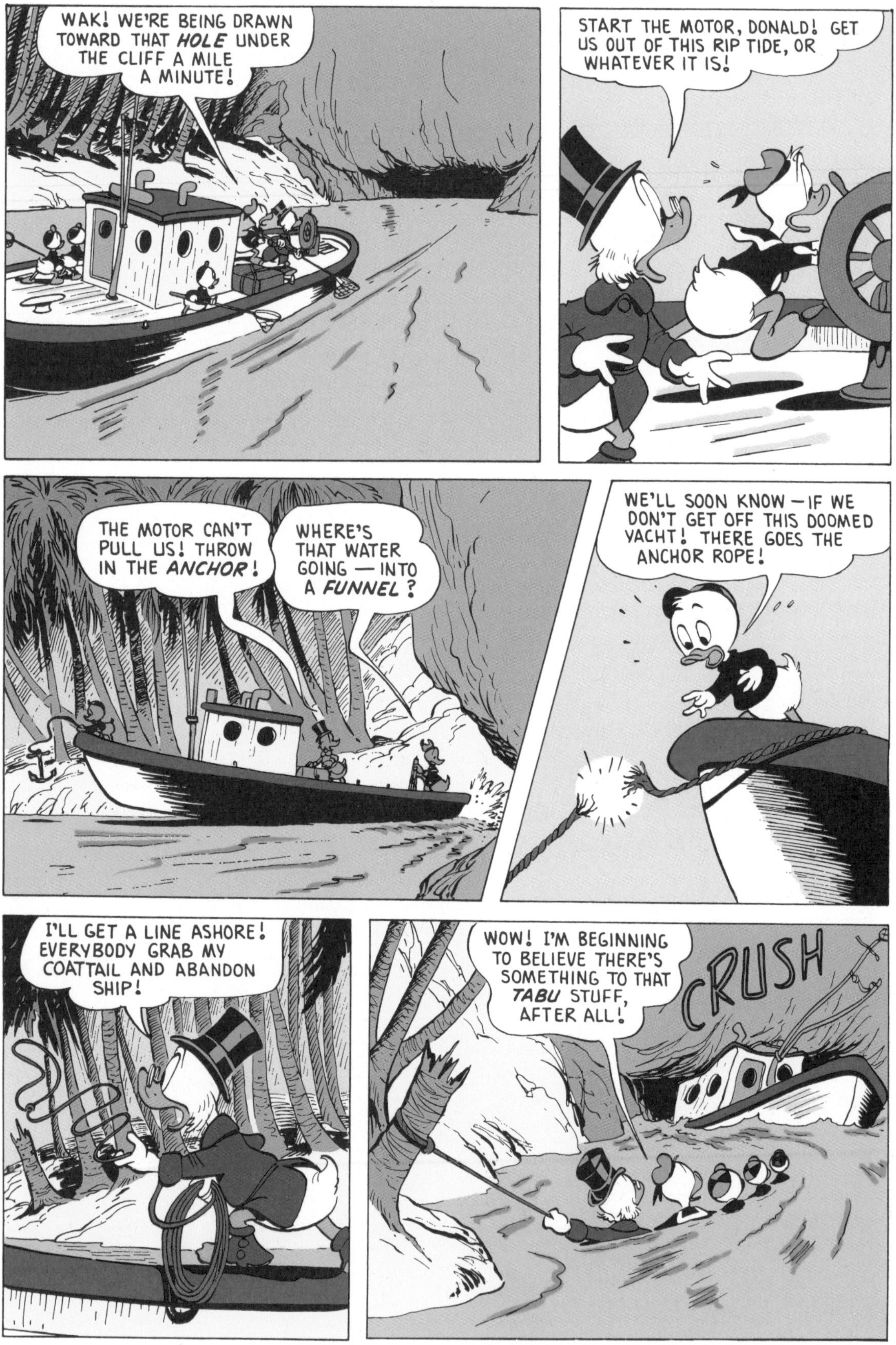
WAK! WE'RE BEING DRAWN TOWARD THAT HOLE UNDER THE CLIFF A MILE A MINUTE!
START THE MOTOR, DONALD! GET US OUT OF THIS RIP TIDE, OR WHATEVER IT IS!
THE MOTOR CAN'T PULL US! THROW IN THE ANCHOR!
WHERE'S THAT WATER GOING — INTO A FUNNEL?
WE'LL SOON KNOW — IF WE DON'T GET OFF THIS DOOMED YACHT! THERE GOES THE ANCHOR ROPE!
I'LL GET A LINE ASHORE! EVERYBODY GRAB MY COATTAIL AND ABANDON SHIP!
WOW! I'M BEGINNING TO BELIEVE THERE'S SOMETHING TO THAT TABU STUFF, AFTER ALL!
CRUSH

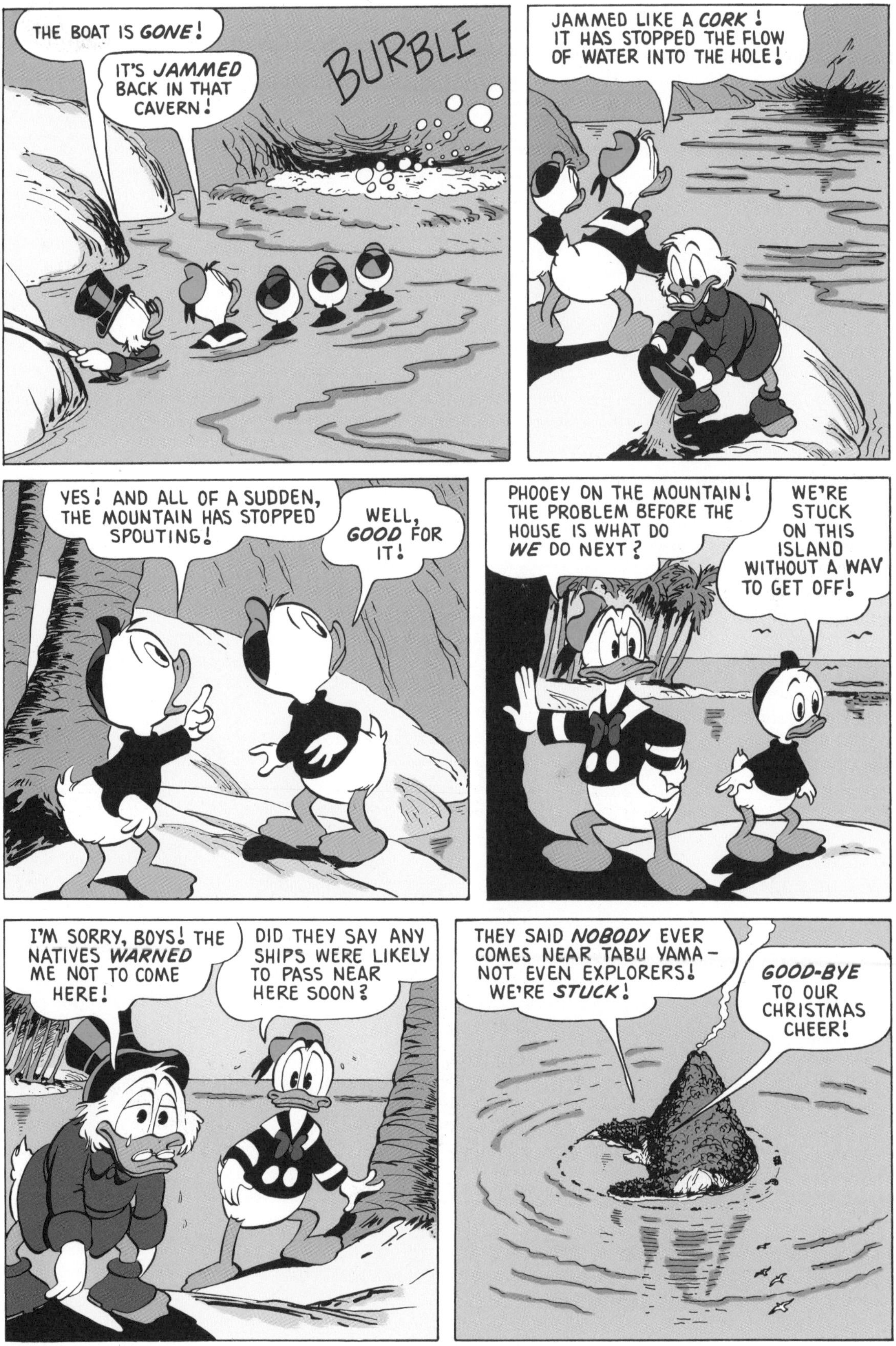
THE BOAT IS GONE!
IT'S JAMMED BACK IN THAT CAVERN!
BURBLE
JAMMED LIKE A CORK! IT HAS STOPPED THE FLOW OF WATER INTO THE HOLE!
YES! AND ALL OF A SUDDEN, THE MOUNTAIN HAS STOPPED SPOUTING!
WELL, GOOD FOR IT!
PHOOEY ON THE MOUNTAIN! THE PROBLEM BEFORE THE HOUSE IS WHAT DO WE DO NEXT?
WE'RE STUCK ON THIS ISLAND WITHOUT A WAY TO GET OFF!
I'M SORRY, BOYS! THE NATIVES WARNED ME NOT TO COME HERE!
DID THEY SAY ANY SHIPS WERE LIKELY TO PASS NEAR HERE SOON?
THEY SAID NOBODY EVER COMES NEAR TABU YAMA— NOT EVEN EXPLORERS! WE'RE STUCK!
GOOD-BYE TO OUR CHRISTMAS CHEER!

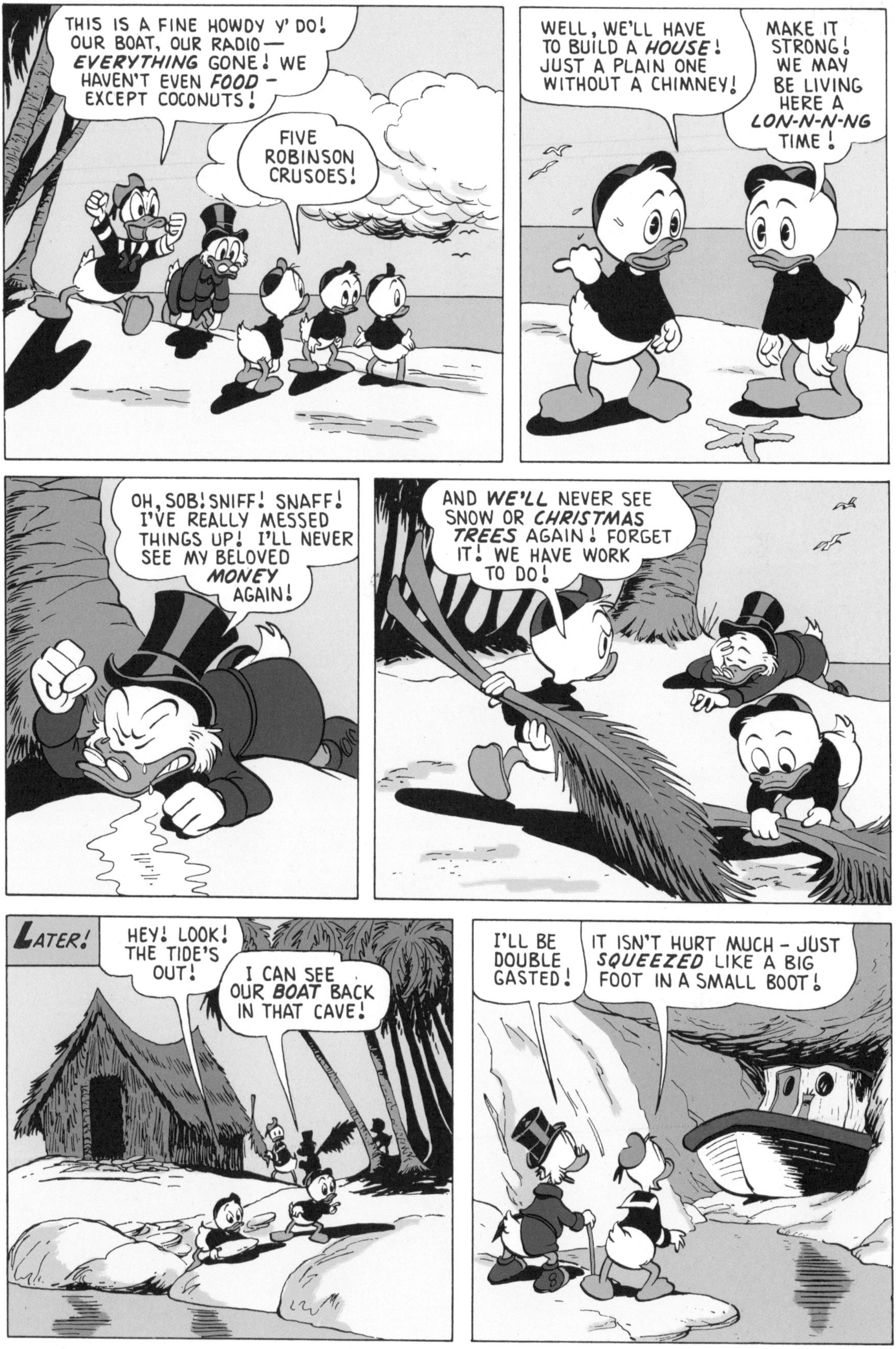
THIS IS A FINE HOWDY Y' DO! OUR BOAT, OUR RADIO— EVERYTHING GONE! WE HAVEN'T EVEN FOOD - EXCEPT COCONUTS!
FIVE ROBINSON CRUSOES!
WELL, WE'LL HAVE TO BUILD A HOUSE! JUST A PLAIN ONE WITHOUT A CHIMNEY!
MAKE IT STRONG! WE MAY BE LIVING HERE A LON-N-N-NG TIME!
OH, SOB! SNIFF! SNAFF! I'VE REALLY MESSED THINGS UP! I'LL NEVER SEE MY BELOVED MONEY AGAIN!
AND WE'LL NEVER SEE SNOW OR CHRISTMAS TREES AGAIN! FORGET IT! WE HAVE WORK TO DO!
LATER!
HEY! LOOK! THE TIDE'S OUT!
I CAN SEE OUR BOAT BACK IN THAT CAVE!
I'LL BE DOUBLE GASTED!
IT ISN'T HURT MUCH - JUST SQUEEZED LIKE A BIG FOOT IN A SMALL BOOT!

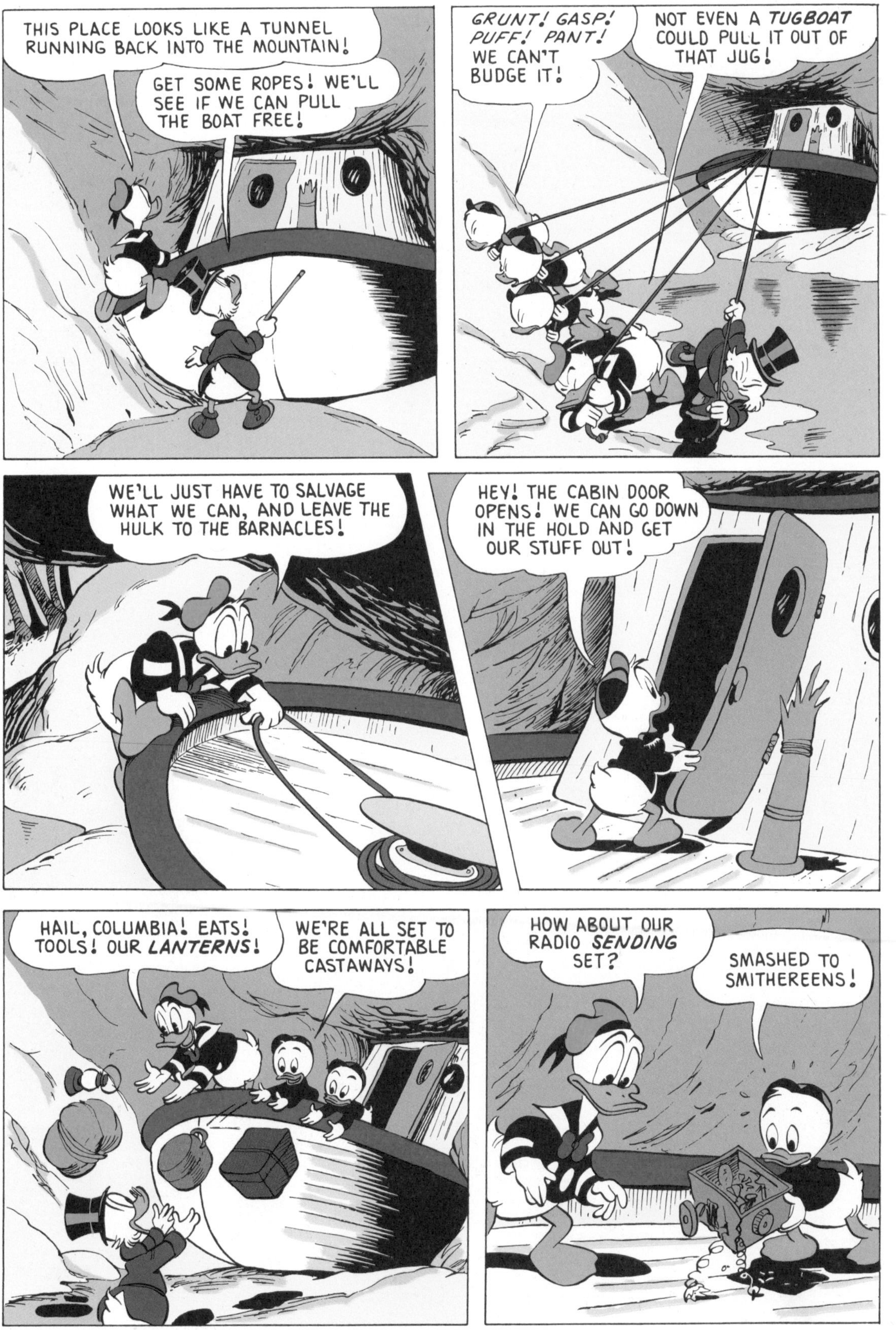
THIS PLACE LOOKS LIKE A TUNNEL RUNNING BACK INTO THE MOUNTAIN!
GET SOME ROPES! WE'LL SEE IF WE CAN PULL THE BOAT FREE!
GRUNT! GASP! PUFF! PANT! WE CAN'T BUDGE IT!
NOT EVEN A TUGBOAT COULD PULL IT OUT OF THAT JUG!
WE'LL JUST HAVE TO SALVAGE WHAT WE CAN, AND LEAVE THE HULK TO THE BARNACLES!
HEY! THE CABIN DOOR OPENS! WE CAN GO DOWN IN THE HOLD AND GET OUR STUFF OUT!
HAIL, COLUMBIA! EATS! TOOLS! OUR LANTERNS!
WE'RE ALL SET TO BE COMFORTABLE CASTAWAYS!
HOW ABOUT OUR RADIO SENDING SET?
SMASHED TO SMITHEREENS!

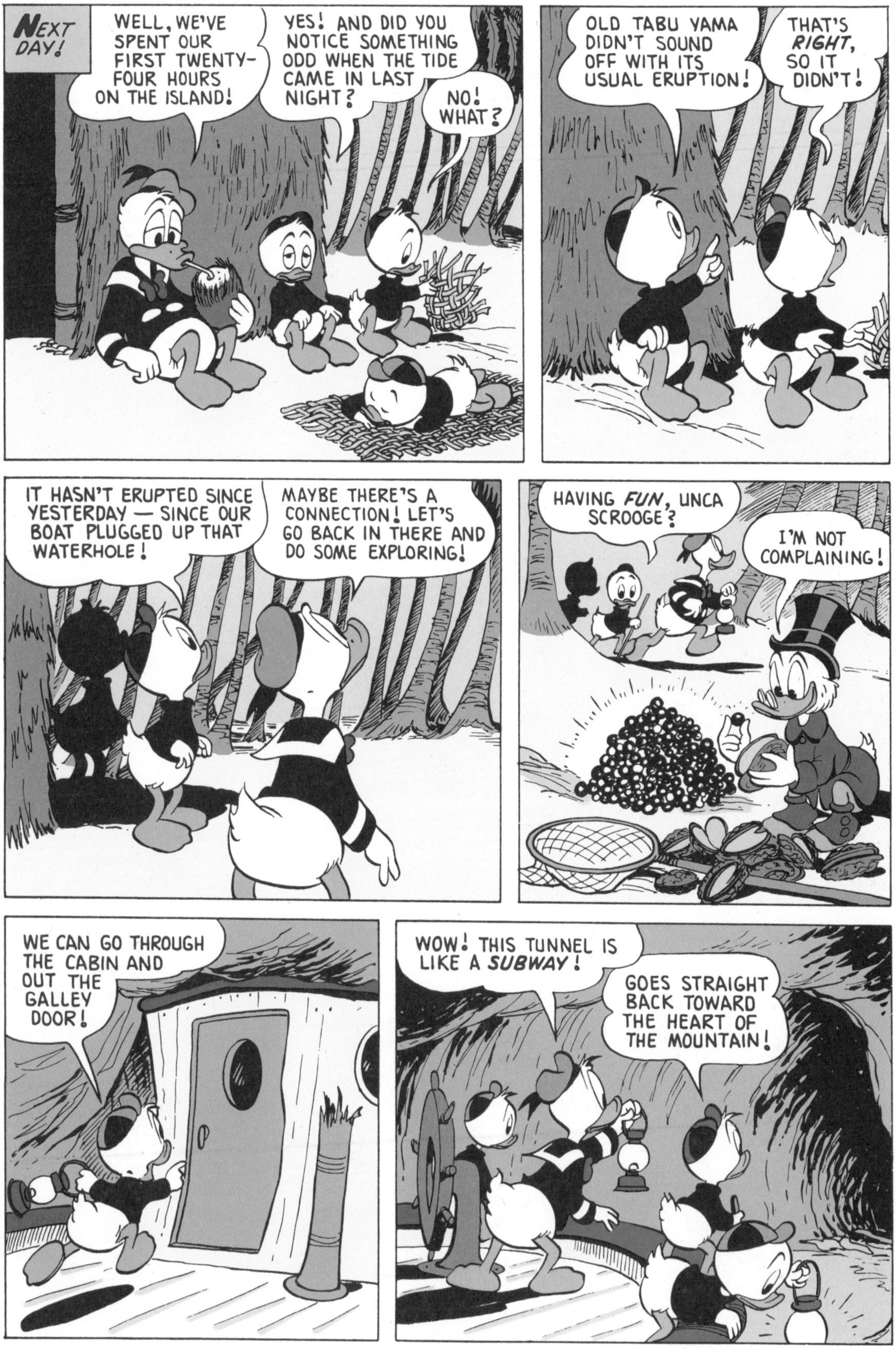
NEXT DAY!
WELL, WE'VE SPENT OUR FIRST TWENTY-FOUR HOURS ON THE ISLAND!
YES! AND DID YOU NOTICE SOMETHING ODD WHEN THE TIDE CAME IN LAST NIGHT?
NO! WHAT?
OLD TABU YAMA DIDN'T SOUND OFF WITH ITS USUAL ERUPTION!
THAT'S *RIGHT*, SO IT DIDN'T!
IT HASN'T ERUPTED SINCE YESTERDAY — SINCE OUR BOAT PLUGGED UP THAT WATERHOLE!
MAYBE THERE'S A CONNECTION! LET'S GO BACK IN THERE AND DO SOME EXPLORING!
HAVING *FUN*, UNCA SCROOGE?
I'M NOT COMPLAINING!
WE CAN GO THROUGH THE CABIN AND OUT THE GALLEY DOOR!
WOW! THIS TUNNEL IS LIKE A *SUBWAY*!
GOES STRAIGHT BACK TOWARD THE HEART OF THE MOUNTAIN!

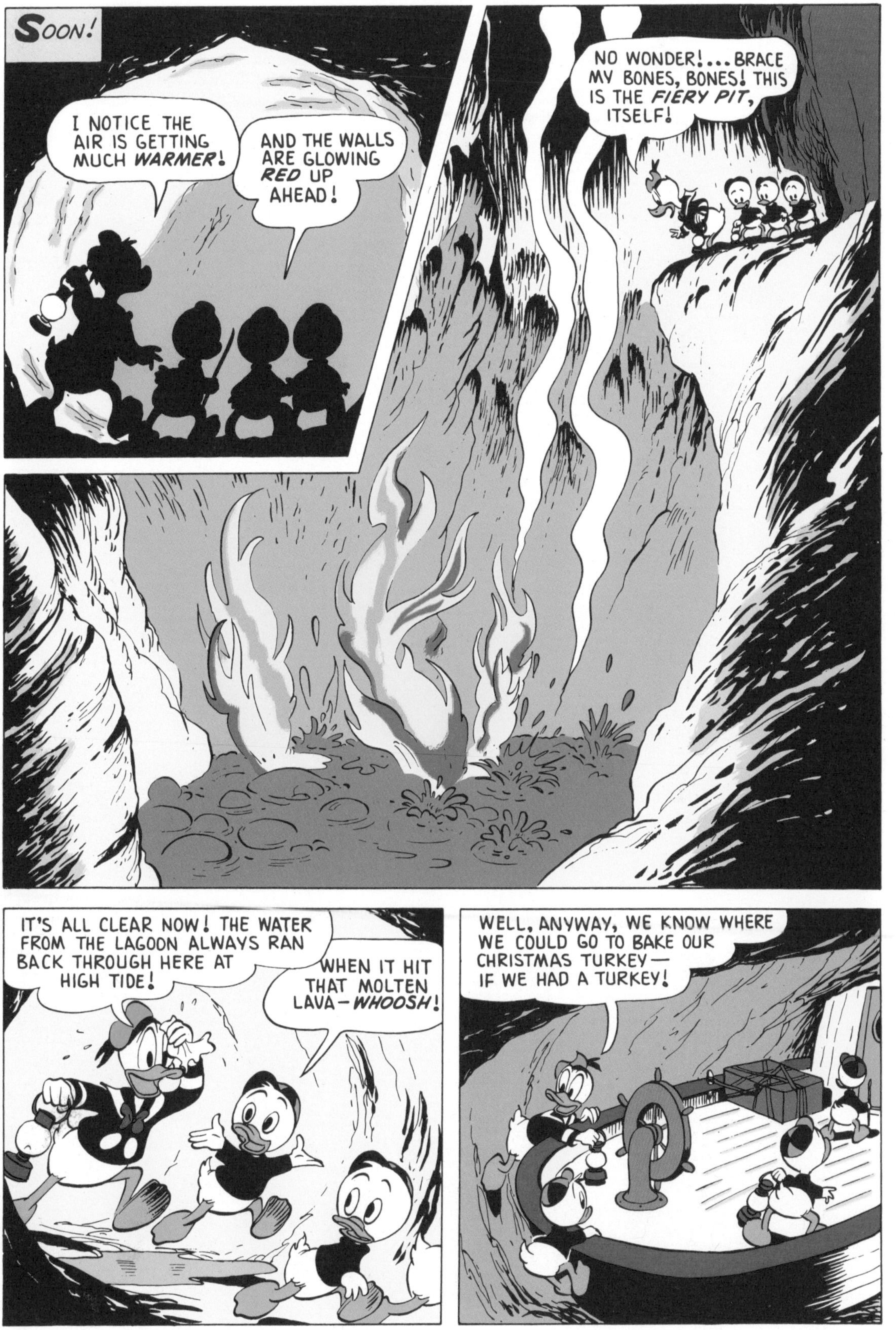
SOON!
I NOTICE THE AIR IS GETTING MUCH WARMER!
AND THE WALLS ARE GLOWING RED UP AHEAD!
NO WONDER!...BRACE MY BONES, BONES! THIS IS THE FIERY PIT, ITSELF!
IT'S ALL CLEAR NOW! THE WATER FROM THE LAGOON ALWAYS RAN BACK THROUGH HERE AT HIGH TIDE!
WHEN IT HIT THAT MOLTEN LAVA—WHOOSH!
WELL, ANYWAY, WE KNOW WHERE WE COULD GO TO BAKE OUR CHRISTMAS TURKEY—IF WE HAD A TURKEY!

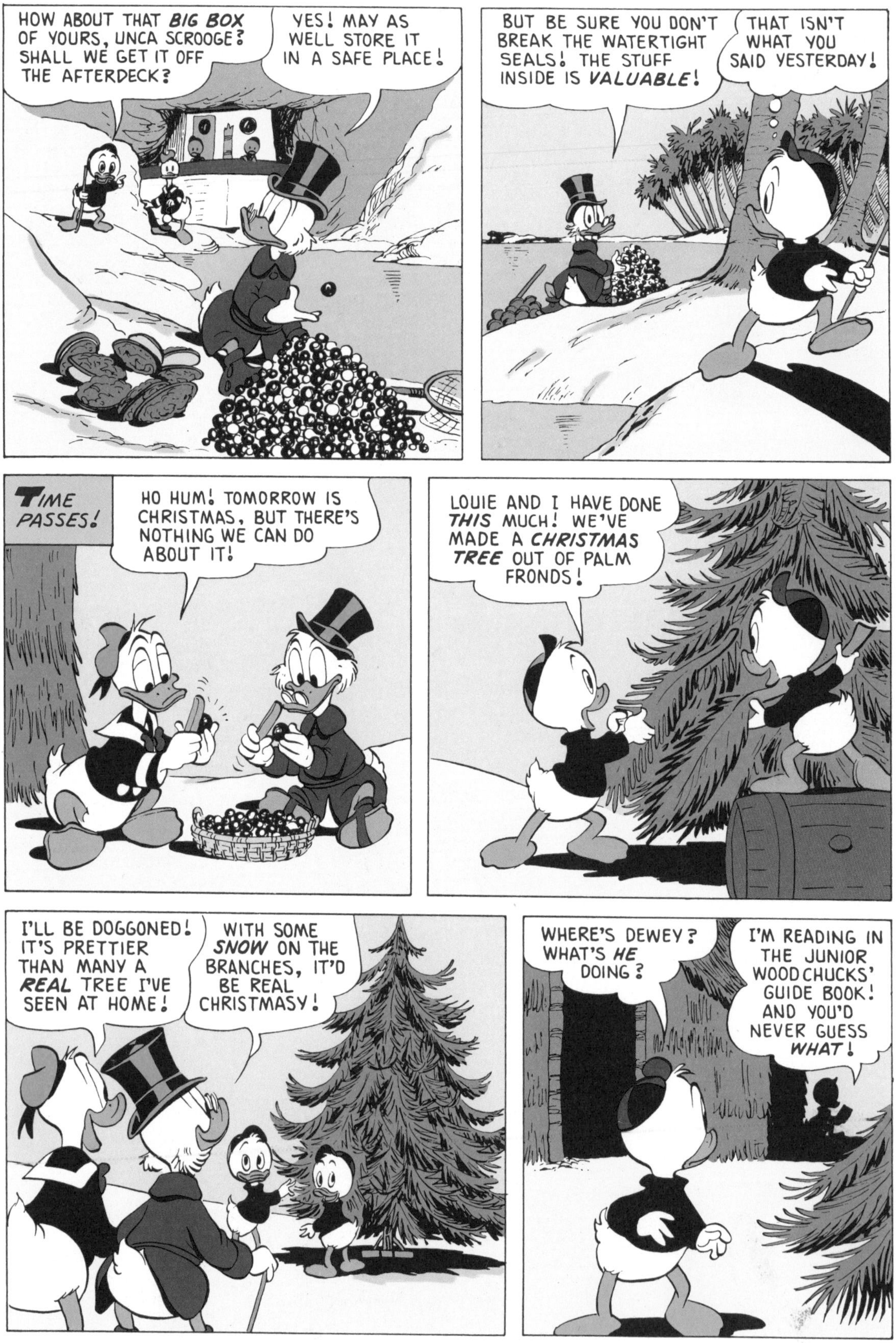

HOW ABOUT THAT BIG BOX OF YOURS, UNCA SCROOGE? SHALL WE GET IT OFF THE AFTERDECK?
YES! MAY AS WELL STORE IT IN A SAFE PLACE!
BUT BE SURE YOU DON'T BREAK THE WATERTIGHT SEALS! THE STUFF INSIDE IS VALUABLE!
THAT ISN'T WHAT YOU SAID YESTERDAY!
TIME PASSES!
HO HUM! TOMORROW IS CHRISTMAS, BUT THERE'S NOTHING WE CAN DO ABOUT IT!
LOUIE AND I HAVE DONE THIS MUCH! WE'VE MADE A CHRISTMAS TREE OUT OF PALM FRONDS!
I'LL BE DOGGONED! IT'S PRETTIER THAN MANY A REAL TREE I'VE SEEN AT HOME!
WITH SOME SNOW ON THE BRANCHES, IT'D BE REAL CHRISTMASY!
WHERE'S DEWEY? WHAT'S HE DOING?
I'M READING IN THE JUNIOR WOODCHUCKS' GUIDE BOOK! AND YOU'D NEVER GUESS WHAT!

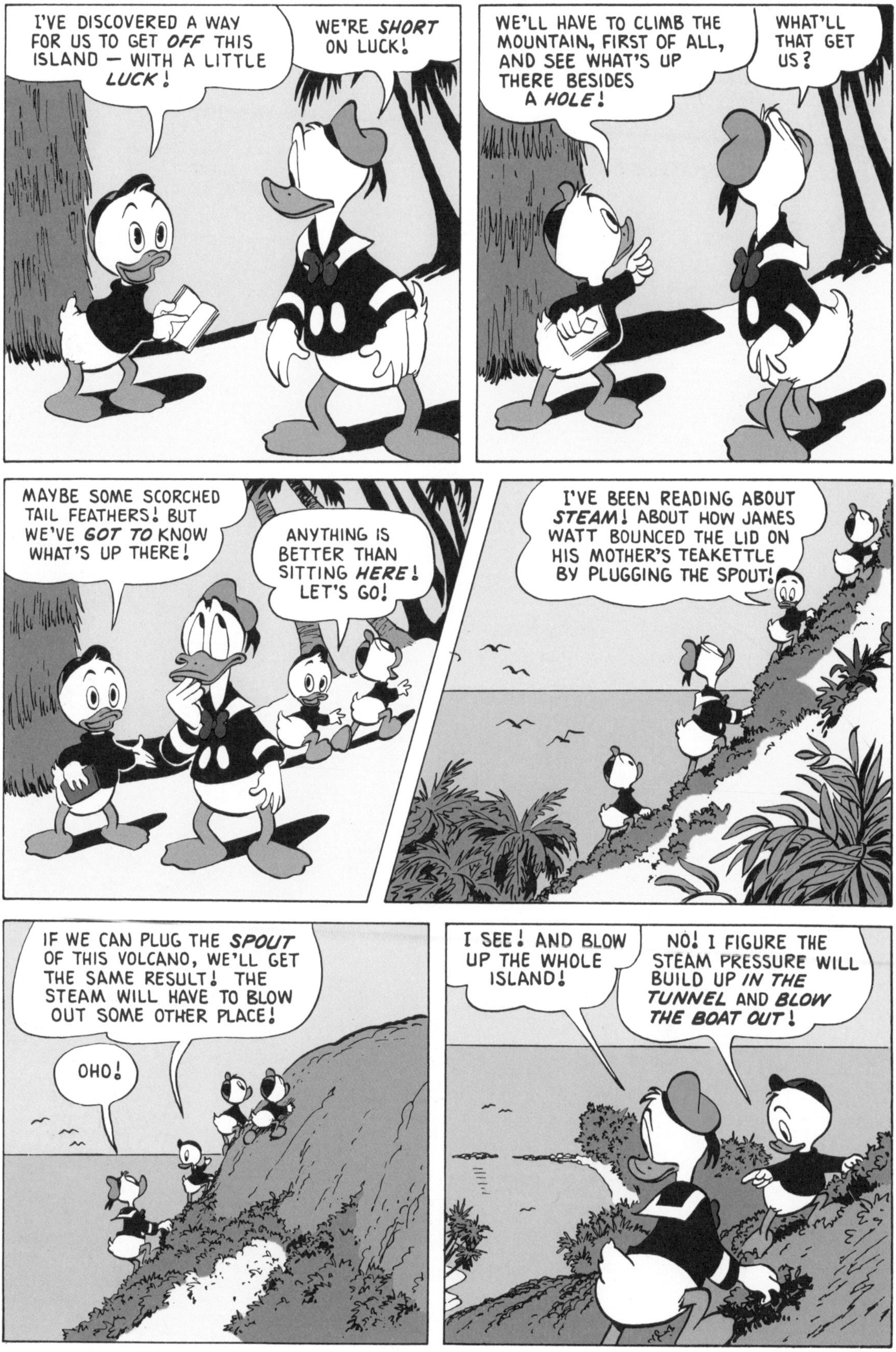
I'VE DISCOVERED A WAY FOR US TO GET OFF THIS ISLAND — WITH A LITTLE LUCK!
WE'RE SHORT ON LUCK!
WE'LL HAVE TO CLIMB THE MOUNTAIN, FIRST OF ALL, AND SEE WHAT'S UP THERE BESIDES A HOLE!
WHAT'LL THAT GET US?
MAYBE SOME SCORCHED TAIL FEATHERS! BUT WE'VE GOT TO KNOW WHAT'S UP THERE!
ANYTHING IS BETTER THAN SITTING HERE! LET'S GO!
I'VE BEEN READING ABOUT STEAM! ABOUT HOW JAMES WATT BOUNCED THE LID ON HIS MOTHER'S TEAKETTLE BY PLUGGING THE SPOUT!
IF WE CAN PLUG THE SPOUT OF THIS VOLCANO, WE'LL GET THE SAME RESULT! THE STEAM WILL HAVE TO BLOW OUT SOME OTHER PLACE!
OHO!
I SEE! AND BLOW UP THE WHOLE ISLAND!
NO! I FIGURE THE STEAM PRESSURE WILL BUILD UP IN THE TUNNEL AND BLOW THE BOAT OUT!

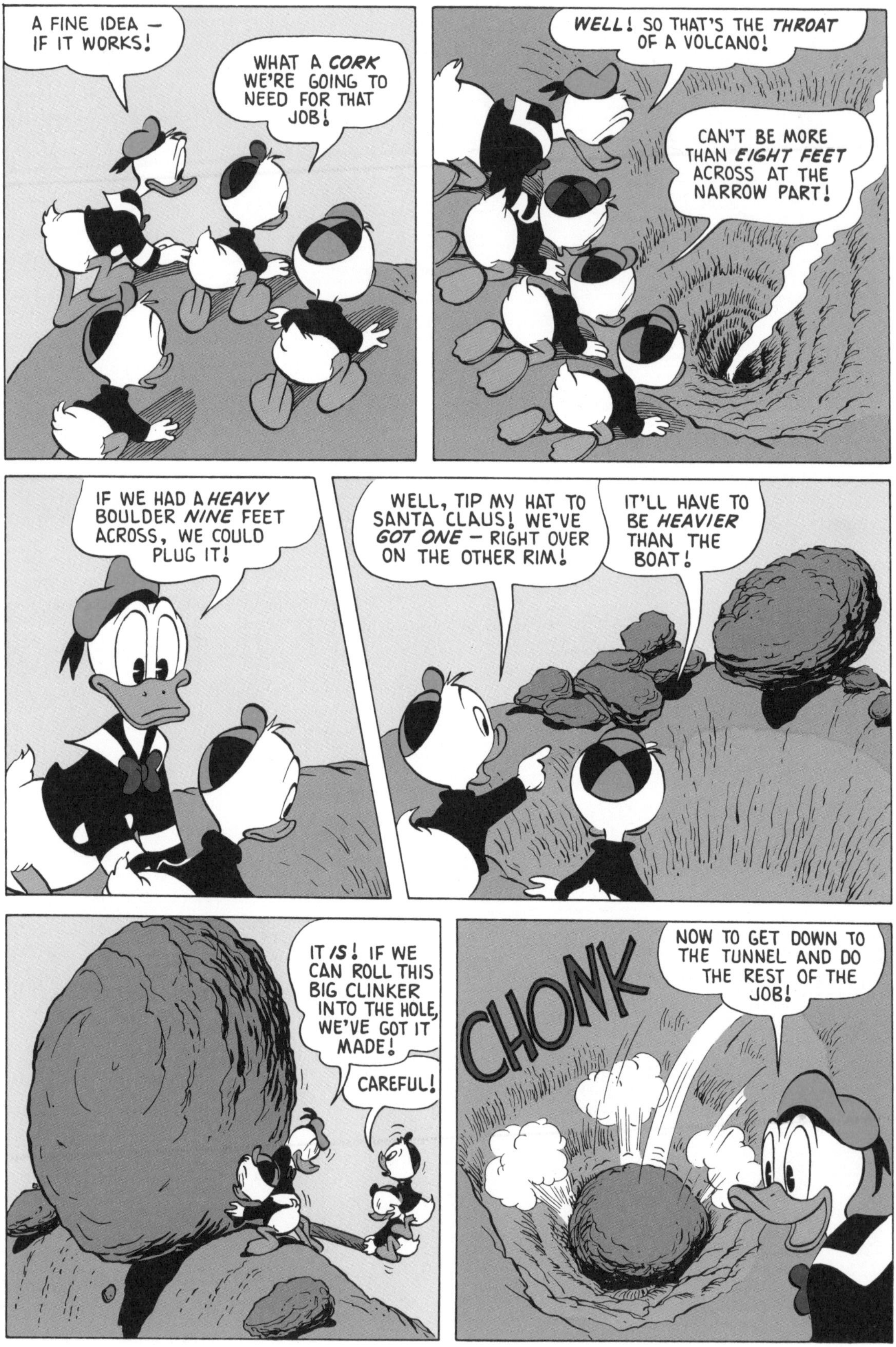
A FINE IDEA — IF IT WORKS!
WHAT A CORK WE'RE GOING TO NEED FOR THAT JOB!
WELL! SO THAT'S THE THROAT OF A VOLCANO!
CAN'T BE MORE THAN EIGHT FEET ACROSS AT THE NARROW PART!
IF WE HAD A HEAVY BOULDER NINE FEET ACROSS, WE COULD PLUG IT!
WELL, TIP MY HAT TO SANTA CLAUS! WE'VE GOT ONE — RIGHT OVER ON THE OTHER RIM!
IT'LL HAVE TO BE HEAVIER THAN THE BOAT!
IT IS! IF WE CAN ROLL THIS BIG CLINKER INTO THE HOLE, WE'VE GOT IT MADE!
CAREFUL!
CHONK
NOW TO GET DOWN TO THE TUNNEL AND DO THE REST OF THE JOB!

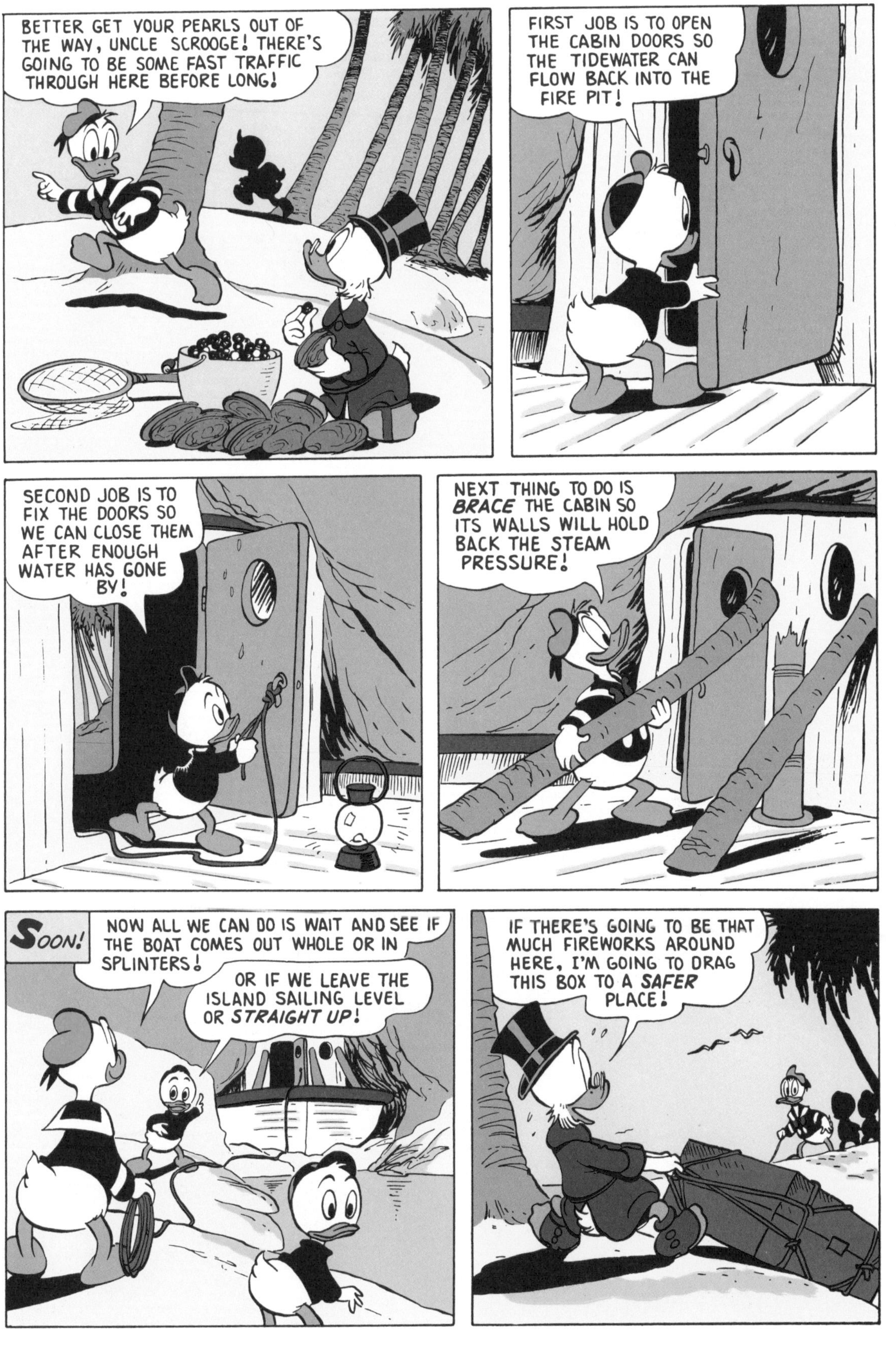
BETTER GET YOUR PEARLS OUT OF THE WAY, UNCLE SCROOGE! THERE'S GOING TO BE SOME FAST TRAFFIC THROUGH HERE BEFORE LONG!
FIRST JOB IS TO OPEN THE CABIN DOORS SO THE TIDEWATER CAN FLOW BACK INTO THE FIRE PIT!
SECOND JOB IS TO FIX THE DOORS SO WE CAN CLOSE THEM AFTER ENOUGH WATER HAS GONE BY!
NEXT THING TO DO IS *BRACE* THE CABIN SO ITS WALLS WILL HOLD BACK THE STEAM PRESSURE!
SOON!
NOW ALL WE CAN DO IS WAIT AND SEE IF THE BOAT COMES OUT WHOLE OR IN SPLINTERS!
OR IF WE LEAVE THE ISLAND SAILING LEVEL OR *STRAIGHT UP*!
IF THERE'S GOING TO BE THAT MUCH FIREWORKS AROUND HERE, I'M GOING TO DRAG THIS BOX TO A *SAFER* PLACE!

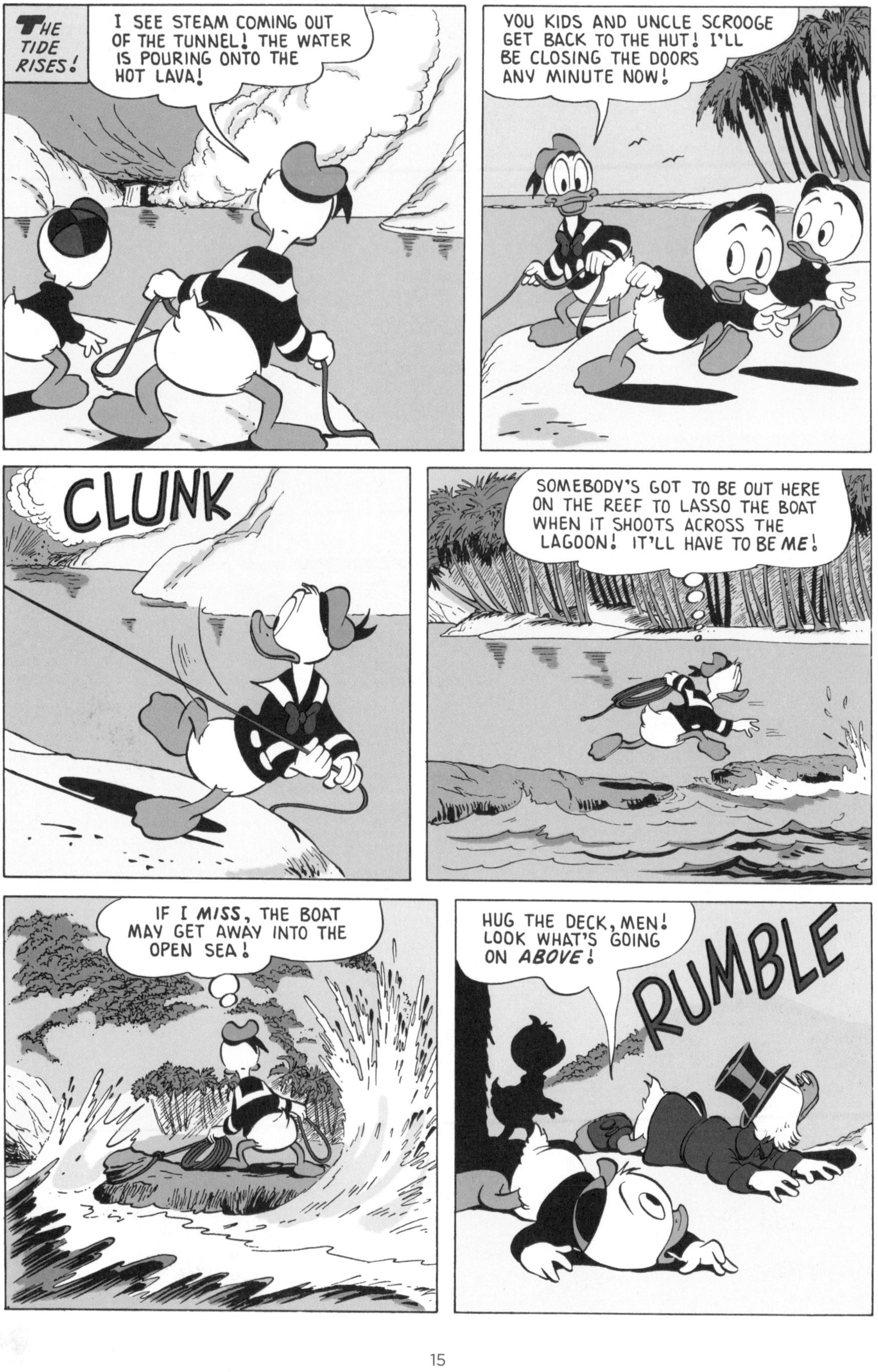
THE TIDE RISES!
I SEE STEAM COMING OUT OF THE TUNNEL! THE WATER IS POURING ONTO THE HOT LAVA!
YOU KIDS AND UNCLE SCROOGE GET BACK TO THE HUT! I'LL BE CLOSING THE DOORS ANY MINUTE NOW!
CLUNK
SOMEBODY'S GOT TO BE OUT HERE ON THE REEF TO LASSO THE BOAT WHEN IT SHOOTS ACROSS THE LAGOON! IT'LL HAVE TO BE ME!
IF I MISS, THE BOAT MAY GET AWAY INTO THE OPEN SEA!
HUG THE DECK, MEN! LOOK WHAT'S GOING ON ABOVE!
RUMBLE

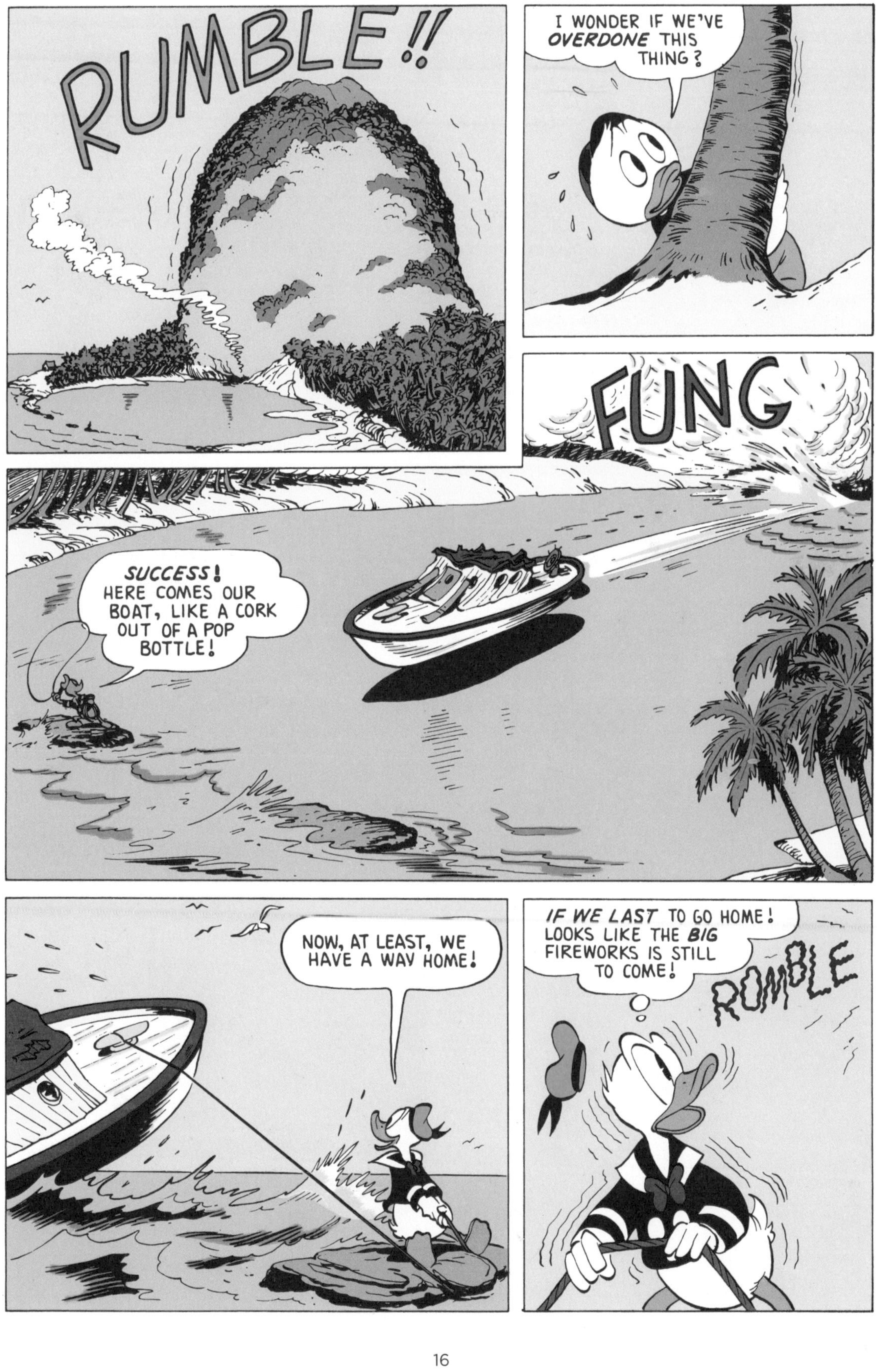
RUMBLE!!
I WONDER IF WE'VE OVERDONE THIS THING?
FUNG
SUCCESS! HERE COMES OUR BOAT, LIKE A CORK OUT OF A POP BOTTLE!
NOW, AT LEAST, WE HAVE A WAY HOME!
IF WE LAST TO GO HOME! LOOKS LIKE THE BIG FIREWORKS IS STILL TO COME!
ROMBLE

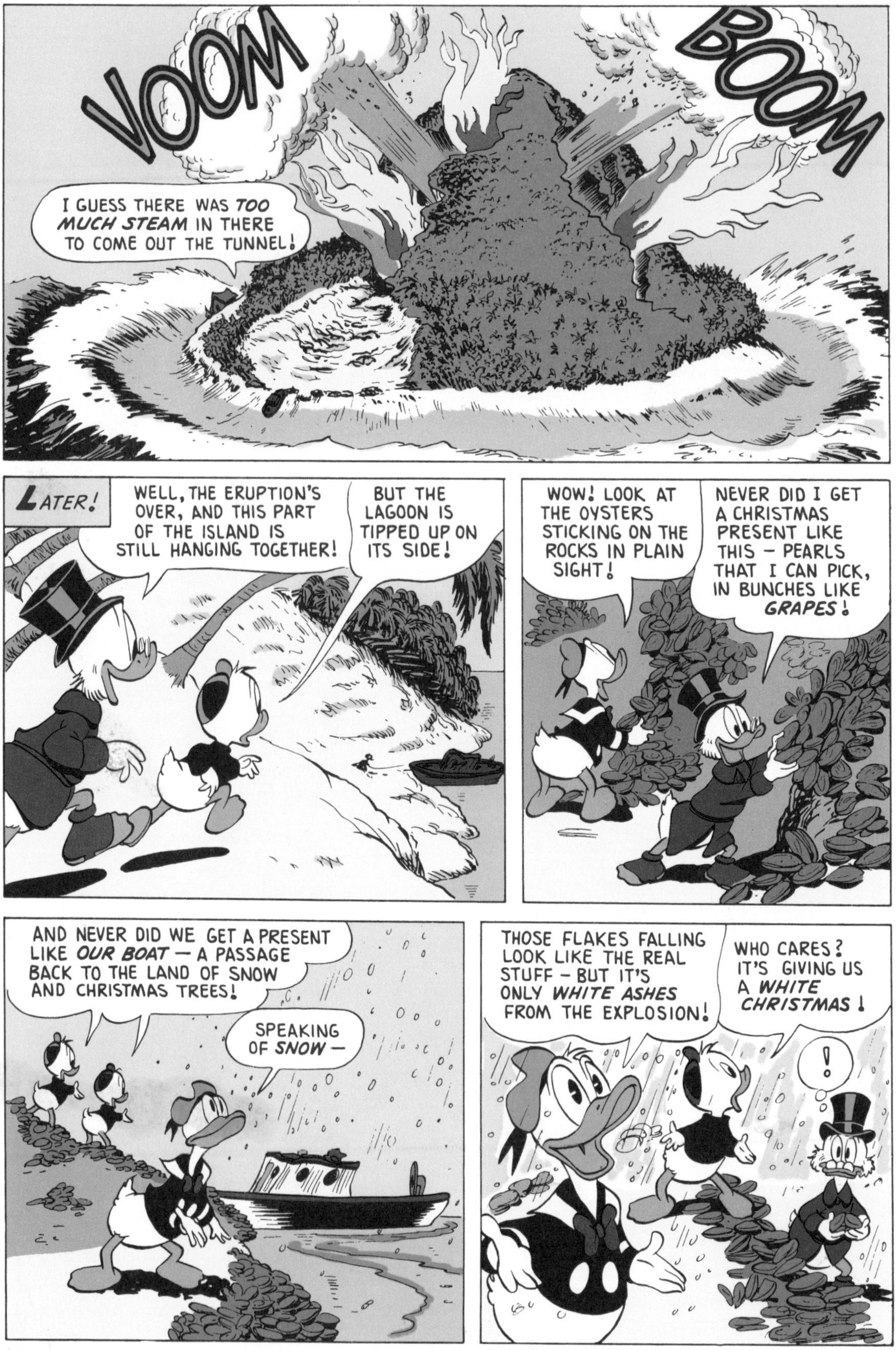
VOOM
BOOM
I GUESS THERE WAS TOO MUCH STEAM IN THERE TO COME OUT THE TUNNEL!
LATER!
WELL, THE ERUPTION'S OVER, AND THIS PART OF THE ISLAND IS STILL HANGING TOGETHER!
BUT THE LAGOON IS TIPPED UP ON ITS SIDE!
WOW! LOOK AT THE OYSTERS STICKING ON THE ROCKS IN PLAIN SIGHT!
NEVER DID I GET A CHRISTMAS PRESENT LIKE THIS — PEARLS THAT I CAN PICK, IN BUNCHES LIKE GRAPES!
AND NEVER DID WE GET A PRESENT LIKE OUR BOAT — A PASSAGE BACK TO THE LAND OF SNOW AND CHRISTMAS TREES!
SPEAKING OF SNOW —
THOSE FLAKES FALLING LOOK LIKE THE REAL STUFF — BUT IT'S ONLY WHITE ASHES FROM THE EXPLOSION!
WHO CARES? IT'S GIVING US A WHITE CHRISTMAS!
!

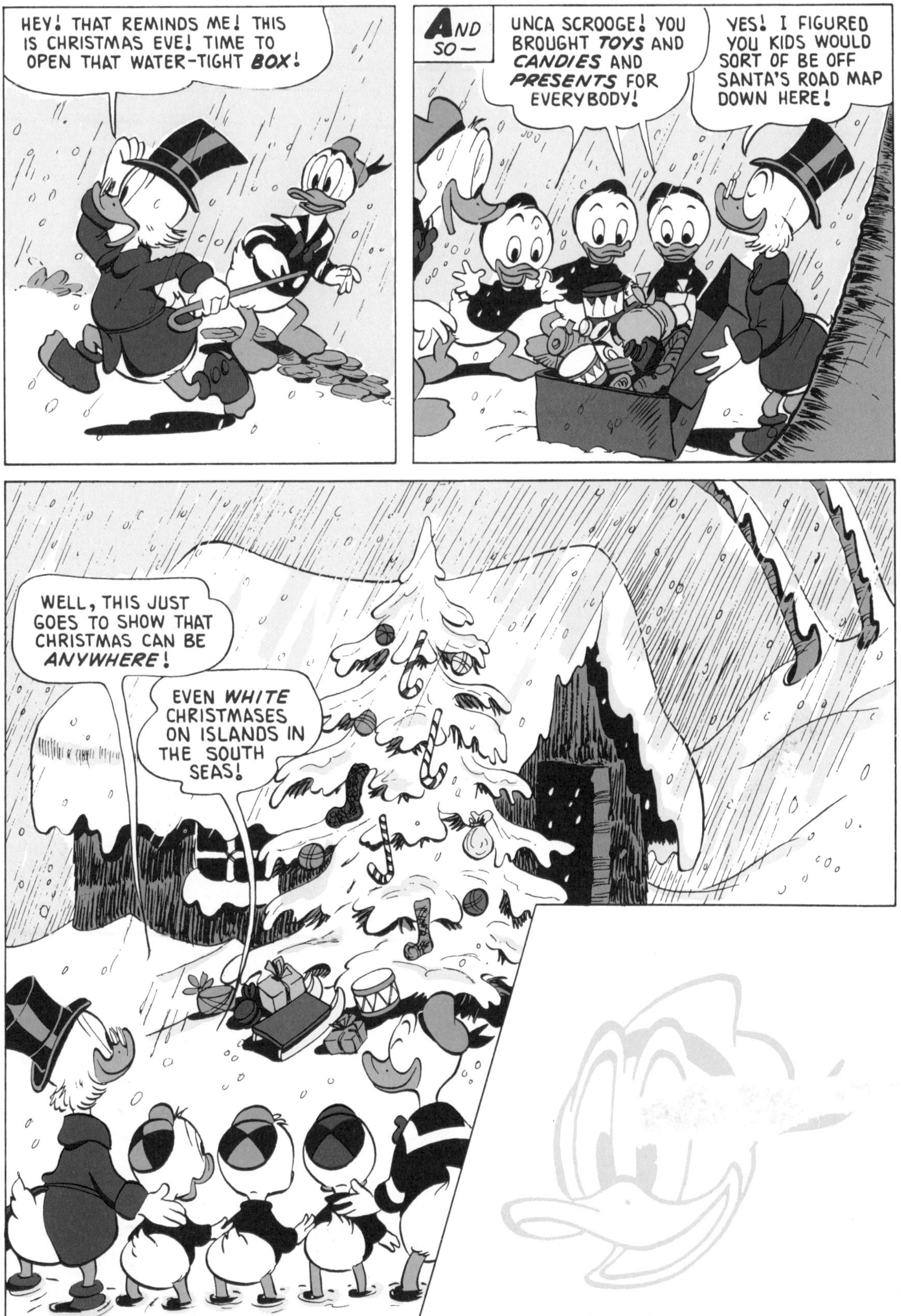
HEY! THAT REMINDS ME! THIS IS CHRISTMAS EVE! TIME TO OPEN THAT WATER-TIGHT BOX!
AND SO—
UNCA SCROOGE! YOU BROUGHT TOYS AND CANDIES AND PRESENTS FOR EVERYBODY!
YES! I FIGURED YOU KIDS WOULD SORT OF BE OFF SANTA'S ROAD MAP DOWN HERE!
WELL, THIS JUST GOES TO SHOW THAT CHRISTMAS CAN BE ANYWHERE!
EVEN WHITE CHRISTMASES ON ISLANDS IN THE SOUTH SEAS!

Publisher and Executive Editor: GARY GROTH
Senior Editor: J. MICHAEL CATRON
Color Editor: SEAN DAVID WILLIAMS
Colorists: RICH TOMMASO, GARY LEACH, SUSAN DAIGLE-LEACH
Series Design: JACOB COVEY
Volume Design: KEELI McCARTHY
Production: PAUL BARESH
Associate Publisher: ERIC REYNOLDS

- -

Fantagraphics Books, Inc.
7563 Lake City Way NE
Seattle WA 98115
(800) 657-1100

Visit us at fantagraphics.com. Follow us on Twitter at @fantagraphics
and on Facebook at facebook.com/fantagraphics.

Special thanks to Thomas Jensen and Kim Weston.

First printing, December 2018
ISBN 978-1-68396-123-9

Printed in The Republic of Korea
Library of Congress Control Number: 2018936467

Now available in this series:

Boxed sets of some titles are available at select locations.

Now available in the *Disney Masters* series:

Walt Disney's

Donald Duck

by Carl Barks

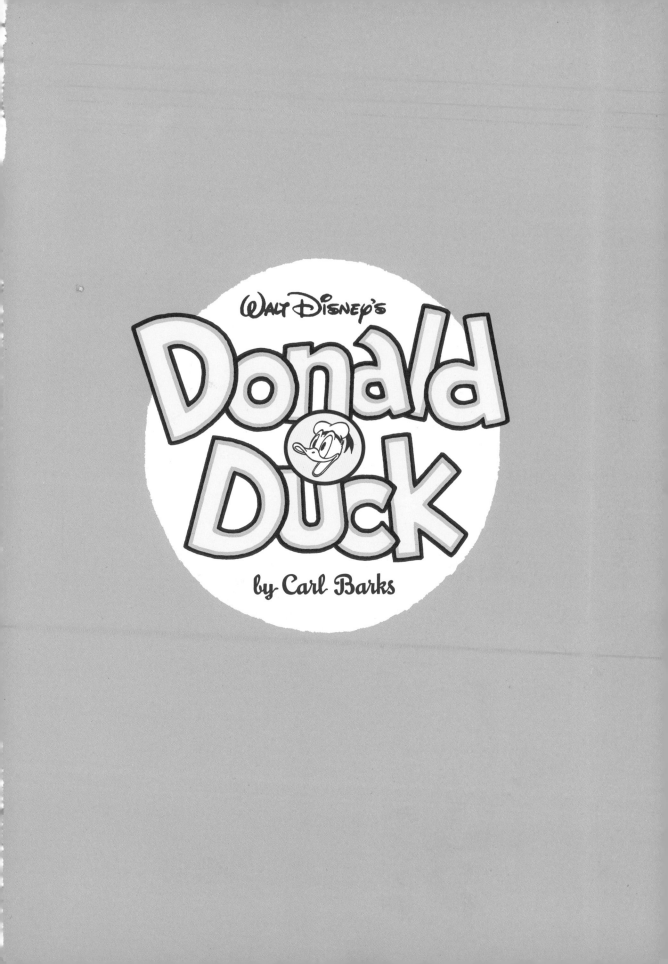

Contents

All comics stories written and drawn by Carl Barks.

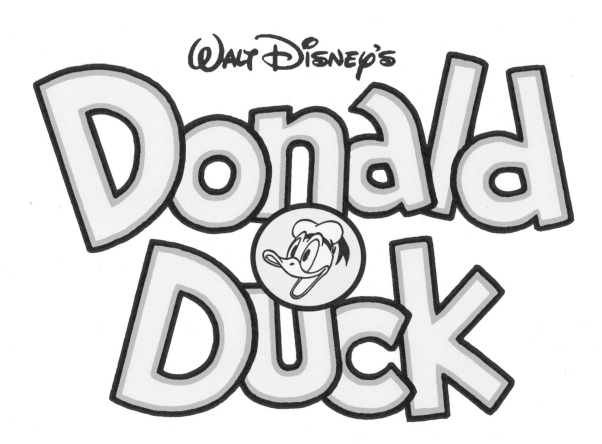

WALT DISNEY'S

Donald Duck

"The Black Pearls of Tabu Yama"

----

by Carl Barks

FANTAGRAPHICS BOOKS
SEATTLE

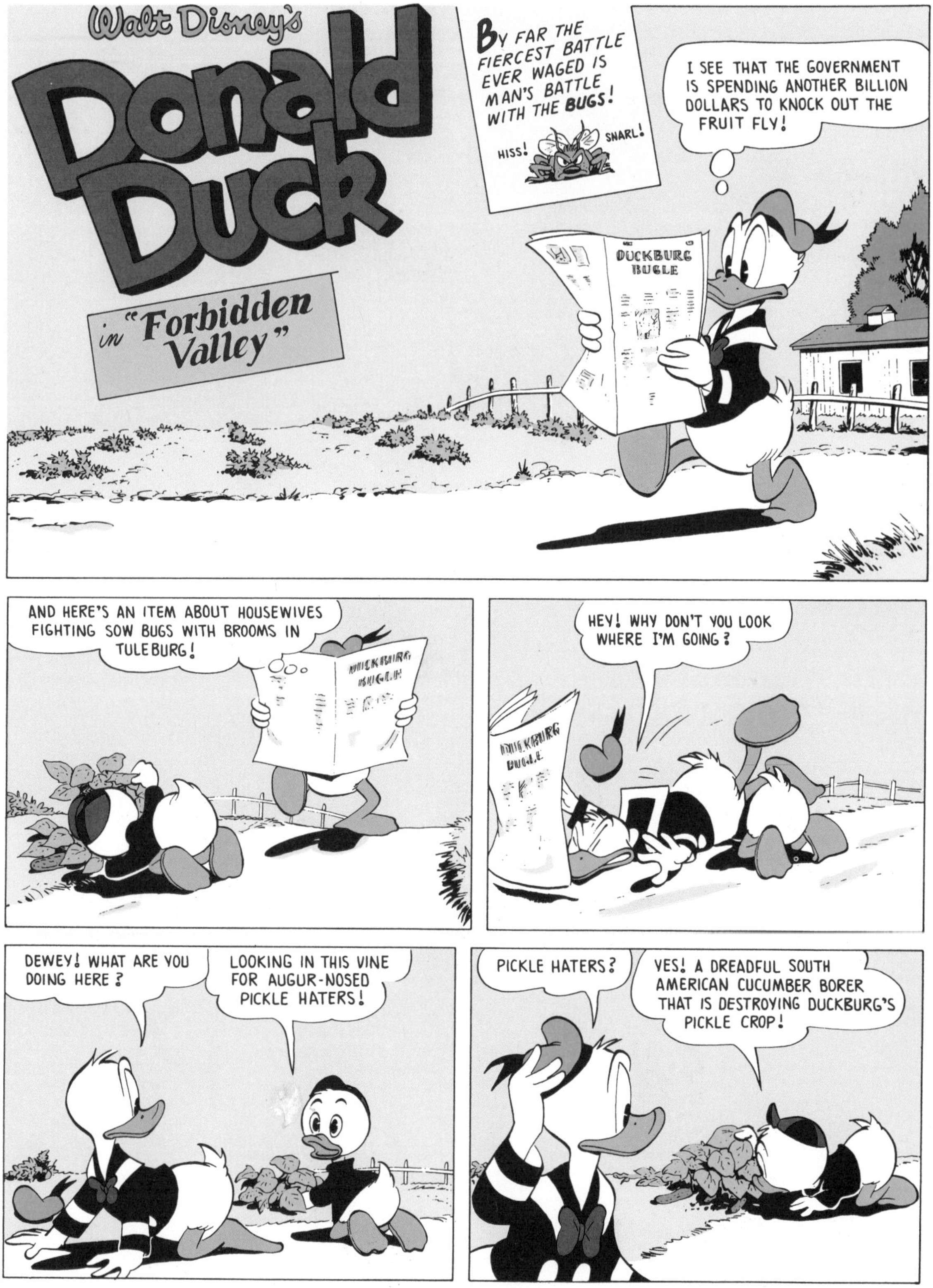
Walt Disney's
Donald Duck
in "Forbidden Valley"
BY FAR THE FIERCEST BATTLE EVER WAGED IS MAN'S BATTLE WITH THE BUGS!
HISS!
SNARL!
I SEE THAT THE GOVERNMENT IS SPENDING ANOTHER BILLION DOLLARS TO KNOCK OUT THE FRUIT FLY!
DUCKBURG BUGLE
AND HERE'S AN ITEM ABOUT HOUSEWIVES FIGHTING SOW BUGS WITH BROOMS IN TULEBURG!
HEY! WHY DON'T YOU LOOK WHERE I'M GOING?
DEWEY! WHAT ARE YOU DOING HERE?
LOOKING IN THIS VINE FOR AUGUR-NOSED PICKLE HATERS!
PICKLE HATERS?
YES! A DREADFUL SOUTH AMERICAN CUCUMBER BORER THAT IS DESTROYING DUCKBURG'S PICKLE CROP!

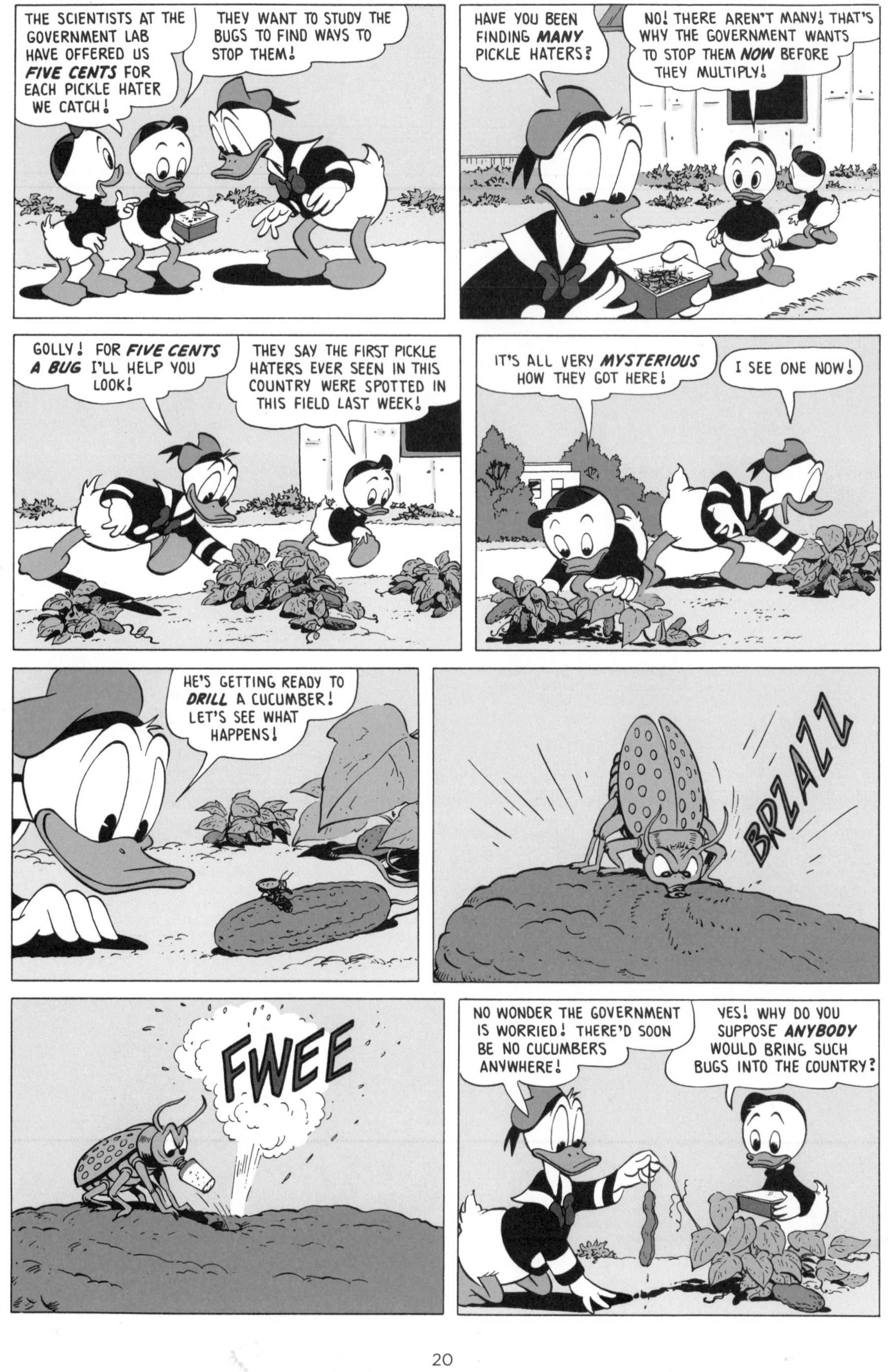
THE SCIENTISTS AT THE GOVERNMENT LAB HAVE OFFERED US FIVE CENTS FOR EACH PICKLE HATER WE CATCH!
THEY WANT TO STUDY THE BUGS TO FIND WAYS TO STOP THEM!
HAVE YOU BEEN FINDING MANY PICKLE HATERS?
NO! THERE AREN'T MANY! THAT'S WHY THE GOVERNMENT WANTS TO STOP THEM NOW BEFORE THEY MULTIPLY!
GOLLY! FOR FIVE CENTS A BUG I'LL HELP YOU LOOK!
THEY SAY THE FIRST PICKLE HATERS EVER SEEN IN THIS COUNTRY WERE SPOTTED IN THIS FIELD LAST WEEK!
IT'S ALL VERY MYSTERIOUS HOW THEY GOT HERE!
I SEE ONE NOW!
HE'S GETTING READY TO DRILL A CUCUMBER! LET'S SEE WHAT HAPPENS!
BRZAZZ
FWEE
NO WONDER THE GOVERNMENT IS WORRIED! THERE'D SOON BE NO CUCUMBERS ANYWHERE!
YES! WHY DO YOU SUPPOSE ANYBODY WOULD BRING SUCH BUGS INTO THE COUNTRY?

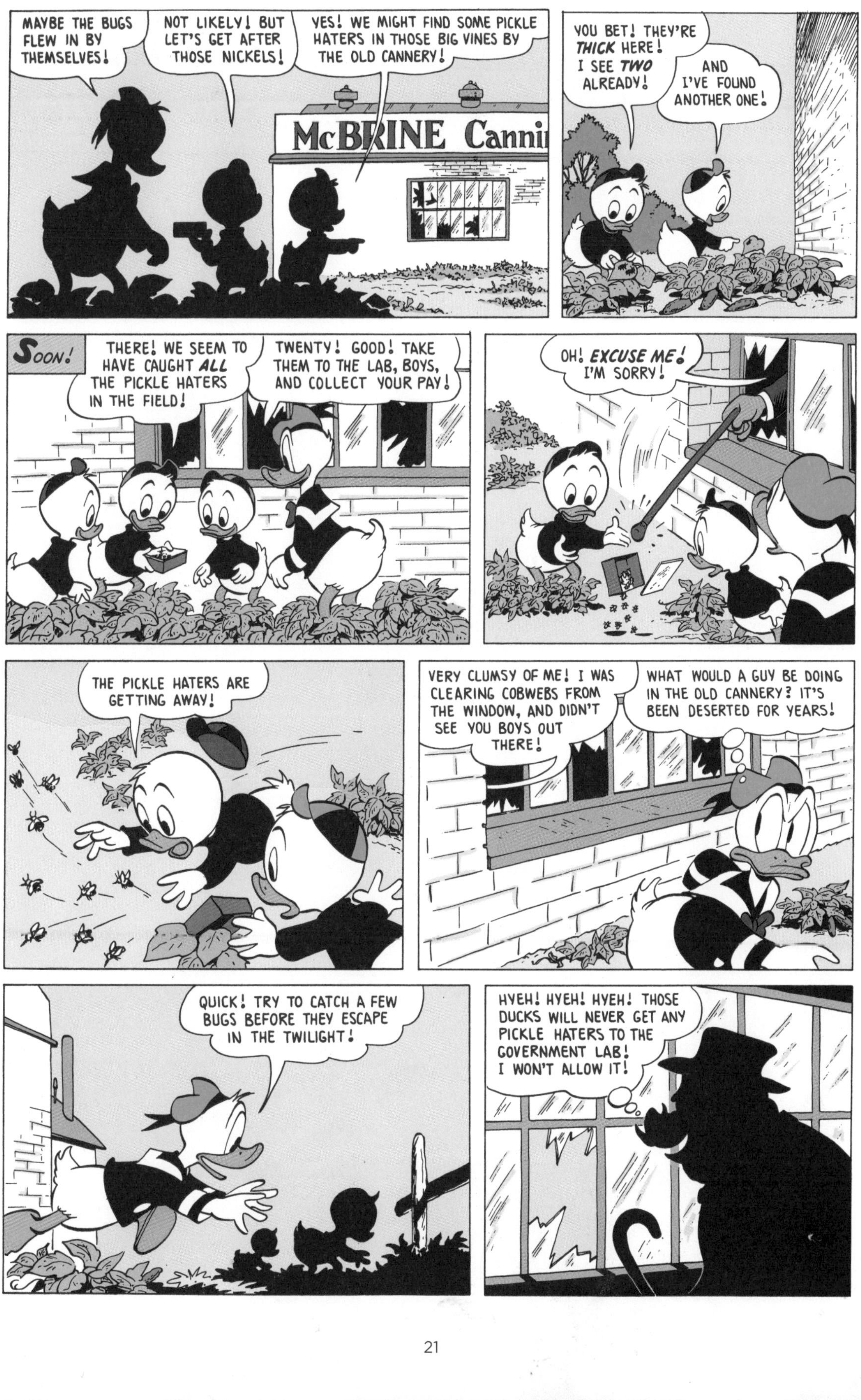
MAYBE THE BUGS FLEW IN BY THEMSELVES!
NOT LIKELY! BUT LET'S GET AFTER THOSE NICKELS!
YES! WE MIGHT FIND SOME PICKLE HATERS IN THOSE BIG VINES BY THE OLD CANNERY!
McBRINE Canni
YOU BET! THEY'RE THICK HERE! I SEE TWO ALREADY!
AND I'VE FOUND ANOTHER ONE!
SOON!
THERE! WE SEEM TO HAVE CAUGHT ALL THE PICKLE HATERS IN THE FIELD!
TWENTY! GOOD! TAKE THEM TO THE LAB, BOYS, AND COLLECT YOUR PAY!
OH! EXCUSE ME! I'M SORRY!
THE PICKLE HATERS ARE GETTING AWAY!
VERY CLUMSY OF ME! I WAS CLEARING COBWEBS FROM THE WINDOW, AND DIDN'T SEE YOU BOYS OUT THERE!
WHAT WOULD A GUY BE DOING IN THE OLD CANNERY? IT'S BEEN DESERTED FOR YEARS!
QUICK! TRY TO CATCH A FEW BUGS BEFORE THEY ESCAPE IN THE TWILIGHT!
HYEH! HYEH! HYEH! THOSE DUCKS WILL NEVER GET ANY PICKLE HATERS TO THE GOVERNMENT LAB! I WON'T ALLOW IT!

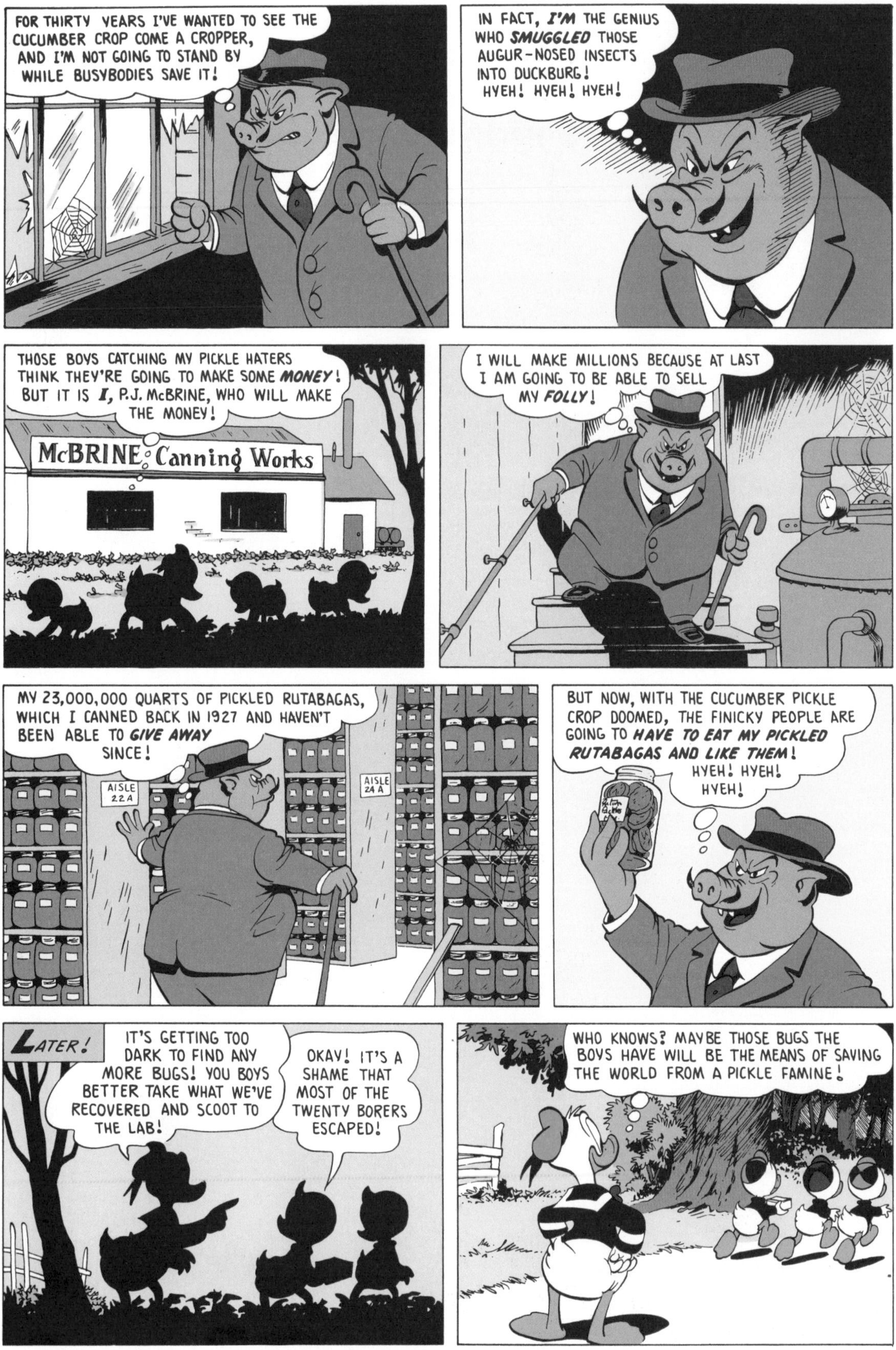
FOR THIRTY YEARS I'VE WANTED TO SEE THE CUCUMBER CROP COME A CROPPER, AND I'M NOT GOING TO STAND BY WHILE BUSYBODIES SAVE IT!
IN FACT, I'M THE GENIUS WHO SMUGGLED THOSE AUGUR-NOSED INSECTS INTO DUCKBURG! HYEH! HYEH! HYEH!
THOSE BOYS CATCHING MY PICKLE HATERS THINK THEY'RE GOING TO MAKE SOME MONEY! BUT IT IS I, P.J. McBRINE, WHO WILL MAKE THE MONEY!
McBRINE Canning Works
I WILL MAKE MILLIONS BECAUSE AT LAST I AM GOING TO BE ABLE TO SELL MY FOLLY!
MY 23,000,000 QUARTS OF PICKLED RUTABAGAS, WHICH I CANNED BACK IN 1927 AND HAVEN'T BEEN ABLE TO GIVE AWAY SINCE!
AISLE 22 A
AISLE 24 A
BUT NOW, WITH THE CUCUMBER PICKLE CROP DOOMED, THE FINICKY PEOPLE ARE GOING TO HAVE TO EAT MY PICKLED RUTABAGAS AND LIKE THEM! HYEH! HYEH! HYEH!
LATER!
IT'S GETTING TOO DARK TO FIND ANY MORE BUGS! YOU BOYS BETTER TAKE WHAT WE'VE RECOVERED AND SCOOT TO THE LAB!
OKAY! IT'S A SHAME THAT MOST OF THE TWENTY BORERS ESCAPED!
WHO KNOWS? MAYBE THOSE BUGS THE BOYS HAVE WILL BE THE MEANS OF SAVING THE WORLD FROM A PICKLE FAMINE!

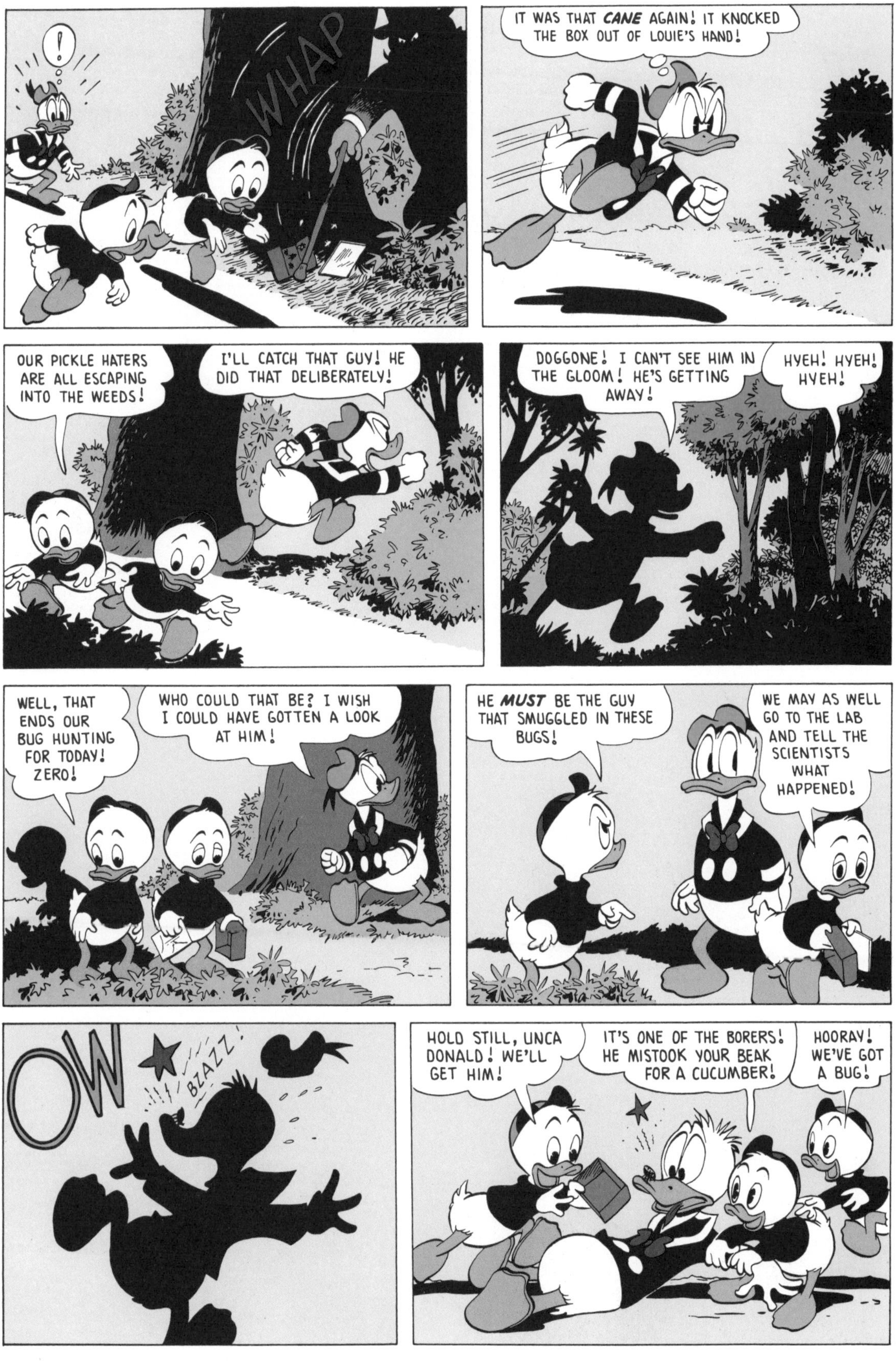
!
WHAP
IT WAS THAT CANE AGAIN! IT KNOCKED THE BOX OUT OF LOUIE'S HAND!
OUR PICKLE HATERS ARE ALL ESCAPING INTO THE WEEDS!
I'LL CATCH THAT GUY! HE DID THAT DELIBERATELY!
DOGGONE! I CAN'T SEE HIM IN THE GLOOM! HE'S GETTING AWAY!
HYEH! HYEH! HYEH!
WELL, THAT ENDS OUR BUG HUNTING FOR TODAY! ZERO!
WHO COULD THAT BE? I WISH I COULD HAVE GOTTEN A LOOK AT HIM!
HE MUST BE THE GUY THAT SMUGGLED IN THESE BUGS!
WE MAY AS WELL GO TO THE LAB AND TELL THE SCIENTISTS WHAT HAPPENED!
OW
BZAZZ!
HOLD STILL, UNCA DONALD! WE'LL GET HIM!
IT'S ONE OF THE BORERS! HE MISTOOK YOUR BEAK FOR A CUCUMBER!
HOORAY! WE'VE GOT A BUG!

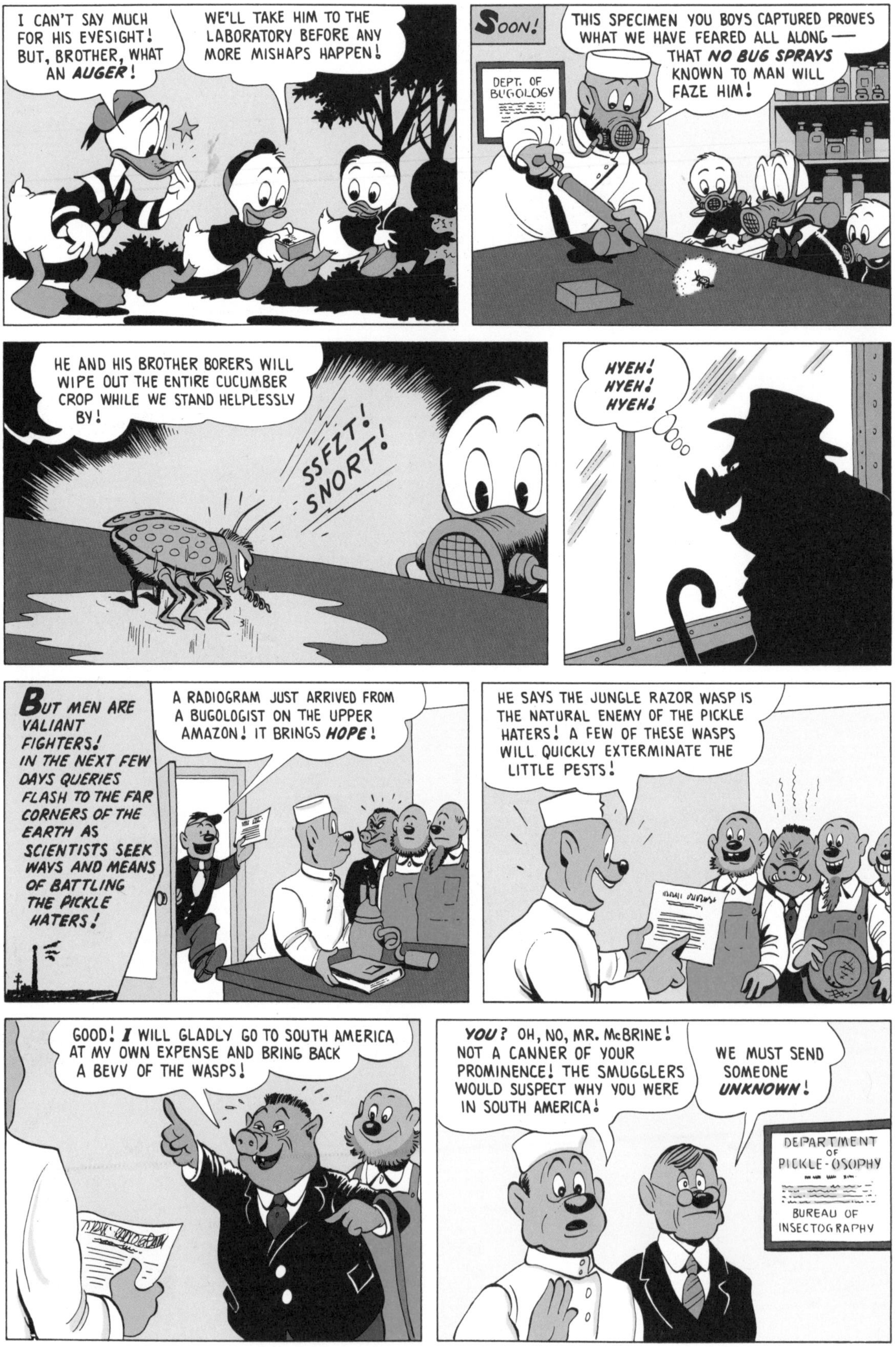
I CAN'T SAY MUCH FOR HIS EYESIGHT! BUT, BROTHER, WHAT AN **AUGER**!
WE'LL TAKE HIM TO THE LABORATORY BEFORE ANY MORE MISHAPS HAPPEN!
SOON!
THIS SPECIMEN YOU BOYS CAPTURED PROVES WHAT WE HAVE FEARED ALL ALONG— THAT **NO BUG SPRAYS** KNOWN TO MAN WILL FAZE HIM!
DEPT. OF BUGOLOGY
HE AND HIS BROTHER BORERS WILL WIPE OUT THE ENTIRE CUCUMBER CROP WHILE WE STAND HELPLESSLY BY!
SSFZT! SNORT!
HYEH! HYEH! HYEH!
BUT MEN ARE VALIANT FIGHTERS! IN THE NEXT FEW DAYS QUERIES FLASH TO THE FAR CORNERS OF THE EARTH AS SCIENTISTS SEEK WAYS AND MEANS OF BATTLING THE PICKLE HATERS!
A RADIOGRAM JUST ARRIVED FROM A BUGOLOGIST ON THE UPPER AMAZON! IT BRINGS **HOPE**!
HE SAYS THE JUNGLE RAZOR WASP IS THE NATURAL ENEMY OF THE PICKLE HATERS! A FEW OF THESE WASPS WILL QUICKLY EXTERMINATE THE LITTLE PESTS!
GOOD! **I** WILL GLADLY GO TO SOUTH AMERICA AT MY OWN EXPENSE AND BRING BACK A BEVY OF THE WASPS!
YOU? OH, NO, MR. McBRINE! NOT A CANNER OF YOUR PROMINENCE! THE SMUGGLERS WOULD SUSPECT WHY YOU WERE IN SOUTH AMERICA!
WE MUST SEND SOMEONE **UNKNOWN**!
DEPARTMENT OF PICKLE-OSOPHY
BUREAU OF INSECTOGRAPHY

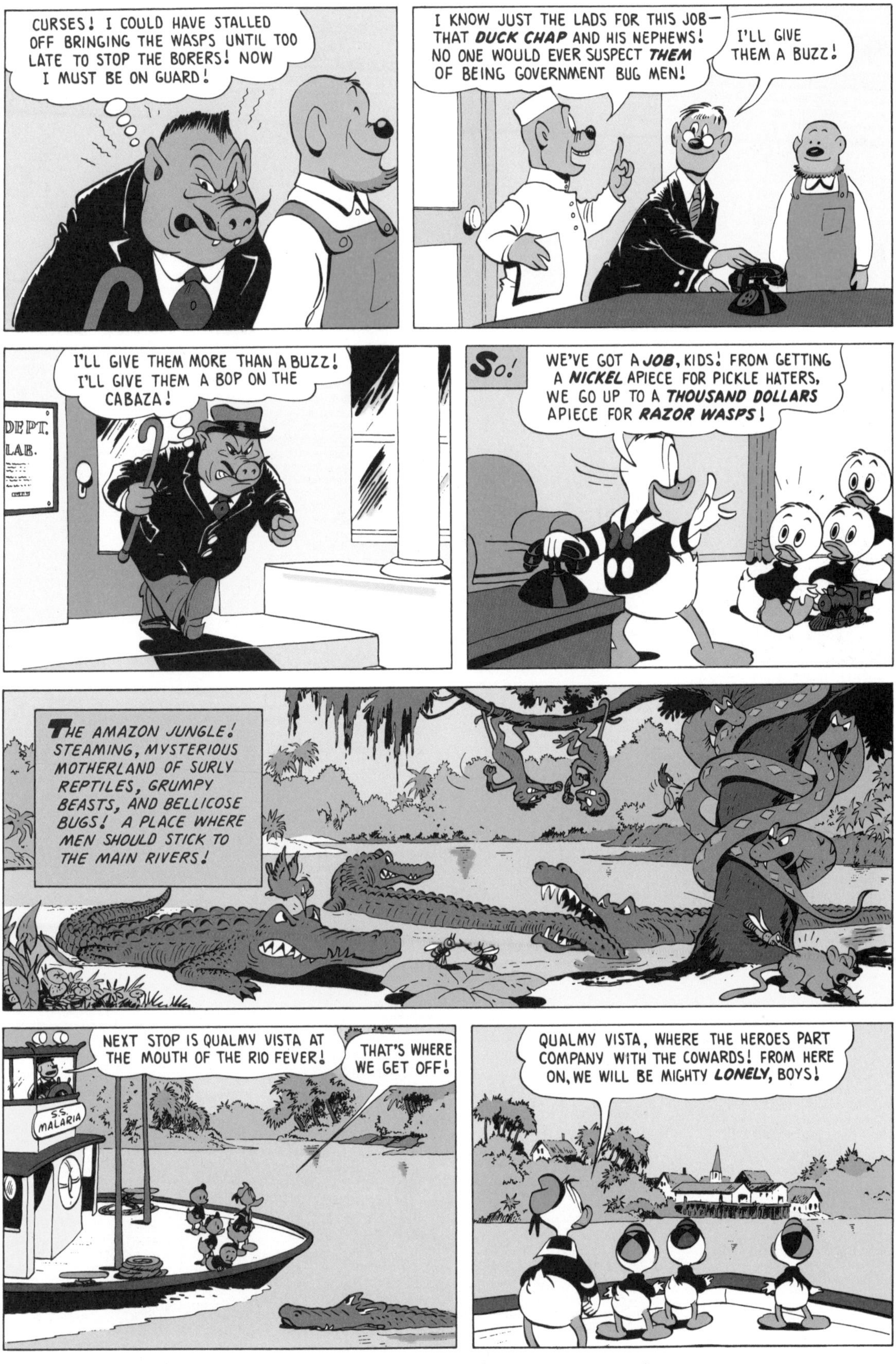
CURSES! I COULD HAVE STALLED OFF BRINGING THE WASPS UNTIL TOO LATE TO STOP THE BORERS! NOW I MUST BE ON GUARD!
I KNOW JUST THE LADS FOR THIS JOB— THAT DUCK CHAP AND HIS NEPHEWS! NO ONE WOULD EVER SUSPECT THEM OF BEING GOVERNMENT BUG MEN!
I'LL GIVE THEM A BUZZ!
I'LL GIVE THEM MORE THAN A BUZZ! I'LL GIVE THEM A BOP ON THE CABAZA!
DEPT. LAB.
SO! WE'VE GOT A JOB, KIDS! FROM GETTING A NICKEL APIECE FOR PICKLE HATERS, WE GO UP TO A THOUSAND DOLLARS APIECE FOR RAZOR WASPS!
THE AMAZON JUNGLE! STEAMING, MYSTERIOUS MOTHERLAND OF SURLY REPTILES, GRUMPY BEASTS, AND BELLICOSE BUGS! A PLACE WHERE MEN SHOULD STICK TO THE MAIN RIVERS!
NEXT STOP IS QUALMY VISTA AT THE MOUTH OF THE RIO FEVER!
THAT'S WHERE WE GET OFF!
S.S. MALARIA
QUALMY VISTA, WHERE THE HEROES PART COMPANY WITH THE COWARDS! FROM HERE ON, WE WILL BE MIGHTY LONELY, BOYS!

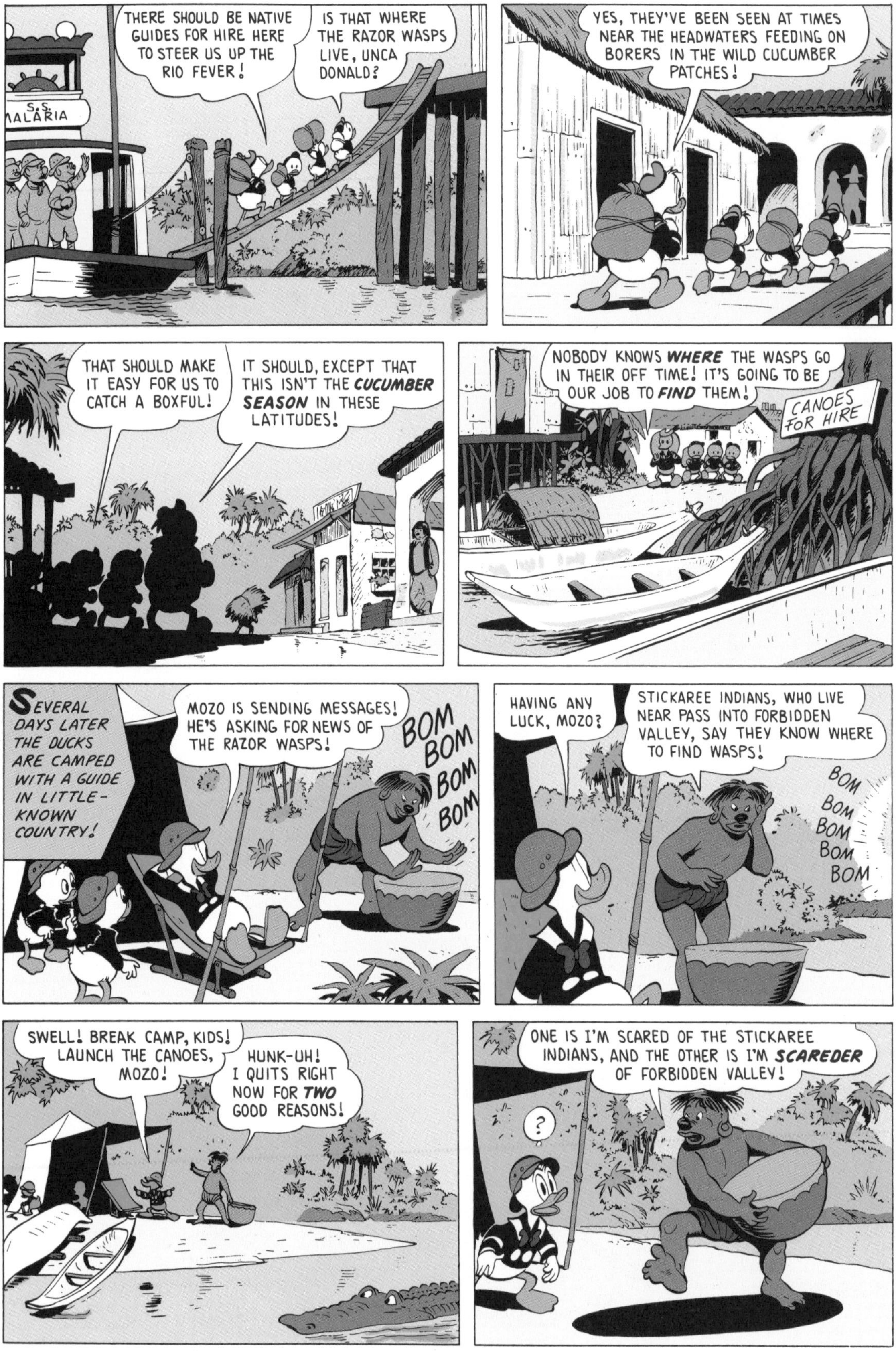
THERE SHOULD BE NATIVE GUIDES FOR HIRE HERE TO STEER US UP THE RIO FEVER!
IS THAT WHERE THE RAZOR WASPS LIVE, UNCA DONALD?
S.S. MALARIA
YES, THEY'VE BEEN SEEN AT TIMES NEAR THE HEADWATERS FEEDING ON BORERS IN THE WILD CUCUMBER PATCHES!
THAT SHOULD MAKE IT EASY FOR US TO CATCH A BOXFUL!
IT SHOULD, EXCEPT THAT THIS ISN'T THE **CUCUMBER SEASON** IN THESE LATITUDES!
NOBODY KNOWS **WHERE** THE WASPS GO IN THEIR OFF TIME! IT'S GOING TO BE OUR JOB TO **FIND** THEM!
CANOES FOR HIRE
SEVERAL DAYS LATER THE DUCKS ARE CAMPED WITH A GUIDE IN LITTLE-KNOWN COUNTRY!
MOZO IS SENDING MESSAGES! HE'S ASKING FOR NEWS OF THE RAZOR WASPS!
BOM BOM BOM BOM
HAVING ANY LUCK, MOZO?
STICKAREE INDIANS, WHO LIVE NEAR PASS INTO FORBIDDEN VALLEY, SAY THEY KNOW WHERE TO FIND WASPS!
BOM BOM BOM BOM BOM
SWELL! BREAK CAMP, KIDS! LAUNCH THE CANOES, MOZO!
HUNK-UH! I QUITS RIGHT NOW FOR **TWO** GOOD REASONS!
ONE IS I'M SCARED OF THE STICKAREE INDIANS, AND THE OTHER IS I'M **SCAREDER** OF FORBIDDEN VALLEY!
?

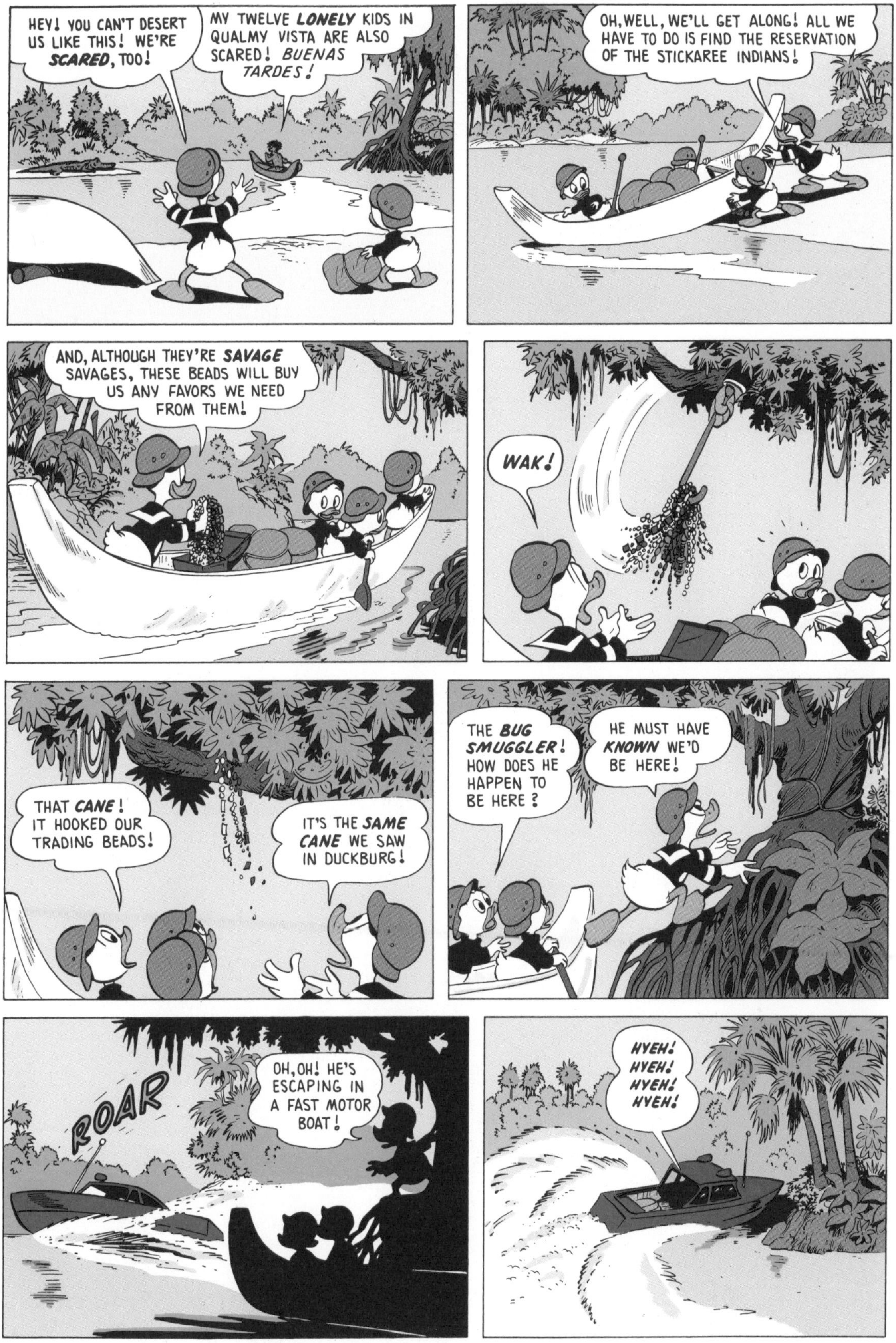
HEY! YOU CAN'T DESERT US LIKE THIS! WE'RE SCARED, TOO!
MY TWELVE LONELY KIDS IN QUALMY VISTA ARE ALSO SCARED! BUENAS TARDES!
OH, WELL, WE'LL GET ALONG! ALL WE HAVE TO DO IS FIND THE RESERVATION OF THE STICKAREE INDIANS!
AND, ALTHOUGH THEY'RE SAVAGE SAVAGES, THESE BEADS WILL BUY US ANY FAVORS WE NEED FROM THEM!
WAK!
THAT CANE! IT HOOKED OUR TRADING BEADS!
IT'S THE SAME CANE WE SAW IN DUCKBURG!
THE BUG SMUGGLER! HOW DOES HE HAPPEN TO BE HERE?
HE MUST HAVE KNOWN WE'D BE HERE!
ROAR
OH, OH! HE'S ESCAPING IN A FAST MOTOR BOAT!
HYEH! HYEH! HYEH! HYEH!

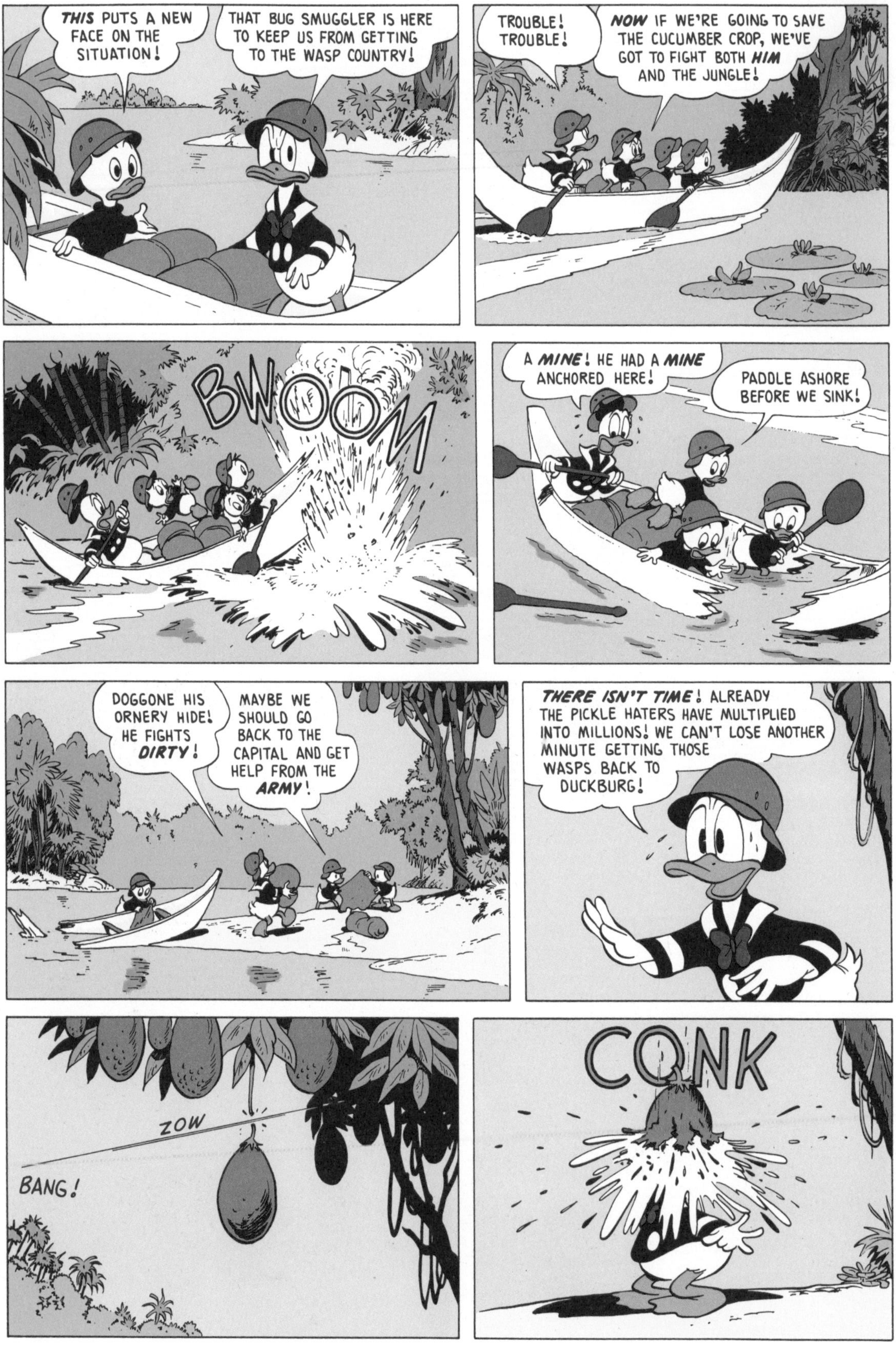
THIS PUTS A NEW FACE ON THE SITUATION!
THAT BUG SMUGGLER IS HERE TO KEEP US FROM GETTING TO THE WASP COUNTRY!
TROUBLE! TROUBLE!
NOW IF WE'RE GOING TO SAVE THE CUCUMBER CROP, WE'VE GOT TO FIGHT BOTH HIM AND THE JUNGLE!
BWOOM
A MINE! HE HAD A MINE ANCHORED HERE!
PADDLE ASHORE BEFORE WE SINK!
DOGGONE HIS ORNERY HIDE! HE FIGHTS DIRTY!
MAYBE WE SHOULD GO BACK TO THE CAPITAL AND GET HELP FROM THE ARMY!
THERE ISN'T TIME! ALREADY THE PICKLE HATERS HAVE MULTIPLIED INTO MILLIONS! WE CAN'T LOSE ANOTHER MINUTE GETTING THOSE WASPS BACK TO DUCKBURG!
ZOW
BANG!
CONK

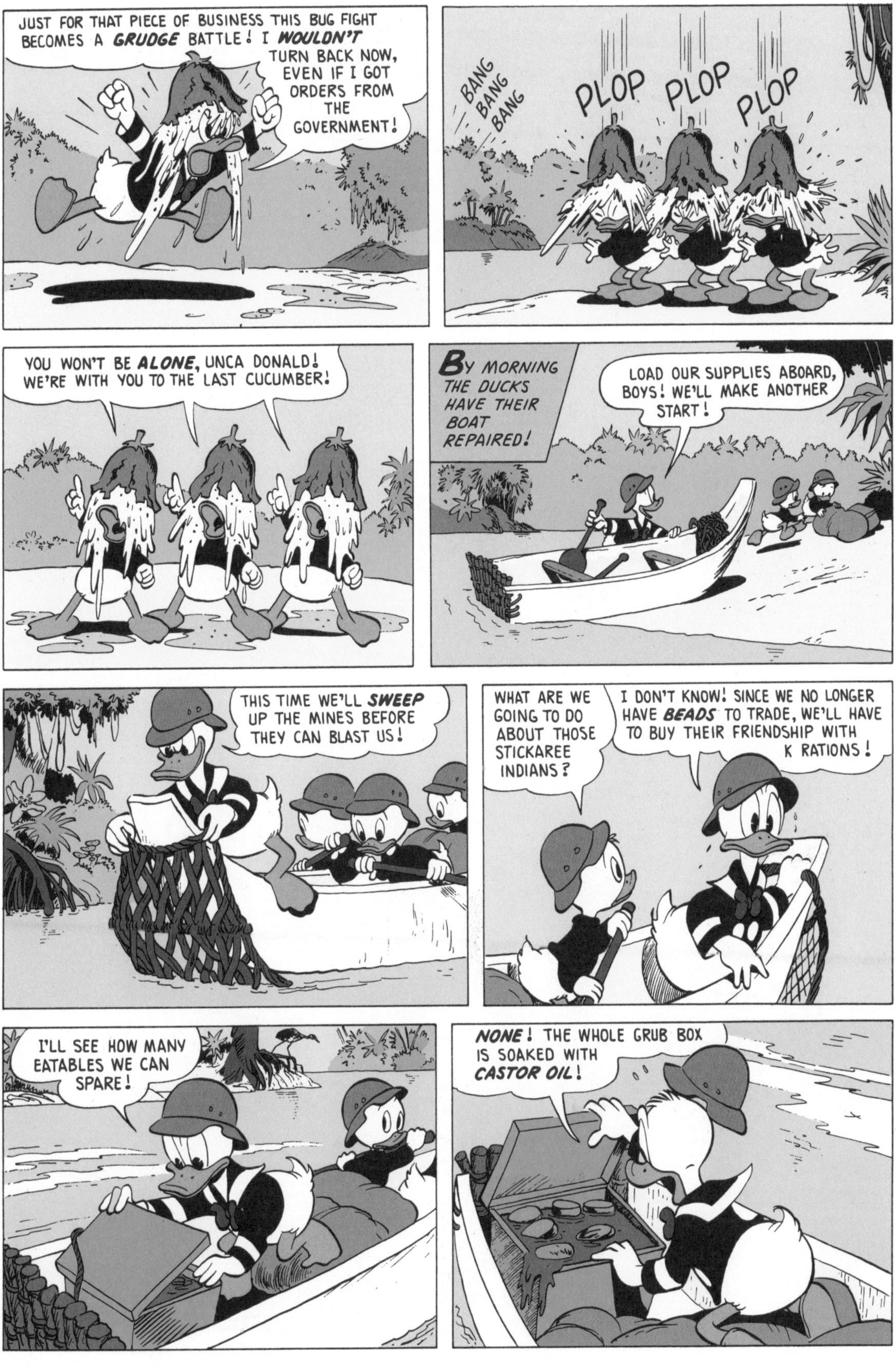

JUST FOR THAT PIECE OF BUSINESS THIS BUG FIGHT BECOMES A **GRUDGE** BATTLE! I **WOULDN'T** TURN BACK NOW, EVEN IF I GOT ORDERS FROM THE GOVERNMENT!
BANG BANG BANG
PLOP PLOP PLOP
YOU WON'T BE **ALONE**, UNCA DONALD! WE'RE WITH YOU TO THE LAST CUCUMBER!
BY MORNING THE DUCKS HAVE THEIR BOAT REPAIRED!
LOAD OUR SUPPLIES ABOARD, BOYS! WE'LL MAKE ANOTHER START!
THIS TIME WE'LL **SWEEP** UP THE MINES BEFORE THEY CAN BLAST US!
WHAT ARE WE GOING TO DO ABOUT THOSE STICKAREE INDIANS?
I DON'T KNOW! SINCE WE NO LONGER HAVE **BEADS** TO TRADE, WE'LL HAVE TO BUY THEIR FRIENDSHIP WITH K RATIONS!
I'LL SEE HOW MANY EATABLES WE CAN SPARE!
NONE! THE WHOLE GRUB BOX IS SOAKED WITH **CASTOR OIL**!

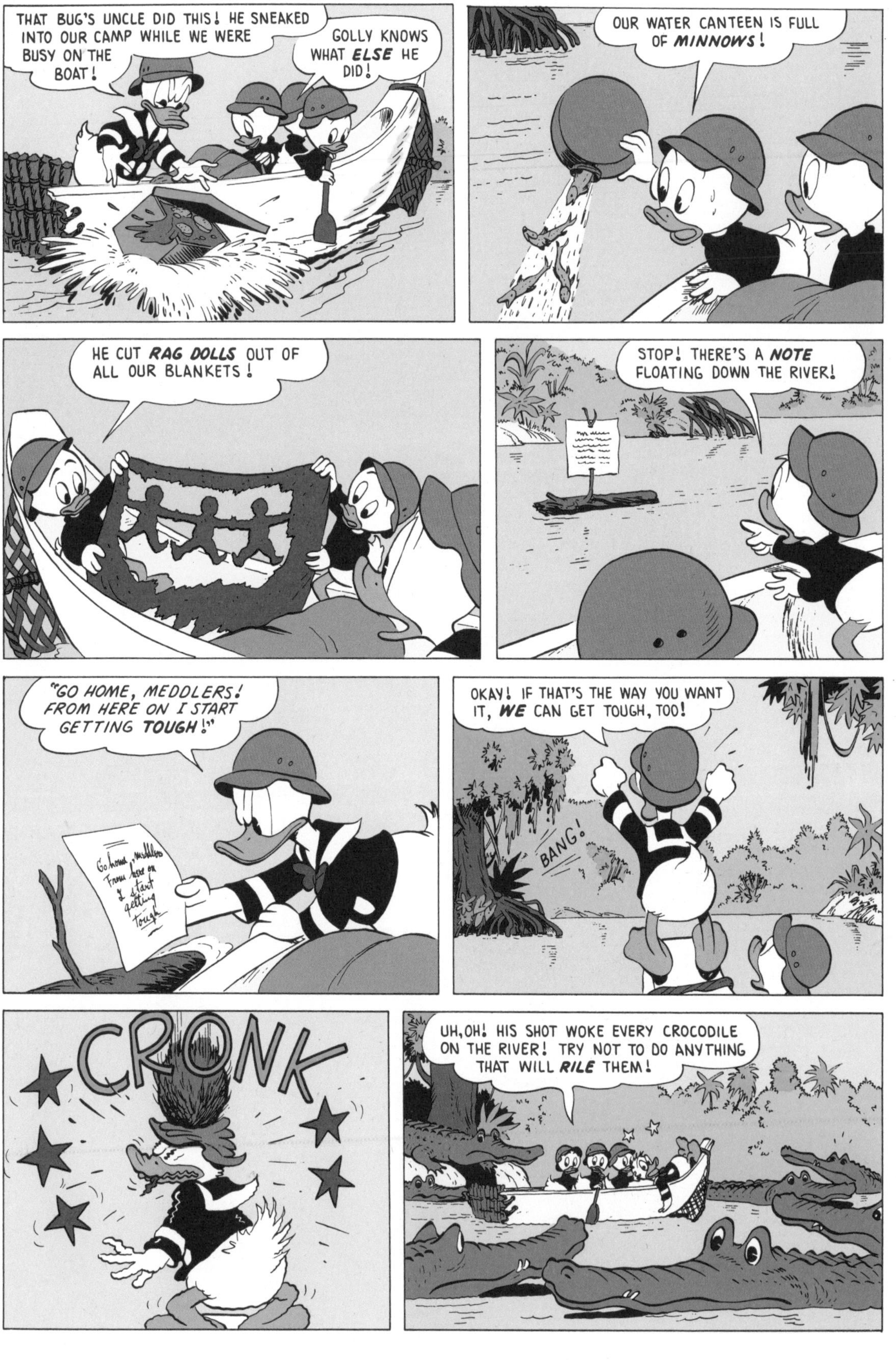
THAT BUG'S UNCLE DID THIS! HE SNEAKED INTO OUR CAMP WHILE WE WERE BUSY ON THE BOAT!
GOLLY KNOWS WHAT ELSE HE DID!
OUR WATER CANTEEN IS FULL OF MINNOWS!
HE CUT RAG DOLLS OUT OF ALL OUR BLANKETS!
STOP! THERE'S A NOTE FLOATING DOWN THE RIVER!
"GO HOME, MEDDLERS! FROM HERE ON I START GETTING TOUGH!"
OKAY! IF THAT'S THE WAY YOU WANT IT, WE CAN GET TOUGH, TOO!
BANG!
CRONK
UH, OH! HIS SHOT WOKE EVERY CROCODILE ON THE RIVER! TRY NOT TO DO ANYTHING THAT WILL RILE THEM!

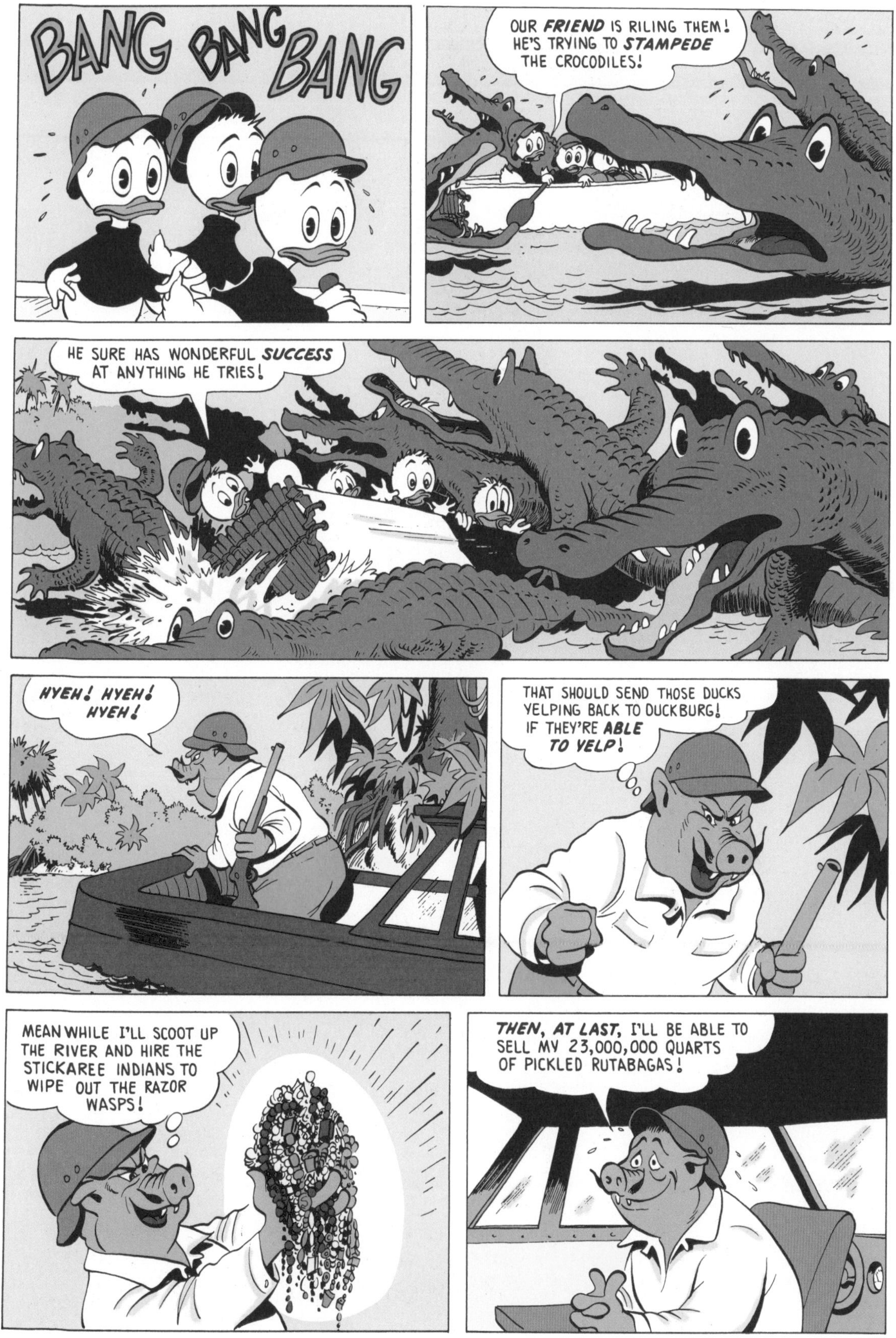

BANG BANG BANG
OUR FRIEND IS RILING THEM! HE'S TRYING TO STAMPEDE THE CROCODILES!
HE SURE HAS WONDERFUL SUCCESS AT ANYTHING HE TRIES!
HYEH! HYEH! HYEH!
THAT SHOULD SEND THOSE DUCKS YELPING BACK TO DUCKBURG! IF THEY'RE ABLE TO VELP!
MEANWHILE I'LL SCOOT UP THE RIVER AND HIRE THE STICKAREE INDIANS TO WIPE OUT THE RAZOR WASPS!
THEN, AT LAST, I'LL BE ABLE TO SELL MY 23,000,000 QUARTS OF PICKLED RUTABAGAS!

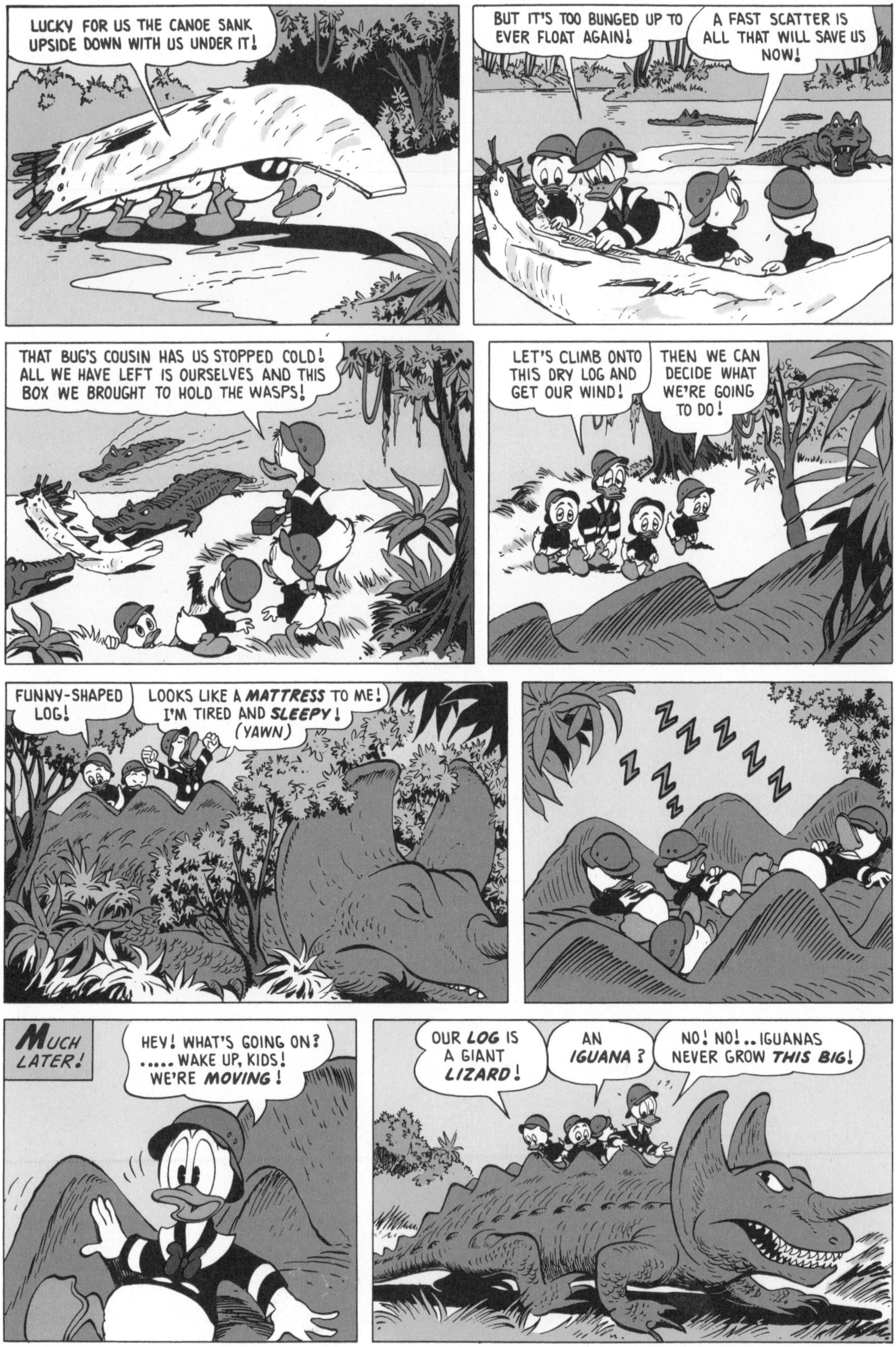
LUCKY FOR US THE CANOE SANK UPSIDE DOWN WITH US UNDER IT!
BUT IT'S TOO BUNGED UP TO EVER FLOAT AGAIN!
A FAST SCATTER IS ALL THAT WILL SAVE US NOW!
THAT BUG'S COUSIN HAS US STOPPED COLD! ALL WE HAVE LEFT IS OURSELVES AND THIS BOX WE BROUGHT TO HOLD THE WASPS!
LET'S CLIMB ONTO THIS DRY LOG AND GET OUR WIND!
THEN WE CAN DECIDE WHAT WE'RE GOING TO DO!
FUNNY-SHAPED LOG!
LOOKS LIKE A MATTRESS TO ME! I'M TIRED AND SLEEPY! (YAWN)
Z Z Z Z Z Z Z Z
MUCH LATER!
HEY! WHAT'S GOING ON? ..... WAKE UP, KIDS! WE'RE MOVING!
OUR LOG IS A GIANT LIZARD!
AN IGUANA?
NO! NO! .. IGUANAS NEVER GROW THIS BIG!

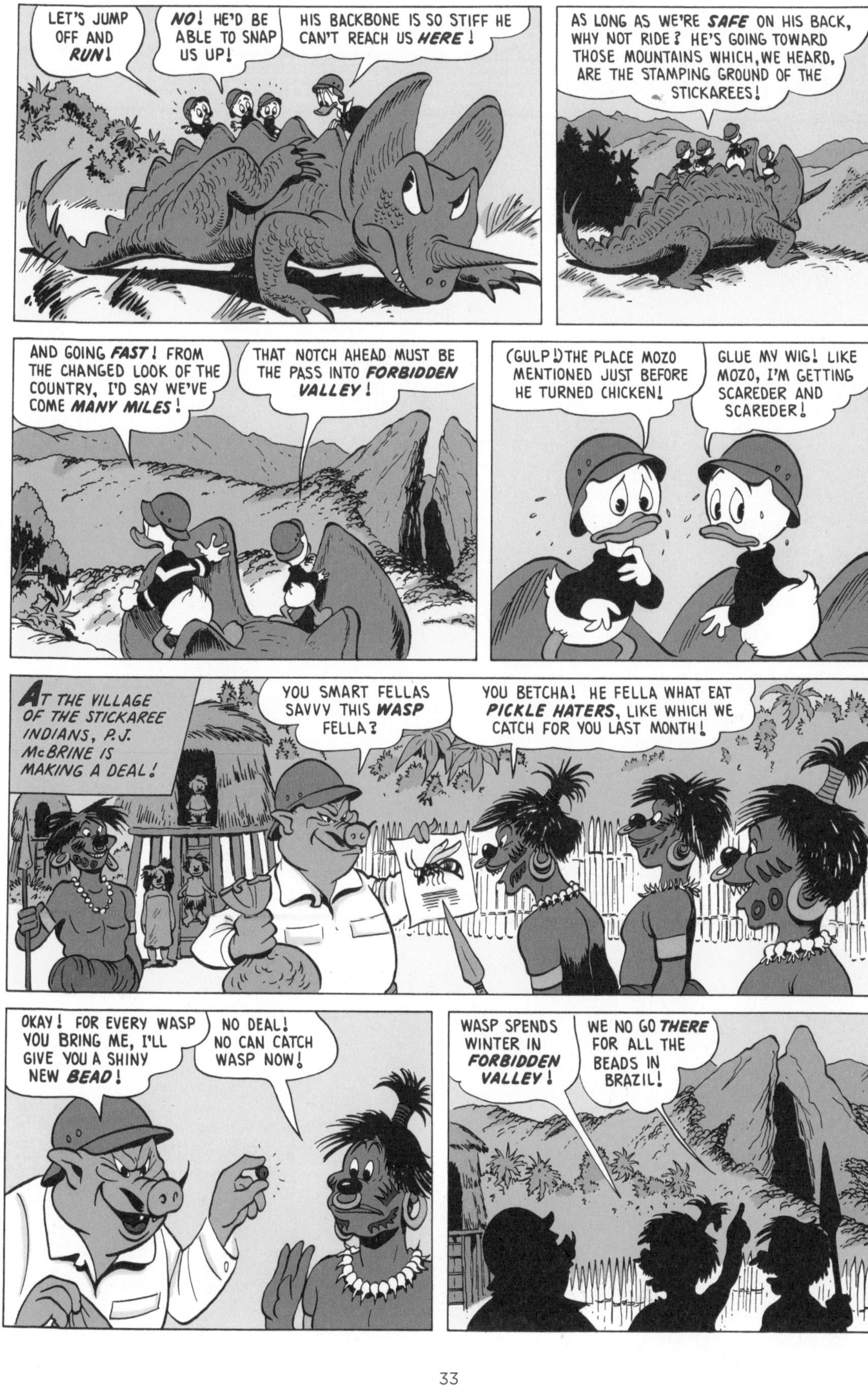
LET'S JUMP OFF AND RUN!
NO! HE'D BE ABLE TO SNAP US UP!
HIS BACKBONE IS SO STIFF HE CAN'T REACH US HERE!
AS LONG AS WE'RE SAFE ON HIS BACK, WHY NOT RIDE? HE'S GOING TOWARD THOSE MOUNTAINS WHICH, WE HEARD, ARE THE STAMPING GROUND OF THE STICKAREES!
AND GOING FAST! FROM THE CHANGED LOOK OF THE COUNTRY, I'D SAY WE'VE COME MANY MILES!
THAT NOTCH AHEAD MUST BE THE PASS INTO FORBIDDEN VALLEY!
(GULP!) THE PLACE MOZO MENTIONED JUST BEFORE HE TURNED CHICKEN!
GLUE MY WIG! LIKE MOZO, I'M GETTING SCAREDER AND SCAREDER!
AT THE VILLAGE OF THE STICKAREE INDIANS, P.J. McBRINE IS MAKING A DEAL!
YOU SMART FELLAS SAVVY THIS WASP FELLA?
YOU BETCHA! HE FELLA WHAT EAT PICKLE HATERS, LIKE WHICH WE CATCH FOR YOU LAST MONTH!
OKAY! FOR EVERY WASP YOU BRING ME, I'LL GIVE YOU A SHINY NEW BEAD!
NO DEAL! NO CAN CATCH WASP NOW!
WASP SPENDS WINTER IN FORBIDDEN VALLEY!
WE NO GO THERE FOR ALL THE BEADS IN BRAZIL!

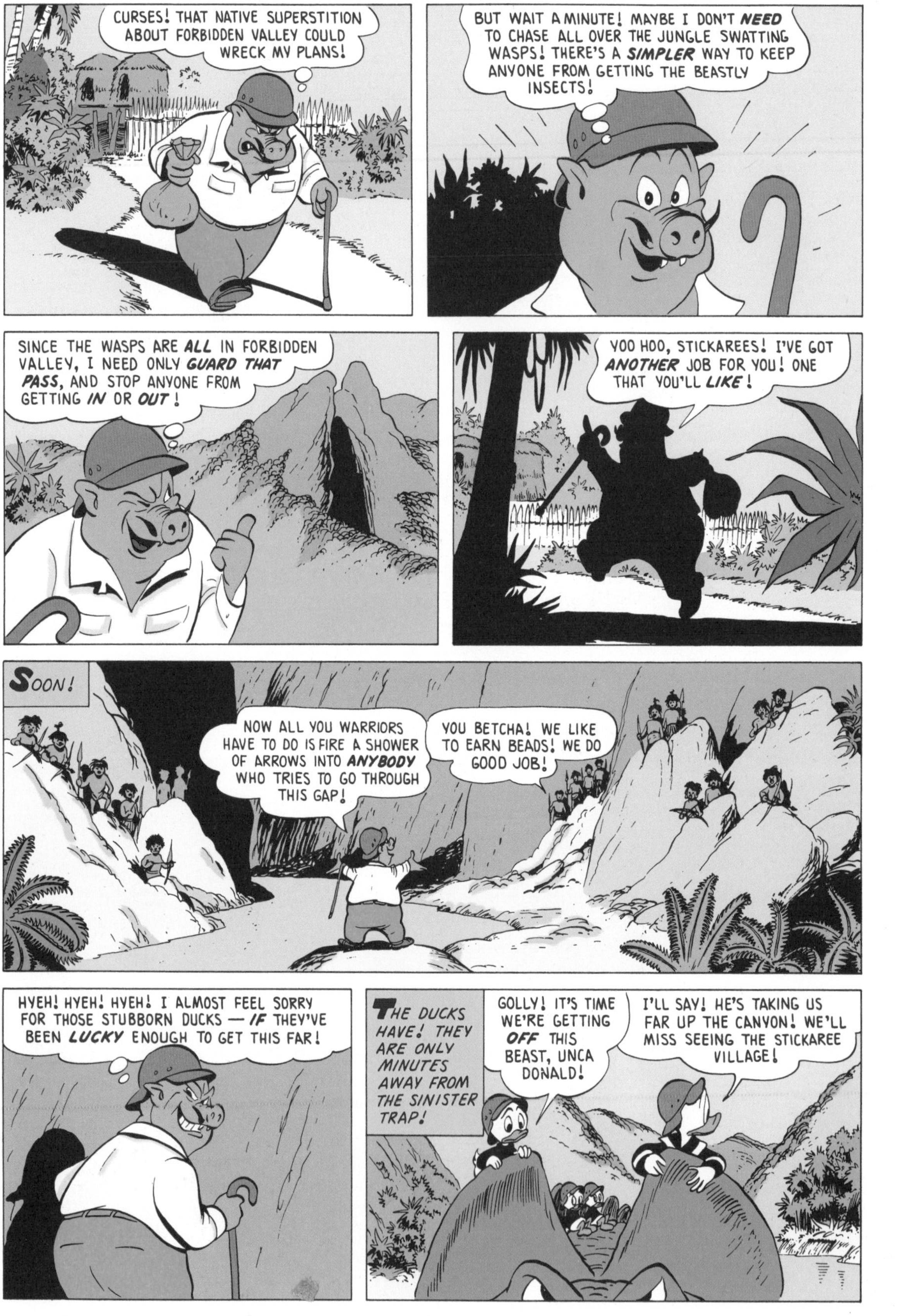
CURSES! THAT NATIVE SUPERSTITION ABOUT FORBIDDEN VALLEY COULD WRECK MY PLANS!
BUT WAIT A MINUTE! MAYBE I DON'T NEED TO CHASE ALL OVER THE JUNGLE SWATTING WASPS! THERE'S A SIMPLER WAY TO KEEP ANYONE FROM GETTING THE BEASTLY INSECTS!
SINCE THE WASPS ARE ALL IN FORBIDDEN VALLEY, I NEED ONLY GUARD THAT PASS, AND STOP ANYONE FROM GETTING IN OR OUT!
YOO HOO, STICKAREES! I'VE GOT ANOTHER JOB FOR YOU! ONE THAT YOU'LL LIKE!
SOON!
NOW ALL YOU WARRIORS HAVE TO DO IS FIRE A SHOWER OF ARROWS INTO ANYBODY WHO TRIES TO GO THROUGH THIS GAP!
YOU BETCHA! WE LIKE TO EARN BEADS! WE DO GOOD JOB!
HYEH! HYEH! HYEH! I ALMOST FEEL SORRY FOR THOSE STUBBORN DUCKS — IF THEY'VE BEEN LUCKY ENOUGH TO GET THIS FAR!
THE DUCKS HAVE! THEY ARE ONLY MINUTES AWAY FROM THE SINISTER TRAP!
GOLLY! IT'S TIME WE'RE GETTING OFF THIS BEAST, UNCA DONALD!
I'LL SAY! HE'S TAKING US FAR UP THE CANYON! WE'LL MISS SEEING THE STICKAREE VILLAGE!

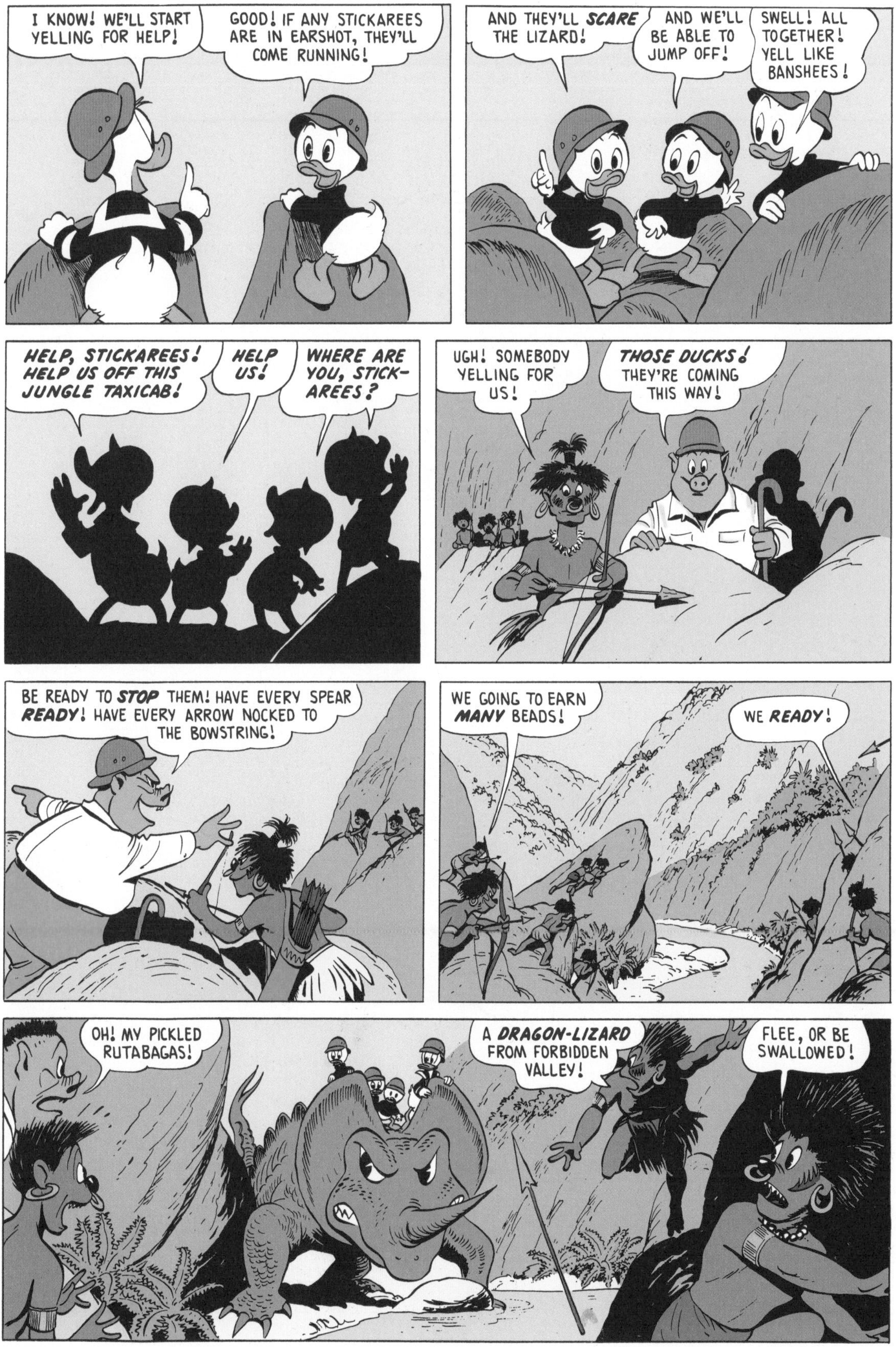
I KNOW! WE'LL START YELLING FOR HELP!
GOOD! IF ANY STICKAREES ARE IN EARSHOT, THEY'LL COME RUNNING!
AND THEY'LL SCARE THE LIZARD!
AND WE'LL BE ABLE TO JUMP OFF!
SWELL! ALL TOGETHER! YELL LIKE BANSHEES!
HELP, STICKAREES! HELP US OFF THIS JUNGLE TAXICAB!
HELP US!
WHERE ARE YOU, STICKAREES?
UGH! SOMEBODY YELLING FOR US!
THOSE DUCKS! THEY'RE COMING THIS WAY!
BE READY TO STOP THEM! HAVE EVERY SPEAR READY! HAVE EVERY ARROW NOCKED TO THE BOWSTRING!
WE GOING TO EARN MANY BEADS!
WE READY!
OH! MY PICKLED RUTABAGAS!
A DRAGON-LIZARD FROM FORBIDDEN VALLEY!
FLEE, OR BE SWALLOWED!

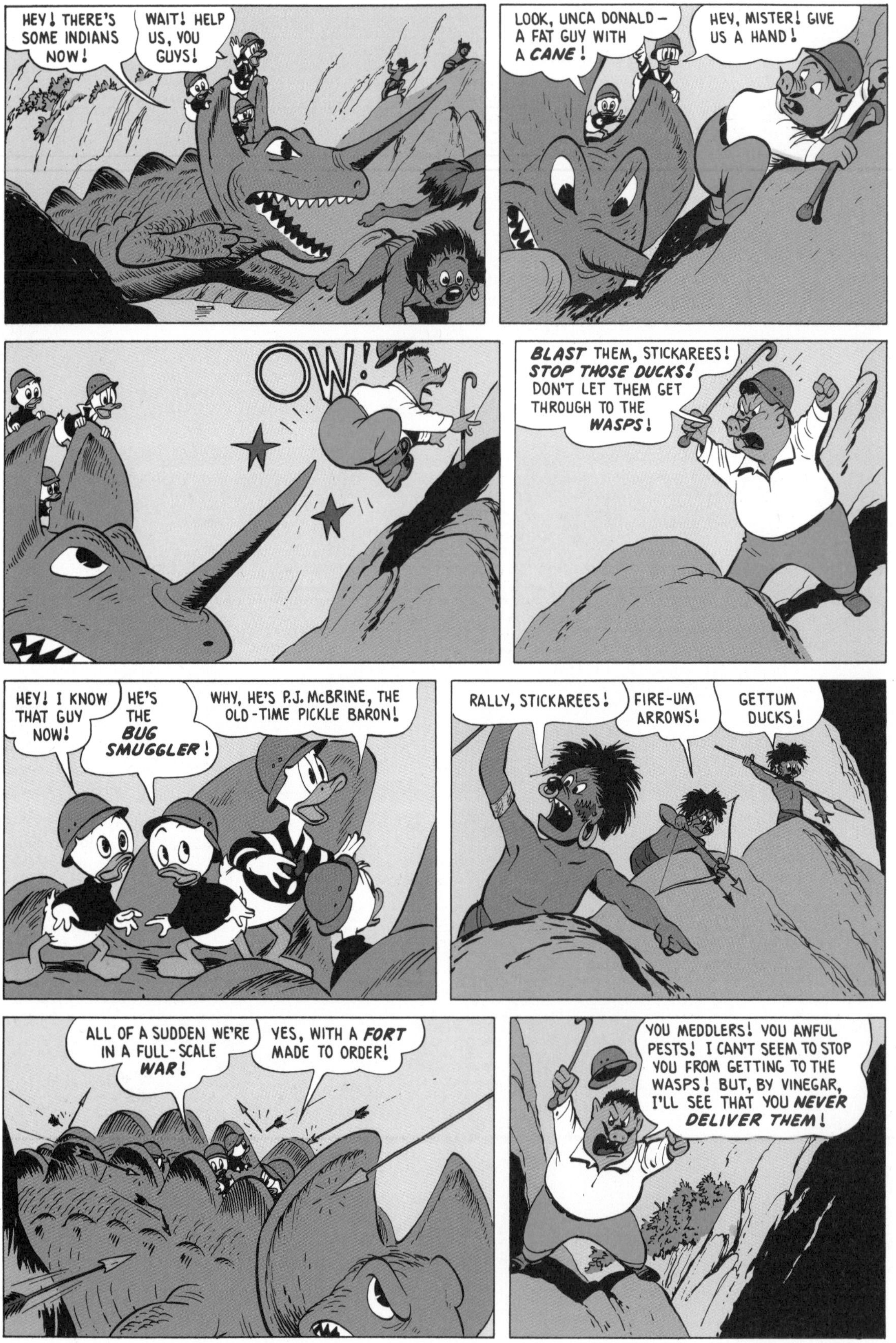
HEY! THERE'S SOME INDIANS NOW!
WAIT! HELP US, YOU GUYS!
LOOK, UNCA DONALD— A FAT GUY WITH A CANE!
HEY, MISTER! GIVE US A HAND!
OW!
BLAST THEM, STICKAREES! STOP THOSE DUCKS! DON'T LET THEM GET THROUGH TO THE WASPS!
HEY! I KNOW THAT GUY NOW!
HE'S THE BUG SMUGGLER!
WHY, HE'S P.J. McBRINE, THE OLD-TIME PICKLE BARON!
RALLY, STICKAREES!
FIRE-UM ARROWS!
GETTUM DUCKS!
ALL OF A SUDDEN WE'RE IN A FULL-SCALE WAR!
YES, WITH A FORT MADE TO ORDER!
YOU MEDDLERS! YOU AWFUL PESTS! I CAN'T SEEM TO STOP YOU FROM GETTING TO THE WASPS! BUT, BY VINEGAR, I'LL SEE THAT YOU NEVER DELIVER THEM!

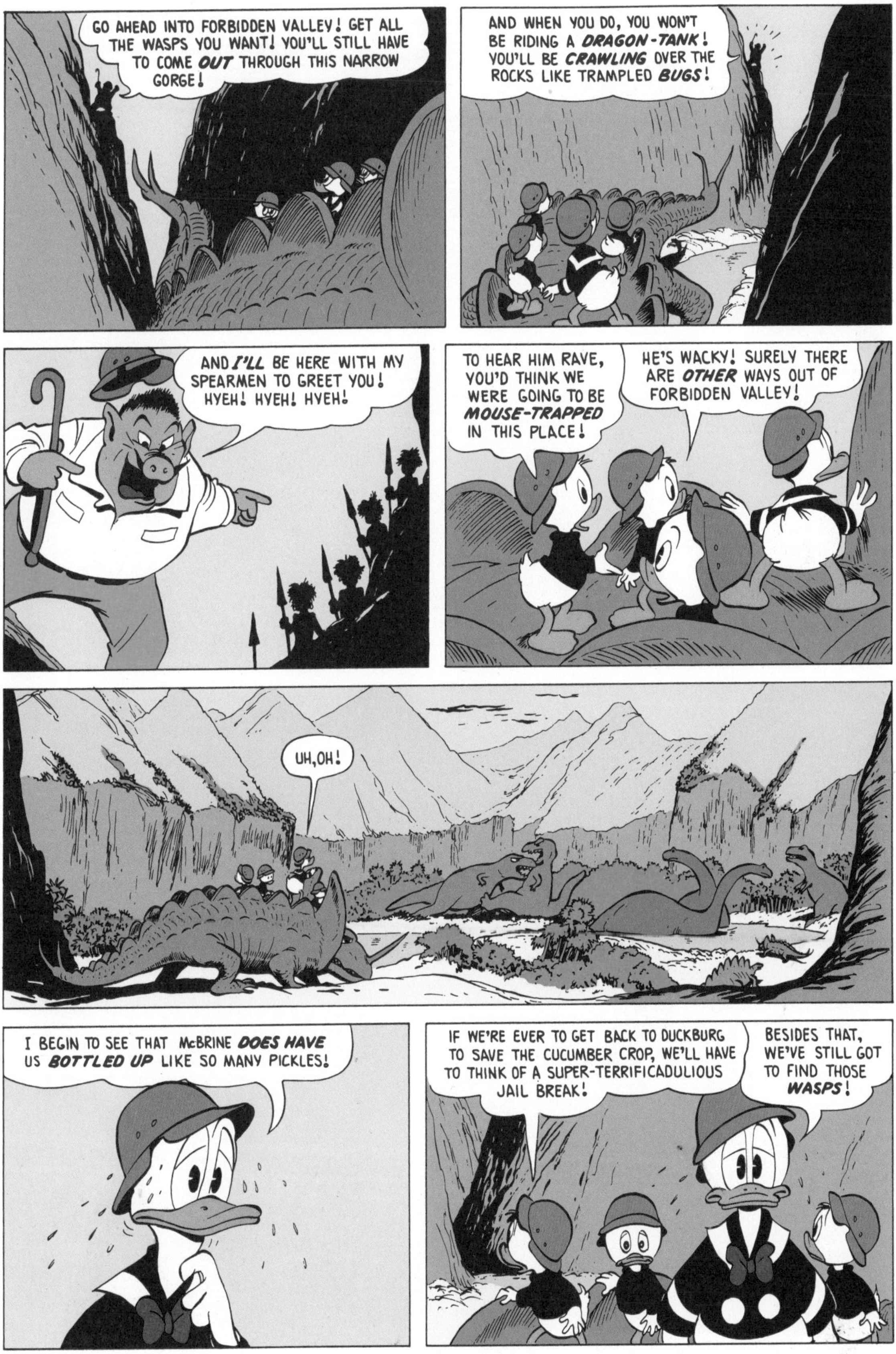

GO AHEAD INTO FORBIDDEN VALLEY! GET ALL THE WASPS YOU WANT! YOU'LL STILL HAVE TO COME **OUT** THROUGH THIS NARROW GORGE!
AND WHEN YOU DO, YOU WON'T BE RIDING A **DRAGON-TANK**! YOU'LL BE **CRAWLING** OVER THE ROCKS LIKE TRAMPLED **BUGS**!
AND **I'LL** BE HERE WITH MY SPEARMEN TO GREET YOU! HYEH! HYEH! HYEH!
TO HEAR HIM RAVE, YOU'D THINK WE WERE GOING TO BE **MOUSE-TRAPPED** IN THIS PLACE!
HE'S WACKY! SURELY THERE ARE **OTHER** WAYS OUT OF FORBIDDEN VALLEY!
UH, OH!
I BEGIN TO SEE THAT McBRINE **DOES HAVE** US **BOTTLED UP** LIKE SO MANY PICKLES!
IF WE'RE EVER TO GET BACK TO DUCKBURG TO SAVE THE CUCUMBER CROP, WE'LL HAVE TO THINK OF A SUPER-TERRIFICADULIOUS JAIL BREAK!
BESIDES THAT, WE'VE STILL GOT TO FIND THOSE **WASPS**!

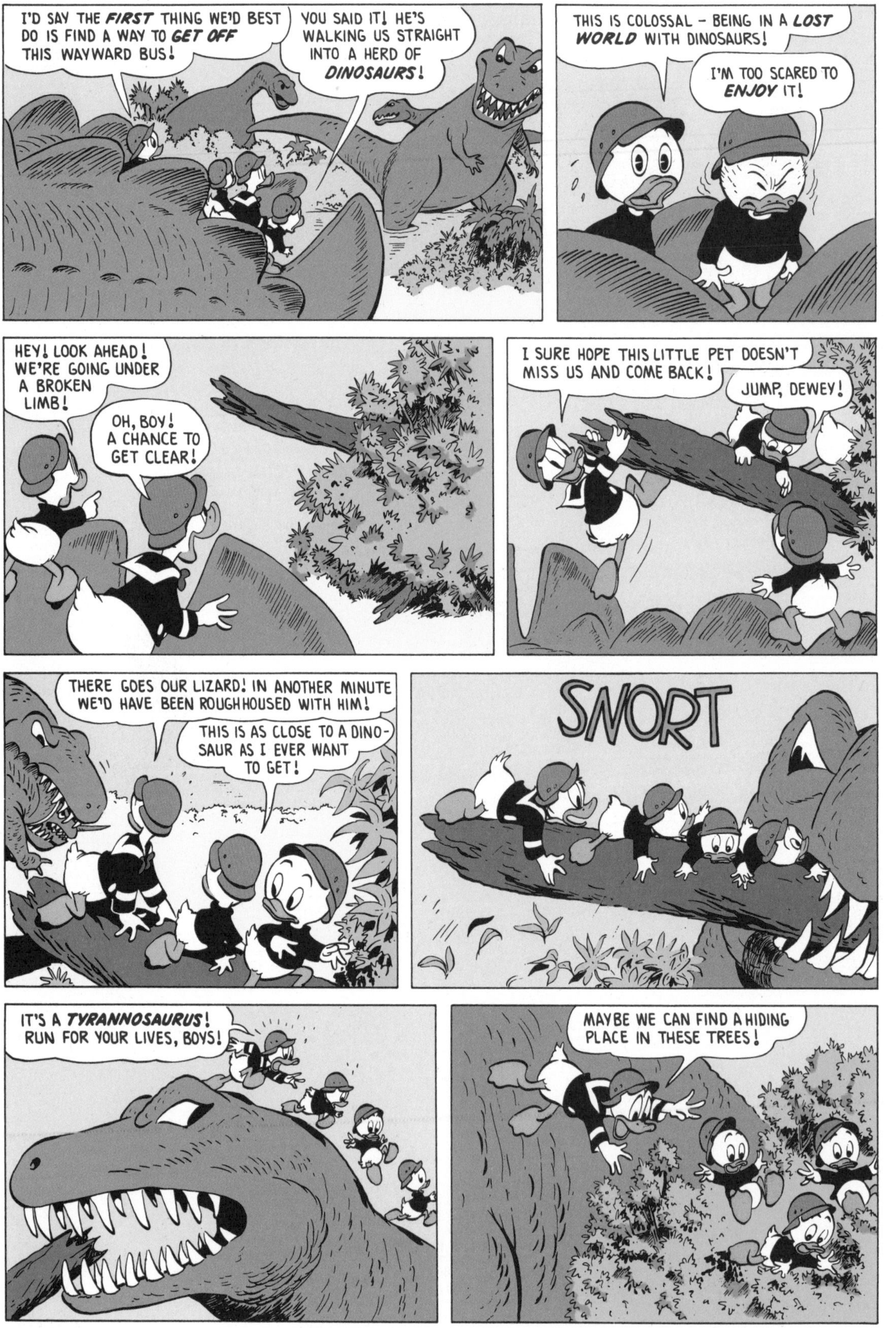

I'D SAY THE *FIRST* THING WE'D BEST DO IS FIND A WAY TO *GET OFF* THIS WAYWARD BUS!
YOU SAID IT! HE'S WALKING US STRAIGHT INTO A HERD OF *DINOSAURS*!
THIS IS COLOSSAL – BEING IN A *LOST WORLD* WITH DINOSAURS!
I'M TOO SCARED TO *ENJOY* IT!
HEY! LOOK AHEAD! WE'RE GOING UNDER A BROKEN LIMB!
OH, BOY! A CHANCE TO GET CLEAR!
I SURE HOPE THIS LITTLE PET DOESN'T MISS US AND COME BACK!
JUMP, DEWEY!
THERE GOES OUR LIZARD! IN ANOTHER MINUTE WE'D HAVE BEEN ROUGHHOUSED WITH HIM!
THIS IS AS CLOSE TO A DINO-SAUR AS I EVER WANT TO GET!
SNORT
IT'S A *TYRANNOSAURUS*! RUN FOR YOUR LIVES, BOYS!
MAYBE WE CAN FIND A HIDING PLACE IN THESE TREES!

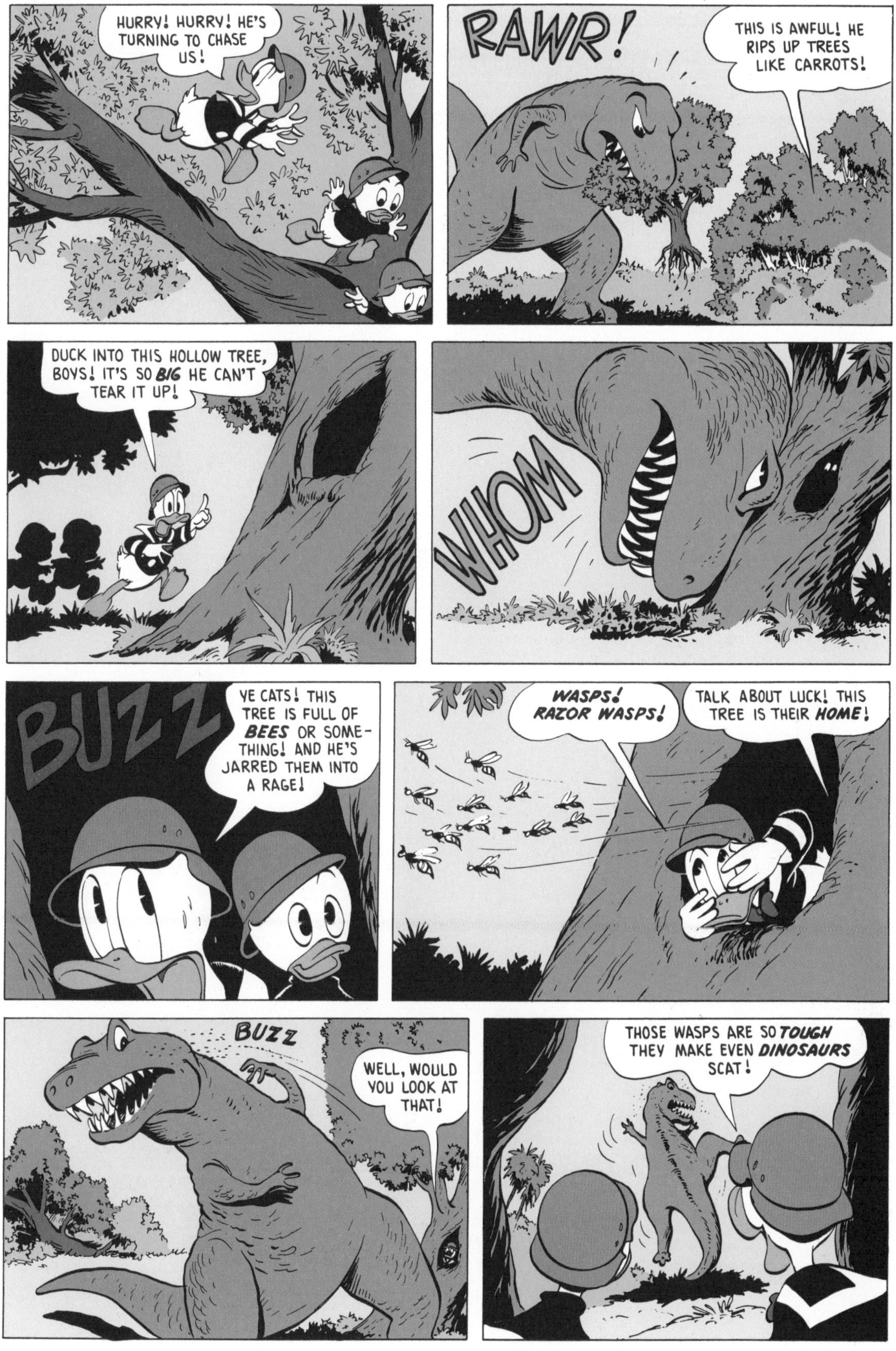
HURRY! HURRY! HE'S TURNING TO CHASE US!
RAWR!
THIS IS AWFUL! HE RIPS UP TREES LIKE CARROTS!
DUCK INTO THIS HOLLOW TREE, BOYS! IT'S SO BIG HE CAN'T TEAR IT UP!
WHOM
BUZZ
YE CATS! THIS TREE IS FULL OF BEES OR SOME-THING! AND HE'S JARRED THEM INTO A RAGE!
WASPS! RAZOR WASPS!
TALK ABOUT LUCK! THIS TREE IS THEIR HOME!
BUZZ
WELL, WOULD YOU LOOK AT THAT!
THOSE WASPS ARE SO TOUGH THEY MAKE EVEN DINOSAURS SCAT!

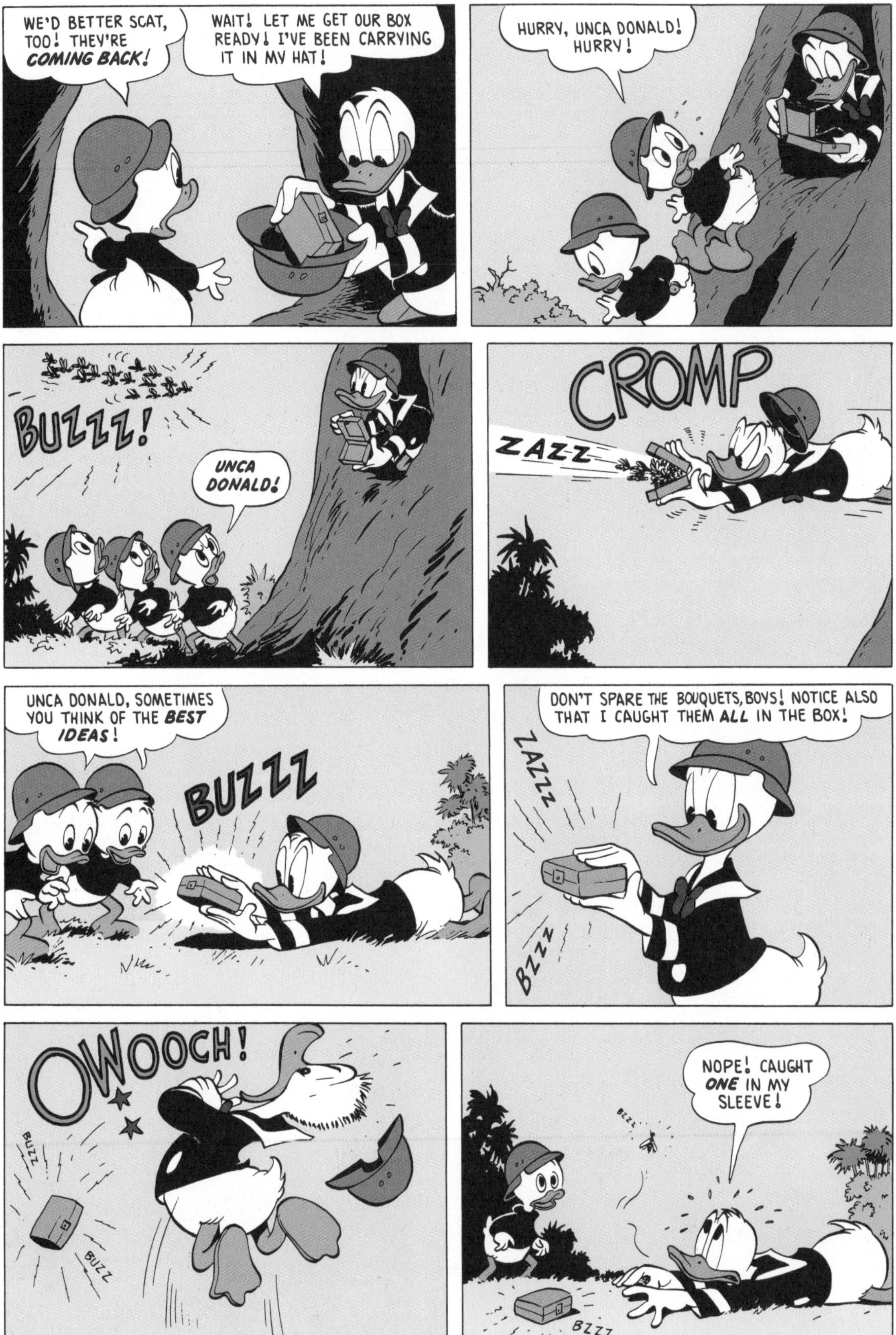

WE'D BETTER SCAT, TOO! THEY'RE COMING BACK!
WAIT! LET ME GET OUR BOX READY! I'VE BEEN CARRYING IT IN MY HAT!
HURRY, UNCA DONALD! HURRY!
BUZZZ!
UNCA DONALD!
CROMP
ZAZZ
UNCA DONALD, SOMETIMES YOU THINK OF THE BEST IDEAS!
BUZZZ
DON'T SPARE THE BOUQUETS, BOYS! NOTICE ALSO THAT I CAUGHT THEM ALL IN THE BOX!
ZAZZZ
BZZZ
OWOOCH!
BUZZ
BUZZ
NOPE! CAUGHT ONE IN MY SLEEVE!
BZZZ
BZZZ

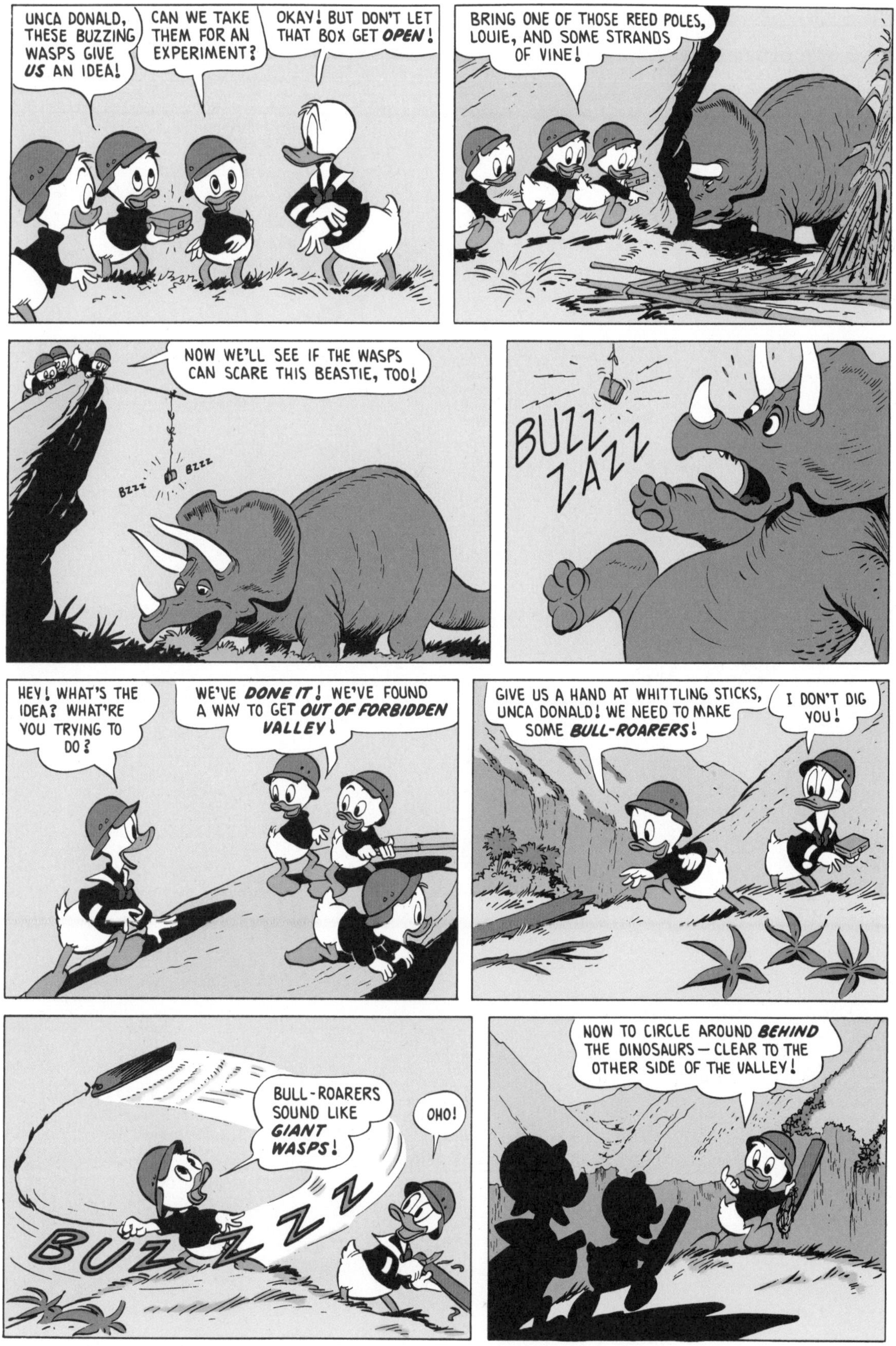
UNCA DONALD, THESE BUZZING WASPS GIVE US AN IDEA!
CAN WE TAKE THEM FOR AN EXPERIMENT?
OKAY! BUT DON'T LET THAT BOX GET OPEN!
BRING ONE OF THOSE REED POLES, LOUIE, AND SOME STRANDS OF VINE!
NOW WE'LL SEE IF THE WASPS CAN SCARE THIS BEASTIE, TOO!
Bzzz
Bzzz
BUZZ ZAZZ
HEY! WHAT'S THE IDEA? WHAT'RE YOU TRYING TO DO?
WE'VE DONE IT! WE'VE FOUND A WAY TO GET OUT OF FORBIDDEN VALLEY!
GIVE US A HAND AT WHITTLING STICKS, UNCA DONALD! WE NEED TO MAKE SOME BULL-ROARERS!
I DON'T DIG YOU!
BULL-ROARERS SOUND LIKE GIANT WASPS!
OHO!
BUZZZZ
NOW TO CIRCLE AROUND BEHIND THE DINOSAURS — CLEAR TO THE OTHER SIDE OF THE VALLEY!

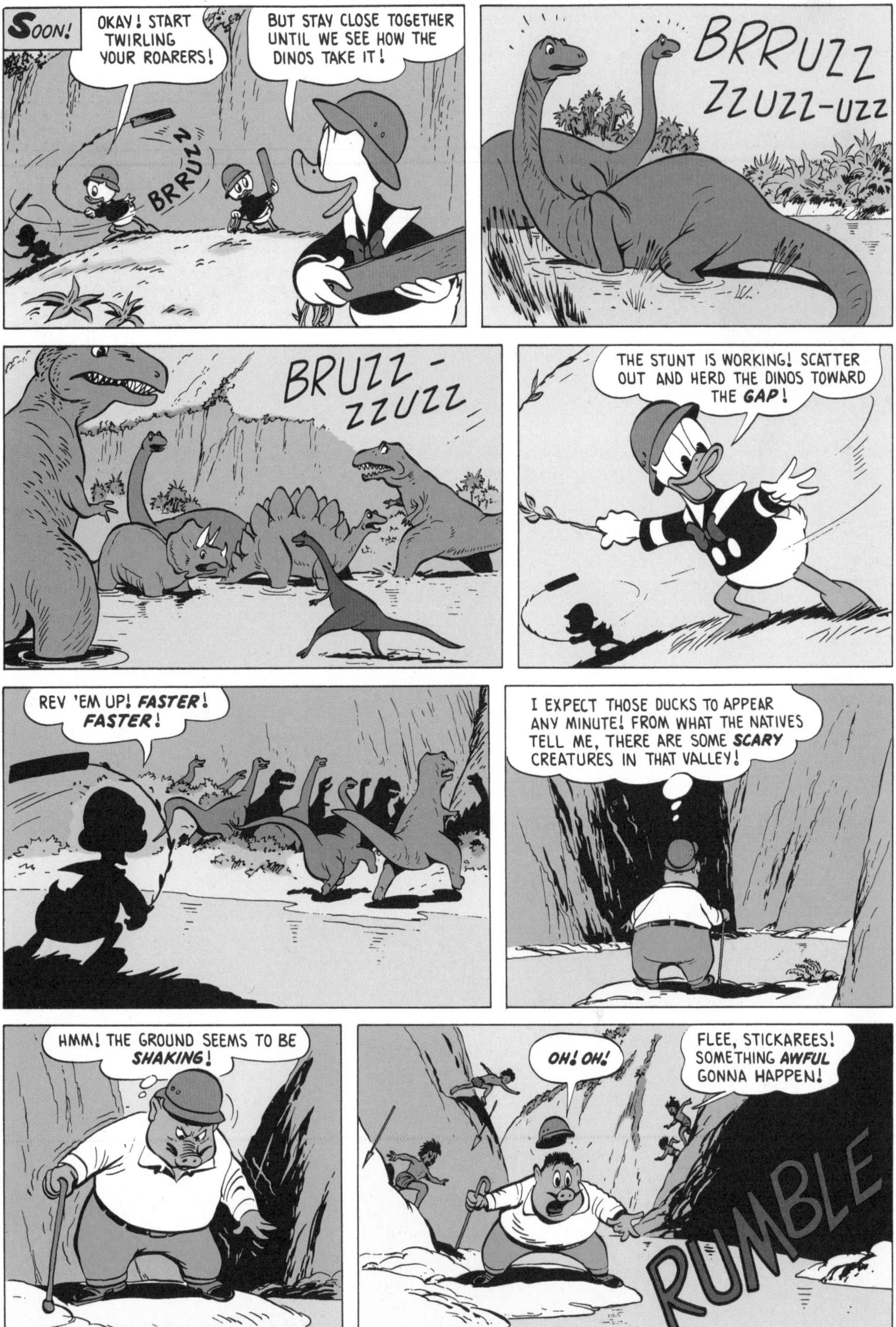
SOON!
OKAY! START TWIRLING YOUR ROARERS!
BUT STAY CLOSE TOGETHER UNTIL WE SEE HOW THE DINOS TAKE IT!
BRRUZZ
BRRUZZ
ZZUZZ-UZZ
BRUZZ-
ZZUZZ
THE STUNT IS WORKING! SCATTER OUT AND HERD THE DINOS TOWARD THE GAP!
REV 'EM UP! FASTER! FASTER!
I EXPECT THOSE DUCKS TO APPEAR ANY MINUTE! FROM WHAT THE NATIVES TELL ME, THERE ARE SOME SCARY CREATURES IN THAT VALLEY!
HMM! THE GROUND SEEMS TO BE SHAKING!
OH! OH!
FLEE, STICKAREES! SOMETHING AWFUL GONNA HAPPEN!
RUMBLE

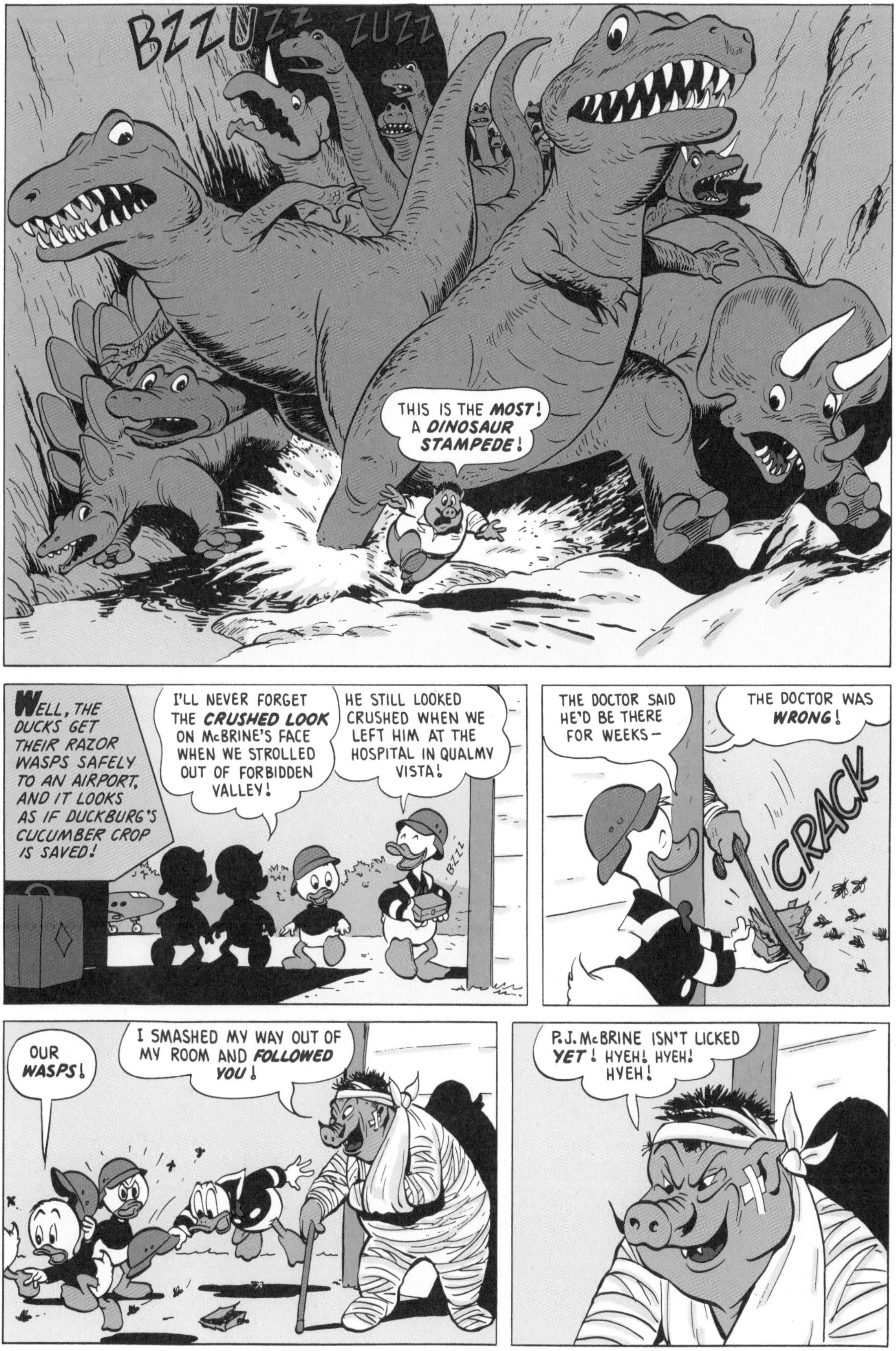
BZZUZZZ ZUZZ
THIS IS THE **MOST**! A **DINOSAUR STAMPEDE**!
WELL, THE DUCKS GET THEIR RAZOR WASPS SAFELY TO AN AIRPORT, AND IT LOOKS AS IF DUCKBURG'S CUCUMBER CROP IS SAVED!
I'LL NEVER FORGET THE **CRUSHED LOOK** ON McBRINE'S FACE WHEN WE STROLLED OUT OF FORBIDDEN VALLEY!
HE STILL LOOKED CRUSHED WHEN WE LEFT HIM AT THE HOSPITAL IN QUALMY VISTA!
BZZZ
THE DOCTOR SAID HE'D BE THERE FOR WEEKS—
THE DOCTOR WAS **WRONG**!
CRACK
OUR **WASPS**!
I SMASHED MY WAY OUT OF MY ROOM AND **FOLLOWED YOU**!
P.J. McBRINE ISN'T LICKED **YET**! HYEH! HYEH! HYEH!

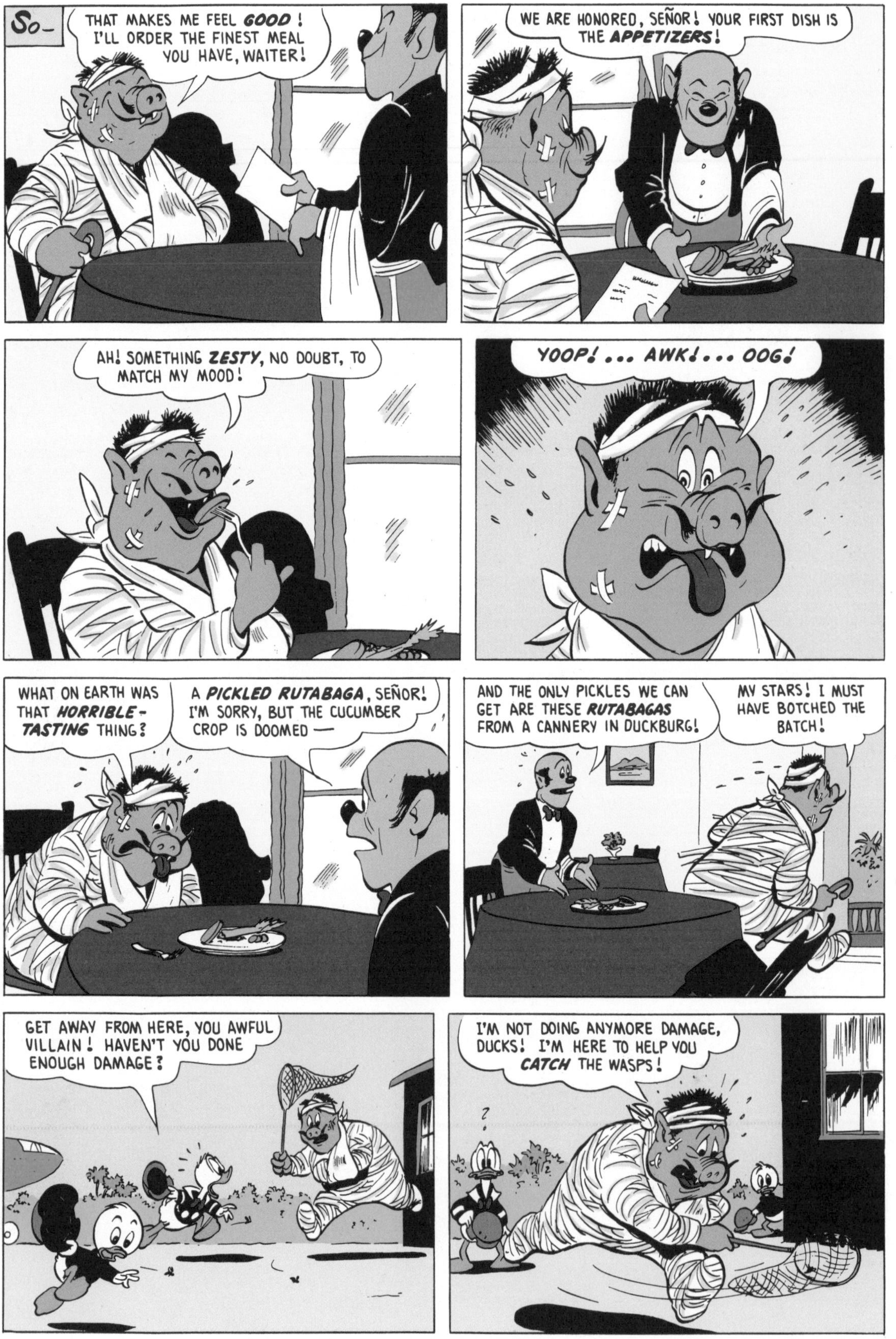
So—
THAT MAKES ME FEEL GOOD! I'LL ORDER THE FINEST MEAL YOU HAVE, WAITER!
WE ARE HONORED, SEÑOR! YOUR FIRST DISH IS THE APPETIZERS!
AH! SOMETHING ZESTY, NO DOUBT, TO MATCH MY MOOD!
YOOP! ... AWK! ... OOG!
WHAT ON EARTH WAS THAT HORRIBLE-TASTING THING?
A PICKLED RUTABAGA, SEÑOR! I'M SORRY, BUT THE CUCUMBER CROP IS DOOMED—
AND THE ONLY PICKLES WE CAN GET ARE THESE RUTABAGAS FROM A CANNERY IN DUCKBURG!
MY STARS! I MUST HAVE BOTCHED THE BATCH!
GET AWAY FROM HERE, YOU AWFUL VILLAIN! HAVEN'T YOU DONE ENOUGH DAMAGE?
I'M NOT DOING ANYMORE DAMAGE, DUCKS! I'M HERE TO HELP YOU CATCH THE WASPS!

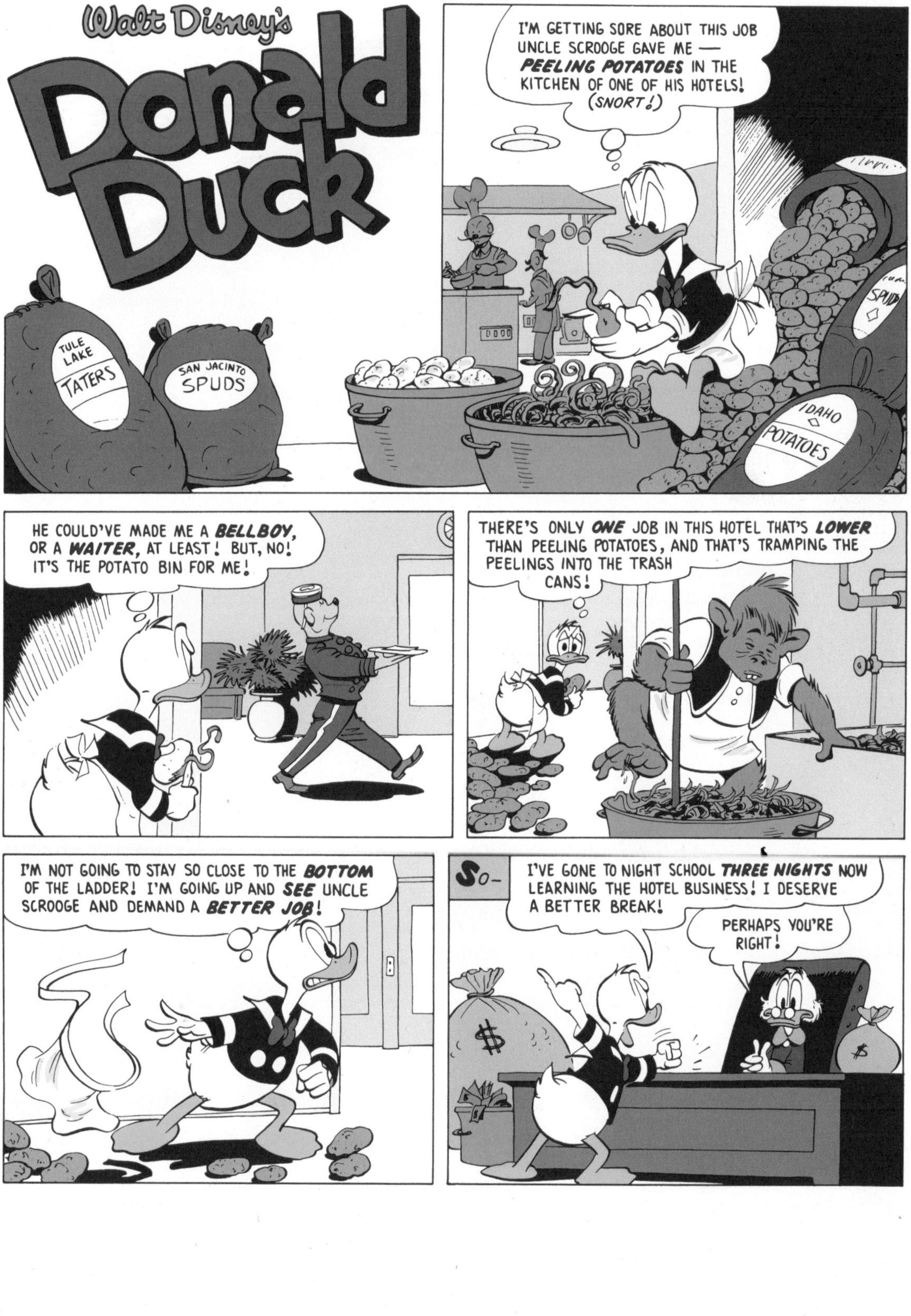
Walt Disney's
Donald Duck
TULE LAKE TATERS
SAN JACINTO SPUDS
I'M GETTING SORE ABOUT THIS JOB UNCLE SCROOGE GAVE ME — PEELING POTATOES IN THE KITCHEN OF ONE OF HIS HOTELS! (SNORT!)
SPUDS
IDAHO POTATOES
HE COULD'VE MADE ME A BELLBOY, OR A WAITER, AT LEAST! BUT, NO! IT'S THE POTATO BIN FOR ME!
THERE'S ONLY ONE JOB IN THIS HOTEL THAT'S LOWER THAN PEELING POTATOES, AND THAT'S TRAMPING THE PEELINGS INTO THE TRASH CANS!
I'M NOT GOING TO STAY SO CLOSE TO THE BOTTOM OF THE LADDER! I'M GOING UP AND SEE UNCLE SCROOGE AND DEMAND A BETTER JOB!
SO—
I'VE GONE TO NIGHT SCHOOL THREE NIGHTS NOW LEARNING THE HOTEL BUSINESS! I DESERVE A BETTER BREAK!
PERHAPS YOU'RE RIGHT!

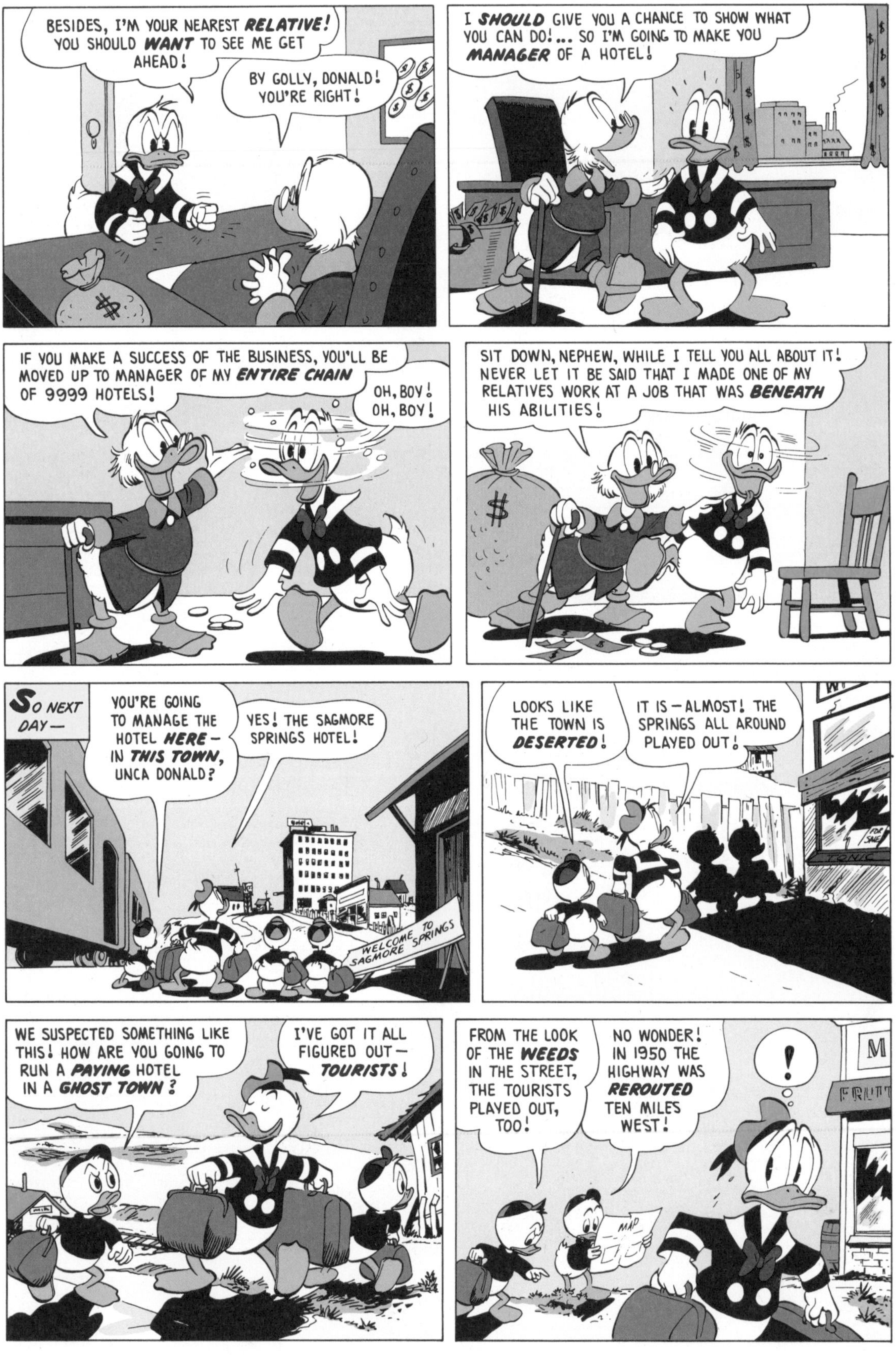
BESIDES, I'M YOUR NEAREST RELATIVE! YOU SHOULD WANT TO SEE ME GET AHEAD!
BY GOLLY, DONALD! YOU'RE RIGHT!
I SHOULD GIVE YOU A CHANCE TO SHOW WHAT YOU CAN DO!... SO I'M GOING TO MAKE YOU MANAGER OF A HOTEL!
IF YOU MAKE A SUCCESS OF THE BUSINESS, YOU'LL BE MOVED UP TO MANAGER OF MY ENTIRE CHAIN OF 9999 HOTELS!
OH, BOY! OH, BOY!
SIT DOWN, NEPHEW, WHILE I TELL YOU ALL ABOUT IT! NEVER LET IT BE SAID THAT I MADE ONE OF MY RELATIVES WORK AT A JOB THAT WAS BENEATH HIS ABILITIES!
SO NEXT DAY—
YOU'RE GOING TO MANAGE THE HOTEL HERE— IN THIS TOWN, UNCA DONALD?
YES! THE SAGMORE SPRINGS HOTEL!
WELCOME TO SAGMORE SPRINGS
LOOKS LIKE THE TOWN IS DESERTED!
IT IS—ALMOST! THE SPRINGS ALL AROUND PLAYED OUT!
FOR SALE
TONIC
WE SUSPECTED SOMETHING LIKE THIS! HOW ARE YOU GOING TO RUN A PAYING HOTEL IN A GHOST TOWN?
I'VE GOT IT ALL FIGURED OUT— TOURISTS!
FROM THE LOOK OF THE WEEDS IN THE STREET, THE TOURISTS PLAYED OUT, TOO!
NO WONDER! IN 1950 THE HIGHWAY WAS REROUTED TEN MILES WEST!
!
MAP
FRUIT

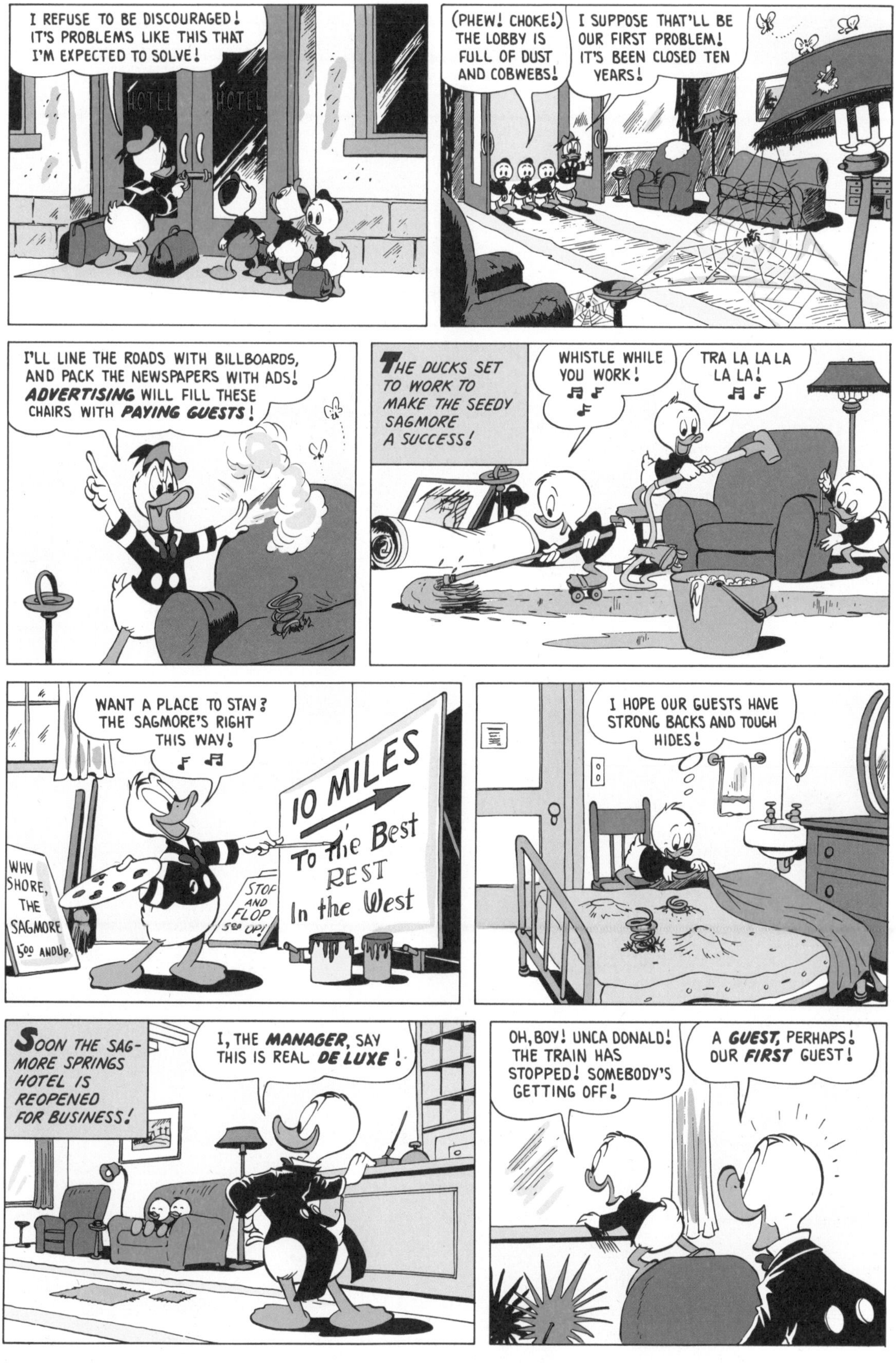

I REFUSE TO BE DISCOURAGED! IT'S PROBLEMS LIKE THIS THAT I'M EXPECTED TO SOLVE!
HOTEL
HOTEL
(PHEW! CHOKE!) THE LOBBY IS FULL OF DUST AND COBWEBS!
I SUPPOSE THAT'LL BE OUR FIRST PROBLEM! IT'S BEEN CLOSED TEN YEARS!
I'LL LINE THE ROADS WITH BILLBOARDS, AND PACK THE NEWSPAPERS WITH ADS! ADVERTISING WILL FILL THESE CHAIRS WITH PAYING GUESTS!
THE DUCKS SET TO WORK TO MAKE THE SEEDY SAGMORE A SUCCESS!
WHISTLE WHILE YOU WORK!
TRA LA LA LA LA LA!
WANT A PLACE TO STAY? THE SAGMORE'S RIGHT THIS WAY!
10 MILES
To the Best REST In the West
WHY SHORE, THE SAGMORE 5.00 AND UP.
STOP AND FLOP 5.00 UP!
I HOPE OUR GUESTS HAVE STRONG BACKS AND TOUGH HIDES!
SOON THE SAGMORE SPRINGS HOTEL IS REOPENED FOR BUSINESS!
I, THE MANAGER, SAY THIS IS REAL DE LUXE!
OH, BOY! UNCA DONALD! THE TRAIN HAS STOPPED! SOMEBODY'S GETTING OFF!
A GUEST, PERHAPS! OUR FIRST GUEST!

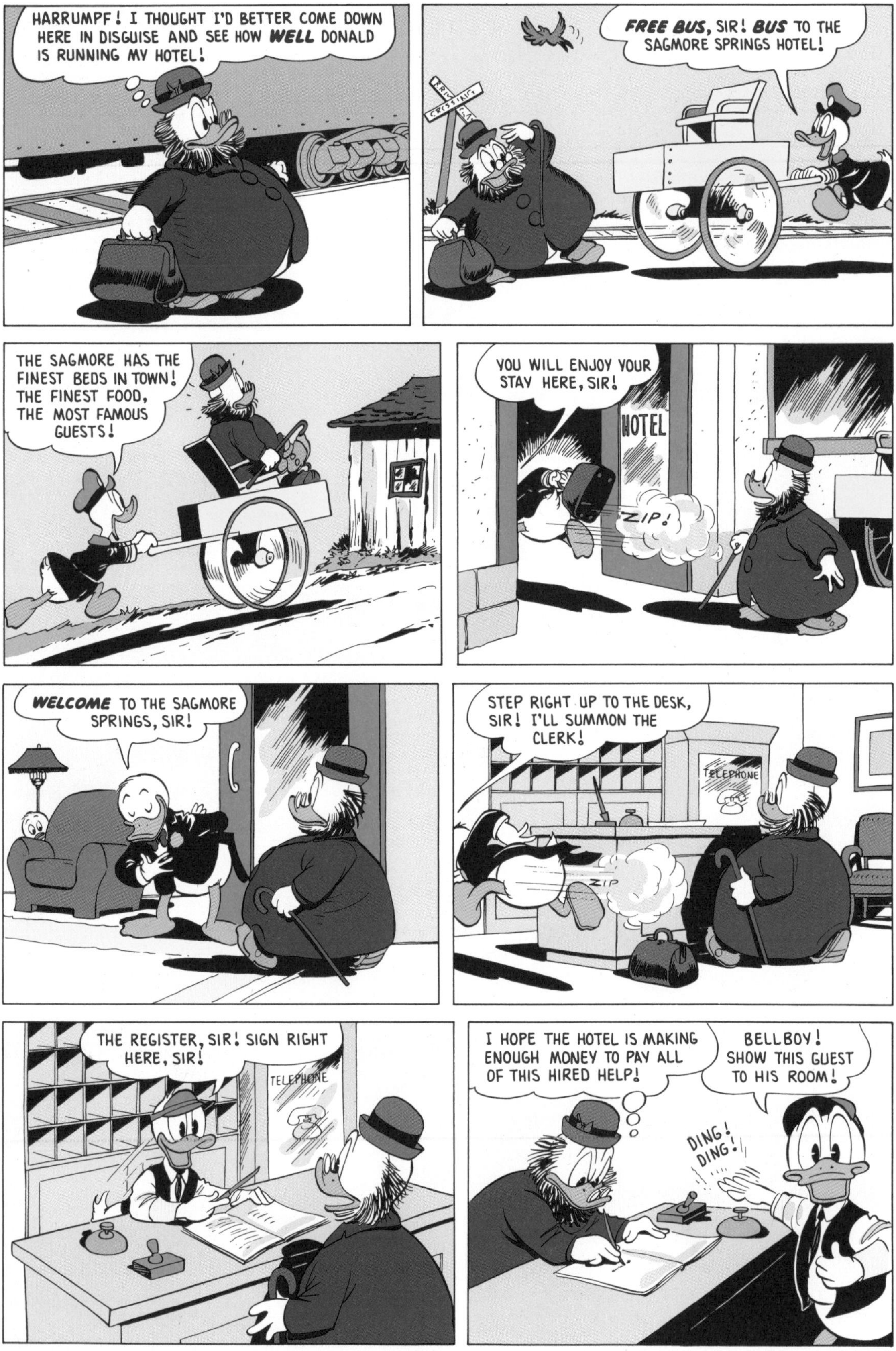
HARRUMPF! I THOUGHT I'D BETTER COME DOWN HERE IN DISGUISE AND SEE HOW WELL DONALD IS RUNNING MY HOTEL!
FREE BUS, SIR! BUS TO THE SAGMORE SPRINGS HOTEL!
THE SAGMORE HAS THE FINEST BEDS IN TOWN! THE FINEST FOOD, THE MOST FAMOUS GUESTS!
YOU WILL ENJOY YOUR STAY HERE, SIR!
HOTEL
ZIP!
WELCOME TO THE SAGMORE SPRINGS, SIR!
STEP RIGHT UP TO THE DESK, SIR! I'LL SUMMON THE CLERK!
TELEPHONE
ZIP
THE REGISTER, SIR! SIGN RIGHT HERE, SIR!
TELEPHONE
I HOPE THE HOTEL IS MAKING ENOUGH MONEY TO PAY ALL OF THIS HIRED HELP!
BELLBOY! SHOW THIS GUEST TO HIS ROOM!
DING! DING!

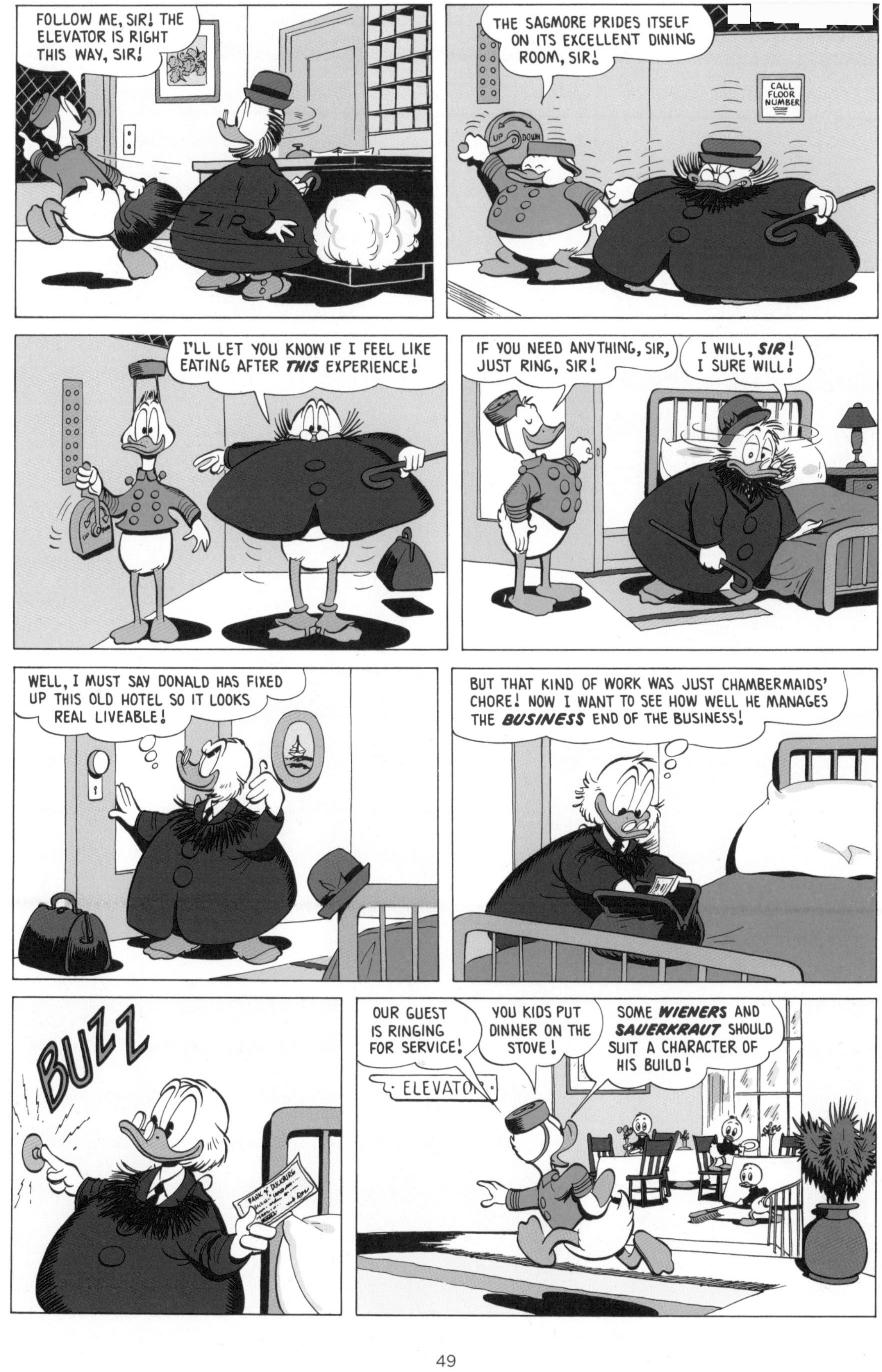
FOLLOW ME, SIR! THE ELEVATOR IS RIGHT THIS WAY, SIR!
ZIP
THE SAGMORE PRIDES ITSELF ON ITS EXCELLENT DINING ROOM, SIR!
UP
DOWN
CALL FLOOR NUMBER
I'LL LET YOU KNOW IF I FEEL LIKE EATING AFTER ***THIS*** EXPERIENCE!
IF YOU NEED ANYTHING, SIR, JUST RING, SIR!
I WILL, ***SIR***! I SURE WILL!
WELL, I MUST SAY DONALD HAS FIXED UP THIS OLD HOTEL SO IT LOOKS REAL LIVEABLE!
BUT THAT KIND OF WORK WAS JUST CHAMBERMAIDS' CHORE! NOW I WANT TO SEE HOW WELL HE MANAGES THE ***BUSINESS*** END OF THE BUSINESS!
BUZZ
OUR GUEST IS RINGING FOR SERVICE!
YOU KIDS PUT DINNER ON THE STOVE!
SOME ***WIENERS*** AND ***SAUERKRAUT*** SHOULD SUIT A CHARACTER OF HIS BUILD!
ELEVATOR

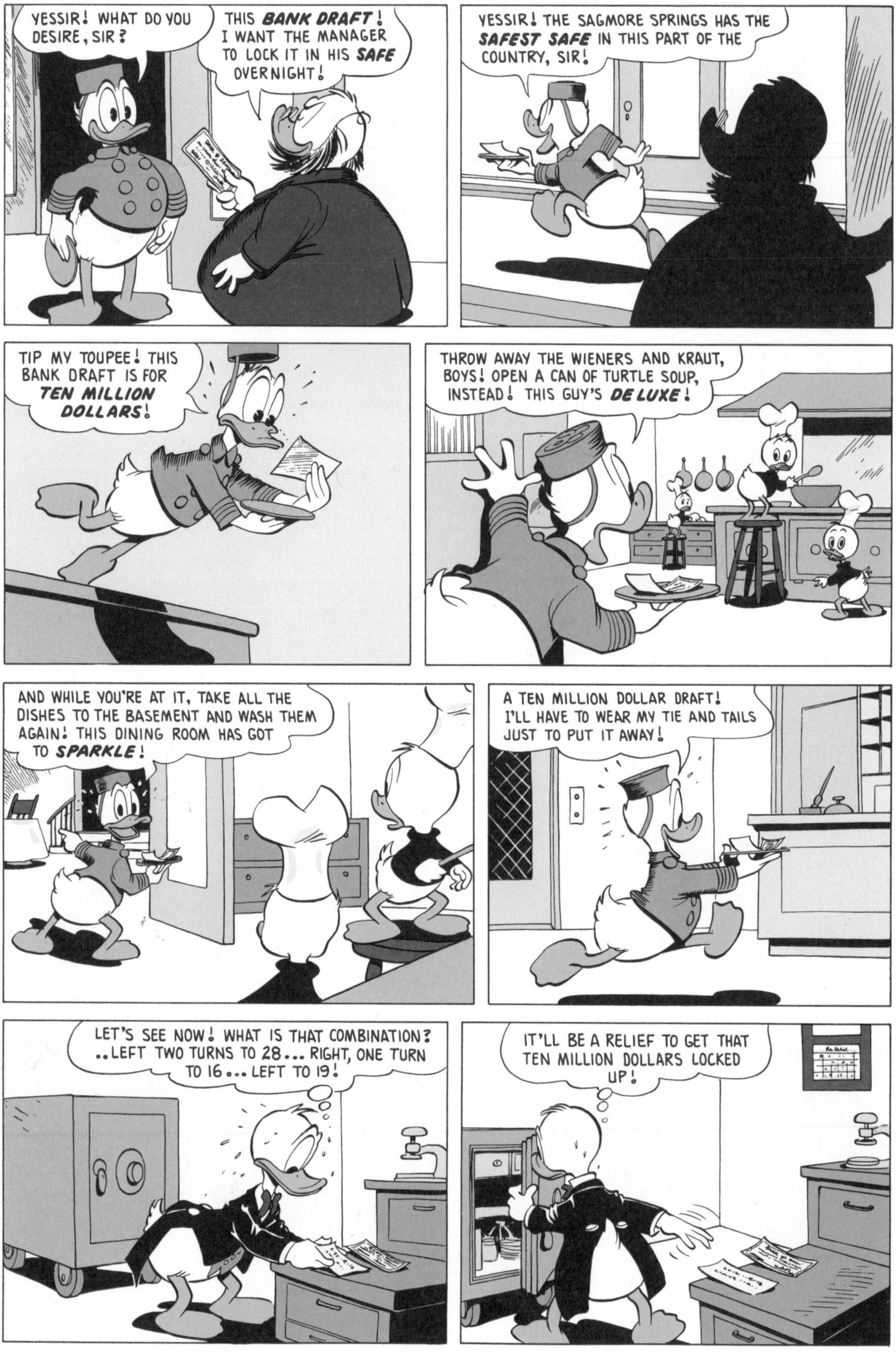

YESSIR! WHAT DO YOU DESIRE, SIR?
THIS BANK DRAFT! I WANT THE MANAGER TO LOCK IT IN HIS SAFE OVERNIGHT!
YESSIR! THE SAGMORE SPRINGS HAS THE SAFEST SAFE IN THIS PART OF THE COUNTRY, SIR!
TIP MY TOUPEE! THIS BANK DRAFT IS FOR TEN MILLION DOLLARS!
THROW AWAY THE WIENERS AND KRAUT, BOYS! OPEN A CAN OF TURTLE SOUP, INSTEAD! THIS GUY'S DE LUXE!
AND WHILE YOU'RE AT IT, TAKE ALL THE DISHES TO THE BASEMENT AND WASH THEM AGAIN! THIS DINING ROOM HAS GOT TO SPARKLE!
A TEN MILLION DOLLAR DRAFT! I'LL HAVE TO WEAR MY TIE AND TAILS JUST TO PUT IT AWAY!
LET'S SEE NOW! WHAT IS THAT COMBINATION? ..LEFT TWO TURNS TO 28... RIGHT, ONE TURN TO 16... LEFT TO 19!
IT'LL BE A RELIEF TO GET THAT TEN MILLION DOLLARS LOCKED UP!

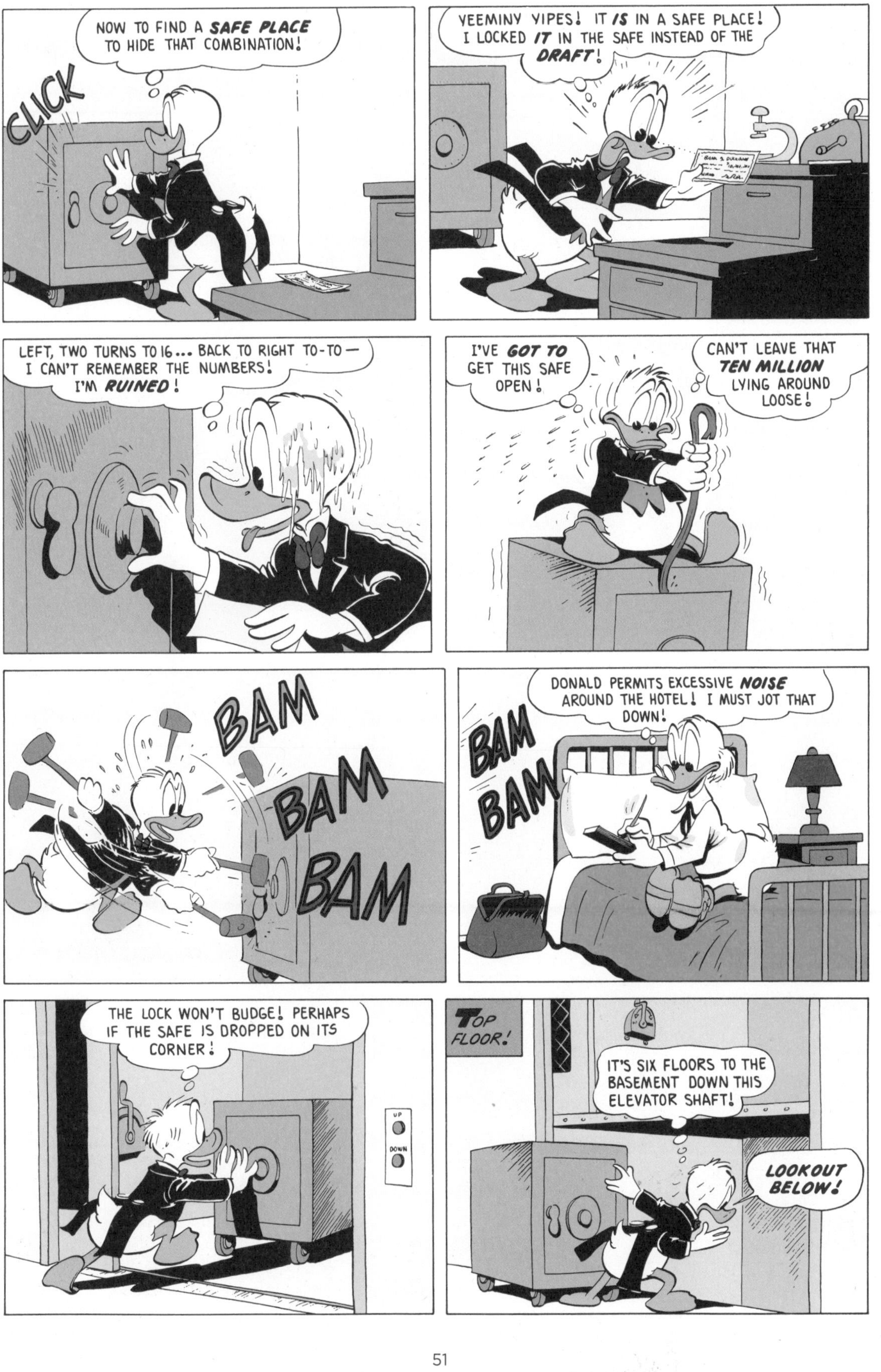
NOW TO FIND A SAFE PLACE TO HIDE THAT COMBINATION!
CLICK
YEEMINY YIPES! IT IS IN A SAFE PLACE! I LOCKED IT IN THE SAFE INSTEAD OF THE DRAFT!
LEFT, TWO TURNS TO 16... BACK TO RIGHT TO-TO— I CAN'T REMEMBER THE NUMBERS! I'M RUINED!
I'VE GOT TO GET THIS SAFE OPEN!
CAN'T LEAVE THAT TEN MILLION LYING AROUND LOOSE!
BAM
BAM
BAM
DONALD PERMITS EXCESSIVE NOISE AROUND THE HOTEL! I MUST JOT THAT DOWN!
BAM
BAM
THE LOCK WON'T BUDGE! PERHAPS IF THE SAFE IS DROPPED ON ITS CORNER!
UP
DOWN
TOP FLOOR!
IT'S SIX FLOORS TO THE BASEMENT DOWN THIS ELEVATOR SHAFT!
LOOKOUT BELOW!

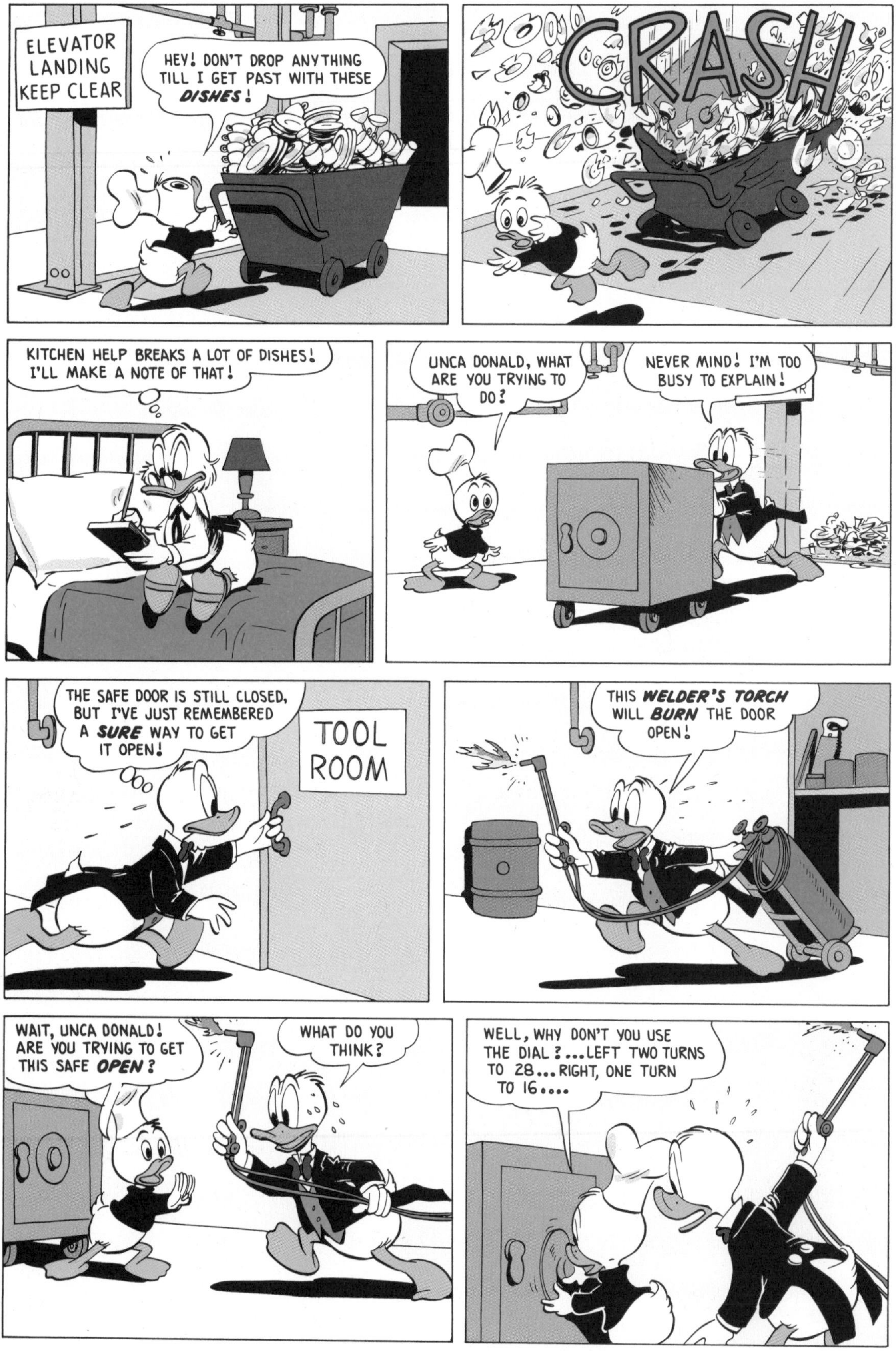

ELEVATOR LANDING KEEP CLEAR
HEY! DON'T DROP ANYTHING TILL I GET PAST WITH THESE **DISHES**!
CRASH
KITCHEN HELP BREAKS A LOT OF DISHES! I'LL MAKE A NOTE OF THAT!
UNCA DONALD, WHAT ARE YOU TRYING TO DO?
NEVER MIND! I'M TOO BUSY TO EXPLAIN!
THE SAFE DOOR IS STILL CLOSED, BUT I'VE JUST REMEMBERED A **SURE** WAY TO GET IT OPEN!
TOOL ROOM
THIS **WELDER'S TORCH** WILL **BURN** THE DOOR OPEN!
WAIT, UNCA DONALD! ARE YOU TRYING TO GET THIS SAFE **OPEN**?
WHAT DO YOU THINK?
WELL, WHY DON'T YOU USE THE DIAL?...LEFT TWO TURNS TO 28...RIGHT, ONE TURN TO 16....

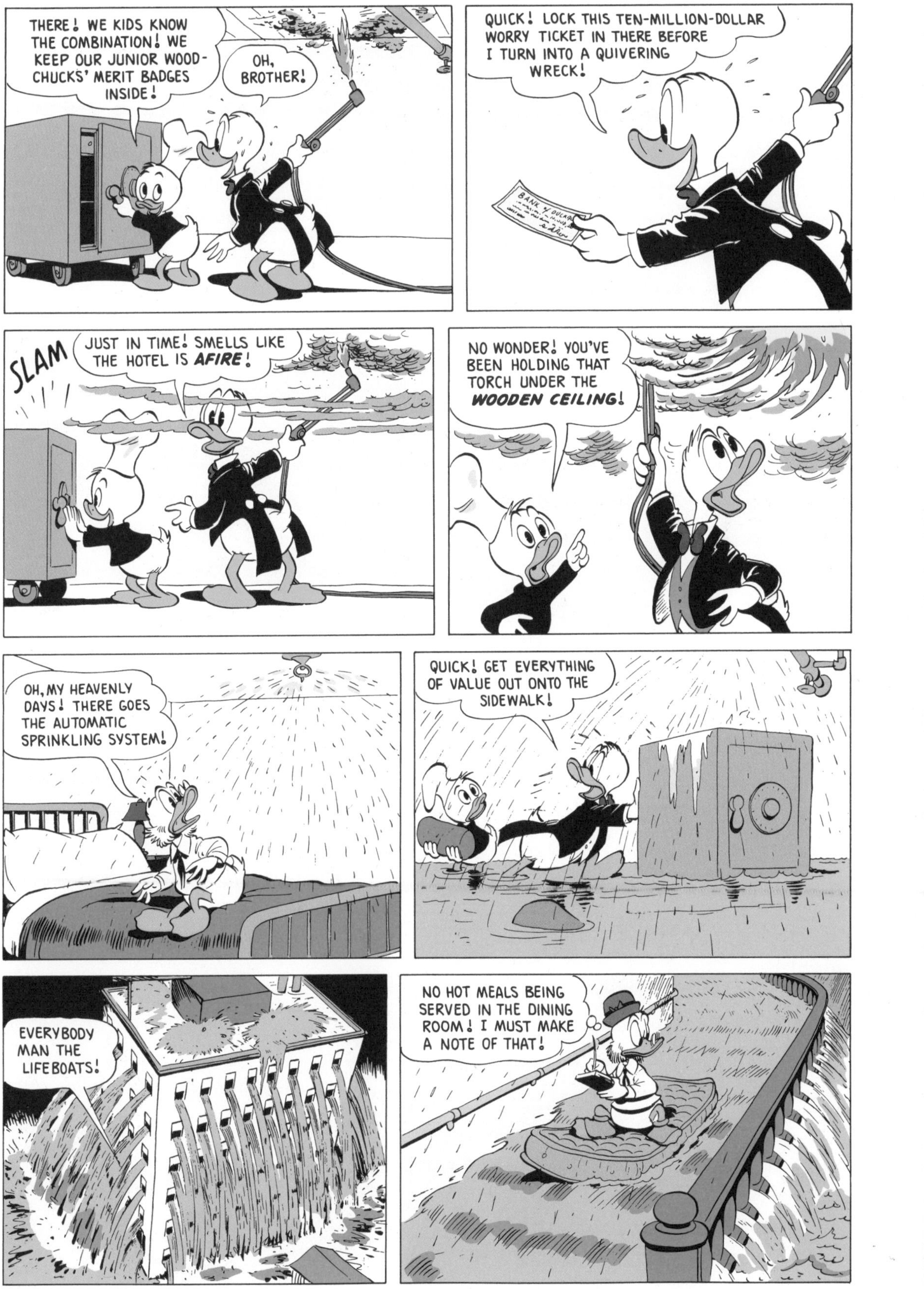
THERE! WE KIDS KNOW THE COMBINATION! WE KEEP OUR JUNIOR WOOD-CHUCKS' MERIT BADGES INSIDE!
OH, BROTHER!
QUICK! LOCK THIS TEN-MILLION-DOLLAR WORRY TICKET IN THERE BEFORE I TURN INTO A QUIVERING WRECK!
SLAM
JUST IN TIME! SMELLS LIKE THE HOTEL IS **AFIRE**!
NO WONDER! YOU'VE BEEN HOLDING THAT TORCH UNDER THE **WOODEN CEILING**!
OH, MY HEAVENLY DAYS! THERE GOES THE AUTOMATIC SPRINKLING SYSTEM!
QUICK! GET EVERYTHING OF VALUE OUT ONTO THE SIDEWALK!
EVERYBODY MAN THE LIFEBOATS!
NO HOT MEALS BEING SERVED IN THE DINING ROOM! I MUST MAKE A NOTE OF THAT!

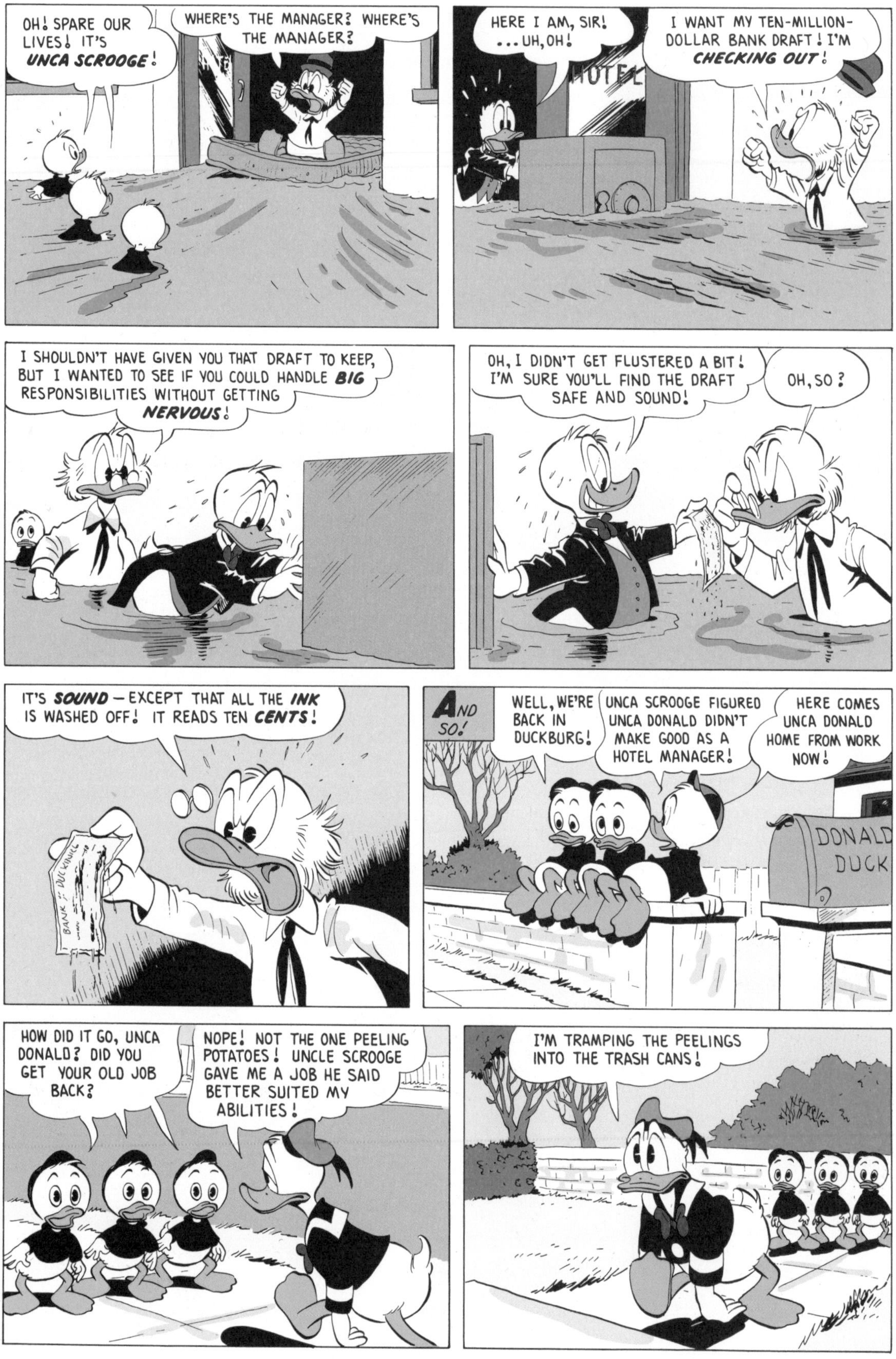
OH! SPARE OUR LIVES! IT'S UNCA SCROOGE!
WHERE'S THE MANAGER? WHERE'S THE MANAGER?
HERE I AM, SIR! ...UH, OH!
I WANT MY TEN-MILLION-DOLLAR BANK DRAFT! I'M CHECKING OUT!
HOTEL
I SHOULDN'T HAVE GIVEN YOU THAT DRAFT TO KEEP, BUT I WANTED TO SEE IF YOU COULD HANDLE BIG RESPONSIBILITIES WITHOUT GETTING NERVOUS!
OH, I DIDN'T GET FLUSTERED A BIT! I'M SURE YOU'LL FIND THE DRAFT SAFE AND SOUND!
OH, SO?
IT'S SOUND — EXCEPT THAT ALL THE INK IS WASHED OFF! IT READS TEN CENTS!
AND SO!
WELL, WE'RE BACK IN DUCKBURG!
UNCA SCROOGE FIGURED UNCA DONALD DIDN'T MAKE GOOD AS A HOTEL MANAGER!
HERE COMES UNCA DONALD HOME FROM WORK NOW!
DONALD DUCK
HOW DID IT GO, UNCA DONALD? DID YOU GET YOUR OLD JOB BACK?
NOPE! NOT THE ONE PEELING POTATOES! UNCLE SCROOGE GAVE ME A JOB HE SAID BETTER SUITED MY ABILITIES!
I'M TRAMPING THE PEELINGS INTO THE TRASH CANS!

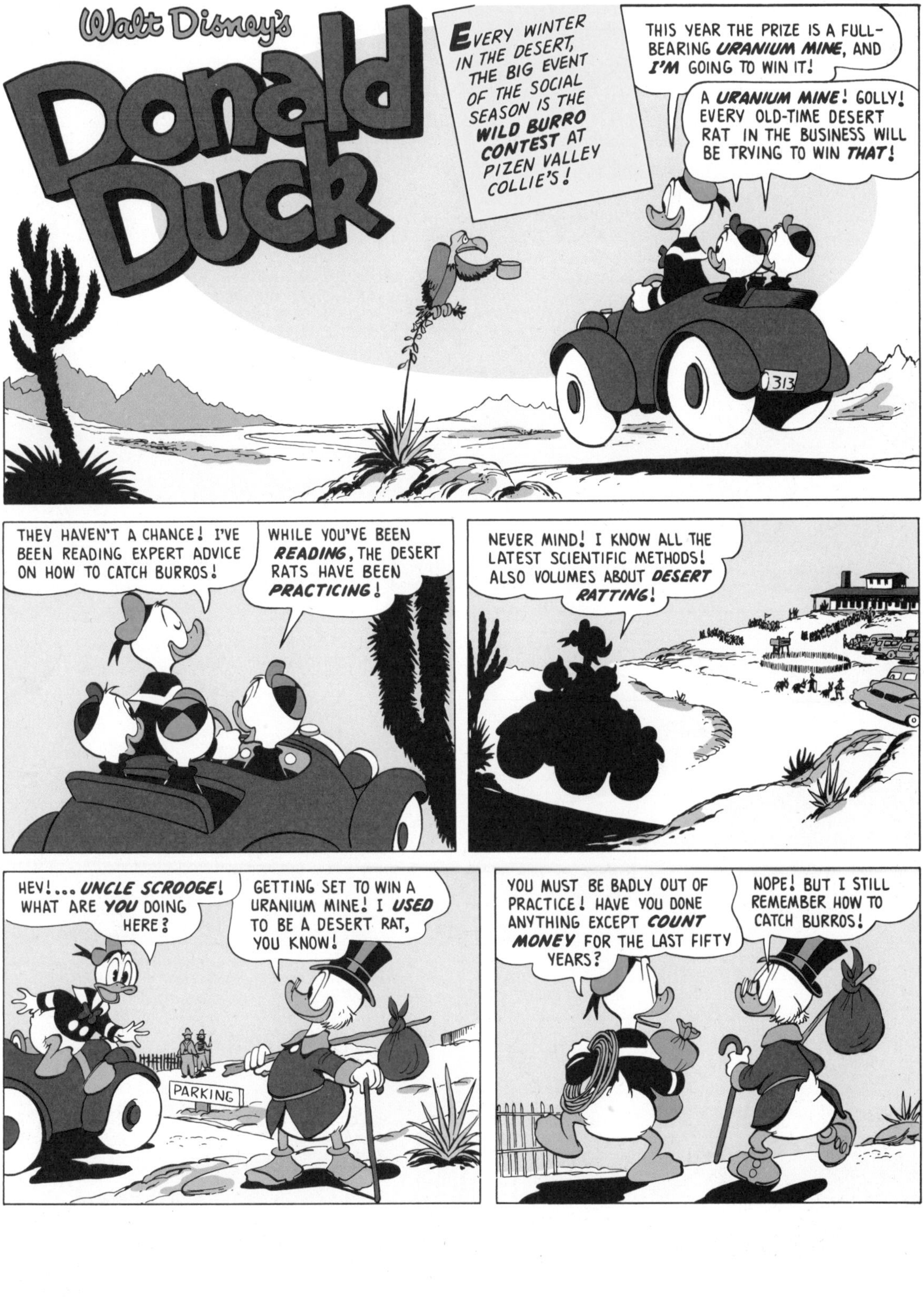
Walt Disney's
Donald Duck
EVERY WINTER IN THE DESERT, THE BIG EVENT OF THE SOCIAL SEASON IS THE WILD BURRO CONTEST AT PIZEN VALLEY COLLIE'S!
THIS YEAR THE PRIZE IS A FULL-BEARING URANIUM MINE, AND I'M GOING TO WIN IT!
A URANIUM MINE! GOLLY! EVERY OLD-TIME DESERT RAT IN THE BUSINESS WILL BE TRYING TO WIN THAT!
313
THEY HAVEN'T A CHANCE! I'VE BEEN READING EXPERT ADVICE ON HOW TO CATCH BURROS!
WHILE YOU'VE BEEN READING, THE DESERT RATS HAVE BEEN PRACTICING!
NEVER MIND! I KNOW ALL THE LATEST SCIENTIFIC METHODS! ALSO VOLUMES ABOUT DESERT RATTING!
HEY!... UNCLE SCROOGE! WHAT ARE YOU DOING HERE?
GETTING SET TO WIN A URANIUM MINE! I USED TO BE A DESERT RAT, YOU KNOW!
PARKING
YOU MUST BE BADLY OUT OF PRACTICE! HAVE YOU DONE ANYTHING EXCEPT COUNT MONEY FOR THE LAST FIFTY YEARS?
NOPE! BUT I STILL REMEMBER HOW TO CATCH BURROS!

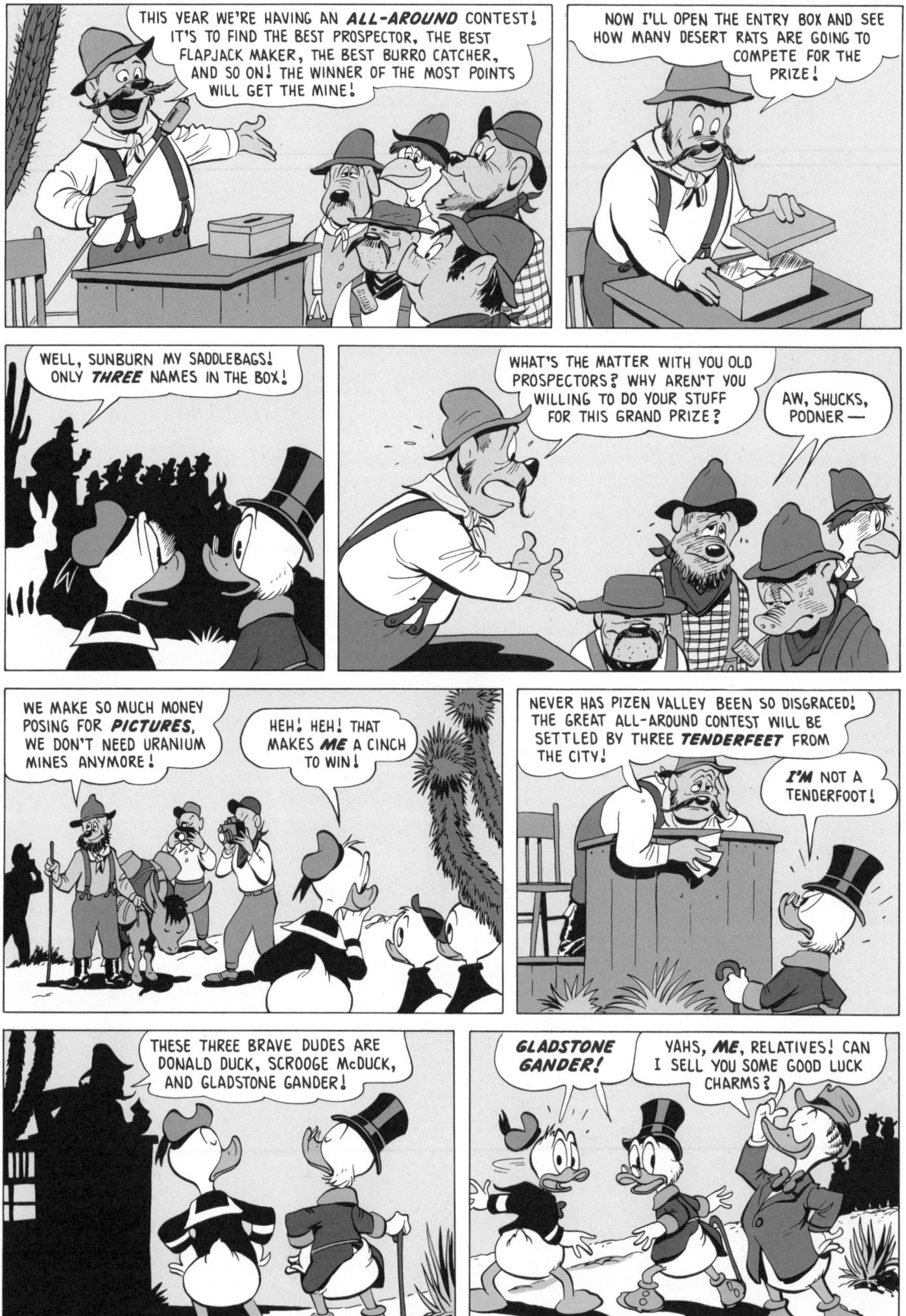
THIS YEAR WE'RE HAVING AN ALL-AROUND CONTEST! IT'S TO FIND THE BEST PROSPECTOR, THE BEST FLAPJACK MAKER, THE BEST BURRO CATCHER, AND SO ON! THE WINNER OF THE MOST POINTS WILL GET THE MINE!
NOW I'LL OPEN THE ENTRY BOX AND SEE HOW MANY DESERT RATS ARE GOING TO COMPETE FOR THE PRIZE!
WELL, SUNBURN MY SADDLEBAGS! ONLY THREE NAMES IN THE BOX!
WHAT'S THE MATTER WITH YOU OLD PROSPECTORS? WHY AREN'T YOU WILLING TO DO YOUR STUFF FOR THIS GRAND PRIZE?
AW, SHUCKS, PODNER —
WE MAKE SO MUCH MONEY POSING FOR PICTURES, WE DON'T NEED URANIUM MINES ANYMORE!
HEH! HEH! THAT MAKES ME A CINCH TO WIN!
NEVER HAS PIZEN VALLEY BEEN SO DISGRACED! THE GREAT ALL-AROUND CONTEST WILL BE SETTLED BY THREE TENDERFEET FROM THE CITY!
I'M NOT A TENDERFOOT!
THESE THREE BRAVE DUDES ARE DONALD DUCK, SCROOGE McDUCK, AND GLADSTONE GANDER!
GLADSTONE GANDER!
YAHS, ME, RELATIVES! CAN I SELL YOU SOME GOOD LUCK CHARMS?

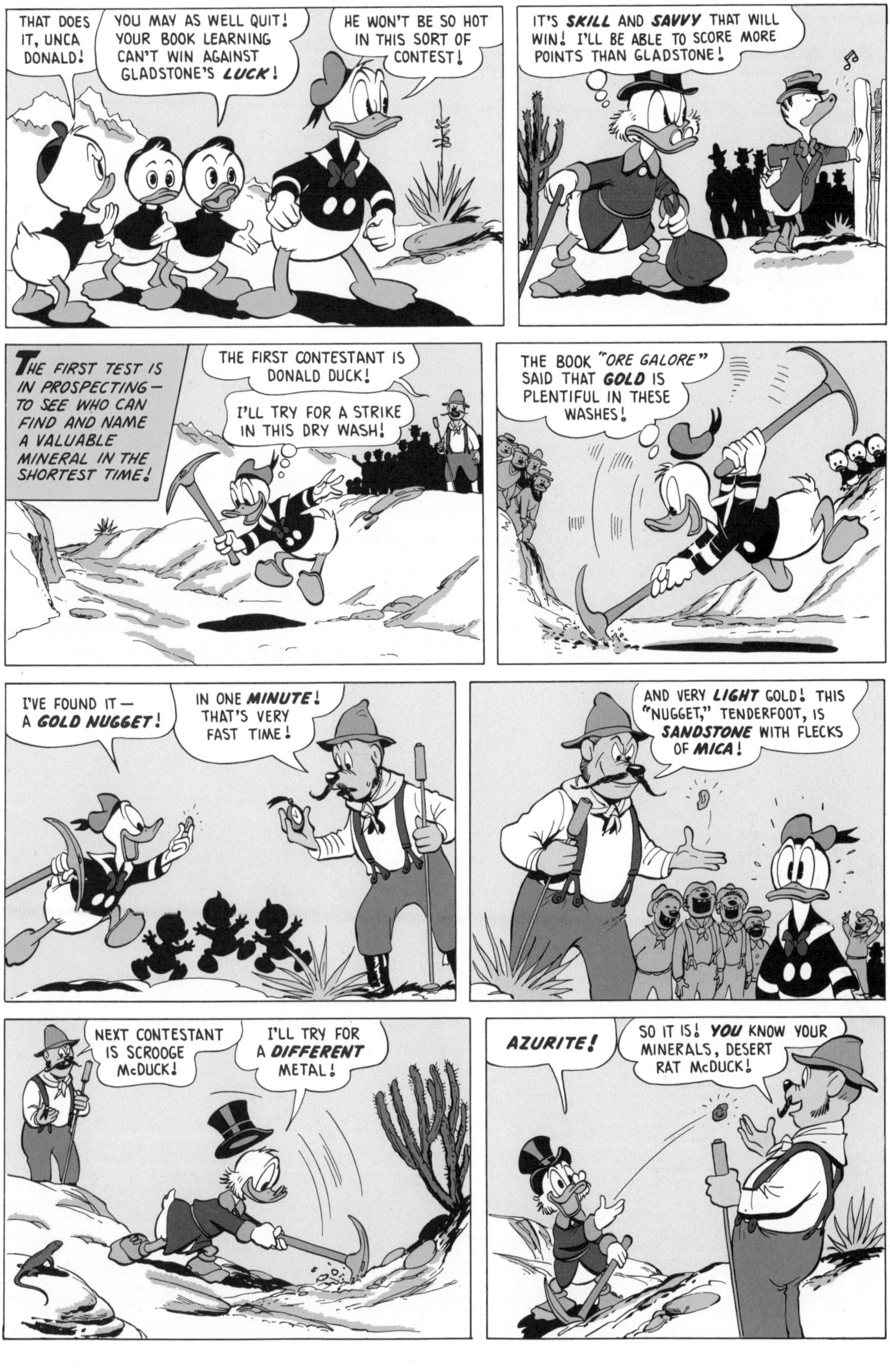
THAT DOES IT, UNCA DONALD!
YOU MAY AS WELL QUIT! YOUR BOOK LEARNING CAN'T WIN AGAINST GLADSTONE'S LUCK!
HE WON'T BE SO HOT IN THIS SORT OF CONTEST!
IT'S SKILL AND SAVVY THAT WILL WIN! I'LL BE ABLE TO SCORE MORE POINTS THAN GLADSTONE!
THE FIRST TEST IS IN PROSPECTING— TO SEE WHO CAN FIND AND NAME A VALUABLE MINERAL IN THE SHORTEST TIME!
THE FIRST CONTESTANT IS DONALD DUCK!
I'LL TRY FOR A STRIKE IN THIS DRY WASH!
THE BOOK "ORE GALORE" SAID THAT GOLD IS PLENTIFUL IN THESE WASHES!
I'VE FOUND IT— A GOLD NUGGET!
IN ONE MINUTE! THAT'S VERY FAST TIME!
AND VERY LIGHT GOLD! THIS "NUGGET," TENDERFOOT, IS SANDSTONE WITH FLECKS OF MICA!
NEXT CONTESTANT IS SCROOGE McDUCK!
I'LL TRY FOR A DIFFERENT METAL!
AZURITE!
SO IT IS! YOU KNOW YOUR MINERALS, DESERT RAT McDUCK!

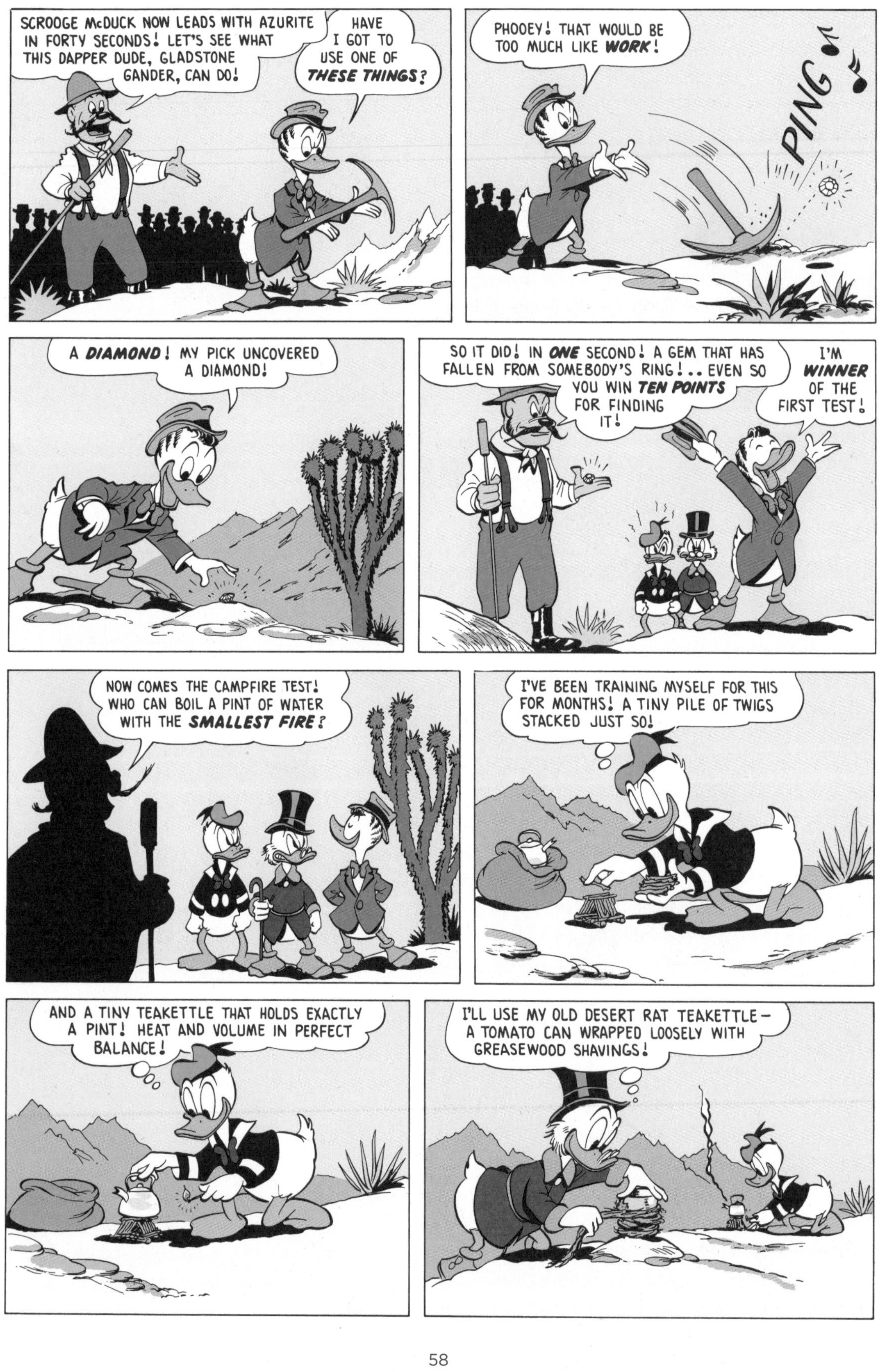
SCROOGE McDUCK NOW LEADS WITH AZURITE IN FORTY SECONDS! LET'S SEE WHAT THIS DAPPER DUDE, GLADSTONE GANDER, CAN DO!
HAVE I GOT TO USE ONE OF **THESE THINGS**?
PHOOEY! THAT WOULD BE TOO MUCH LIKE **WORK**!
PING
A **DIAMOND**! MY PICK UNCOVERED A DIAMOND!
SO IT DID! IN **ONE** SECOND! A GEM THAT HAS FALLEN FROM SOMEBODY'S RING!.. EVEN SO YOU WIN **TEN POINTS** FOR FINDING IT!
I'M **WINNER** OF THE FIRST TEST!
NOW COMES THE CAMPFIRE TEST! WHO CAN BOIL A PINT OF WATER WITH THE **SMALLEST FIRE**?
I'VE BEEN TRAINING MYSELF FOR THIS FOR MONTHS! A TINY PILE OF TWIGS STACKED JUST SO!
AND A TINY TEAKETTLE THAT HOLDS EXACTLY A PINT! HEAT AND VOLUME IN PERFECT BALANCE!
I'LL USE MY OLD DESERT RAT TEAKETTLE— A TOMATO CAN WRAPPED LOOSELY WITH GREASEWOOD SHAVINGS!

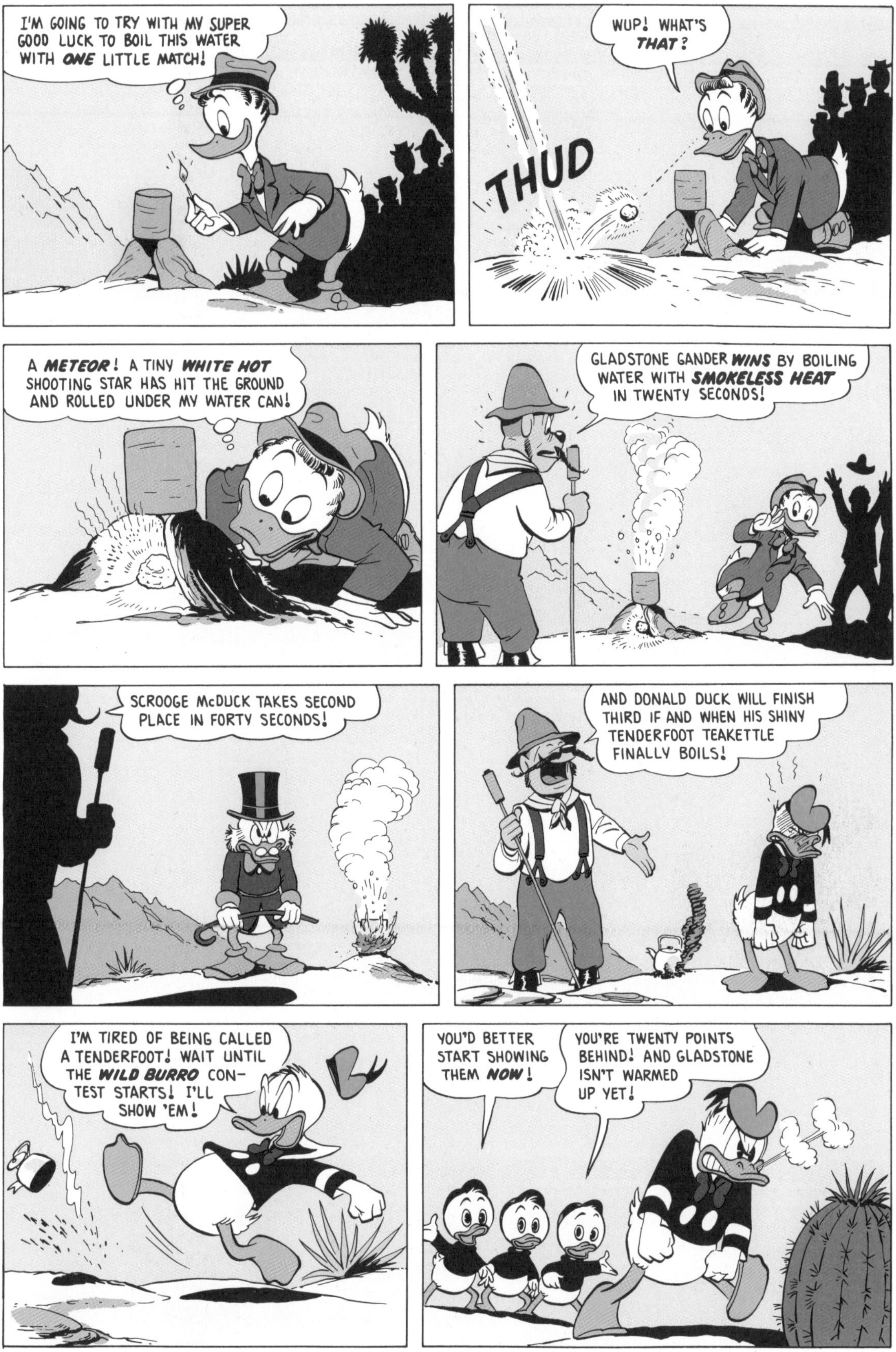
I'M GOING TO TRY WITH MY SUPER GOOD LUCK TO BOIL THIS WATER WITH ONE LITTLE MATCH!
WUP! WHAT'S THAT?
THUD
A METEOR! A TINY WHITE HOT SHOOTING STAR HAS HIT THE GROUND AND ROLLED UNDER MY WATER CAN!
GLADSTONE GANDER WINS BY BOILING WATER WITH SMOKELESS HEAT IN TWENTY SECONDS!
SCROOGE McDUCK TAKES SECOND PLACE IN FORTY SECONDS!
AND DONALD DUCK WILL FINISH THIRD IF AND WHEN HIS SHINY TENDERFOOT TEAKETTLE FINALLY BOILS!
I'M TIRED OF BEING CALLED A TENDERFOOT! WAIT UNTIL THE WILD BURRO CONTEST STARTS! I'LL SHOW 'EM!
YOU'D BETTER START SHOWING THEM NOW!
YOU'RE TWENTY POINTS BEHIND! AND GLADSTONE ISN'T WARMED UP YET!

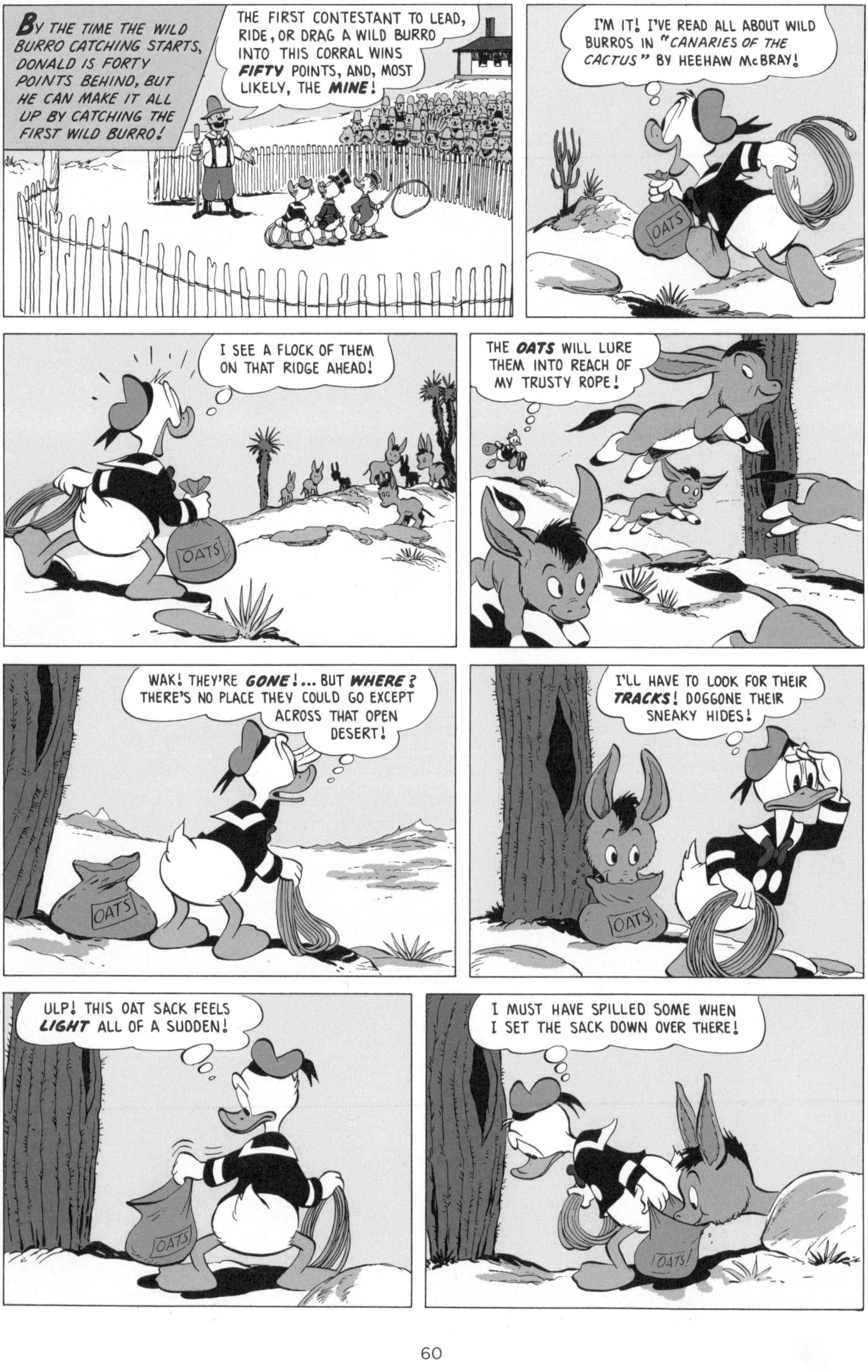
BY THE TIME THE WILD BURRO CATCHING STARTS, DONALD IS FORTY POINTS BEHIND, BUT HE CAN MAKE IT ALL UP BY CATCHING THE FIRST WILD BURRO!
THE FIRST CONTESTANT TO LEAD, RIDE, OR DRAG A WILD BURRO INTO THIS CORRAL WINS FIFTY POINTS, AND, MOST LIKELY, THE MINE!
I'M IT! I'VE READ ALL ABOUT WILD BURROS IN "CANARIES OF THE CACTUS" BY HEEHAW McBRAY!
OATS
I SEE A FLOCK OF THEM ON THAT RIDGE AHEAD!
OATS
THE OATS WILL LURE THEM INTO REACH OF MY TRUSTY ROPE!
WAK! THEY'RE GONE!... BUT WHERE? THERE'S NO PLACE THEY COULD GO EXCEPT ACROSS THAT OPEN DESERT!
OATS
I'LL HAVE TO LOOK FOR THEIR TRACKS! DOGGONE THEIR SNEAKY HIDES!
OATS
ULP! THIS OAT SACK FEELS LIGHT ALL OF A SUDDEN!
OATS
I MUST HAVE SPILLED SOME WHEN I SET THE SACK DOWN OVER THERE!
OATS

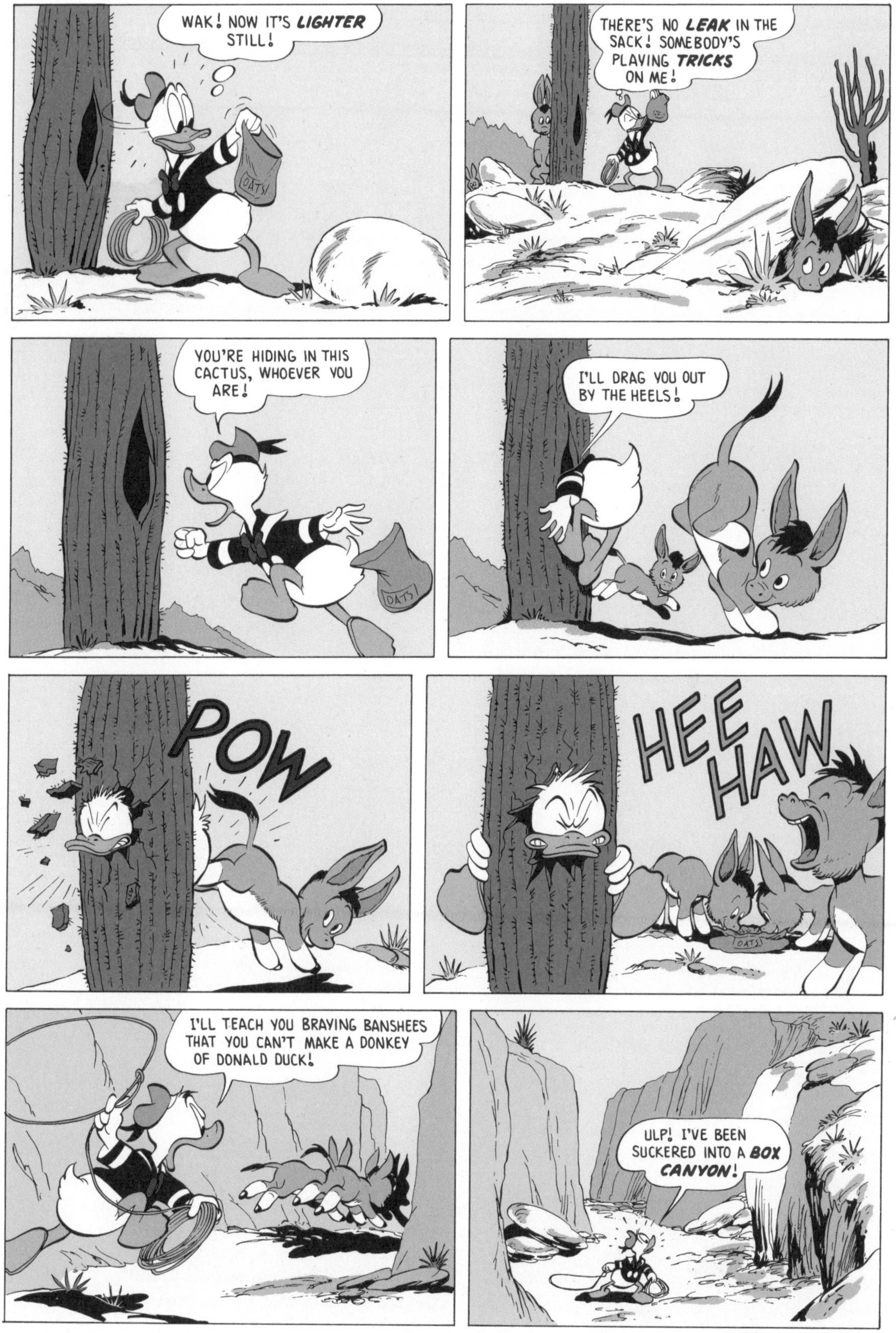
WAK! NOW IT'S **LIGHTER** STILL!
OATS
THERE'S NO **LEAK** IN THE SACK! SOMEBODY'S PLAYING **TRICKS** ON ME!
YOU'RE HIDING IN THIS CACTUS, WHOEVER YOU ARE!
OATS
I'LL DRAG YOU OUT BY THE HEELS!
POW
HEE HAW
OATS
I'LL TEACH YOU BRAYING BANSHEES THAT YOU CAN'T MAKE A DONKEY OF DONALD DUCK!
ULP! I'VE BEEN SUCKERED INTO A **BOX CANYON**!

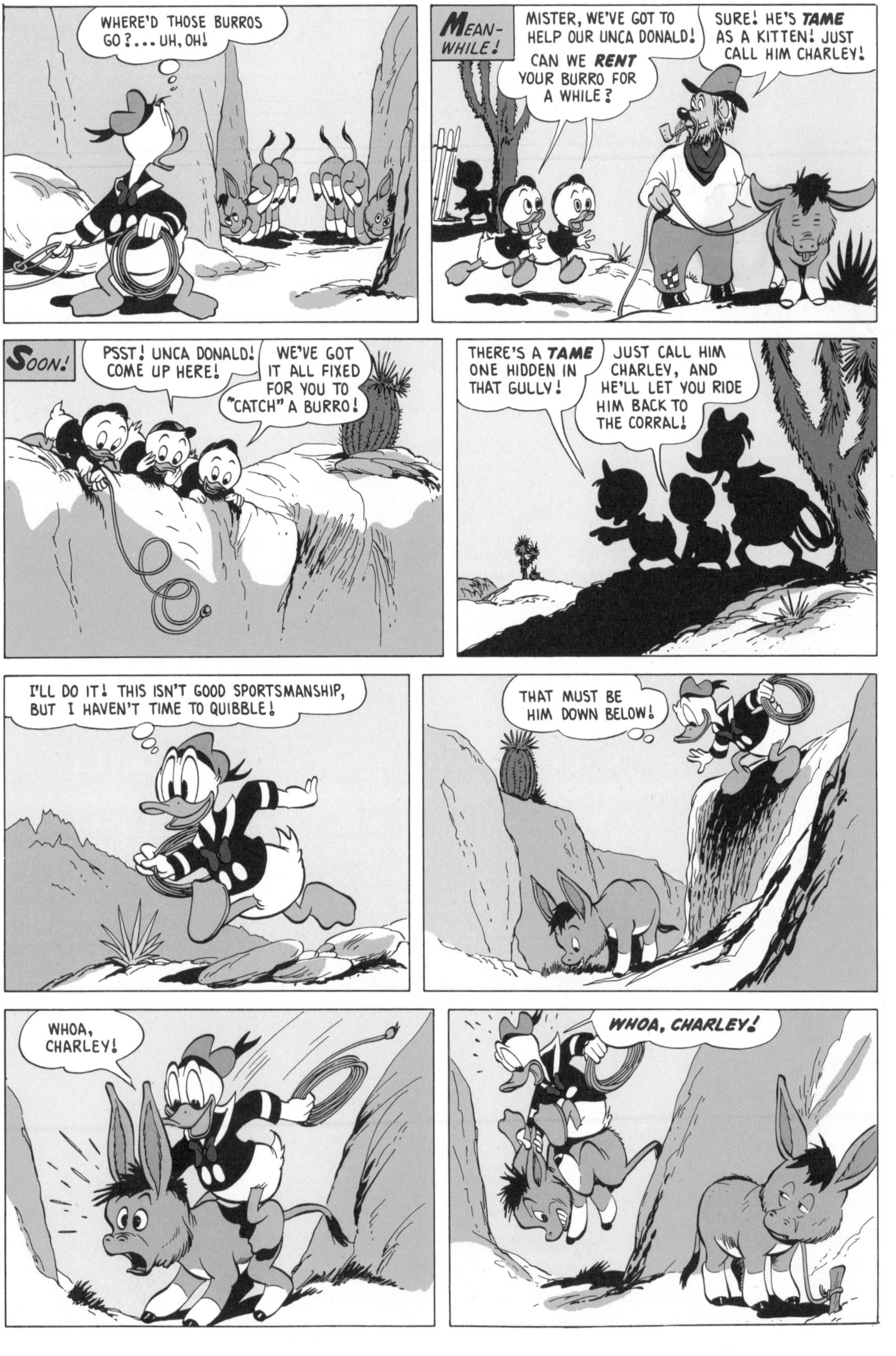

WHERE'D THOSE BURROS GO?... UH, OH!
MEAN-WHILE!
MISTER, WE'VE GOT TO HELP OUR UNCA DONALD!
CAN WE RENT YOUR BURRO FOR A WHILE?
SURE! HE'S TAME AS A KITTEN! JUST CALL HIM CHARLEY!
SOON!
PSST! UNCA DONALD! COME UP HERE!
WE'VE GOT IT ALL FIXED FOR YOU TO "CATCH" A BURRO!
THERE'S A TAME ONE HIDDEN IN THAT GULLY!
JUST CALL HIM CHARLEY, AND HE'LL LET YOU RIDE HIM BACK TO THE CORRAL!
I'LL DO IT! THIS ISN'T GOOD SPORTSMANSHIP, BUT I HAVEN'T TIME TO QUIBBLE!
THAT MUST BE HIM DOWN BELOW!
WHOA, CHARLEY!
WHOA, CHARLEY!

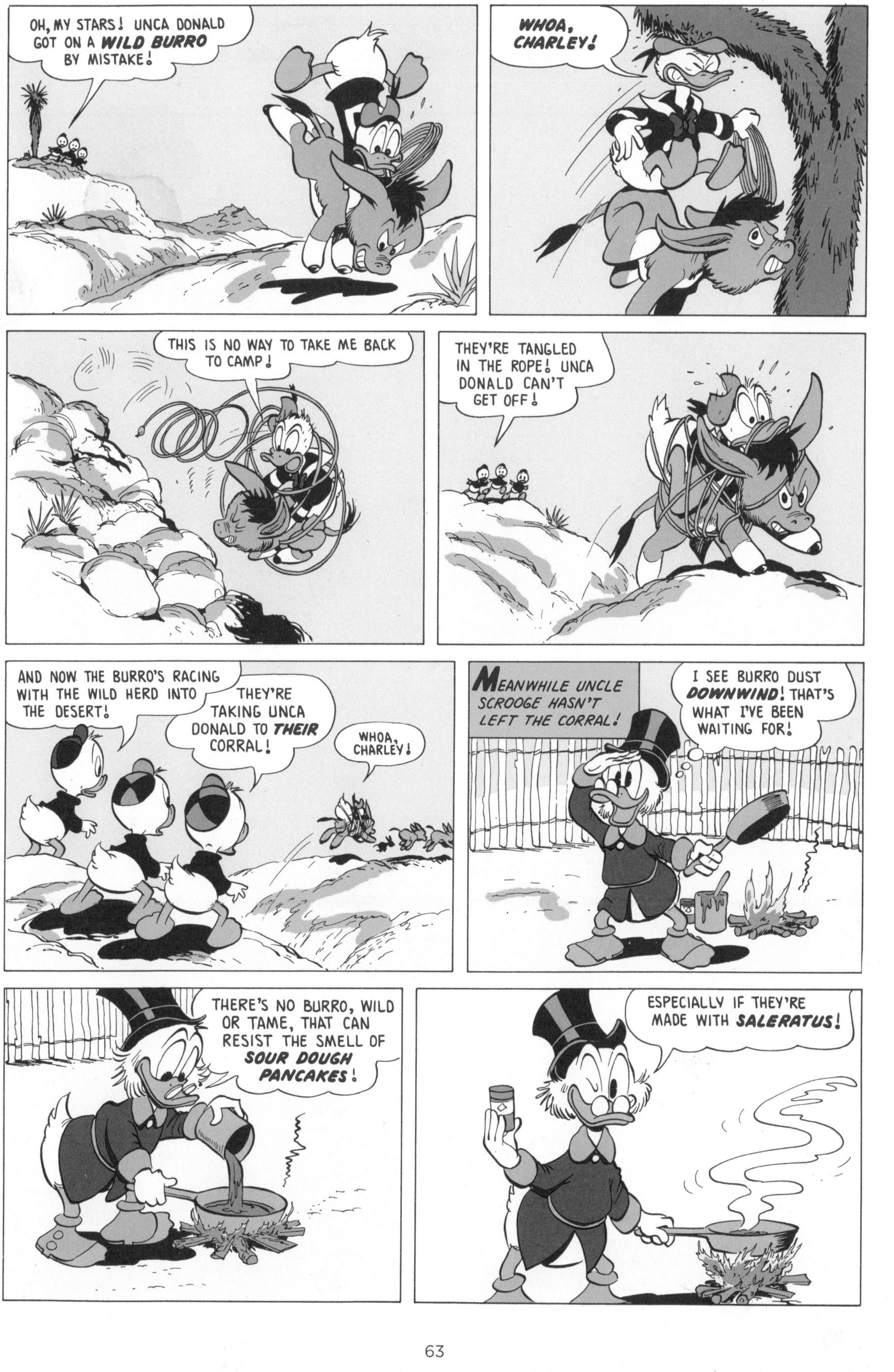

OH, MY STARS! UNCA DONALD GOT ON A **WILD BURRO** BY MISTAKE!
WHOA, CHARLEY!
THIS IS NO WAY TO TAKE ME BACK TO CAMP!
THEY'RE TANGLED IN THE ROPE! UNCA DONALD CAN'T GET OFF!
AND NOW THE BURRO'S RACING WITH THE WILD HERD INTO THE DESERT!
THEY'RE TAKING UNCA DONALD TO **THEIR** CORRAL!
WHOA, CHARLEY!
MEANWHILE UNCLE SCROOGE HASN'T LEFT THE CORRAL!
I SEE BURRO DUST **DOWNWIND**! THAT'S WHAT I'VE BEEN WAITING FOR!
THERE'S NO BURRO, WILD OR TAME, THAT CAN RESIST THE SMELL OF **SOUR DOUGH PANCAKES**!
ESPECIALLY IF THEY'RE MADE WITH **SALERATUS**!

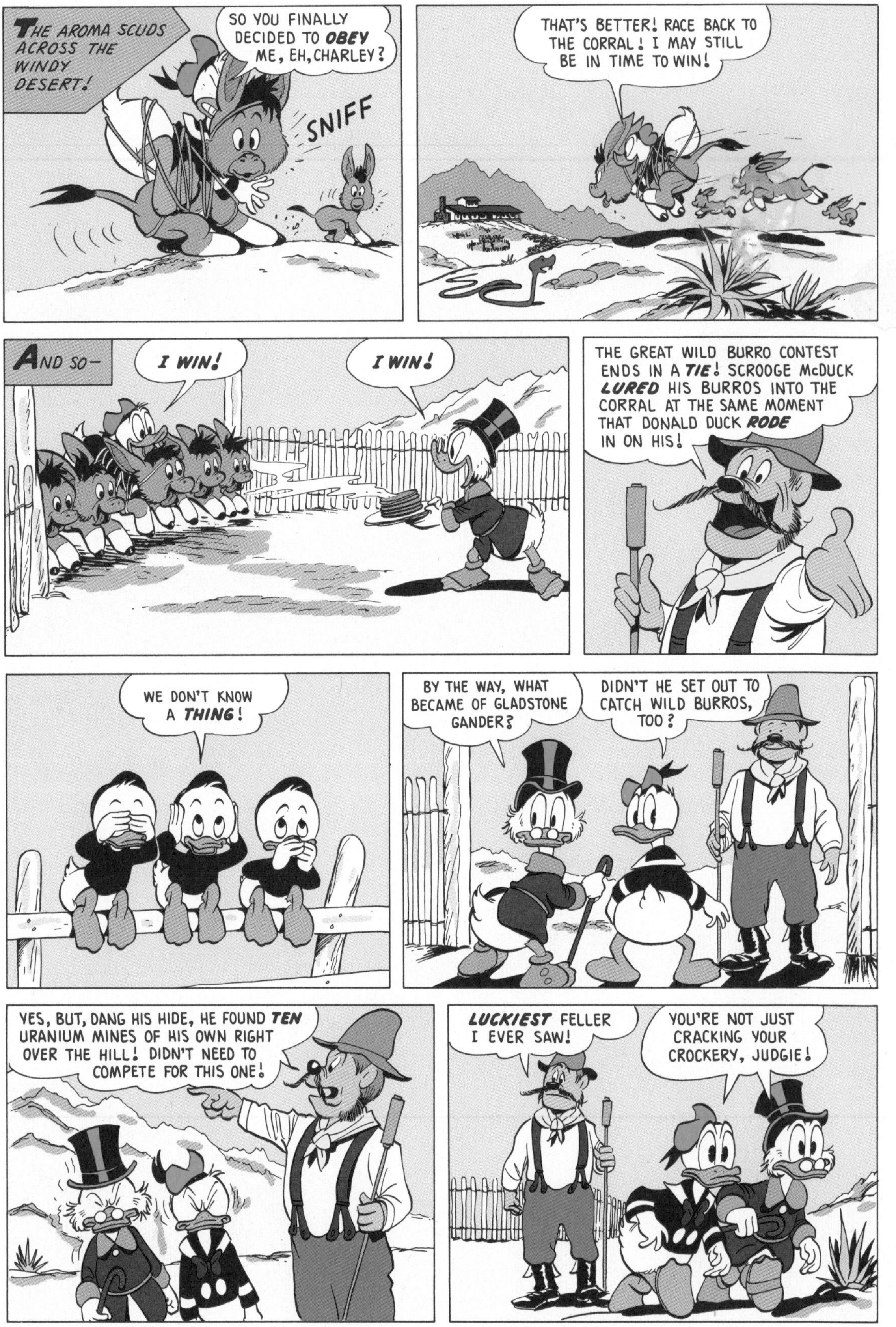

THE AROMA SCUDS ACROSS THE WINDY DESERT!
SO YOU FINALLY DECIDED TO OBEY ME, EH, CHARLEY?
SNIFF
THAT'S BETTER! RACE BACK TO THE CORRAL! I MAY STILL BE IN TIME TO WIN!
AND SO—
I WIN!
I WIN!
THE GREAT WILD BURRO CONTEST ENDS IN A TIE! SCROOGE McDUCK LURED HIS BURROS INTO THE CORRAL AT THE SAME MOMENT THAT DONALD DUCK RODE IN ON HIS!
WE DON'T KNOW A THING!
BY THE WAY, WHAT BECAME OF GLADSTONE GANDER?
DIDN'T HE SET OUT TO CATCH WILD BURROS, TOO?
YES, BUT, DANG HIS HIDE, HE FOUND TEN URANIUM MINES OF HIS OWN RIGHT OVER THE HILL! DIDN'T NEED TO COMPETE FOR THIS ONE!
LUCKIEST FELLER I EVER SAW!
YOU'RE NOT JUST CRACKING YOUR CROCKERY, JUDGIE!

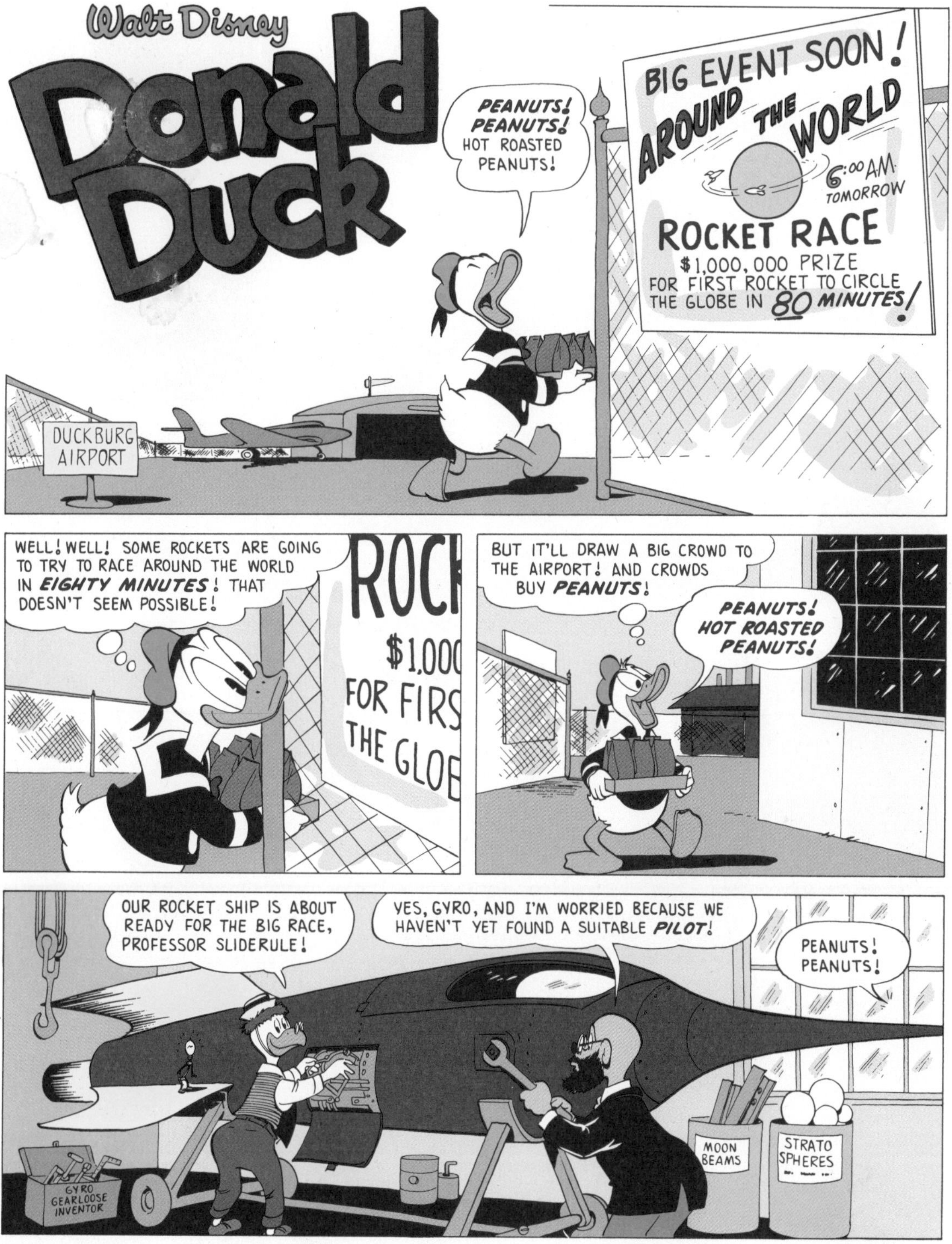
Walt Disney
Donald Duck
PEANUTS! PEANUTS! HOT ROASTED PEANUTS!
BIG EVENT SOON! AROUND THE WORLD 6:00 A.M. TOMORROW ROCKET RACE $1,000,000 PRIZE FOR FIRST ROCKET TO CIRCLE THE GLOBE IN 80 MINUTES!
DUCKBURG AIRPORT
WELL! WELL! SOME ROCKETS ARE GOING TO TRY TO RACE AROUND THE WORLD IN EIGHTY MINUTES! THAT DOESN'T SEEM POSSIBLE!
ROCK $1,000 FOR FIRS THE GLOBE
BUT IT'LL DRAW A BIG CROWD TO THE AIRPORT! AND CROWDS BUY PEANUTS!
PEANUTS! HOT ROASTED PEANUTS!
OUR ROCKET SHIP IS ABOUT READY FOR THE BIG RACE, PROFESSOR SLIDERULE!
YES, GYRO, AND I'M WORRIED BECAUSE WE HAVEN'T YET FOUND A SUITABLE PILOT!
PEANUTS! PEANUTS!
GYRO GEARLOOSE INVENTOR
MOON BEAMS
STRATO SPHERES

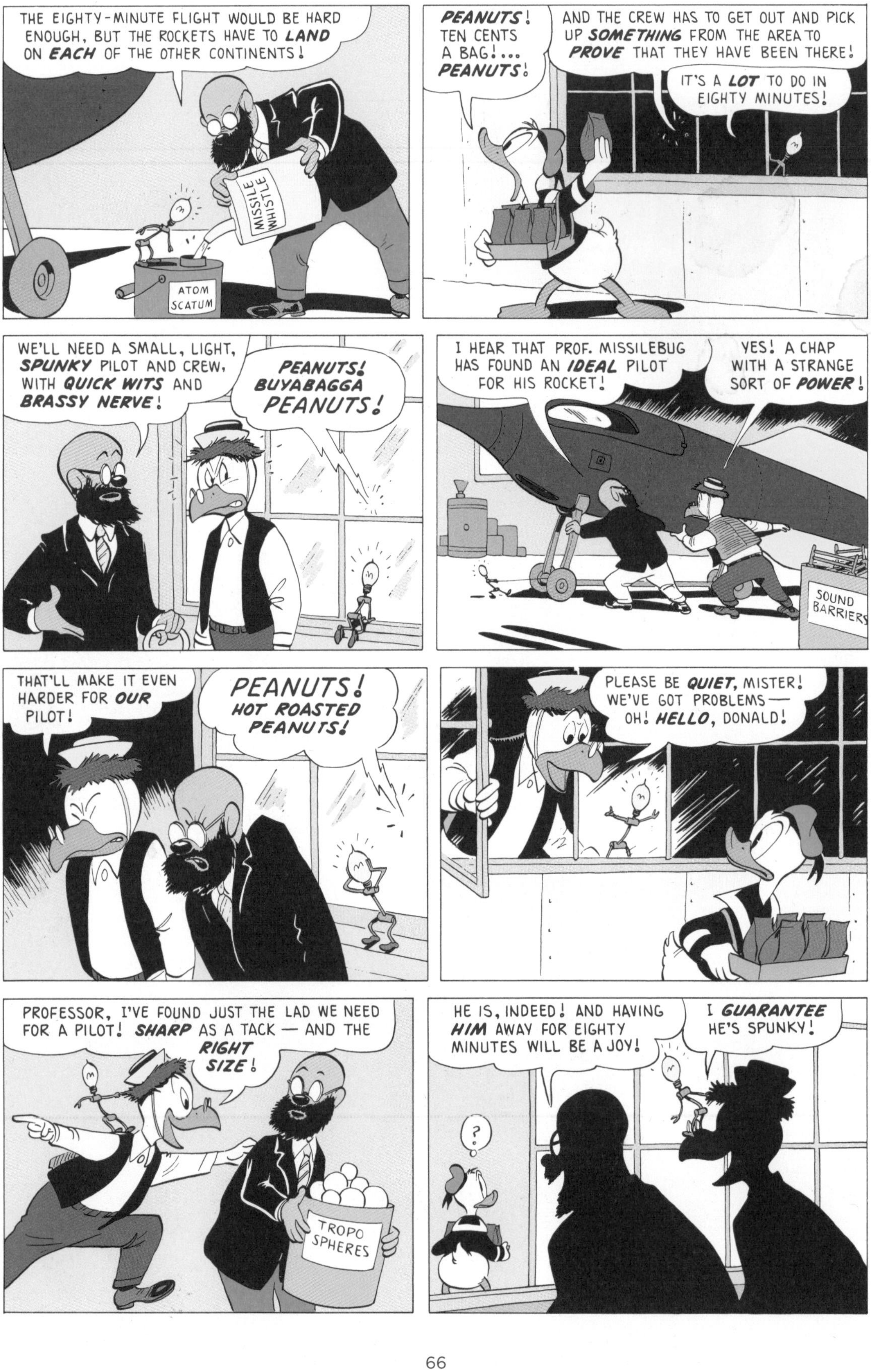
THE EIGHTY-MINUTE FLIGHT WOULD BE HARD ENOUGH, BUT THE ROCKETS HAVE TO **LAND** ON **EACH** OF THE OTHER CONTINENTS!
MISSILE WHISTLE
ATOM SCATUM
PEANUTS! TEN CENTS A BAG!... **PEANUTS**!
AND THE CREW HAS TO GET OUT AND PICK UP **SOMETHING** FROM THE AREA TO **PROVE** THAT THEY HAVE BEEN THERE!
IT'S A **LOT** TO DO IN EIGHTY MINUTES!
WE'LL NEED A SMALL, LIGHT, **SPUNKY** PILOT AND CREW, WITH **QUICK WITS** AND **BRASSY NERVE**!
PEANUTS! BUYABAGGA PEANUTS!
I HEAR THAT PROF. MISSILEBUG HAS FOUND AN **IDEAL** PILOT FOR HIS ROCKET!
YES! A CHAP WITH A STRANGE SORT OF **POWER**!
SOUND BARRIERS
THAT'LL MAKE IT EVEN HARDER FOR **OUR** PILOT!
PEANUTS! **HOT ROASTED PEANUTS!**
PLEASE BE **QUIET**, MISTER! WE'VE GOT PROBLEMS— OH! **HELLO**, DONALD!
PROFESSOR, I'VE FOUND JUST THE LAD WE NEED FOR A PILOT! **SHARP** AS A TACK — AND THE **RIGHT SIZE**!
TROPO SPHERES
HE IS, INDEED! AND HAVING **HIM** AWAY FOR EIGHTY MINUTES WILL BE A JOY!
I **GUARANTEE** HE'S SPUNKY!
?

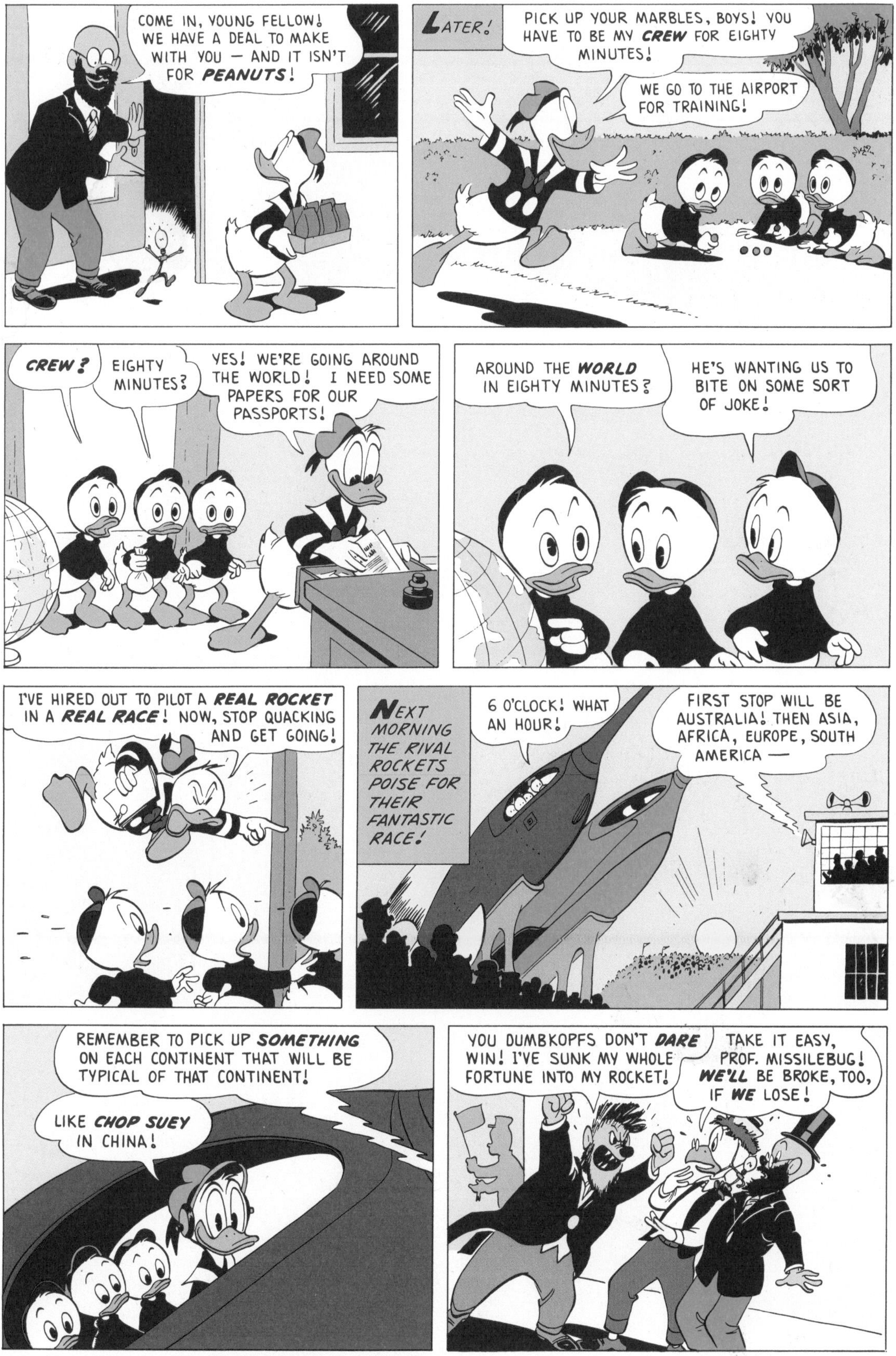
COME IN, YOUNG FELLOW! WE HAVE A DEAL TO MAKE WITH YOU — AND IT ISN'T FOR PEANUTS!
LATER!
PICK UP YOUR MARBLES, BOYS! YOU HAVE TO BE MY CREW FOR EIGHTY MINUTES!
WE GO TO THE AIRPORT FOR TRAINING!
CREW?
EIGHTY MINUTES?
YES! WE'RE GOING AROUND THE WORLD! I NEED SOME PAPERS FOR OUR PASSPORTS!
AROUND THE WORLD IN EIGHTY MINUTES?
HE'S WANTING US TO BITE ON SOME SORT OF JOKE!
I'VE HIRED OUT TO PILOT A REAL ROCKET IN A REAL RACE! NOW, STOP QUACKING AND GET GOING!
NEXT MORNING THE RIVAL ROCKETS POISE FOR THEIR FANTASTIC RACE!
6 O'CLOCK! WHAT AN HOUR!
FIRST STOP WILL BE AUSTRALIA! THEN ASIA, AFRICA, EUROPE, SOUTH AMERICA —
REMEMBER TO PICK UP SOMETHING ON EACH CONTINENT THAT WILL BE TYPICAL OF THAT CONTINENT!
LIKE CHOP SUEY IN CHINA!
YOU DUMBKOPFS DON'T DARE WIN! I'VE SUNK MY WHOLE FORTUNE INTO MY ROCKET!
TAKE IT EASY, PROF. MISSILEBUG! WE'LL BE BROKE, TOO, IF WE LOSE!

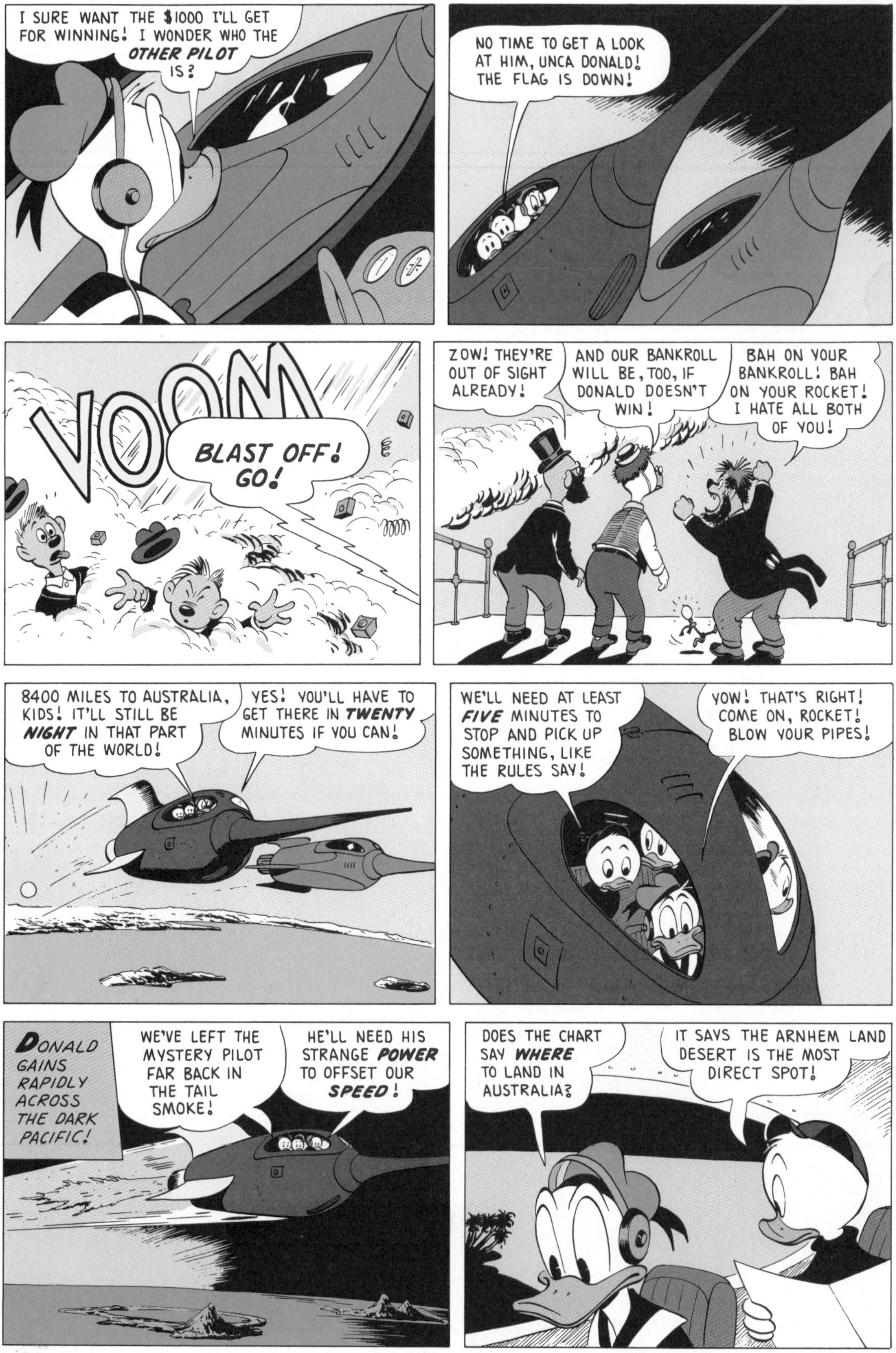
I SURE WANT THE $1000 I'LL GET FOR WINNING! I WONDER WHO THE OTHER PILOT IS?
NO TIME TO GET A LOOK AT HIM, UNCA DONALD! THE FLAG IS DOWN!
VOOM
BLAST OFF! GO!
ZOW! THEY'RE OUT OF SIGHT ALREADY!
AND OUR BANKROLL WILL BE, TOO, IF DONALD DOESN'T WIN!
BAH ON YOUR BANKROLL! BAH ON YOUR ROCKET! I HATE ALL BOTH OF YOU!
8400 MILES TO AUSTRALIA, KIDS! IT'LL STILL BE NIGHT IN THAT PART OF THE WORLD!
YES! YOU'LL HAVE TO GET THERE IN TWENTY MINUTES IF YOU CAN!
WE'LL NEED AT LEAST FIVE MINUTES TO STOP AND PICK UP SOMETHING, LIKE THE RULES SAY!
YOW! THAT'S RIGHT! COME ON, ROCKET! BLOW YOUR PIPES!
DONALD GAINS RAPIDLY ACROSS THE DARK PACIFIC!
WE'VE LEFT THE MYSTERY PILOT FAR BACK IN THE TAIL SMOKE!
HE'LL NEED HIS STRANGE POWER TO OFFSET OUR SPEED!
DOES THE CHART SAY WHERE TO LAND IN AUSTRALIA?
IT SAYS THE ARNHEM LAND DESERT IS THE MOST DIRECT SPOT!

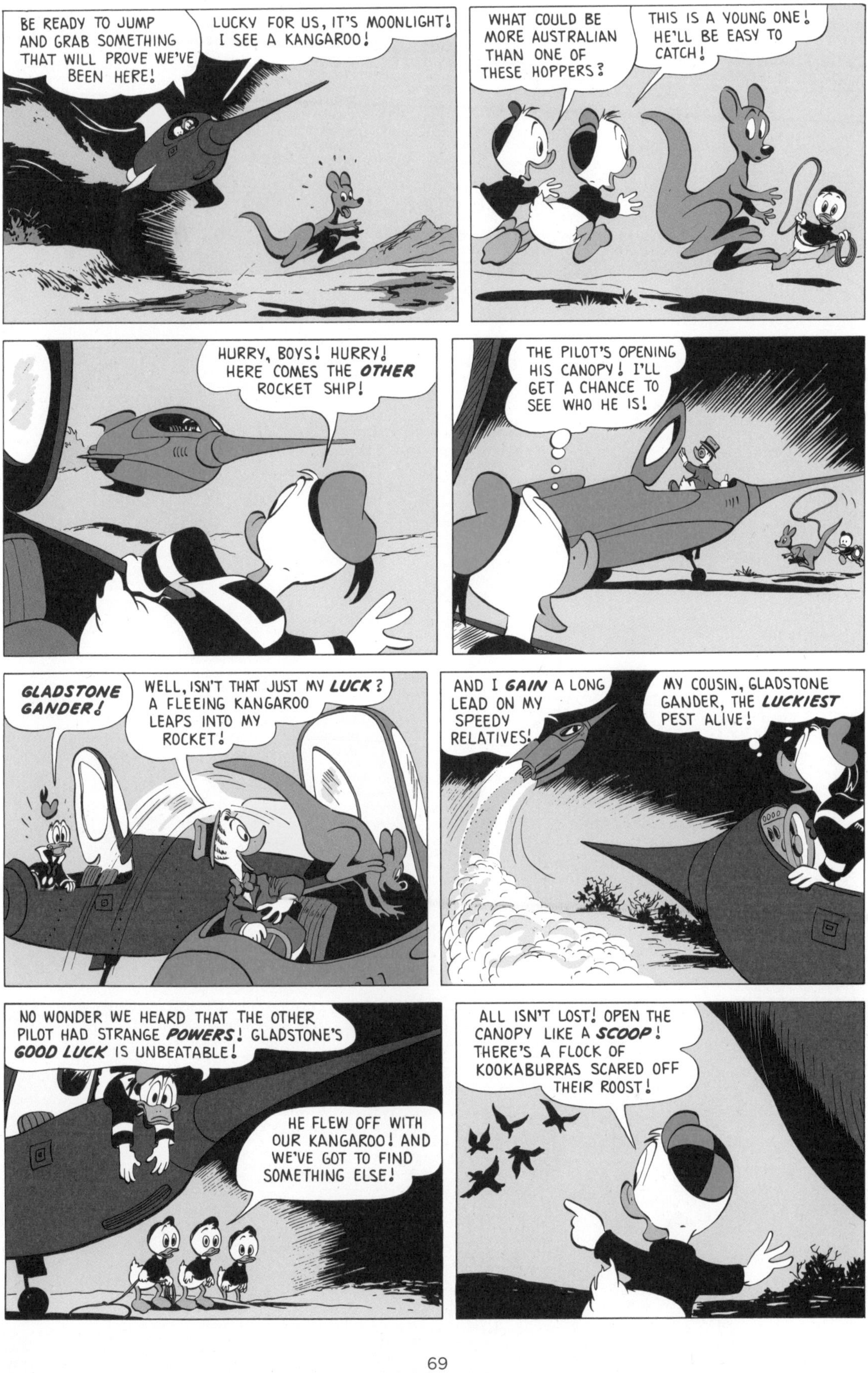
BE READY TO JUMP AND GRAB SOMETHING THAT WILL PROVE WE'VE BEEN HERE!
LUCKY FOR US, IT'S MOONLIGHT! I SEE A KANGAROO!
WHAT COULD BE MORE AUSTRALIAN THAN ONE OF THESE HOPPERS?
THIS IS A YOUNG ONE! HE'LL BE EASY TO CATCH!
HURRY, BOYS! HURRY! HERE COMES THE **OTHER** ROCKET SHIP!
THE PILOT'S OPENING HIS CANOPY! I'LL GET A CHANCE TO SEE WHO HE IS!
GLADSTONE GANDER!
WELL, ISN'T THAT JUST MY **LUCK**? A FLEEING KANGAROO LEAPS INTO MY ROCKET!
AND I **GAIN** A LONG LEAD ON MY SPEEDY RELATIVES!
MY COUSIN, GLADSTONE GANDER, THE **LUCKIEST** PEST ALIVE!
NO WONDER WE HEARD THAT THE OTHER PILOT HAD STRANGE **POWERS**! GLADSTONE'S **GOOD LUCK** IS UNBEATABLE!
HE FLEW OFF WITH OUR KANGAROO! AND WE'VE GOT TO FIND SOMETHING ELSE!
ALL ISN'T LOST! OPEN THE CANOPY LIKE A **SCOOP**! THERE'S A FLOCK OF KOOKABURRAS SCARED OFF THEIR ROOST!

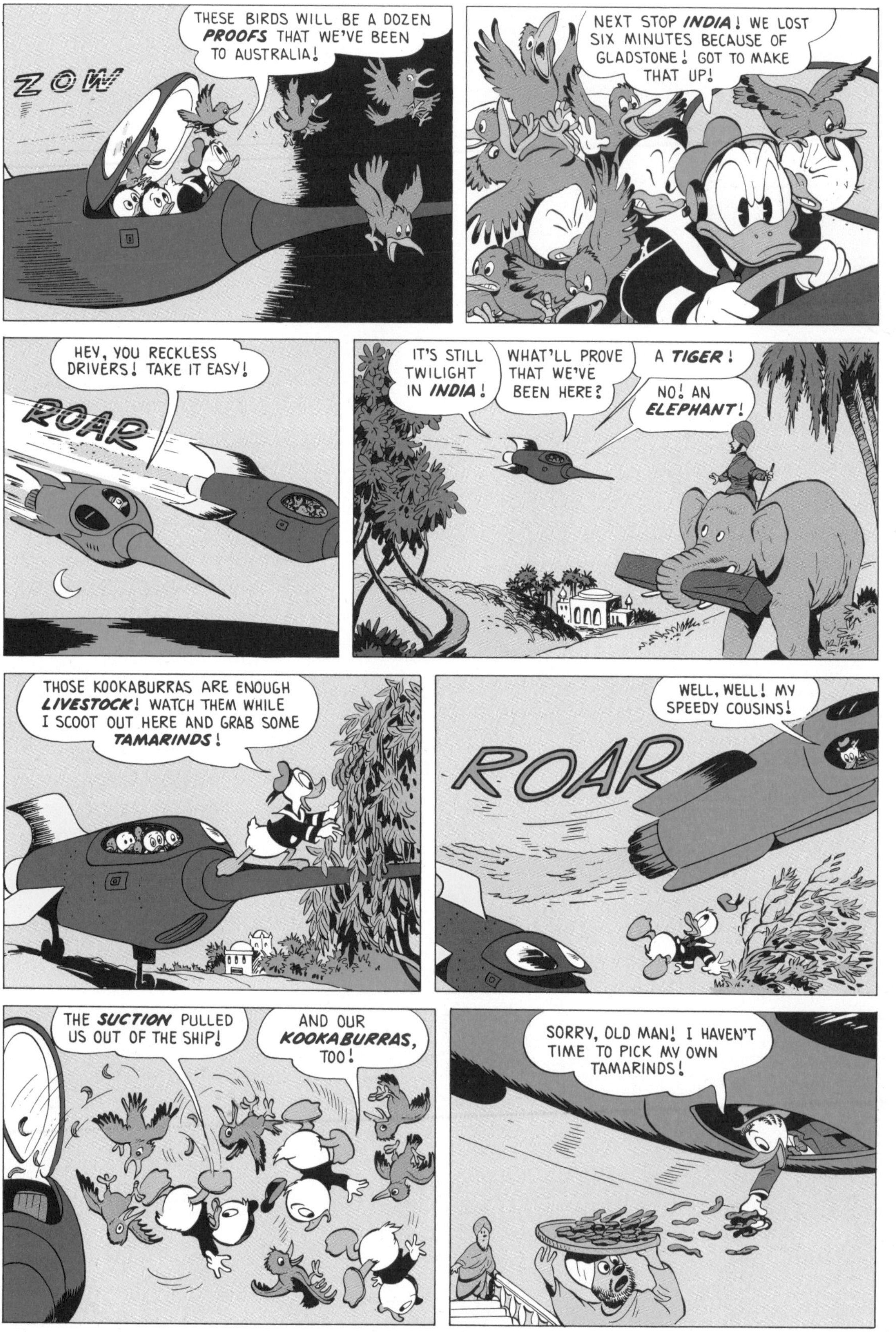
THESE BIRDS WILL BE A DOZEN PROOFS THAT WE'VE BEEN TO AUSTRALIA!
ZOW
NEXT STOP INDIA! WE LOST SIX MINUTES BECAUSE OF GLADSTONE! GOT TO MAKE THAT UP!
HEY, YOU RECKLESS DRIVERS! TAKE IT EASY!
ROAR
IT'S STILL TWILIGHT IN INDIA!
WHAT'LL PROVE THAT WE'VE BEEN HERE?
A TIGER!
NO! AN ELEPHANT!
THOSE KOOKABURRAS ARE ENOUGH LIVESTOCK! WATCH THEM WHILE I SCOOT OUT HERE AND GRAB SOME TAMARINDS!
WELL, WELL! MY SPEEDY COUSINS!
ROAR
THE SUCTION PULLED US OUT OF THE SHIP!
AND OUR KOOKABURRAS, TOO!
SORRY, OLD MAN! I HAVEN'T TIME TO PICK MY OWN TAMARINDS!

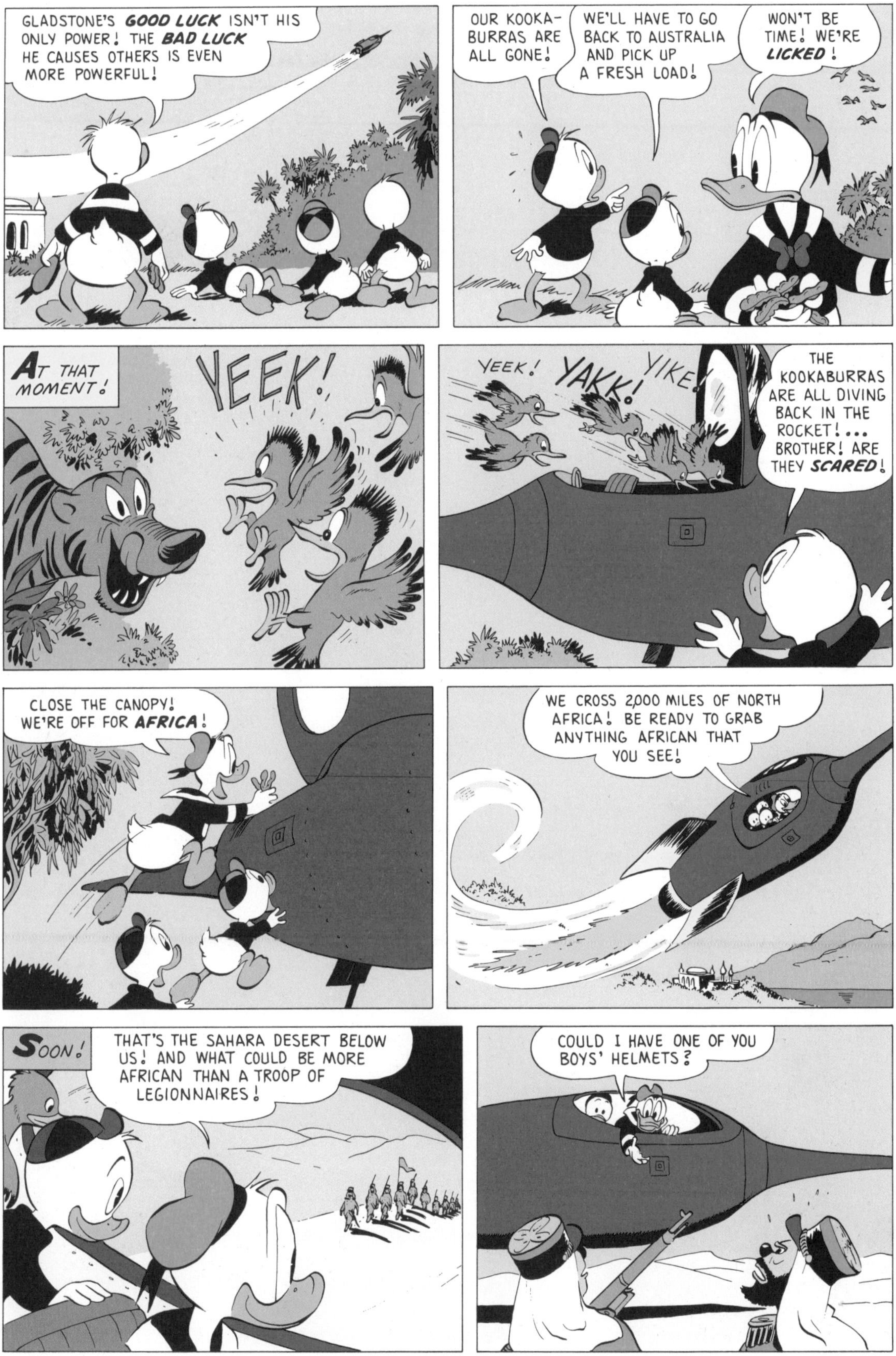
GLADSTONE'S GOOD LUCK ISN'T HIS ONLY POWER! THE BAD LUCK HE CAUSES OTHERS IS EVEN MORE POWERFUL!
OUR KOOKA-BURRAS ARE ALL GONE!
WE'LL HAVE TO GO BACK TO AUSTRALIA AND PICK UP A FRESH LOAD!
WON'T BE TIME! WE'RE LICKED!
AT THAT MOMENT!
YEEK!
YEEK! YAKK! YIKE!
THE KOOKABURRAS ARE ALL DIVING BACK IN THE ROCKET!... BROTHER! ARE THEY SCARED!
CLOSE THE CANOPY! WE'RE OFF FOR AFRICA!
WE CROSS 2,000 MILES OF NORTH AFRICA! BE READY TO GRAB ANYTHING AFRICAN THAT YOU SEE!
SOON!
THAT'S THE SAHARA DESERT BELOW US! AND WHAT COULD BE MORE AFRICAN THAN A TROOP OF LEGIONNAIRES!
COULD I HAVE ONE OF YOU BOYS' HELMETS?

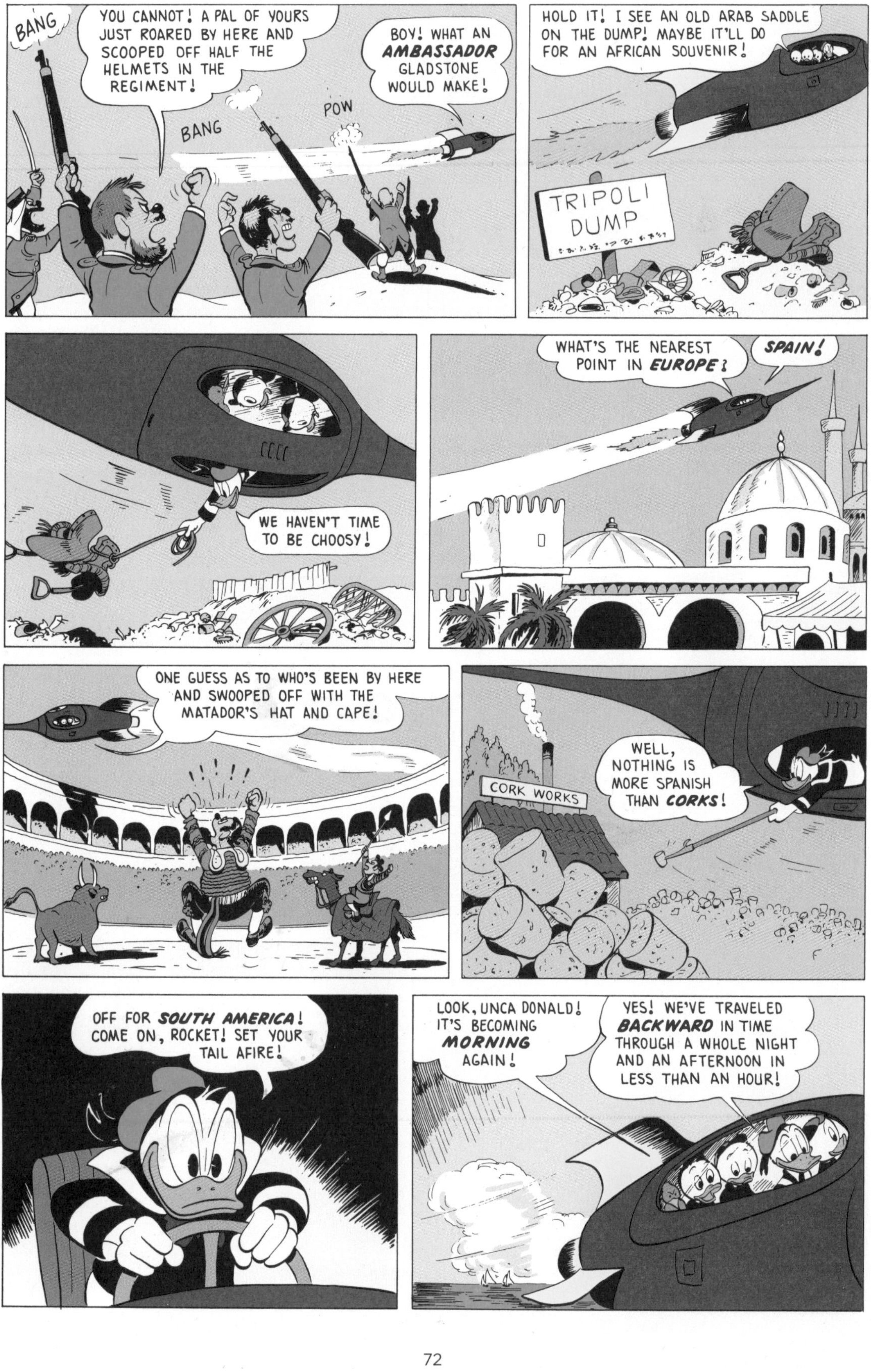
BANG
YOU CANNOT! A PAL OF YOURS JUST ROARED BY HERE AND SCOOPED OFF HALF THE HELMETS IN THE REGIMENT!
BANG
POW
BOY! WHAT AN **AMBASSADOR** GLADSTONE WOULD MAKE!
HOLD IT! I SEE AN OLD ARAB SADDLE ON THE DUMP! MAYBE IT'LL DO FOR AN AFRICAN SOUVENIR!
TRIPOLI DUMP
WE HAVEN'T TIME TO BE CHOOSY!
WHAT'S THE NEAREST POINT IN **EUROPE**?
SPAIN!
ONE GUESS AS TO WHO'S BEEN BY HERE AND SWOOPED OFF WITH THE MATADOR'S HAT AND CAPE!
CORK WORKS
WELL, NOTHING IS MORE SPANISH THAN **CORKS**!
OFF FOR **SOUTH AMERICA**! COME ON, ROCKET! SET YOUR TAIL AFIRE!
LOOK, UNCA DONALD! IT'S BECOMING **MORNING** AGAIN!
YES! WE'VE TRAVELED **BACKWARD** IN TIME THROUGH A WHOLE NIGHT AND AN AFTERNOON IN LESS THAN AN HOUR!

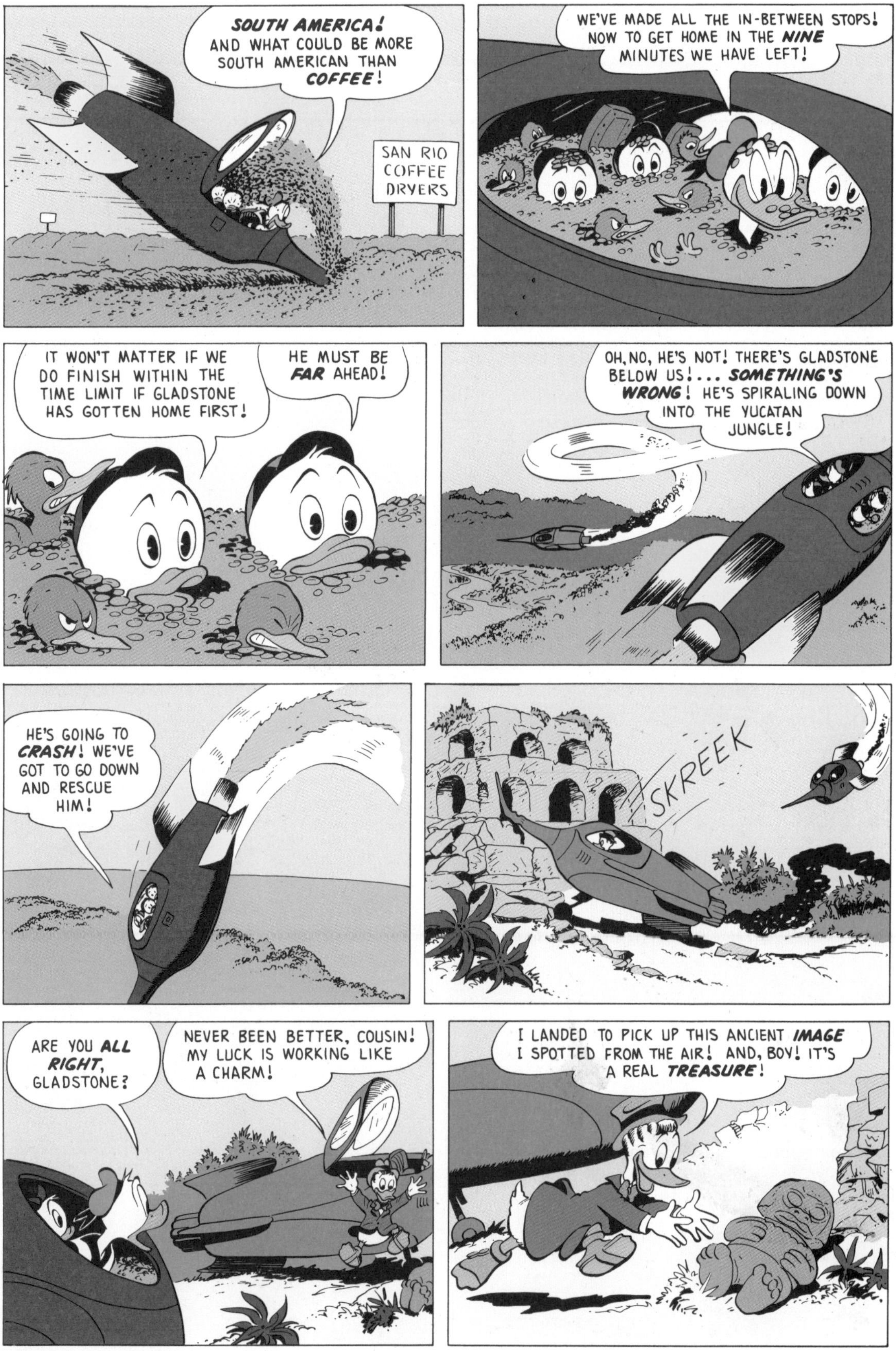
SOUTH AMERICA! AND WHAT COULD BE MORE SOUTH AMERICAN THAN COFFEE!
SAN RIO COFFEE DRYERS
WE'VE MADE ALL THE IN-BETWEEN STOPS! NOW TO GET HOME IN THE NINE MINUTES WE HAVE LEFT!
IT WON'T MATTER IF WE DO FINISH WITHIN THE TIME LIMIT IF GLADSTONE HAS GOTTEN HOME FIRST!
HE MUST BE FAR AHEAD!
OH, NO, HE'S NOT! THERE'S GLADSTONE BELOW US!... SOMETHING'S WRONG! HE'S SPIRALING DOWN INTO THE YUCATAN JUNGLE!
HE'S GOING TO CRASH! WE'VE GOT TO GO DOWN AND RESCUE HIM!
SKREEK
ARE YOU ALL RIGHT, GLADSTONE?
NEVER BEEN BETTER, COUSIN! MY LUCK IS WORKING LIKE A CHARM!
I LANDED TO PICK UP THIS ANCIENT IMAGE I SPOTTED FROM THE AIR! AND, BOY! IT'S A REAL TREASURE!

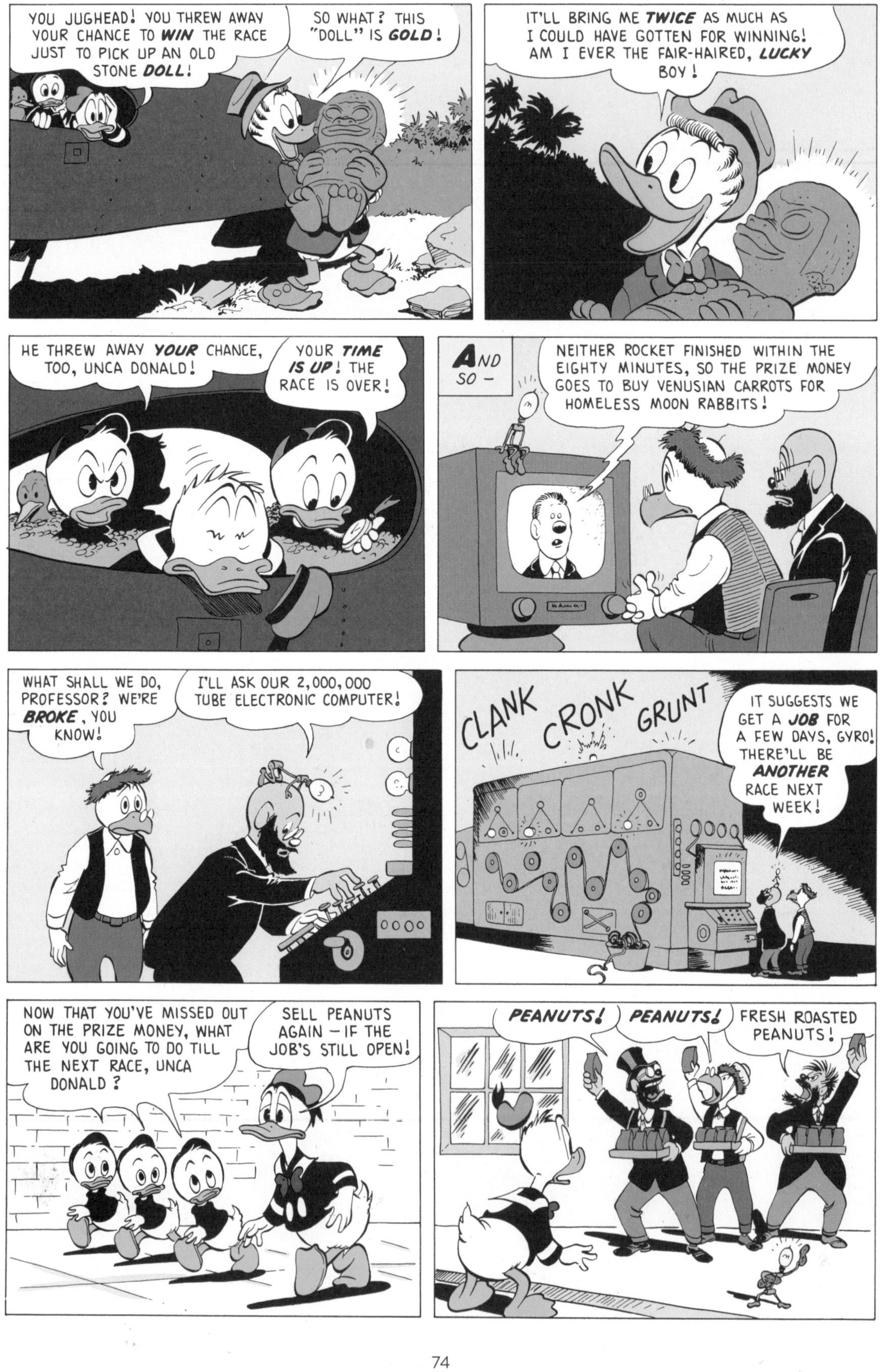

YOU JUGHEAD! YOU THREW AWAY YOUR CHANCE TO **WIN** THE RACE JUST TO PICK UP AN OLD STONE **DOLL**!
SO WHAT? THIS "DOLL" IS **GOLD**!
IT'LL BRING ME **TWICE** AS MUCH AS I COULD HAVE GOTTEN FOR WINNING! AM I EVER THE FAIR-HAIRED, **LUCKY** BOY!
HE THREW AWAY **YOUR** CHANCE, TOO, UNCA DONALD!
YOUR **TIME IS UP**! THE RACE IS OVER!
AND SO –
NEITHER ROCKET FINISHED WITHIN THE EIGHTY MINUTES, SO THE PRIZE MONEY GOES TO BUY VENUSIAN CARROTS FOR HOMELESS MOON RABBITS!
WHAT SHALL WE DO, PROFESSOR? WE'RE **BROKE**, YOU KNOW!
I'LL ASK OUR 2,000,000 TUBE ELECTRONIC COMPUTER!
CLANK
CRONK
GRUNT
IT SUGGESTS WE GET A **JOB** FOR A FEW DAYS, GYRO! THERE'LL BE **ANOTHER** RACE NEXT WEEK!
NOW THAT YOU'VE MISSED OUT ON THE PRIZE MONEY, WHAT ARE YOU GOING TO DO TILL THE NEXT RACE, UNCA DONALD?
SELL PEANUTS AGAIN – IF THE JOB'S STILL OPEN!
PEANUTS!
PEANUTS!
FRESH ROASTED PEANUTS!

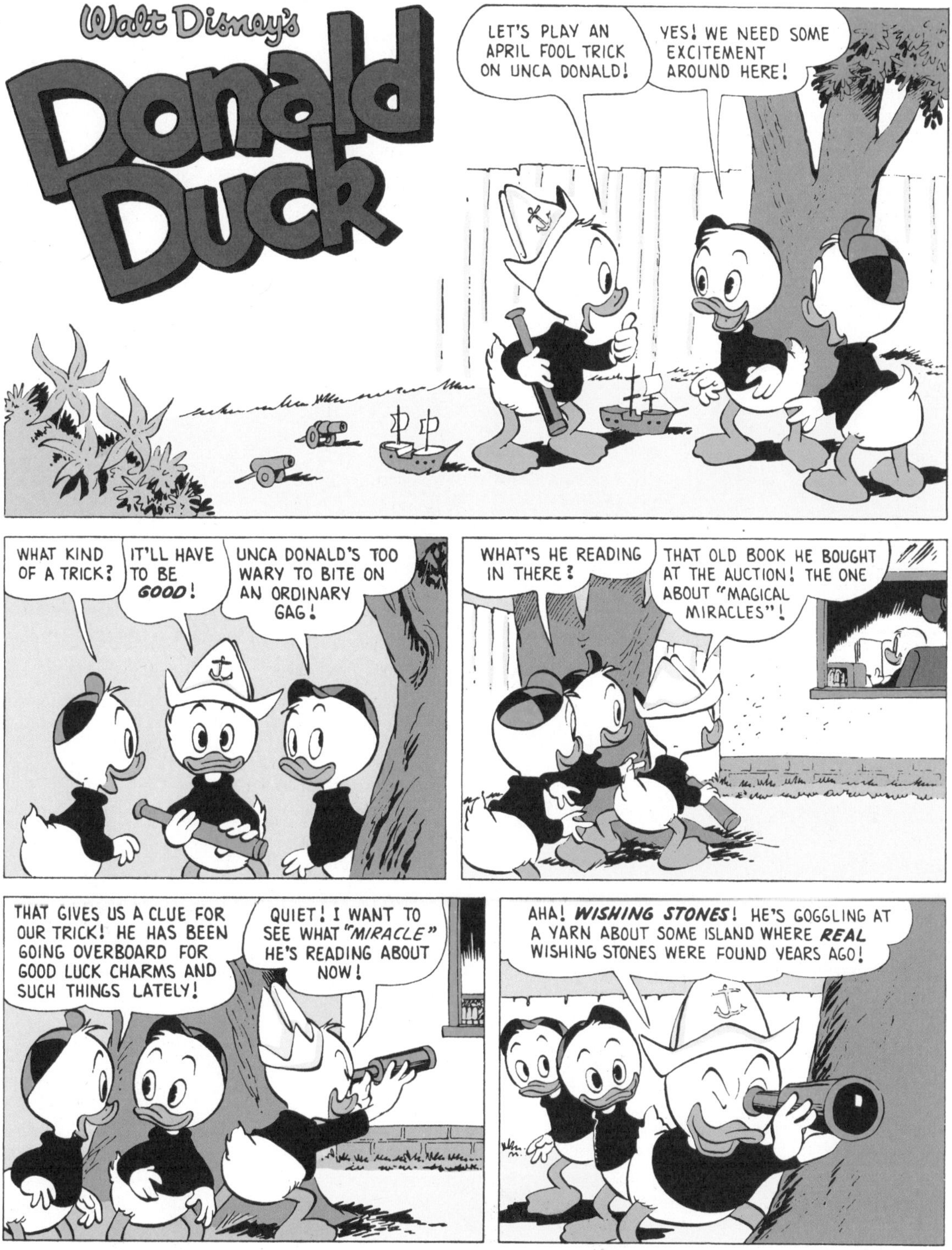
Walt Disney's
Donald Duck
LET'S PLAY AN APRIL FOOL TRICK ON UNCA DONALD!
YES! WE NEED SOME EXCITEMENT AROUND HERE!
WHAT KIND OF A TRICK?
IT'LL HAVE TO BE ***GOOD***!
UNCA DONALD'S TOO WARY TO BITE ON AN ORDINARY GAG!
WHAT'S HE READING IN THERE?
THAT OLD BOOK HE BOUGHT AT THE AUCTION! THE ONE ABOUT "MAGICAL MIRACLES"!
THAT GIVES US A CLUE FOR OUR TRICK! HE HAS BEEN GOING OVERBOARD FOR GOOD LUCK CHARMS AND SUCH THINGS LATELY!
QUIET! I WANT TO SEE WHAT "*MIRACLE*" HE'S READING ABOUT NOW!
AHA! ***WISHING STONES***! HE'S GOGGLING AT A YARN ABOUT SOME ISLAND WHERE ***REAL*** WISHING STONES WERE FOUND YEARS AGO!

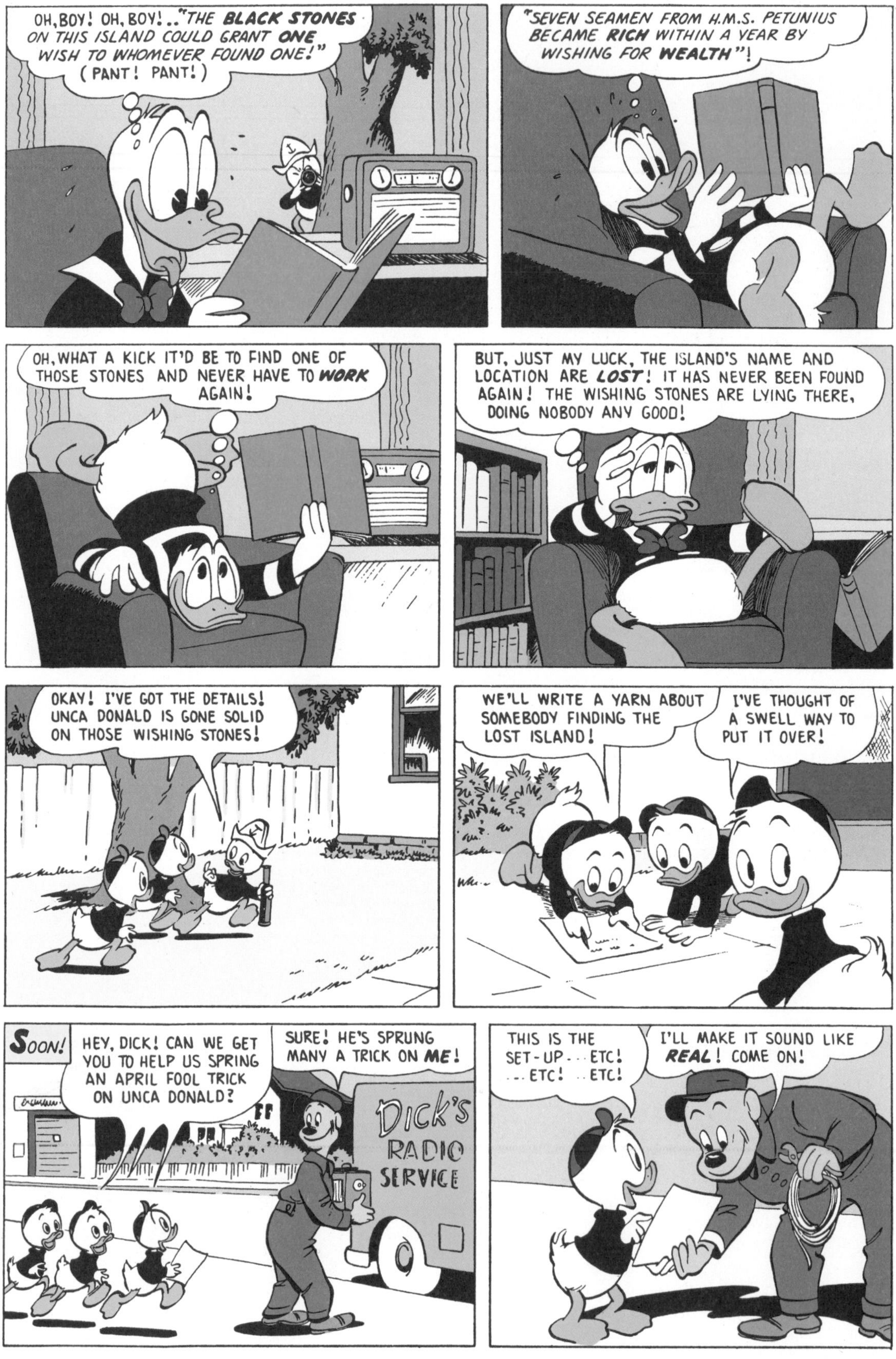
OH, BOY! OH, BOY! .."THE BLACK STONES ON THIS ISLAND COULD GRANT ONE WISH TO WHOMEVER FOUND ONE!" (PANT! PANT!)
"SEVEN SEAMEN FROM H.M.S. PETUNIUS BECAME RICH WITHIN A YEAR BY WISHING FOR WEALTH"!
OH, WHAT A KICK IT'D BE TO FIND ONE OF THOSE STONES AND NEVER HAVE TO WORK AGAIN!
BUT, JUST MY LUCK, THE ISLAND'S NAME AND LOCATION ARE LOST! IT HAS NEVER BEEN FOUND AGAIN! THE WISHING STONES ARE LYING THERE, DOING NOBODY ANY GOOD!
OKAY! I'VE GOT THE DETAILS! UNCA DONALD IS GONE SOLID ON THOSE WISHING STONES!
WE'LL WRITE A YARN ABOUT SOMEBODY FINDING THE LOST ISLAND!
I'VE THOUGHT OF A SWELL WAY TO PUT IT OVER!
SOON!
HEY, DICK! CAN WE GET YOU TO HELP US SPRING AN APRIL FOOL TRICK ON UNCA DONALD?
SURE! HE'S SPRUNG MANY A TRICK ON ME!
DICK'S RADIO SERVICE
THIS IS THE SET-UP... ETC! ...ETC! ..ETC!
I'LL MAKE IT SOUND LIKE REAL! COME ON!

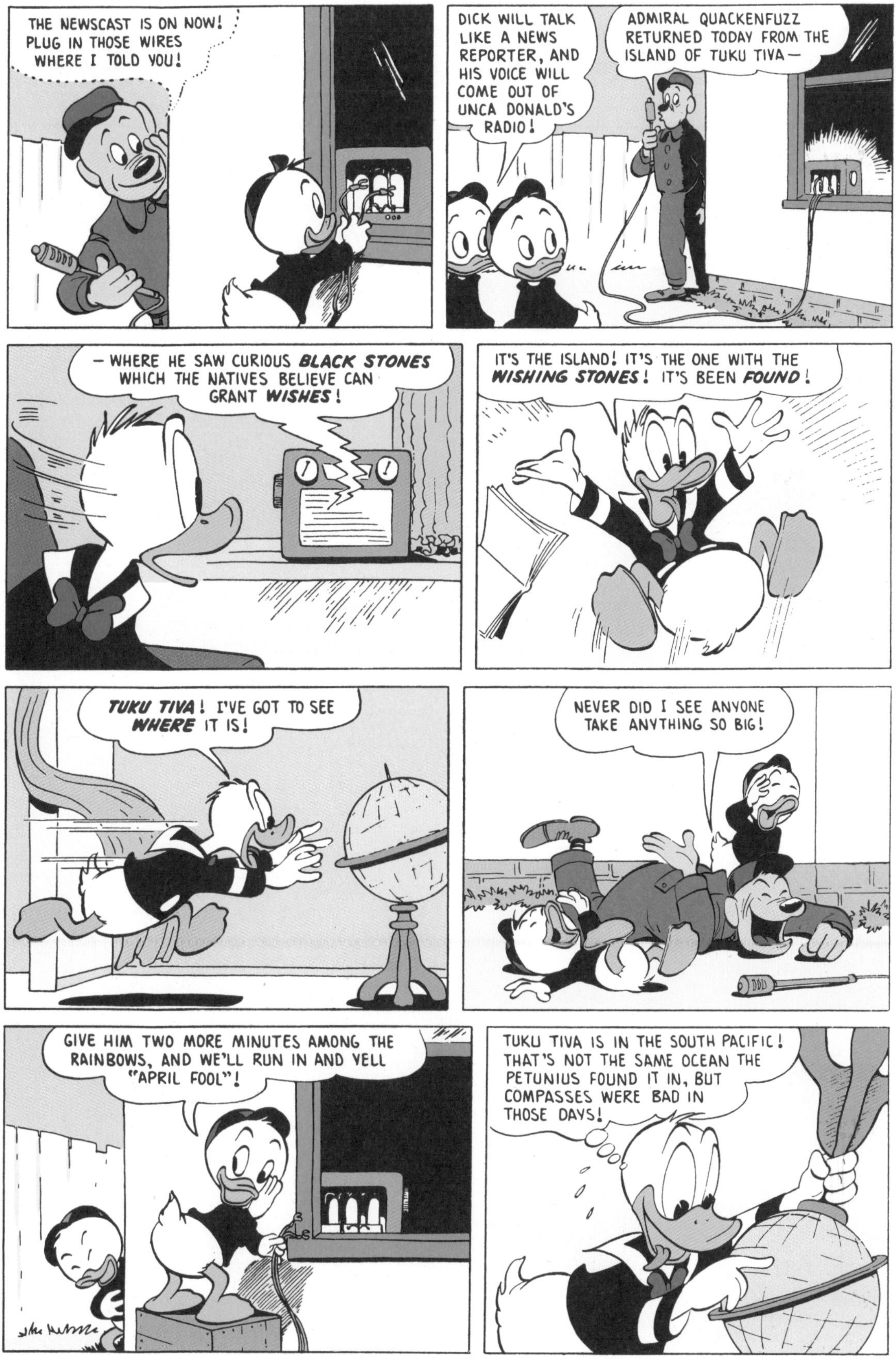
THE NEWSCAST IS ON NOW! PLUG IN THOSE WIRES WHERE I TOLD YOU!
DICK WILL TALK LIKE A NEWS REPORTER, AND HIS VOICE WILL COME OUT OF UNCA DONALD'S RADIO!
ADMIRAL QUACKENFUZZ RETURNED TODAY FROM THE ISLAND OF TUKU TIVA—
—WHERE HE SAW CURIOUS BLACK STONES WHICH THE NATIVES BELIEVE CAN GRANT WISHES!
IT'S THE ISLAND! IT'S THE ONE WITH THE WISHING STONES! IT'S BEEN FOUND!
TUKU TIVA! I'VE GOT TO SEE WHERE IT IS!
NEVER DID I SEE ANYONE TAKE ANYTHING SO BIG!
GIVE HIM TWO MORE MINUTES AMONG THE RAINBOWS, AND WE'LL RUN IN AND YELL "APRIL FOOL"!
TUKU TIVA IS IN THE SOUTH PACIFIC! THAT'S NOT THE SAME OCEAN THE PETUNIUS FOUND IT IN, BUT COMPASSES WERE BAD IN THOSE DAYS!

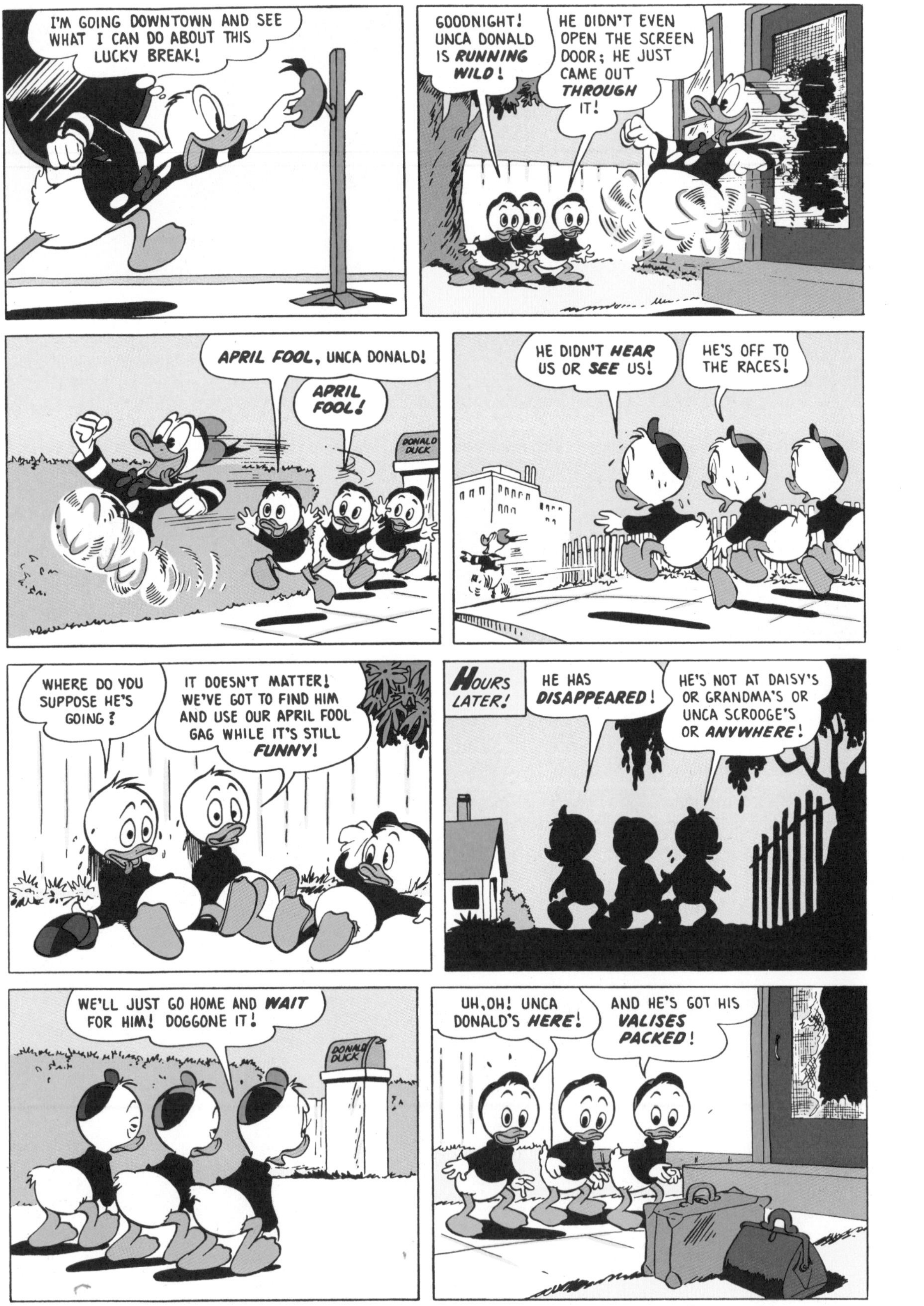
I'M GOING DOWNTOWN AND SEE WHAT I CAN DO ABOUT THIS LUCKY BREAK!
GOODNIGHT! UNCA DONALD IS RUNNING WILD!
HE DIDN'T EVEN OPEN THE SCREEN DOOR; HE JUST CAME OUT THROUGH IT!
APRIL FOOL, UNCA DONALD!
APRIL FOOL!
DONALD DUCK
HE DIDN'T HEAR US OR SEE US!
HE'S OFF TO THE RACES!
WHERE DO YOU SUPPOSE HE'S GOING?
IT DOESN'T MATTER! WE'VE GOT TO FIND HIM AND USE OUR APRIL FOOL GAG WHILE IT'S STILL FUNNY!
HOURS LATER!
HE HAS DISAPPEARED!
HE'S NOT AT DAISY'S OR GRANDMA'S OR UNCA SCROOGE'S OR ANYWHERE!
WE'LL JUST GO HOME AND WAIT FOR HIM! DOGGONE IT!
DONALD DUCK
UH, OH! UNCA DONALD'S HERE!
AND HE'S GOT HIS VALISES PACKED!

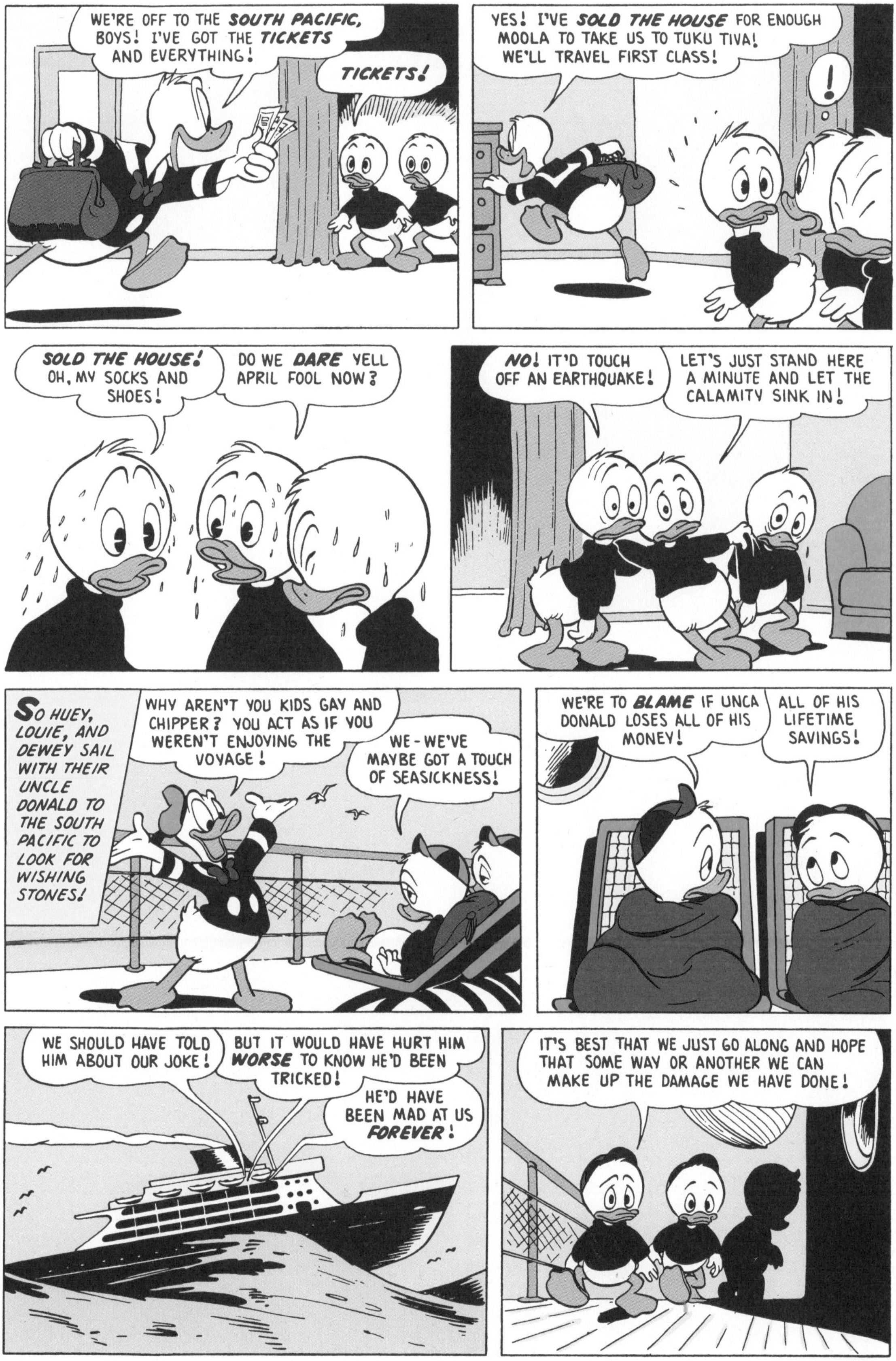
WE'RE OFF TO THE SOUTH PACIFIC, BOYS! I'VE GOT THE TICKETS AND EVERYTHING!
TICKETS!
YES! I'VE SOLD THE HOUSE FOR ENOUGH MOOLA TO TAKE US TO TUKU TIVA! WE'LL TRAVEL FIRST CLASS!
!
SOLD THE HOUSE! OH, MY SOCKS AND SHOES!
DO WE DARE YELL APRIL FOOL NOW?
NO! IT'D TOUCH OFF AN EARTHQUAKE!
LET'S JUST STAND HERE A MINUTE AND LET THE CALAMITY SINK IN!
SO HUEY, LOUIE, AND DEWEY SAIL WITH THEIR UNCLE DONALD TO THE SOUTH PACIFIC TO LOOK FOR WISHING STONES!
WHY AREN'T YOU KIDS GAY AND CHIPPER? YOU ACT AS IF YOU WEREN'T ENJOYING THE VOYAGE!
WE-WE'VE MAYBE GOT A TOUCH OF SEASICKNESS!
WE'RE TO BLAME IF UNCA DONALD LOSES ALL OF HIS MONEY!
ALL OF HIS LIFETIME SAVINGS!
WE SHOULD HAVE TOLD HIM ABOUT OUR JOKE!
BUT IT WOULD HAVE HURT HIM WORSE TO KNOW HE'D BEEN TRICKED!
HE'D HAVE BEEN MAD AT US FOREVER!
IT'S BEST THAT WE JUST GO ALONG AND HOPE THAT SOME WAY OR ANOTHER WE CAN MAKE UP THE DAMAGE WE HAVE DONE!

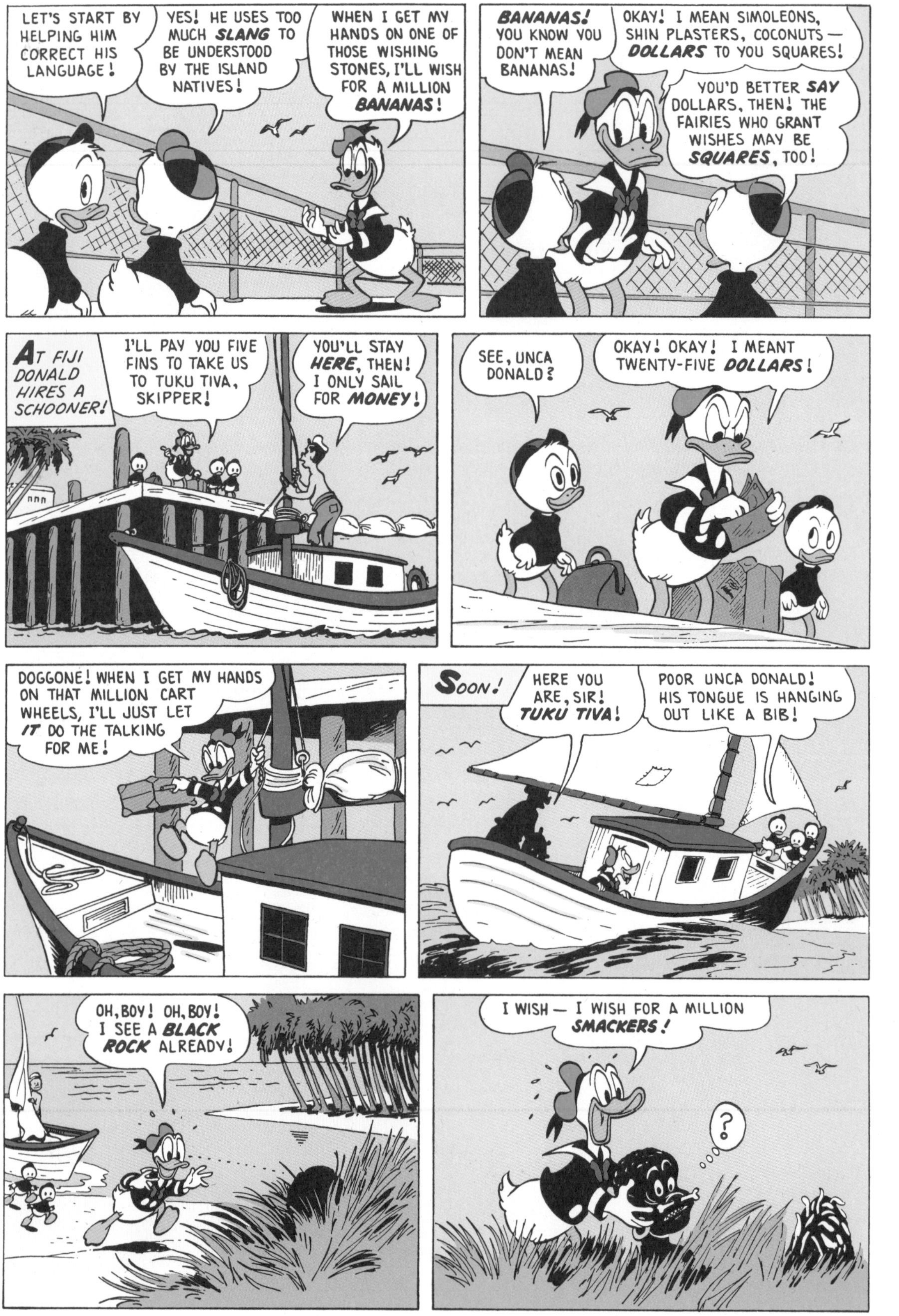
LET'S START BY HELPING HIM CORRECT HIS LANGUAGE!
YES! HE USES TOO MUCH SLANG TO BE UNDERSTOOD BY THE ISLAND NATIVES!
WHEN I GET MY HANDS ON ONE OF THOSE WISHING STONES, I'LL WISH FOR A MILLION BANANAS!
BANANAS! YOU KNOW YOU DON'T MEAN BANANAS!
OKAY! I MEAN SIMOLEONS, SHIN PLASTERS, COCONUTS — DOLLARS TO YOU SQUARES!
YOU'D BETTER SAY DOLLARS, THEN! THE FAIRIES WHO GRANT WISHES MAY BE SQUARES, TOO!
AT FIJI DONALD HIRES A SCHOONER!
I'LL PAY YOU FIVE FINS TO TAKE US TO TUKU TIVA, SKIPPER!
YOU'LL STAY HERE, THEN! I ONLY SAIL FOR MONEY!
SEE, UNCA DONALD?
OKAY! OKAY! I MEANT TWENTY-FIVE DOLLARS!
DOGGONE! WHEN I GET MY HANDS ON THAT MILLION CART WHEELS, I'LL JUST LET IT DO THE TALKING FOR ME!
SOON!
HERE YOU ARE, SIR! TUKU TIVA!
POOR UNCA DONALD! HIS TONGUE IS HANGING OUT LIKE A BIB!
OH, BOY! OH, BOY! I SEE A BLACK ROCK ALREADY!
I WISH — I WISH FOR A MILLION SMACKERS!
?

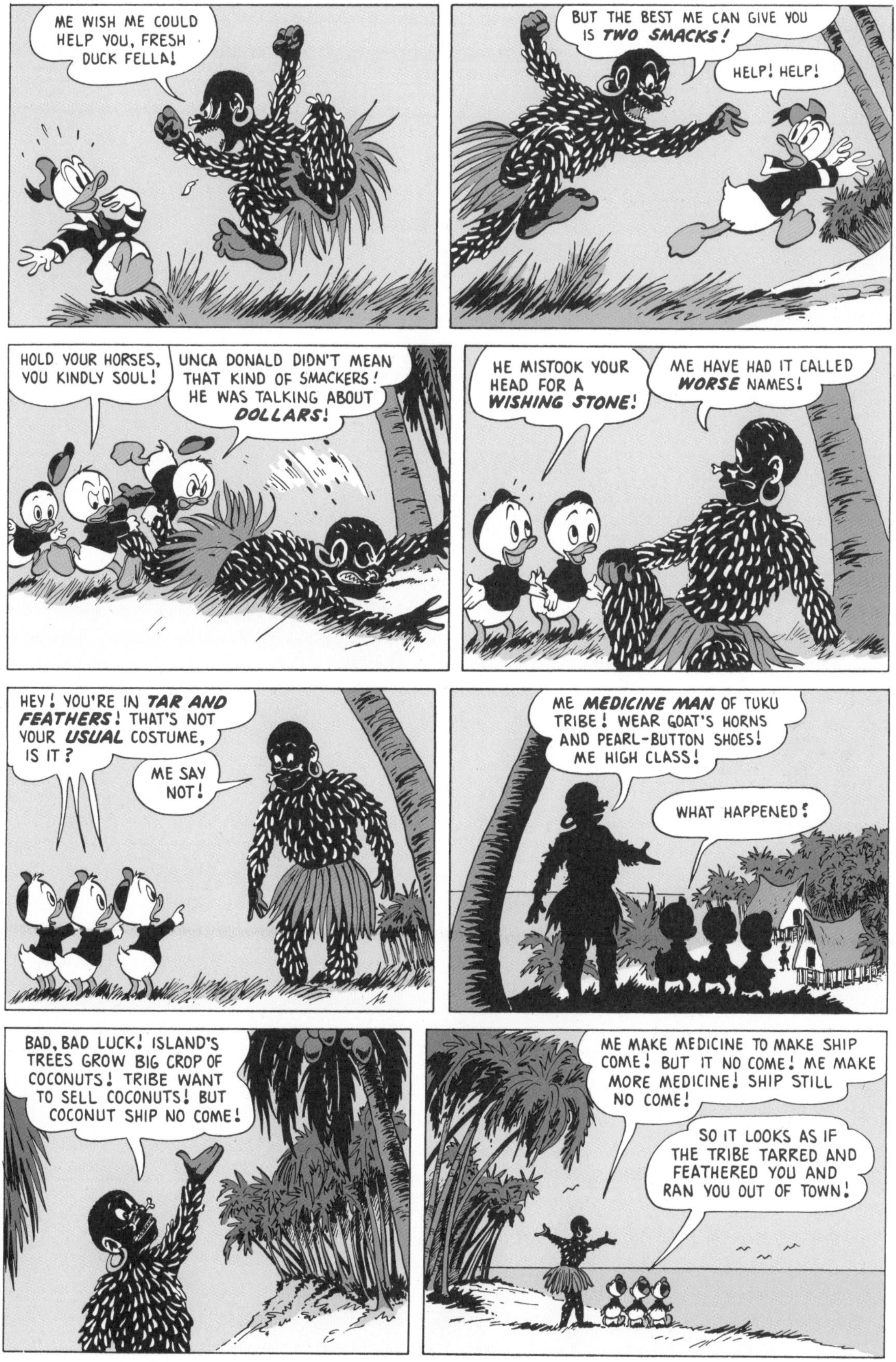
ME WISH ME COULD HELP YOU, FRESH DUCK FELLA!
BUT THE BEST ME CAN GIVE YOU IS TWO SMACKS!
HELP! HELP!
HOLD YOUR HORSES, YOU KINDLY SOUL!
UNCA DONALD DIDN'T MEAN THAT KIND OF SMACKERS! HE WAS TALKING ABOUT DOLLARS!
HE MISTOOK YOUR HEAD FOR A WISHING STONE!
ME HAVE HAD IT CALLED WORSE NAMES!
HEY! YOU'RE IN TAR AND FEATHERS! THAT'S NOT YOUR USUAL COSTUME, IS IT?
ME SAY NOT!
ME MEDICINE MAN OF TUKU TRIBE! WEAR GOAT'S HORNS AND PEARL-BUTTON SHOES! ME HIGH CLASS!
WHAT HAPPENED?
BAD, BAD LUCK! ISLAND'S TREES GROW BIG CROP OF COCONUTS! TRIBE WANT TO SELL COCONUTS! BUT COCONUT SHIP NO COME!
ME MAKE MEDICINE TO MAKE SHIP COME! BUT IT NO COME! ME MAKE MORE MEDICINE! SHIP STILL NO COME!
SO IT LOOKS AS IF THE TRIBE TARRED AND FEATHERED YOU AND RAN YOU OUT OF TOWN!

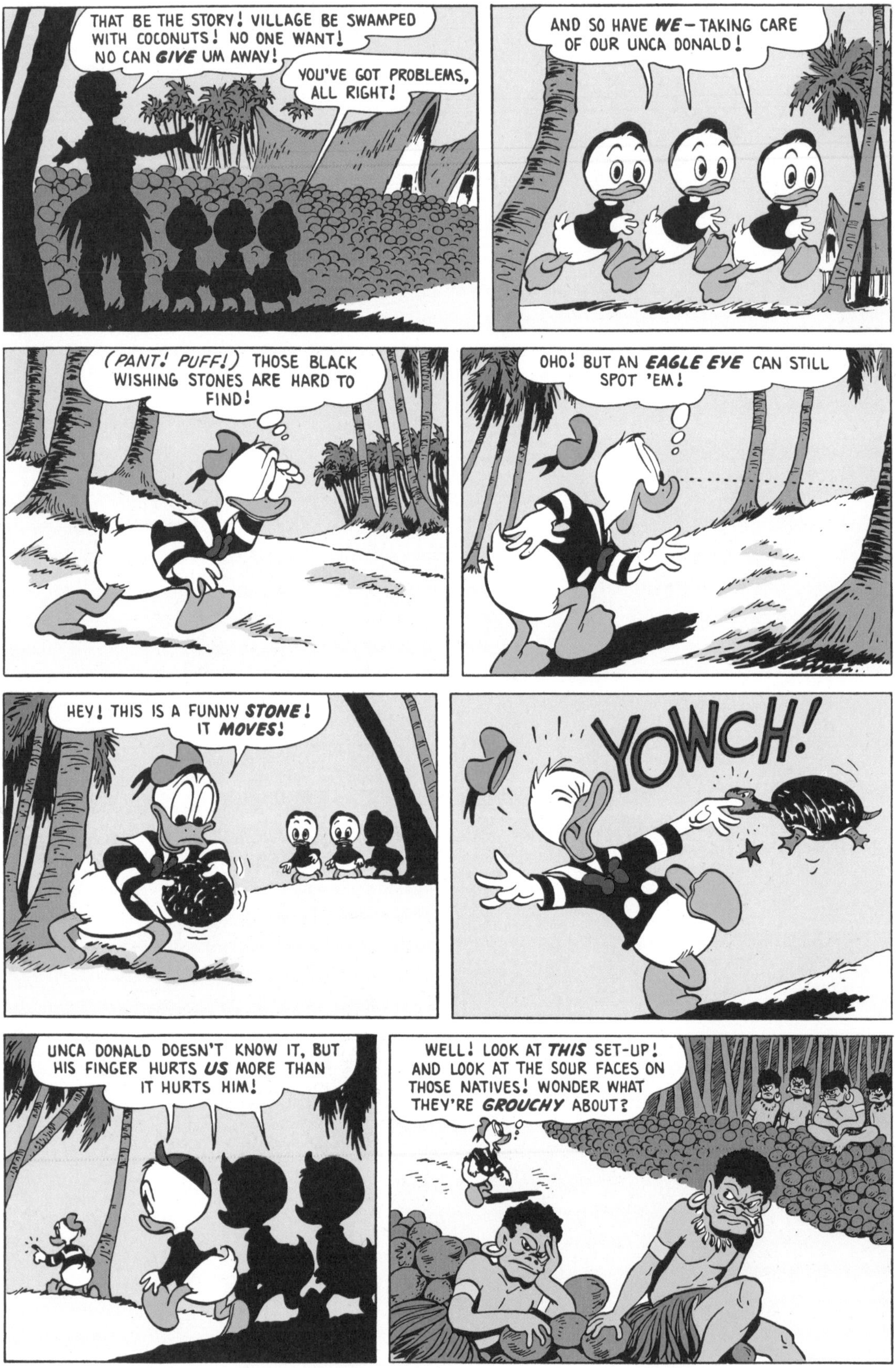
THAT BE THE STORY! VILLAGE BE SWAMPED WITH COCONUTS! NO ONE WANT! NO CAN GIVE UM AWAY!
YOU'VE GOT PROBLEMS, ALL RIGHT!
AND SO HAVE WE—TAKING CARE OF OUR UNCA DONALD!
(PANT! PUFF!) THOSE BLACK WISHING STONES ARE HARD TO FIND!
OHO! BUT AN EAGLE EYE CAN STILL SPOT 'EM!
HEY! THIS IS A FUNNY STONE! IT MOVES!
YOWCH!
UNCA DONALD DOESN'T KNOW IT, BUT HIS FINGER HURTS US MORE THAN IT HURTS HIM!
WELL! LOOK AT THIS SET-UP! AND LOOK AT THE SOUR FACES ON THOSE NATIVES! WONDER WHAT THEY'RE GROUCHY ABOUT?

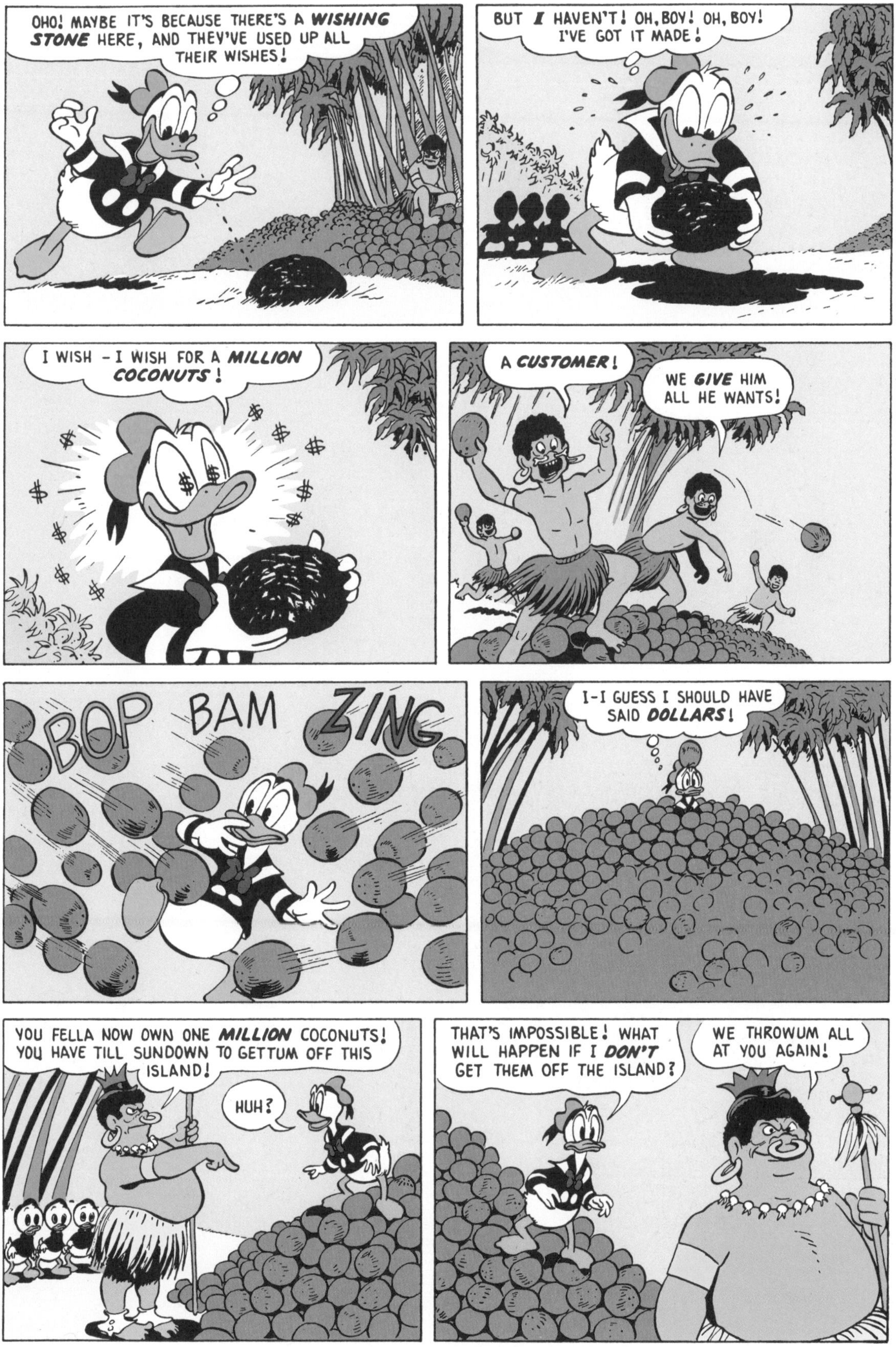
OHO! MAYBE IT'S BECAUSE THERE'S A WISHING STONE HERE, AND THEY'VE USED UP ALL THEIR WISHES!
BUT I HAVEN'T! OH, BOY! OH, BOY! I'VE GOT IT MADE!
I WISH - I WISH FOR A MILLION COCONUTS!
A CUSTOMER!
WE GIVE HIM ALL HE WANTS!
BOP
BAM
ZING
I-I GUESS I SHOULD HAVE SAID DOLLARS!
YOU FELLA NOW OWN ONE MILLION COCONUTS! YOU HAVE TILL SUNDOWN TO GETTUM OFF THIS ISLAND!
HUH?
THAT'S IMPOSSIBLE! WHAT WILL HAPPEN IF I DON'T GET THEM OFF THE ISLAND?
WE THROWUM ALL AT YOU AGAIN!

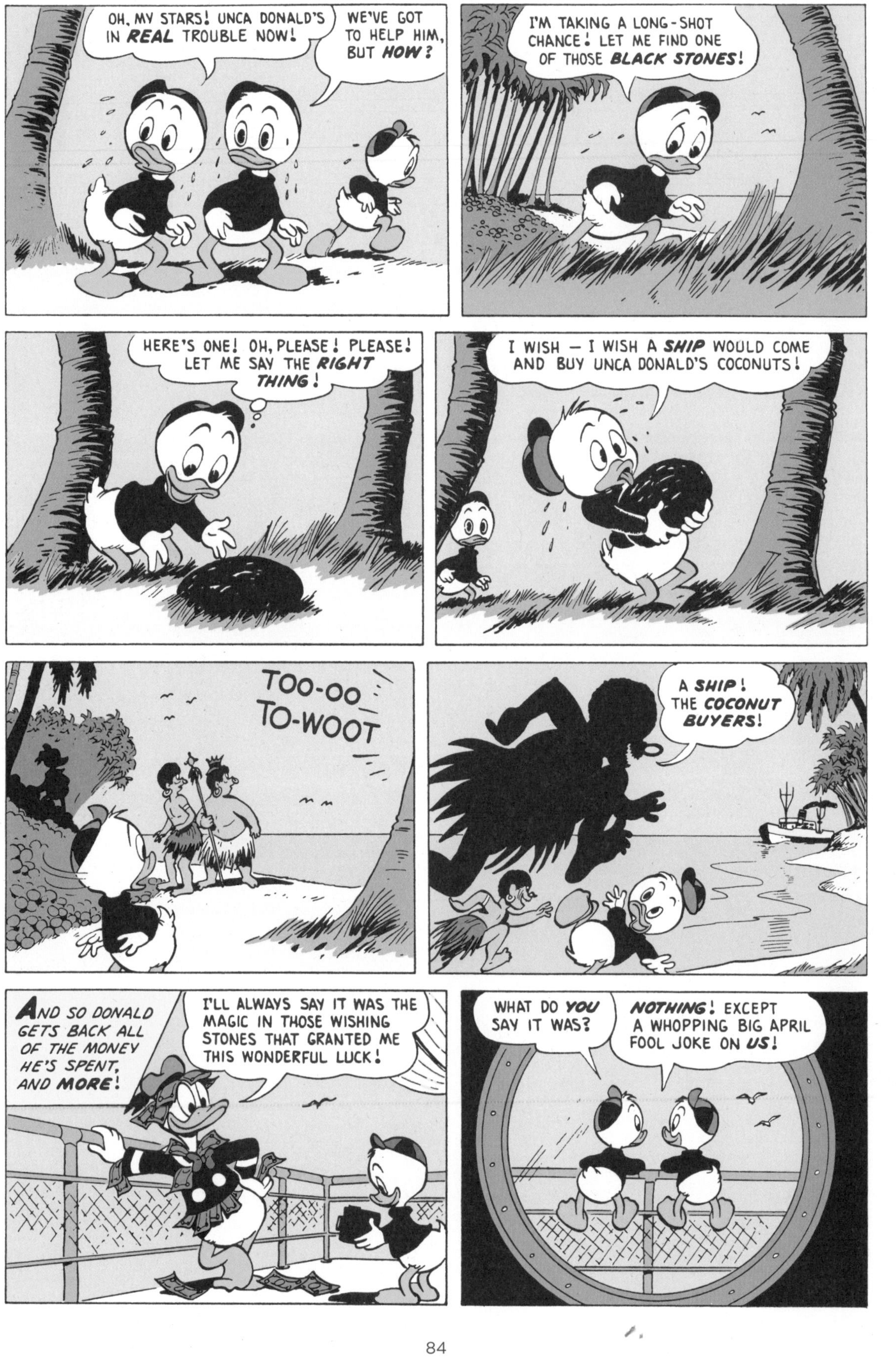
OH, MY STARS! UNCA DONALD'S IN REAL TROUBLE NOW!
WE'VE GOT TO HELP HIM, BUT HOW?
I'M TAKING A LONG-SHOT CHANCE! LET ME FIND ONE OF THOSE BLACK STONES!
HERE'S ONE! OH, PLEASE! PLEASE! LET ME SAY THE RIGHT THING!
I WISH — I WISH A SHIP WOULD COME AND BUY UNCA DONALD'S COCONUTS!
TOO-OO TO-WOOT
A SHIP! THE COCONUT BUYERS!
AND SO DONALD GETS BACK ALL OF THE MONEY HE'S SPENT, AND MORE!
I'LL ALWAYS SAY IT WAS THE MAGIC IN THOSE WISHING STONES THAT GRANTED ME THIS WONDERFUL LUCK!
WHAT DO YOU SAY IT WAS?
NOTHING! EXCEPT A WHOPPING BIG APRIL FOOL JOKE ON US!

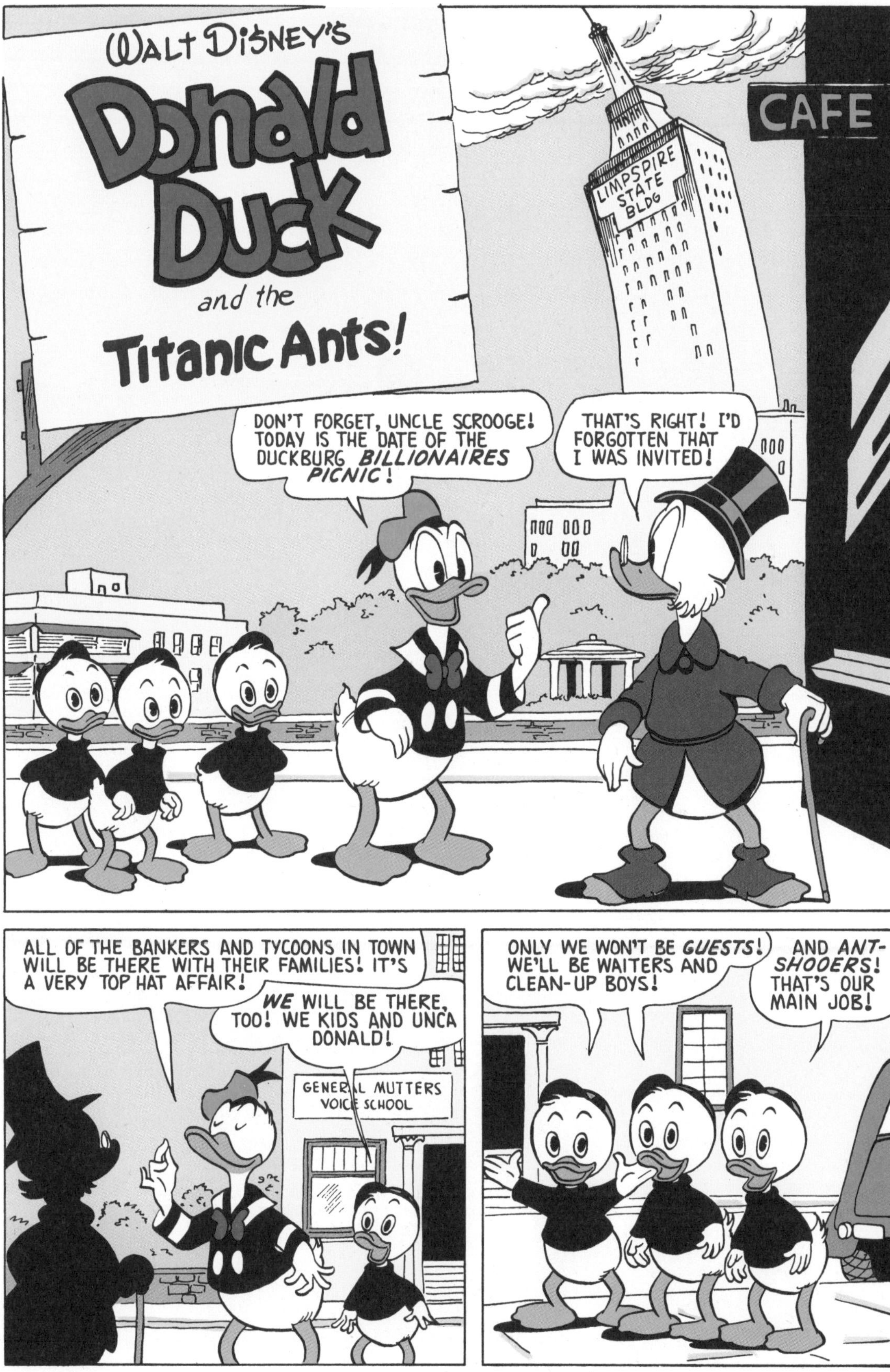
WALT DISNEY'S
Donald Duck
and the
Titanic Ants!
CAFE
LIMPSPIRE STATE BLDG
DON'T FORGET, UNCLE SCROOGE! TODAY IS THE DATE OF THE DUCKBURG BILLIONAIRES PICNIC!
THAT'S RIGHT! I'D FORGOTTEN THAT I WAS INVITED!
ALL OF THE BANKERS AND TYCOONS IN TOWN WILL BE THERE WITH THEIR FAMILIES! IT'S A VERY TOP HAT AFFAIR!
WE WILL BE THERE, TOO! WE KIDS AND UNCA DONALD!
GENERAL MUTTERS VOICE SCHOOL
ONLY WE WON'T BE GUESTS! WE'LL BE WAITERS AND CLEAN-UP BOYS!
AND ANT-SHOOERS! THAT'S OUR MAIN JOB!

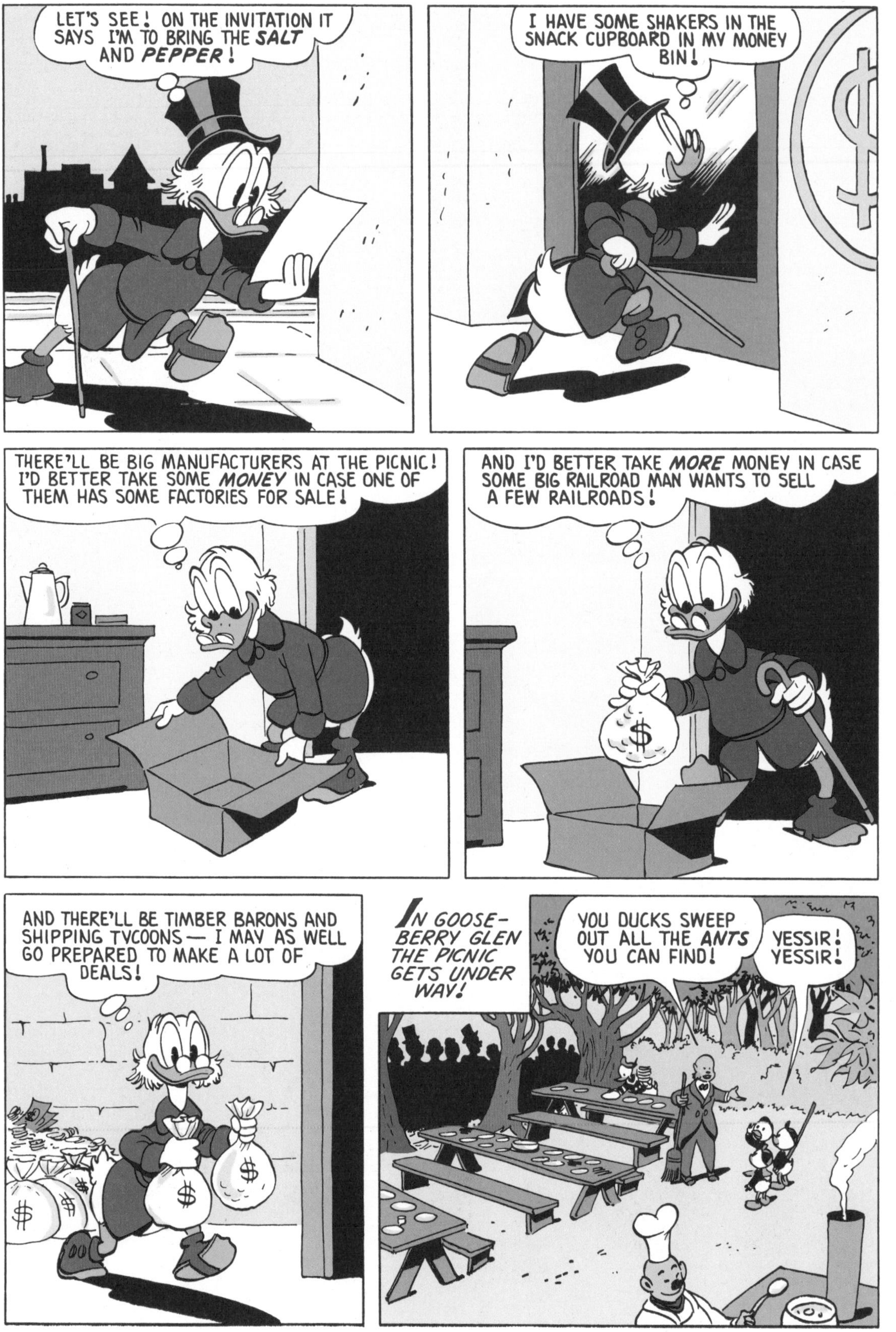
LET'S SEE! ON THE INVITATION IT SAYS I'M TO BRING THE SALT AND PEPPER!
I HAVE SOME SHAKERS IN THE SNACK CUPBOARD IN MY MONEY BIN!
THERE'LL BE BIG MANUFACTURERS AT THE PICNIC! I'D BETTER TAKE SOME MONEY IN CASE ONE OF THEM HAS SOME FACTORIES FOR SALE!
AND I'D BETTER TAKE MORE MONEY IN CASE SOME BIG RAILROAD MAN WANTS TO SELL A FEW RAILROADS!
AND THERE'LL BE TIMBER BARONS AND SHIPPING TYCOONS — I MAY AS WELL GO PREPARED TO MAKE A LOT OF DEALS!
IN GOOSEBERRY GLEN THE PICNIC GETS UNDER WAY!
YOU DUCKS SWEEP OUT ALL THE ANTS YOU CAN FIND!
YESSIR! YESSIR!

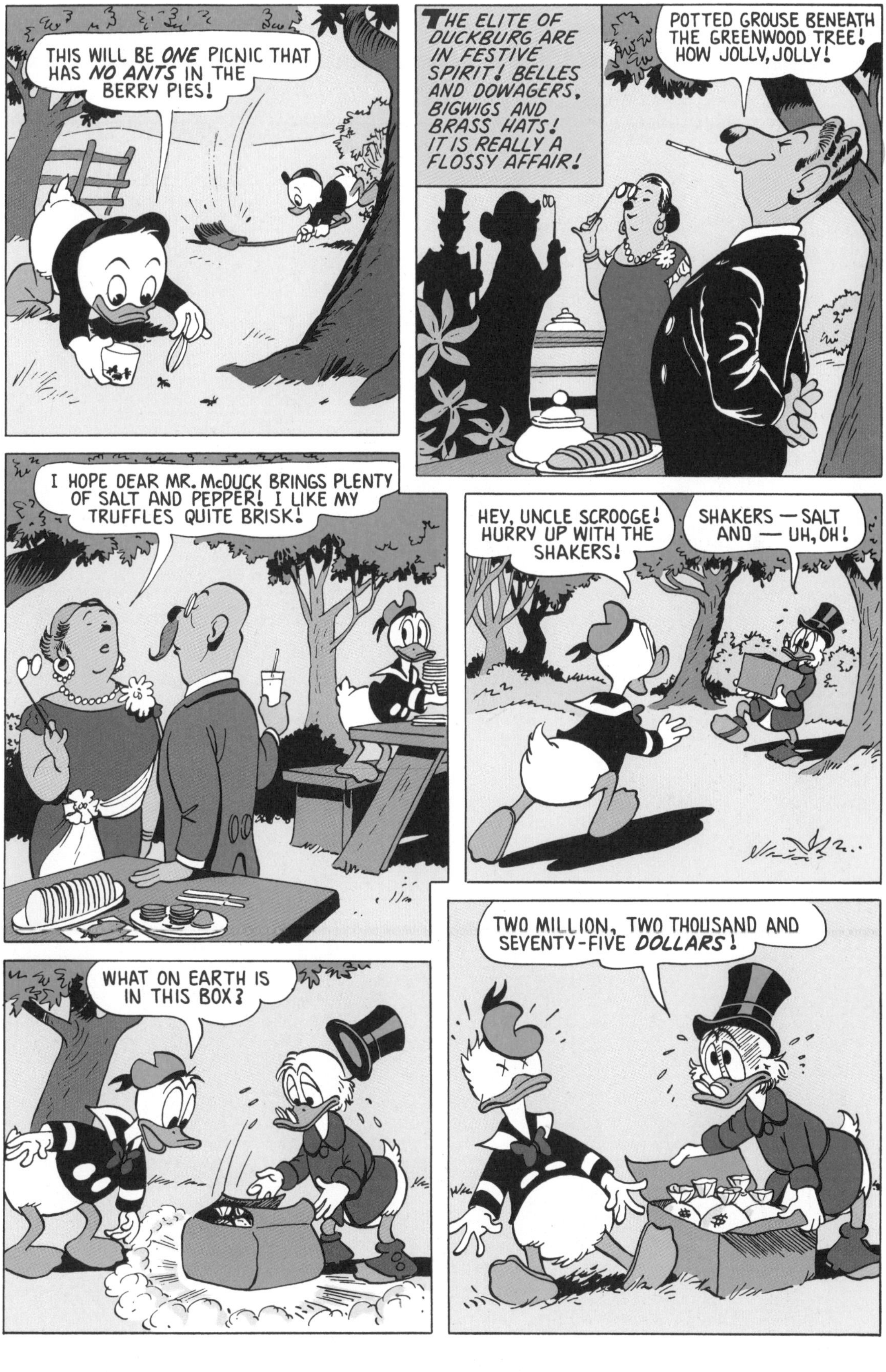

THIS WILL BE *ONE* PICNIC THAT HAS *NO ANTS* IN THE BERRY PIES!
THE ELITE OF DUCKBURG ARE IN FESTIVE SPIRIT! BELLES AND DOWAGERS, BIGWIGS AND BRASS HATS! IT IS REALLY A FLOSSY AFFAIR!
POTTED GROUSE BENEATH THE GREENWOOD TREE! HOW JOLLY, JOLLY!
I HOPE DEAR MR. McDUCK BRINGS PLENTY OF SALT AND PEPPER! I LIKE MY TRUFFLES QUITE BRISK!
HEY, UNCLE SCROOGE! HURRY UP WITH THE SHAKERS!
SHAKERS — SALT AND — UH, OH!
WHAT ON EARTH IS IN THIS BOX?
TWO MILLION, TWO THOUSAND AND SEVENTY-FIVE *DOLLARS*!

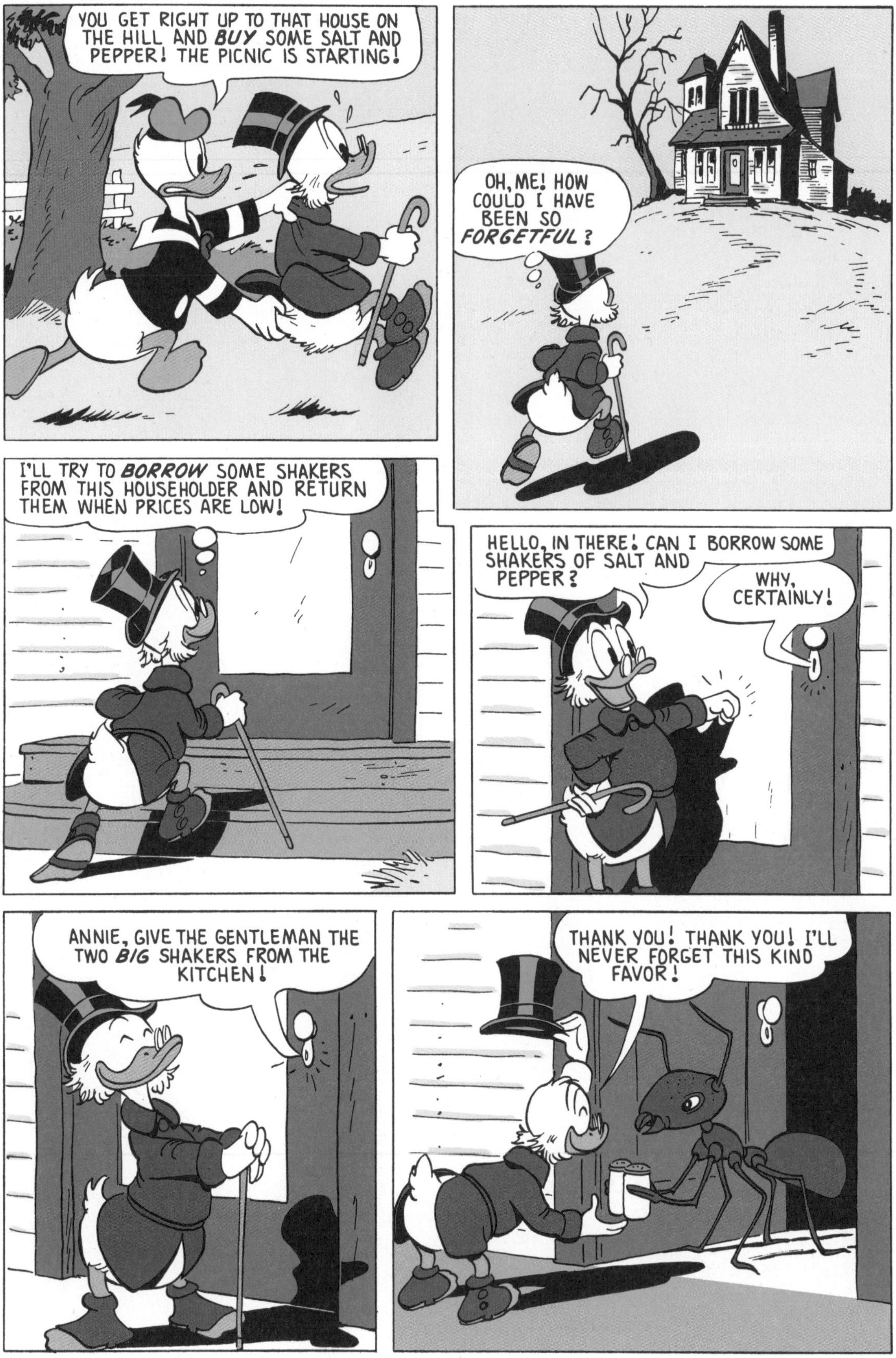
YOU GET RIGHT UP TO THAT HOUSE ON THE HILL AND BUY SOME SALT AND PEPPER! THE PICNIC IS STARTING!
OH, ME! HOW COULD I HAVE BEEN SO FORGETFUL?
I'LL TRY TO BORROW SOME SHAKERS FROM THIS HOUSEHOLDER AND RETURN THEM WHEN PRICES ARE LOW!
HELLO, IN THERE! CAN I BORROW SOME SHAKERS OF SALT AND PEPPER?
WHY, CERTAINLY!
ANNIE, GIVE THE GENTLEMAN THE TWO BIG SHAKERS FROM THE KITCHEN!
THANK YOU! THANK YOU! I'LL NEVER FORGET THIS KIND FAVOR!

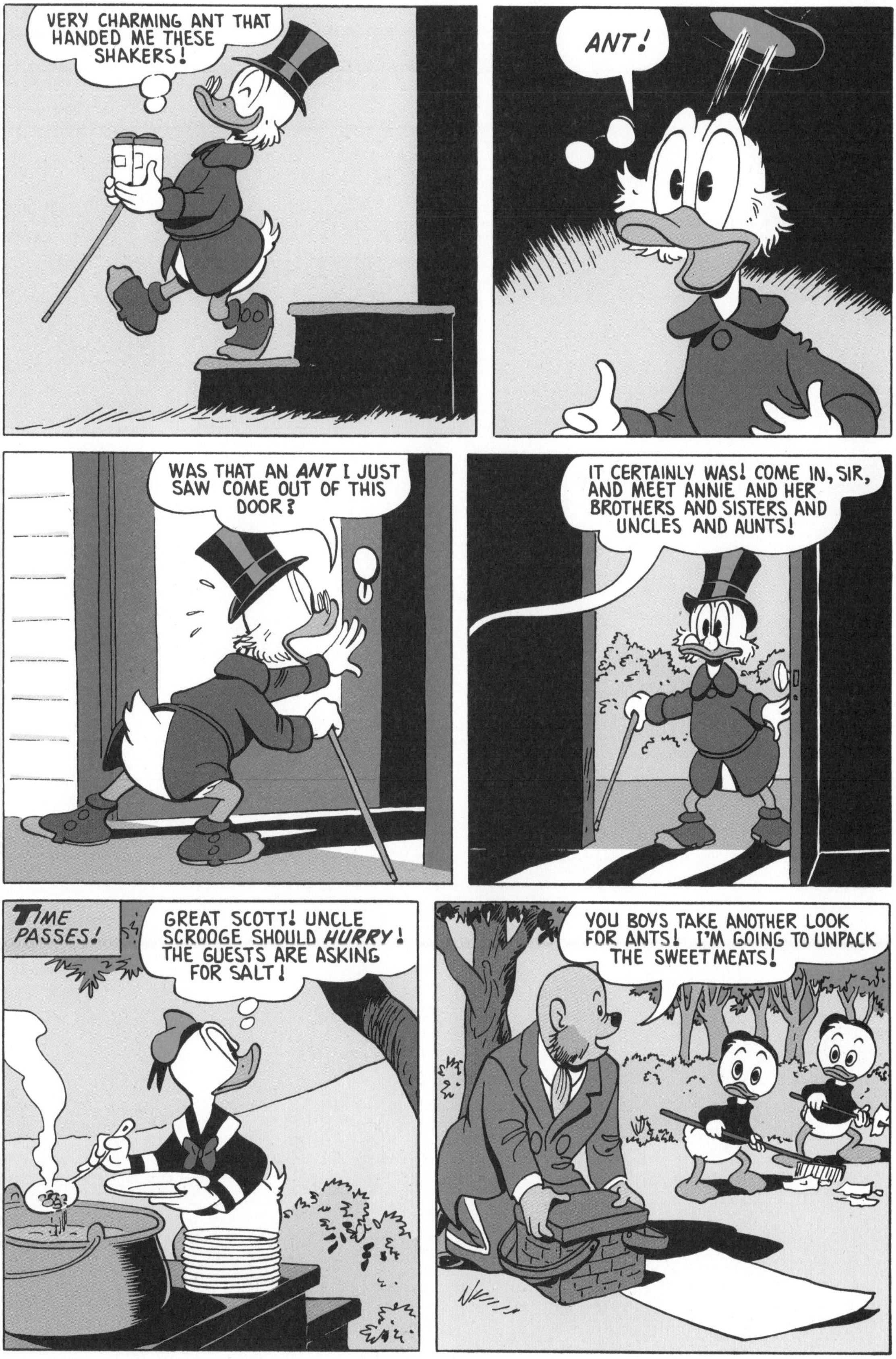
VERY CHARMING ANT THAT HANDED ME THESE SHAKERS!
ANT!
WAS THAT AN ANT I JUST SAW COME OUT OF THIS DOOR?
IT CERTAINLY WAS! COME IN, SIR, AND MEET ANNIE AND HER BROTHERS AND SISTERS AND UNCLES AND AUNTS!
TIME PASSES!
GREAT SCOTT! UNCLE SCROOGE SHOULD HURRY! THE GUESTS ARE ASKING FOR SALT!
YOU BOYS TAKE ANOTHER LOOK FOR ANTS! I'M GOING TO UNPACK THE SWEETMEATS!

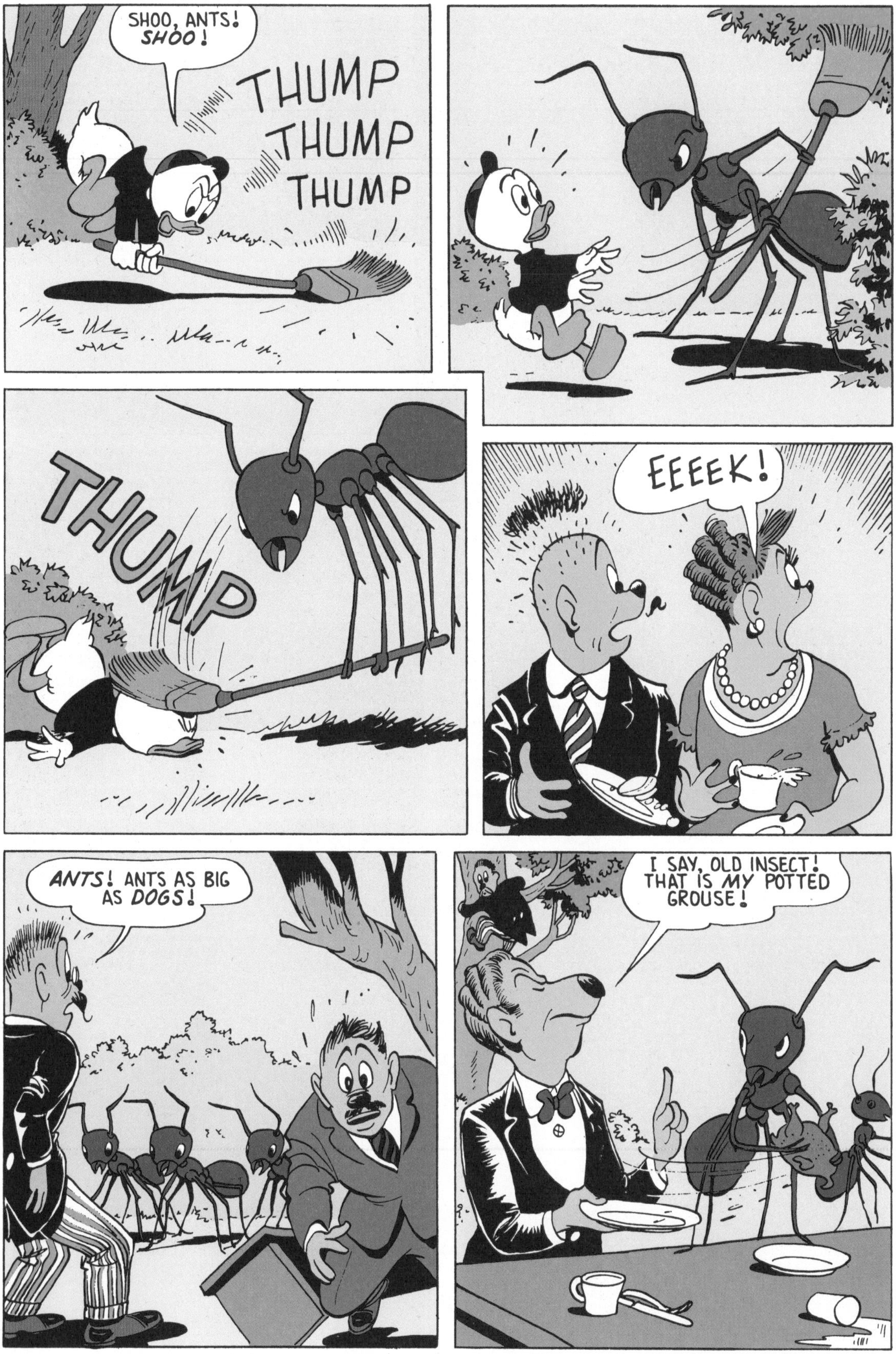
SHOO, ANTS! SHOO!
THUMP THUMP THUMP
THUMP
EEEEK!
ANTS! ANTS AS BIG AS DOGS!
I SAY, OLD INSECT! THAT IS MY POTTED GROUSE!

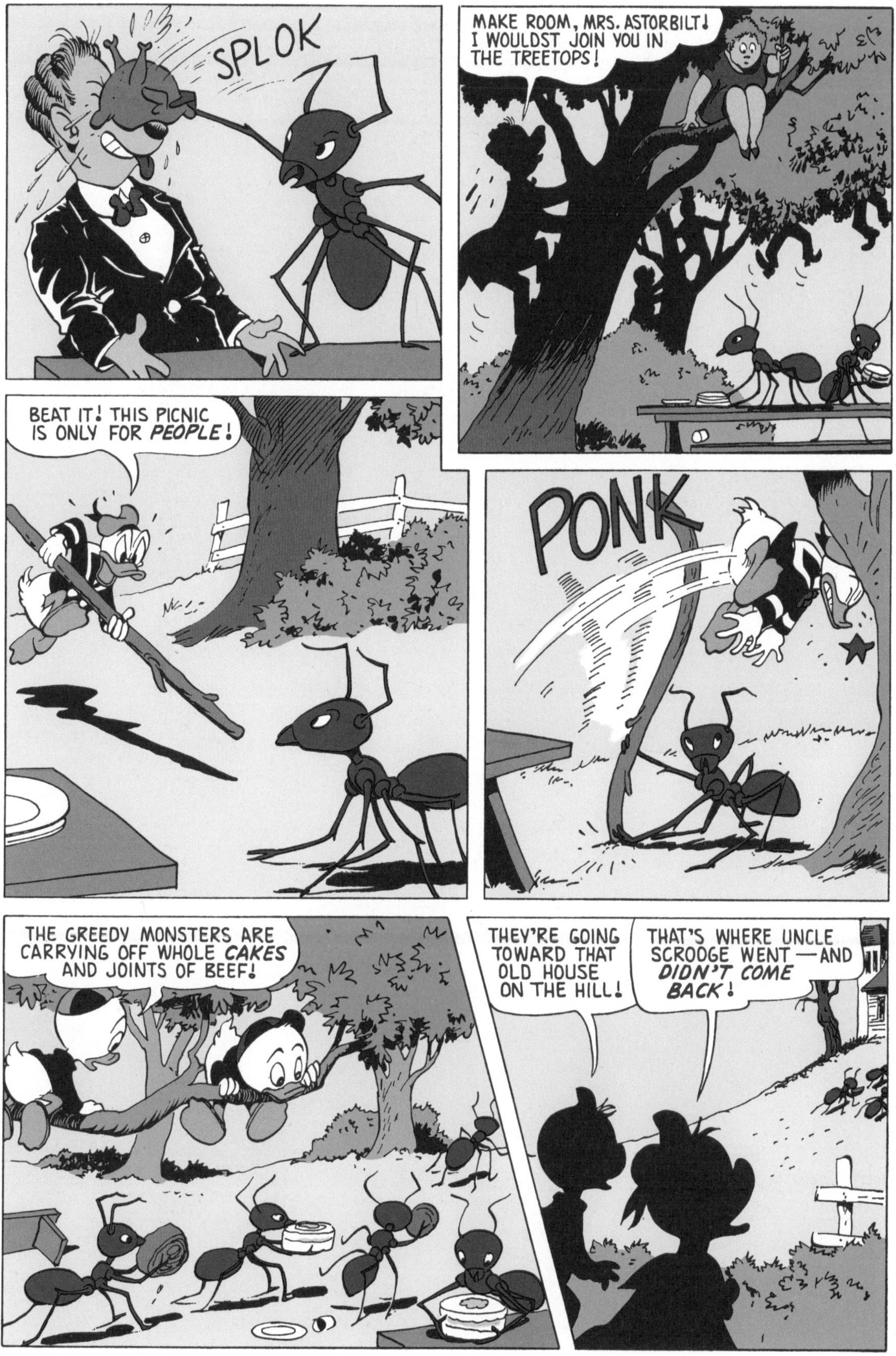
SPLOK
MAKE ROOM, MRS. ASTORBILT! I WOULDST JOIN YOU IN THE TREETOPS!
BEAT IT! THIS PICNIC IS ONLY FOR *PEOPLE*!
PONK
THE GREEDY MONSTERS ARE CARRYING OFF WHOLE *CAKES* AND JOINTS OF BEEF!
THEY'RE GOING TOWARD THAT OLD HOUSE ON THE HILL!
THAT'S WHERE UNCLE SCROOGE WENT — AND *DIDN'T COME BACK*!

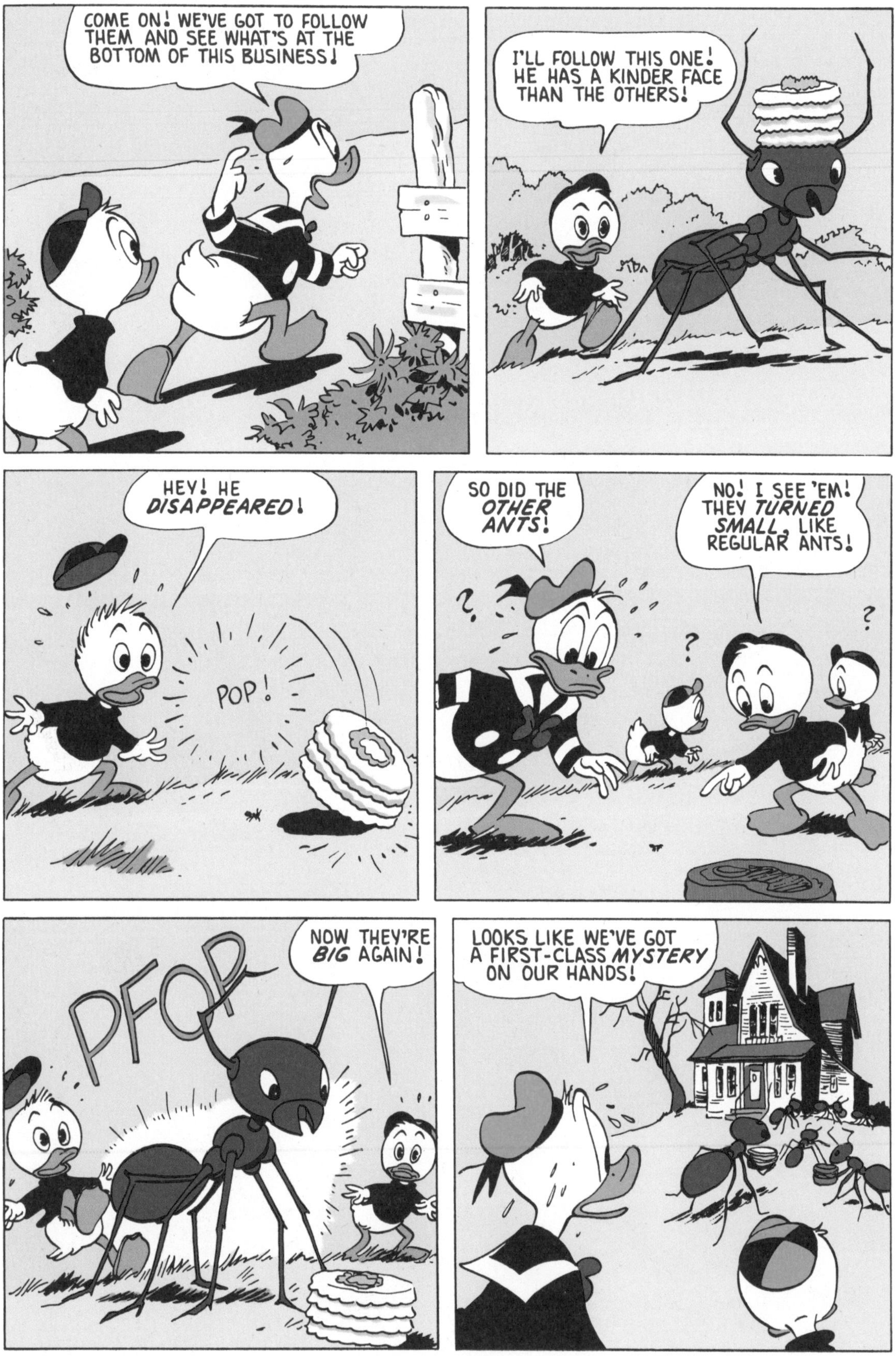
COME ON! WE'VE GOT TO FOLLOW THEM AND SEE WHAT'S AT THE BOTTOM OF THIS BUSINESS!
I'LL FOLLOW THIS ONE! HE HAS A KINDER FACE THAN THE OTHERS!
HEY! HE *DISAPPEARED*!
POP!
SO DID THE *OTHER ANTS*!
NO! I SEE 'EM! THEY *TURNED SMALL*, LIKE REGULAR ANTS!
PFOP
NOW THEY'RE *BIG* AGAIN!
LOOKS LIKE WE'VE GOT A FIRST-CLASS *MYSTERY* ON OUR HANDS!

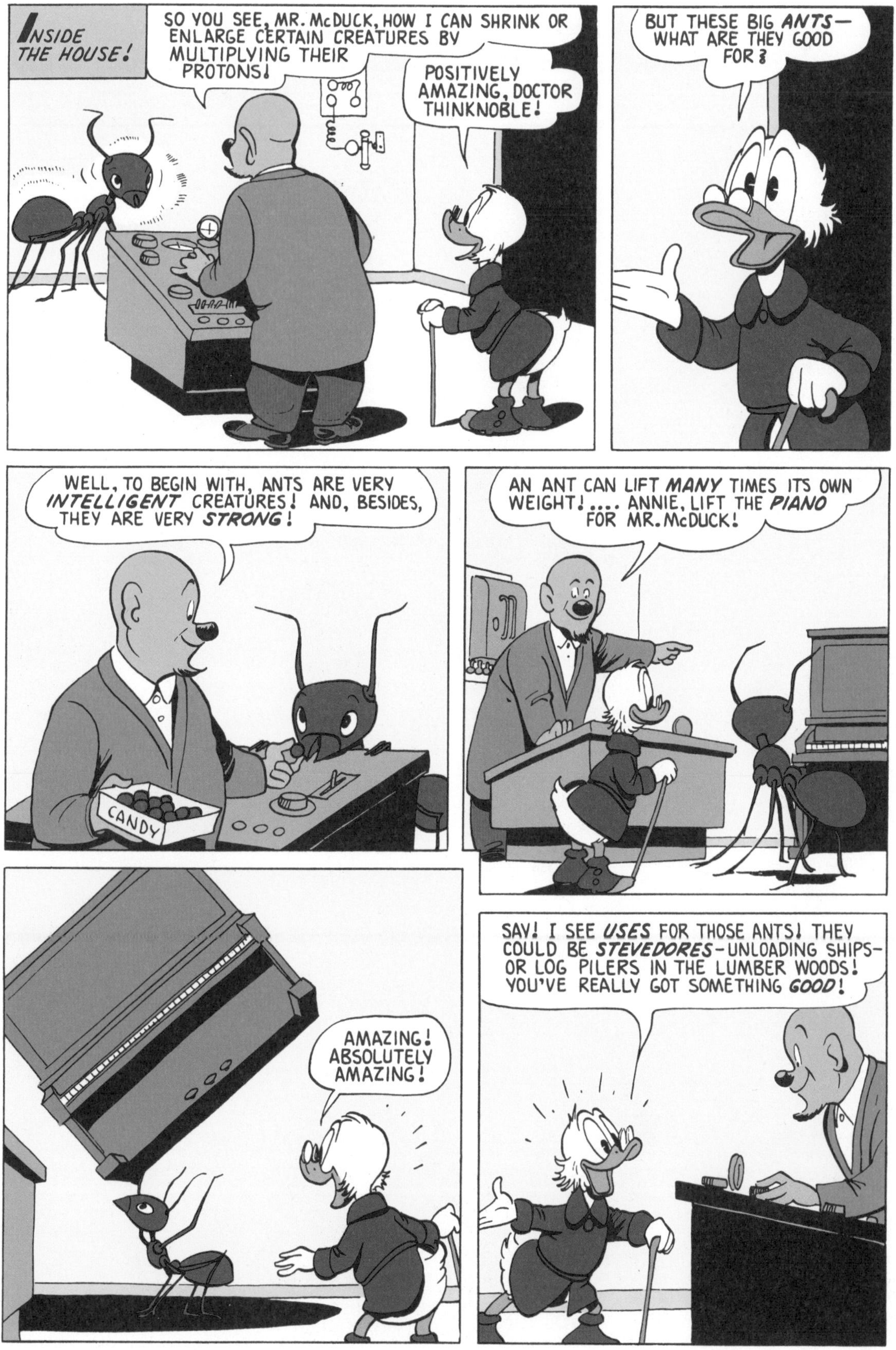
INSIDE THE HOUSE!
SO YOU SEE, MR. McDUCK, HOW I CAN SHRINK OR ENLARGE CERTAIN CREATURES BY MULTIPLYING THEIR PROTONS!
POSITIVELY AMAZING, DOCTOR THINKNOBLE!
BUT THESE BIG ANTS— WHAT ARE THEY GOOD FOR?
WELL, TO BEGIN WITH, ANTS ARE VERY INTELLIGENT CREATURES! AND, BESIDES, THEY ARE VERY STRONG!
CANDY
AN ANT CAN LIFT MANY TIMES ITS OWN WEIGHT! .... ANNIE, LIFT THE PIANO FOR MR. McDUCK!
AMAZING! ABSOLUTELY AMAZING!
SAY! I SEE USES FOR THOSE ANTS! THEY COULD BE STEVEDORES - UNLOADING SHIPS- OR LOG PILERS IN THE LUMBER WOODS! YOU'VE REALLY GOT SOMETHING GOOD!

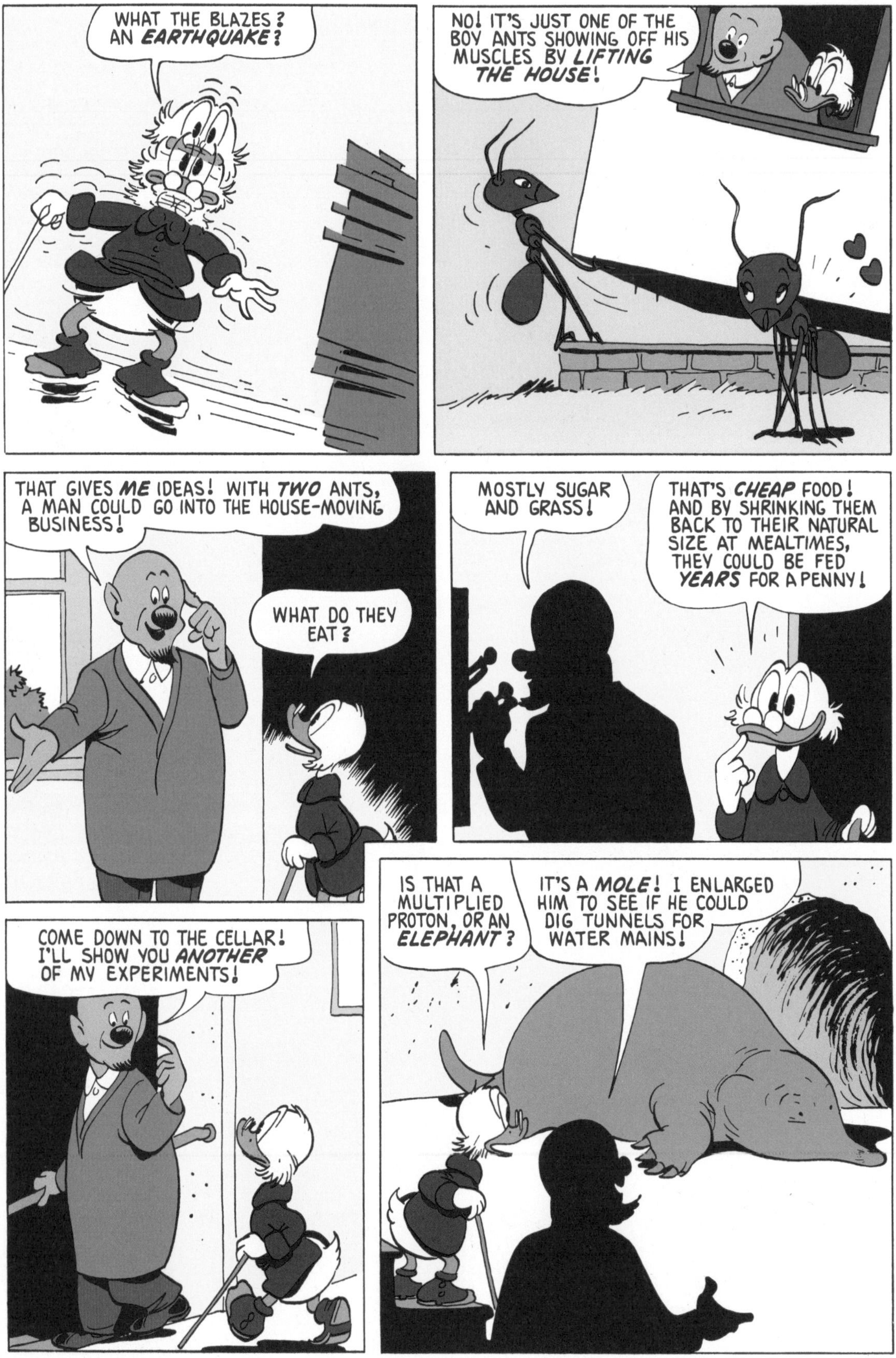
WHAT THE BLAZES? AN EARTHQUAKE?
NO! IT'S JUST ONE OF THE BOY ANTS SHOWING OFF HIS MUSCLES BY LIFTING THE HOUSE!
THAT GIVES ME IDEAS! WITH TWO ANTS, A MAN COULD GO INTO THE HOUSE-MOVING BUSINESS!
WHAT DO THEY EAT?
MOSTLY SUGAR AND GRASS!
THAT'S CHEAP FOOD! AND BY SHRINKING THEM BACK TO THEIR NATURAL SIZE AT MEALTIMES, THEY COULD BE FED YEARS FOR A PENNY!
COME DOWN TO THE CELLAR! I'LL SHOW YOU ANOTHER OF MY EXPERIMENTS!
IS THAT A MULTIPLIED PROTON, OR AN ELEPHANT?
IT'S A MOLE! I ENLARGED HIM TO SEE IF HE COULD DIG TUNNELS FOR WATER MAINS!

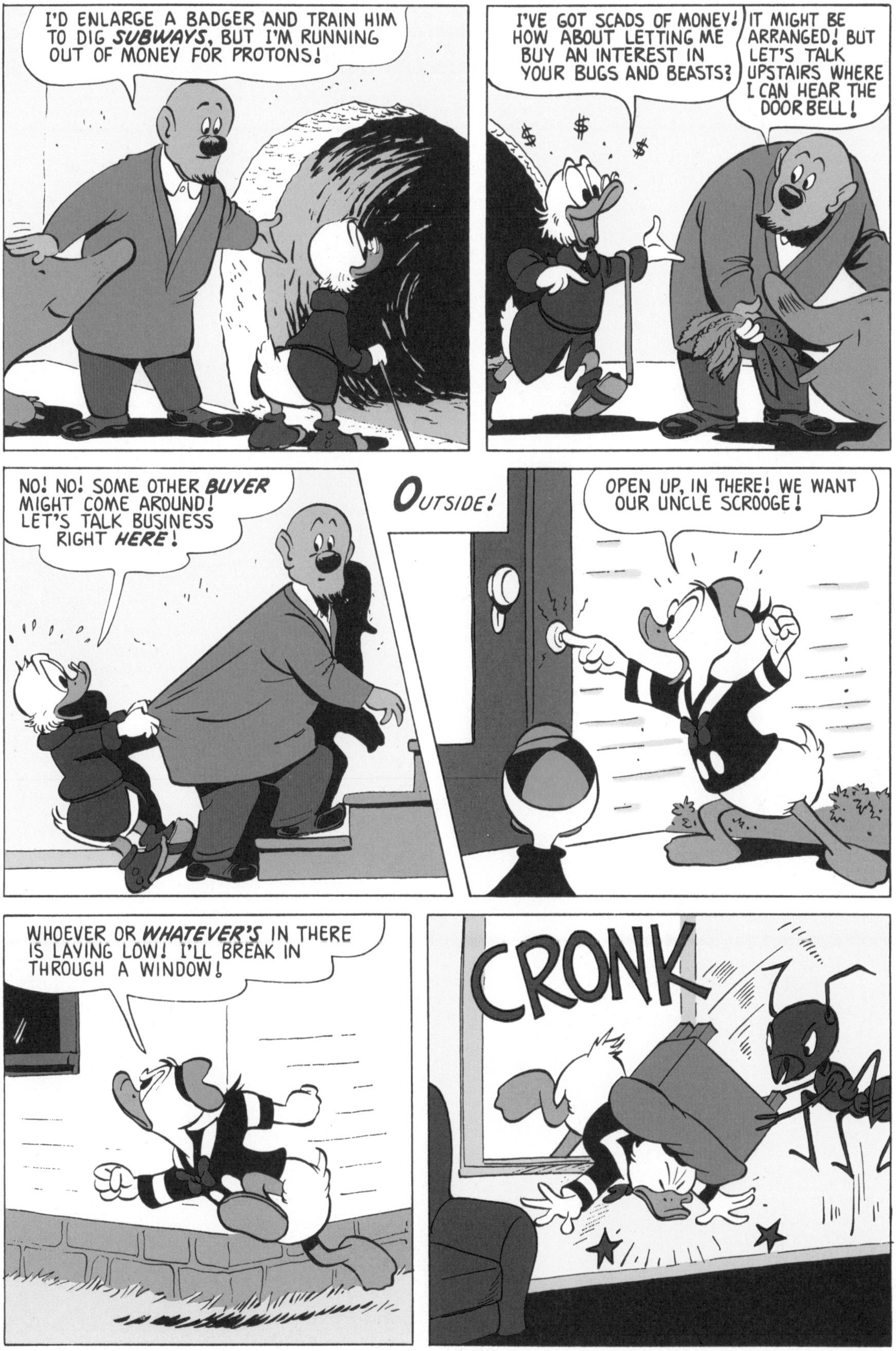
I'D ENLARGE A BADGER AND TRAIN HIM TO DIG SUBWAYS, BUT I'M RUNNING OUT OF MONEY FOR PROTONS!
I'VE GOT SCADS OF MONEY! HOW ABOUT LETTING ME BUY AN INTEREST IN YOUR BUGS AND BEASTS?
IT MIGHT BE ARRANGED! BUT LET'S TALK UPSTAIRS WHERE I CAN HEAR THE DOORBELL!
NO! NO! SOME OTHER BUYER MIGHT COME AROUND! LET'S TALK BUSINESS RIGHT HERE!
OUTSIDE!
OPEN UP, IN THERE! WE WANT OUR UNCLE SCROOGE!
WHOEVER OR WHATEVER'S IN THERE IS LAYING LOW! I'LL BREAK IN THROUGH A WINDOW!
CRONK

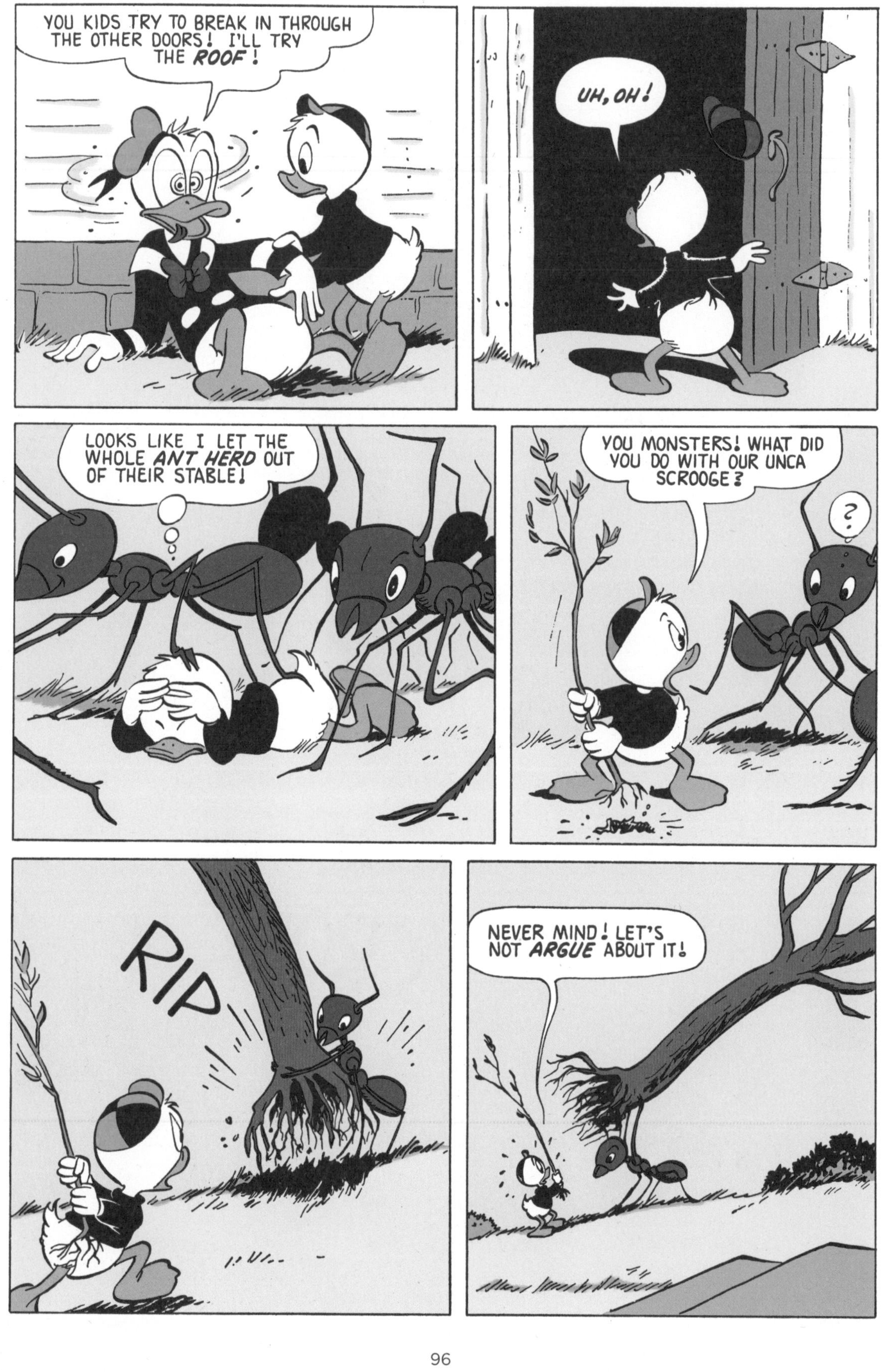
YOU KIDS TRY TO BREAK IN THROUGH THE OTHER DOORS! I'LL TRY THE ROOF!
UH, OH!
LOOKS LIKE I LET THE WHOLE ANT HERD OUT OF THEIR STABLE!
YOU MONSTERS! WHAT DID YOU DO WITH OUR UNCA SCROOGE?
?
RIP
NEVER MIND! LET'S NOT ARGUE ABOUT IT!

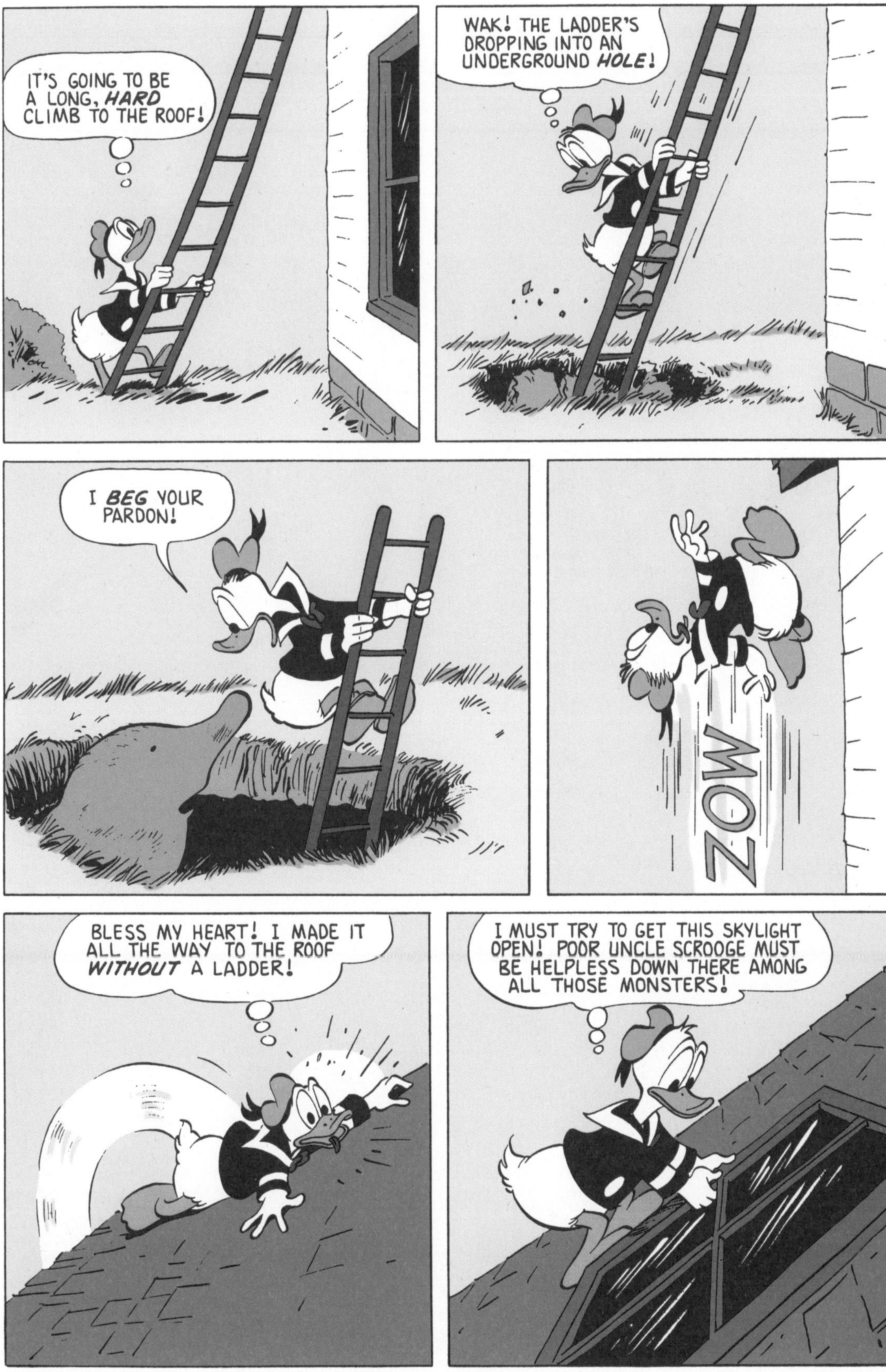
IT'S GOING TO BE A LONG, HARD CLIMB TO THE ROOF!
WAK! THE LADDER'S DROPPING INTO AN UNDERGROUND HOLE!
I BEG YOUR PARDON!
ZOW
BLESS MY HEART! I MADE IT ALL THE WAY TO THE ROOF WITHOUT A LADDER!
I MUST TRY TO GET THIS SKYLIGHT OPEN! POOR UNCLE SCROOGE MUST BE HELPLESS DOWN THERE AMONG ALL THOSE MONSTERS!

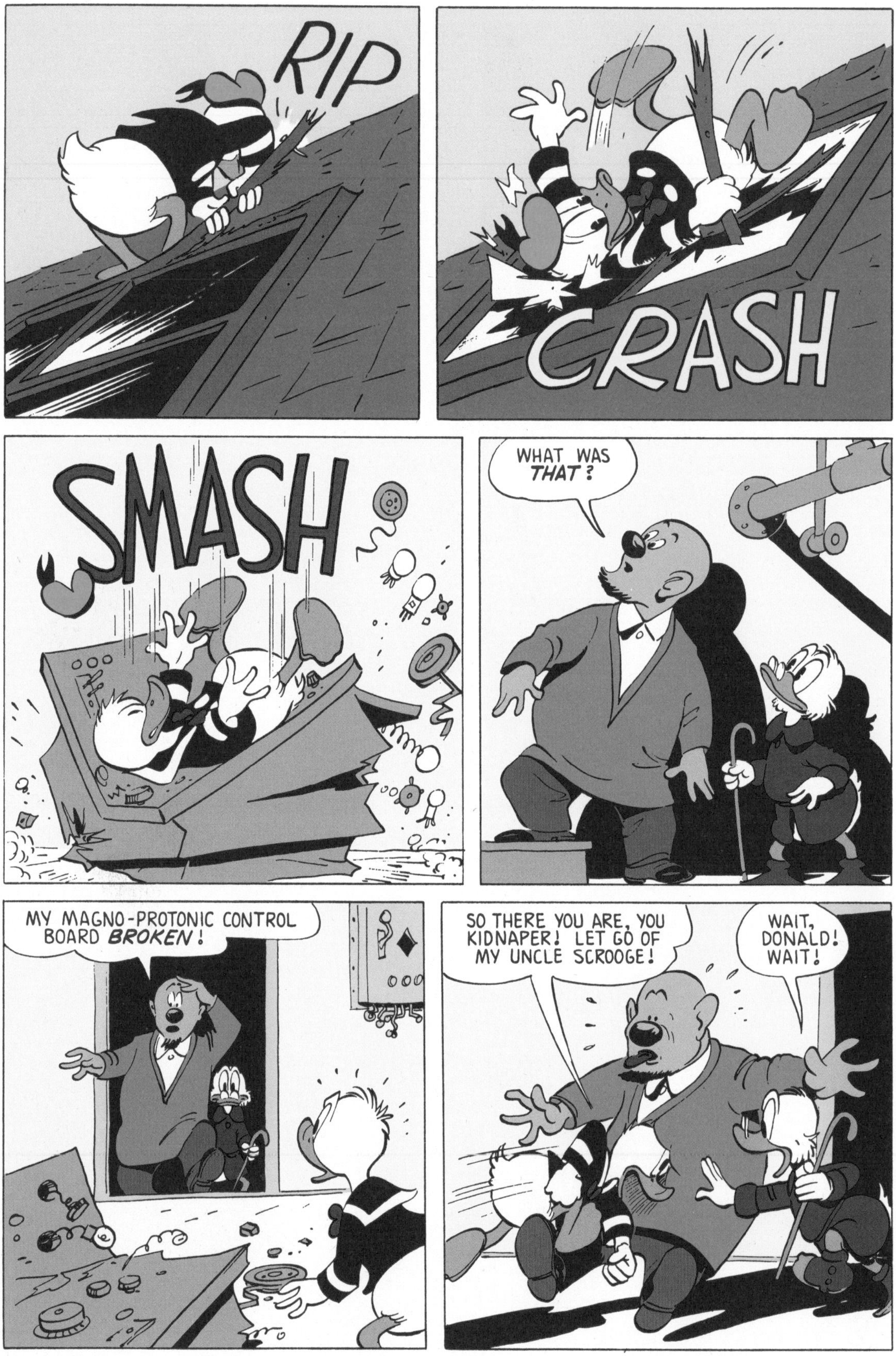
RIP
CRASH
SMASH
WHAT WAS THAT?
MY MAGNO-PROTONIC CONTROL BOARD BROKEN!
SO THERE YOU ARE, YOU KIDNAPER! LET GO OF MY UNCLE SCROOGE!
WAIT, DONALD! WAIT!

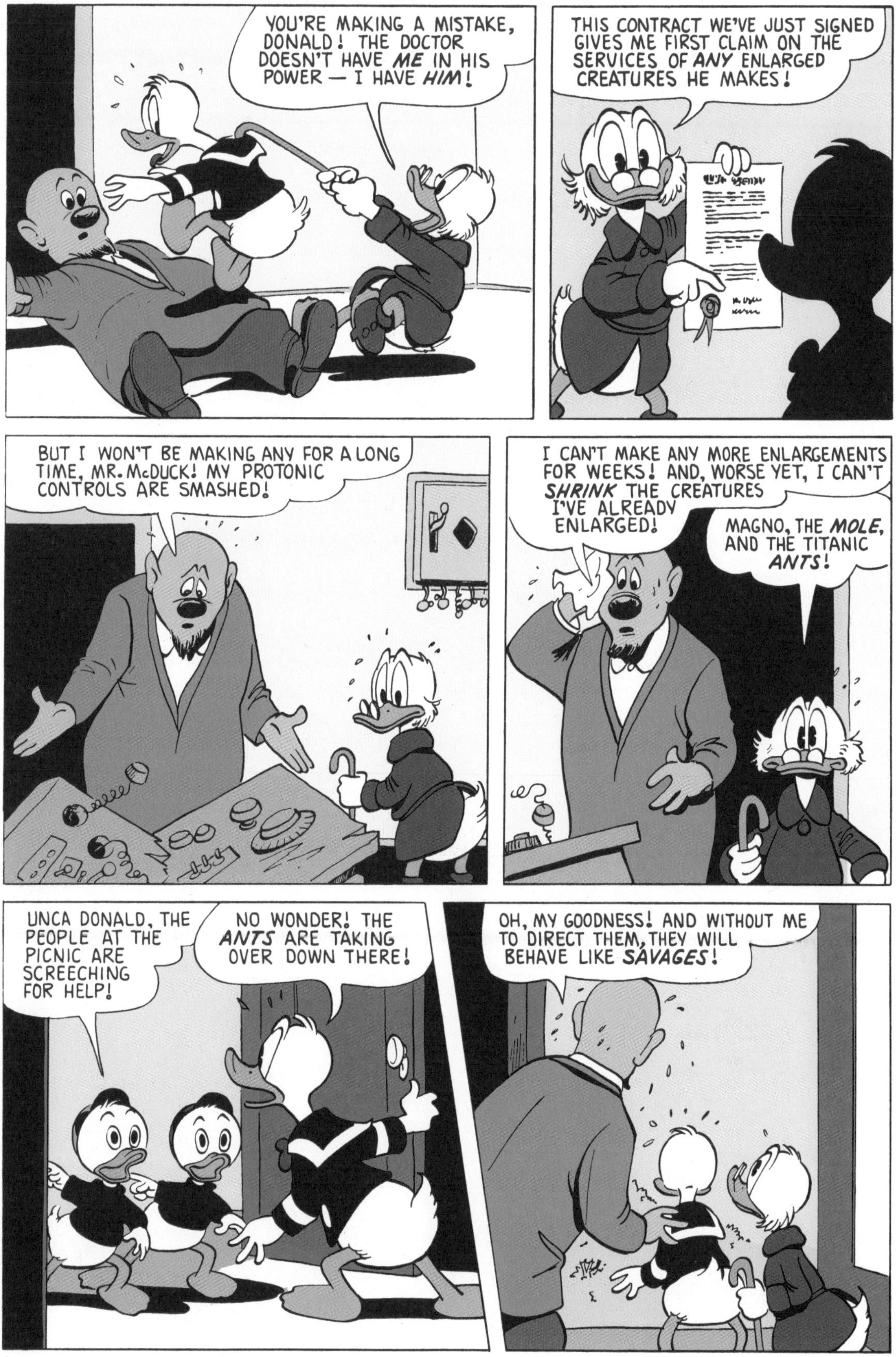
YOU'RE MAKING A MISTAKE, DONALD! THE DOCTOR DOESN'T HAVE *ME* IN HIS POWER — I HAVE *HIM*!
THIS CONTRACT WE'VE JUST SIGNED GIVES ME FIRST CLAIM ON THE SERVICES OF *ANY* ENLARGED CREATURES HE MAKES!
BUT I WON'T BE MAKING ANY FOR A LONG TIME, MR. McDUCK! MY PROTONIC CONTROLS ARE SMASHED!
I CAN'T MAKE ANY MORE ENLARGEMENTS FOR WEEKS! AND, WORSE YET, I CAN'T *SHRINK* THE CREATURES I'VE ALREADY ENLARGED!
MAGNO, THE *MOLE*, AND THE TITANIC *ANTS*!
UNCA DONALD, THE PEOPLE AT THE PICNIC ARE SCREECHING FOR HELP!
NO WONDER! THE *ANTS* ARE TAKING OVER DOWN THERE!
OH, MY GOODNESS! AND WITHOUT ME TO DIRECT THEM, THEY WILL BEHAVE LIKE *SAVAGES*!

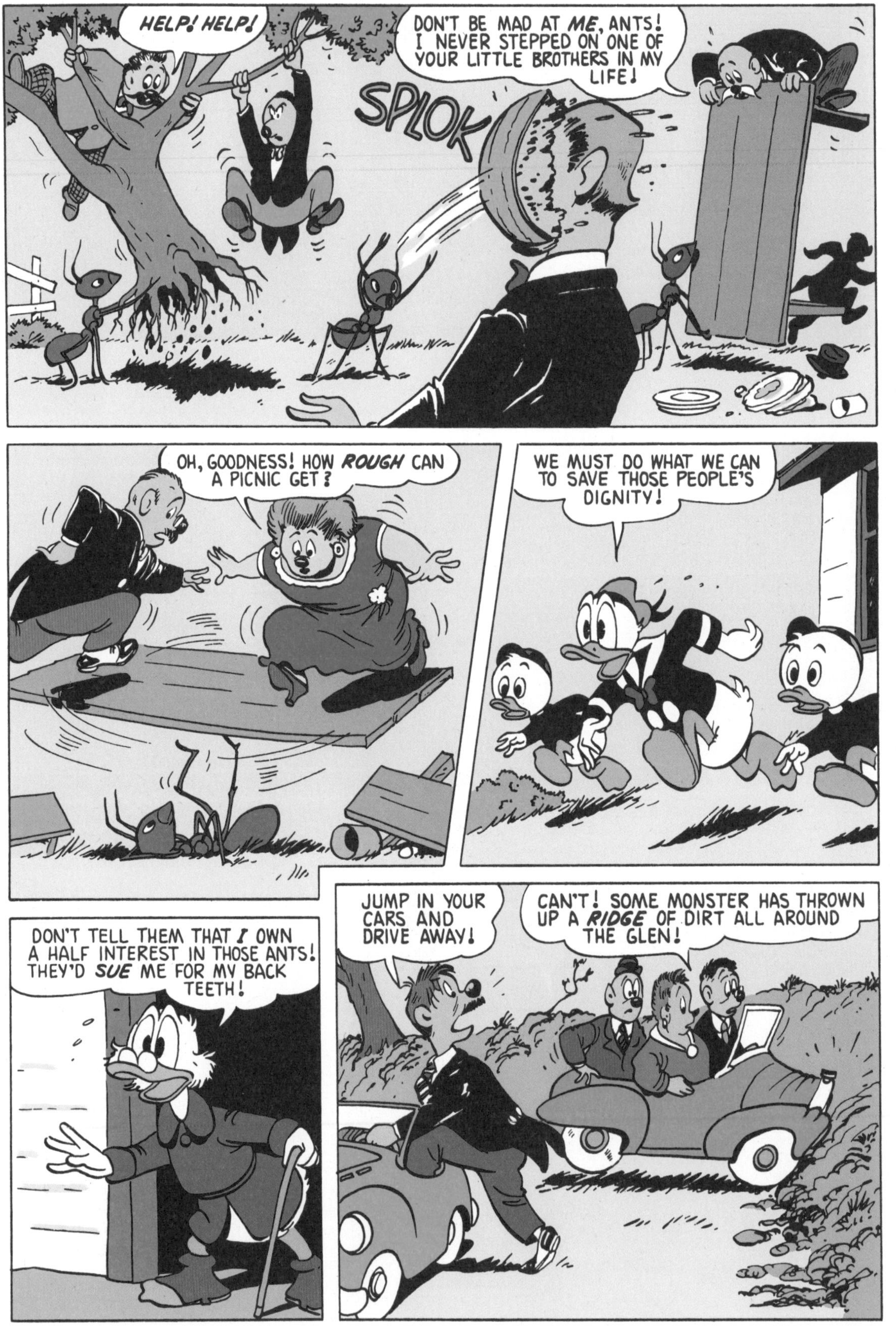
HELP! HELP!
DON'T BE MAD AT *ME*, ANTS! I NEVER STEPPED ON ONE OF YOUR LITTLE BROTHERS IN MY LIFE!
SPLOK
OH, GOODNESS! HOW *ROUGH* CAN A PICNIC GET?
WE MUST DO WHAT WE CAN TO SAVE THOSE PEOPLE'S DIGNITY!
DON'T TELL THEM THAT *I* OWN A HALF INTEREST IN THOSE ANTS! THEY'D *SUE* ME FOR MY BACK TEETH!
JUMP IN YOUR CARS AND DRIVE AWAY!
CAN'T! SOME MONSTER HAS THROWN UP A *RIDGE* OF DIRT ALL AROUND THE GLEN!

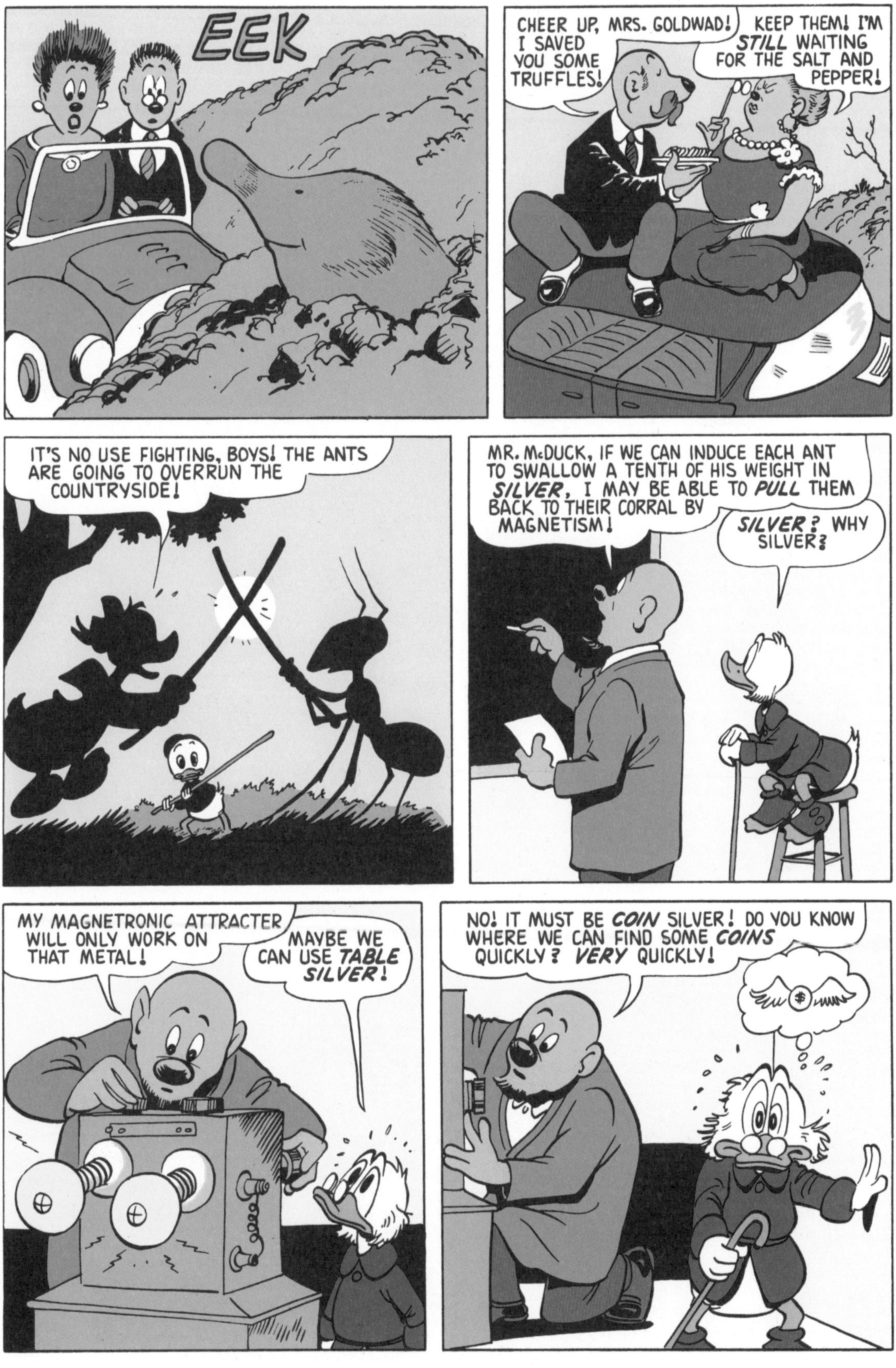
EEK
CHEER UP, MRS. GOLDWAD! I SAVED YOU SOME TRUFFLES!
KEEP THEM! I'M STILL WAITING FOR THE SALT AND PEPPER!
IT'S NO USE FIGHTING, BOYS! THE ANTS ARE GOING TO OVERRUN THE COUNTRYSIDE!
MR. McDUCK, IF WE CAN INDUCE EACH ANT TO SWALLOW A TENTH OF HIS WEIGHT IN SILVER, I MAY BE ABLE TO PULL THEM BACK TO THEIR CORRAL BY MAGNETISM!
SILVER? WHY SILVER?
MY MAGNETRONIC ATTRACTER WILL ONLY WORK ON THAT METAL!
MAYBE WE CAN USE TABLE SILVER!
NO! IT MUST BE COIN SILVER! DO YOU KNOW WHERE WE CAN FIND SOME COINS QUICKLY? VERY QUICKLY!

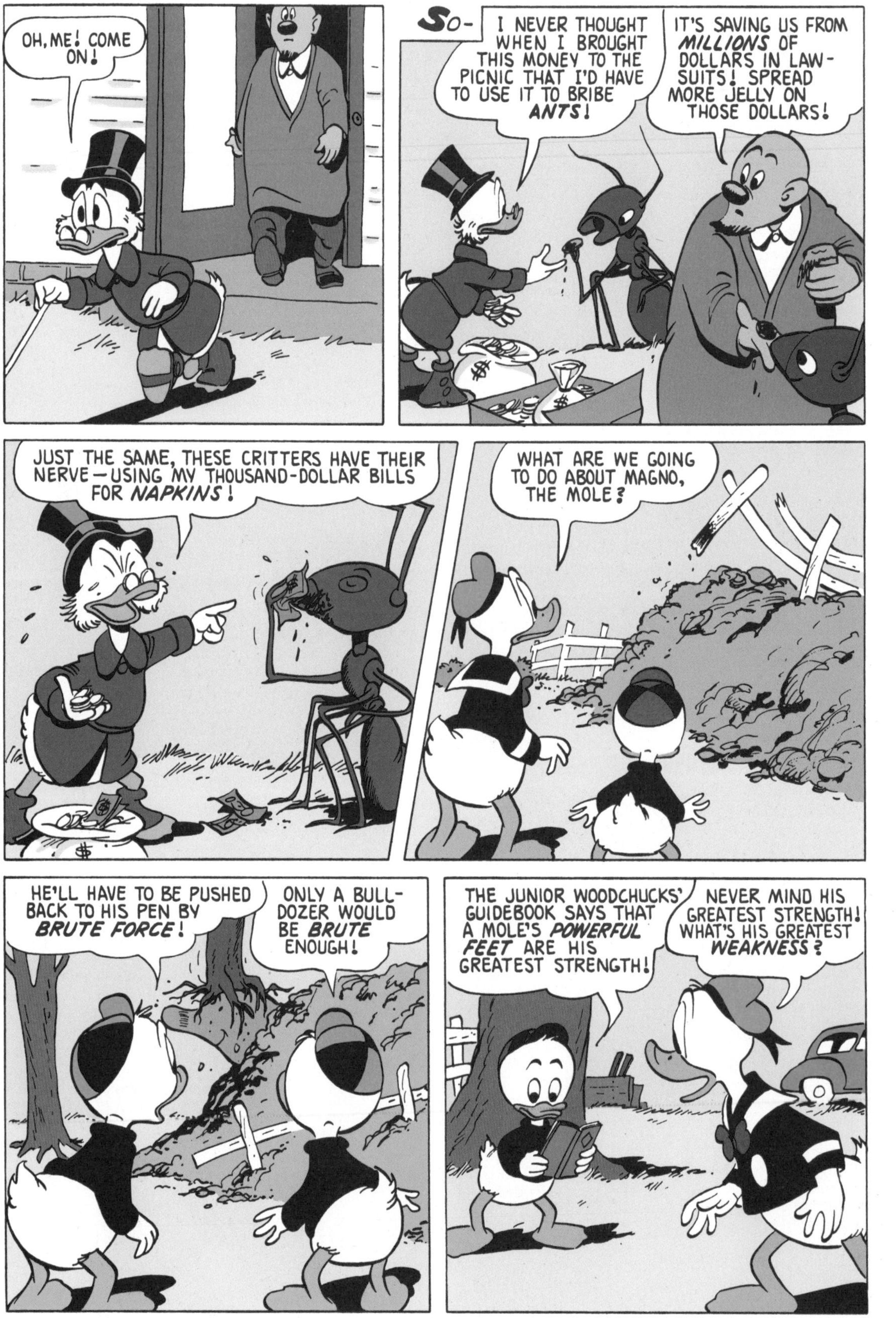
OH, ME! COME ON!
SO-
I NEVER THOUGHT WHEN I BROUGHT THIS MONEY TO THE PICNIC THAT I'D HAVE TO USE IT TO BRIBE *ANTS*!
IT'S SAVING US FROM *MILLIONS* OF DOLLARS IN LAW-SUITS! SPREAD MORE JELLY ON THOSE DOLLARS!
JUST THE SAME, THESE CRITTERS HAVE THEIR NERVE—USING MY THOUSAND-DOLLAR BILLS FOR *NAPKINS*!
WHAT ARE WE GOING TO DO ABOUT MAGNO, THE MOLE?
HE'LL HAVE TO BE PUSHED BACK TO HIS PEN BY *BRUTE FORCE*!
ONLY A BULL-DOZER WOULD BE *BRUTE* ENOUGH!
THE JUNIOR WOODCHUCKS' GUIDEBOOK SAYS THAT A MOLE'S *POWERFUL FEET* ARE HIS GREATEST STRENGTH!
NEVER MIND HIS GREATEST STRENGTH! WHAT'S HIS GREATEST *WEAKNESS*?

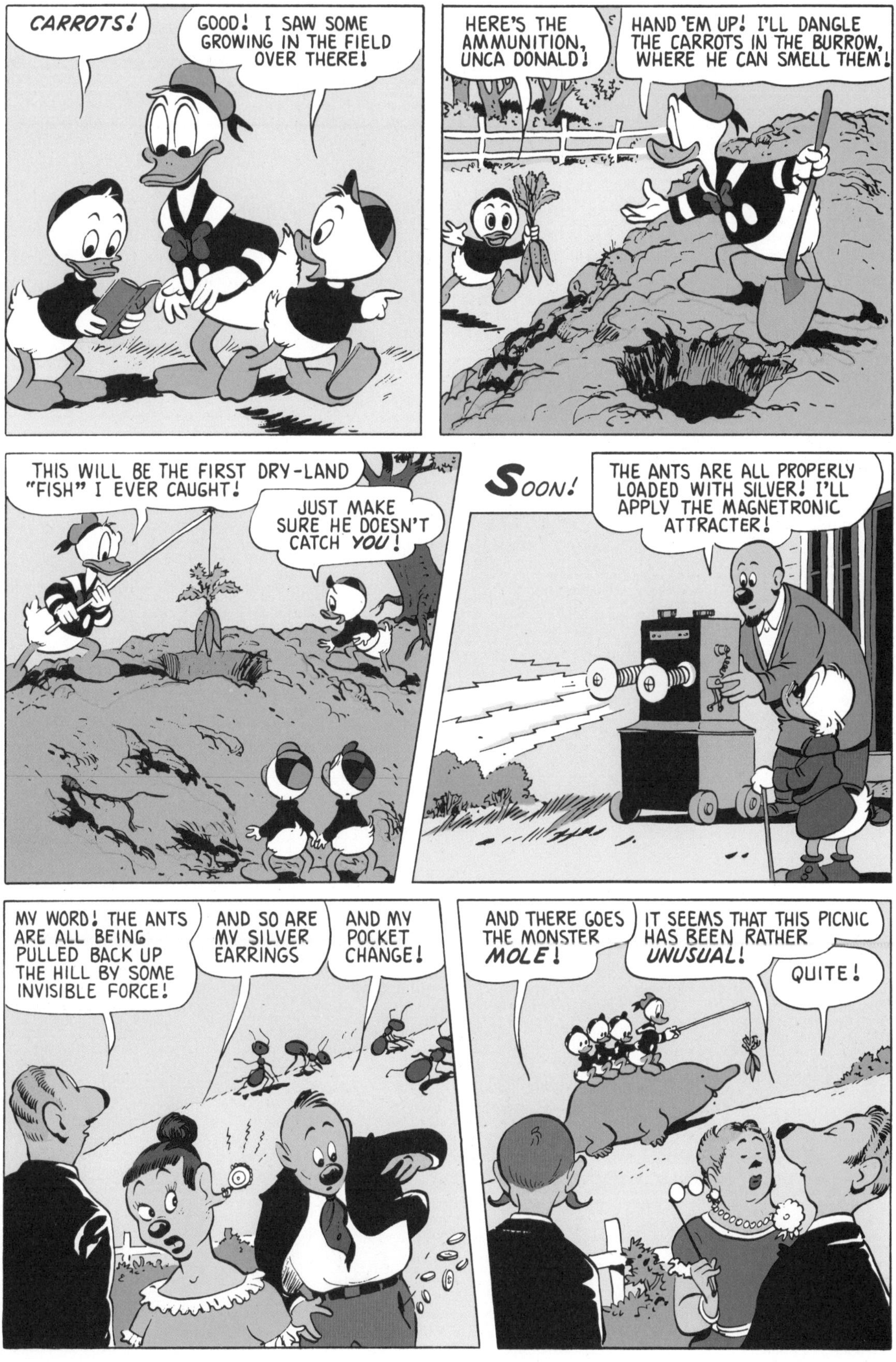
CARROTS!
GOOD! I SAW SOME GROWING IN THE FIELD OVER THERE!
HERE'S THE AMMUNITION, UNCA DONALD!
HAND 'EM UP! I'LL DANGLE THE CARROTS IN THE BURROW, WHERE HE CAN SMELL THEM!
THIS WILL BE THE FIRST DRY-LAND "FISH" I EVER CAUGHT!
JUST MAKE SURE HE DOESN'T CATCH YOU!
SOON!
THE ANTS ARE ALL PROPERLY LOADED WITH SILVER! I'LL APPLY THE MAGNETRONIC ATTRACTER!
MY WORD! THE ANTS ARE ALL BEING PULLED BACK UP THE HILL BY SOME INVISIBLE FORCE!
AND SO ARE MY SILVER EARRINGS
AND MY POCKET CHANGE!
AND THERE GOES THE MONSTER MOLE!
IT SEEMS THAT THIS PICNIC HAS BEEN RATHER UNUSUAL!
QUITE!

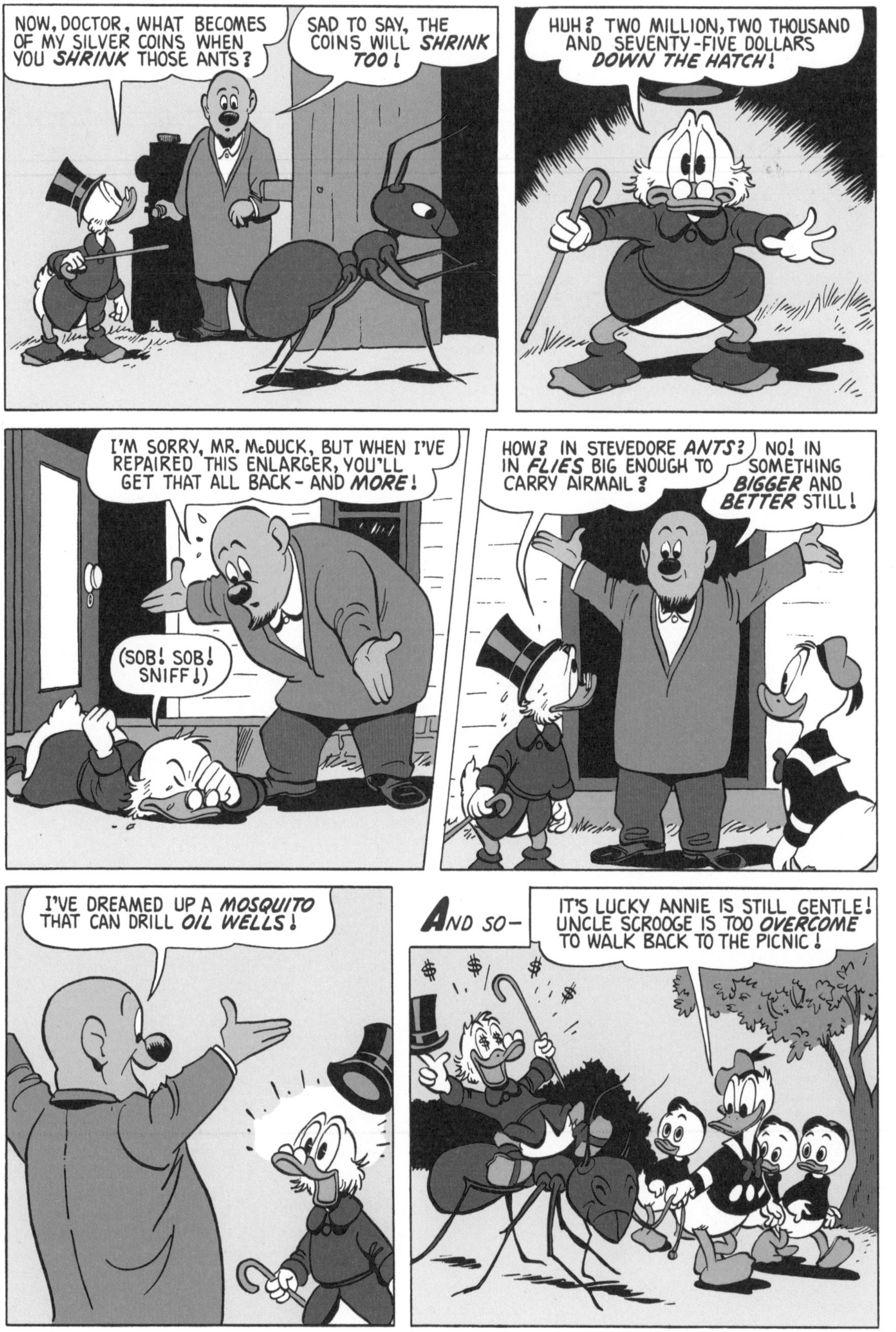

NOW, DOCTOR, WHAT BECOMES OF MY SILVER COINS WHEN YOU SHRINK THOSE ANTS?
SAD TO SAY, THE COINS WILL SHRINK TOO!
HUH? TWO MILLION, TWO THOUSAND AND SEVENTY-FIVE DOLLARS DOWN THE HATCH!
I'M SORRY, MR. McDUCK, BUT WHEN I'VE REPAIRED THIS ENLARGER, YOU'LL GET THAT ALL BACK - AND MORE!
(SOB! SOB! SNIFF!)
HOW? IN STEVEDORE ANTS? IN FLIES BIG ENOUGH TO CARRY AIRMAIL?
NO! IN SOMETHING BIGGER AND BETTER STILL!
I'VE DREAMED UP A MOSQUITO THAT CAN DRILL OIL WELLS!
AND SO-
IT'S LUCKY ANNIE IS STILL GENTLE! UNCLE SCROOGE IS TOO OVERCOME TO WALK BACK TO THE PICNIC!

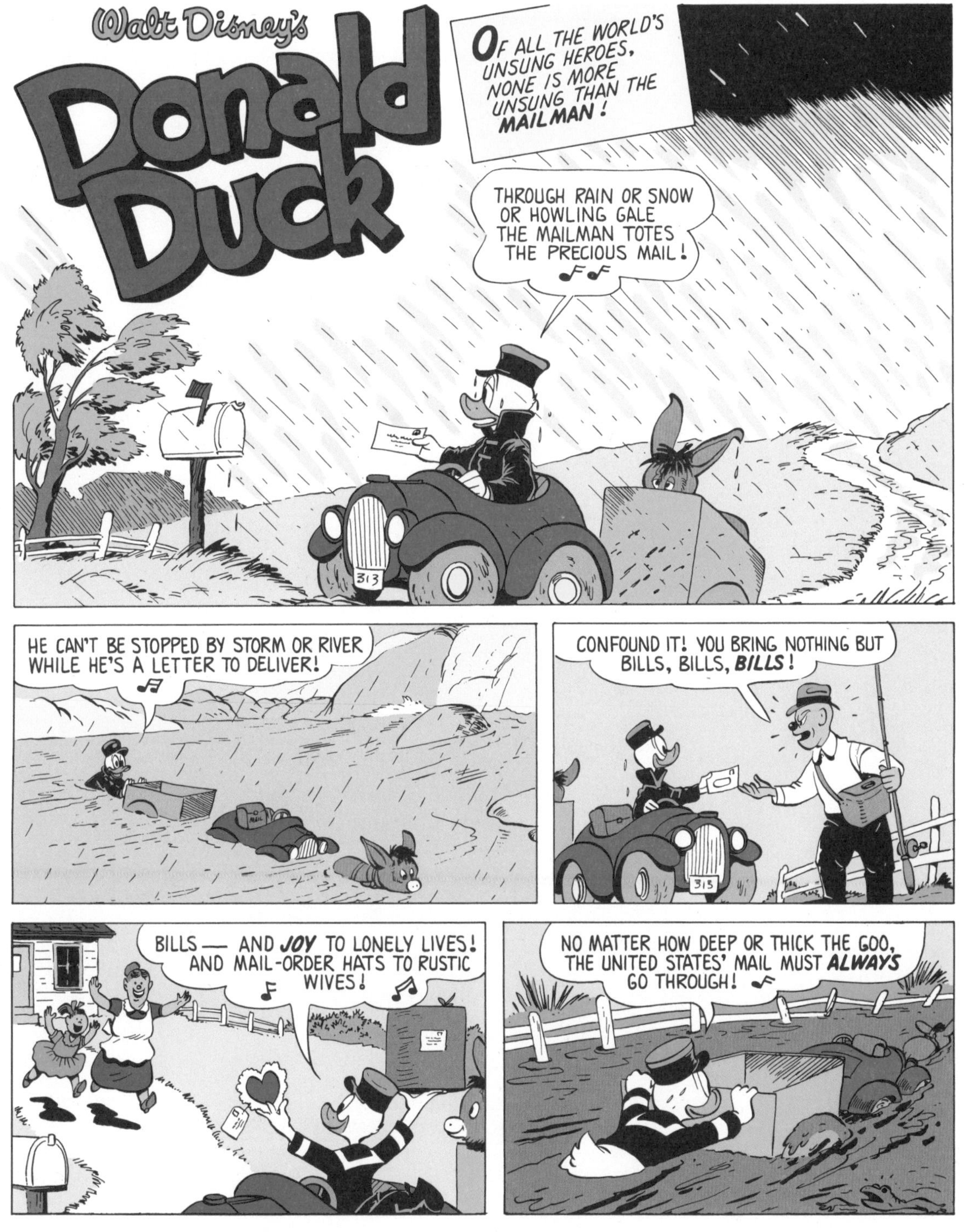
Walt Disney's
Donald Duck
OF ALL THE WORLD'S UNSUNG HEROES, NONE IS MORE UNSUNG THAN THE MAILMAN!
THROUGH RAIN OR SNOW OR HOWLING GALE THE MAILMAN TOTES THE PRECIOUS MAIL!
313
HE CAN'T BE STOPPED BY STORM OR RIVER WHILE HE'S A LETTER TO DELIVER!
CONFOUND IT! YOU BRING NOTHING BUT BILLS, BILLS, BILLS!
313
BILLS — AND JOY TO LONELY LIVES! AND MAIL-ORDER HATS TO RUSTIC WIVES!
NO MATTER HOW DEEP OR THICK THE GOO, THE UNITED STATES' MAIL MUST ALWAYS GO THROUGH!

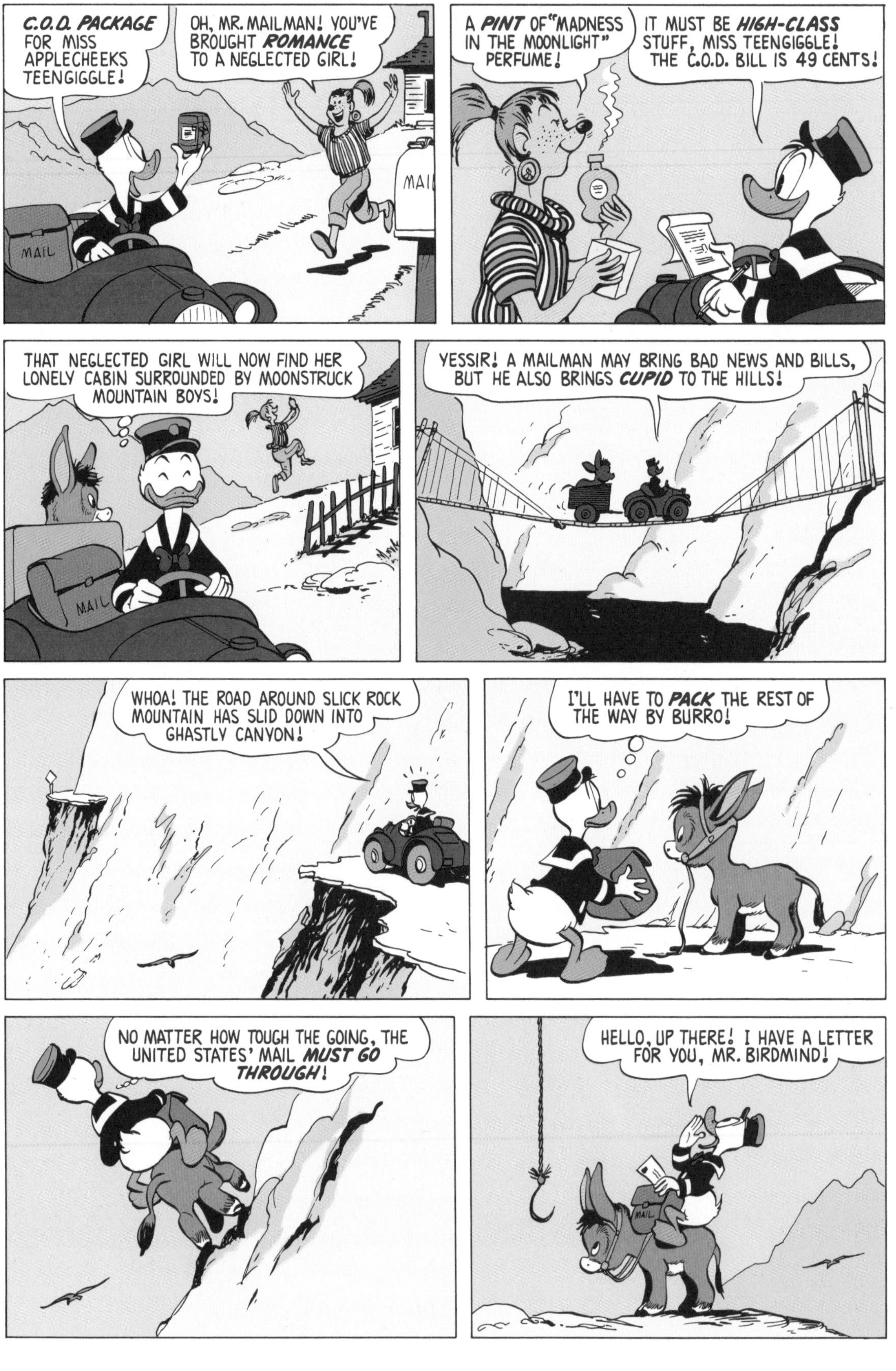
C.O.D. PACKAGE FOR MISS APPLECHEEKS TEENGIGGLE!
OH, MR. MAILMAN! YOU'VE BROUGHT ROMANCE TO A NEGLECTED GIRL!
MAIL
MAIL
A PINT OF "MADNESS IN THE MOONLIGHT" PERFUME!
IT MUST BE HIGH-CLASS STUFF, MISS TEENGIGGLE! THE C.O.D. BILL IS 49 CENTS!
THAT NEGLECTED GIRL WILL NOW FIND HER LONELY CABIN SURROUNDED BY MOONSTRUCK MOUNTAIN BOYS!
MAIL
YESSIR! A MAILMAN MAY BRING BAD NEWS AND BILLS, BUT HE ALSO BRINGS CUPID TO THE HILLS!
WHOA! THE ROAD AROUND SLICK ROCK MOUNTAIN HAS SLID DOWN INTO GHASTLY CANYON!
I'LL HAVE TO PACK THE REST OF THE WAY BY BURRO!
NO MATTER HOW TOUGH THE GOING, THE UNITED STATES' MAIL MUST GO THROUGH!
HELLO, UP THERE! I HAVE A LETTER FOR YOU, MR. BIRDMIND!
MAIL

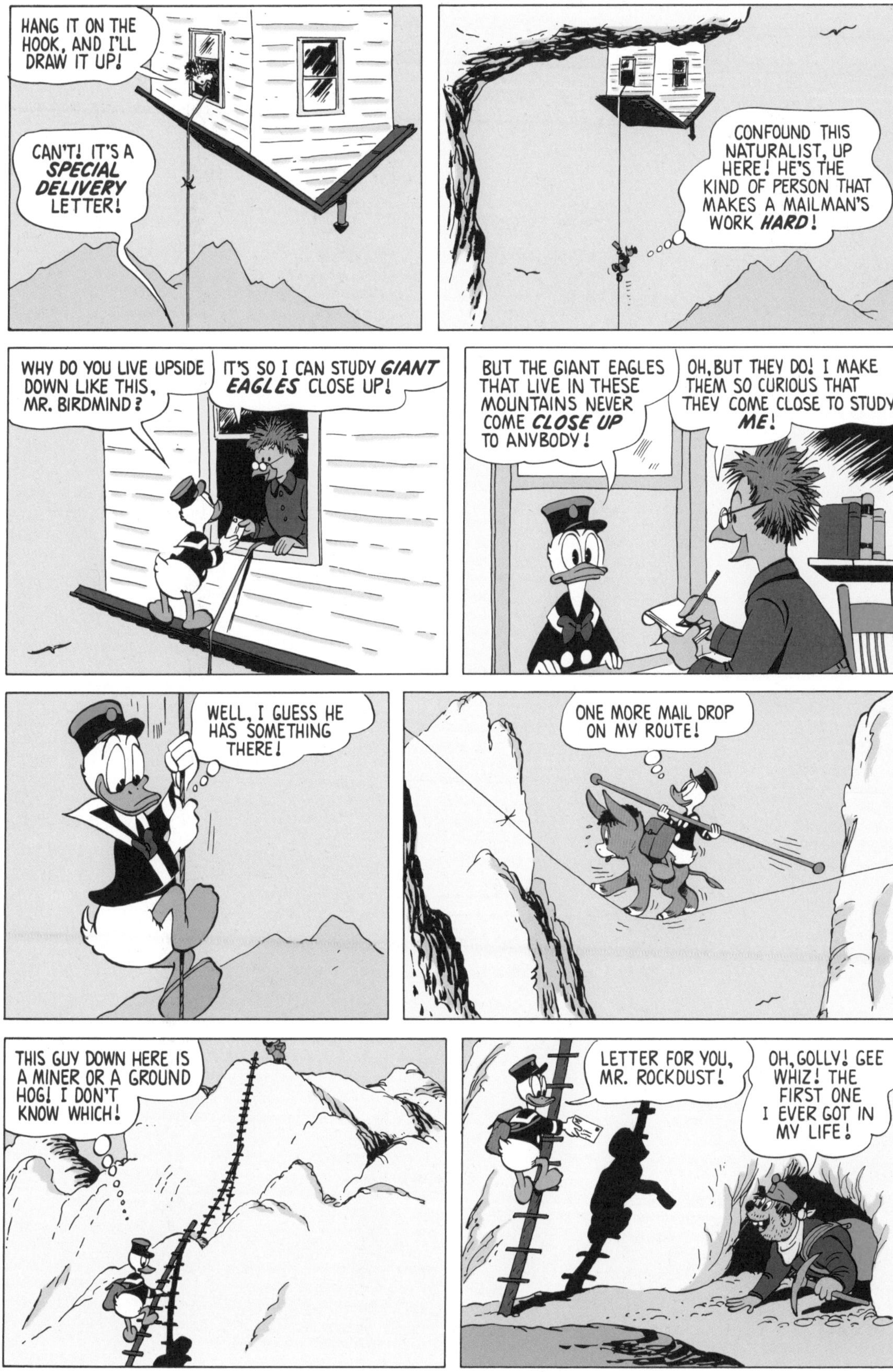
HANG IT ON THE HOOK, AND I'LL DRAW IT UP!
CAN'T! IT'S A SPECIAL DELIVERY LETTER!
CONFOUND THIS NATURALIST, UP HERE! HE'S THE KIND OF PERSON THAT MAKES A MAILMAN'S WORK HARD!
WHY DO YOU LIVE UPSIDE DOWN LIKE THIS, MR. BIRDMIND?
IT'S SO I CAN STUDY GIANT EAGLES CLOSE UP!
BUT THE GIANT EAGLES THAT LIVE IN THESE MOUNTAINS NEVER COME CLOSE UP TO ANYBODY!
OH, BUT THEY DO! I MAKE THEM SO CURIOUS THAT THEY COME CLOSE TO STUDY ME!
WELL, I GUESS HE HAS SOMETHING THERE!
ONE MORE MAIL DROP ON MY ROUTE!
THIS GUY DOWN HERE IS A MINER OR A GROUND HOG! I DON'T KNOW WHICH!
LETTER FOR YOU, MR. ROCKDUST!
OH, GOLLY! GEE WHIZ! THE FIRST ONE I EVER GOT IN MY LIFE!

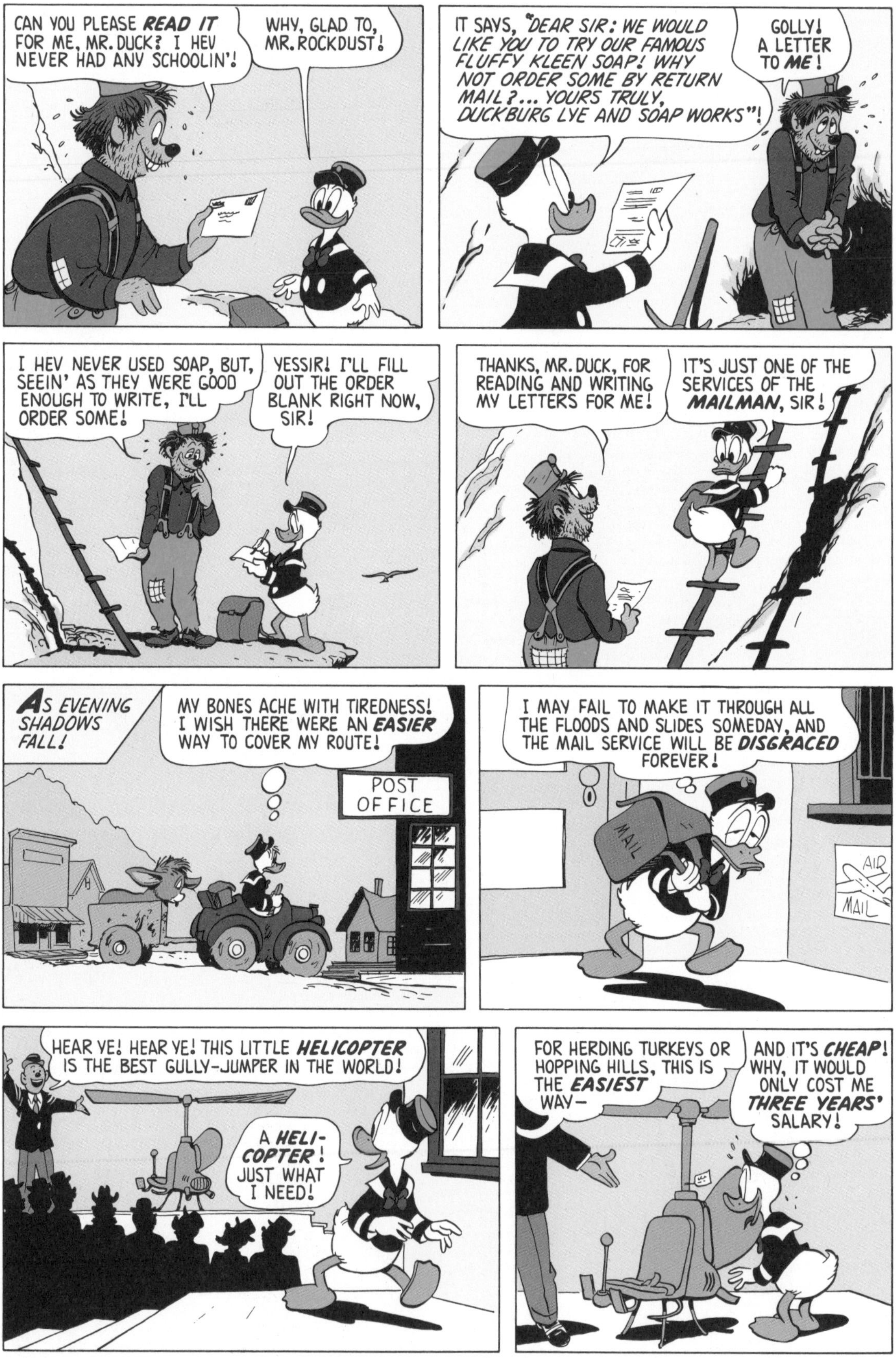

CAN YOU PLEASE READ IT FOR ME, MR. DUCK? I HEV NEVER HAD ANY SCHOOLIN'!
WHY, GLAD TO, MR. ROCKDUST!
IT SAYS, "DEAR SIR: WE WOULD LIKE YOU TO TRY OUR FAMOUS FLUFFY KLEEN SOAP! WHY NOT ORDER SOME BY RETURN MAIL?... YOURS TRULY, DUCKBURG LYE AND SOAP WORKS"!
GOLLY! A LETTER TO ME!
I HEV NEVER USED SOAP, BUT, SEEIN' AS THEY WERE GOOD ENOUGH TO WRITE, I'LL ORDER SOME!
YESSIR! I'LL FILL OUT THE ORDER BLANK RIGHT NOW, SIR!
THANKS, MR. DUCK, FOR READING AND WRITING MY LETTERS FOR ME!
IT'S JUST ONE OF THE SERVICES OF THE MAILMAN, SIR!
AS EVENING SHADOWS FALL!
MY BONES ACHE WITH TIREDNESS! I WISH THERE WERE AN EASIER WAY TO COVER MY ROUTE!
POST OFFICE
I MAY FAIL TO MAKE IT THROUGH ALL THE FLOODS AND SLIDES SOMEDAY, AND THE MAIL SERVICE WILL BE DISGRACED FOREVER!
MAIL
AIR MAIL
HEAR YE! HEAR YE! THIS LITTLE HELICOPTER IS THE BEST GULLY-JUMPER IN THE WORLD!
A HELI-COPTER! JUST WHAT I NEED!
FOR HERDING TURKEYS OR HOPPING HILLS, THIS IS THE EASIEST WAY—
AND IT'S CHEAP! WHY, IT WOULD ONLY COST ME THREE YEARS' SALARY!

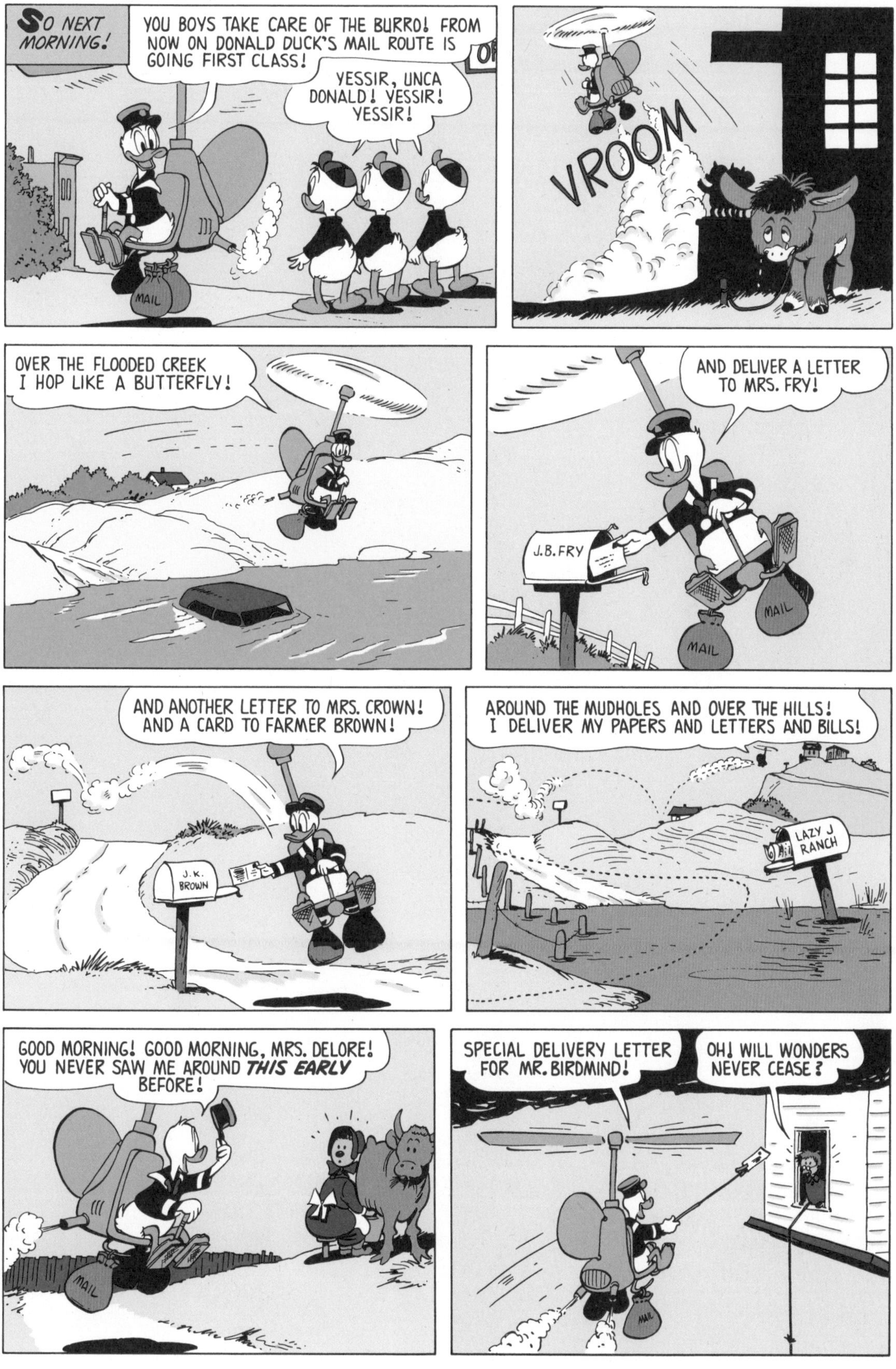
SO NEXT MORNING!
YOU BOYS TAKE CARE OF THE BURRO! FROM NOW ON DONALD DUCK'S MAIL ROUTE IS GOING FIRST CLASS!
YESSIR, UNCA DONALD! YESSIR! YESSIR!
MAIL
VROOM
OVER THE FLOODED CREEK I HOP LIKE A BUTTERFLY!
AND DELIVER A LETTER TO MRS. FRY!
J.B. FRY
MAIL
MAIL
AND ANOTHER LETTER TO MRS. CROWN! AND A CARD TO FARMER BROWN!
J.K. BROWN
AROUND THE MUDHOLES AND OVER THE HILLS! I DELIVER MY PAPERS AND LETTERS AND BILLS!
LAZY J RANCH
GOOD MORNING! GOOD MORNING, MRS. DELORE! YOU NEVER SAW ME AROUND ***THIS EARLY*** BEFORE!
MAIL
SPECIAL DELIVERY LETTER FOR MR. BIRDMIND!
OH! WILL WONDERS NEVER CEASE?
MAIL

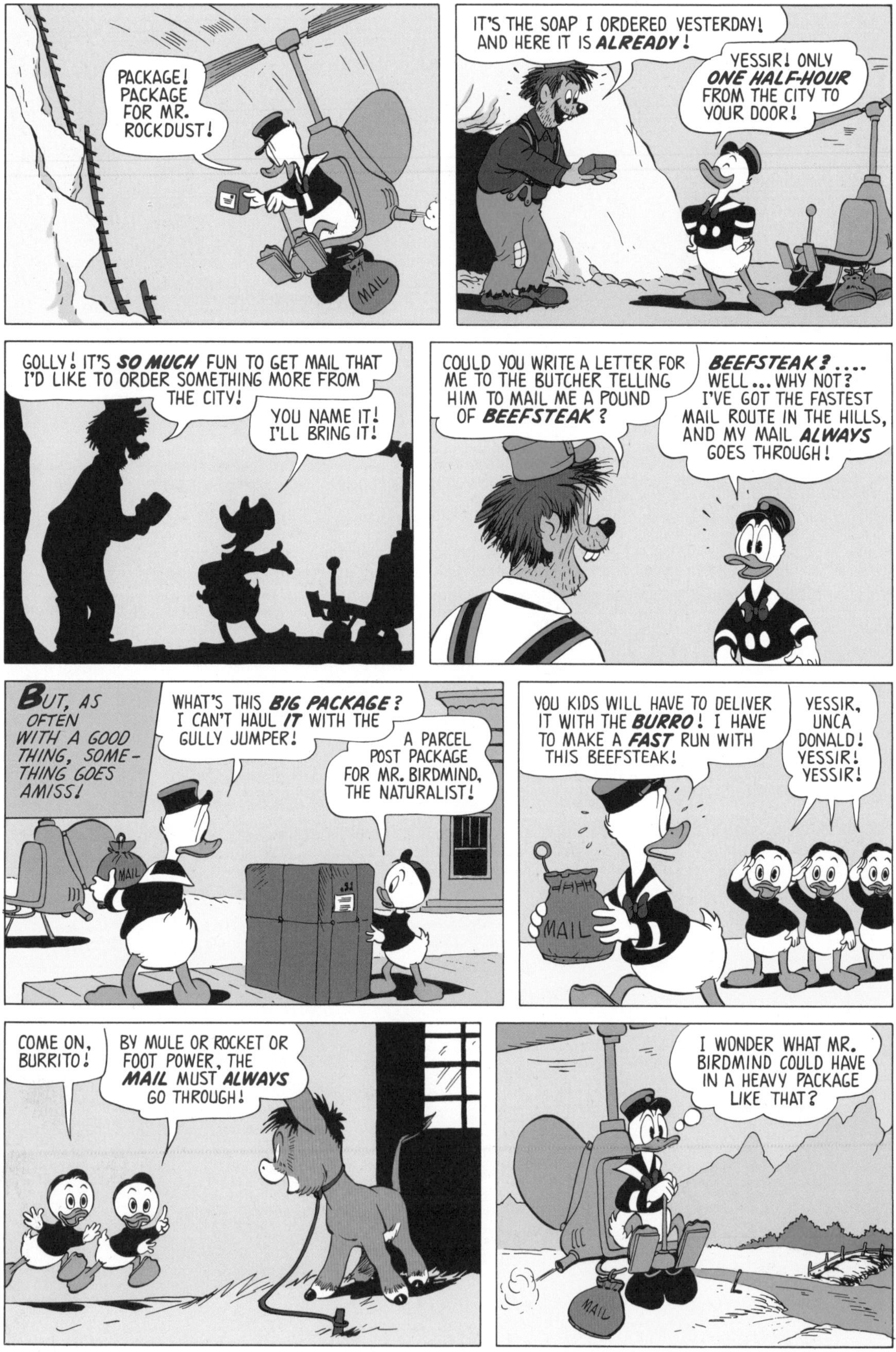
PACKAGE! PACKAGE FOR MR. ROCKDUST!
IT'S THE SOAP I ORDERED YESTERDAY! AND HERE IT IS ALREADY!
YESSIR! ONLY ONE HALF-HOUR FROM THE CITY TO YOUR DOOR!
GOLLY! IT'S SO MUCH FUN TO GET MAIL THAT I'D LIKE TO ORDER SOMETHING MORE FROM THE CITY!
YOU NAME IT! I'LL BRING IT!
COULD YOU WRITE A LETTER FOR ME TO THE BUTCHER TELLING HIM TO MAIL ME A POUND OF BEEFSTEAK?
BEEFSTEAK? .... WELL ... WHY NOT? I'VE GOT THE FASTEST MAIL ROUTE IN THE HILLS, AND MY MAIL ALWAYS GOES THROUGH!
BUT, AS OFTEN WITH A GOOD THING, SOMETHING GOES AMISS!
WHAT'S THIS BIG PACKAGE? I CAN'T HAUL IT WITH THE GULLY JUMPER!
A PARCEL POST PACKAGE FOR MR. BIRDMIND, THE NATURALIST!
YOU KIDS WILL HAVE TO DELIVER IT WITH THE BURRO! I HAVE TO MAKE A FAST RUN WITH THIS BEEFSTEAK!
YESSIR, UNCA DONALD! YESSIR! YESSIR!
MAIL
COME ON, BURRITO!
BY MULE OR ROCKET OR FOOT POWER, THE MAIL MUST ALWAYS GO THROUGH!
I WONDER WHAT MR. BIRDMIND COULD HAVE IN A HEAVY PACKAGE LIKE THAT?
MAIL

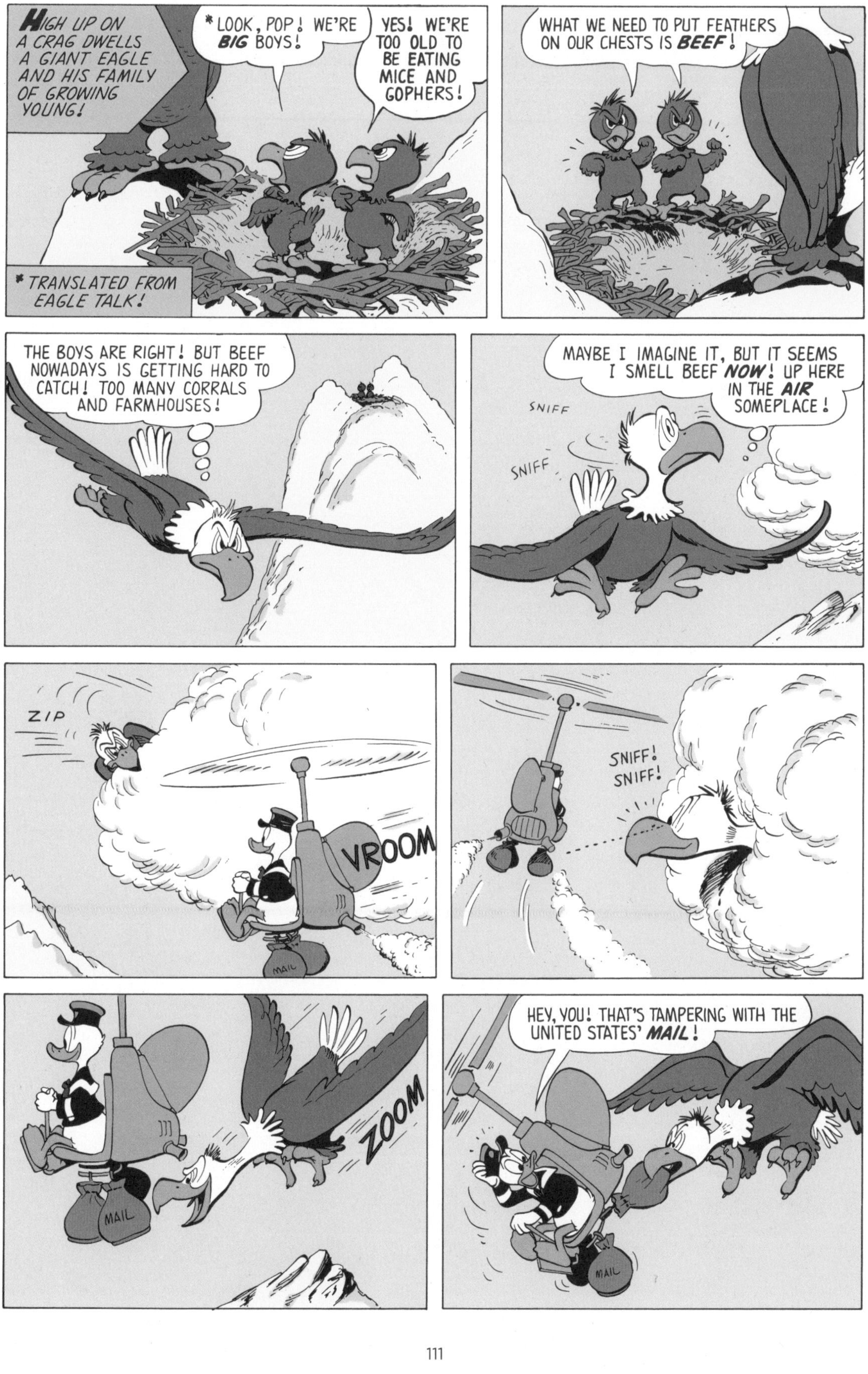
HIGH UP ON A CRAG DWELLS A GIANT EAGLE AND HIS FAMILY OF GROWING YOUNG!
*LOOK, POP! WE'RE BIG BOYS!
YES! WE'RE TOO OLD TO BE EATING MICE AND GOPHERS!
*TRANSLATED FROM EAGLE TALK!
WHAT WE NEED TO PUT FEATHERS ON OUR CHESTS IS BEEF!
THE BOYS ARE RIGHT! BUT BEEF NOWADAYS IS GETTING HARD TO CATCH! TOO MANY CORRALS AND FARMHOUSES!
MAYBE I IMAGINE IT, BUT IT SEEMS I SMELL BEEF NOW! UP HERE IN THE AIR SOMEPLACE!
SNIFF
SNIFF
ZIP
VROOM
MAIL
SNIFF! SNIFF!
MAIL
ZOOM
HEY, YOU! THAT'S TAMPERING WITH THE UNITED STATES' MAIL!
MAIL

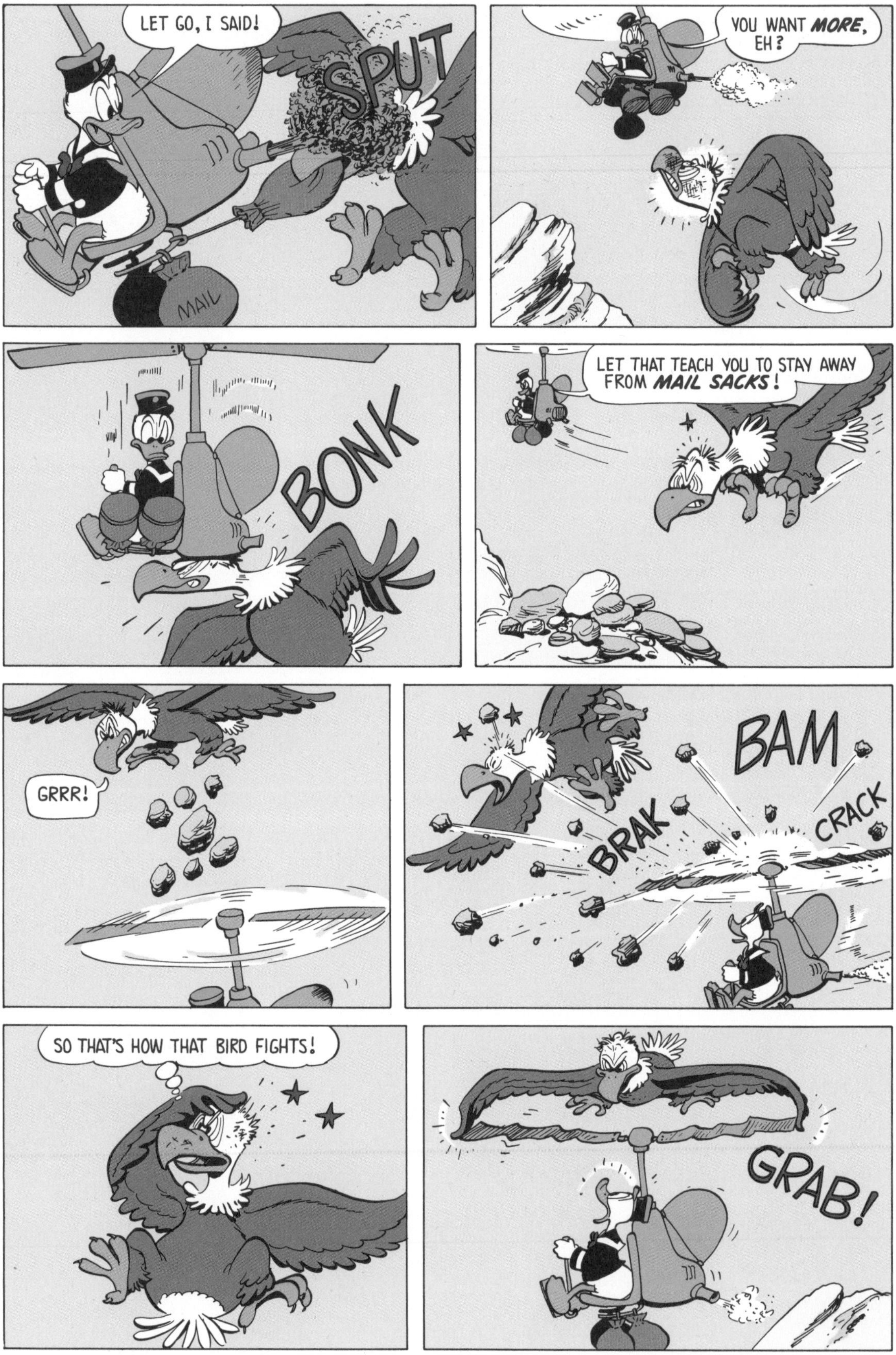

LET GO, I SAID!
SPUT
YOU WANT MORE, EH?
BONK
LET THAT TEACH YOU TO STAY AWAY FROM MAIL SACKS!
GRRR!
BAM
BRAK
CRACK
SO THAT'S HOW THAT BIRD FIGHTS!
GRAB!

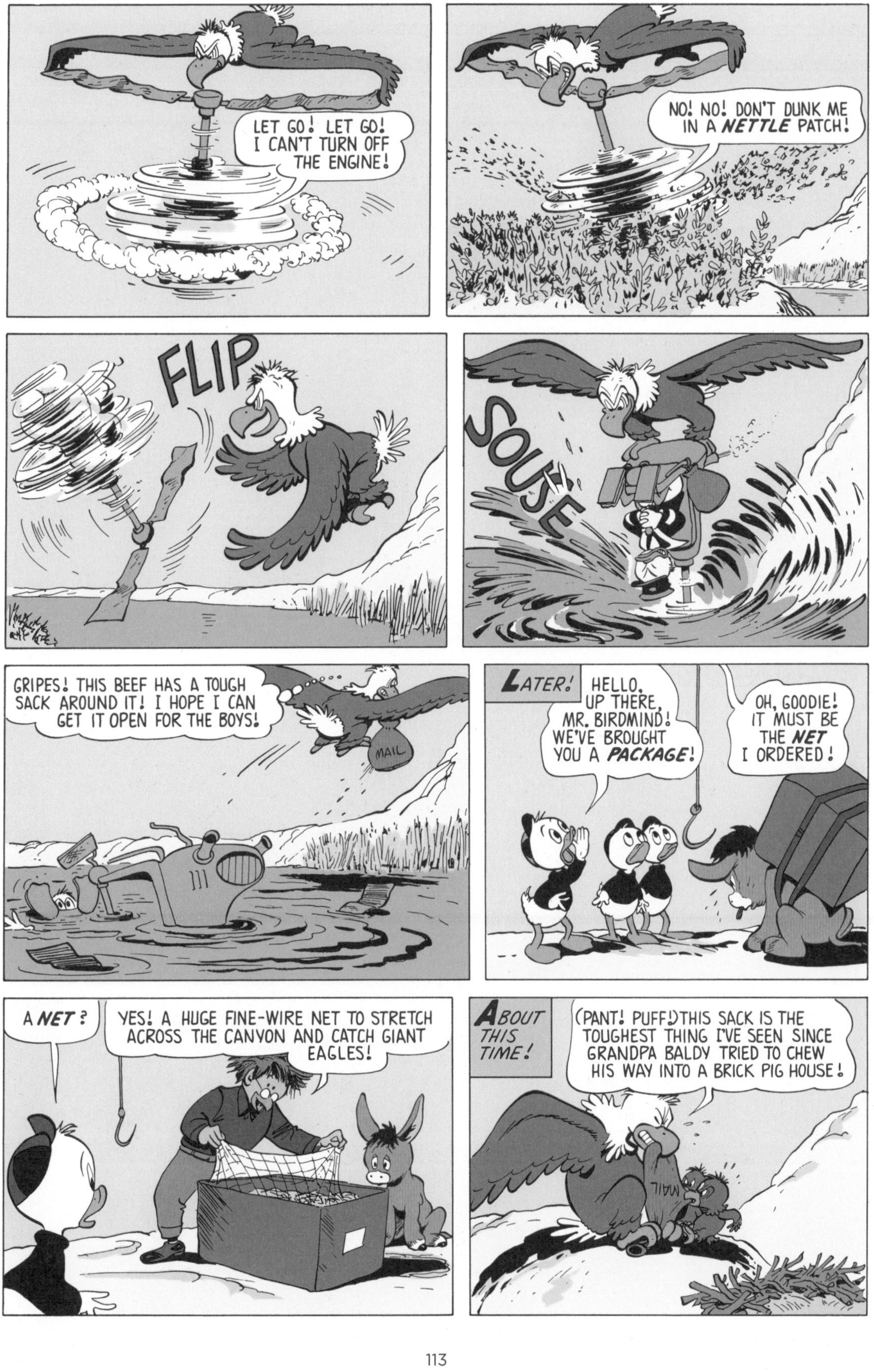
LET GO! LET GO! I CAN'T TURN OFF THE ENGINE!
NO! NO! DON'T DUNK ME IN A NETTLE PATCH!
FLIP
SOUSE
GRIPES! THIS BEEF HAS A TOUGH SACK AROUND IT! I HOPE I CAN GET IT OPEN FOR THE BOYS!
MAIL
LATER!
HELLO, UP THERE, MR. BIRDMIND! WE'VE BROUGHT YOU A PACKAGE!
OH, GOODIE! IT MUST BE THE NET I ORDERED!
A NET?
YES! A HUGE FINE-WIRE NET TO STRETCH ACROSS THE CANYON AND CATCH GIANT EAGLES!
ABOUT THIS TIME!
(PANT! PUFF!) THIS SACK IS THE TOUGHEST THING I'VE SEEN SINCE GRANDPA BALDY TRIED TO CHEW HIS WAY INTO A BRICK PIG HOUSE!
MAIL

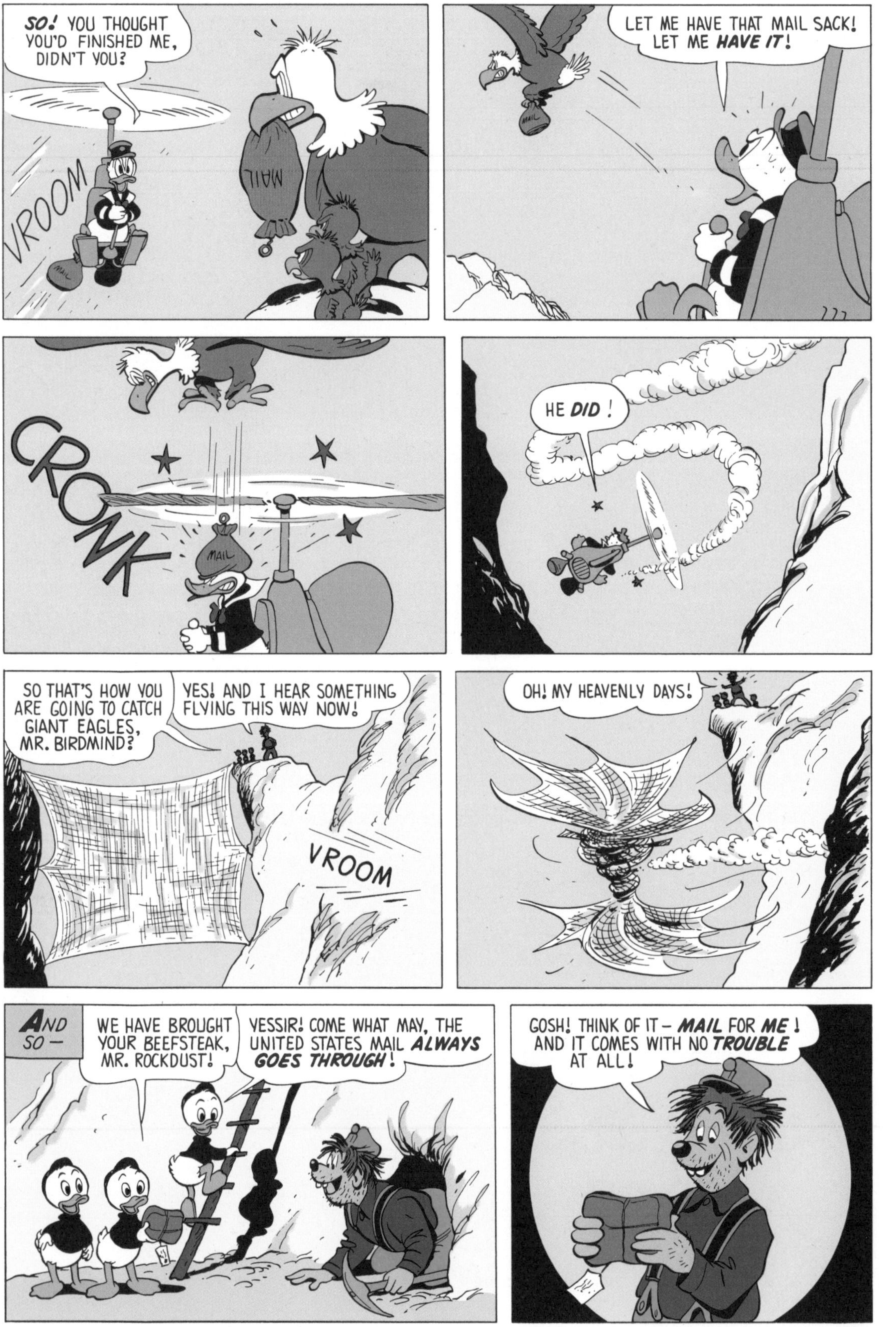
SO! YOU THOUGHT YOU'D FINISHED ME, DIDN'T YOU?
VROOM
MAIL
LET ME HAVE THAT MAIL SACK! LET ME HAVE IT!
MAIL
CRONK
MAIL
HE DID!
SO THAT'S HOW YOU ARE GOING TO CATCH GIANT EAGLES, MR. BIRDMIND?
YES! AND I HEAR SOMETHING FLYING THIS WAY NOW!
VROOM
OH! MY HEAVENLY DAYS!
AND SO—
WE HAVE BROUGHT YOUR BEEFSTEAK, MR. ROCKDUST!
YESSIR! COME WHAT MAY, THE UNITED STATES MAIL ALWAYS GOES THROUGH!
GOSH! THINK OF IT – MAIL FOR ME! AND IT COMES WITH NO TROUBLE AT ALL!

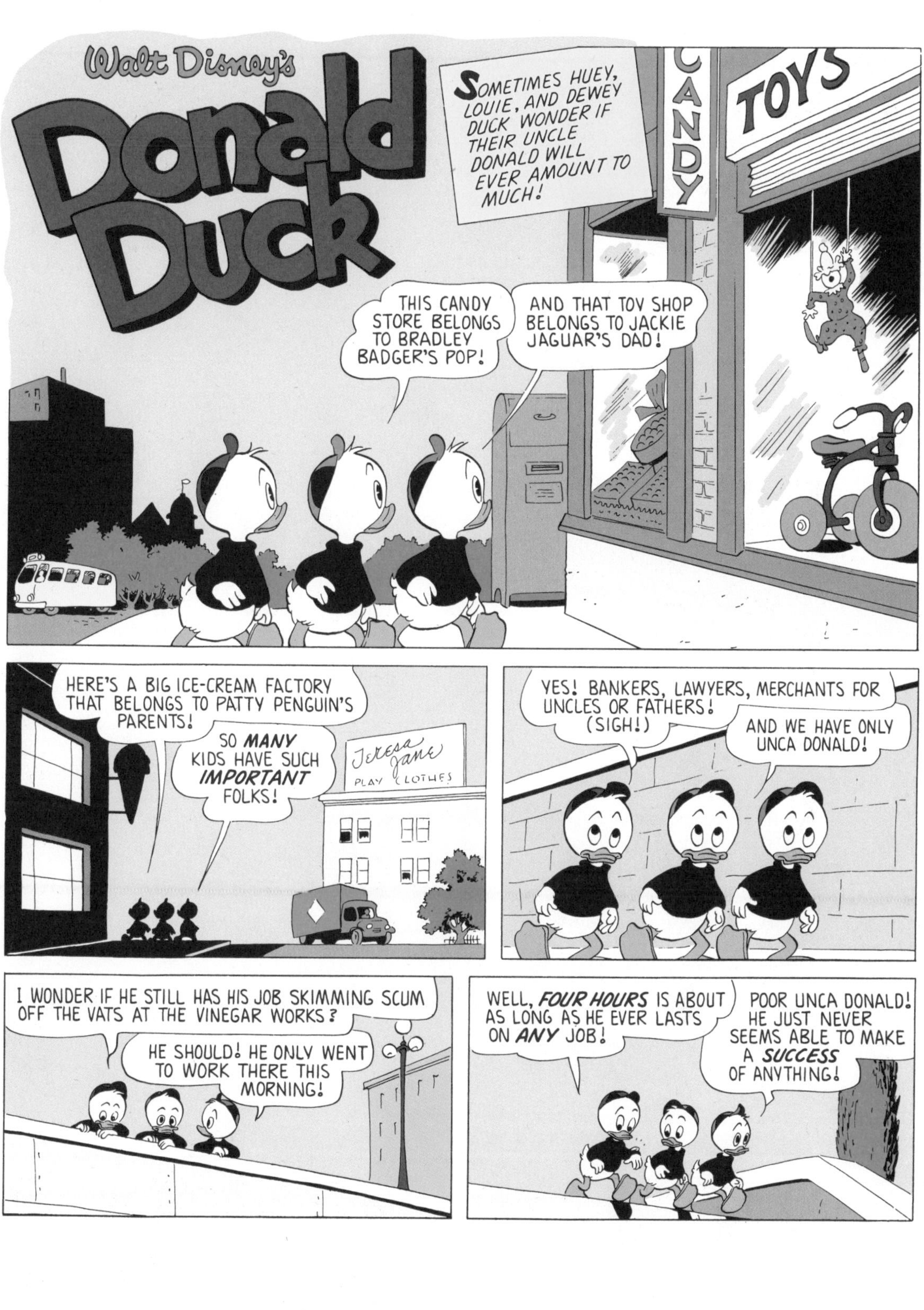
Walt Disney's
Donald Duck
SOMETIMES HUEY, LOUIE, AND DEWEY DUCK WONDER IF THEIR UNCLE DONALD WILL EVER AMOUNT TO MUCH!
CANDY
TOYS
THIS CANDY STORE BELONGS TO BRADLEY BADGER'S POP!
AND THAT TOY SHOP BELONGS TO JACKIE JAGUAR'S DAD!
HERE'S A BIG ICE-CREAM FACTORY THAT BELONGS TO PATTY PENGUIN'S PARENTS!
SO *MANY* KIDS HAVE SUCH *IMPORTANT* FOLKS!
PLAY CLOTHES
YES! BANKERS, LAWYERS, MERCHANTS FOR UNCLES OR FATHERS! (SIGH!)
AND WE HAVE ONLY UNCA DONALD!
I WONDER IF HE STILL HAS HIS JOB SKIMMING SCUM OFF THE VATS AT THE VINEGAR WORKS?
HE SHOULD! HE ONLY WENT TO WORK THERE THIS MORNING!
WELL, *FOUR HOURS* IS ABOUT AS LONG AS HE EVER LASTS ON *ANY* JOB!
POOR UNCA DONALD! HE JUST NEVER SEEMS ABLE TO MAKE A *SUCCESS* OF ANYTHING!

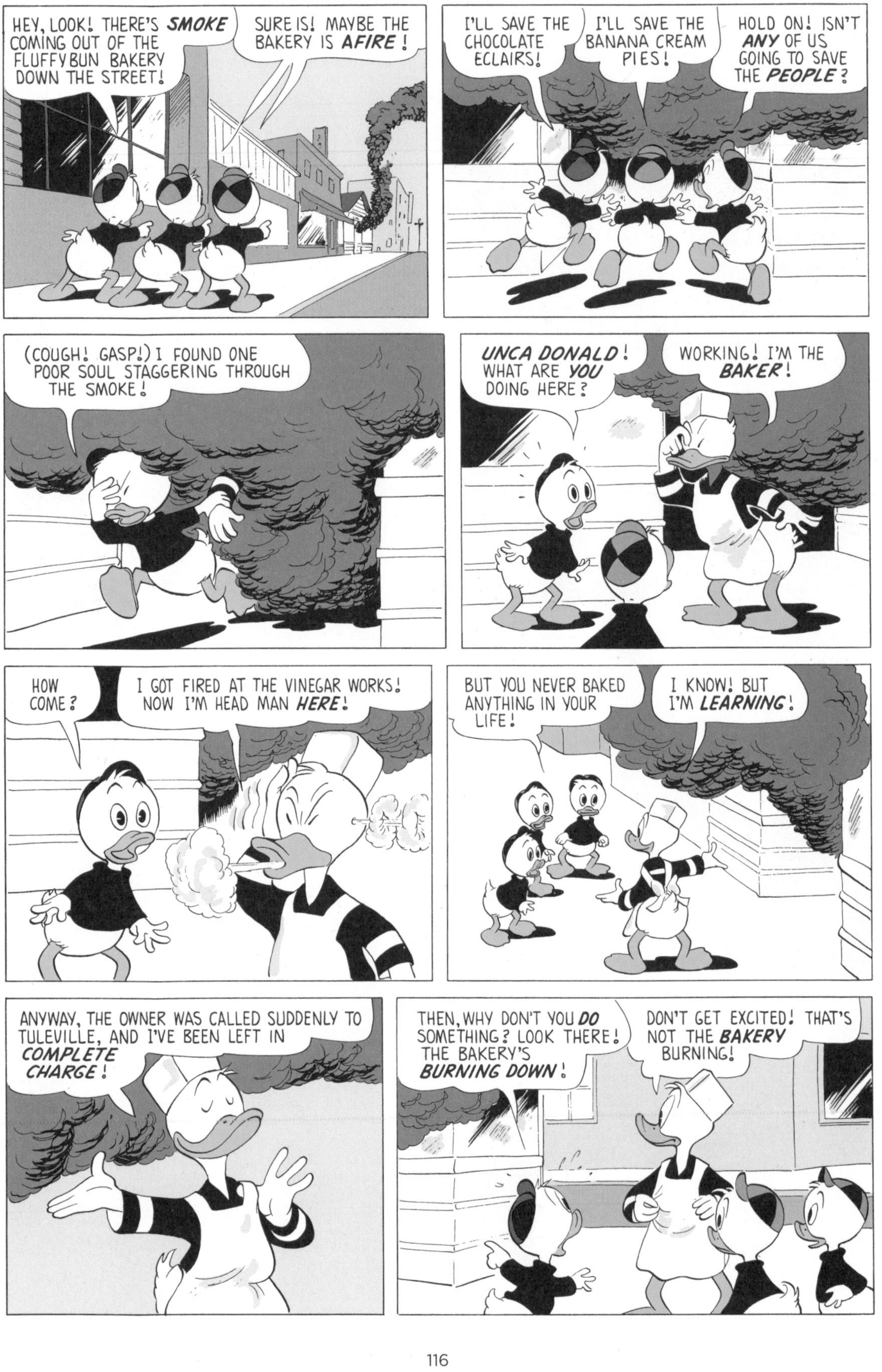

HEY, LOOK! THERE'S **SMOKE** COMING OUT OF THE FLUFFYBUN BAKERY DOWN THE STREET!
SURE IS! MAYBE THE BAKERY IS **AFIRE**!
I'LL SAVE THE CHOCOLATE ECLAIRS!
I'LL SAVE THE BANANA CREAM PIES!
HOLD ON! ISN'T **ANY** OF US GOING TO SAVE THE **PEOPLE**?
(COUGH! GASP!) I FOUND ONE POOR SOUL STAGGERING THROUGH THE SMOKE!
UNCA DONALD! WHAT ARE **YOU** DOING HERE?
WORKING! I'M THE **BAKER**!
HOW COME?
I GOT FIRED AT THE VINEGAR WORKS! NOW I'M HEAD MAN **HERE**!
BUT YOU NEVER BAKED ANYTHING IN YOUR LIFE!
I KNOW! BUT I'M **LEARNING**!
ANYWAY, THE OWNER WAS CALLED SUDDENLY TO TULEVILLE, AND I'VE BEEN LEFT IN **COMPLETE CHARGE**!
THEN, WHY DON'T YOU **DO** SOMETHING? LOOK THERE! THE BAKERY'S **BURNING DOWN**!
DON'T GET EXCITED! THAT'S NOT THE **BAKERY** BURNING!

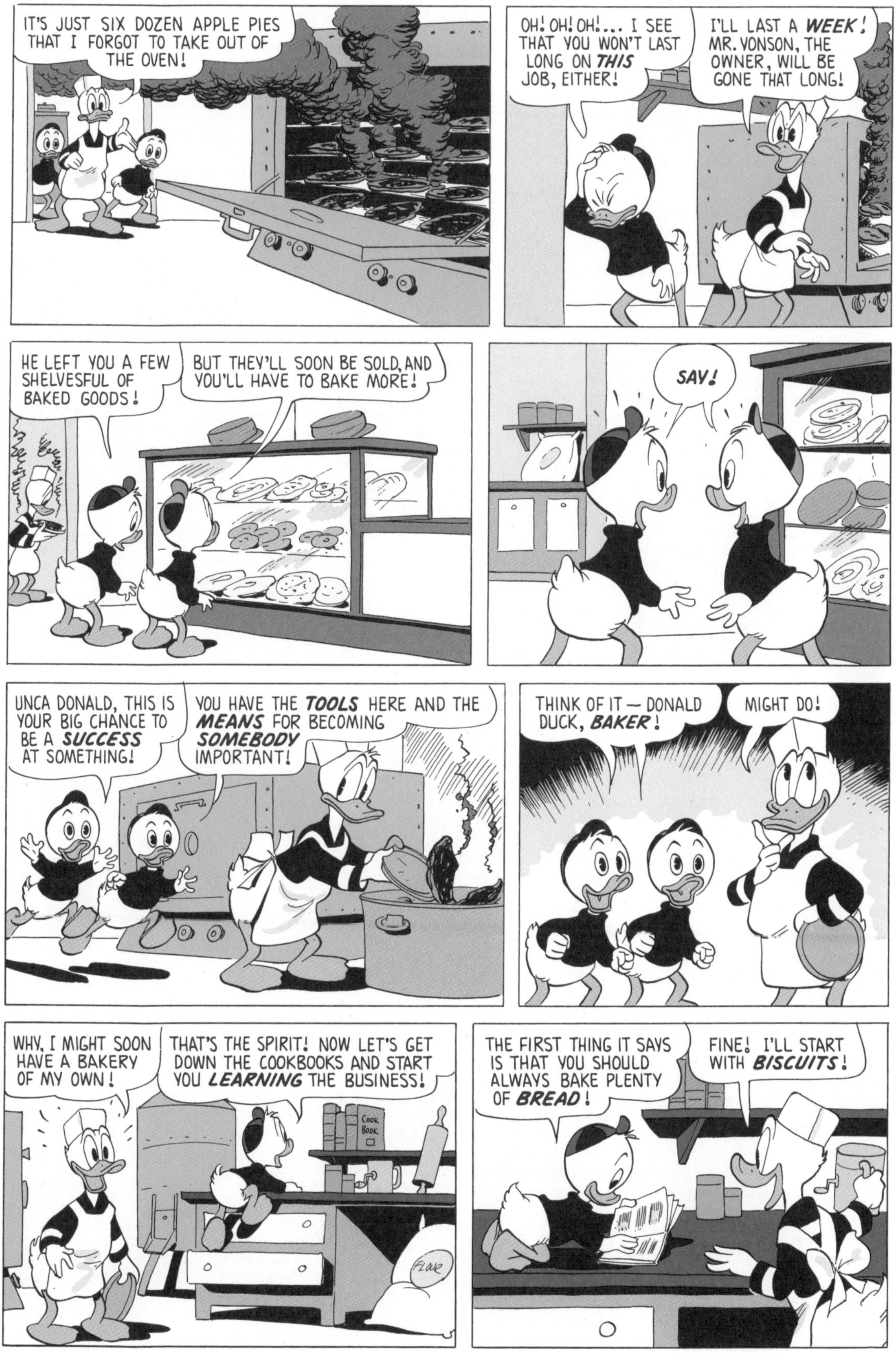
IT'S JUST SIX DOZEN APPLE PIES THAT I FORGOT TO TAKE OUT OF THE OVEN!
OH! OH! OH!... I SEE THAT YOU WON'T LAST LONG ON **THIS** JOB, EITHER!
I'LL LAST A **WEEK**! MR. VONSON, THE OWNER, WILL BE GONE THAT LONG!
HE LEFT YOU A FEW SHELVESFUL OF BAKED GOODS!
BUT THEY'LL SOON BE SOLD, AND YOU'LL HAVE TO BAKE MORE!
SAY!
UNCA DONALD, THIS IS YOUR BIG CHANCE TO BE A **SUCCESS** AT SOMETHING!
YOU HAVE THE **TOOLS** HERE AND THE **MEANS** FOR BECOMING **SOMEBODY** IMPORTANT!
THINK OF IT — DONALD DUCK, **BAKER**!
MIGHT DO!
WHY, I MIGHT SOON HAVE A BAKERY OF MY OWN!
THAT'S THE SPIRIT! NOW LET'S GET DOWN THE COOKBOOKS AND START YOU **LEARNING** THE BUSINESS!
COOK BOOK
FLOUR
THE FIRST THING IT SAYS IS THAT YOU SHOULD ALWAYS BAKE PLENTY OF **BREAD**!
FINE! I'LL START WITH **BISCUITS**!

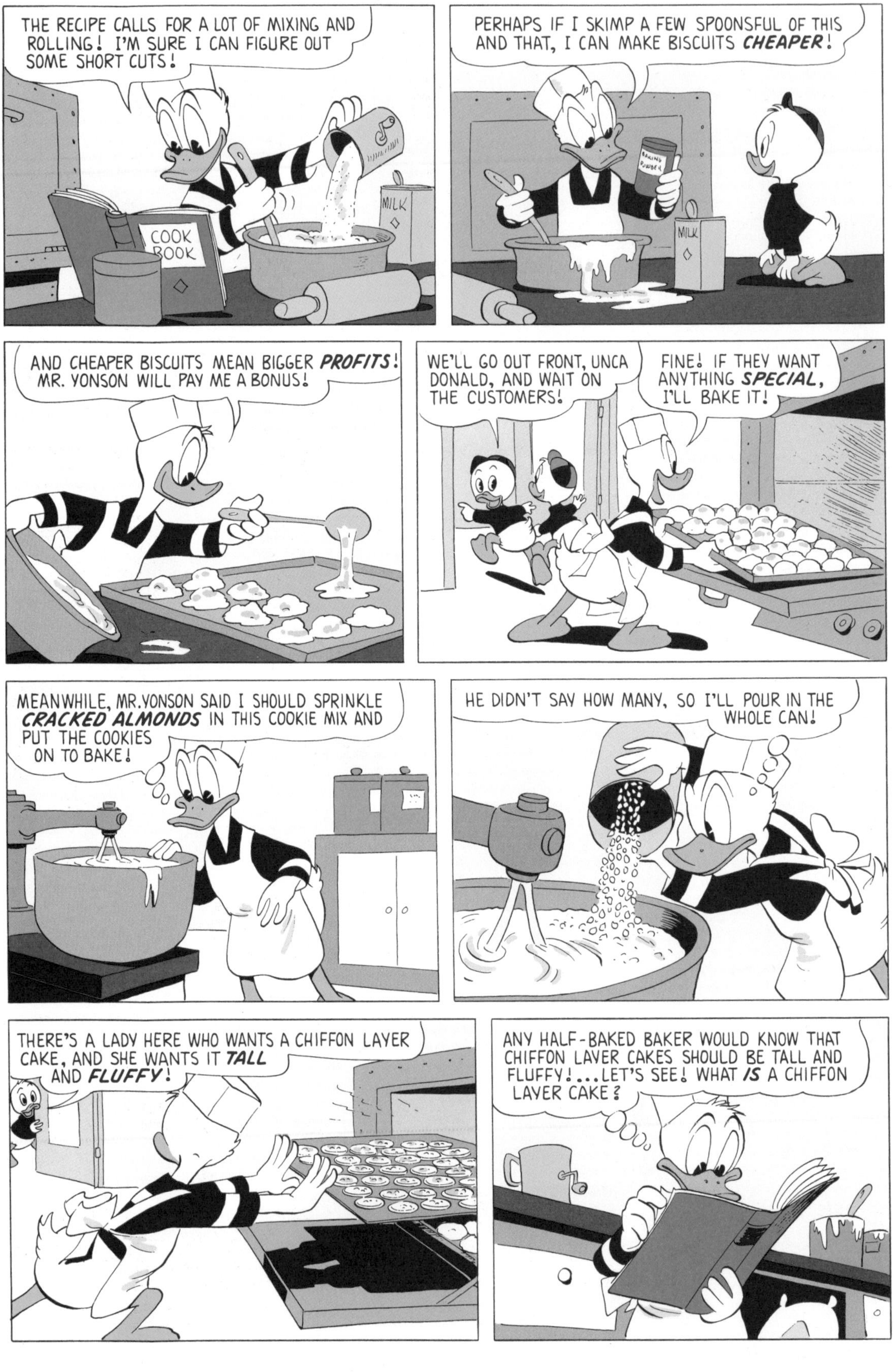
THE RECIPE CALLS FOR A LOT OF MIXING AND ROLLING! I'M SURE I CAN FIGURE OUT SOME SHORT CUTS!
COOK BOOK
MILK
PERHAPS IF I SKIMP A FEW SPOONSFUL OF THIS AND THAT, I CAN MAKE BISCUITS **CHEAPER**!
MILK
AND CHEAPER BISCUITS MEAN BIGGER **PROFITS**! MR. YONSON WILL PAY ME A BONUS!
WE'LL GO OUT FRONT, UNCA DONALD, AND WAIT ON THE CUSTOMERS!
FINE! IF THEY WANT ANYTHING **SPECIAL**, I'LL BAKE IT!
MEANWHILE, MR. YONSON SAID I SHOULD SPRINKLE **CRACKED ALMONDS** IN THIS COOKIE MIX AND PUT THE COOKIES ON TO BAKE!
HE DIDN'T SAY HOW MANY, SO I'LL POUR IN THE WHOLE CAN!
THERE'S A LADY HERE WHO WANTS A CHIFFON LAYER CAKE, AND SHE WANTS IT **TALL** AND **FLUFFY**!
ANY HALF-BAKED BAKER WOULD KNOW THAT CHIFFON LAYER CAKES SHOULD BE TALL AND FLUFFY! ...LET'S SEE! WHAT **IS** A CHIFFON LAYER CAKE?

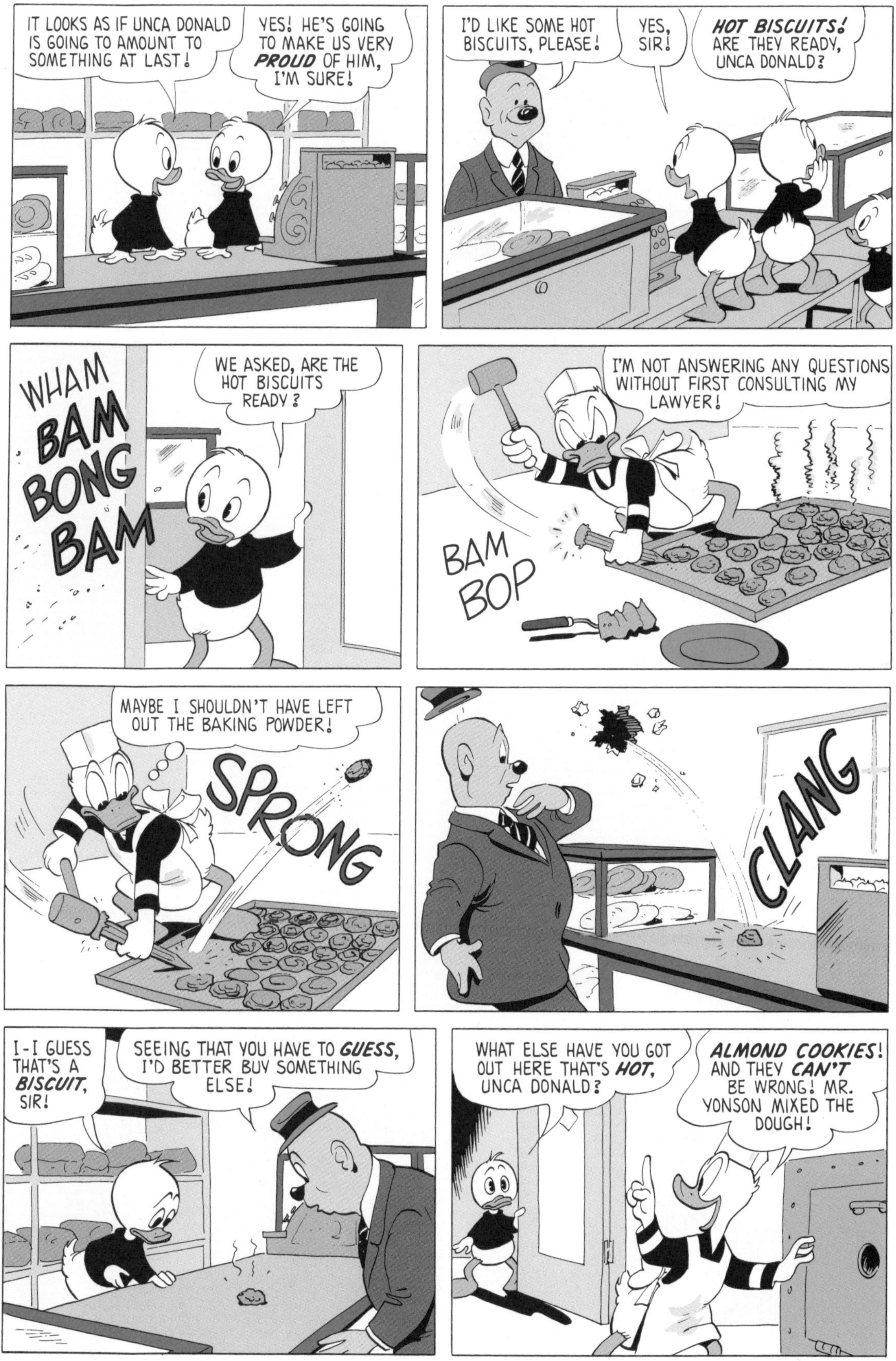
IT LOOKS AS IF UNCA DONALD IS GOING TO AMOUNT TO SOMETHING AT LAST!
YES! HE'S GOING TO MAKE US VERY PROUD OF HIM, I'M SURE!
I'D LIKE SOME HOT BISCUITS, PLEASE!
YES, SIR!
HOT BISCUITS! ARE THEY READY, UNCA DONALD?
WHAM BAM BONG BAM
WE ASKED, ARE THE HOT BISCUITS READY?
I'M NOT ANSWERING ANY QUESTIONS WITHOUT FIRST CONSULTING MY LAWYER!
BAM BOP
MAYBE I SHOULDN'T HAVE LEFT OUT THE BAKING POWDER!
SPRONG
CLANG
I-I GUESS THAT'S A BISCUIT, SIR!
SEEING THAT YOU HAVE TO GUESS, I'D BETTER BUY SOMETHING ELSE!
WHAT ELSE HAVE YOU GOT OUT HERE THAT'S HOT, UNCA DONALD?
ALMOND COOKIES! AND THEY CAN'T BE WRONG! MR. YONSON MIXED THE DOUGH!

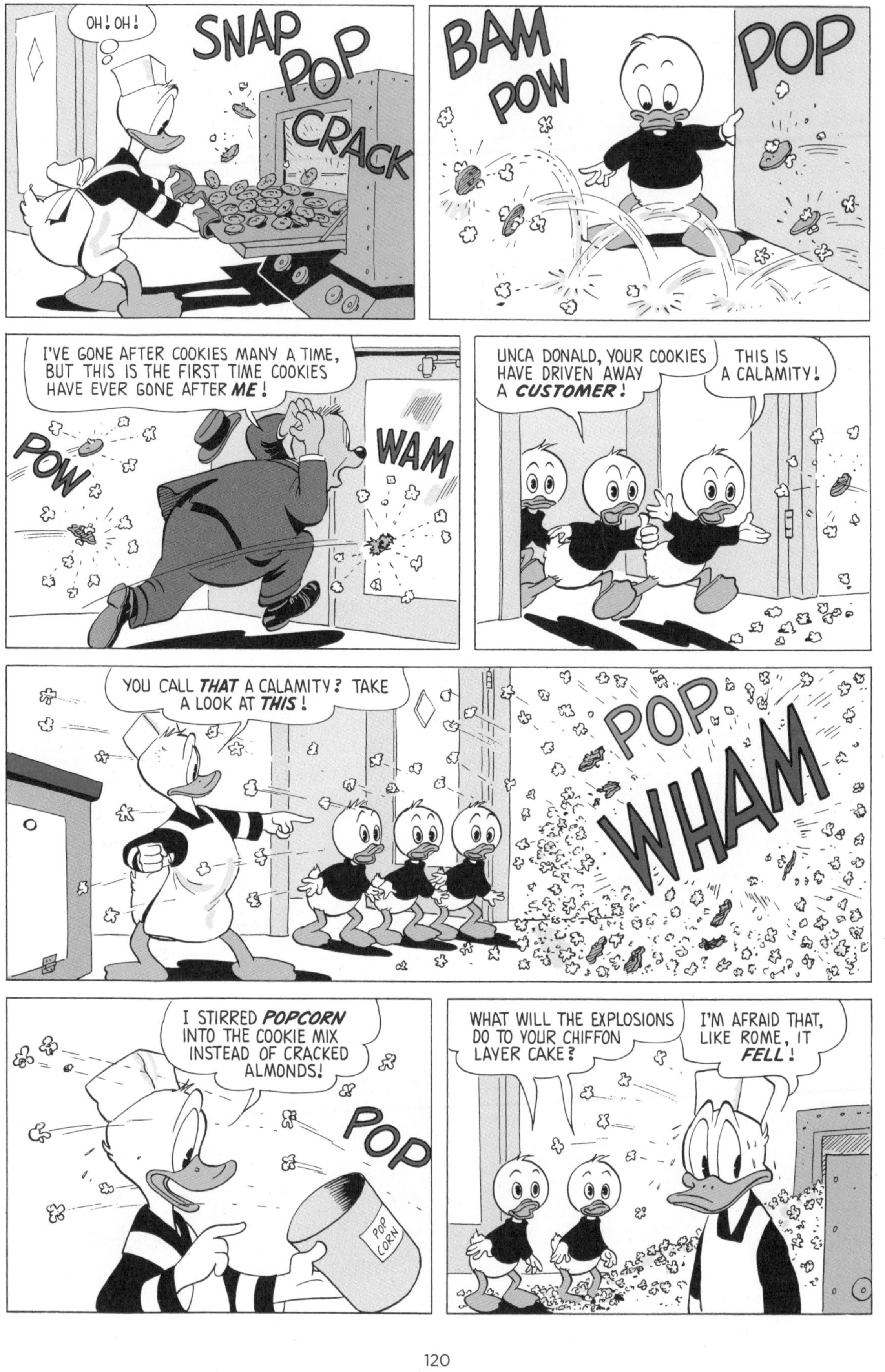
OH! OH!
SNAP
POP
CRACK
BAM
POW
POP
I'VE GONE AFTER COOKIES MANY A TIME, BUT THIS IS THE FIRST TIME COOKIES HAVE EVER GONE AFTER **ME**!
POW
WAM
UNCA DONALD, YOUR COOKIES HAVE DRIVEN AWAY A ***CUSTOMER***!
THIS IS A CALAMITY!
YOU CALL ***THAT*** A CALAMITY? TAKE A LOOK AT ***THIS***!
POP
WHAM
I STIRRED ***POPCORN*** INTO THE COOKIE MIX INSTEAD OF CRACKED ALMONDS!
POP
POP CORN
WHAT WILL THE EXPLOSIONS DO TO YOUR CHIFFON LAYER CAKE?
I'M AFRAID THAT, LIKE ROME, IT ***FELL***!

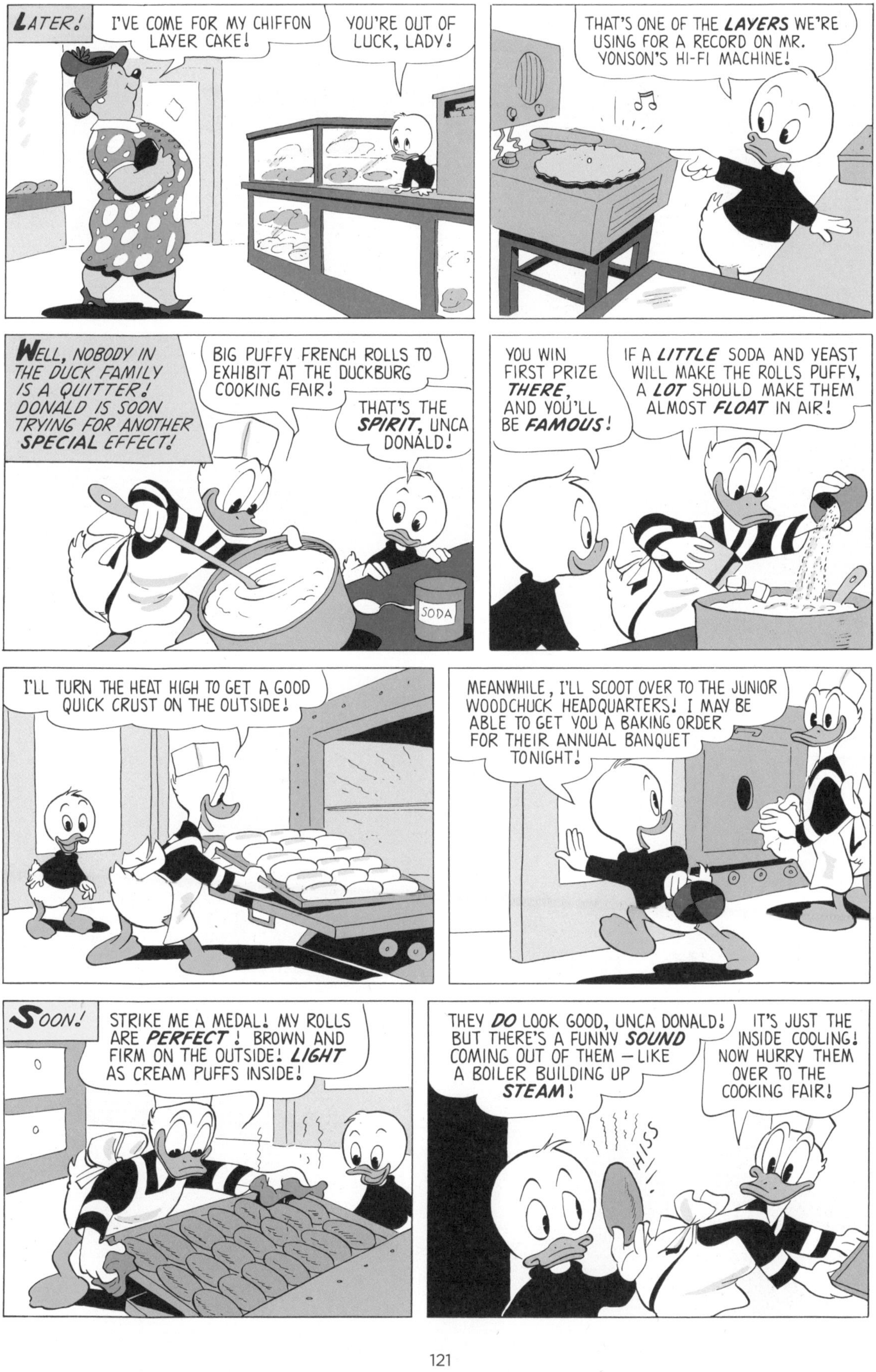
LATER!
I'VE COME FOR MY CHIFFON LAYER CAKE!
YOU'RE OUT OF LUCK, LADY!
THAT'S ONE OF THE LAYERS WE'RE USING FOR A RECORD ON MR. YONSON'S HI-FI MACHINE!
WELL, NOBODY IN THE DUCK FAMILY IS A QUITTER! DONALD IS SOON TRYING FOR ANOTHER SPECIAL EFFECT!
BIG PUFFY FRENCH ROLLS TO EXHIBIT AT THE DUCKBURG COOKING FAIR!
THAT'S THE SPIRIT, UNCA DONALD!
SODA
YOU WIN FIRST PRIZE THERE, AND YOU'LL BE FAMOUS!
IF A LITTLE SODA AND YEAST WILL MAKE THE ROLLS PUFFY, A LOT SHOULD MAKE THEM ALMOST FLOAT IN AIR!
I'LL TURN THE HEAT HIGH TO GET A GOOD QUICK CRUST ON THE OUTSIDE!
MEANWHILE, I'LL SCOOT OVER TO THE JUNIOR WOODCHUCK HEADQUARTERS! I MAY BE ABLE TO GET YOU A BAKING ORDER FOR THEIR ANNUAL BANQUET TONIGHT!
SOON!
STRIKE ME A MEDAL! MY ROLLS ARE PERFECT! BROWN AND FIRM ON THE OUTSIDE! LIGHT AS CREAM PUFFS INSIDE!
THEY DO LOOK GOOD, UNCA DONALD! BUT THERE'S A FUNNY SOUND COMING OUT OF THEM — LIKE A BOILER BUILDING UP STEAM!
HISS
IT'S JUST THE INSIDE COOLING! NOW HURRY THEM OVER TO THE COOKING FAIR!

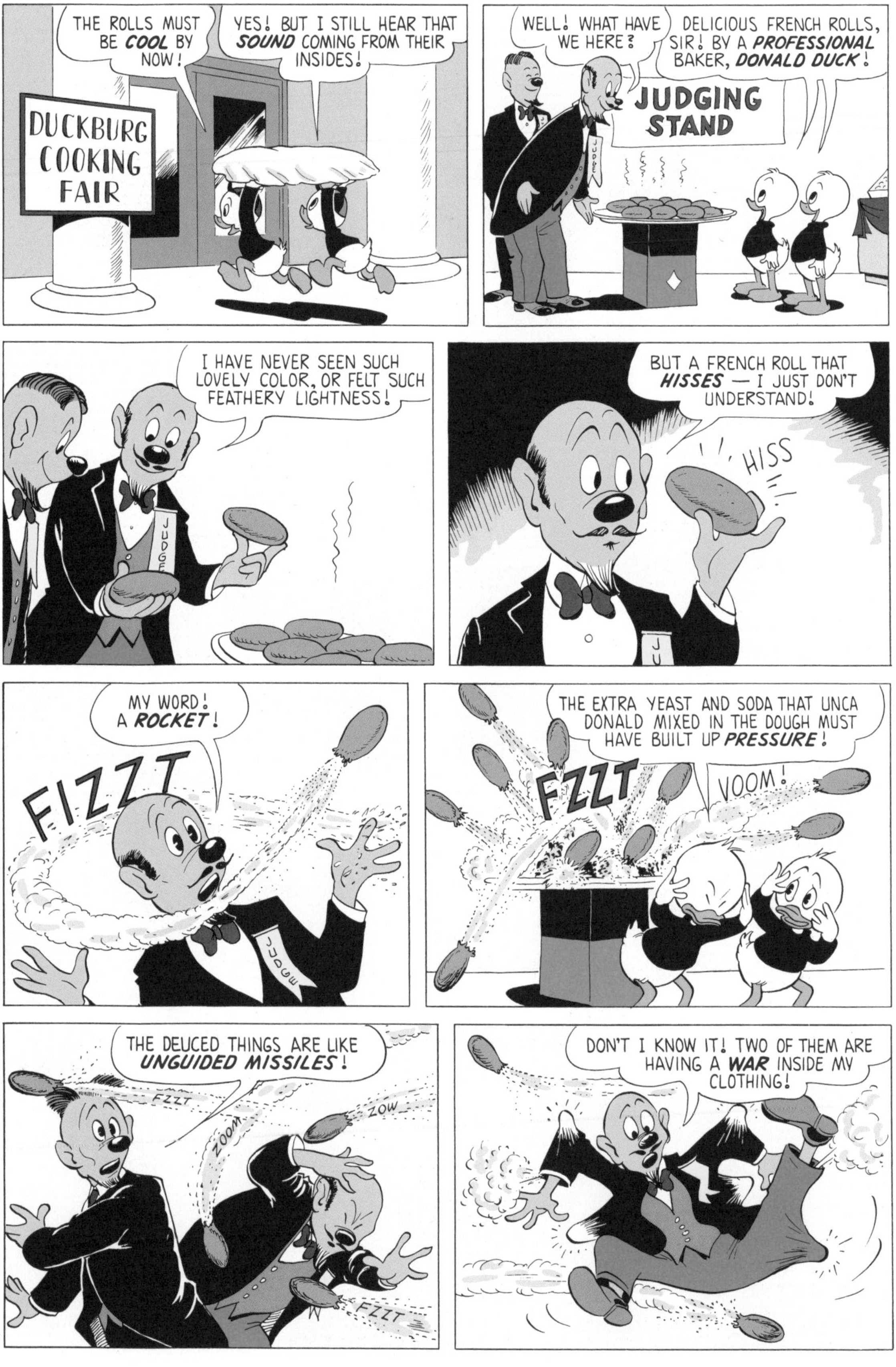
THE ROLLS MUST BE COOL BY NOW!
YES! BUT I STILL HEAR THAT SOUND COMING FROM THEIR INSIDES!
DUCKBURG COOKING FAIR
WELL! WHAT HAVE WE HERE?
DELICIOUS FRENCH ROLLS, SIR! BY A PROFESSIONAL BAKER, DONALD DUCK!
JUDGING STAND
JUDGE
I HAVE NEVER SEEN SUCH LOVELY COLOR, OR FELT SUCH FEATHERY LIGHTNESS!
BUT A FRENCH ROLL THAT HISSES — I JUST DON'T UNDERSTAND!
HISS
MY WORD! A ROCKET!
FIZZT
THE EXTRA YEAST AND SODA THAT UNCA DONALD MIXED IN THE DOUGH MUST HAVE BUILT UP PRESSURE!
FZZT
VOOM!
THE DEUCED THINGS ARE LIKE UNGUIDED MISSILES!
FZZT
ZOOM
ZOW
FZZT
DON'T I KNOW IT! TWO OF THEM ARE HAVING A WAR INSIDE MY CLOTHING!

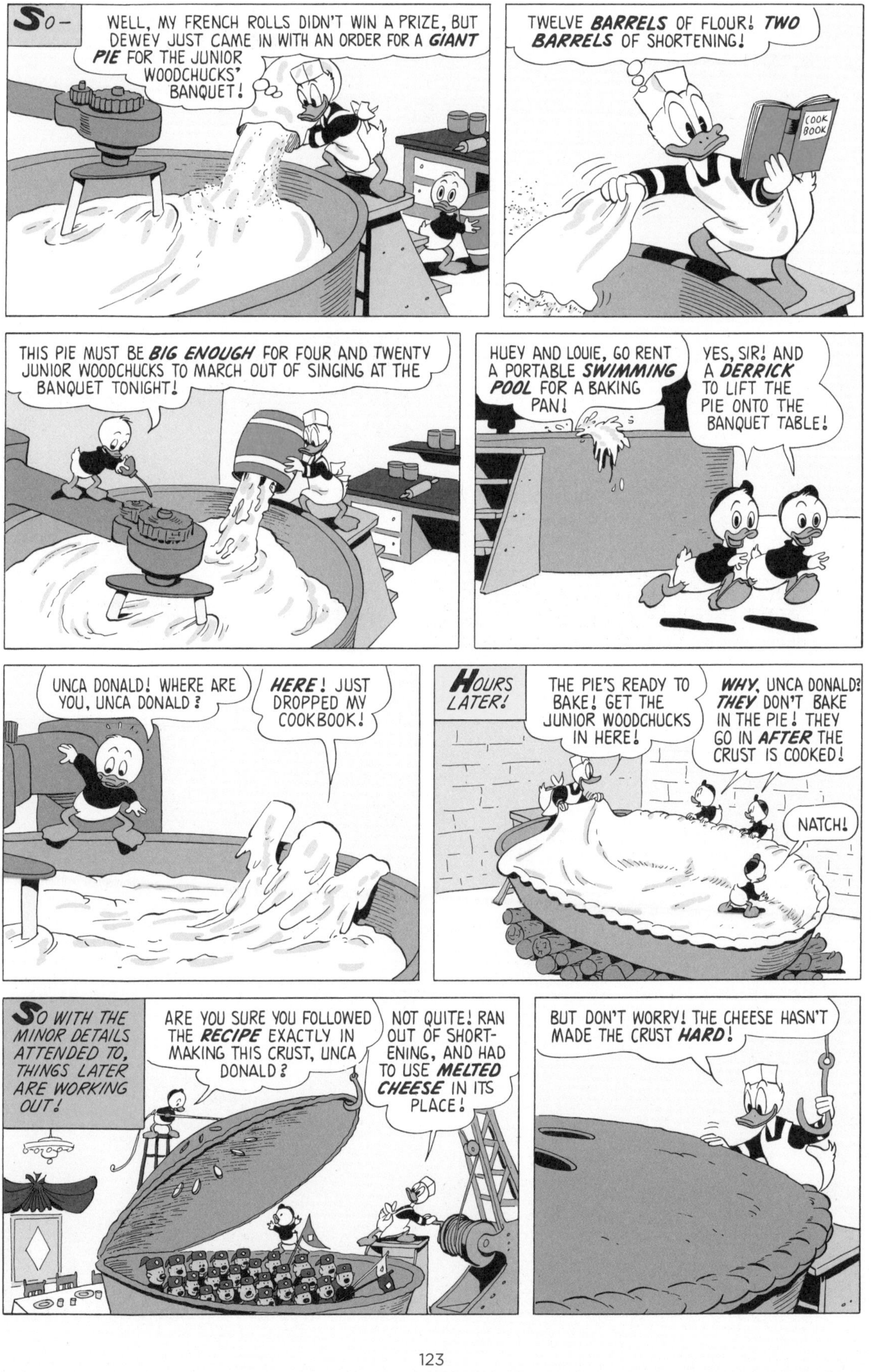

SO—
WELL, MY FRENCH ROLLS DIDN'T WIN A PRIZE, BUT DEWEY JUST CAME IN WITH AN ORDER FOR A GIANT PIE FOR THE JUNIOR WOODCHUCKS' BANQUET!
TWELVE BARRELS OF FLOUR! TWO BARRELS OF SHORTENING!
COOK BOOK
THIS PIE MUST BE BIG ENOUGH FOR FOUR AND TWENTY JUNIOR WOODCHUCKS TO MARCH OUT OF SINGING AT THE BANQUET TONIGHT!
HUEY AND LOUIE, GO RENT A PORTABLE SWIMMING POOL FOR A BAKING PAN!
YES, SIR! AND A DERRICK TO LIFT THE PIE ONTO THE BANQUET TABLE!
UNCA DONALD! WHERE ARE YOU, UNCA DONALD?
HERE! JUST DROPPED MY COOKBOOK!
HOURS LATER!
THE PIE'S READY TO BAKE! GET THE JUNIOR WOODCHUCKS IN HERE!
WHY, UNCA DONALD? THEY DON'T BAKE IN THE PIE! THEY GO IN AFTER THE CRUST IS COOKED!
NATCH!
SO WITH THE MINOR DETAILS ATTENDED TO, THINGS LATER ARE WORKING OUT!
ARE YOU SURE YOU FOLLOWED THE RECIPE EXACTLY IN MAKING THIS CRUST, UNCA DONALD?
NOT QUITE! RAN OUT OF SHORTENING, AND HAD TO USE MELTED CHEESE IN ITS PLACE!
BUT DON'T WORRY! THE CHEESE HASN'T MADE THE CRUST HARD!

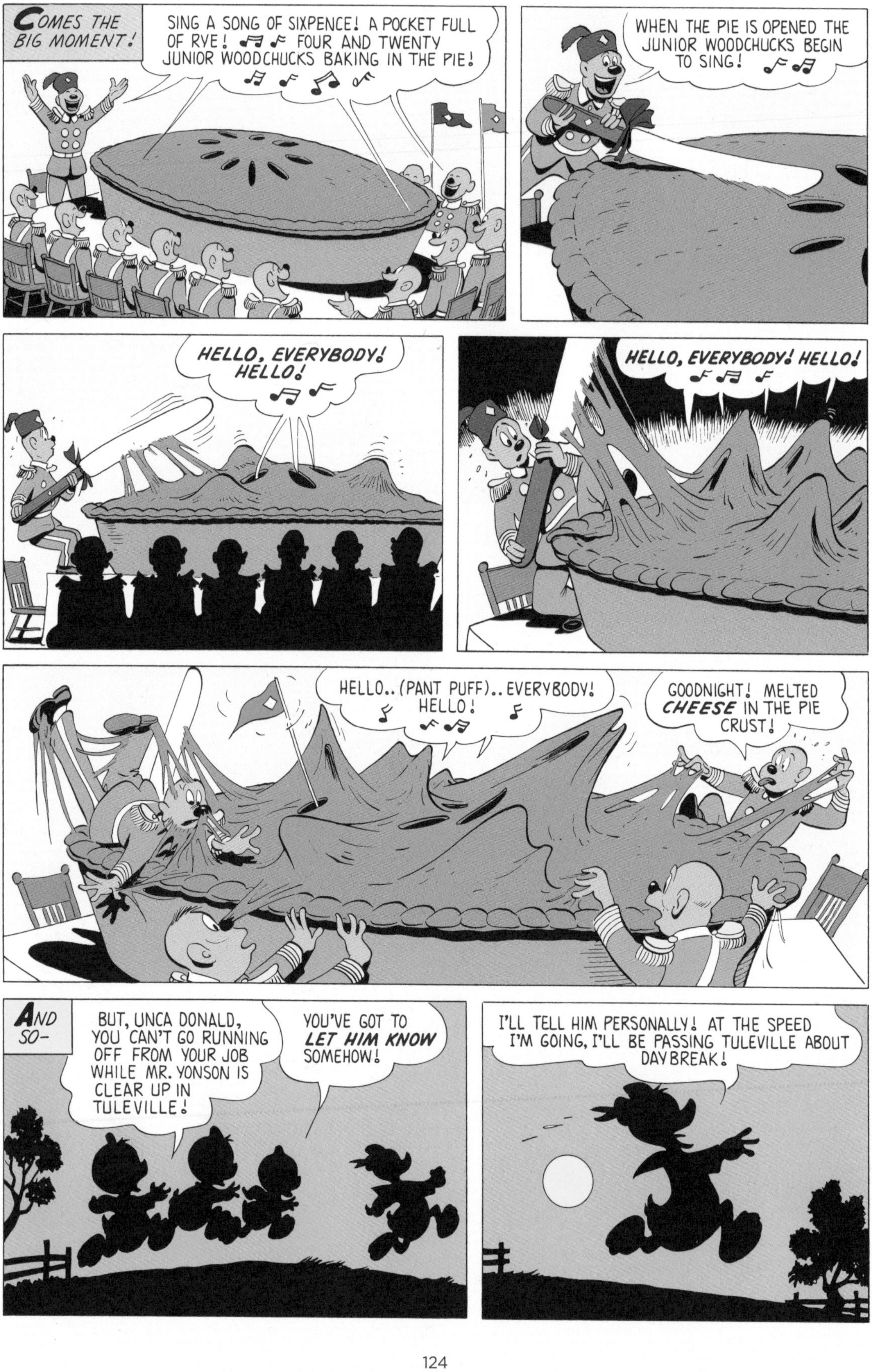
COMES THE BIG MOMENT!
SING A SONG OF SIXPENCE! A POCKET FULL OF RYE! FOUR AND TWENTY JUNIOR WOODCHUCKS BAKING IN THE PIE!
WHEN THE PIE IS OPENED THE JUNIOR WOODCHUCKS BEGIN TO SING!
HELLO, EVERYBODY! HELLO!
HELLO, EVERYBODY! HELLO!
HELLO.. (PANT PUFF).. EVERYBODY! HELLO!
GOODNIGHT! MELTED CHEESE IN THE PIE CRUST!
AND SO-
BUT, UNCA DONALD, YOU CAN'T GO RUNNING OFF FROM YOUR JOB WHILE MR. YONSON IS CLEAR UP IN TULEVILLE!
YOU'VE GOT TO LET HIM KNOW SOMEHOW!
I'LL TELL HIM PERSONALLY! AT THE SPEED I'M GOING, I'LL BE PASSING TULEVILLE ABOUT DAYBREAK!

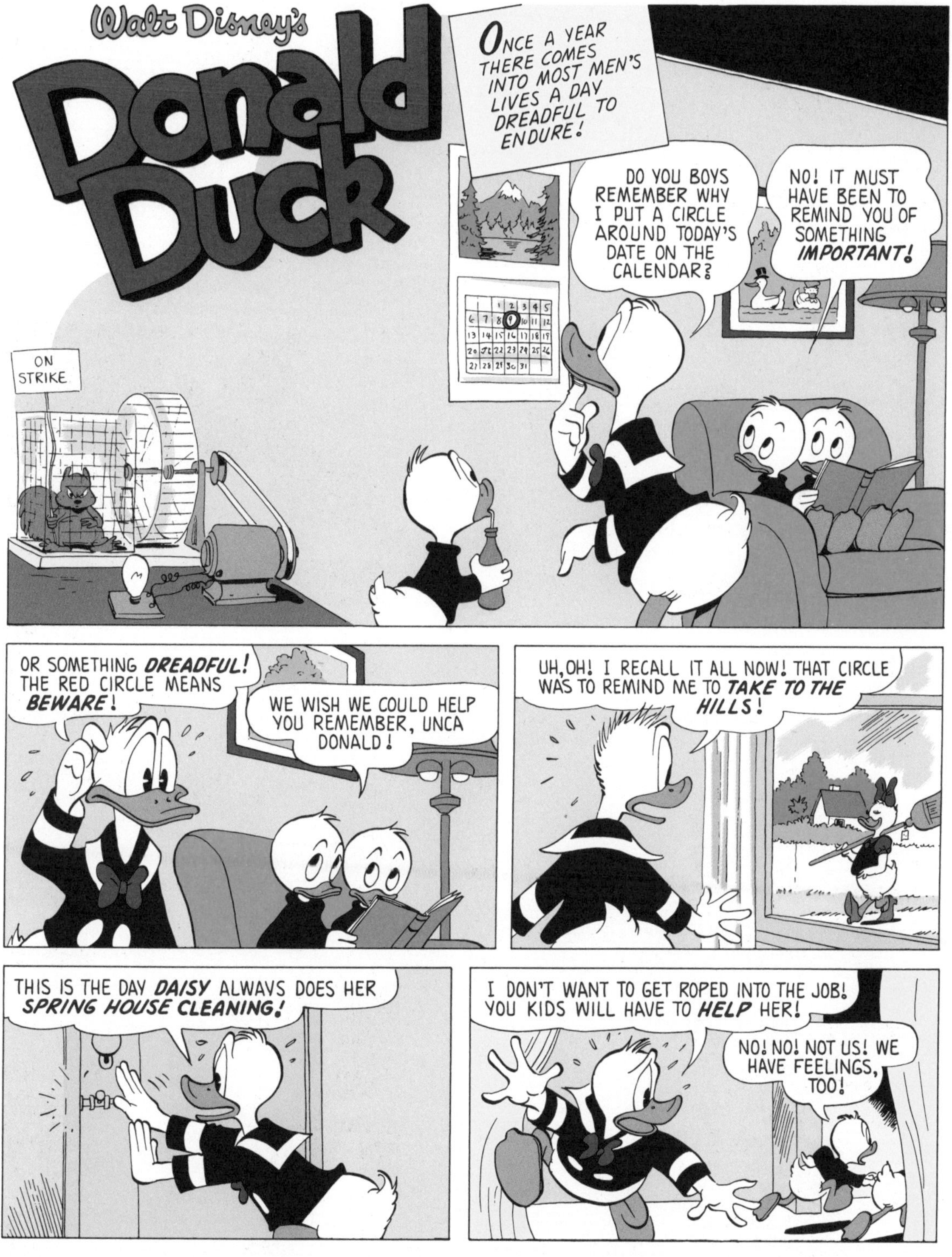

Walt Disney's
Donald Duck
ONCE A YEAR THERE COMES INTO MOST MEN'S LIVES A DAY DREADFUL TO ENDURE!
ON STRIKE
DO YOU BOYS REMEMBER WHY I PUT A CIRCLE AROUND TODAY'S DATE ON THE CALENDAR?
NO! IT MUST HAVE BEEN TO REMIND YOU OF SOMETHING IMPORTANT!
OR SOMETHING DREADFUL! THE RED CIRCLE MEANS BEWARE!
WE WISH WE COULD HELP YOU REMEMBER, UNCA DONALD!
UH, OH! I RECALL IT ALL NOW! THAT CIRCLE WAS TO REMIND ME TO TAKE TO THE HILLS!
THIS IS THE DAY DAISY ALWAYS DOES HER SPRING HOUSE CLEANING!
I DON'T WANT TO GET ROPED INTO THE JOB! YOU KIDS WILL HAVE TO HELP HER!
NO! NO! NOT US! WE HAVE FEELINGS, TOO!

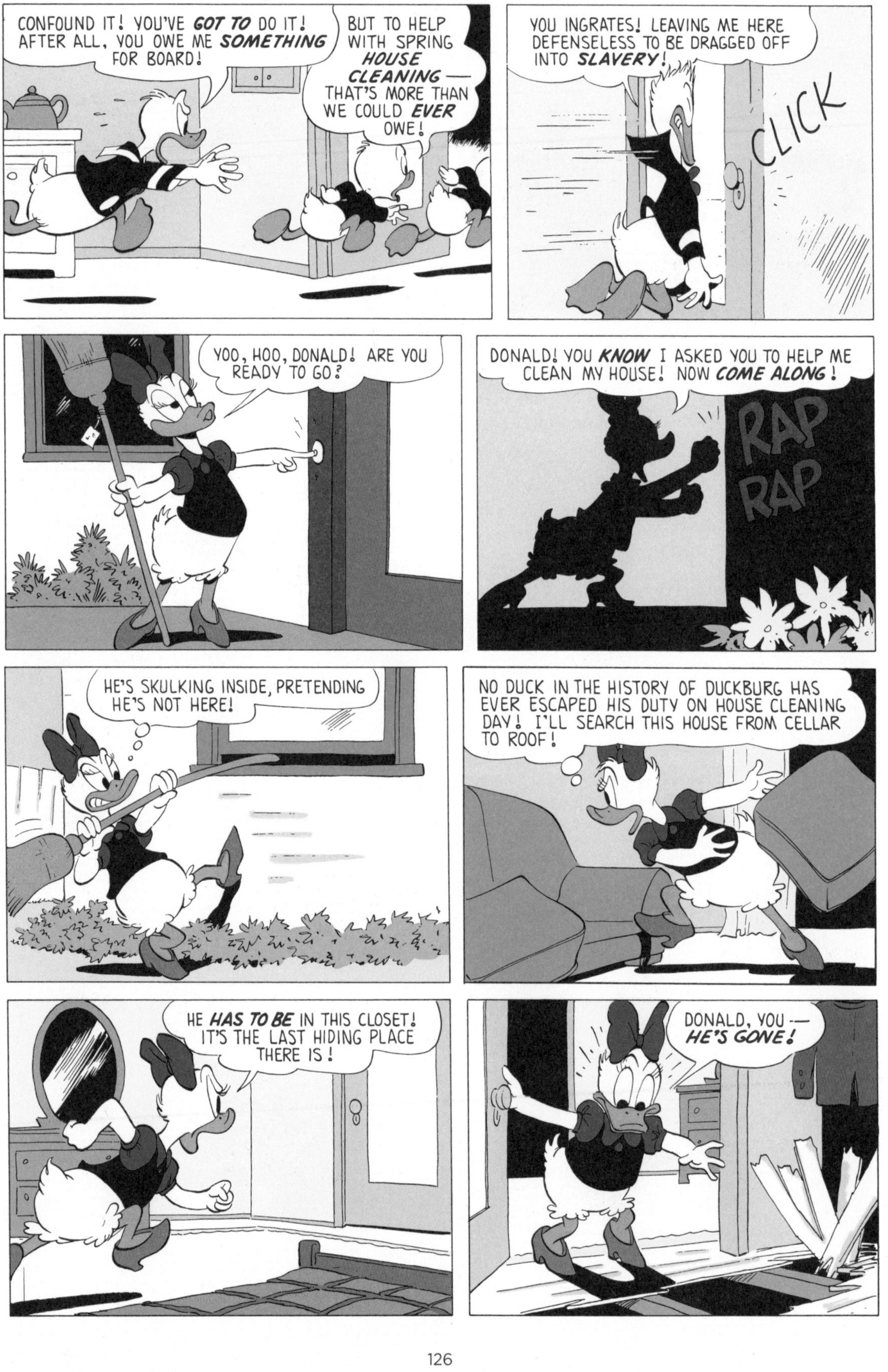
CONFOUND IT! YOU'VE GOT TO DO IT! AFTER ALL, YOU OWE ME SOMETHING FOR BOARD!
BUT TO HELP WITH SPRING HOUSE CLEANING — THAT'S MORE THAN WE COULD EVER OWE!
YOU INGRATES! LEAVING ME HERE DEFENSELESS TO BE DRAGGED OFF INTO SLAVERY!
CLICK
YOO, HOO, DONALD! ARE YOU READY TO GO?
DONALD! YOU KNOW I ASKED YOU TO HELP ME CLEAN MY HOUSE! NOW COME ALONG!
RAP RAP
HE'S SKULKING INSIDE, PRETENDING HE'S NOT HERE!
NO DUCK IN THE HISTORY OF DUCKBURG HAS EVER ESCAPED HIS DUTY ON HOUSE CLEANING DAY! I'LL SEARCH THIS HOUSE FROM CELLAR TO ROOF!
HE HAS TO BE IN THIS CLOSET! IT'S THE LAST HIDING PLACE THERE IS!
DONALD, YOU — HE'S GONE!

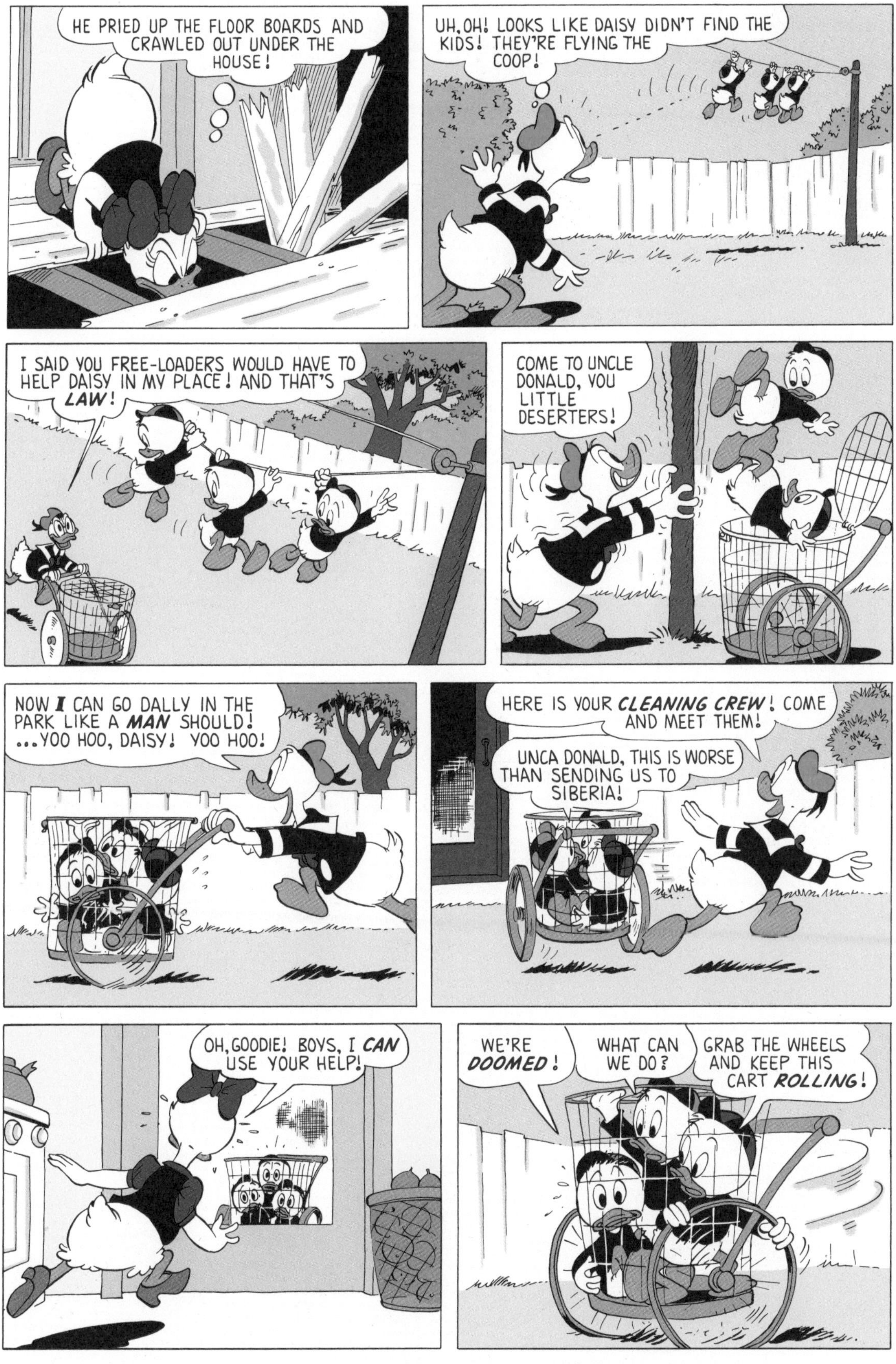
HE PRIED UP THE FLOOR BOARDS AND CRAWLED OUT UNDER THE HOUSE!
UH, OH! LOOKS LIKE DAISY DIDN'T FIND THE KIDS! THEY'RE FLYING THE COOP!
I SAID YOU FREE-LOADERS WOULD HAVE TO HELP DAISY IN MY PLACE! AND THAT'S LAW!
COME TO UNCLE DONALD, YOU LITTLE DESERTERS!
NOW I CAN GO DALLY IN THE PARK LIKE A MAN SHOULD! ...YOO HOO, DAISY! YOO HOO!
HERE IS YOUR CLEANING CREW! COME AND MEET THEM!
UNCA DONALD, THIS IS WORSE THAN SENDING US TO SIBERIA!
OH, GOODIE! BOYS, I CAN USE YOUR HELP!
WE'RE DOOMED!
WHAT CAN WE DO?
GRAB THE WHEELS AND KEEP THIS CART ROLLING!

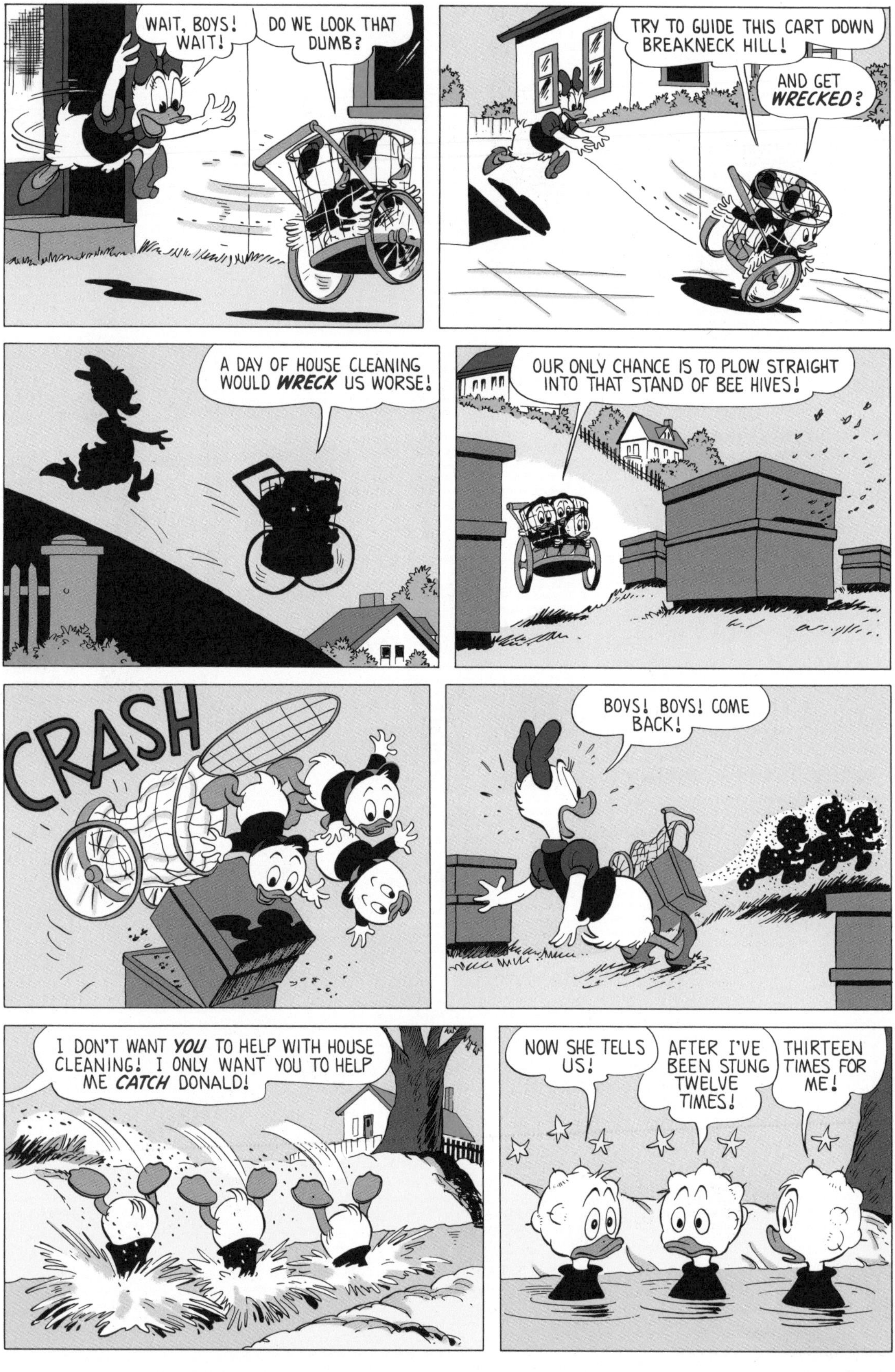

WAIT, BOYS! WAIT!
DO WE LOOK THAT DUMB?
TRY TO GUIDE THIS CART DOWN BREAKNECK HILL!
AND GET **WRECKED**?
A DAY OF HOUSE CLEANING WOULD **WRECK** US WORSE!
OUR ONLY CHANCE IS TO PLOW STRAIGHT INTO THAT STAND OF BEE HIVES!
CRASH
BOYS! BOYS! COME BACK!
I DON'T WANT **YOU** TO HELP WITH HOUSE CLEANING! I ONLY WANT YOU TO HELP ME **CATCH** DONALD!
NOW SHE TELLS US!
AFTER I'VE BEEN STUNG TWELVE TIMES!
THIRTEEN TIMES FOR ME!

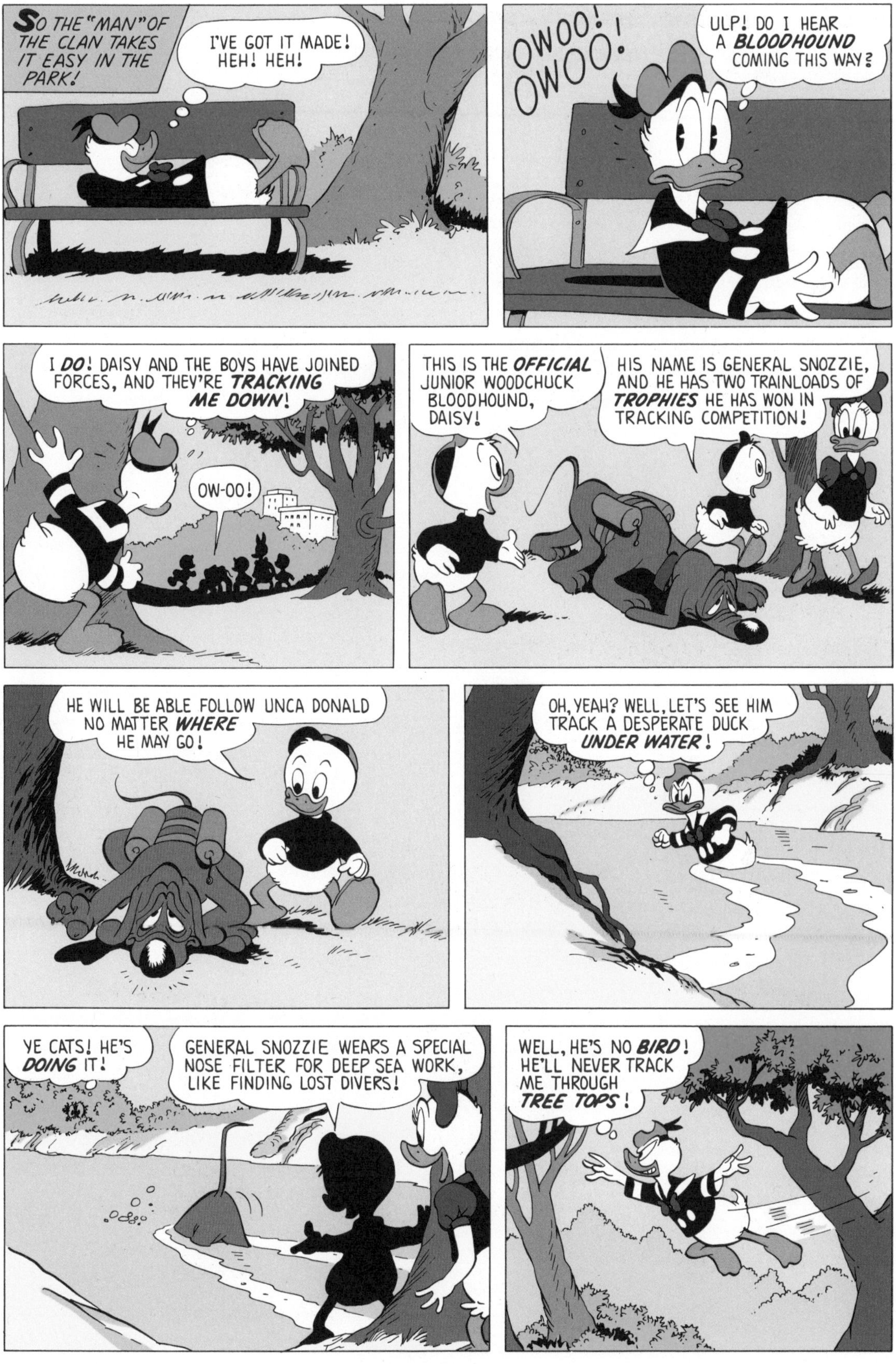
SO THE "MAN" OF THE CLAN TAKES IT EASY IN THE PARK!
I'VE GOT IT MADE! HEH! HEH!
OWOO! OWOO!
ULP! DO I HEAR A BLOODHOUND COMING THIS WAY?
I DO! DAISY AND THE BOYS HAVE JOINED FORCES, AND THEY'RE TRACKING ME DOWN!
OW-OO!
THIS IS THE OFFICIAL JUNIOR WOODCHUCK BLOODHOUND, DAISY!
HIS NAME IS GENERAL SNOZZIE, AND HE HAS TWO TRAINLOADS OF TROPHIES HE HAS WON IN TRACKING COMPETITION!
HE WILL BE ABLE FOLLOW UNCA DONALD NO MATTER WHERE HE MAY GO!
OH, YEAH? WELL, LET'S SEE HIM TRACK A DESPERATE DUCK UNDER WATER!
YE CATS! HE'S DOING IT!
GENERAL SNOZZIE WEARS A SPECIAL NOSE FILTER FOR DEEP SEA WORK, LIKE FINDING LOST DIVERS!
WELL, HE'S NO BIRD! HE'LL NEVER TRACK ME THROUGH TREE TOPS!

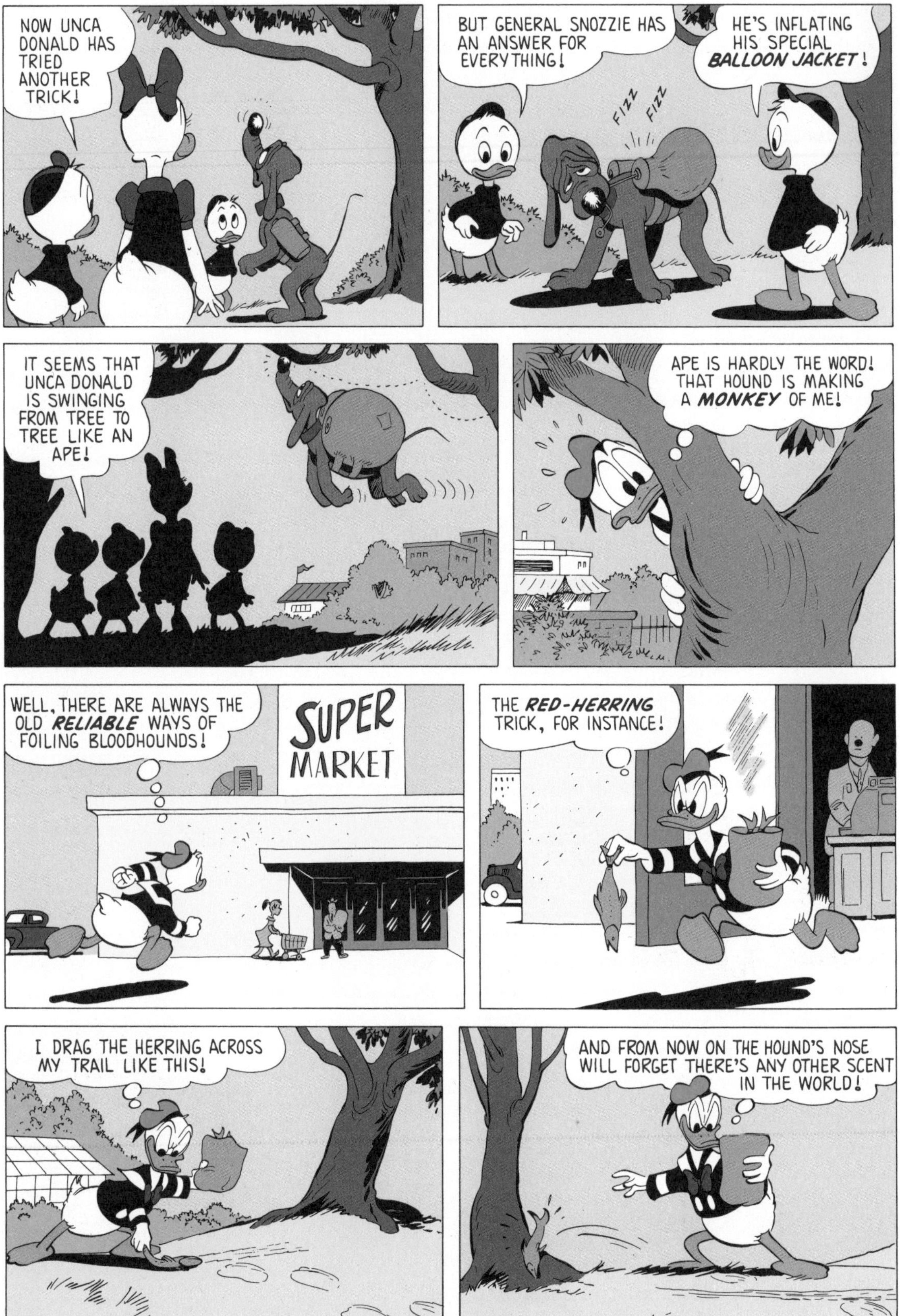
NOW UNCA DONALD HAS TRIED ANOTHER TRICK!
BUT GENERAL SNOZZIE HAS AN ANSWER FOR EVERYTHING!
HE'S INFLATING HIS SPECIAL BALLOON JACKET!
FIZZ FIZZ
IT SEEMS THAT UNCA DONALD IS SWINGING FROM TREE TO TREE LIKE AN APE!
APE IS HARDLY THE WORD! THAT HOUND IS MAKING A MONKEY OF ME!
WELL, THERE ARE ALWAYS THE OLD RELIABLE WAYS OF FOILING BLOODHOUNDS!
SUPER MARKET
THE RED-HERRING TRICK, FOR INSTANCE!
I DRAG THE HERRING ACROSS MY TRAIL LIKE THIS!
AND FROM NOW ON THE HOUND'S NOSE WILL FORGET THERE'S ANY OTHER SCENT IN THE WORLD!

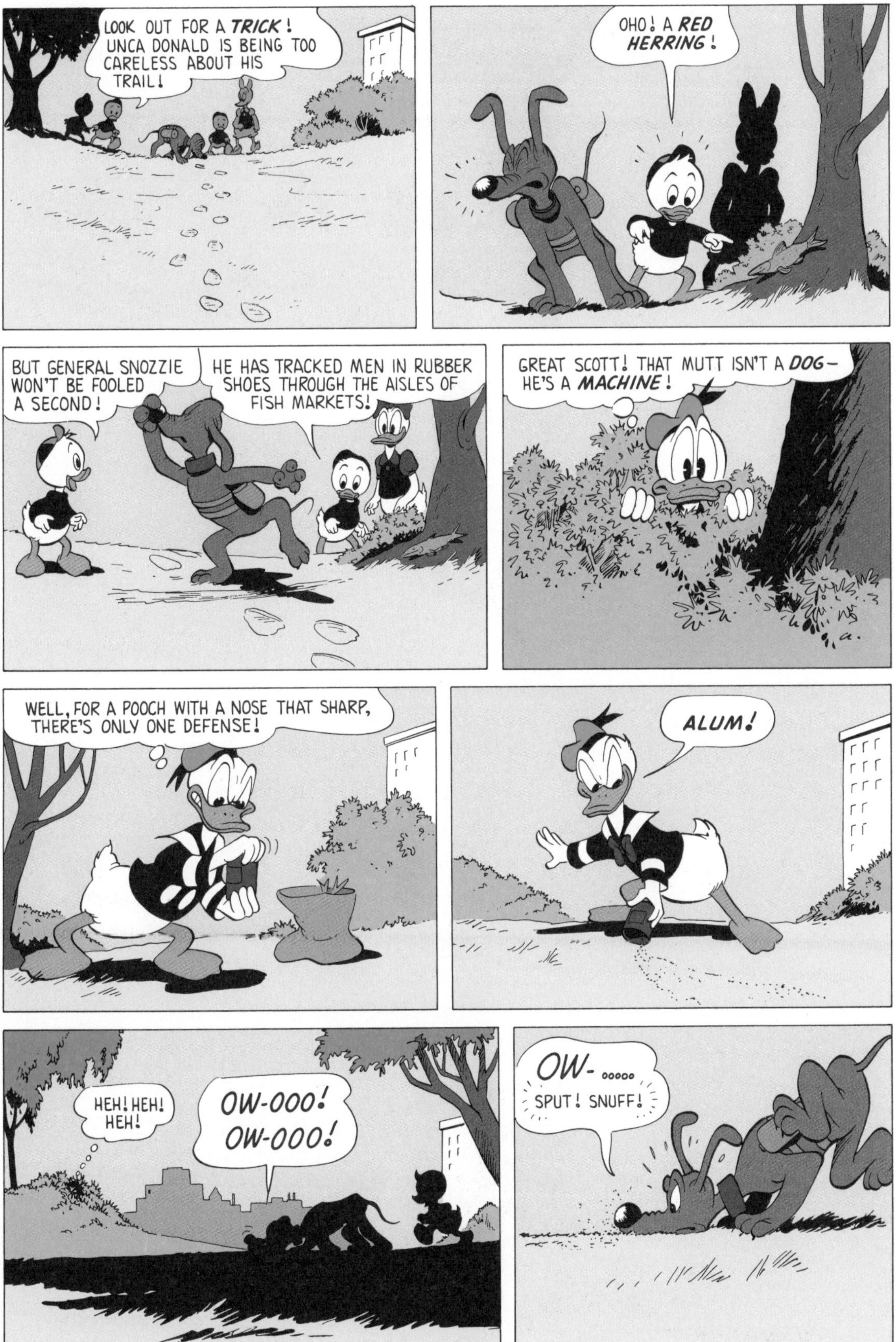
LOOK OUT FOR A TRICK! UNCA DONALD IS BEING TOO CARELESS ABOUT HIS TRAIL!
OHO! A RED HERRING!
BUT GENERAL SNOZZIE WON'T BE FOOLED A SECOND!
HE HAS TRACKED MEN IN RUBBER SHOES THROUGH THE AISLES OF FISH MARKETS!
GREAT SCOTT! THAT MUTT ISN'T A DOG— HE'S A MACHINE!
WELL, FOR A POOCH WITH A NOSE THAT SHARP, THERE'S ONLY ONE DEFENSE!
ALUM!
HEH! HEH! HEH!
OW-OOO! OW-OOO!
OW-.....
SPUT! SNUFF!

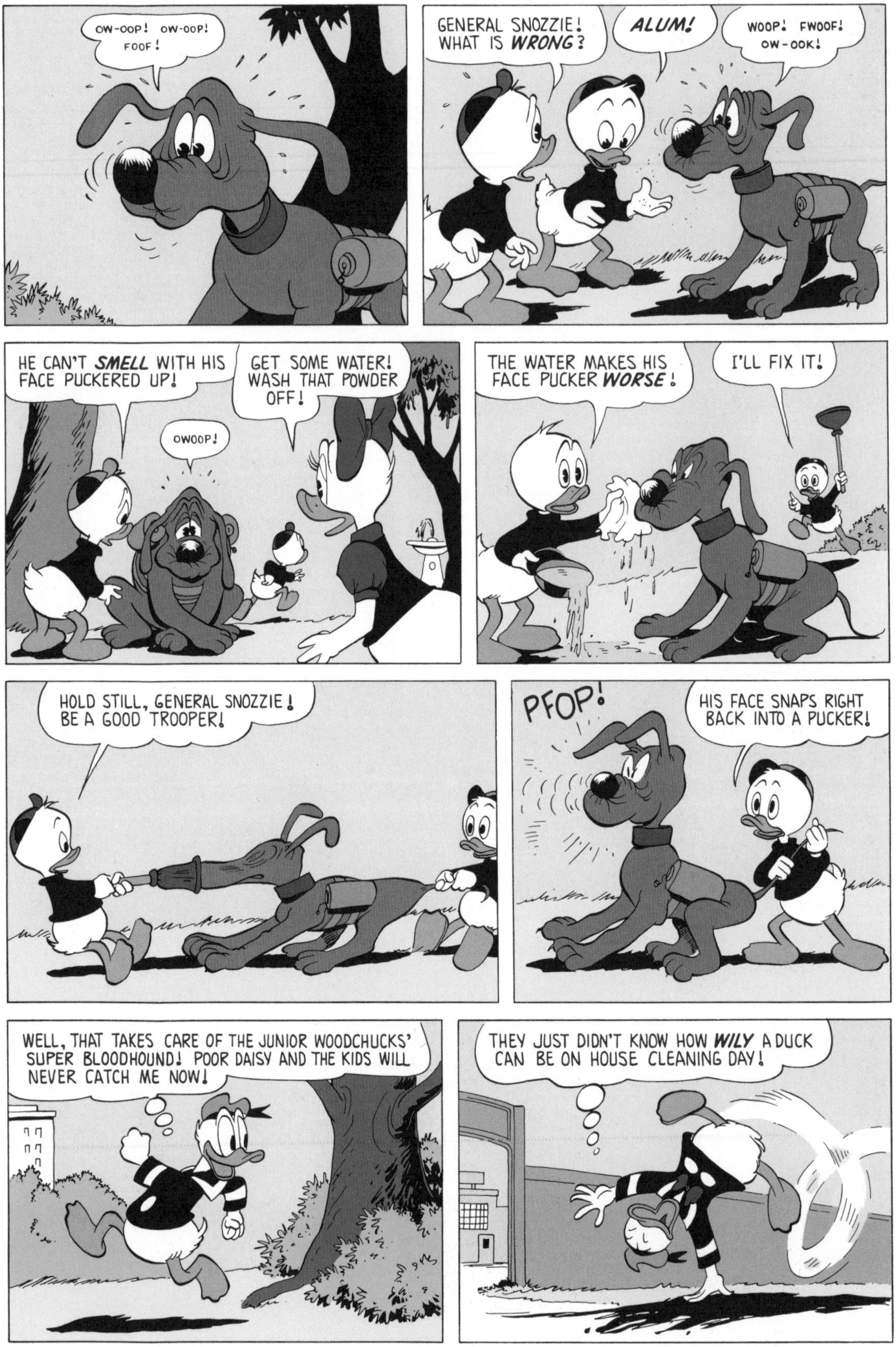

OW-OOP! OW-OOP! FOOF!
GENERAL SNOZZIE! WHAT IS WRONG?
ALUM!
WOOP! FWOOF! OW-OOK!
HE CAN'T SMELL WITH HIS FACE PUCKERED UP!
GET SOME WATER! WASH THAT POWDER OFF!
OWOOP!
THE WATER MAKES HIS FACE PUCKER WORSE!
I'LL FIX IT!
HOLD STILL, GENERAL SNOZZIE! BE A GOOD TROOPER!
PFOP!
HIS FACE SNAPS RIGHT BACK INTO A PUCKER!
WELL, THAT TAKES CARE OF THE JUNIOR WOODCHUCKS' SUPER BLOODHOUND! POOR DAISY AND THE KIDS WILL NEVER CATCH ME NOW!
THEY JUST DIDN'T KNOW HOW WILY A DUCK CAN BE ON HOUSE CLEANING DAY!

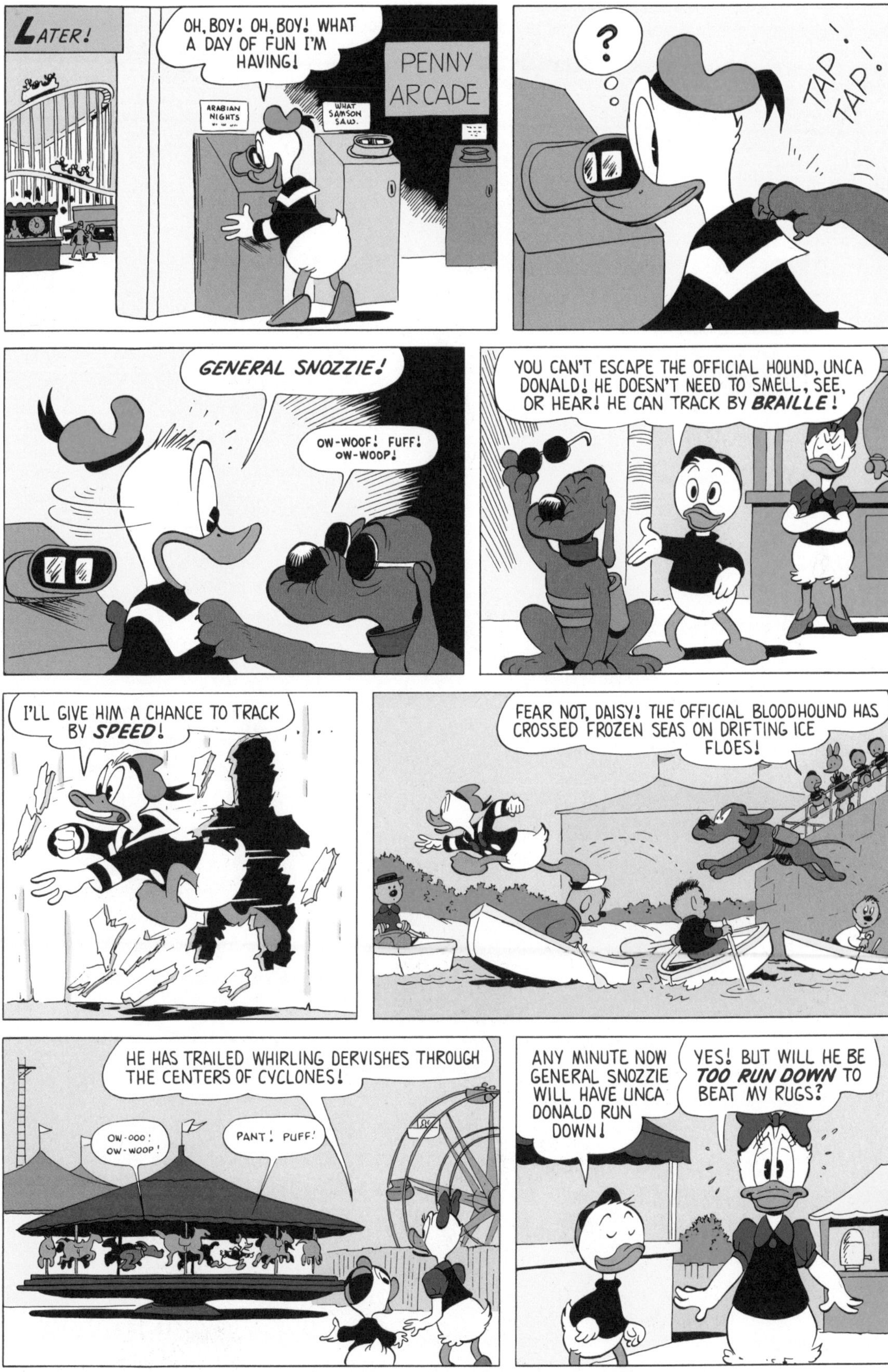
LATER!
OH, BOY! OH, BOY! WHAT A DAY OF FUN I'M HAVING!
PENNY ARCADE
ARABIAN NIGHTS
WHAT SAMSON SAW.
?
TAP! TAP!
GENERAL SNOZZIE!
OW-WOOF! FUFF! OW-WOOP!
YOU CAN'T ESCAPE THE OFFICIAL HOUND, UNCA DONALD! HE DOESN'T NEED TO SMELL, SEE, OR HEAR! HE CAN TRACK BY BRAILLE!
I'LL GIVE HIM A CHANCE TO TRACK BY SPEED!
FEAR NOT, DAISY! THE OFFICIAL BLOODHOUND HAS CROSSED FROZEN SEAS ON DRIFTING ICE FLOES!
HE HAS TRAILED WHIRLING DERVISHES THROUGH THE CENTERS OF CYCLONES!
OW-OOO! OW-WOOP!
PANT! PUFF!
ANY MINUTE NOW GENERAL SNOZZIE WILL HAVE UNCA DONALD RUN DOWN!
YES! BUT WILL HE BE TOO RUN DOWN TO BEAT MY RUGS?

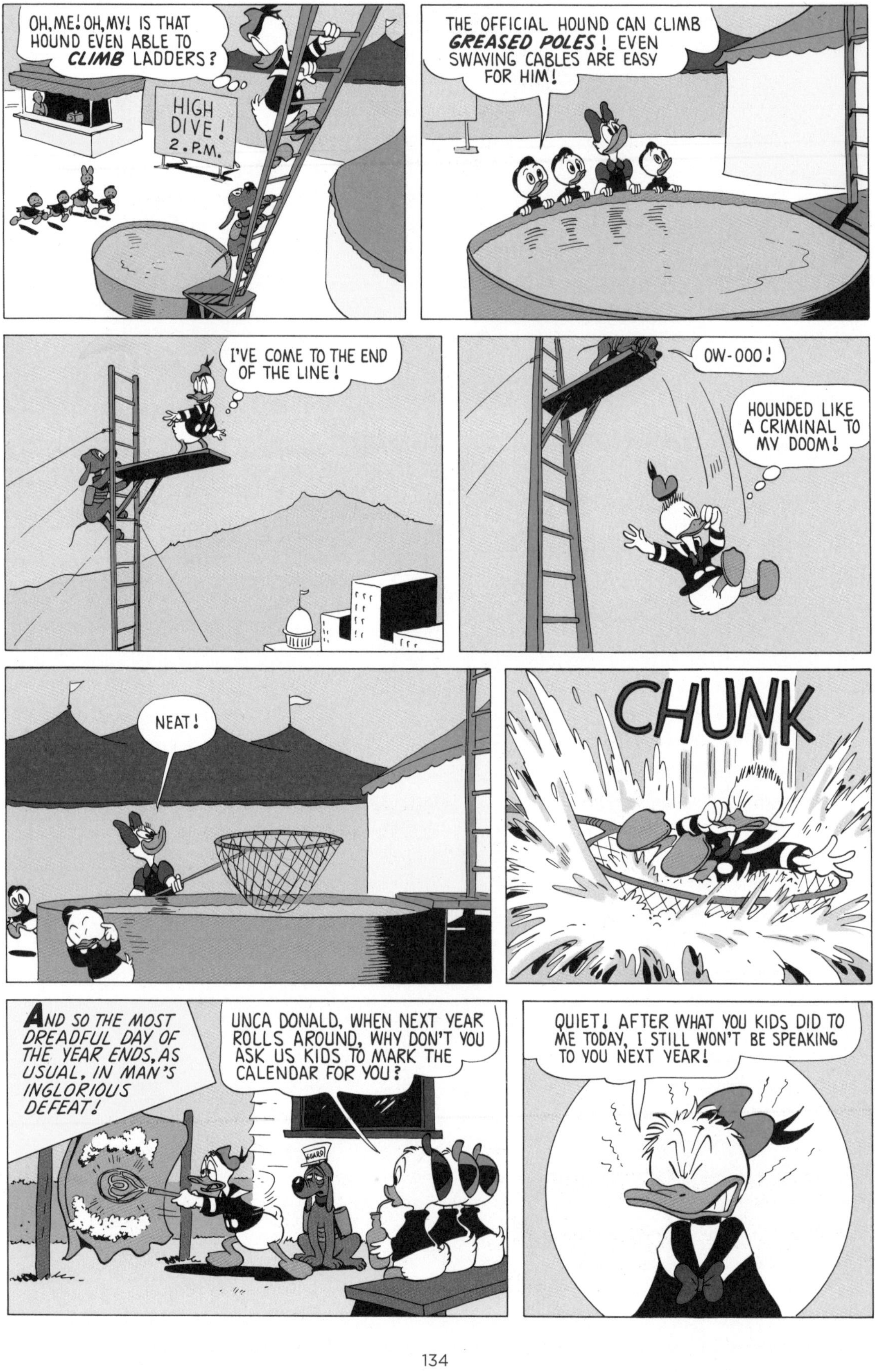
OH, ME! OH, MY! IS THAT HOUND EVEN ABLE TO CLIMB LADDERS?
HIGH DIVE! 2 P.M.
THE OFFICIAL HOUND CAN CLIMB GREASED POLES! EVEN SWAYING CABLES ARE EASY FOR HIM!
I'VE COME TO THE END OF THE LINE!
OW-OOO!
HOUNDED LIKE A CRIMINAL TO MY DOOM!
NEAT!
CHUNK
AND SO THE MOST DREADFUL DAY OF THE YEAR ENDS, AS USUAL, IN MAN'S INGLORIOUS DEFEAT!
UNCA DONALD, WHEN NEXT YEAR ROLLS AROUND, WHY DON'T YOU ASK US KIDS TO MARK THE CALENDAR FOR YOU?
GUARD
QUIET! AFTER WHAT YOU KIDS DID TO ME TODAY, I STILL WON'T BE SPEAKING TO YOU NEXT YEAR!

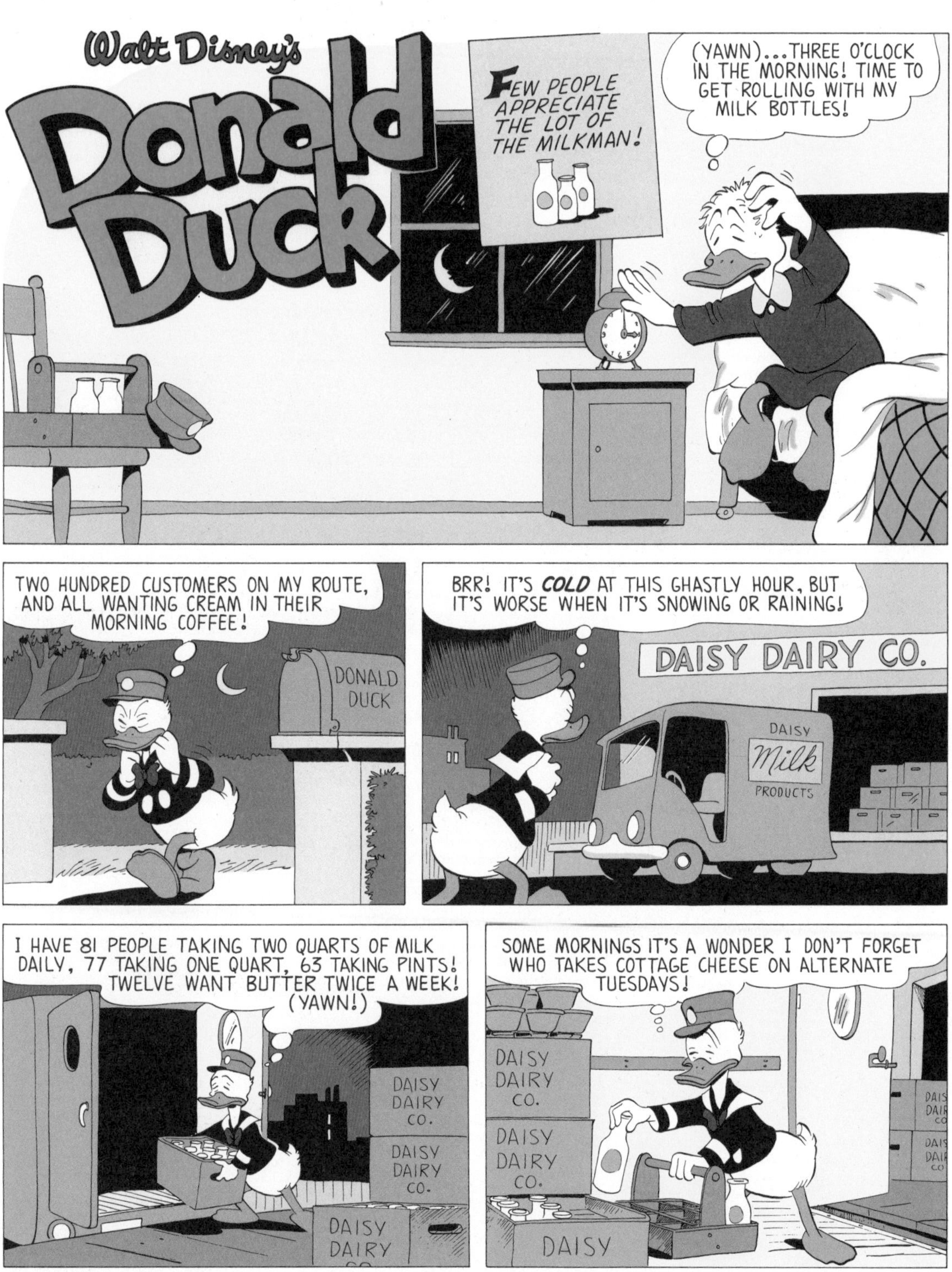
Walt Disney's
Donald Duck
FEW PEOPLE APPRECIATE THE LOT OF THE MILKMAN!
(YAWN)...THREE O'CLOCK IN THE MORNING! TIME TO GET ROLLING WITH MY MILK BOTTLES!
TWO HUNDRED CUSTOMERS ON MY ROUTE, AND ALL WANTING CREAM IN THEIR MORNING COFFEE!
DONALD DUCK
BRR! IT'S COLD AT THIS GHASTLY HOUR, BUT IT'S WORSE WHEN IT'S SNOWING OR RAINING!
DAISY DAIRY CO.
DAISY Milk PRODUCTS
I HAVE 81 PEOPLE TAKING TWO QUARTS OF MILK DAILY, 77 TAKING ONE QUART, 63 TAKING PINTS! TWELVE WANT BUTTER TWICE A WEEK! (YAWN!)
DAISY DAIRY CO.
DAISY DAIRY CO.
DAISY DAIRY
SOME MORNINGS IT'S A WONDER I DON'T FORGET WHO TAKES COTTAGE CHEESE ON ALTERNATE TUESDAYS!
DAISY DAIRY CO.
DAISY DAIRY CO.
DAISY

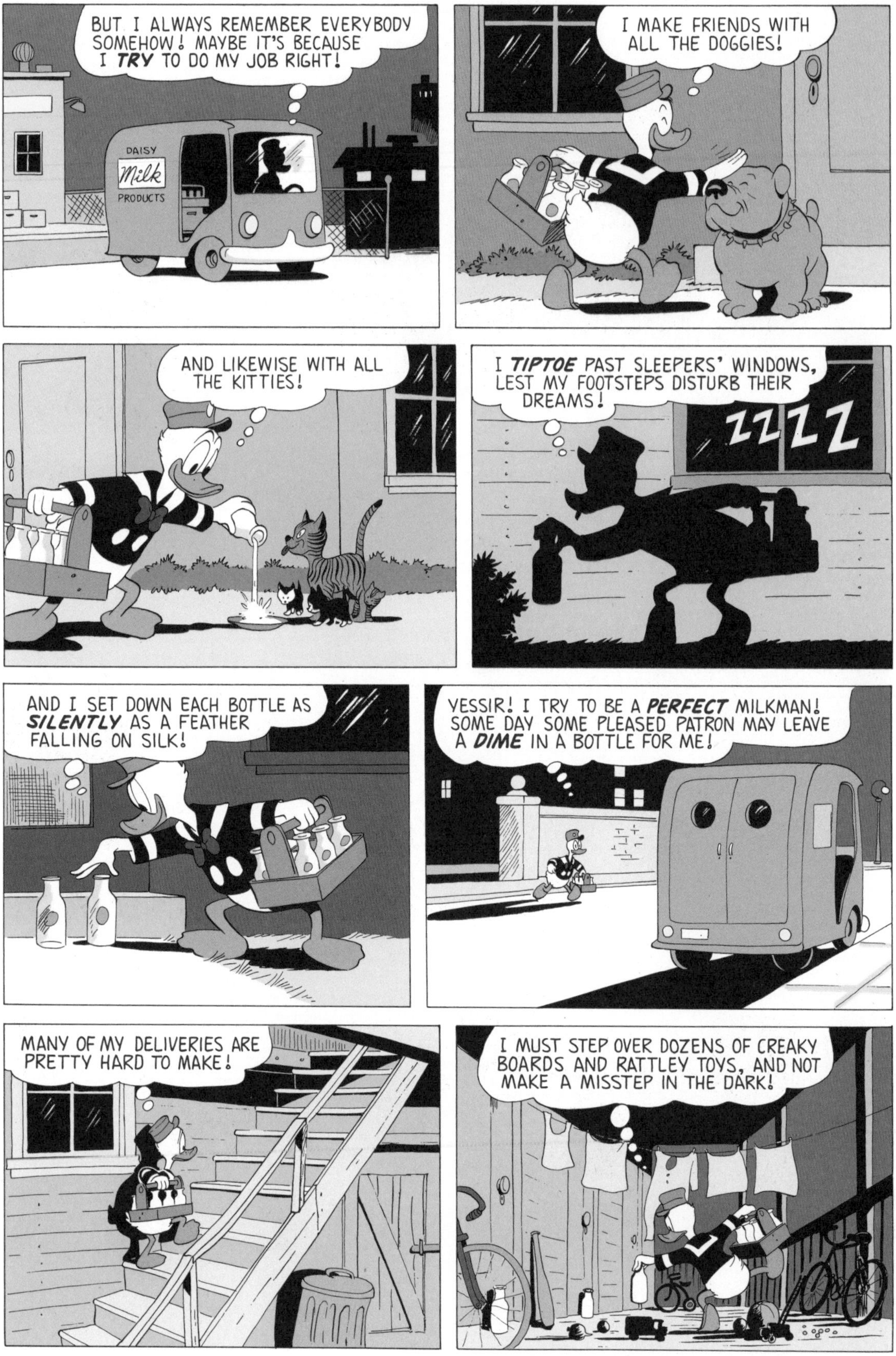
BUT I ALWAYS REMEMBER EVERYBODY SOMEHOW! MAYBE IT'S BECAUSE I **TRY** TO DO MY JOB RIGHT!
DAISY Milk PRODUCTS
I MAKE FRIENDS WITH ALL THE DOGGIES!
AND LIKEWISE WITH ALL THE KITTIES!
I **TIPTOE** PAST SLEEPERS' WINDOWS, LEST MY FOOTSTEPS DISTURB THEIR DREAMS!
ZZZZ
AND I SET DOWN EACH BOTTLE AS **SILENTLY** AS A FEATHER FALLING ON SILK!
YESSIR! I TRY TO BE A **PERFECT** MILKMAN! SOME DAY SOME PLEASED PATRON MAY LEAVE A **DIME** IN A BOTTLE FOR ME!
MANY OF MY DELIVERIES ARE PRETTY HARD TO MAKE!
I MUST STEP OVER DOZENS OF CREAKY BOARDS AND RATTLEY TOYS, AND NOT MAKE A MISSTEP IN THE DARK!

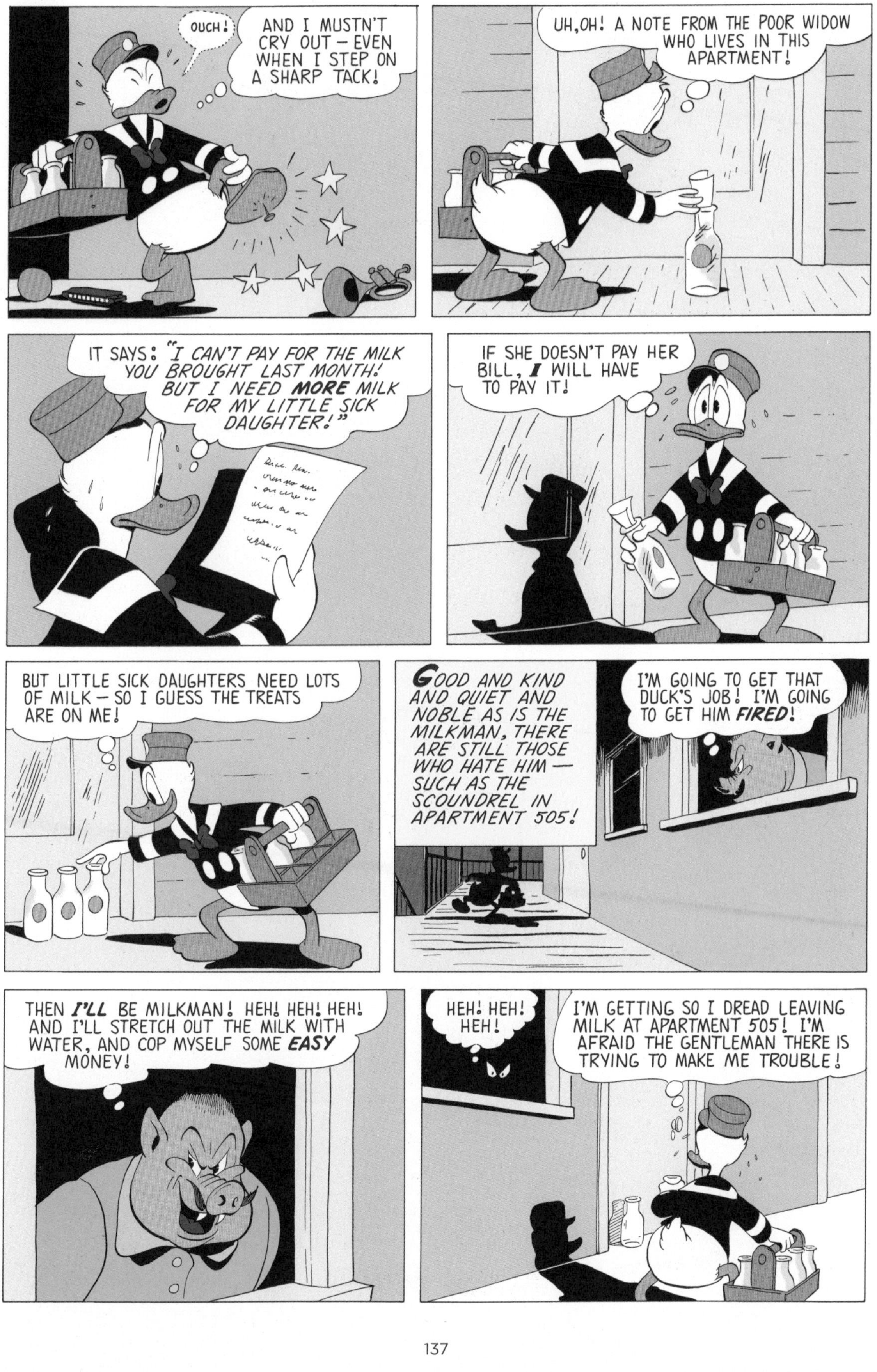
OUCH!
AND I MUSTN'T CRY OUT — EVEN WHEN I STEP ON A SHARP TACK!
UH, OH! A NOTE FROM THE POOR WIDOW WHO LIVES IN THIS APARTMENT!
IT SAYS: "I CAN'T PAY FOR THE MILK YOU BROUGHT LAST MONTH! BUT I NEED MORE MILK FOR MY LITTLE SICK DAUGHTER!"
IF SHE DOESN'T PAY HER BILL, I WILL HAVE TO PAY IT!
BUT LITTLE SICK DAUGHTERS NEED LOTS OF MILK — SO I GUESS THE TREATS ARE ON ME!
GOOD AND KIND AND QUIET AND NOBLE AS IS THE MILKMAN, THERE ARE STILL THOSE WHO HATE HIM — SUCH AS THE SCOUNDREL IN APARTMENT 505!
I'M GOING TO GET THAT DUCK'S JOB! I'M GOING TO GET HIM FIRED!
THEN I'LL BE MILKMAN! HEH! HEH! HEH! AND I'LL STRETCH OUT THE MILK WITH WATER, AND COP MYSELF SOME EASY MONEY!
HEH! HEH! HEH!
I'M GETTING SO I DREAD LEAVING MILK AT APARTMENT 505! I'M AFRAID THE GENTLEMAN THERE IS TRYING TO MAKE ME TROUBLE!

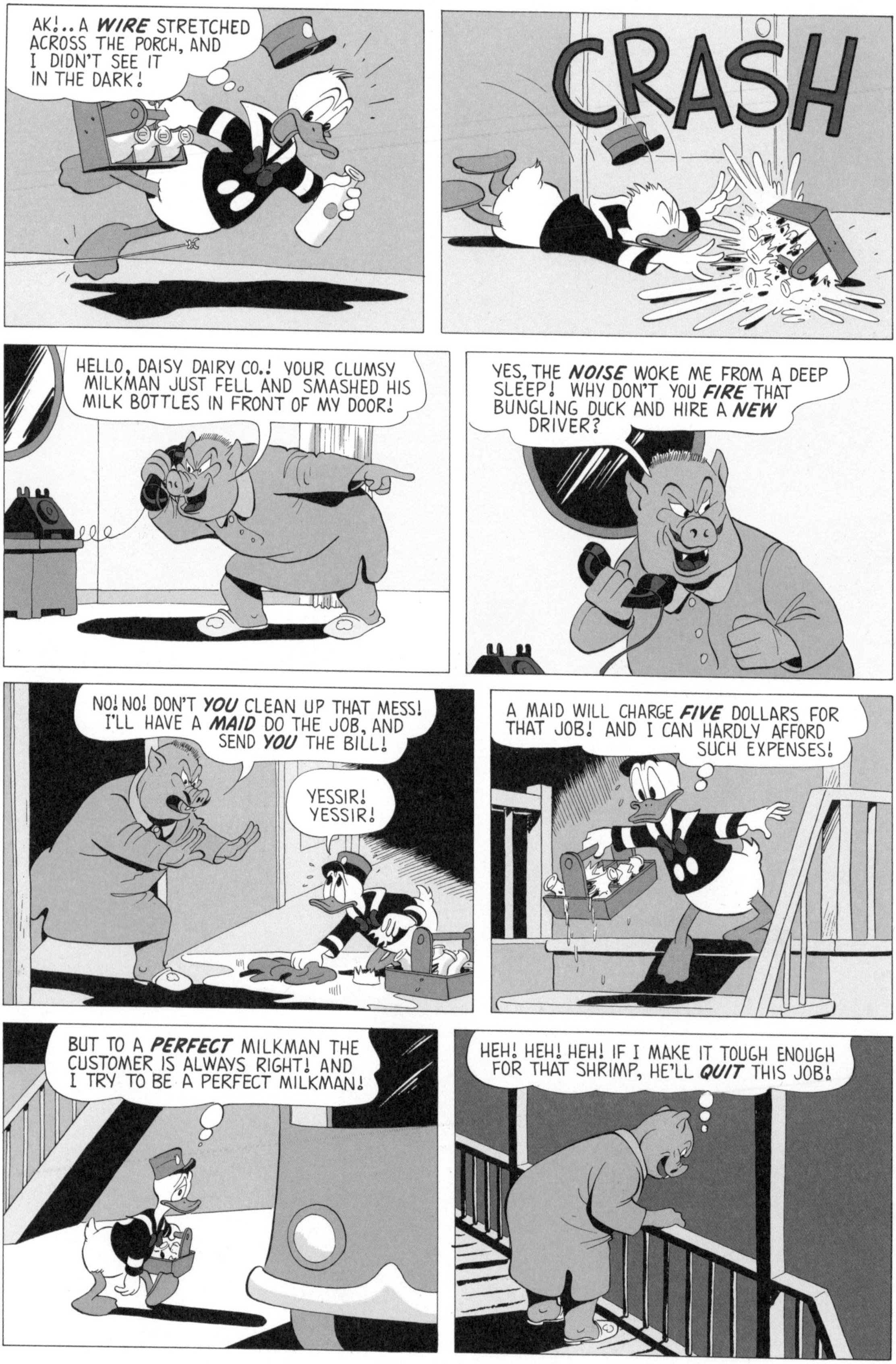
AK!..A WIRE STRETCHED ACROSS THE PORCH, AND I DIDN'T SEE IT IN THE DARK!
CRASH
HELLO, DAISY DAIRY CO.! YOUR CLUMSY MILKMAN JUST FELL AND SMASHED HIS MILK BOTTLES IN FRONT OF MY DOOR!
YES, THE NOISE WOKE ME FROM A DEEP SLEEP! WHY DON'T YOU FIRE THAT BUNGLING DUCK AND HIRE A NEW DRIVER?
NO! NO! DON'T YOU CLEAN UP THAT MESS! I'LL HAVE A MAID DO THE JOB, AND SEND YOU THE BILL!
YESSIR! YESSIR!
A MAID WILL CHARGE FIVE DOLLARS FOR THAT JOB! AND I CAN HARDLY AFFORD SUCH EXPENSES!
BUT TO A PERFECT MILKMAN THE CUSTOMER IS ALWAYS RIGHT! AND I TRY TO BE A PERFECT MILKMAN!
HEH! HEH! HEH! IF I MAKE IT TOUGH ENOUGH FOR THAT SHRIMP, HE'LL QUIT THIS JOB!

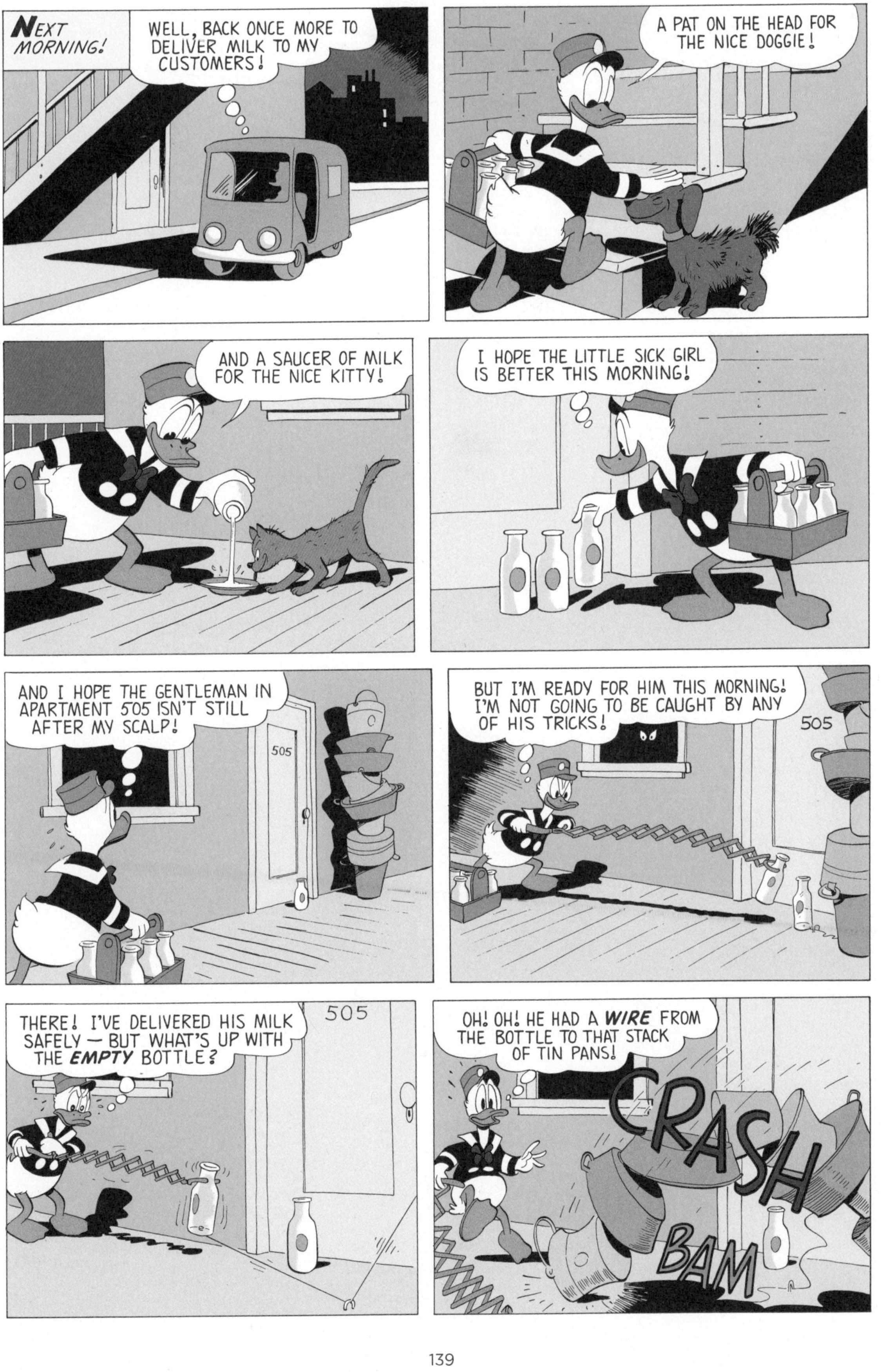
NEXT MORNING!
WELL, BACK ONCE MORE TO DELIVER MILK TO MY CUSTOMERS!
A PAT ON THE HEAD FOR THE NICE DOGGIE!
AND A SAUCER OF MILK FOR THE NICE KITTY!
I HOPE THE LITTLE SICK GIRL IS BETTER THIS MORNING!
AND I HOPE THE GENTLEMAN IN APARTMENT 505 ISN'T STILL AFTER MY SCALP!
505
BUT I'M READY FOR HIM THIS MORNING! I'M NOT GOING TO BE CAUGHT BY ANY OF HIS TRICKS!
505
THERE! I'VE DELIVERED HIS MILK SAFELY — BUT WHAT'S UP WITH THE EMPTY BOTTLE?
505
OH! OH! HE HAD A WIRE FROM THE BOTTLE TO THAT STACK OF TIN PANS!
CRASH
BAM

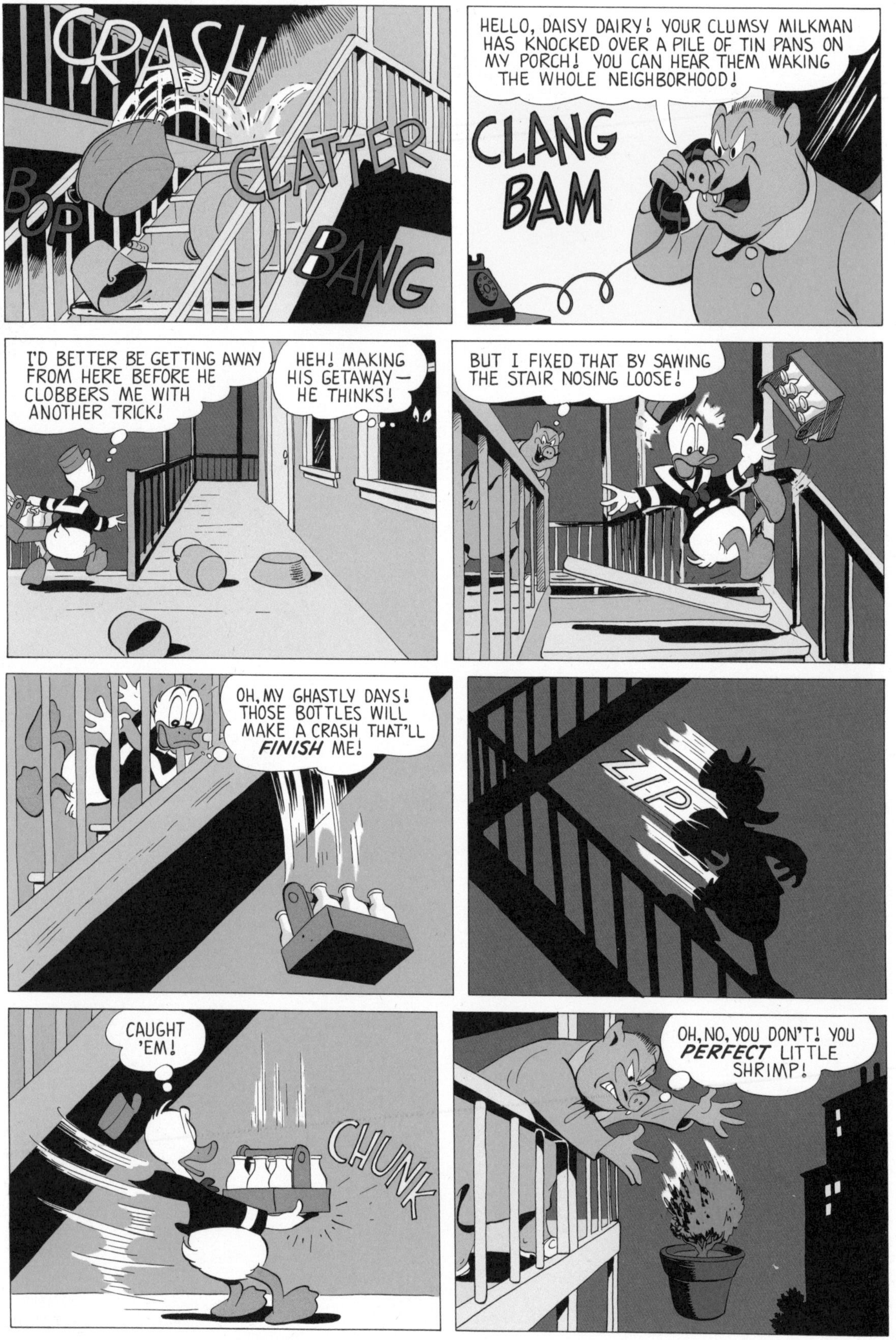
CRASH
BOP
CLATTER
BANG
HELLO, DAISY DAIRY! YOUR CLUMSY MILKMAN HAS KNOCKED OVER A PILE OF TIN PANS ON MY PORCH! YOU CAN HEAR THEM WAKING THE WHOLE NEIGHBORHOOD!
CLANG
BAM
I'D BETTER BE GETTING AWAY FROM HERE BEFORE HE CLOBBERS ME WITH ANOTHER TRICK!
HEH! MAKING HIS GETAWAY— HE THINKS!
BUT I FIXED THAT BY SAWING THE STAIR NOSING LOOSE!
OH, MY GHASTLY DAYS! THOSE BOTTLES WILL MAKE A CRASH THAT'LL FINISH ME!
ZIP
CAUGHT 'EM!
CHUNK
OH, NO, YOU DON'T! YOU PERFECT LITTLE SHRIMP!

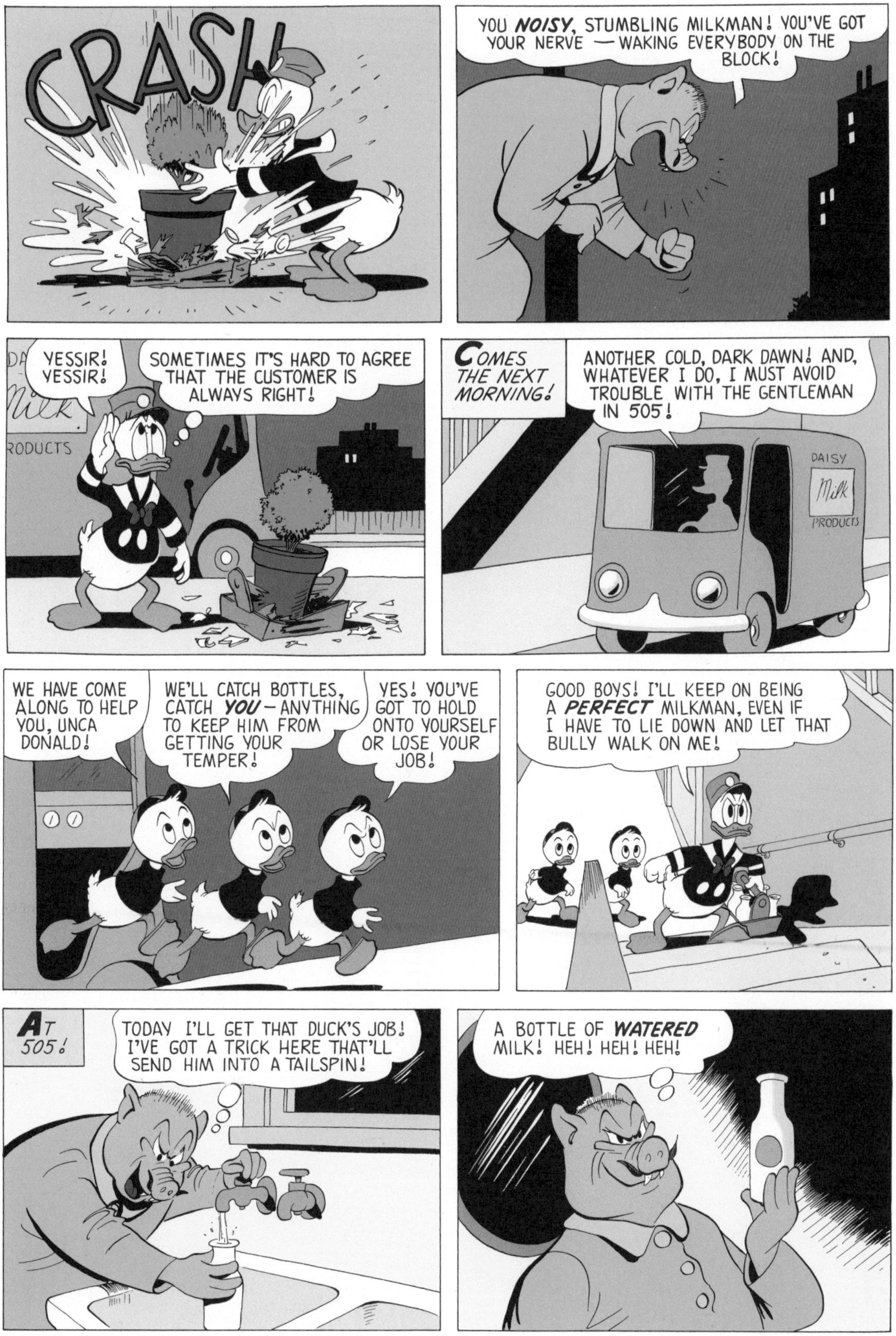
CRASH
YOU NOISY, STUMBLING MILKMAN! YOU'VE GOT YOUR NERVE — WAKING EVERYBODY ON THE BLOCK!
YESSIR! YESSIR!
SOMETIMES IT'S HARD TO AGREE THAT THE CUSTOMER IS ALWAYS RIGHT!
COMES THE NEXT MORNING!
ANOTHER COLD, DARK DAWN! AND, WHATEVER I DO, I MUST AVOID TROUBLE WITH THE GENTLEMAN IN 505!
DAISY Milk PRODUCTS
WE HAVE COME ALONG TO HELP YOU, UNCA DONALD!
WE'LL CATCH BOTTLES, CATCH YOU — ANYTHING TO KEEP HIM FROM GETTING YOUR TEMPER!
YES! YOU'VE GOT TO HOLD ONTO YOURSELF OR LOSE YOUR JOB!
GOOD BOYS! I'LL KEEP ON BEING A PERFECT MILKMAN, EVEN IF I HAVE TO LIE DOWN AND LET THAT BULLY WALK ON ME!
AT 505!
TODAY I'LL GET THAT DUCK'S JOB! I'VE GOT A TRICK HERE THAT'LL SEND HIM INTO A TAILSPIN!
A BOTTLE OF WATERED MILK! HEH! HEH! HEH!

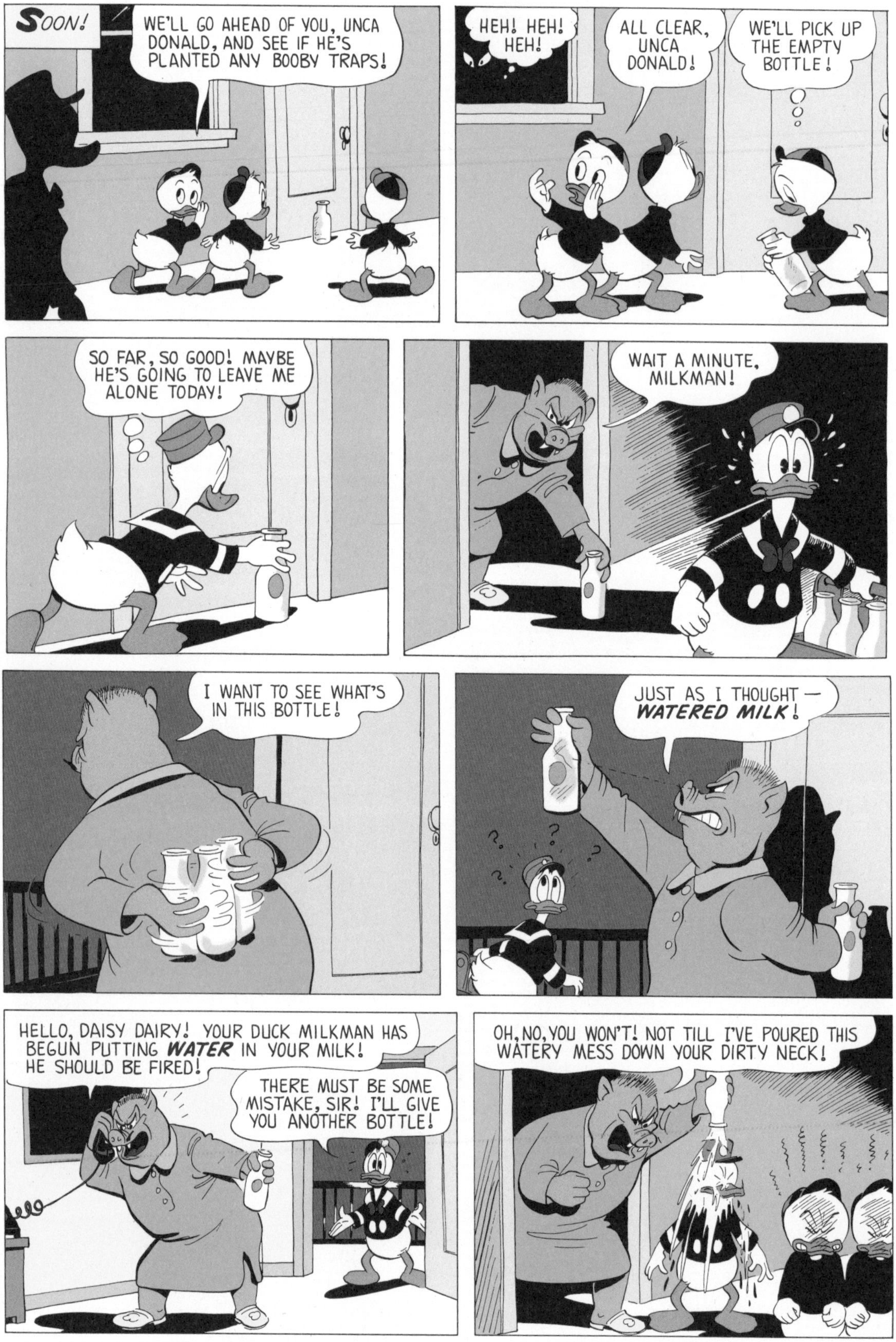
SOON!
WE'LL GO AHEAD OF YOU, UNCA DONALD, AND SEE IF HE'S PLANTED ANY BOOBY TRAPS!
HEH! HEH! HEH!
ALL CLEAR, UNCA DONALD!
WE'LL PICK UP THE EMPTY BOTTLE!
SO FAR, SO GOOD! MAYBE HE'S GOING TO LEAVE ME ALONE TODAY!
WAIT A MINUTE, MILKMAN!
I WANT TO SEE WHAT'S IN THIS BOTTLE!
JUST AS I THOUGHT — WATERED MILK!
HELLO, DAISY DAIRY! YOUR DUCK MILKMAN HAS BEGUN PUTTING WATER IN YOUR MILK! HE SHOULD BE FIRED!
THERE MUST BE SOME MISTAKE, SIR! I'LL GIVE YOU ANOTHER BOTTLE!
OH, NO, YOU WON'T! NOT TILL I'VE POURED THIS WATERY MESS DOWN YOUR DIRTY NECK!

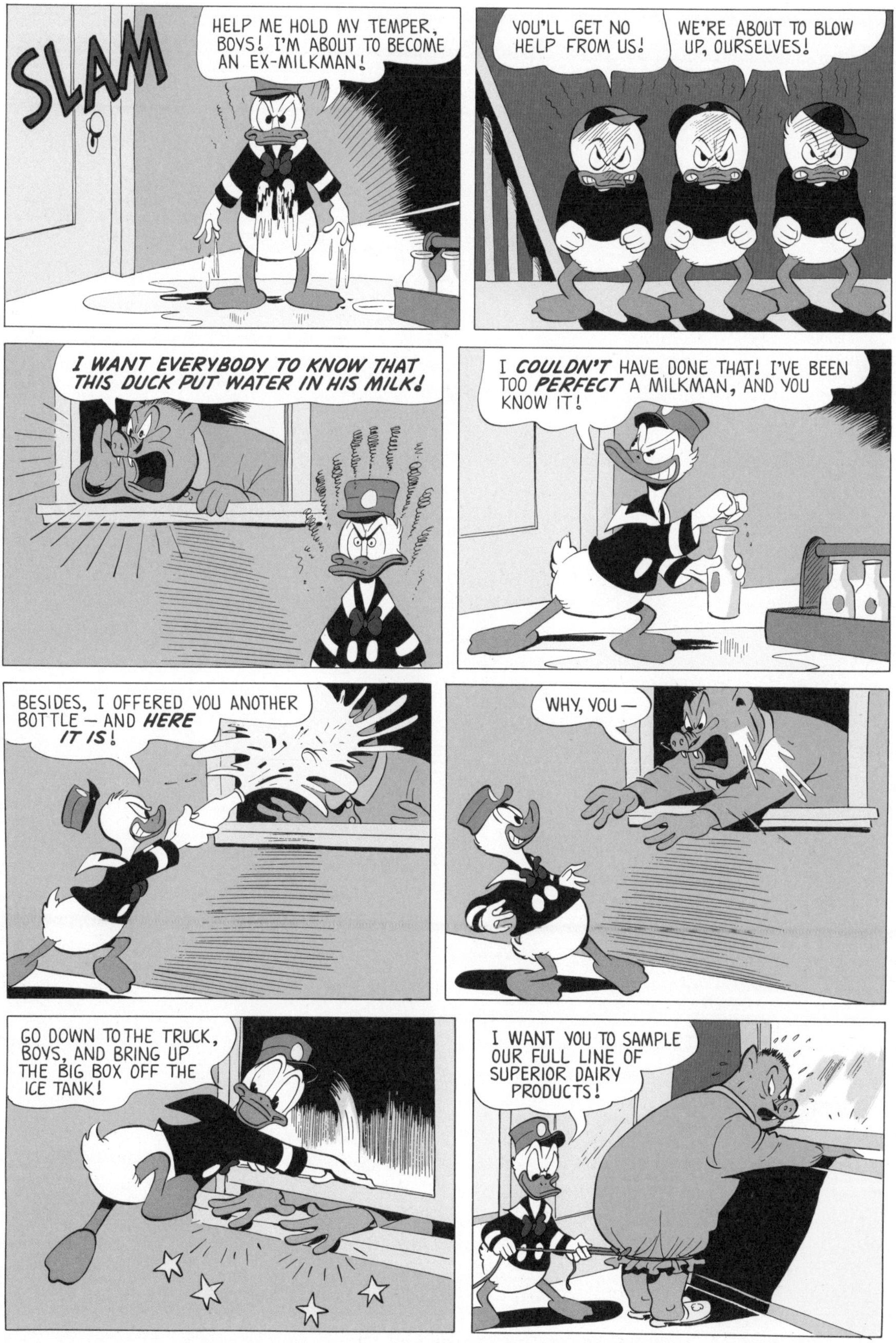
SLAM
HELP ME HOLD MY TEMPER, BOYS! I'M ABOUT TO BECOME AN EX-MILKMAN!
YOU'LL GET NO HELP FROM US!
WE'RE ABOUT TO BLOW UP, OURSELVES!
I WANT EVERYBODY TO KNOW THAT THIS DUCK PUT WATER IN HIS MILK!
I COULDN'T HAVE DONE THAT! I'VE BEEN TOO PERFECT A MILKMAN, AND YOU KNOW IT!
BESIDES, I OFFERED YOU ANOTHER BOTTLE — AND HERE IT IS!
WHY, YOU —
GO DOWN TO THE TRUCK, BOYS, AND BRING UP THE BIG BOX OFF THE ICE TANK!
I WANT YOU TO SAMPLE OUR FULL LINE OF SUPERIOR DAIRY PRODUCTS!

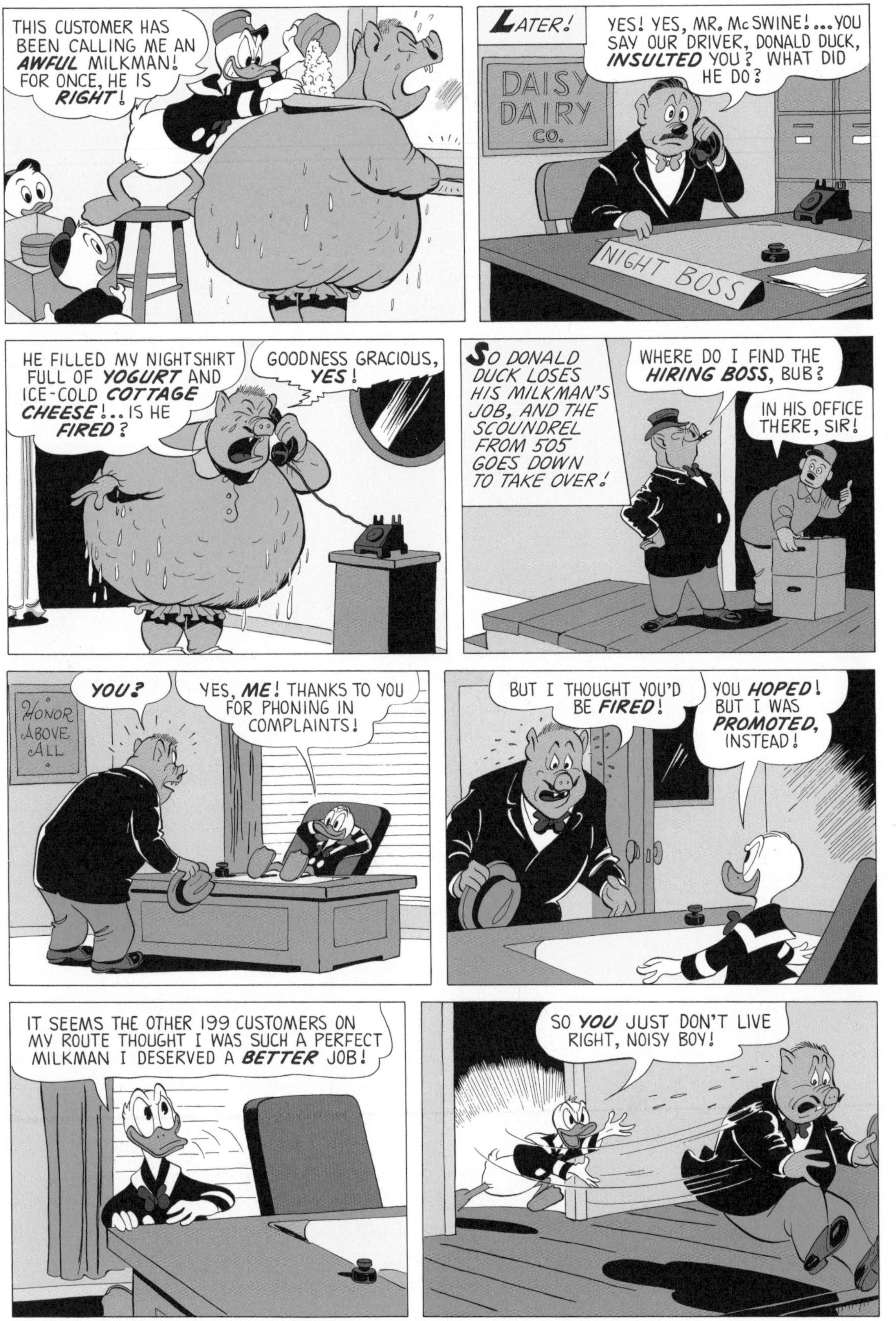
THIS CUSTOMER HAS BEEN CALLING ME AN AWFUL MILKMAN! FOR ONCE, HE IS RIGHT!
LATER!
YES! YES, MR. McSWINE! ...YOU SAY OUR DRIVER, DONALD DUCK, INSULTED YOU? WHAT DID HE DO?
DAISY DAIRY CO.
NIGHT BOSS
HE FILLED MY NIGHTSHIRT FULL OF YOGURT AND ICE-COLD COTTAGE CHEESE!.. IS HE FIRED?
GOODNESS GRACIOUS, YES!
SO DONALD DUCK LOSES HIS MILKMAN'S JOB, AND THE SCOUNDREL FROM 505 GOES DOWN TO TAKE OVER!
WHERE DO I FIND THE HIRING BOSS, BUB?
IN HIS OFFICE THERE, SIR!
HONOR ABOVE ALL
YOU?
YES, ME! THANKS TO YOU FOR PHONING IN COMPLAINTS!
BUT I THOUGHT YOU'D BE FIRED!
YOU HOPED! BUT I WAS PROMOTED, INSTEAD!
IT SEEMS THE OTHER 199 CUSTOMERS ON MY ROUTE THOUGHT I WAS SUCH A PERFECT MILKMAN I DESERVED A BETTER JOB!
SO YOU JUST DON'T LIVE RIGHT, NOISY BOY!

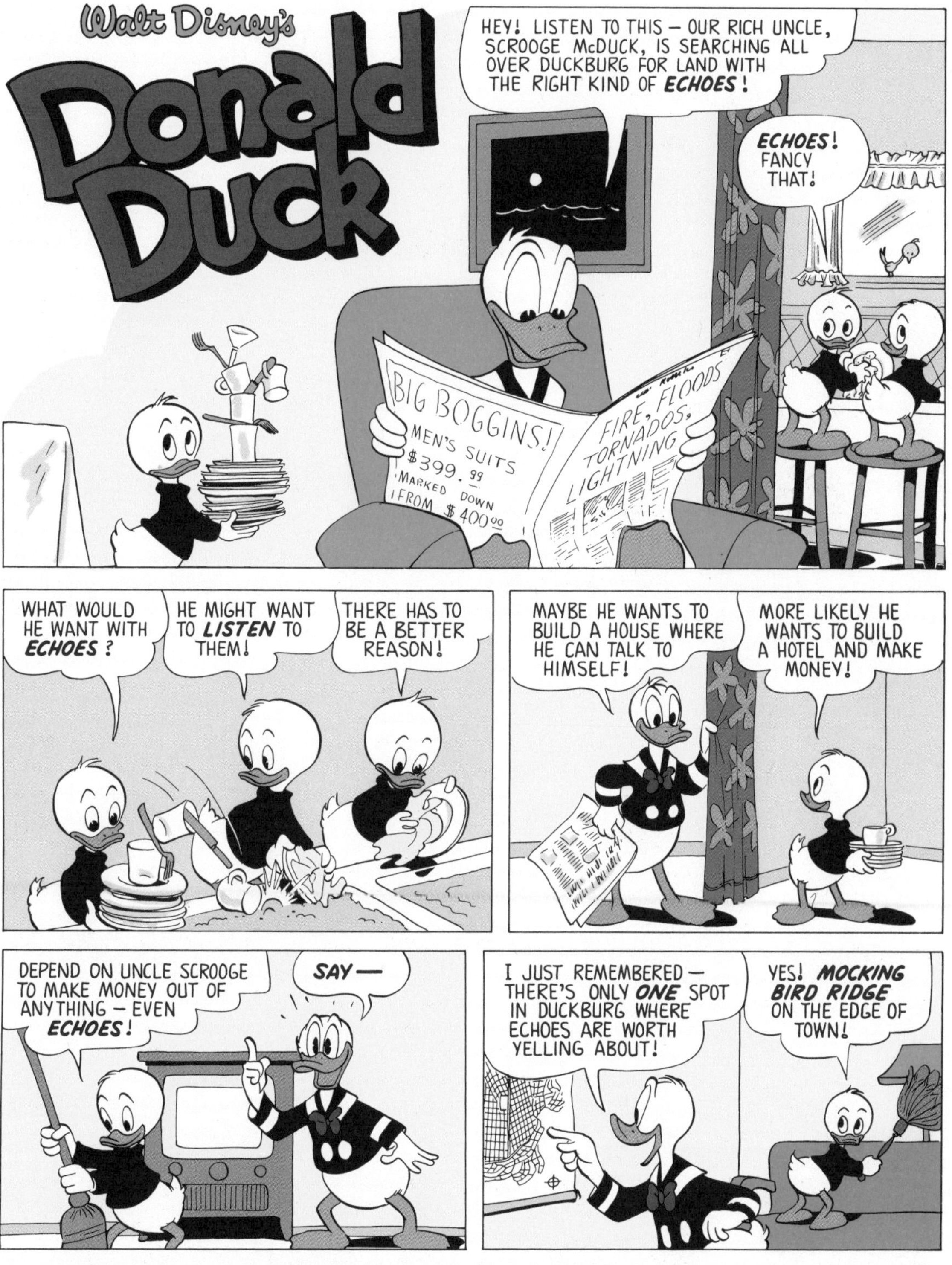
Walt Disney's
Donald Duck
HEY! LISTEN TO THIS — OUR RICH UNCLE, SCROOGE McDUCK, IS SEARCHING ALL OVER DUCKBURG FOR LAND WITH THE RIGHT KIND OF ECHOES!
ECHOES! FANCY THAT!
BIG BOGGINS! MEN'S SUITS $399.99 MARKED DOWN FROM $400.00
FIRE, FLOODS TORNADOS, LIGHTNING
WHAT WOULD HE WANT WITH ECHOES?
HE MIGHT WANT TO LISTEN TO THEM!
THERE HAS TO BE A BETTER REASON!
MAYBE HE WANTS TO BUILD A HOUSE WHERE HE CAN TALK TO HIMSELF!
MORE LIKELY HE WANTS TO BUILD A HOTEL AND MAKE MONEY!
DEPEND ON UNCLE SCROOGE TO MAKE MONEY OUT OF ANYTHING — EVEN ECHOES!
SAY —
I JUST REMEMBERED — THERE'S ONLY ONE SPOT IN DUCKBURG WHERE ECHOES ARE WORTH YELLING ABOUT!
YES! MOCKING BIRD RIDGE ON THE EDGE OF TOWN!

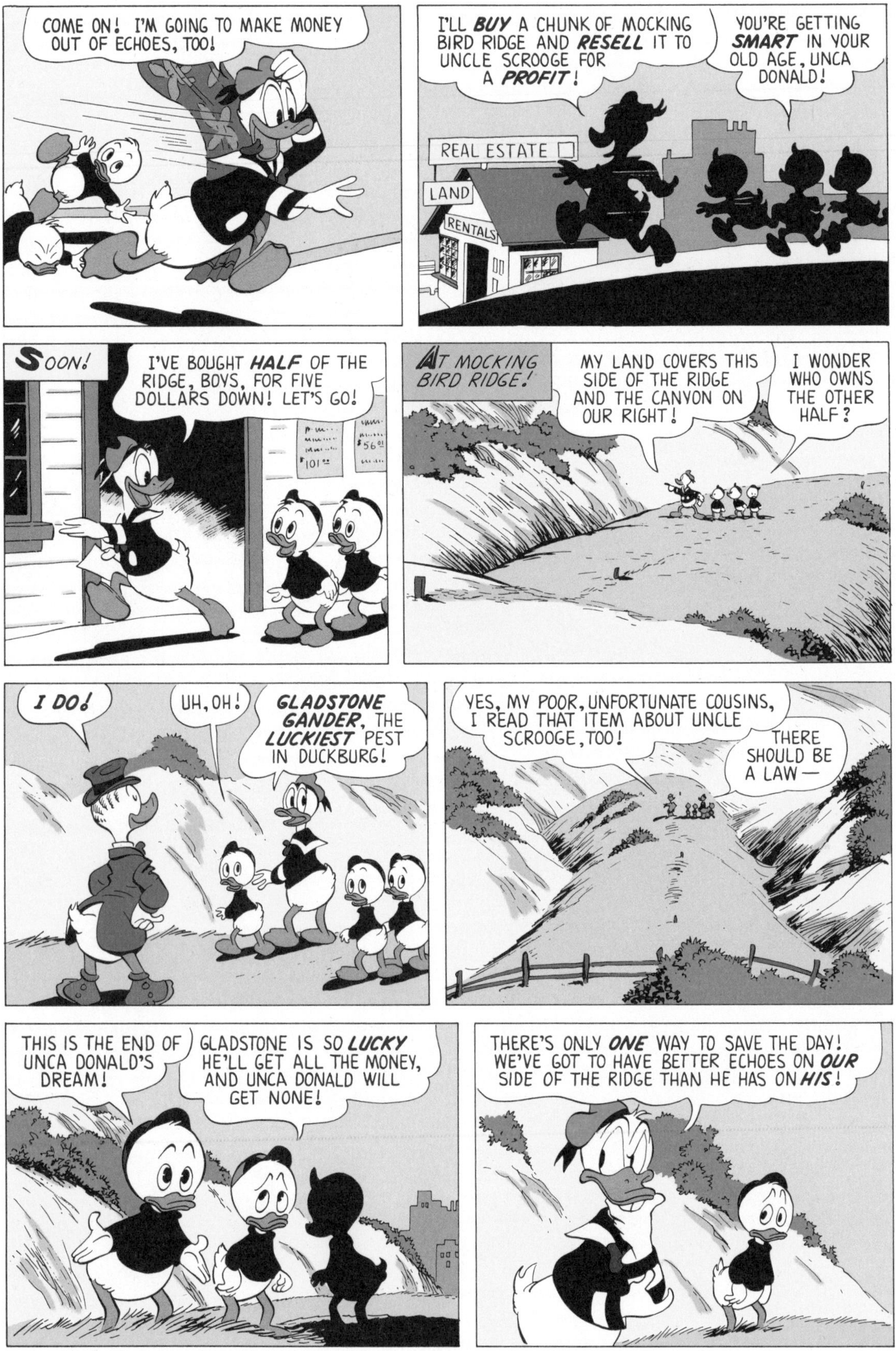

COME ON! I'M GOING TO MAKE MONEY OUT OF ECHOES, TOO!
I'LL **BUY** A CHUNK OF MOCKING BIRD RIDGE AND **RESELL** IT TO UNCLE SCROOGE FOR A **PROFIT**!
YOU'RE GETTING **SMART** IN YOUR OLD AGE, UNCA DONALD!
REAL ESTATE
LAND
RENTALS
SOON!
I'VE BOUGHT **HALF** OF THE RIDGE, BOYS, FOR FIVE DOLLARS DOWN! LET'S GO!
AT MOCKING BIRD RIDGE!
MY LAND COVERS THIS SIDE OF THE RIDGE AND THE CANYON ON OUR RIGHT!
I WONDER WHO OWNS THE OTHER HALF?
I DO!
UH, OH!
GLADSTONE GANDER, THE **LUCKIEST** PEST IN DUCKBURG!
YES, MY POOR, UNFORTUNATE COUSINS, I READ THAT ITEM ABOUT UNCLE SCROOGE, TOO!
THERE SHOULD BE A LAW—
THIS IS THE END OF UNCA DONALD'S DREAM!
GLADSTONE IS SO **LUCKY** HE'LL GET ALL THE MONEY, AND UNCA DONALD WILL GET NONE!
THERE'S ONLY **ONE** WAY TO SAVE THE DAY! WE'VE GOT TO HAVE BETTER ECHOES ON **OUR** SIDE OF THE RIDGE THAN HE HAS ON **HIS**!

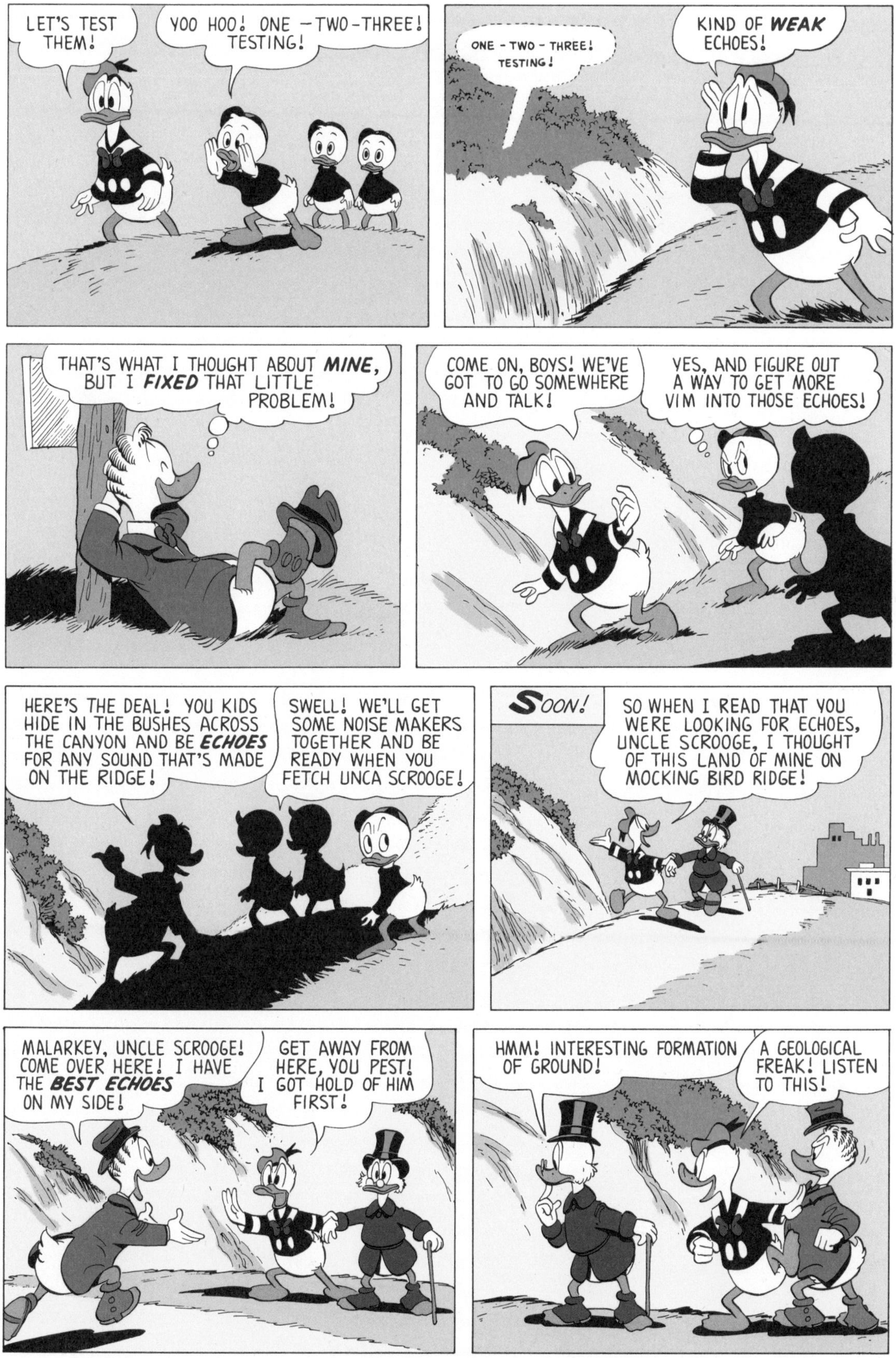
LET'S TEST THEM!
YOO HOO! ONE —TWO—THREE! TESTING!
ONE - TWO - THREE! TESTING!
KIND OF WEAK ECHOES!
THAT'S WHAT I THOUGHT ABOUT MINE, BUT I FIXED THAT LITTLE PROBLEM!
COME ON, BOYS! WE'VE GOT TO GO SOMEWHERE AND TALK!
YES, AND FIGURE OUT A WAY TO GET MORE VIM INTO THOSE ECHOES!
HERE'S THE DEAL! YOU KIDS HIDE IN THE BUSHES ACROSS THE CANYON AND BE ECHOES FOR ANY SOUND THAT'S MADE ON THE RIDGE!
SWELL! WE'LL GET SOME NOISE MAKERS TOGETHER AND BE READY WHEN YOU FETCH UNCA SCROOGE!
SOON!
SO WHEN I READ THAT YOU WERE LOOKING FOR ECHOES, UNCLE SCROOGE, I THOUGHT OF THIS LAND OF MINE ON MOCKING BIRD RIDGE!
MALARKEY, UNCLE SCROOGE! COME OVER HERE! I HAVE THE BEST ECHOES ON MY SIDE!
GET AWAY FROM HERE, YOU PEST! I GOT HOLD OF HIM FIRST!
HMM! INTERESTING FORMATION OF GROUND!
A GEOLOGICAL FREAK! LISTEN TO THIS!

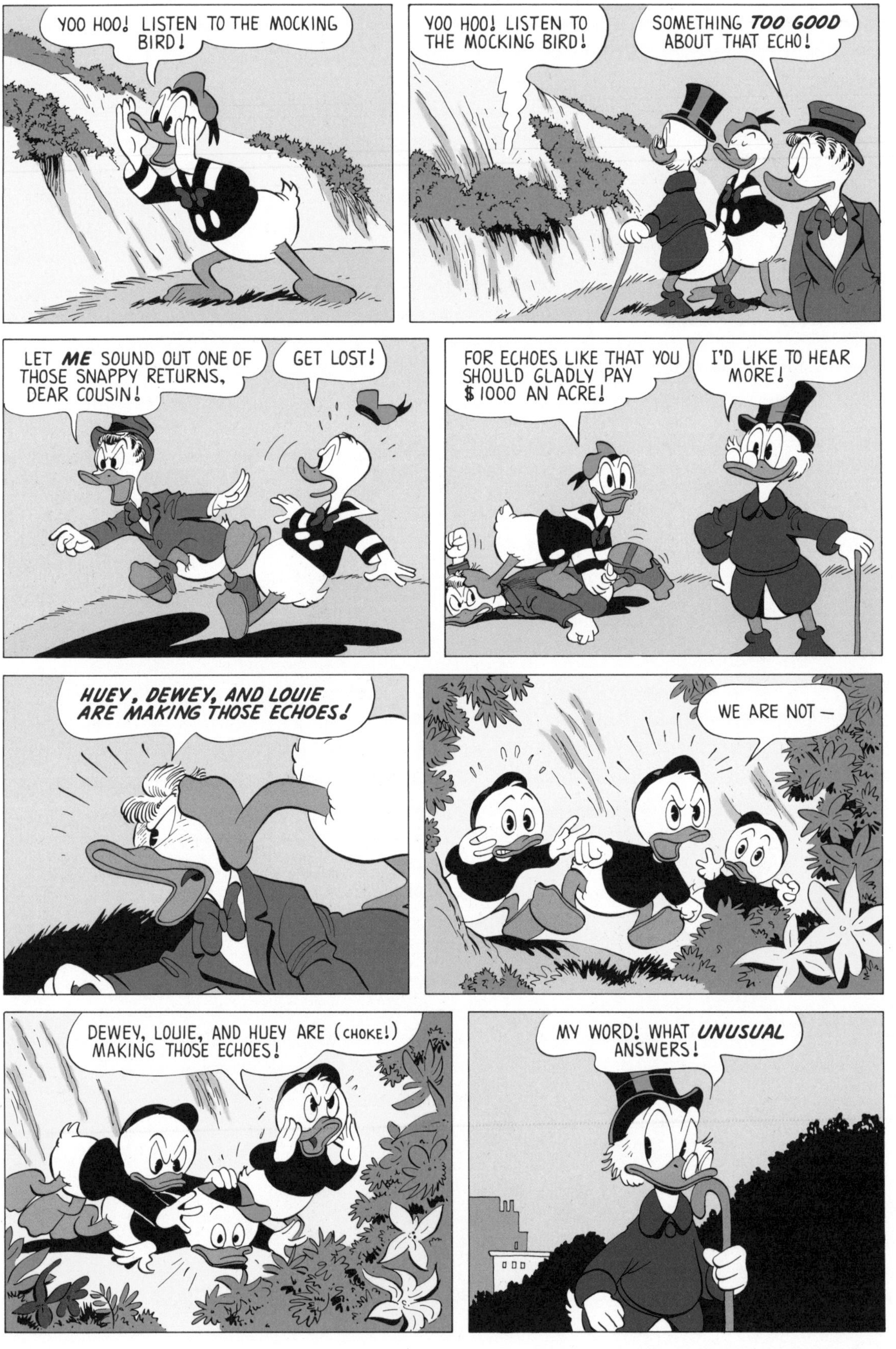
YOO HOO! LISTEN TO THE MOCKING BIRD!
YOO HOO! LISTEN TO THE MOCKING BIRD!
SOMETHING TOO GOOD ABOUT THAT ECHO!
LET ME SOUND OUT ONE OF THOSE SNAPPY RETURNS, DEAR COUSIN!
GET LOST!
FOR ECHOES LIKE THAT YOU SHOULD GLADLY PAY $1000 AN ACRE!
I'D LIKE TO HEAR MORE!
HUEY, DEWEY, AND LOUIE ARE MAKING THOSE ECHOES!
WE ARE NOT—
DEWEY, LOUIE, AND HUEY ARE (CHOKE!) MAKING THOSE ECHOES!
MY WORD! WHAT UNUSUAL ANSWERS!

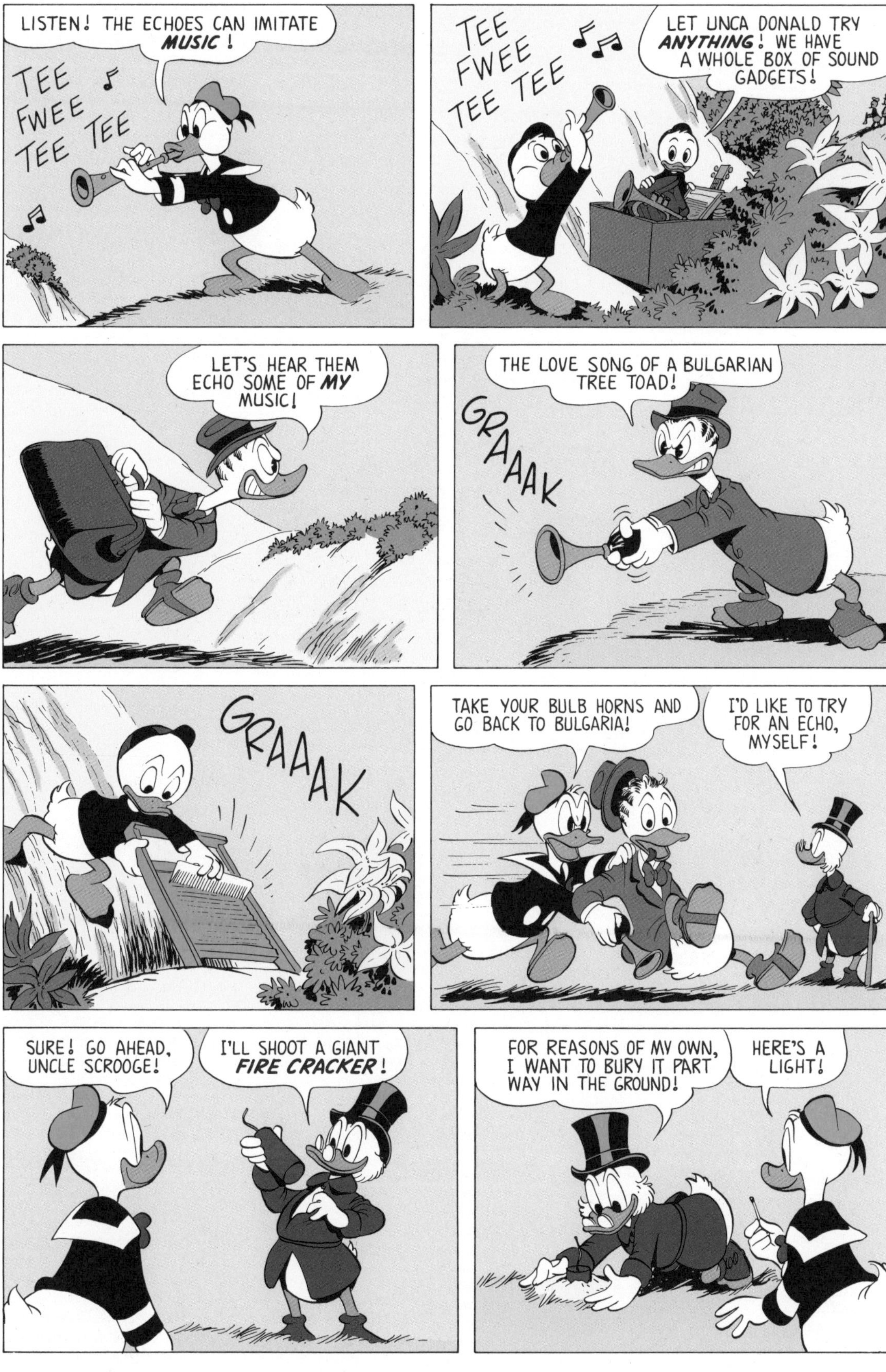
LISTEN! THE ECHOES CAN IMITATE MUSIC!
TEE FWEE TEE TEE
TEE FWEE TEE TEE
LET UNCA DONALD TRY ANYTHING! WE HAVE A WHOLE BOX OF SOUND GADGETS!
LET'S HEAR THEM ECHO SOME OF MY MUSIC!
THE LOVE SONG OF A BULGARIAN TREE TOAD!
GRAAAK
GRAAAK
TAKE YOUR BULB HORNS AND GO BACK TO BULGARIA!
I'D LIKE TO TRY FOR AN ECHO, MYSELF!
SURE! GO AHEAD, UNCLE SCROOGE!
I'LL SHOOT A GIANT FIRE CRACKER!
FOR REASONS OF MY OWN, I WANT TO BURY IT PART WAY IN THE GROUND!
HERE'S A LIGHT!

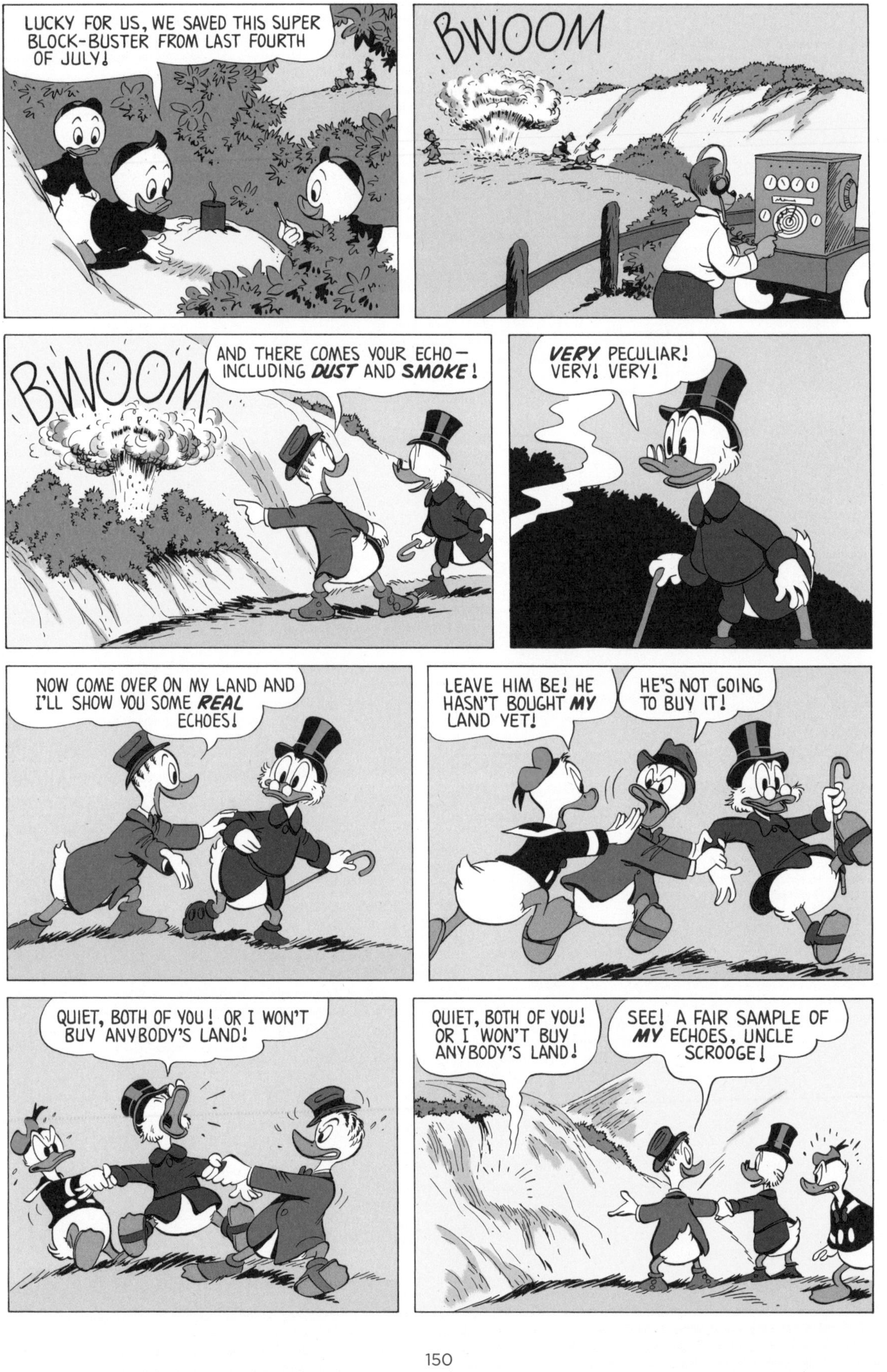
LUCKY FOR US, WE SAVED THIS SUPER BLOCK-BUSTER FROM LAST FOURTH OF JULY!
BWOOM
BWOOM
AND THERE COMES YOUR ECHO— INCLUDING DUST AND SMOKE!
VERY PECULIAR! VERY! VERY!
NOW COME OVER ON MY LAND AND I'LL SHOW YOU SOME REAL ECHOES!
LEAVE HIM BE! HE HASN'T BOUGHT MY LAND YET!
HE'S NOT GOING TO BUY IT!
QUIET, BOTH OF YOU! OR I WON'T BUY ANYBODY'S LAND!
QUIET, BOTH OF YOU! OR I WON'T BUY ANYBODY'S LAND!
SEE! A FAIR SAMPLE OF MY ECHOES, UNCLE SCROOGE!

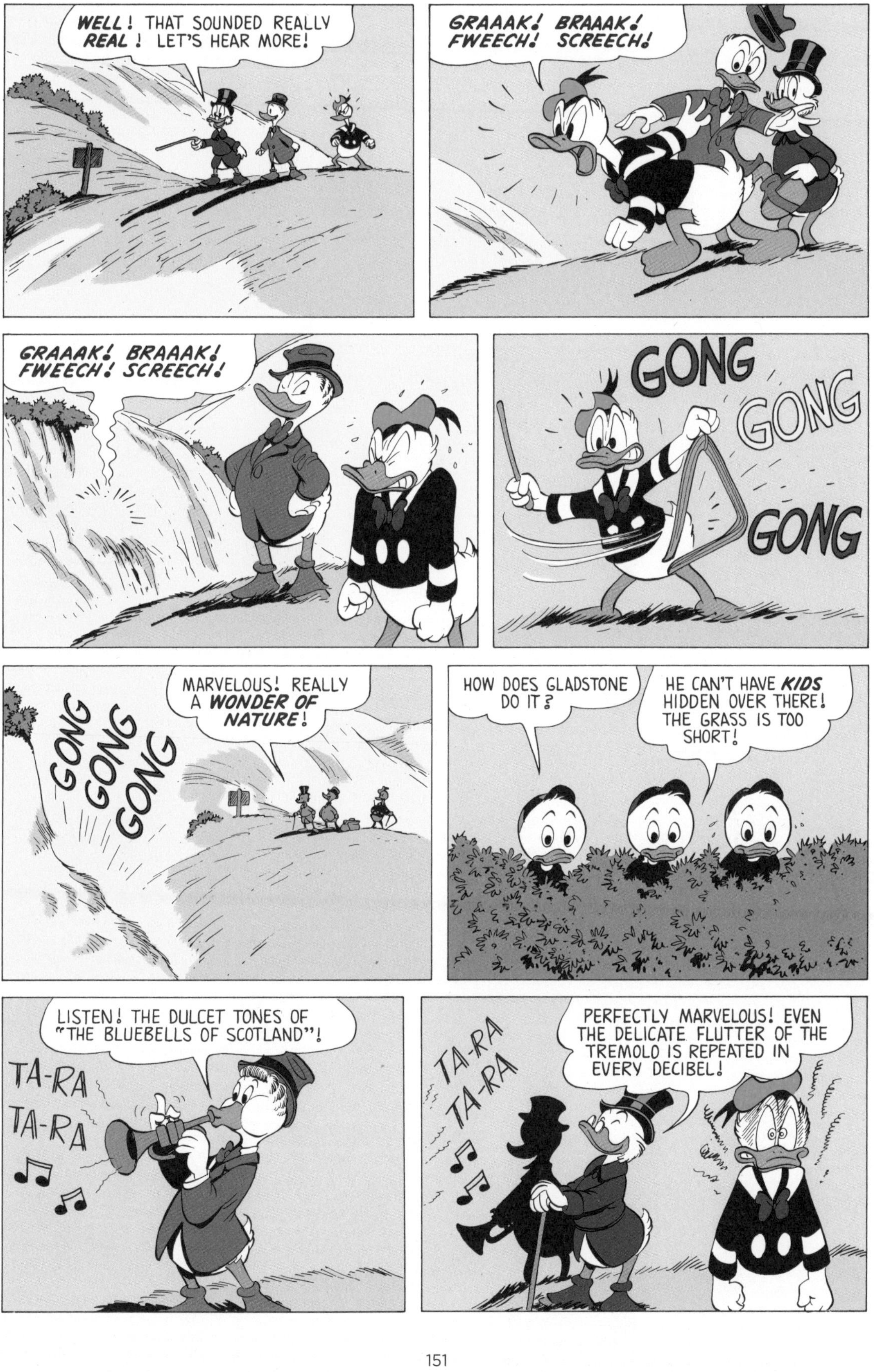
WELL! THAT SOUNDED REALLY REAL! LET'S HEAR MORE!
GRAAAK! BRAAAK! FWEECH! SCREECH!
GRAAAK! BRAAAK! FWEECH! SCREECH!
GONG
GONG
GONG
GONG GONG GONG
MARVELOUS! REALLY A WONDER OF NATURE!
HOW DOES GLADSTONE DO IT?
HE CAN'T HAVE KIDS HIDDEN OVER THERE! THE GRASS IS TOO SHORT!
LISTEN! THE DULCET TONES OF "THE BLUEBELLS OF SCOTLAND"!
TA-RA TA-RA
TA-RA TA-RA
PERFECTLY MARVELOUS! EVEN THE DELICATE FLUTTER OF THE TREMOLO IS REPEATED IN EVERY DECIBEL!

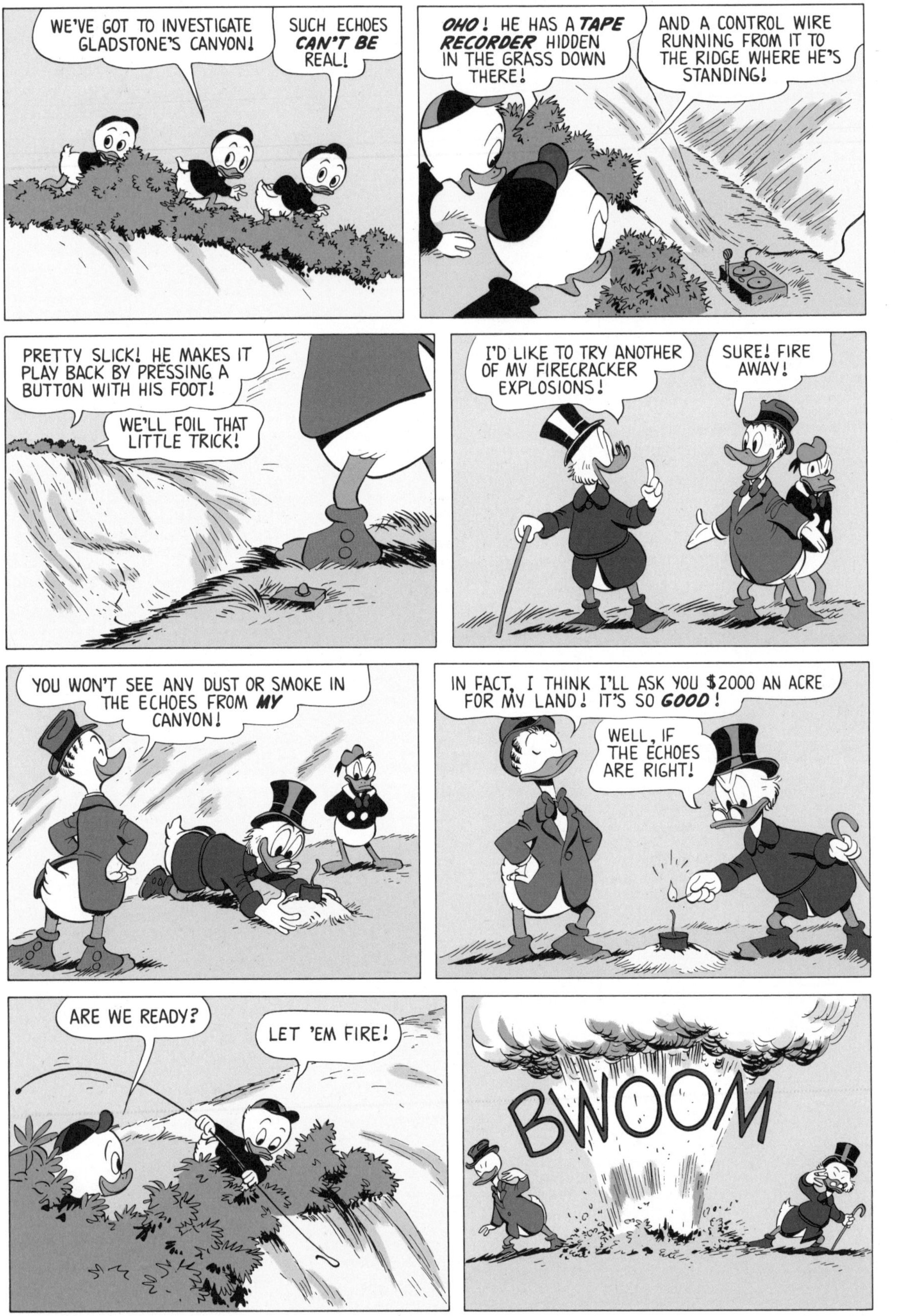
WE'VE GOT TO INVESTIGATE GLADSTONE'S CANYON!
SUCH ECHOES CAN'T BE REAL!
OHO! HE HAS A TAPE RECORDER HIDDEN IN THE GRASS DOWN THERE!
AND A CONTROL WIRE RUNNING FROM IT TO THE RIDGE WHERE HE'S STANDING!
PRETTY SLICK! HE MAKES IT PLAY BACK BY PRESSING A BUTTON WITH HIS FOOT!
WE'LL FOIL THAT LITTLE TRICK!
I'D LIKE TO TRY ANOTHER OF MY FIRECRACKER EXPLOSIONS!
SURE! FIRE AWAY!
YOU WON'T SEE ANY DUST OR SMOKE IN THE ECHOES FROM MY CANYON!
IN FACT, I THINK I'LL ASK YOU $2000 AN ACRE FOR MY LAND! IT'S SO GOOD!
WELL, IF THE ECHOES ARE RIGHT!
ARE WE READY?
LET 'EM FIRE!
BWOOM

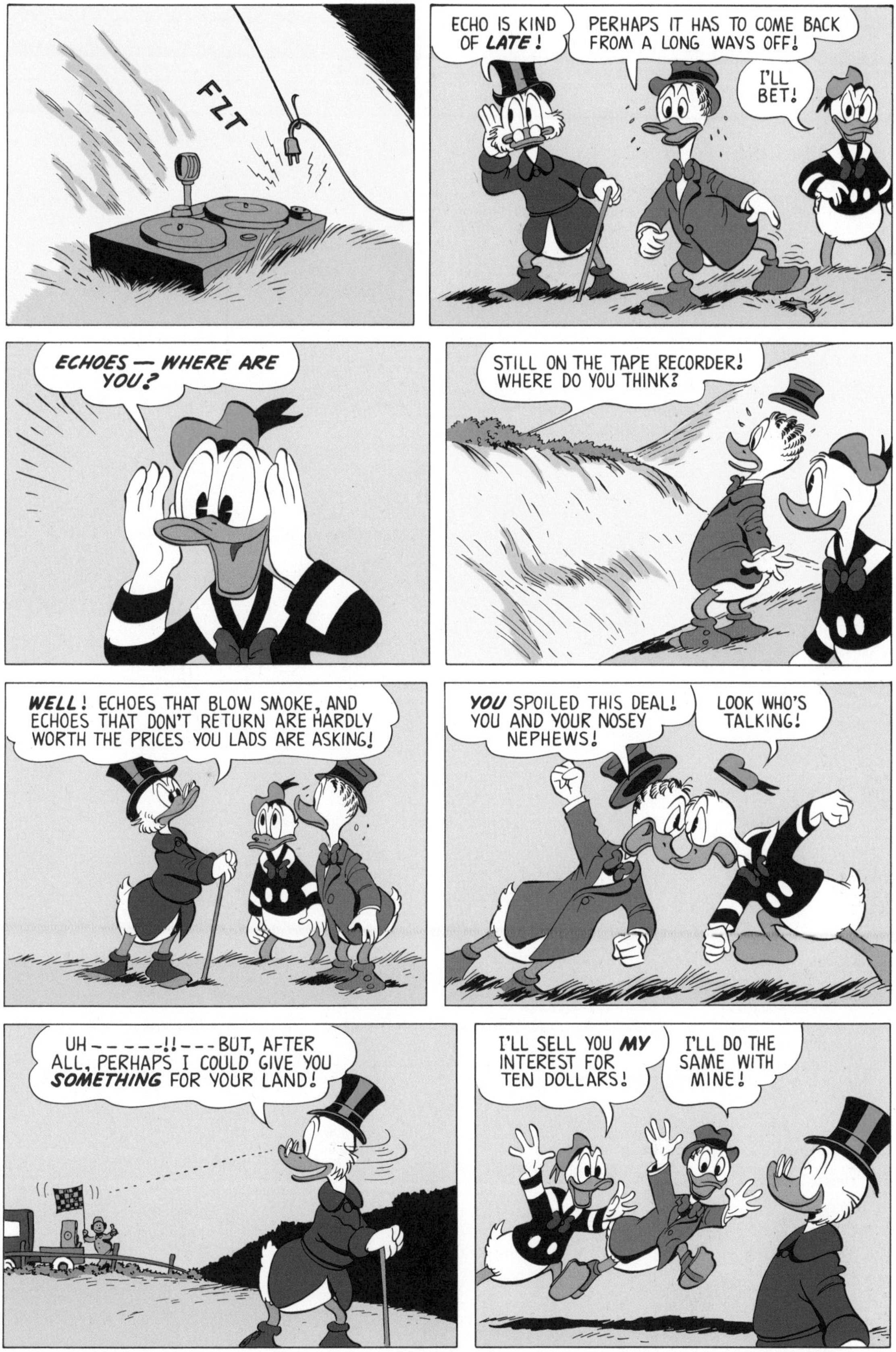
FZT
ECHO IS KIND OF LATE!
PERHAPS IT HAS TO COME BACK FROM A LONG WAYS OFF!
I'LL BET!
ECHOES — WHERE ARE YOU?
STILL ON THE TAPE RECORDER! WHERE DO YOU THINK?
WELL! ECHOES THAT BLOW SMOKE, AND ECHOES THAT DON'T RETURN ARE HARDLY WORTH THE PRICES YOU LADS ARE ASKING!
YOU SPOILED THIS DEAL! YOU AND YOUR NOSEY NEPHEWS!
LOOK WHO'S TALKING!
UH -----!!---BUT, AFTER ALL, PERHAPS I COULD GIVE YOU SOMETHING FOR YOUR LAND!
I'LL SELL YOU MY INTEREST FOR TEN DOLLARS!
I'LL DO THE SAME WITH MINE!

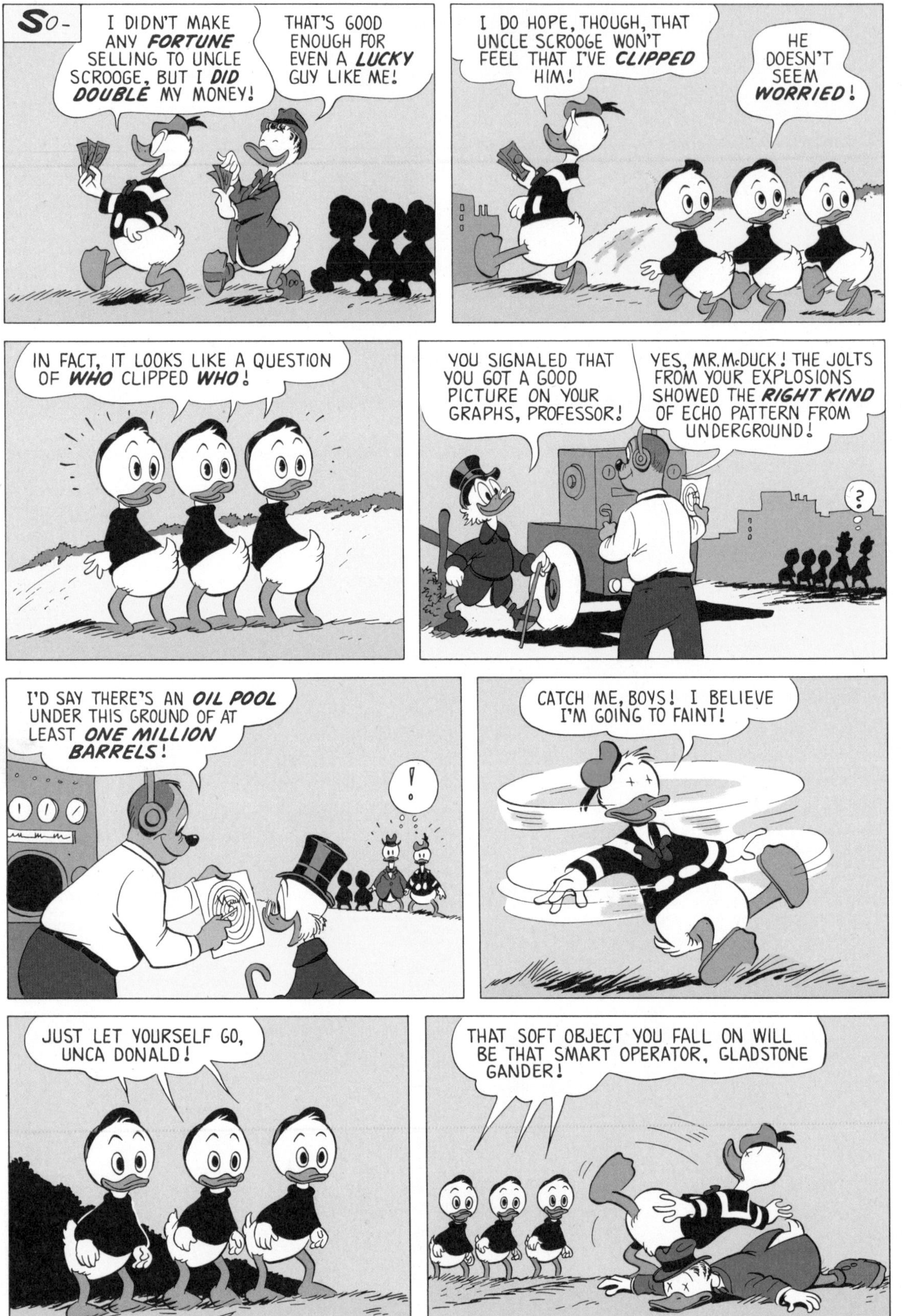

SO-
I DIDN'T MAKE ANY FORTUNE SELLING TO UNCLE SCROOGE, BUT I DID DOUBLE MY MONEY!
THAT'S GOOD ENOUGH FOR EVEN A LUCKY GUY LIKE ME!
I DO HOPE, THOUGH, THAT UNCLE SCROOGE WON'T FEEL THAT I'VE CLIPPED HIM!
HE DOESN'T SEEM WORRIED!
IN FACT, IT LOOKS LIKE A QUESTION OF WHO CLIPPED WHO!
YOU SIGNALED THAT YOU GOT A GOOD PICTURE ON YOUR GRAPHS, PROFESSOR!
YES, MR. McDUCK! THE JOLTS FROM YOUR EXPLOSIONS SHOWED THE RIGHT KIND OF ECHO PATTERN FROM UNDERGROUND!
?
I'D SAY THERE'S AN OIL POOL UNDER THIS GROUND OF AT LEAST ONE MILLION BARRELS!
!
CATCH ME, BOYS! I BELIEVE I'M GOING TO FAINT!
JUST LET YOURSELF GO, UNCA DONALD!
THAT SOFT OBJECT YOU FALL ON WILL BE THAT SMART OPERATOR, GLADSTONE GANDER!

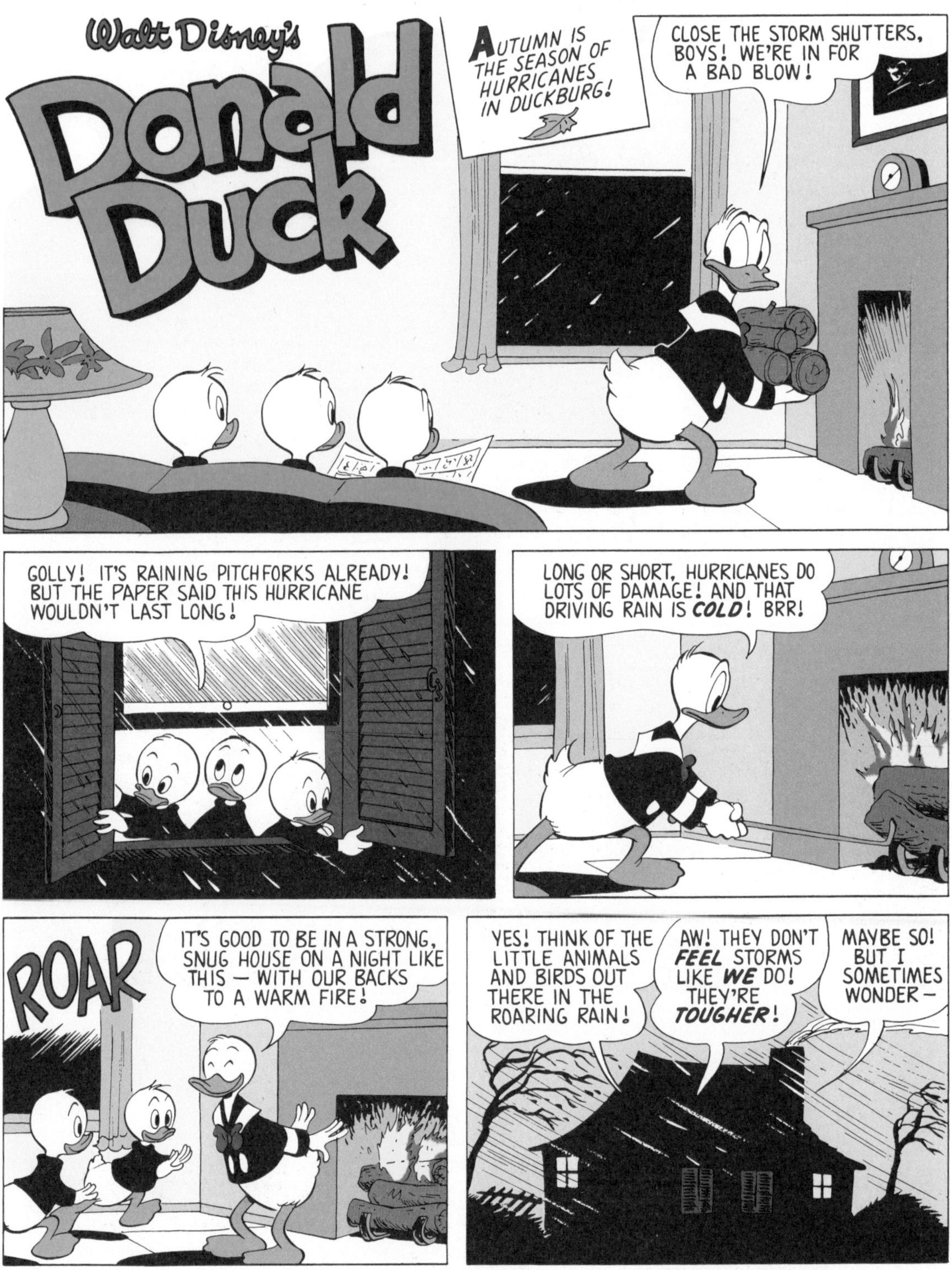
Walt Disney's
Donald Duck
AUTUMN IS THE SEASON OF HURRICANES IN DUCKBURG!
CLOSE THE STORM SHUTTERS, BOYS! WE'RE IN FOR A BAD BLOW!
GOLLY! IT'S RAINING PITCHFORKS ALREADY! BUT THE PAPER SAID THIS HURRICANE WOULDN'T LAST LONG!
LONG OR SHORT, HURRICANES DO LOTS OF DAMAGE! AND THAT DRIVING RAIN IS COLD! BRR!
ROAR
IT'S GOOD TO BE IN A STRONG, SNUG HOUSE ON A NIGHT LIKE THIS — WITH OUR BACKS TO A WARM FIRE!
YES! THINK OF THE LITTLE ANIMALS AND BIRDS OUT THERE IN THE ROARING RAIN!
AW! THEY DON'T FEEL STORMS LIKE WE DO! THEY'RE TOUGHER!
MAYBE SO! BUT I SOMETIMES WONDER—

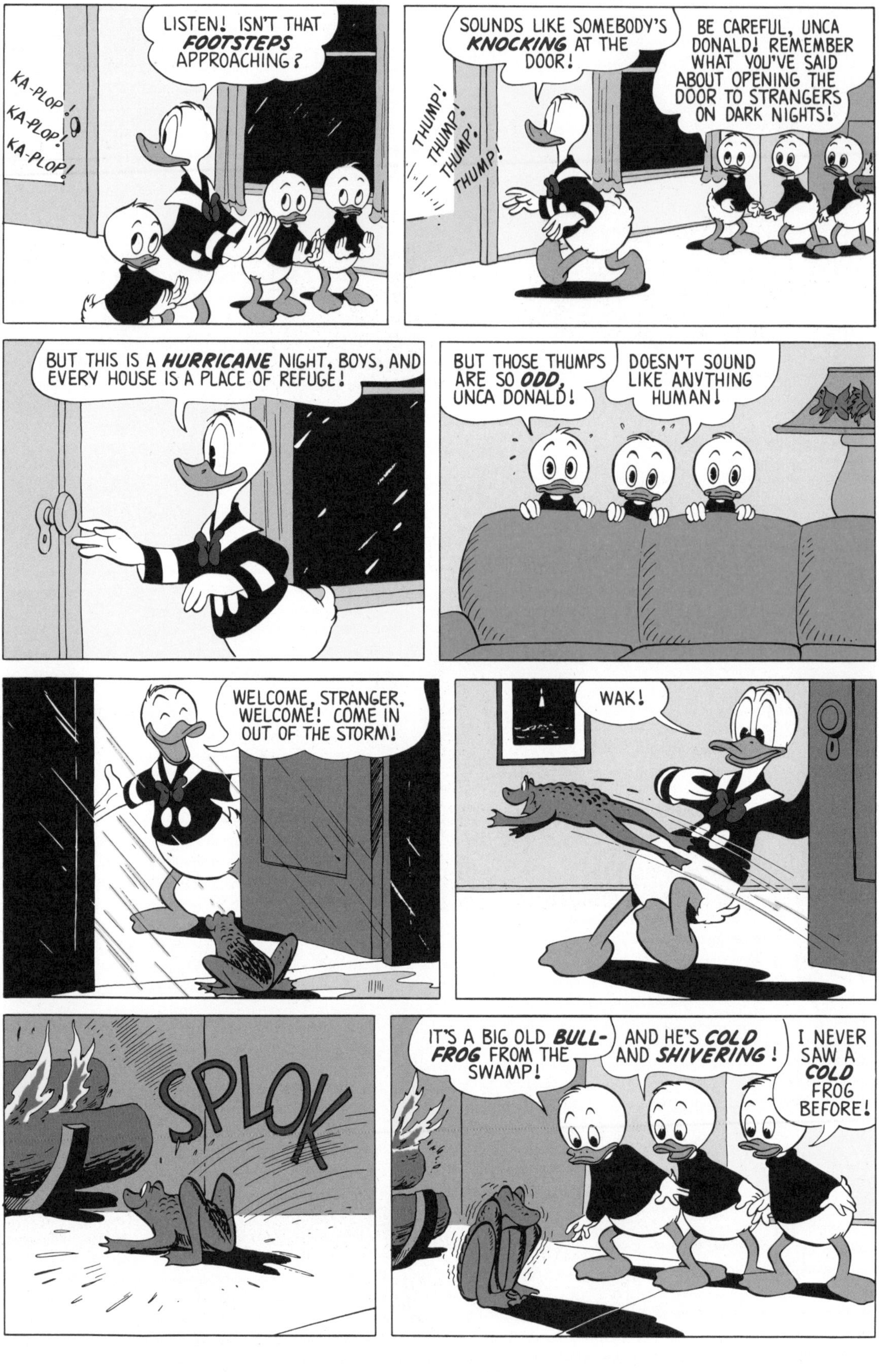

LISTEN! ISN'T THAT FOOTSTEPS APPROACHING?
KA-PLOP! KA-PLOP! KA-PLOP!
SOUNDS LIKE SOMEBODY'S KNOCKING AT THE DOOR!
BE CAREFUL, UNCA DONALD! REMEMBER WHAT YOU'VE SAID ABOUT OPENING THE DOOR TO STRANGERS ON DARK NIGHTS!
THUMP! THUMP! THUMP! THUMP!
BUT THIS IS A HURRICANE NIGHT, BOYS, AND EVERY HOUSE IS A PLACE OF REFUGE!
BUT THOSE THUMPS ARE SO ODD, UNCA DONALD!
DOESN'T SOUND LIKE ANYTHING HUMAN!
WELCOME, STRANGER, WELCOME! COME IN OUT OF THE STORM!
WAK!
SPLOK
IT'S A BIG OLD BULL-FROG FROM THE SWAMP!
AND HE'S COLD AND SHIVERING!
I NEVER SAW A COLD FROG BEFORE!

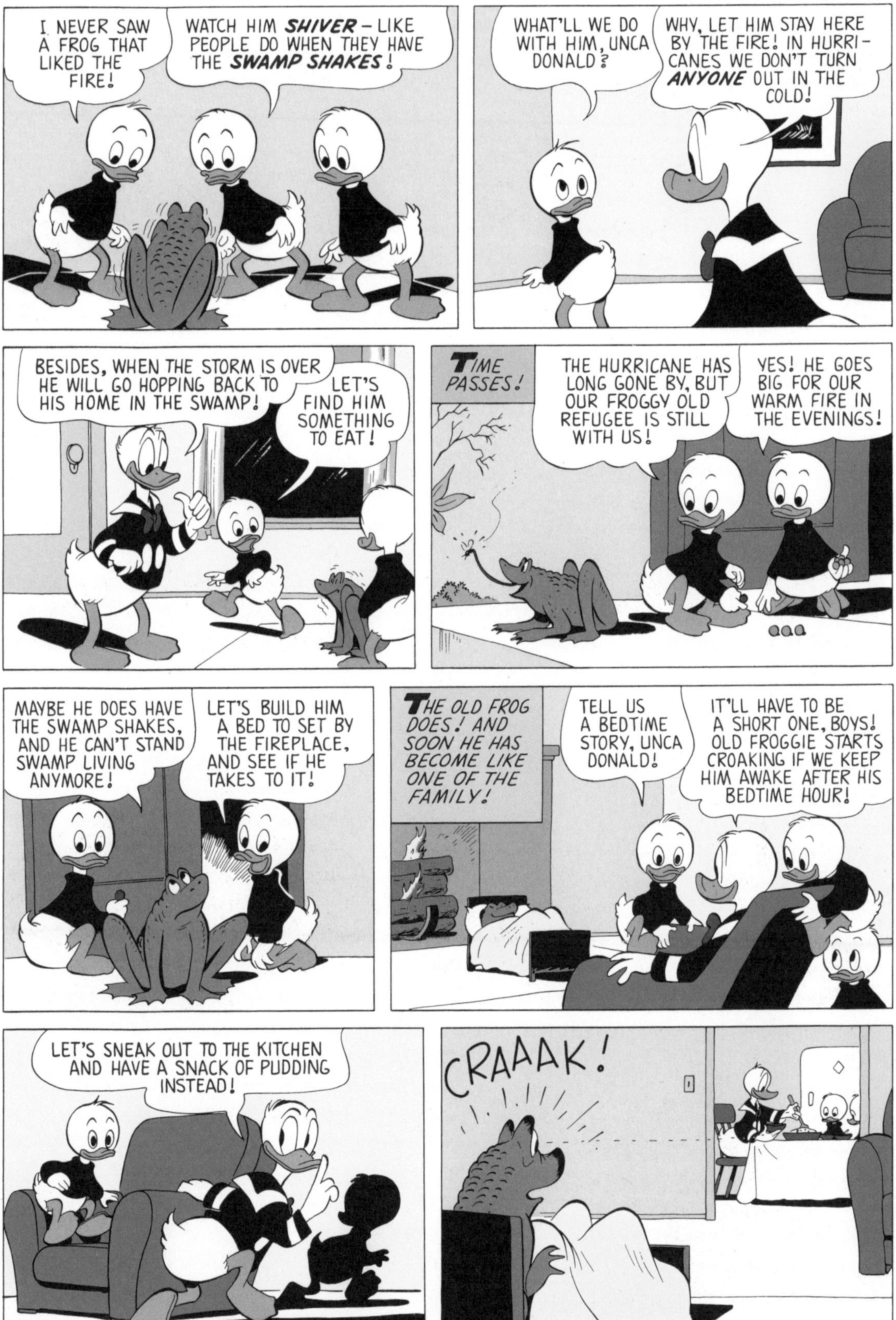
I NEVER SAW A FROG THAT LIKED THE FIRE!
WATCH HIM SHIVER – LIKE PEOPLE DO WHEN THEY HAVE THE SWAMP SHAKES!
WHAT'LL WE DO WITH HIM, UNCA DONALD?
WHY, LET HIM STAY HERE BY THE FIRE! IN HURRICANES WE DON'T TURN ANYONE OUT IN THE COLD!
BESIDES, WHEN THE STORM IS OVER HE WILL GO HOPPING BACK TO HIS HOME IN THE SWAMP!
LET'S FIND HIM SOMETHING TO EAT!
TIME PASSES!
THE HURRICANE HAS LONG GONE BY, BUT OUR FROGGY OLD REFUGEE IS STILL WITH US!
YES! HE GOES BIG FOR OUR WARM FIRE IN THE EVENINGS!
MAYBE HE DOES HAVE THE SWAMP SHAKES, AND HE CAN'T STAND SWAMP LIVING ANYMORE!
LET'S BUILD HIM A BED TO SET BY THE FIREPLACE, AND SEE IF HE TAKES TO IT!
THE OLD FROG DOES! AND SOON HE HAS BECOME LIKE ONE OF THE FAMILY!
TELL US A BEDTIME STORY, UNCA DONALD!
IT'LL HAVE TO BE A SHORT ONE, BOYS! OLD FROGGIE STARTS CROAKING IF WE KEEP HIM AWAKE AFTER HIS BEDTIME HOUR!
LET'S SNEAK OUT TO THE KITCHEN AND HAVE A SNACK OF PUDDING INSTEAD!
CRAAAK!

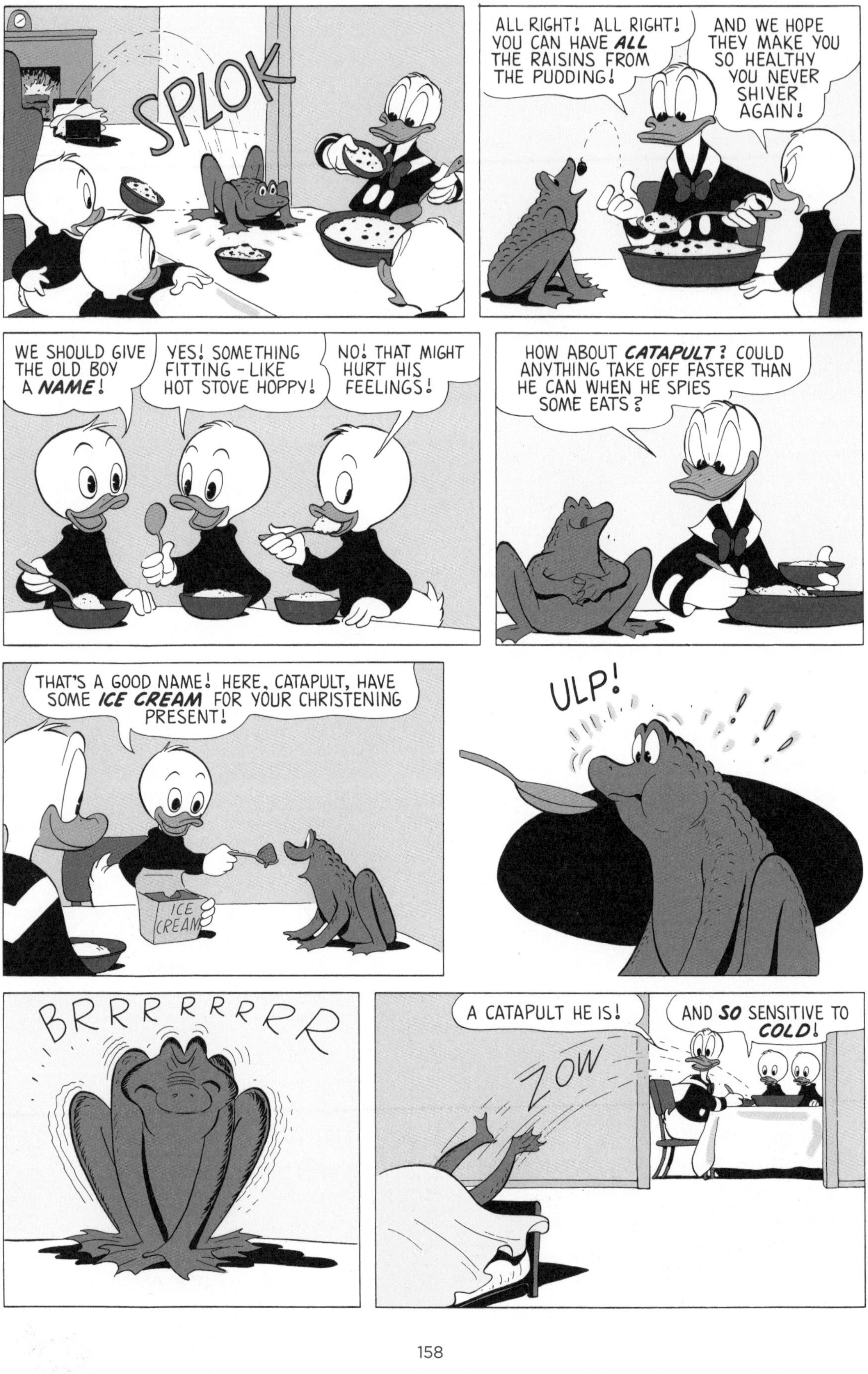

SPLOK
ALL RIGHT! ALL RIGHT! YOU CAN HAVE ALL THE RAISINS FROM THE PUDDING!
AND WE HOPE THEY MAKE YOU SO HEALTHY YOU NEVER SHIVER AGAIN!
WE SHOULD GIVE THE OLD BOY A NAME!
YES! SOMETHING FITTING - LIKE HOT STOVE HOPPY!
NO! THAT MIGHT HURT HIS FEELINGS!
HOW ABOUT CATAPULT? COULD ANYTHING TAKE OFF FASTER THAN HE CAN WHEN HE SPIES SOME EATS?
THAT'S A GOOD NAME! HERE, CATAPULT, HAVE SOME ICE CREAM FOR YOUR CHRISTENING PRESENT!
ICE CREAM
ULP!
BRRRRRRRR
A CATAPULT HE IS!
AND SO SENSITIVE TO COLD!
ZOW

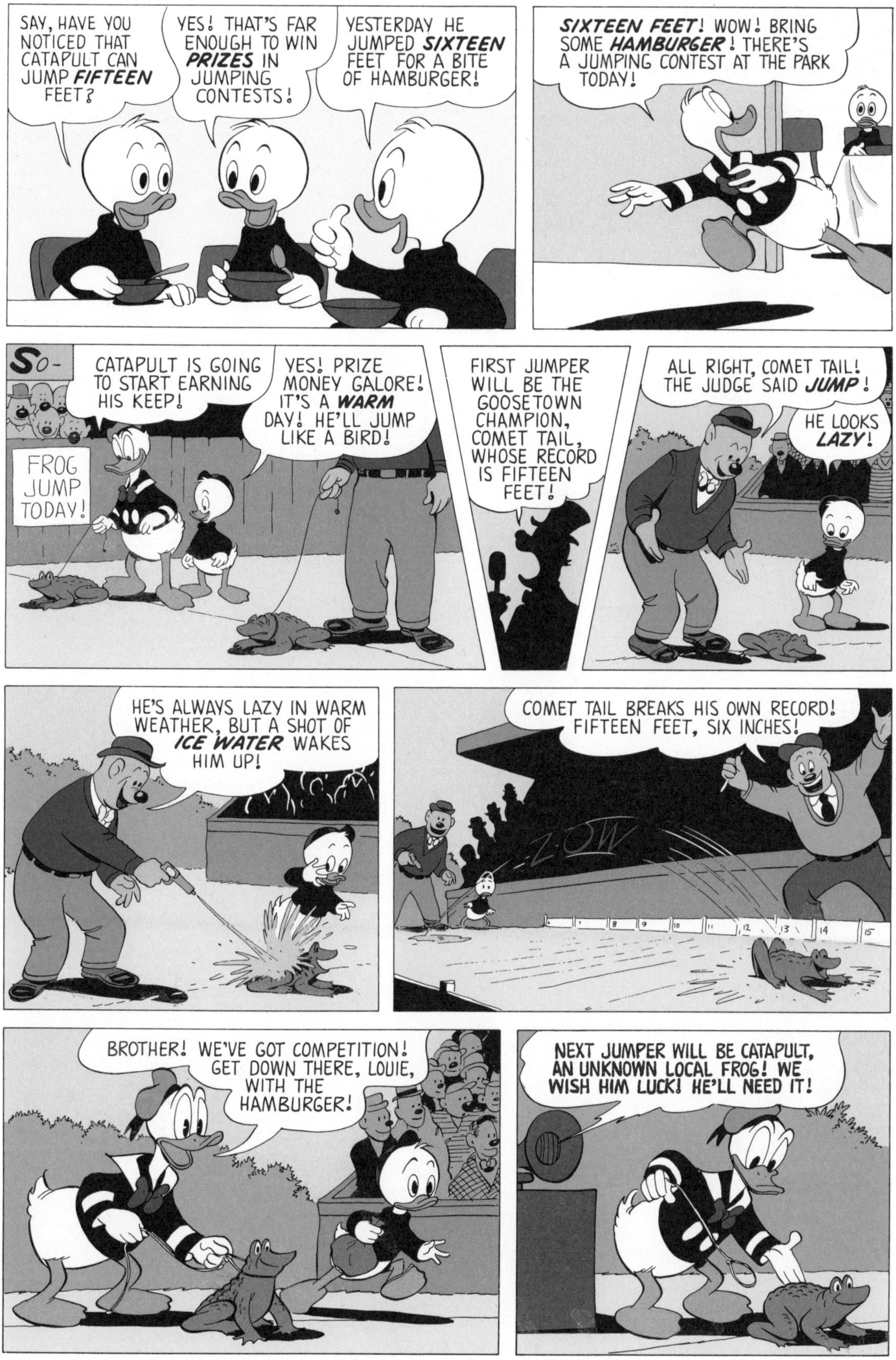
SAY, HAVE YOU NOTICED THAT CATAPULT CAN JUMP FIFTEEN FEET?
YES! THAT'S FAR ENOUGH TO WIN PRIZES IN JUMPING CONTESTS!
YESTERDAY HE JUMPED SIXTEEN FEET FOR A BITE OF HAMBURGER!
SIXTEEN FEET! WOW! BRING SOME HAMBURGER! THERE'S A JUMPING CONTEST AT THE PARK TODAY!
SO-
CATAPULT IS GOING TO START EARNING HIS KEEP!
YES! PRIZE MONEY GALORE! IT'S A WARM DAY! HE'LL JUMP LIKE A BIRD!
FROG JUMP TODAY!
FIRST JUMPER WILL BE THE GOOSETOWN CHAMPION, COMET TAIL, WHOSE RECORD IS FIFTEEN FEET!
ALL RIGHT, COMET TAIL! THE JUDGE SAID JUMP!
HE LOOKS LAZY!
HE'S ALWAYS LAZY IN WARM WEATHER, BUT A SHOT OF ICE WATER WAKES HIM UP!
COMET TAIL BREAKS HIS OWN RECORD! FIFTEEN FEET, SIX INCHES!
Z-O-W
BROTHER! WE'VE GOT COMPETITION! GET DOWN THERE, LOUIE, WITH THE HAMBURGER!
NEXT JUMPER WILL BE CATAPULT, AN UNKNOWN LOCAL FROG! WE WISH HIM LUCK! HE'LL NEED IT!

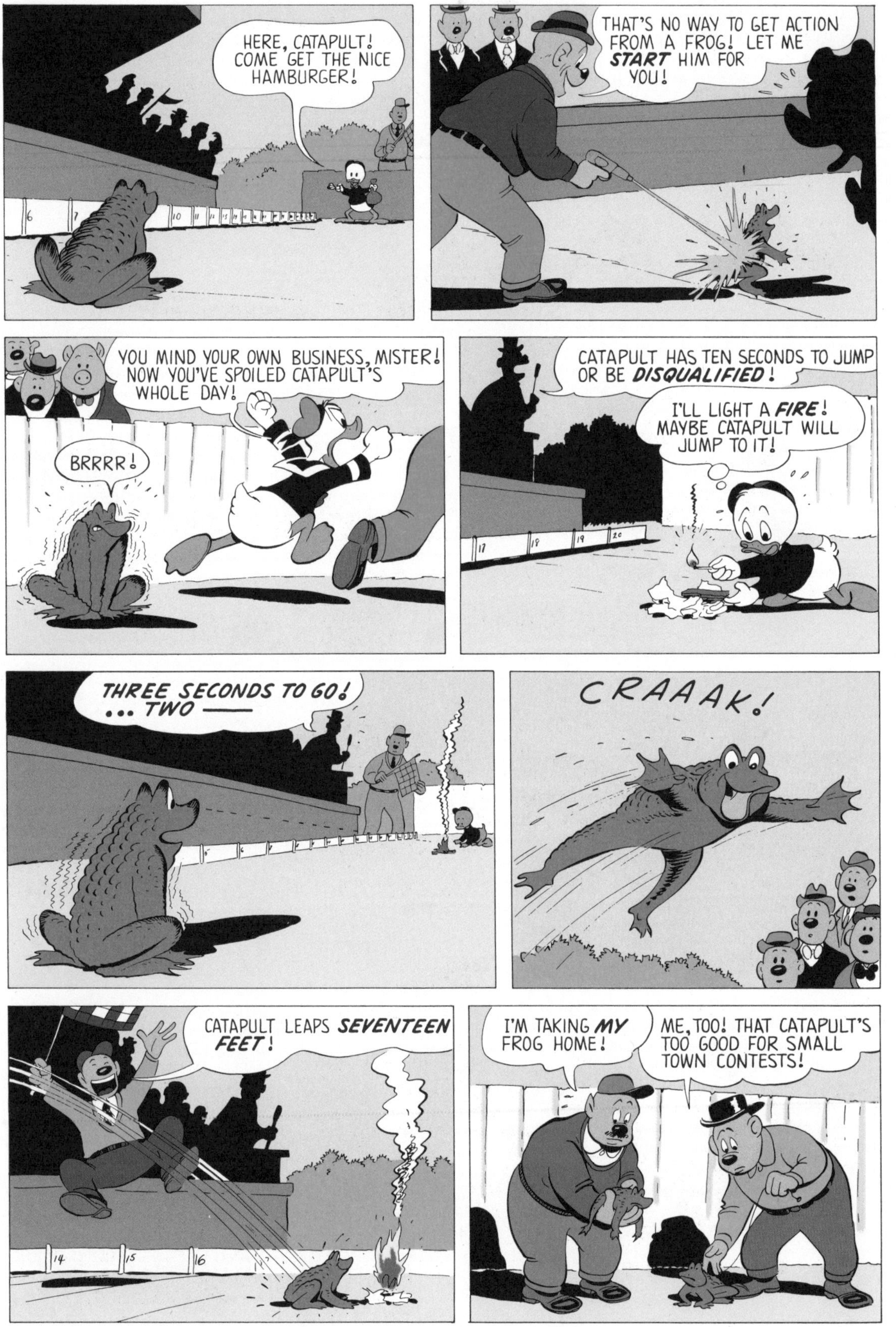
HERE, CATAPULT! COME GET THE NICE HAMBURGER!
THAT'S NO WAY TO GET ACTION FROM A FROG! LET ME START HIM FOR YOU!
YOU MIND YOUR OWN BUSINESS, MISTER! NOW YOU'VE SPOILED CATAPULT'S WHOLE DAY!
BRRRR!
CATAPULT HAS TEN SECONDS TO JUMP OR BE DISQUALIFIED!
I'LL LIGHT A FIRE! MAYBE CATAPULT WILL JUMP TO IT!
THREE SECONDS TO GO! ... TWO ——
CRAAAK!
CATAPULT LEAPS SEVENTEEN FEET!
I'M TAKING MY FROG HOME!
ME, TOO! THAT CATAPULT'S TOO GOOD FOR SMALL TOWN CONTESTS!

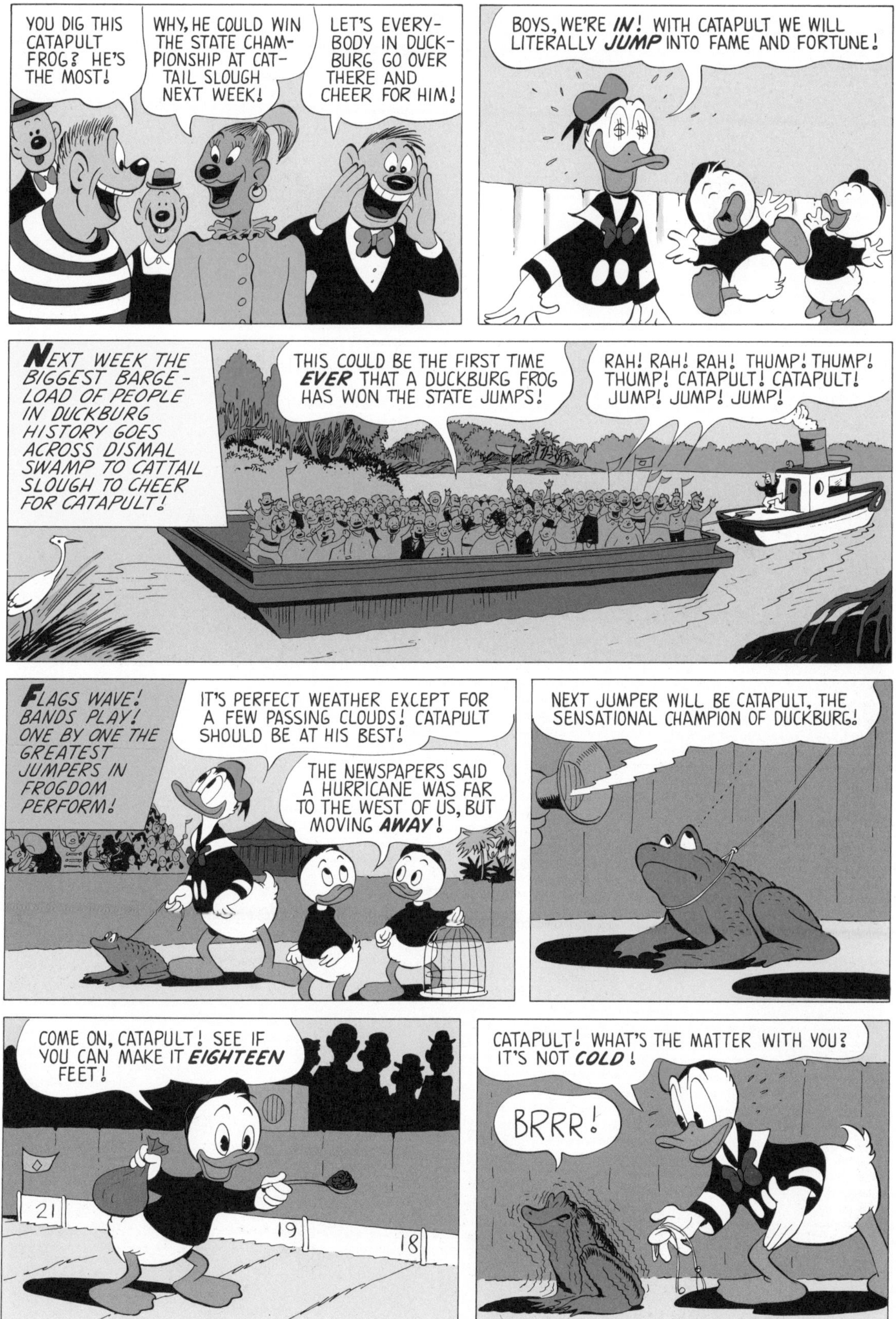
YOU DIG THIS CATAPULT FROG? HE'S THE MOST!
WHY, HE COULD WIN THE STATE CHAMPIONSHIP AT CATTAIL SLOUGH NEXT WEEK!
LET'S EVERYBODY IN DUCKBURG GO OVER THERE AND CHEER FOR HIM!
BOYS, WE'RE IN! WITH CATAPULT WE WILL LITERALLY JUMP INTO FAME AND FORTUNE!
NEXT WEEK THE BIGGEST BARGE-LOAD OF PEOPLE IN DUCKBURG HISTORY GOES ACROSS DISMAL SWAMP TO CATTAIL SLOUGH TO CHEER FOR CATAPULT!
THIS COULD BE THE FIRST TIME EVER THAT A DUCKBURG FROG HAS WON THE STATE JUMPS!
RAH! RAH! RAH! THUMP! THUMP! THUMP! CATAPULT! CATAPULT! JUMP! JUMP! JUMP!
FLAGS WAVE! BANDS PLAY! ONE BY ONE THE GREATEST JUMPERS IN FROGDOM PERFORM!
IT'S PERFECT WEATHER EXCEPT FOR A FEW PASSING CLOUDS! CATAPULT SHOULD BE AT HIS BEST!
THE NEWSPAPERS SAID A HURRICANE WAS FAR TO THE WEST OF US, BUT MOVING AWAY!
NEXT JUMPER WILL BE CATAPULT, THE SENSATIONAL CHAMPION OF DUCKBURG!
COME ON, CATAPULT! SEE IF YOU CAN MAKE IT EIGHTEEN FEET!
21
19
18
CATAPULT! WHAT'S THE MATTER WITH YOU? IT'S NOT COLD!
BRRR!

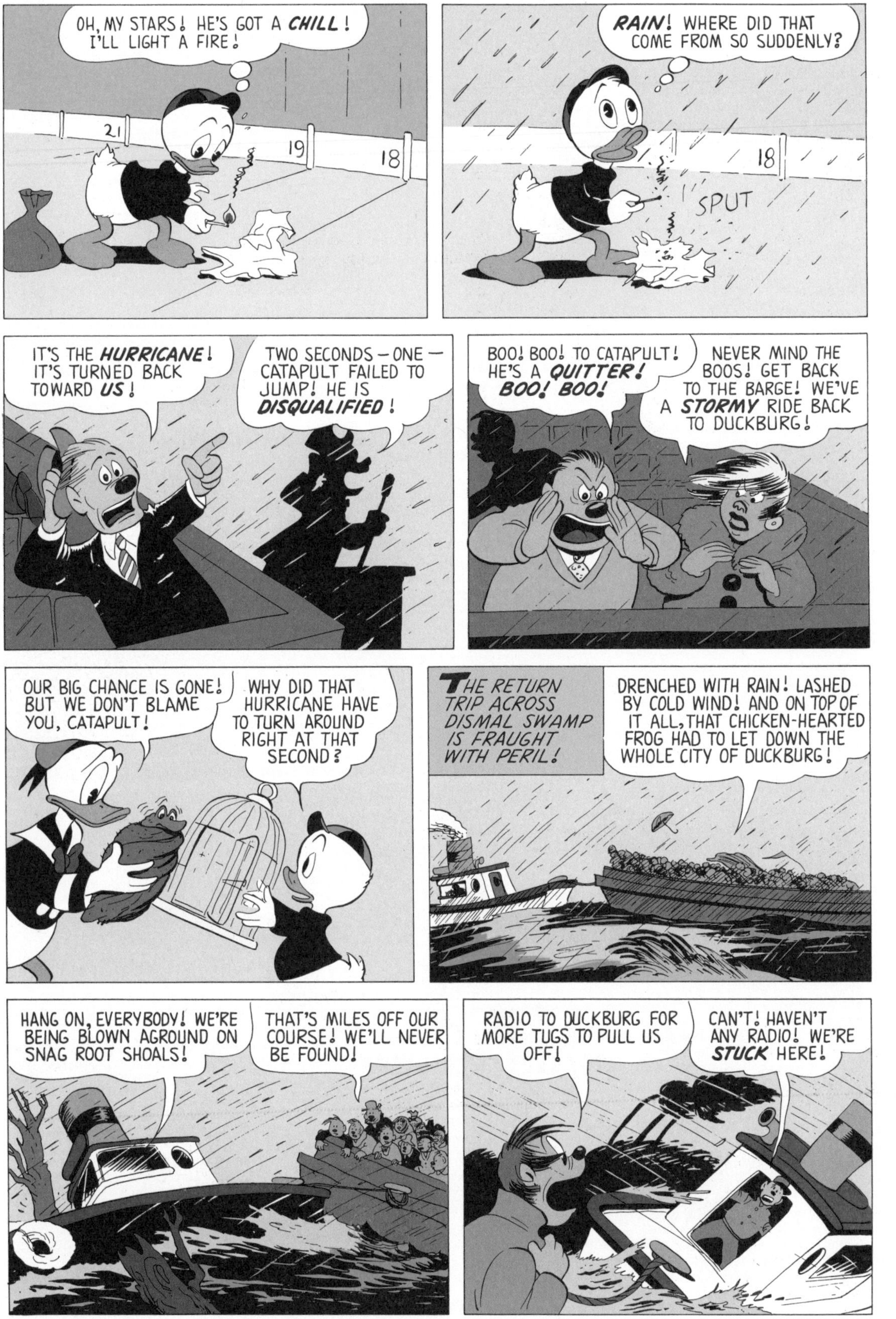
OH, MY STARS! HE'S GOT A CHILL! I'LL LIGHT A FIRE!
21
19
18
RAIN! WHERE DID THAT COME FROM SO SUDDENLY?
18
SPUT
IT'S THE HURRICANE! IT'S TURNED BACK TOWARD US!
TWO SECONDS – ONE – CATAPULT FAILED TO JUMP! HE IS DISQUALIFIED!
BOO! BOO! TO CATAPULT! HE'S A QUITTER! BOO! BOO!
NEVER MIND THE BOOS! GET BACK TO THE BARGE! WE'VE A STORMY RIDE BACK TO DUCKBURG!
OUR BIG CHANCE IS GONE! BUT WE DON'T BLAME YOU, CATAPULT!
WHY DID THAT HURRICANE HAVE TO TURN AROUND RIGHT AT THAT SECOND?
THE RETURN TRIP ACROSS DISMAL SWAMP IS FRAUGHT WITH PERIL!
DRENCHED WITH RAIN! LASHED BY COLD WIND! AND ON TOP OF IT ALL, THAT CHICKEN-HEARTED FROG HAD TO LET DOWN THE WHOLE CITY OF DUCKBURG!
HANG ON, EVERYBODY! WE'RE BEING BLOWN AGROUND ON SNAG ROOT SHOALS!
THAT'S MILES OFF OUR COURSE! WE'LL NEVER BE FOUND!
RADIO TO DUCKBURG FOR MORE TUGS TO PULL US OFF!
CAN'T! HAVEN'T ANY RADIO! WE'RE STUCK HERE!

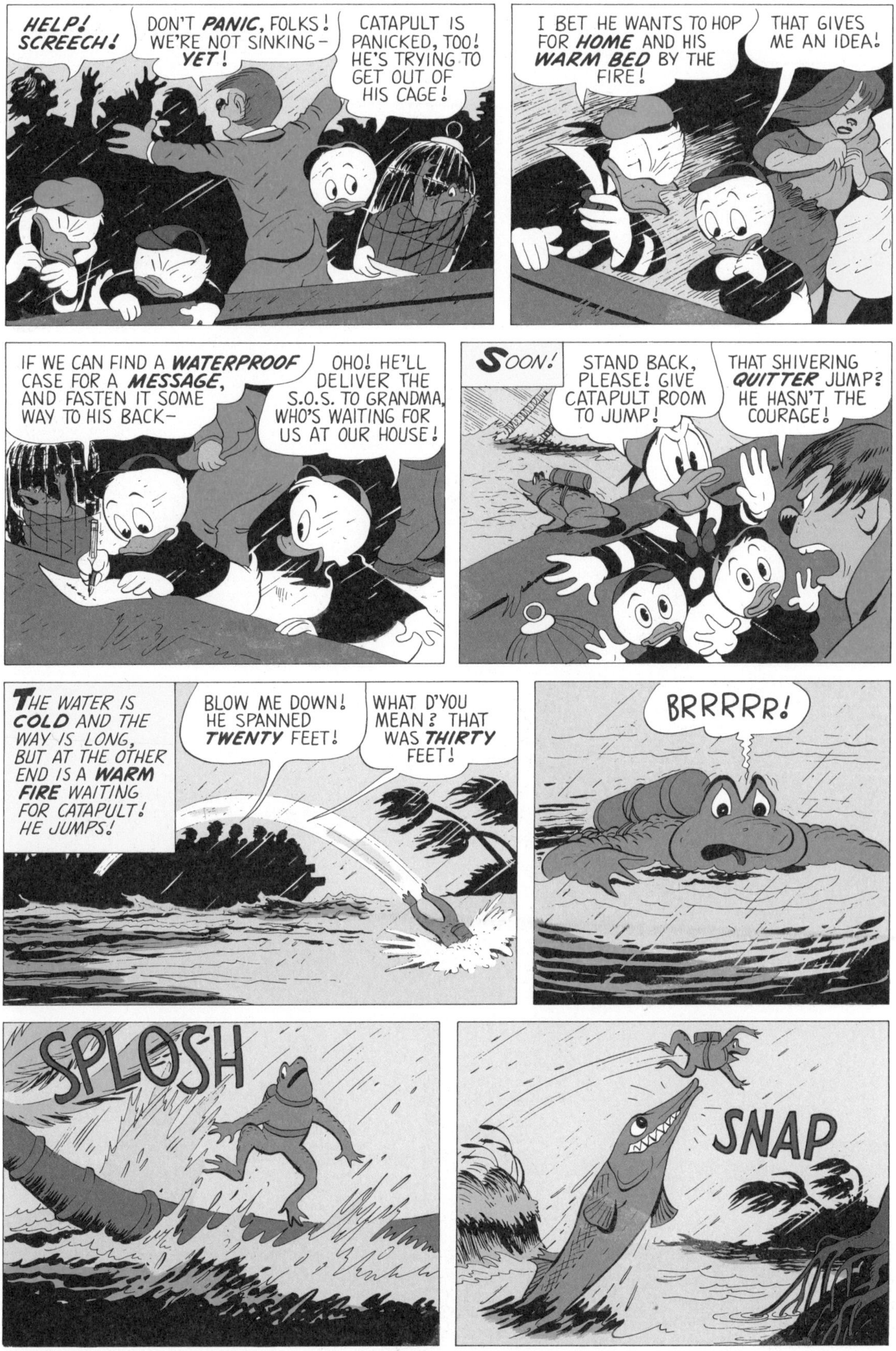
HELP! SCREECH!
DON'T PANIC, FOLKS! WE'RE NOT SINKING– YET!
CATAPULT IS PANICKED, TOO! HE'S TRYING TO GET OUT OF HIS CAGE!
I BET HE WANTS TO HOP FOR HOME AND HIS WARM BED BY THE FIRE!
THAT GIVES ME AN IDEA!
IF WE CAN FIND A WATERPROOF CASE FOR A MESSAGE, AND FASTEN IT SOME WAY TO HIS BACK–
OHO! HE'LL DELIVER THE S.O.S. TO GRANDMA, WHO'S WAITING FOR US AT OUR HOUSE!
SOON!
STAND BACK, PLEASE! GIVE CATAPULT ROOM TO JUMP!
THAT SHIVERING QUITTER JUMP? HE HASN'T THE COURAGE!
THE WATER IS COLD AND THE WAY IS LONG, BUT AT THE OTHER END IS A WARM FIRE WAITING FOR CATAPULT! HE JUMPS!
BLOW ME DOWN! HE SPANNED TWENTY FEET!
WHAT D'YOU MEAN? THAT WAS THIRTY FEET!
BRRRRR!
SPLOSH
SNAP

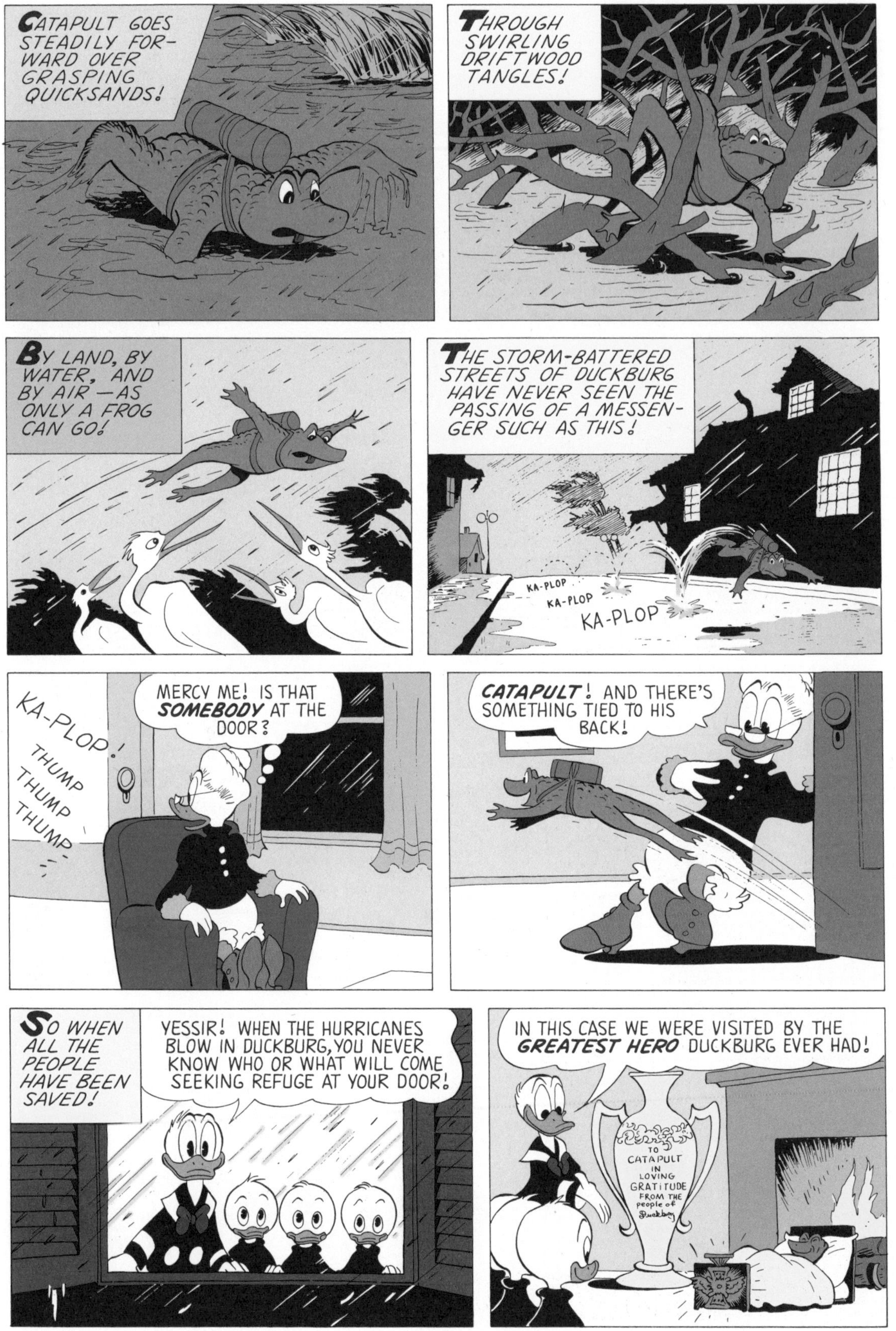
CATAPULT GOES STEADILY FORWARD OVER GRASPING QUICKSANDS!
THROUGH SWIRLING DRIFTWOOD TANGLES!
BY LAND, BY WATER, AND BY AIR—AS ONLY A FROG CAN GO!
THE STORM-BATTERED STREETS OF DUCKBURG HAVE NEVER SEEN THE PASSING OF A MESSENGER SUCH AS THIS!
KA-PLOP
KA-PLOP
KA-PLOP
KA-PLOP!
THUMP THUMP THUMP
MERCY ME! IS THAT SOMEBODY AT THE DOOR?
CATAPULT! AND THERE'S SOMETHING TIED TO HIS BACK!
SO WHEN ALL THE PEOPLE HAVE BEEN SAVED!
YESSIR! WHEN THE HURRICANES BLOW IN DUCKBURG, YOU NEVER KNOW WHO OR WHAT WILL COME SEEKING REFUGE AT YOUR DOOR!
IN THIS CASE WE WERE VISITED BY THE GREATEST HERO DUCKBURG EVER HAD!
TO CATAPULT IN LOVING GRATITUDE FROM THE people of Duckburg

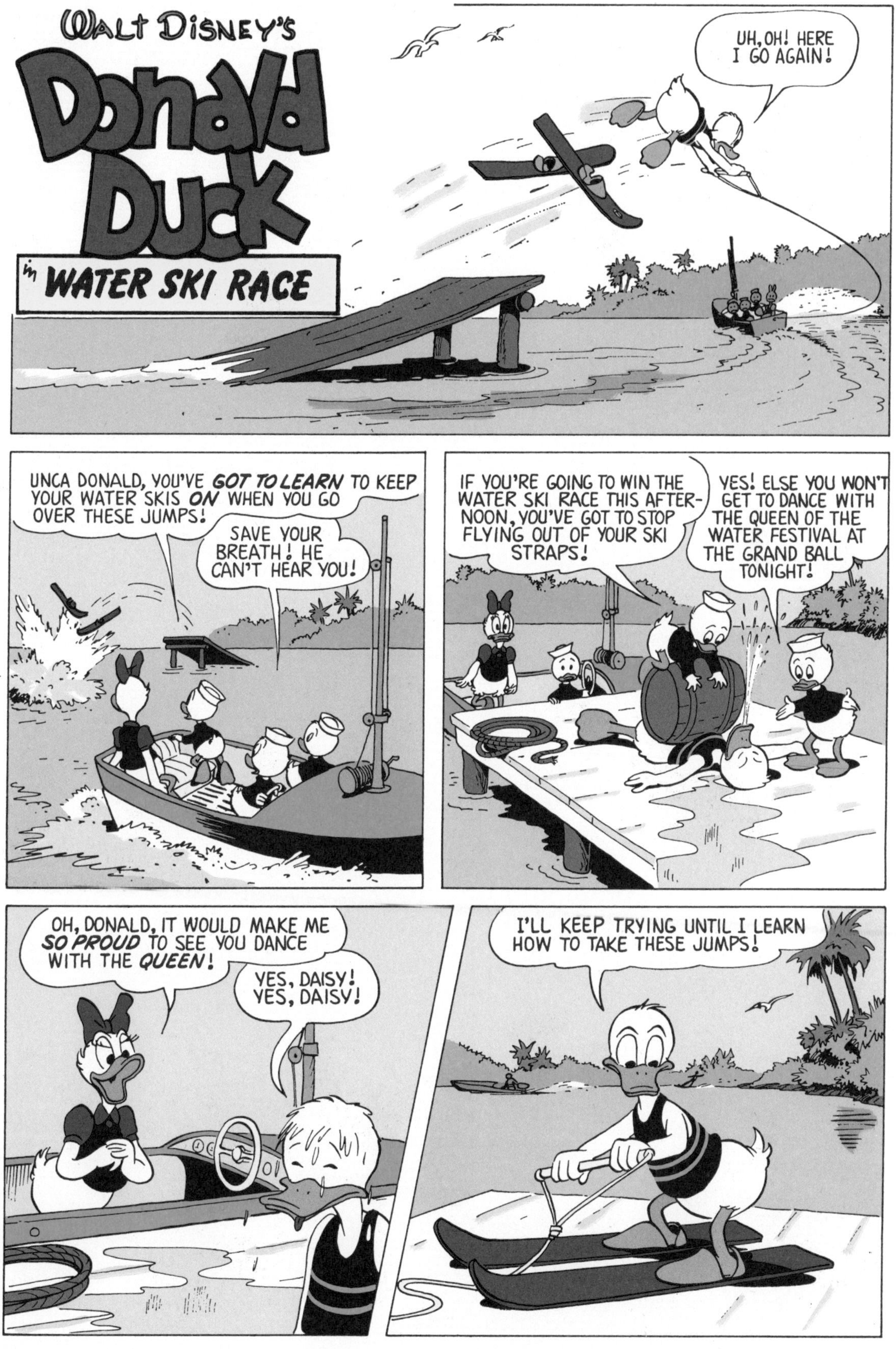

WALT DISNEY'S
Donald Duck
in WATER SKI RACE
UH, OH! HERE I GO AGAIN!
UNCA DONALD, YOU'VE GOT TO LEARN TO KEEP YOUR WATER SKIS ON WHEN YOU GO OVER THESE JUMPS!
SAVE YOUR BREATH! HE CAN'T HEAR YOU!
IF YOU'RE GOING TO WIN THE WATER SKI RACE THIS AFTER-NOON, YOU'VE GOT TO STOP FLYING OUT OF YOUR SKI STRAPS!
YES! ELSE YOU WON'T GET TO DANCE WITH THE QUEEN OF THE WATER FESTIVAL AT THE GRAND BALL TONIGHT!
OH, DONALD, IT WOULD MAKE ME SO PROUD TO SEE YOU DANCE WITH THE QUEEN!
YES, DAISY! YES, DAISY!
I'LL KEEP TRYING UNTIL I LEARN HOW TO TAKE THESE JUMPS!

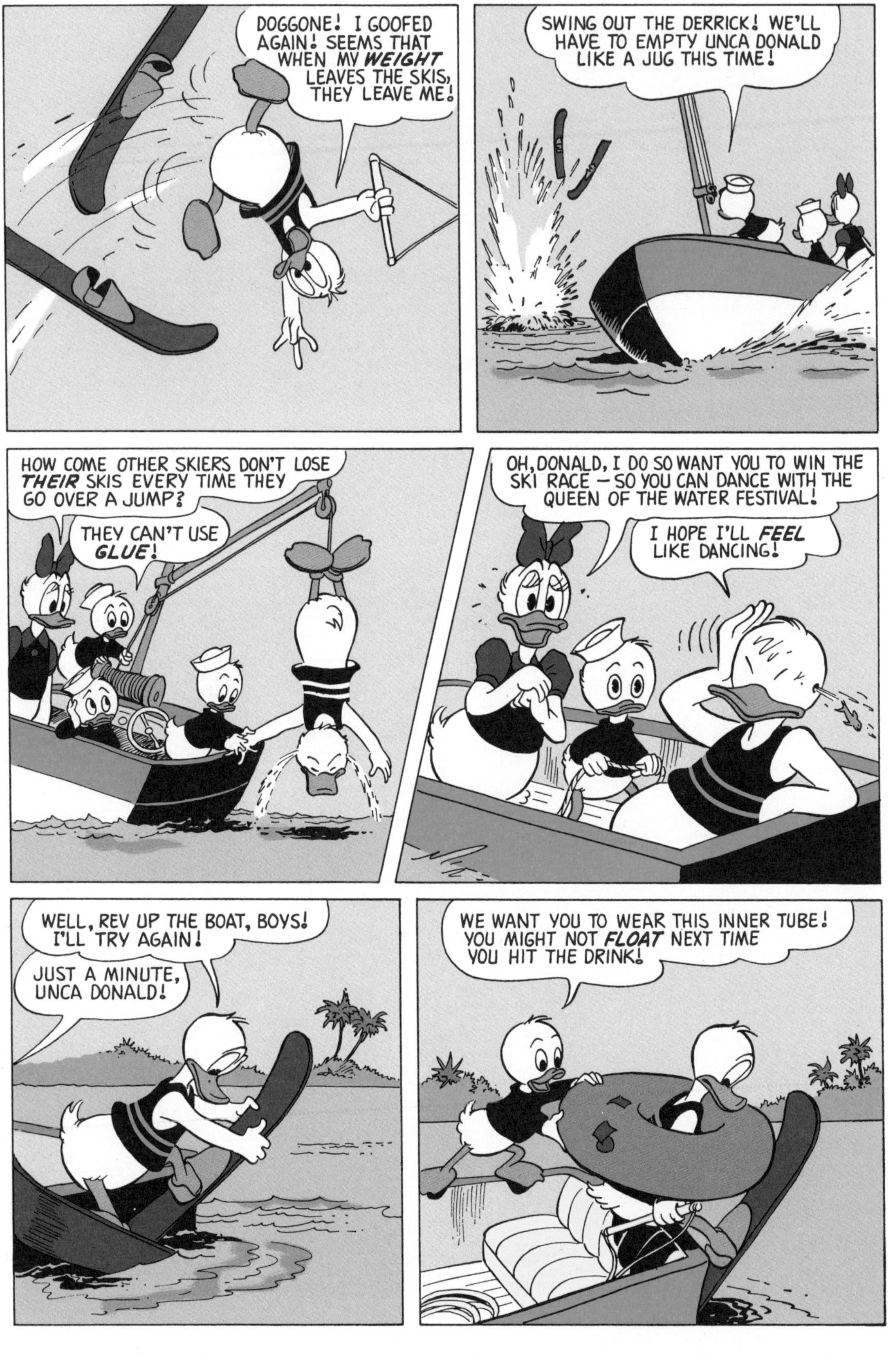
DOGGONE! I GOOFED AGAIN! SEEMS THAT WHEN MY WEIGHT LEAVES THE SKIS, THEY LEAVE ME!
SWING OUT THE DERRICK! WE'LL HAVE TO EMPTY UNCA DONALD LIKE A JUG THIS TIME!
HOW COME OTHER SKIERS DON'T LOSE THEIR SKIS EVERY TIME THEY GO OVER A JUMP?
THEY CAN'T USE GLUE!
OH, DONALD, I DO SO WANT YOU TO WIN THE SKI RACE — SO YOU CAN DANCE WITH THE QUEEN OF THE WATER FESTIVAL!
I HOPE I'LL FEEL LIKE DANCING!
WELL, REV UP THE BOAT, BOYS! I'LL TRY AGAIN!
JUST A MINUTE, UNCA DONALD!
WE WANT YOU TO WEAR THIS INNER TUBE! YOU MIGHT NOT FLOAT NEXT TIME YOU HIT THE DRINK!

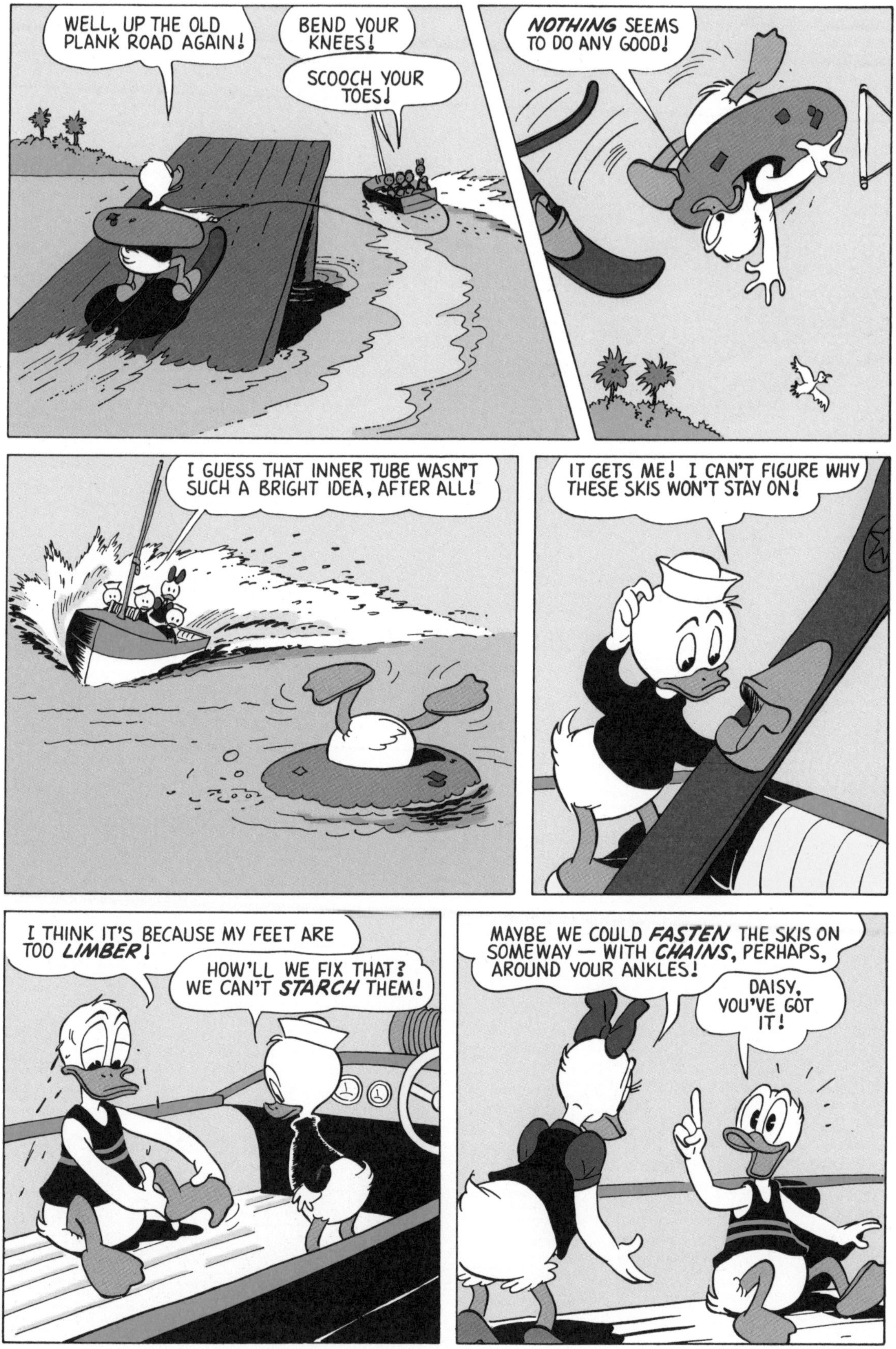
WELL, UP THE OLD PLANK ROAD AGAIN!
BEND YOUR KNEES!
SCOOCH YOUR TOES!
NOTHING SEEMS TO DO ANY GOOD!
I GUESS THAT INNER TUBE WASN'T SUCH A BRIGHT IDEA, AFTER ALL!
IT GETS ME! I CAN'T FIGURE WHY THESE SKIS WON'T STAY ON!
I THINK IT'S BECAUSE MY FEET ARE TOO LIMBER!
HOW'LL WE FIX THAT? WE CAN'T STARCH THEM!
MAYBE WE COULD FASTEN THE SKIS ON SOMEWAY — WITH CHAINS, PERHAPS, AROUND YOUR ANKLES!
DAISY, YOU'VE GOT IT!

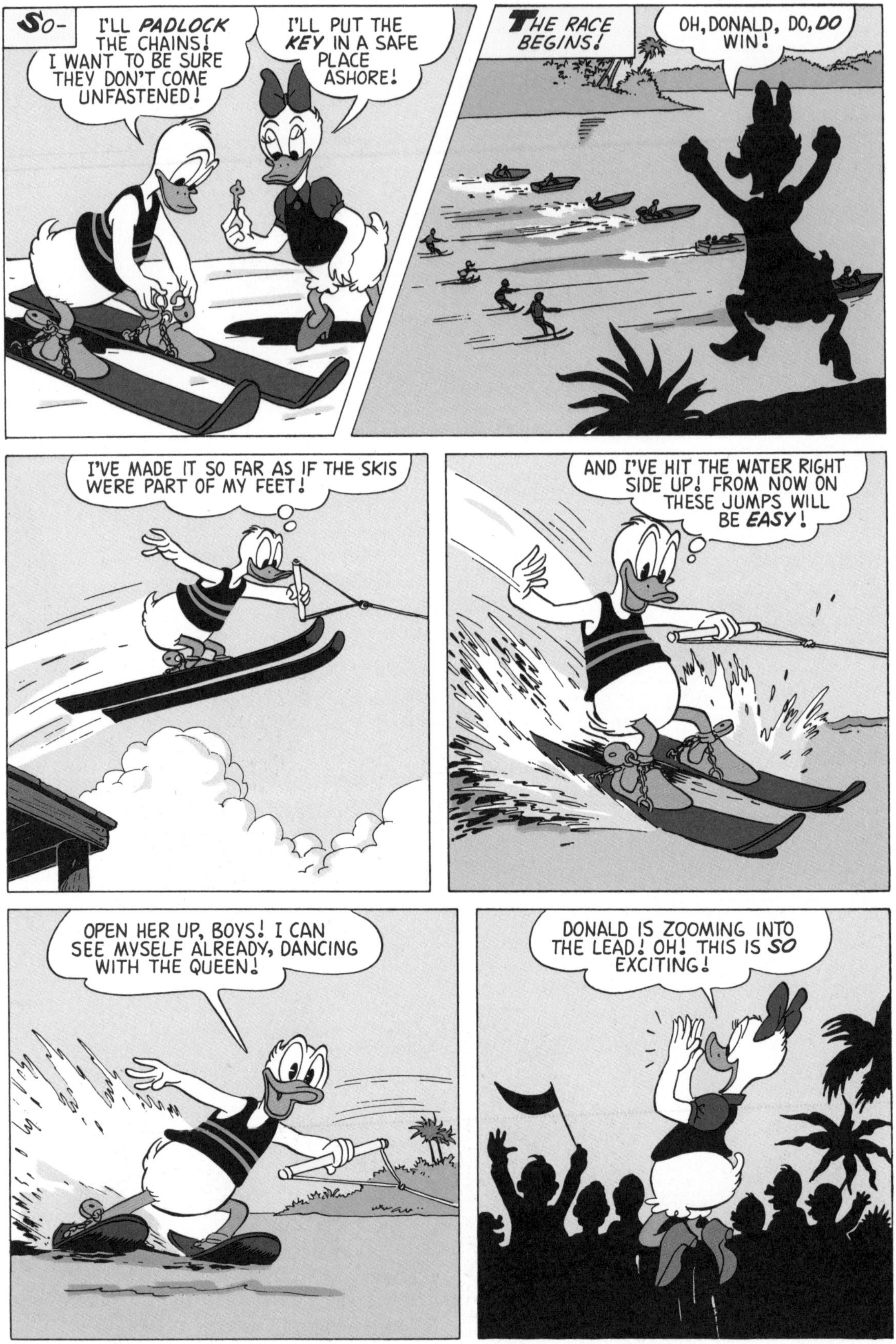
SO-
I'LL PADLOCK THE CHAINS! I WANT TO BE SURE THEY DON'T COME UNFASTENED!
I'LL PUT THE KEY IN A SAFE PLACE ASHORE!
THE RACE BEGINS!
OH, DONALD, DO, DO WIN!
I'VE MADE IT SO FAR AS IF THE SKIS WERE PART OF MY FEET!
AND I'VE HIT THE WATER RIGHT SIDE UP! FROM NOW ON THESE JUMPS WILL BE EASY!
OPEN HER UP, BOYS! I CAN SEE MYSELF ALREADY, DANCING WITH THE QUEEN!
DONALD IS ZOOMING INTO THE LEAD! OH! THIS IS SO EXCITING!

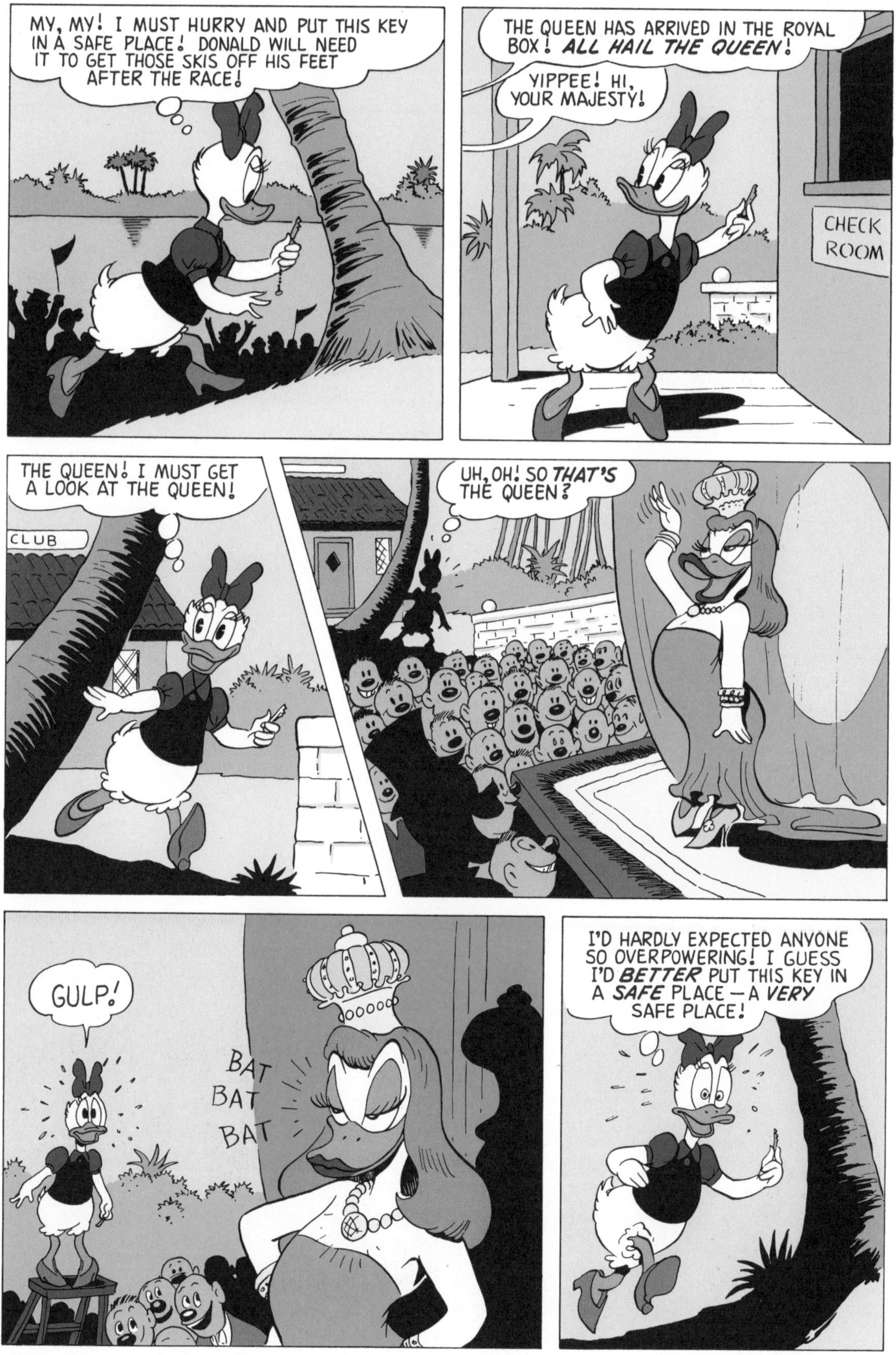
MY, MY! I MUST HURRY AND PUT THIS KEY IN A SAFE PLACE! DONALD WILL NEED IT TO GET THOSE SKIS OFF HIS FEET AFTER THE RACE!
THE QUEEN HAS ARRIVED IN THE ROYAL BOX! ALL HAIL THE QUEEN!
YIPPEE! HI, YOUR MAJESTY!
CHECK ROOM
THE QUEEN! I MUST GET A LOOK AT THE QUEEN!
CLUB
UH, OH! SO THAT'S THE QUEEN?
GULP!
BAT BAT BAT
I'D HARDLY EXPECTED ANYONE SO OVERPOWERING! I GUESS I'D BETTER PUT THIS KEY IN A SAFE PLACE — A VERY SAFE PLACE!

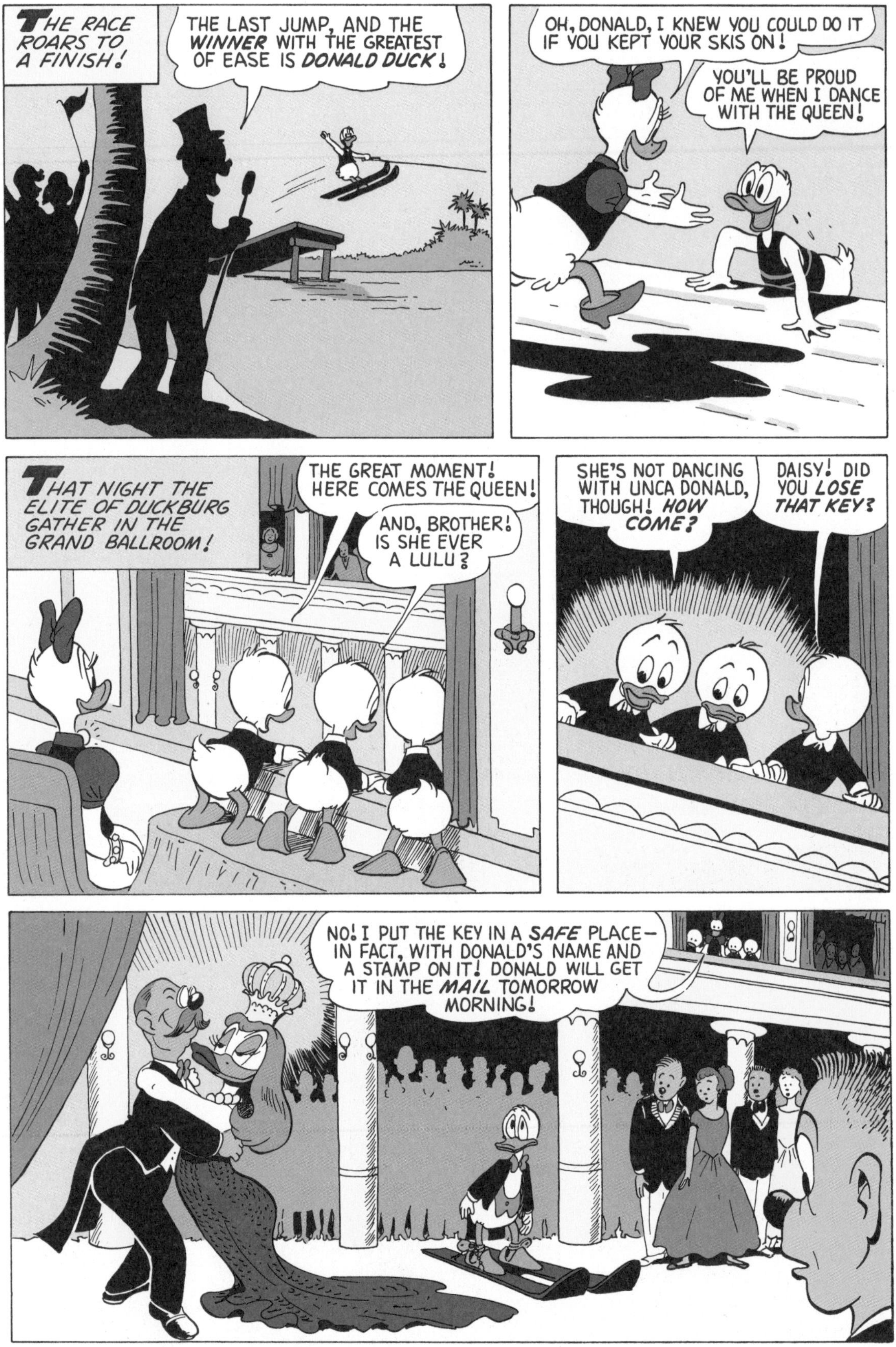
THE RACE ROARS TO A FINISH!
THE LAST JUMP, AND THE WINNER WITH THE GREATEST OF EASE IS DONALD DUCK!
OH, DONALD, I KNEW YOU COULD DO IT IF YOU KEPT YOUR SKIS ON!
YOU'LL BE PROUD OF ME WHEN I DANCE WITH THE QUEEN!
THAT NIGHT THE ELITE OF DUCKBURG GATHER IN THE GRAND BALLROOM!
THE GREAT MOMENT! HERE COMES THE QUEEN!
AND, BROTHER! IS SHE EVER A LULU?
SHE'S NOT DANCING WITH UNCA DONALD, THOUGH! HOW COME?
DAISY! DID YOU LOSE THAT KEY?
NO! I PUT THE KEY IN A SAFE PLACE—IN FACT, WITH DONALD'S NAME AND A STAMP ON IT! DONALD WILL GET IT IN THE MAIL TOMORROW MORNING!

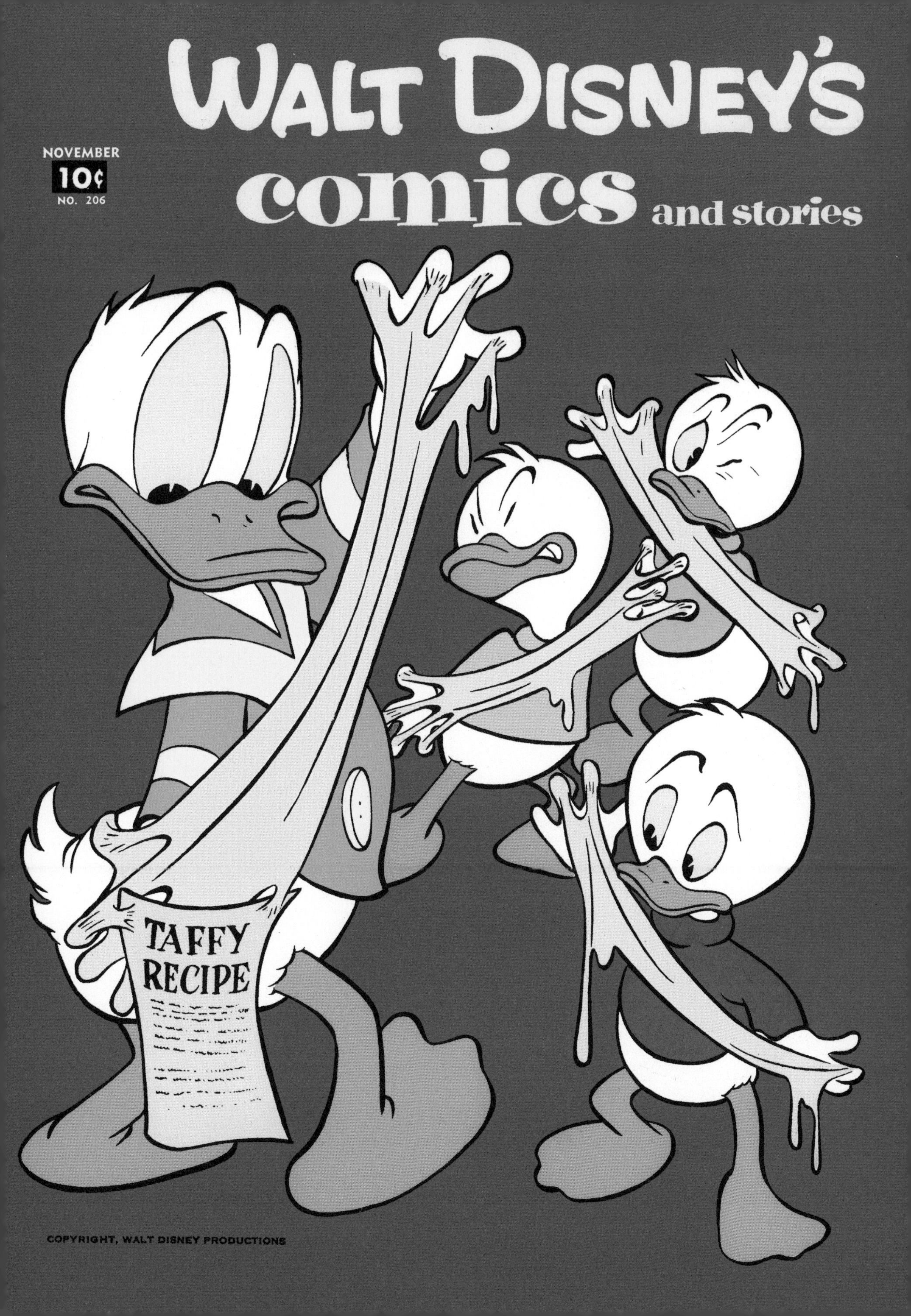
WALT DISNEY'S
NOVEMBER
10¢
NO. 206
comics
and stories
TAFFY
RECIPE
COPYRIGHT, WALT DISNEY PRODUCTIONS

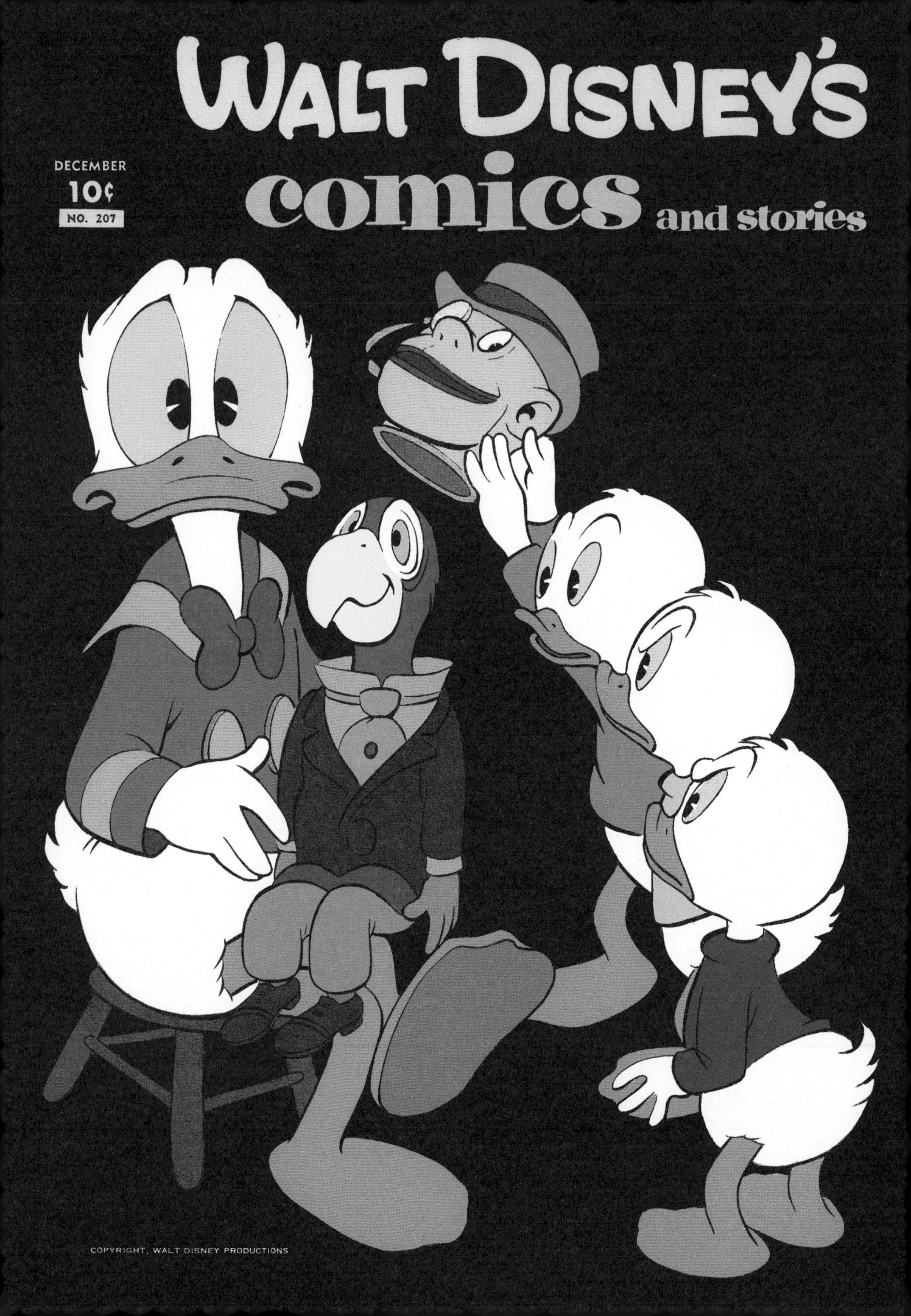
WALT DISNEY'S
comics and stories
DECEMBER
10¢
NO. 207
COPYRIGHT, WALT DISNEY PRODUCTIONS

Story Notes

THE BLACK PEARLS OF TABU YAMA p. 1

Now here's a truly intriguing Barksian oddball. For starters, unlike most other Barks stories, the look of "The Black Pearls of Tabu Yama" is significantly different because The Duck Man opens up his page layouts to give us a tale told in a three-tier panel grid (six panels per page) instead of his usual four tiers (eight panels per page). It's the first of three such stories in this volume, along with "Donald Duck and the Titanic Ants" and "Water Ski Race," about which more later.

Like the tale's titular island itself, "The Black Pearls of Tabu Yama" is rarely explored alongside the rest of Carl Barks's output, though it blends two familiar scenarios: a globe-trotting treasure hunt and a farcical deconstruction of Christmas.

Barks's Christmas stories run the gamut from nearly Victorian meditations on privilege and poverty like "A Christmas for Shacktown" (*Walt Disney's Donald Duck: "A Christmas for Shacktown,"* Volume 11 in this series) to madcap remixes like "The Hammy Camel" (*Walt Disney's Donald Duck: "The Ghost Sheriff of Last Gasp,"* Volume 15). Of course, his most important yuletide romp, 1947's "Christmas on Bear Mountain" (*Walt Disney's Donald Duck: "Christmas on Bear Mountain,"* Volume 5), introduced Scrooge McDuck as a midcentury riff on Dickens's converted curmudgeon.

By the time Barks parks his swashducklers in Tabu Yama, Uncle Scrooge's shift from sour miser to gleeful explorer provides the story's best gag. To emphasize Scrooge's mellower side, Barks includes several moments where the marooned tycoon whiles away his shipwrecked holiday stockpiling black pearls.

Scrooge's innocent excitement finds its counterpoint in similar panels where his savvy nephews are hard at work weaving palm mats for their makeshift shelter. Barks's industrious child focuses on survival while his childlike industrialist happily hoards fairly useless marble-sized treasure. The contrast subtly suggests how much Scrooge's character has softened over the years.

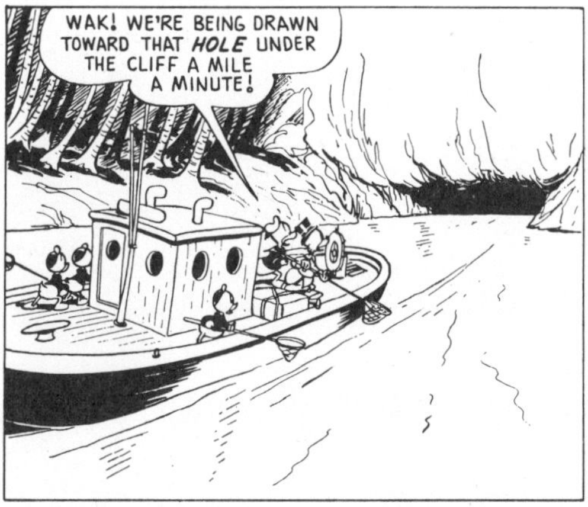
WAK! WE'RE BEING DRAWN TOWARD THAT *HOLE* UNDER THE CLIFF A MILE A MINUTE!

Meanwhile, the "lashed," "locked," and "waterproofed" evidence of Scrooge's Christmas Eve generosity is kept secret until absolutely necessary.

If any one character shines in this kooky Christmas calamity, though, it is Donald, whose ornery oratory labels the ordeal a "tabu snafu." While references to Robinson Crusoe's resourcefulness and James Watt's ingenuity arise around him, Donald prefers thoroughly modernized gratification. He cracks wise about tasty turkeys, oversized clinkers, pop bottles, "fast traffic," and subway tunnels to better cope with their predicament. He even invokes parliamentary procedure while the Ducks brainstorm their way to freedom. But his best line comes as they salvage the gear that will make them more "comfortable castaways." "Hail Columbia!" he

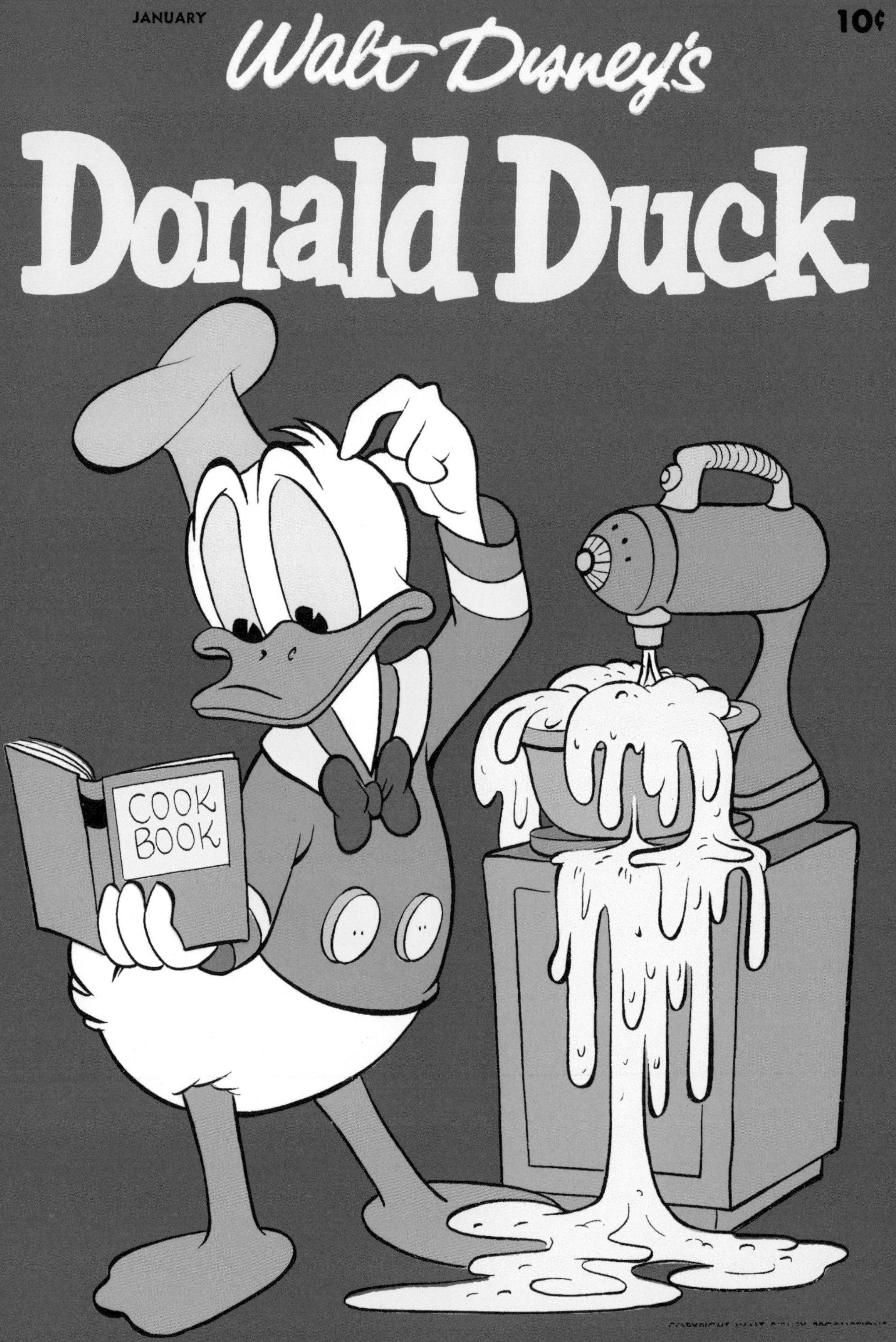
JANUARY
10¢
Walt Disney's
Donald Duck
COOK BOOK

shouts joyfully, "Eats! Tools! Our *lanterns!*" For Donald, primitive adversity is the best possible reason to indulge in American convenience!

This story also provides one of Donald's most exciting moments in Barksian comics. His daring effort to lasso the rocketing boat while the island explodes around them is a thrilling gambit, and his deliberate interior monologue emphasizes the scene's steam-powered hilarity.

The mysterious island of Tabu Yama itself is a compelling "character" of sorts. Barks renders the island's topography in richly contoured panels with repeated swaths of palm and coconut groves. His own fascination with geology and physics informs every frame as the Ducks dissect Tabu Yama's pneumatic anatomy.

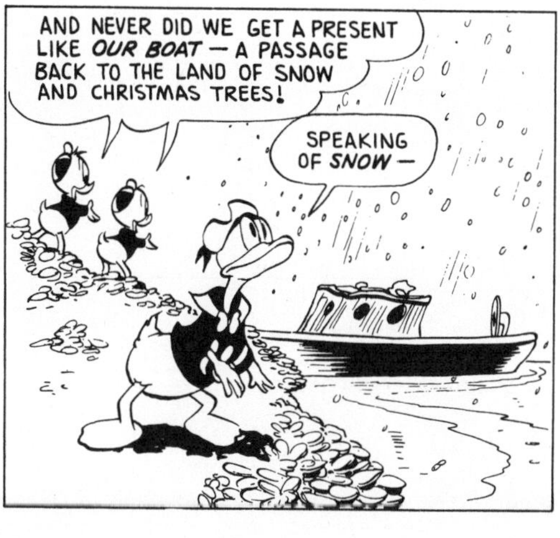
AND NEVER DID WE GET A PRESENT LIKE OUR BOAT — A PASSAGE BACK TO THE LAND OF SNOW AND CHRISTMAS TREES!
SPEAKING OF SNOW —

The final island-cracking upheaval also suggests that Barks's complex natural world deserves further eco-environmental criticism, especially with regard to the constant mischief his colonizing characters leave behind. In this case, a once-beautiful ecosystem is left "hanging together" with its "lagoon tipped up on its side." It's a strange, violent, and somewhat worrisome conclusion for a Christmas story, where ash rains down like snow on a fake holiday ornament.

Though Scrooge calls the pearls his greatest Christmas present, Barks leaves readers wondering a bit about the larger costs and compromises of Christmas in Disney's post-colonial Adventureland.

— DANIEL YEZBICK

FORBIDDEN VALLEY p. 19

"Forbidden Valley" is an anomaly in the Carl Barks canon. It's his first long Donald Duck story in years and one in which Uncle Scrooge doesn't tag along and drive the action. If it seems to echo earlier adventures, that's because it's a reworking of "Darkest Africa" (*Walt Disney's Donald Duck: "The Old Castle's Secret,"* Volume 6). That earlier story is an anomaly itself. Unlike other stories during Barks's golden period, it appears rushed, with sloppy inking and finishes that look as though someone else dabbed them in while Barks was out of the room. For a story about something as silly as a butterfly hunt, "Darkest Africa" also suffers from some truly terrifying stakes and imagery, with the Ducks in constant mortal danger.

Rarely was a later remake superior in every way to Barks's earlier original, but that is certainly the case with "Forbidden Valley." It's a farce from the get-go: Duckburg's pickle

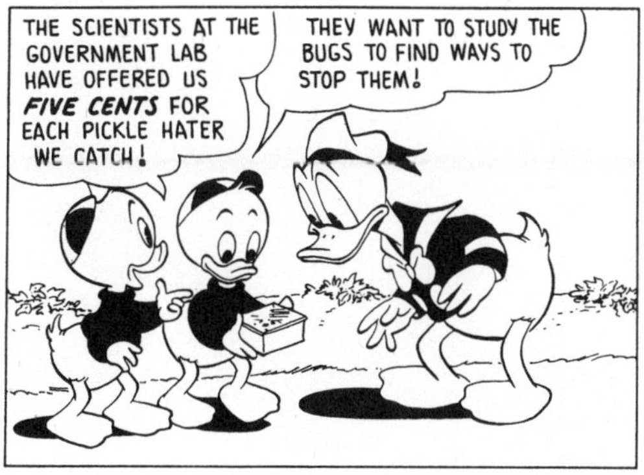
THE SCIENTISTS AT THE GOVERNMENT LAB HAVE OFFERED US FIVE CENTS FOR EACH PICKLE HATER WE CATCH!
THEY WANT TO STUDY THE BUGS TO FIND WAYS TO STOP THEM!

crop faces extinction due to the mysterious South American Augur-Nosed Pickle Haters. The only way to eliminate them is their natural enemy, the Jungle Razor Wasp. Donald and his nephews embark on a journey to the Amazon to bring back a swarm of those wasps alive.

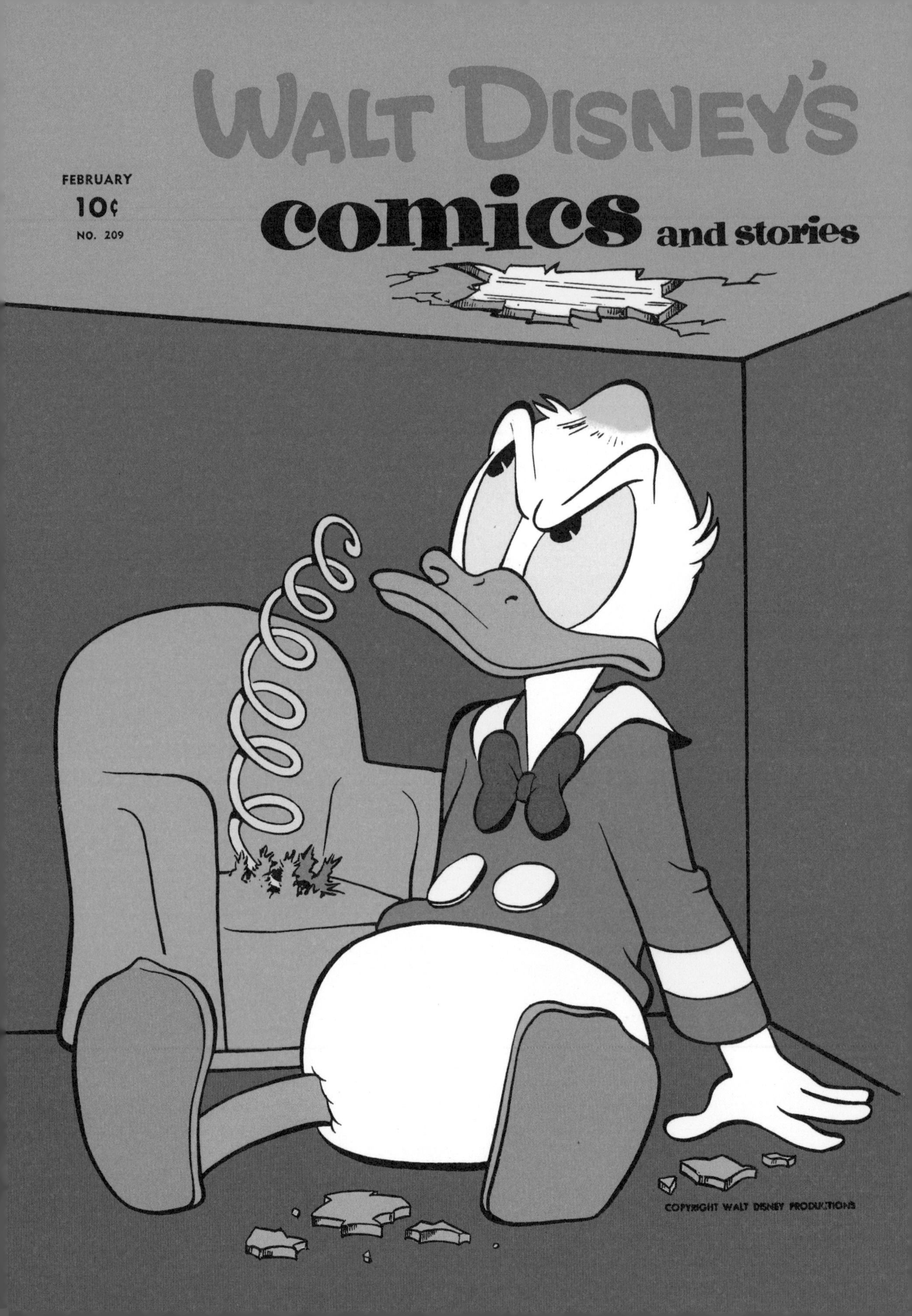
WALT DISNEY'S
FEBRUARY
10¢
NO. 209
comics and stories
COPYRIGHT WALT DISNEY PRODUCTIONS

One P. J. McBrine, the crooked canner who brought the Pickle Haters to Duckburg in the first place, stalks and sabotages them every step of the way. And why? To correct his folly: canning 23,000,000 quarts of pickled rutabagas that he can't even give away. "But now, with the cucumber pickle crop doomed, the finicky people are going to *have to eat my pickled rutabagas and like them!* Hyeh! Hyeh! Hyeh!"

Yes, it's a silly concept, but Barks handles it with a balance lacking in the earlier story. McBrine does his best to wreck the Ducks' efforts, but we're never too concerned about our heroes' safety since the adventure goes so far over the top.

And what could possibly bring this bug hunt to a fever pitch? Turns out the wasps' winter home is the Forbidden Valley of the title, where dinosaurs still thrive. Barks smartly has the Ducks spend only six pages there in order to give his farce a fittingly farcical climax. And upon their seemingly victorious return to Duckburg, Barks treats us to an inevitably ironic (and hysterical) conclusion.

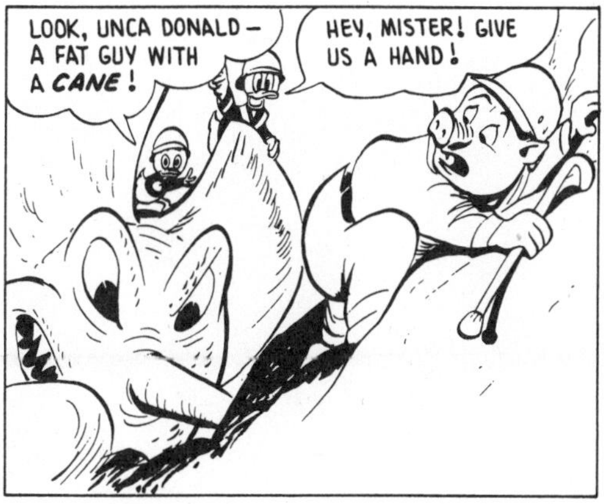
LOOK, UNCA DONALD — A FAT GUY WITH A *CANE*!
HEY, MISTER! GIVE US A HAND!

The pig-faced "P. J. McBrine" will resurface under various aliases, his most frequent one being "Argus McSwine" (most fans have simply termed him "the Pig Villain"). McBrine/McSwine proves to be a natural for Donald and Scrooge stories that require a self-centered, snobbish, and vindictive adversary. And what better character to fill that role than a pig, right?

— THAD KOMOROWSKI

SAGMORE SPRINGS HOTEL p. 45

A look at the brief biography in the back of this book reveals several of the non-cartooning occupations Carl Barks held during his lifetime. They make for a labor-intensive lot, without much call for executive expertise. Such arduous employment might help explain how Barks could so easily display a fundamental understanding of tough jobs while neither routinely scorning nor romanticizing hard work. Through his Duck, he could convincingly convey empathy for the working stiff while not ignoring the commonplace shortcomings of same.

"Sagmore Springs Hotel" presents that balance. It's difficult not to root for Donald with his exuberance, industriousness, and can-do spirit (bolstered by every single one of those three night classes in hotel administration). His critical failing — the beginning of his downfall — is but a single moment of forgetfulness, an experience too familiar to us all.

Barks's evenhandedness extends to the other end of the economic spectrum as well. Scrooge is not some cardboard class antagonist. Sure, he coolly jots down notes on imperfections even when floating at flood stage

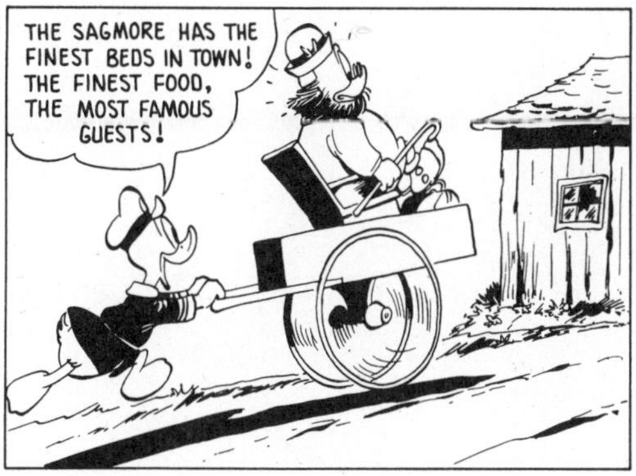
THE SAGMORE HAS THE FINEST BEDS IN TOWN! THE FINEST FOOD, THE MOST FAMOUS GUESTS!

down the hotel stairs as calmly as if on the tamest Disneyland ride in the Magic Kingdom. Yes, his remark about "chambermaids' chore" is harsh, especially as we've seen how madly Donald has been scrambling.

WALT DISNEY'S comics and stories

MAY
10¢
NO. 212

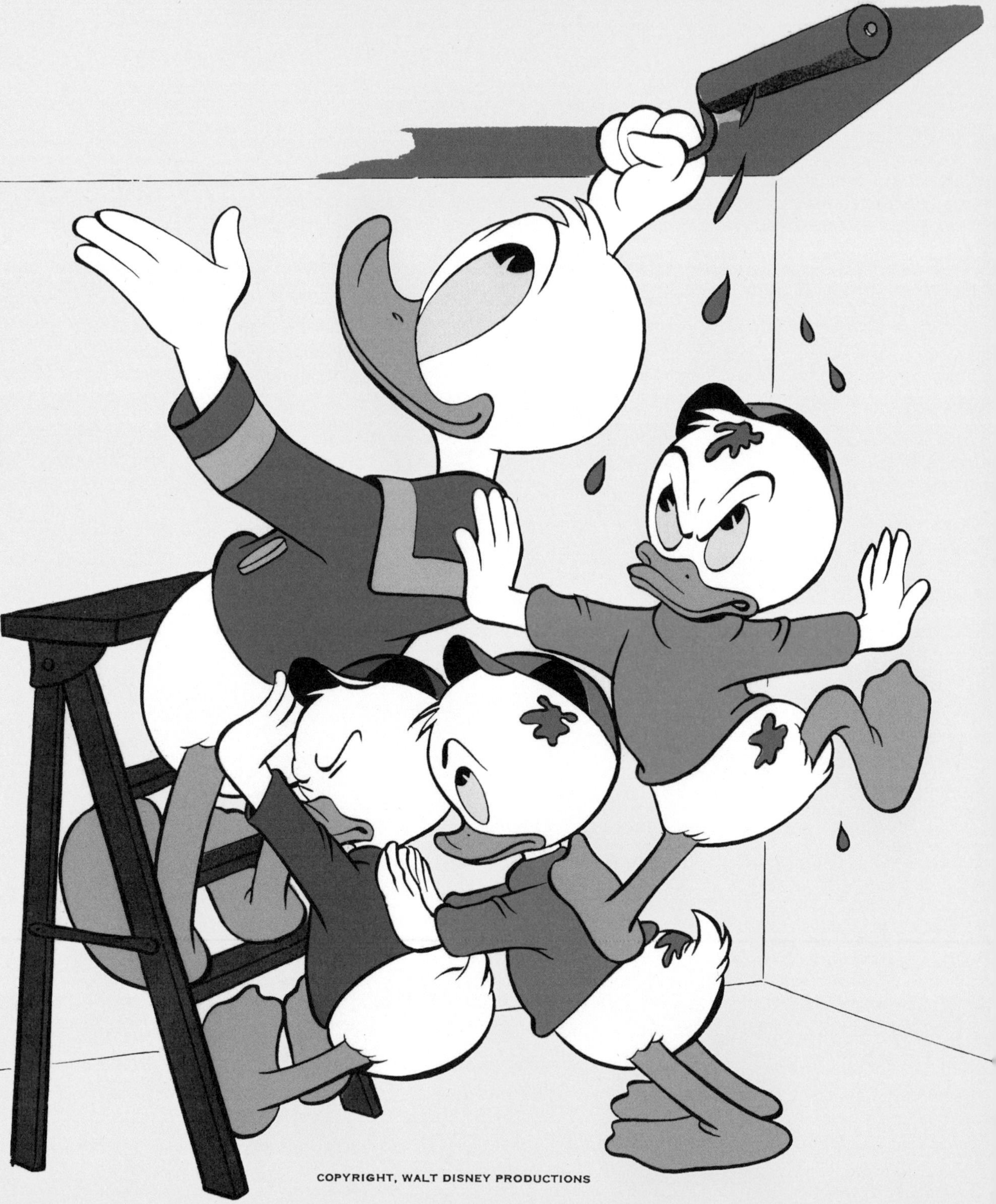

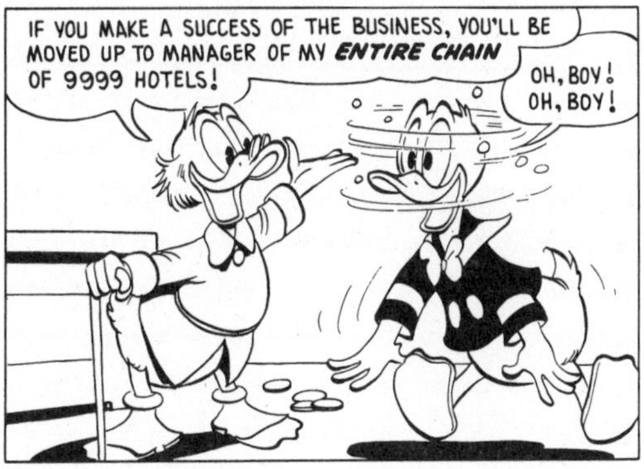
IF YOU MAKE A SUCCESS OF THE BUSINESS, YOU'LL BE MOVED UP TO MANAGER OF MY *ENTIRE CHAIN* OF 9999 HOTELS!
OH, BOY! OH, BOY!

But Scrooge is committed in his own way, too. He has shown an honest willingness to help his nephew raise his station and has a vested interest in that success. In testing Donald, he has anticipated exactly the quality that hobbles his nephew's managerial potential: his incapacitating jitters when facing outsized responsibilities.

Giving a fair shake to the foibles and aptitudes of both labor and management can be challenging. Making it amusing is a harder job still.

— RICH KREINER

THE TENDERFOOT TRAP p. 55

While Donald regularly vies against Scrooge or Gladstone, he seldom finds himself in direct competition with both at the same time, as he does in "The Tenderfoot Trap."

Worse, Donald is something of an odd man out, as Carl Barks frames the desert tournament as a comedic contest of the classic "nature versus nurture" debate. Gladstone personifies the former, blessed with his preposterously good luck, while Scrooge represents a lifetime of developed abilities and hard-won skills: the talents he has nurtured.

Against such avatars, the profoundly mortal Donald can muster only book learning to augment his dogged determination and his willingness to bend the rules. It hardly matters. Gladstone, as is his custom, thoroughly demolishes the notion of a level playing field just as effectively as he annihilates any "debate" on theoretical matters.

Note, though, how carefully Barks constructs each character's approach to his challenges (and the ultimate solutions) to be consistent with each character's strengths. In that way, each makes his own "luck" — but, of course, it all still conspires to heighten Donald's frustration and physical discomfort.

This story additionally stands out for the narrowed color palate of its backgrounds. Panels are awash in shades of sun-bleached

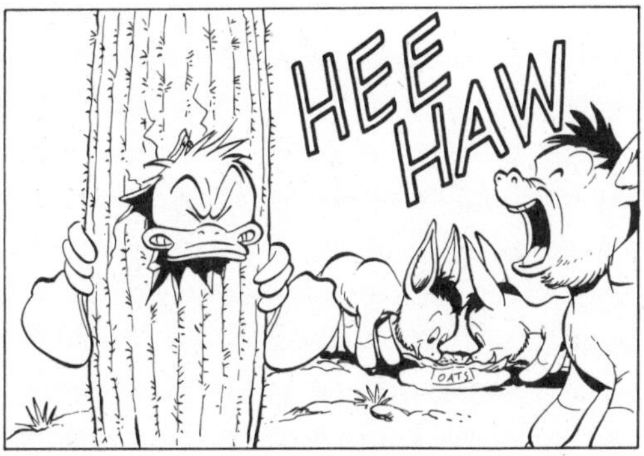
HEE HAW
OATS

yellows and desert tans. This relative uniformity is highly unusual for Barks, who — setting a story in outer space, under the sea, or wherever — offers, as a matter of course, greater contrasts by varying the scenes, environments, and dominant hues. Yet there is no sense of monotony or constraint here, thanks to the vital characters and the pervasive warm browns that remind of oven-baked treats.

And saleratus? It's a potash-based, carbon-rich bicarbonate used in baking powders, which surely must smell better than it sounds.

— RICH KREINER

ROCKET RACE AROUND THE WORLD p. 65

Just as he did in "Forbidden Valley" in this volume, and would do again during the 1950s and 1960s, Carl Barks recycles elements of an earlier plot for "Rocket Race Around the World." The countdown to blast off here is much the same as an earlier Barks story, "Rocket Race to the Moon" (*Walt Disney's*

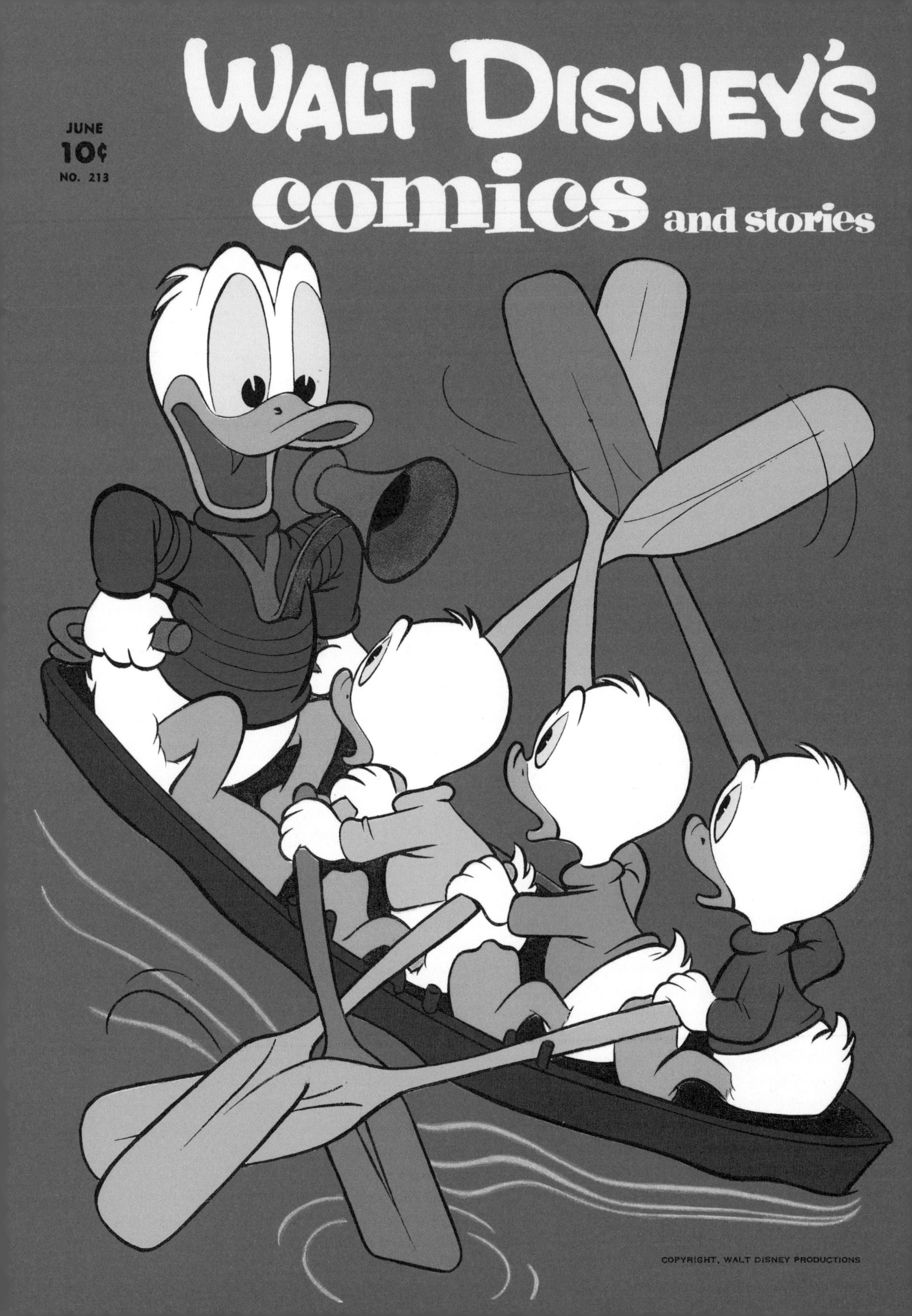
WALT DISNEY'S
JUNE
10¢
NO. 213
comics and stories
COPYRIGHT, WALT DISNEY PRODUCTIONS

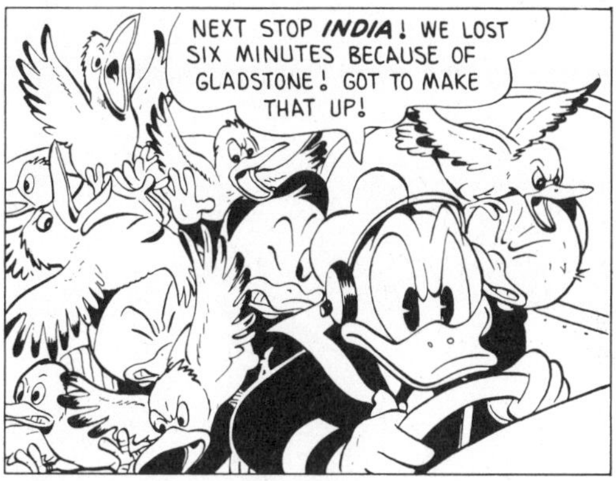
NEXT STOP *INDIA*! WE LOST SIX MINUTES BECAUSE OF GLADSTONE! GOT TO MAKE THAT UP!

Donald Duck: "The Old Castle's Secret," Volume 6). In that story, paperboy Donald passes by a laboratory where Professors Cosmic and Gamma are adding the final touches to a rocket ship that the Duck will end up piloting on a round trip to the Moon in competition against Baron de Sleezy.

In this case, peanut seller Donald gets involved in a race in a rocket ship that has just been assembled by Gyro Gearloose and Professor Sliderule, against their rival, the German-accented Prof. Missilebug (a parody of Wernher von Braun).

Barks was smart enough to alter the plot here so that it feels original to his readers. His nephews accompany Donald in this race around the world, and their competitor is none other than their exaggeratedly lucky cousin, Gladstone Gander (who had only just made his debut five months before the earlier rocket race story was published).

Only technically do both rocket races end without a winner. In the first story, neither Donald nor Baron de Sleezy gain anything after their rocket ships blow up. In "Rocket Race Around the World," Donald and the kids are on track to win, but they lose because Donald chooses to rescue Gladstone, whose own ship appears to crash in the Yucatan jungle. Barks is pretty cynical here, as not only is Donald's good deed not rewarded, but he is humiliated by Gladstone, who, despite also losing, makes more from the discovery of an ancient golden idol than he would have if he'd won the race.

The two stories also have very similar endings in that, in a typical reversal of roles, the scientists from the earlier one and the rocket ship owners here end up broke — selling newspapers and peanuts, respectively — basically stealing Donald's job.

— ALBERTO BECATTINI

WISHING STONE ISLAND p. 75

When Huey, Dewey, and Louie concoct an April Fool's gag based on Donald's belief in a mythological artifact, it turns out to have tangible consequences and apparently brings Donald real fortune in the end. Donald's insistence on using slang terms to refer to money, the perpetual object of his desire, and the literal interpretation of those metaphors by the

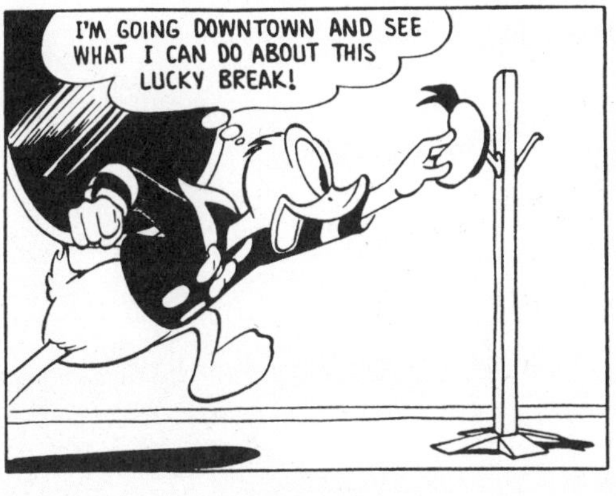
I'M GOING DOWNTOWN AND SEE WHAT I CAN DO ABOUT THIS LUCKY BREAK!

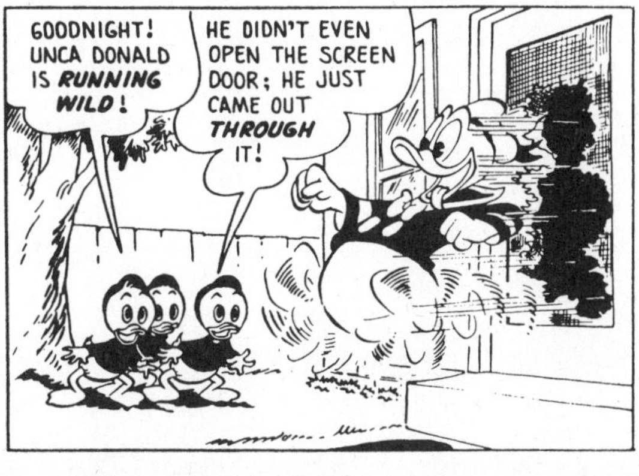
GOODNIGHT! UNCA DONALD IS *RUNNING WILD*!
HE DIDN'T EVEN OPEN THE SCREEN DOOR; HE JUST CAME OUT *THROUGH* IT!

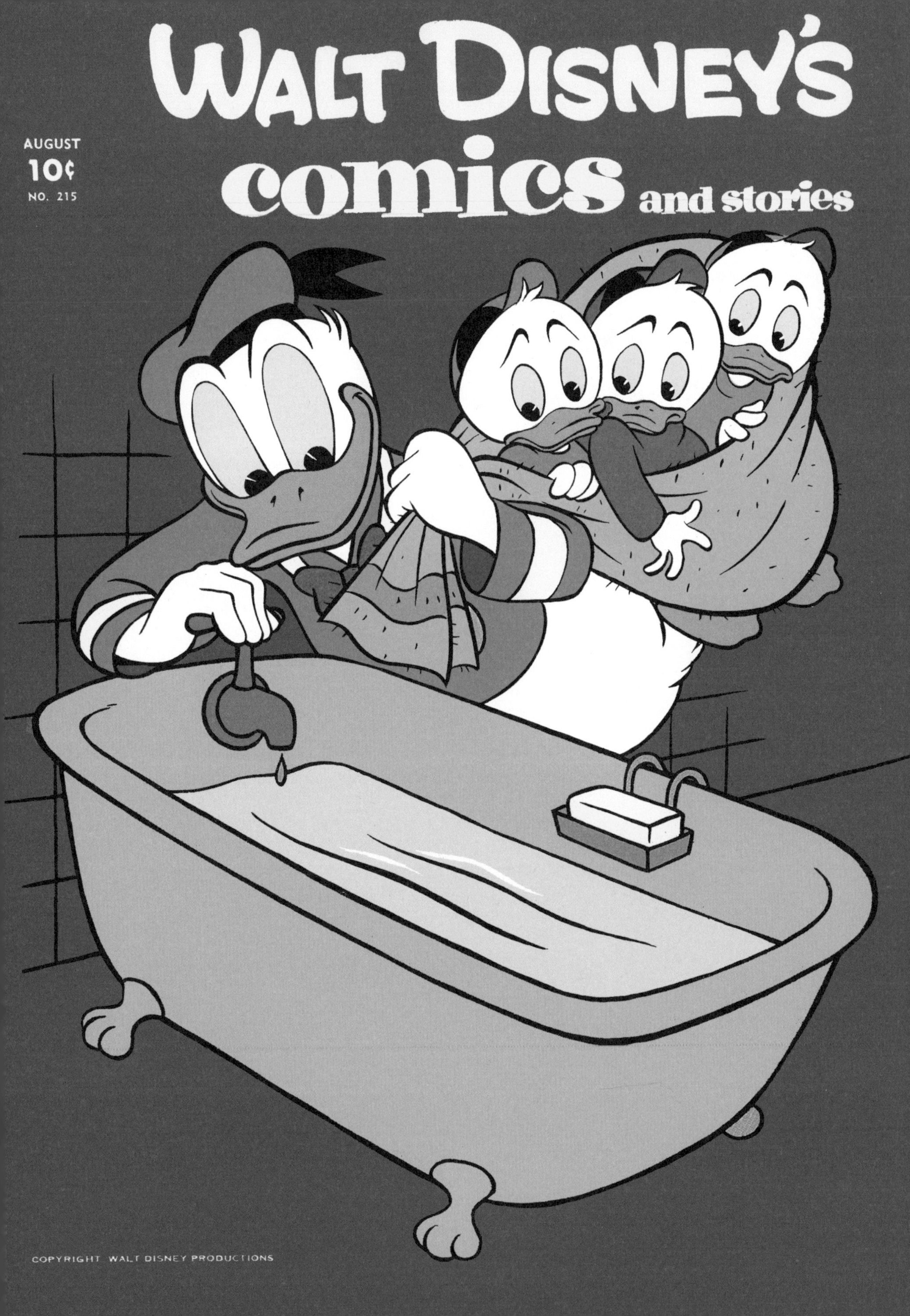
WALT DISNEY'S
AUGUST
10¢
NO. 215
comics and stories
COPYRIGHT WALT DISNEY PRODUCTIONS

people around him is the kind of semantic humor that particularly appeals to young readers whose laughter Barks was courting.

As was often the case at this point in his career, Barks's template for this story was an earlier one, "Donald Mines His Own Business" (*Walt Disney's Donald Duck: "Christmas on Bear Mountain,"* Volume 5), in which the nephews draw a map of imagined treasure that leads Donald to a real gold mine. A fake map is similarly instrumental in Barks's masterpiece "Luck of the North" (*Walt Disney's Donald Duck: "Trail of the Unicorn,"* Volume 8).

As in those stories, the twisting of make-believe and reality, as if on a Moebius strip, brings us toward closure. It remains unclear whether the absurd happenstance that drives both humor and plot reveals a karmic order that punishes or rewards the protagonists for the relative morality of their behavior or merely reflects existential meaninglessness. This story would imply the latter.

It is a loosely structured agglomeration of fragmentary fancies and bizarre whims. The idea of magic wishing stones came from Barks's eldest daughter, Peggy (1923–1963), who would occasionally send him ideas. The radio gag was inspired by a practical joke he remembered Nick George, his colleague at Disney Animation during the war, playing on their supervisor, Harry Reeves, using a radio transmitter.

As he would often do, Barks taps into the Western imaginary by locating the source of Donald's material desire in a far-off, exotic locale. Donald's error of mistaking the head of an island native in the tall grass for a wishing stone is disturbing and borderline grotesque far in excess of the plot itself. This racialist cliché is simultaneously enhanced and subverted by the medicine man being in tarred- and-feathered blackface, which obscures the grass skirt and pierced ears of his "real" appearance as a Pacific Islander stereotype.

There is no karmic order here, only the irony of chance. Our desires and prejudices, it seems, are what tethers us in the face of absurdity. Reflecting on the story's creation, Barks brings this point home by letting us look through the magic mirror of the final panel's porthole, assuring us that it has all been "A whopping big April Fool joke on *us!*"

— MATTHIAS WIVEL

DONALD DUCK AND THE TITANIC ANTS! p. 85

Some readers will find "Donald Duck and the Titanic Ants" a lightweight 20-pager filled with enjoyable and ephemeral gags, while others will attempt to read some elaborate socio-political commentary into this disastrous picnic for the super-rich.

In 1974, three Italian authors — Piero Marovelli, Elvio Paolini, and Giulio Saccomano — wrote a book on Carl Barks in which they interpreted this story as a Marxist parable: Uncle Scrooge and the picnicking tycoons are the capitalists who hold the economic power; the unnamed scientist represents the pure researcher who loses his innocence after being seduced by money; and the ants are the working class, which rebels against the capital that enslaves it but which can be pacified with salary increases (the jelly-coated silver coins).

This extremely politicized reading is typical of the era in which that book was written, but seems excessive to us — and only remotely

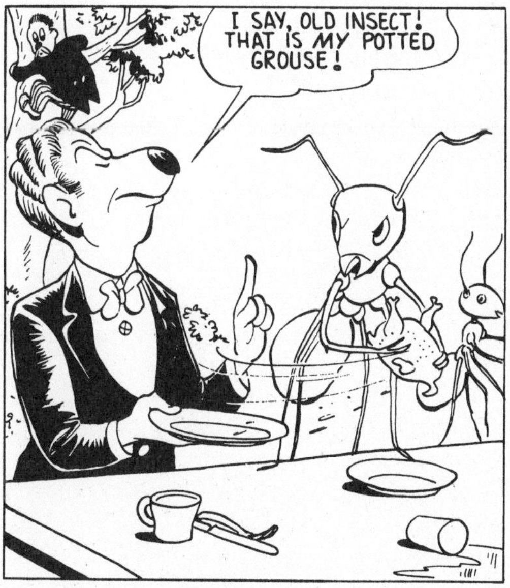
I SAY, OLD INSECT! THAT IS MY POTTED GROUSE!

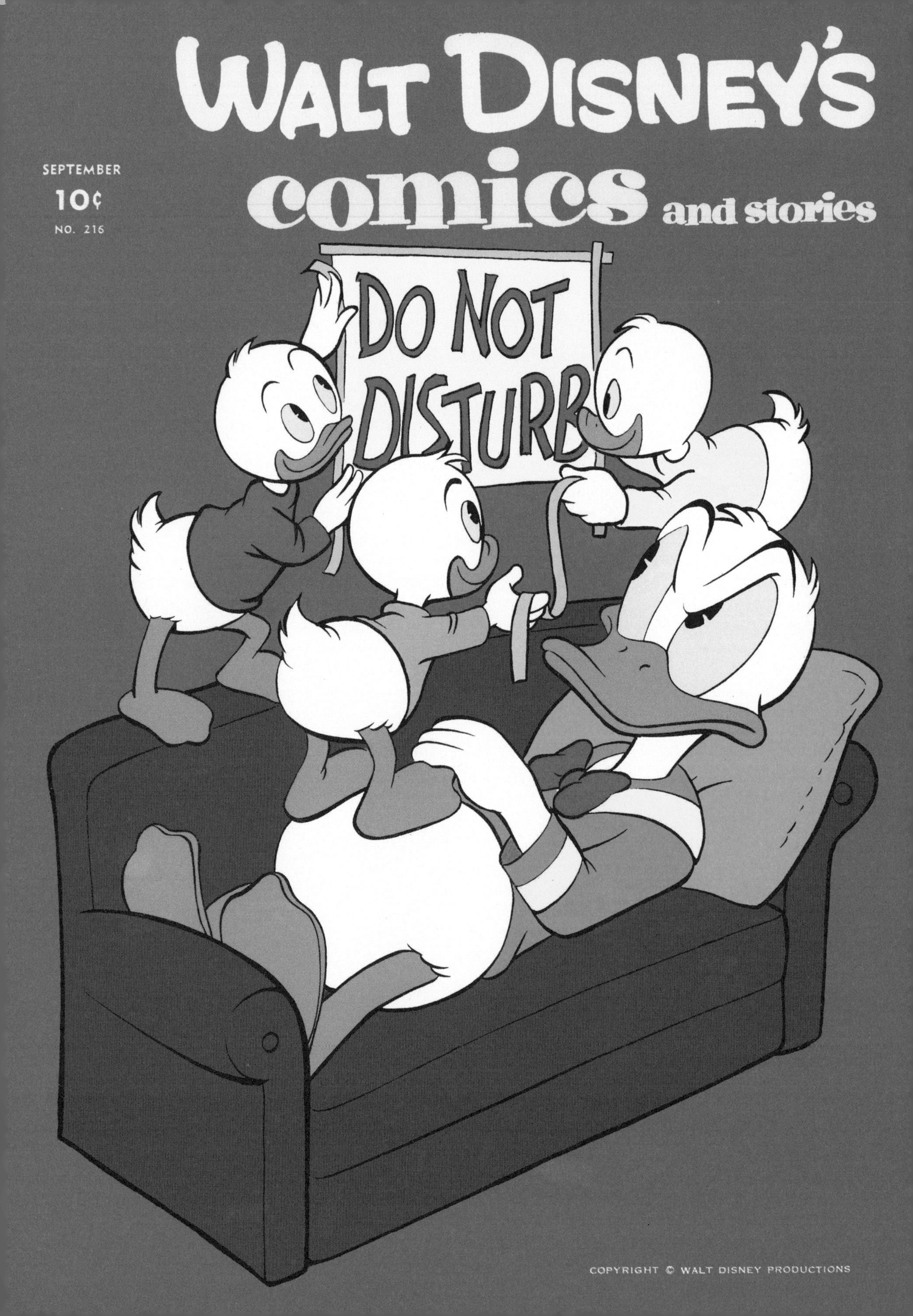

WALT DISNEY'S
comics and stories
SEPTEMBER
10¢
NO. 216
DO NOT DISTURB
COPYRIGHT © WALT DISNEY PRODUCTIONS

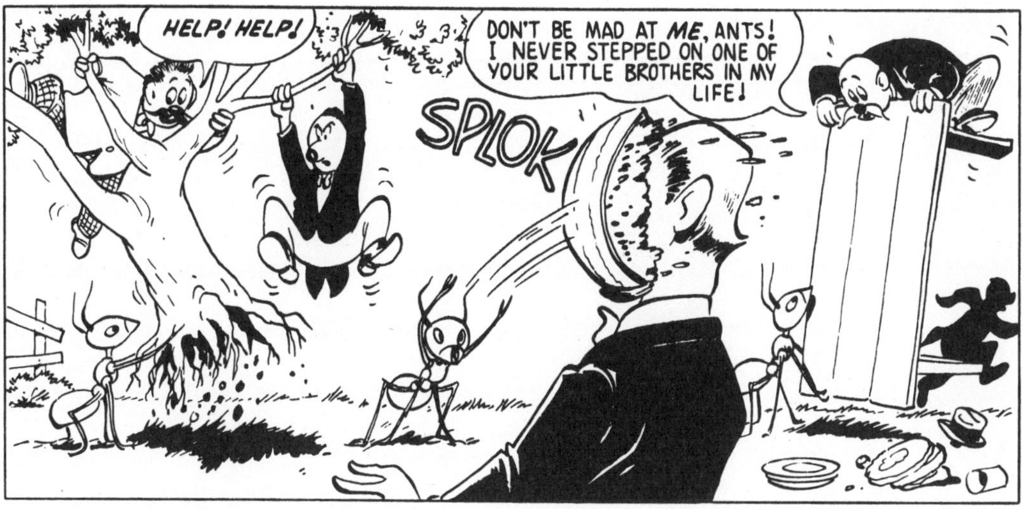
HELP! HELP!
DON'T BE MAD AT *ME*, ANTS! I NEVER STEPPED ON ONE OF YOUR LITTLE BROTHERS IN MY LIFE!
SPLOK

connected to the story that Barks actually wrote. The most amusing evidence that such far-fetched interpretations have very little foundation in the stories they discuss is the fact that two other authors, Chilean this time, Ariel Dorfman and Armand Mattelart, had already published a book three years earlier in which they accused Barks (and Disney comics more generally) of championing the opposite of Marxism, namely capitalism and imperialism. Biased critics will read whatever they want into the work they discuss.

We believe Barks was a million miles from promoting either ideology when he was writing his masterpieces. Such a discussion does, however, inspire us to fantasize about Barks's unconscious inspiration for his gags.

Barks (perhaps a free-spirited anarchist at heart?) pokes fun at the tics and idiosyncrasies of the wealthy — Scrooge is stingy with pennies but lavish with sacks of millions; the snob lady with her eyes closed in disdain cares only about the salt and pepper on her truffles, oblivious to the fact that the ants have reduced the picnic area to a war zone.

As in several other short stories, Barks playfully disrupts a hypocritical and ridiculous equilibrium (the picnic of the super rich) with an unexpected and tumultuous disturbance (the giant ants). He enjoys making fun of the tycoons — piercing their bubble of omnipotence and revealing their human flaws and weaknesses. This resonates with his undeclared but evident love for the utopian preindustrial societies that frequently appear in his other works.

And his fondness for exceptionally clever scientists whose zany inventions grow out of control in typical "sorcerer's apprentice" fashion is not a surprise when we consider the second most significant character (after Scrooge, of course) that Barks introduced into the Duckburg universe, namely Gyro Gearloose.

— LEONARDO GORI AND
FRANCESCO STAJANO

THE PERSISTENT POSTMAN p. 105

Many cartoonists looking for an idea might go to a joke book. Carl Barks went to the want ads. This little off-the-cuff tour de force is practically a theme and motif index.

You have both aspects of Donald Duck — Donald the adventurer and Donald the Santayana fanatic, redoubling his efforts even when his initial aim is forgotten. You have the conviction that there is no such thing as a laborsaving device. You have the apolitical conservative view that considers each new thing to be both inevitable and undesirable. You have the habitual aggression of the natural world.

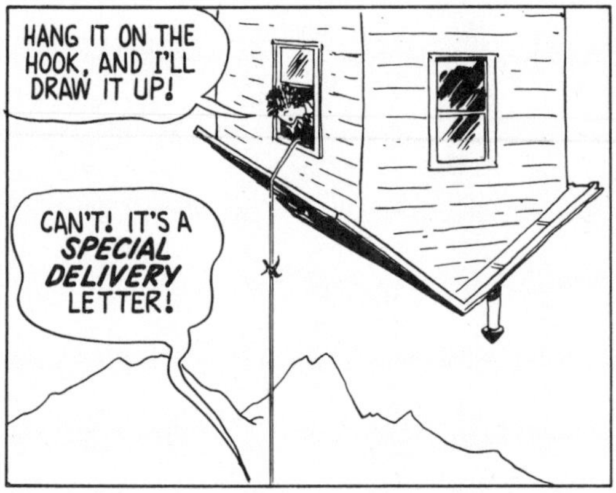
HANG IT ON THE HOOK, AND I'LL DRAW IT UP!
CAN'T! IT'S A *SPECIAL DELIVERY* LETTER!

You have the demonstration that an image need not twirl through a projector to be a moving picture.

And you have the little gift that you wouldn't even have been expecting from him — the delightful strain of "Neither snow nor rain nor heat nor gloom of night" doggerel running through the story.

That the real United States Postal Service creed does not actually rhyme is neither a concern nor an impediment.

— R. FIORE

THE HALF-BAKED BAKER p. 115

Carl Barks didn't always go back to his earlier comic book stories to recycle plots. In "The Half-Baked Baker," he reaches back to one of the Donald Duck animated shorts he had contributed to as a story man at the Disney Studio from 1936 to 1942. The short in question is *Chef Donald* (released December 5, 1941), in which the Duck is listening to a radio cooking program while mixing up a batch of waffles. Unfortunately, he gets distracted and accidentally adds rubber cement to the batter instead of baking powder.

Barks's comic book story has a more elaborate plot than the cartoon short, involving the nephews as well as a few Duckburgians. Unlike other 10-pagers, it does not follow the development of what Barks fans often refer to as the "brittle-mastery-of-Donald-Duck syndrome." Here, Donald has not acquired a mastery of some special ability that his pride and arrogance will ultimately turn into disaster.

The story opens with the nephews lamenting that their uncle is a failure, and the smoke coming out of the Fluffybun Bakery looks ominous. Nor does Donald have any previous experience as a baker. Though he is willing to learn, he is sloppy and hasty at preparing biscuits, and, just like in the animated short, he mixes in the wrong ingredients, stirring popcorn into the cookie batter instead of cracked almonds.

As often occurs in Barks's 10-pagers, Donald's awkwardness as a baker reaches its acme in the final part of the story, where as many as 40 Junior Woodchucks get stuck because of the melted cheese (instead of shortening) the Duck has used to make his giant pie. In this respect, the ending is similar to that of *Chef Donald*, where Donald himself gets stuck — before running out to take his revenge on the radio cooking program host.

— ALBERTO BECATTINI

DODGING MISS DAISY p. 125

Why doesn't Donald just tell Daisy to beat her own stupid rugs?

Common sense goes out the window on this day of lunacy that finds Donald manically evading Daisy's ploy to force him to participate in her spring cleaning. Barks, too, throws out the characterization and plotting he honed so beautifully in the 1950s 10-pagers in favor of a romp that harkens back to the artist's gag-and-violence filled days as a story man for animated cartoons.

"Dodging Miss Daisy" specifically recalls director Tex Avery's "little guy is always there" cartoons with Droopy Dog, not quite coincidentally, since Barks wrote and drew two stories with Avery's character (christened "Happy Hound") for the MGM *Our Gang Comics* in 1944. Indeed, the sallow-faced General Snozzie, the official Junior Woodchuck bloodhound that makes his debut in this story, slightly resembles Barks's rendition of Droopy. What goes around ...

Daisy's unusual presence on every page still doesn't give her more to do than in other stories where she's a framing device in a few panels. This may be the very story critics have in mind when they discuss the inherent misogyny of the Daisy Duck character throughout Disney comics history. She's not a character at all, just pure savagery, which is Barks's point — she's not here to be anything but a savage, inescapable injustice that aims to torture Donald.

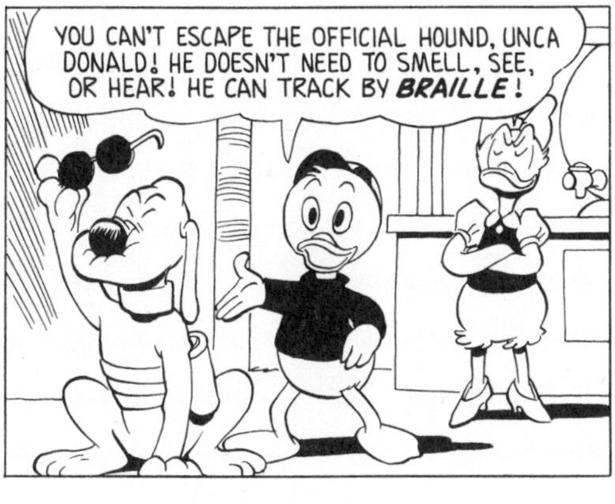
YOU CAN'T ESCAPE THE OFFICIAL HOUND, UNCA DONALD! HE DOESN'T NEED TO SMELL, SEE, OR HEAR! HE CAN TRACK BY *BRAILLE*!

Earlier Barks stories, notably "You Can't Guess" (*Walt Disney's Donald Duck: "The Pixilated Parrot,"* Volume 9) and "A Christmas for Shacktown" (*Walt Disney's Donald Duck: "A Christmas for Shacktown,"* Volume 11) gave Daisy some warmth and depth, but let's face it: nice isn't funny. The meaner and more preposterous Donald's relationship with Daisy is, the more hilarious it is, as "Dodging Miss Daisy" epitomizes.

Even if it does ignore the obvious: why doesn't he just tell her to beat her own stupid rugs?

— THAD KOMOROWSKI

DONALD THE MILKMAN p. 135

A Carl Barks story first published in Europe?

That's what happened with "Donald the Milkman," which was originally intended to appear (most likely) in *Walt Disney's Comics and Stories* #215 in 1958. But it didn't actually see print until sixteen years later, in The Netherlands, in *Donald Duck* #47, November 22, 1974. U.S. readers had to wait another sixteen years, until *Walt Disney's Comics and Stories* #550, August 1990, to finally get to read it.

Why? Our main clue is Barks's comment in his work records: "this story was shelved because Donald was too mean to the villain."

In fact, "Donald the Milkman" is one of Barks's more moralistic tales, full of his old-fashioned values. But you can read it here and judge for yourself.

Donald delivers milk for the Daisy Dairy Co., and he tries to be the "perfect milkman": he remembers all his 200 customers' desiderata (who wants how much milk, butter, cottage cheese, etc., and how often), makes friends with their pets, and even pays out of his own pocket for the milk that a poor widow needs for her "little sick daughter."

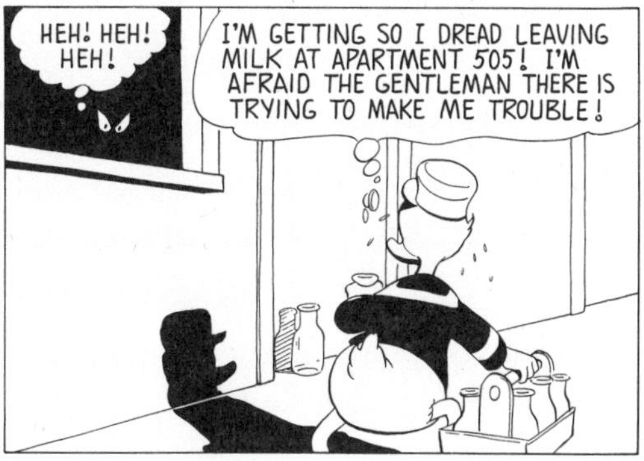
HEH! HEH! HEH!
I'M GETTING SO I DREAD LEAVING MILK AT APARTMENT 505! I'M AFRAID THE GENTLEMAN THERE IS TRYING TO MAKE ME TROUBLE!

In Barks's 10-pagers, Donald is generally the best at what he does, whatever job he chooses, but he becomes too confident, and that hubris (what the ancient Greeks called a "challenge to the gods") leads to his ultimate downfall.

But this story doesn't follow the "brittle-mastery-of-Donald-Duck syndrome." Instead, Donald has a foe — an anthropomorphic pig of the type often used by Barks for villains, whom we later learn is named McSwine. He wants to get Donald fired so he can take the job, "stretch out the milk with water, and cop ... some *easy* money."

Actually, his motivation seems futile — there are certainly more remunerative (if less honest) jobs than milkman. Probably McSwine envies Donald's dedication to a job that is often considered humble, since McSwine knows in his heart that he is good at nothing. But that doesn't stop him from setting all kinds of noisy traps for Donald to trip and wake the neighborhood.

In the end, Donald gets righteously angry and fills the nightshirt McSwine is wearing with "yogurt and ice-cold cottage cheese!," a scene that Barks's editor deemed to be too rude, thus the rejection of the story. But instead of being fired, Donald is promoted and gets an office at Daisy Dairy Co.

The moral of the story: try to do your best, no matter how humble your job might seem, and you will be rewarded.

Too old-fashioned? Probably. But not bad advice.

— STEFANO PRIARONE

BATTLE OF THE ECHOES p. 145

In a contest between Donald and his rival, Gladstone Gander, the winner is all but preordained to be Scrooge. This story is loosely based on the earlier "Managing the Echo System" (*Walt Disney's Donald Duck: "Lost in the Andes,"* Volume 7) that played on the conceit of artificially generated echoes, and which made fun of the proto-beatnik "nature boy" movements of the late 1940s.

In "Battle of the Echoes," the satire is directed at the would-be land speculators of the 1950s, as the suburban boom explodes and everyone imagines that every patch of land on the outskirts of town will soon be worth a fortune. The postwar housing boom had found gold in worthless farmland outside many major urban centers, as white flight drove returning GIs and their families out into new suburbs, which were sprouting like mushrooms.

Of course, the topography of Duckburg does not lend itself to suburban sprawl. In addition to Mocking Bird Ridge, the site of the action of this tale, other Barks tales tell us the outskirts of town are dotted with a canyon (Wildwood), a bluff (Pizen), a hollow (Red Ant), and a Glenn (Wildwood) — all making it more suited to a tourist destination than suburban development. For that reason, Donald and the boys, and even the troublesome Gladstone, all assume Scrooge's interest in the land is because he is looking to develop a hotel.

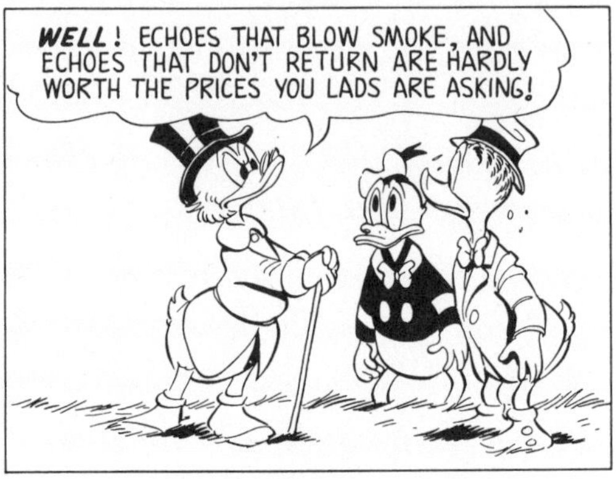
WELL! ECHOES THAT BLOW SMOKE, AND ECHOES THAT DON'T RETURN ARE HARDLY WORTH THE PRICES YOU LADS ARE ASKING!

Where the earlier story pits the nephews against Donald, this story unites the four of them against Gladstone in a contest of artificial echoes. In the end, Donald and Gladstone manage to double their meager $5 investment, but Scrooge, of course, walks away with the postwar speculator's dream of a major oilfield — all the more invaluable as Texas's golden age begins to wind down.

As happens so often, the amateurs do the professional speculator's work for him, and the unimaginably wealthy get wealthier still.

— JARED GARDNER

OLD FROGGIE CATAPULT p. 155

In the early animated cartoons, Donald Duck was almost always an irascible troublemaker. Though often a menace in Barks's comics as well, Donald can sometimes be, as the cartoonist noted, "too generous," an excess that, like his many other flaws, could generate a tale's plot and comedy.

"Old Froggie Catapult" features an unusual Donald. Exceptionally generous, he shows an unwavering concern for others. (He deviates from this affect only for a single panel, when, at the thought of future "fame and fortune," his eyeballs turn into dollar signs.) But in no sense is he too generous — his kindness never backfires and turns into comedy, though readers familiar with him might expect it to.

In Barks's stories, the nephews typically represent the most ecologically minded Ducks. But in this tale, Donald plays the role of relentlessly benevolent ecological exemplar. He displays a hypersensitivity to the story's suffering hero, viewing animals as emotional — even ethical — creatures deserving of compassion. Though Barks once dismissed the emerging environmental movement as "ecological bushwa," "Old Froggie Catapult" is a decidedly pro-animal fable. In tales such as

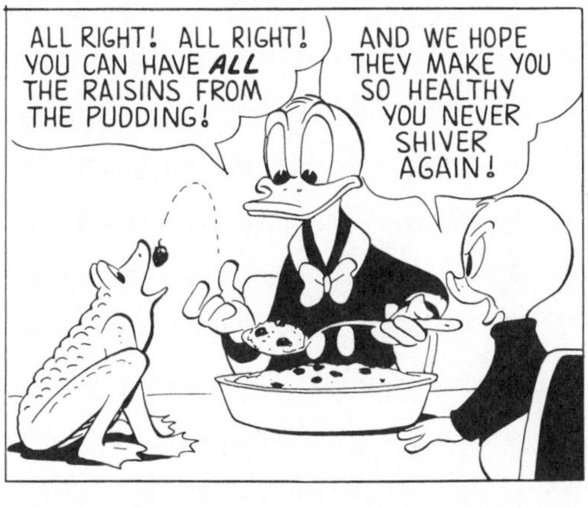
ALL RIGHT! ALL RIGHT! YOU CAN HAVE ALL THE RAISINS FROM THE PUDDING!
AND WE HOPE THEY MAKE YOU SO HEALTHY YOU NEVER SHIVER AGAIN!

"Darkest Africa" (*Walt Disney's Donald Duck: "The Old Castle's Secret,"* Volume 6), Barks employs animals solely in service of the plot's needs — and they pay a price for it.

But here, those who mistreat animals, such as the men who shoot water at frogs to motivate them — in contrast to the Ducks, who use non-violent incentives — are villains. The story celebrates human-animal similarity and reciprocity. Just as Donald saves the frog, the frog saves the Ducks and dozens of others from drowning in a hurricane, despite the fact that he dreads cold water.

Barks would likely see his comics' representations of animals as driven by a storyteller's practical needs rather than moral or ecological concerns. As the cartoonist often said, he changed a character's traits and habits when necessary to generate a plot, keep the gags moving, or catch readers off guard. As this story shows, a supremely generous Donald can be as unexpected and interesting as his familiar petulant self.

— KEN PARILLE

WATER SKI RACE p. 165

"Water Ski Race" is an amusing but minor entry in the Barks canon, designed primarily around the ridiculousness of its final image of Donald Duck in formalwear with skis on his feet.

The first three pages — fully one-half of its story — establish the obstacle that Donald and his nephews must overcome: will Donald learn to keep his skis on so he'll have a chance to win the race and earn a dance with the Queen of the Water Festival? This information is presented in two full word balloons on page 1, panel 3 (p. 165), but Barks nevertheless shows Donald wiping out no less than three times in the first three pages, repeating in visual terms the problem he strives to solve.

There are other redundancies in the story, too: on page 2, panel 3 (p. 166), a nephew says that other skiers "can't use glue" to keep their skis on, and this joke is rerun — with "starch" instead of "glue" — on page 3 (p. 167). Why the repetition? Maybe Barks liked drawing, again and again, the antic panels of Donald in the air, his body flailing and his skis flying away at all angles from his body.

And how silly is it for one Duck to plop an inner tube around the middle of another because, "You might not float next time you hit the drink!"?

The second half of "Water Ski Race" is based on an odd characterization of Daisy, who doesn't have the common-sense knowledge that Festival Queens (Water and otherwise) are apt to be pretty girls. "I'd hardly expected someone so overpowering!" she implausibly muses on page 5 (p. 169), revealing the jealousy necessary to keep Donald locked into his skis for the punch line. And so a story that begins with Donald's graceless water skiing ends with an elegant dance that, alas, excludes him.

— CRAIG FISCHER

UNMIXING A MIX-UP

As we did in the previous book in this series, we present the stories in this volume in what might seem a curiously different order than the publication sequence shown on the last page. That's because, with the exception of this volume's lead story, "The Black Pearls of Tabu Yama," we have opted to publish these stories in the order in which Barks wrote and drew them.

Barks's records show that he was submitting his stories on time, at his usual pace, and Barks scholars do not know why the release of these stories was so mixed up. We have restored the order of the stories here to better show the flow of Barks's creative output.

For those keeping track of this peculiar period of Barks releases, Barks wrote and drew "The Black Pearls of Tabu Yama" just after "The Tenderfoot Trap" and before "Wishing Stone Island." Additionally, he submitted "The Persistent Postman," "Dodging Miss Daisy," and "The Half-Baked Baker" all on the same date, listing them in his records in a way that leads some to speculate that they were drawn in that order. We present them here in the order in which they originally saw print, relative to one another.

One more note about "The Black Pearls of Tabu Yama" — the final panel of that story as originally published was not by Carl Barks, but, rather, was a non-Barks illustration of Santa Claus introducing the next story in the comic book. Since Barks had nothing to do with that segue, and since it certainly doesn't introduce the next story in *this* book, we give you the final page of "The Black Pearls of Tabu Yama" with a cheery bit of additional Barks art to punctuate the end of the story.

— J. MICHAEL CATRON

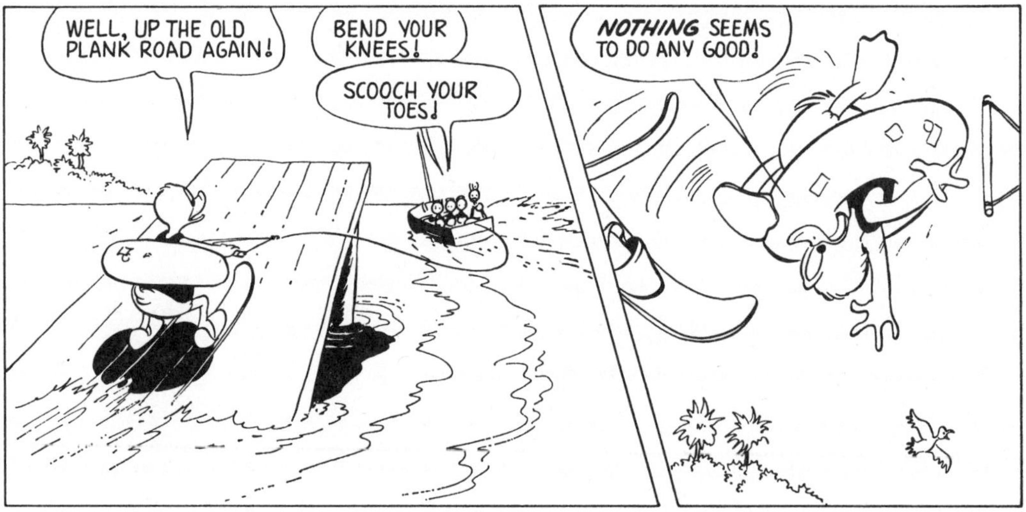
WELL, UP THE OLD PLANK ROAD AGAIN!
BEND YOUR KNEES!
SCOOCH YOUR TOES!
NOTHING SEEMS TO DO ANY GOOD!

Carl Barks
LIFE AMONG THE DUCKS

by DONALD AULT

ABOVE: *Carl Barks at the 1982 San Diego Comic-Con. Photo by Alan Light.*

"I was a real misfit," Carl Barks said, thinking back over an early life of hard labor — as a farmer, a logger, a mule-skinner, a rivet heater, and a printing press feeder — before he was hired as a full-time cartoonist for an obscure risqué magazine in 1931.

Barks was born in 1901 and (mostly) raised in Merrill, Oregon. He had always wanted to be a cartoonist, but everything that happened to him in his early years seemed to stand in his way. He suffered a significant hearing loss after a bout with the measles. His mother died. He had to leave school after the eighth grade. His father suffered a mental breakdown. His older brother was whisked off to World War I.

His first marriage, in 1921, was to a woman who was unsympathetic to his dreams and who ultimately bore two children "by accident," as Barks phrased it. The two divorced in 1930.

In 1931, he pulled up stakes from Merrill and headed to Minnesota, leaving his mother-in-law, whom he trusted more than his wife, in charge of his children.

Arriving in Minneapolis, he went to work for the *Calgary Eye-Opener*, that risqué magazine. He thought he would finally be drawing cartoons full time, but the editor and most of the staff were alcoholics, so Barks ended up running the whole show.

In 1935 he took "a great gamble" and, on the strength of some cartoons he'd submitted in response to an advertisement from the Disney Studio, he moved to California and entered an animation trial period. He was soon promoted to "story man" in Disney's Donald Duck animation unit, where he made significant contributions to 36 Donald cartoon shorts between 1936 and 1942, including helping to create Huey, Dewey, and Louie for "Donald's Nephews" in 1938. Ultimately, though, he grew dissatisfied. The production of animated cartoons "by committee," as he described it, stifled his imagination.

For that and other reasons, in 1942 he left Disney to run a chicken farm. But when he was offered a chance by Western Publishing to write and illustrate a new series of Donald Duck comic book stories, he jumped at it. The comic book format suited him, and the quality of his work persuaded the editors to grant him a freedom and autonomy he'd never known and that few others were ever granted. He would go on to write and draw more than 6,000 pages in over 500 stories and uncounted hundreds of covers between 1942 and 1966 for Western's Dell and Gold Key imprints.

Barks had almost no formal art training. He had taught himself how to draw by imitating his early favorite artists — Winsor McCay (*Little Nemo*), Frederick Opper (*Happy Hooligan*), Elzie Segar (*Popeye*), and Floyd Gottfredson (*Mickey Mouse*).

He taught himself how to write well by going back to the grammar books he had shunned in school, making up jingles and rhymes, and inventing other linguistic exercises to get a natural feel for the rhythm and dialogue of sequential narrative.

Barks married again in 1938, but that union ended disastrously in divorce in 1951. In 1954, Barks married Margaret Wynnfred Williams, known as Garé, who soon began assisting him by lettering and inking backgrounds on his comic book work. They remained happily together until her death in 1993.

He did his work in the California desert and often mailed his stories in to the office. He worked his stories over and over "backward and forward." Barks was not a vain man, but he had confidence in his talent. He knew what hard work was, and he knew that he'd put his best efforts into every story he produced.

On those occasions when he did go into Western's offices he would "just dare anybody to see if they could improve on it." His confidence was justified. His work was largely responsible for some of the best-selling comic books in the world — *Walt Disney's Comics and Stories* and *Uncle Scrooge*.

Because Western's policy was to keep their writers and artists anonymous, readers never knew the name of the "good duck artist" — but they could spot the superiority of his work. When fans determined to solve the mystery of his anonymity finally tracked him down (not unlike an adventure Huey, Dewey, and Louie might embark upon), Barks was quite happy to correspond and otherwise communicate with his legion of aficionados.

Given all the obstacles of his early years and the dark days that haunted him off and on for the rest of his life, it's remarkable that he laughed so easily and loved to make others laugh.

In the process of expanding Donald Duck's character far beyond the hot-tempered Donald of animation, Barks created a moveable locale (Duckburg) and a cast of dynamic characters: Scrooge McDuck, the Beagle Boys, Gladstone Gander, Gyro Gearloose, the Junior Woodchucks. And there were hundreds of others who made only one memorable appearance in the engaging, imaginative, and unpredictable comedy-adventures that he wrote and drew from scratch for nearly a quarter of a century.

Among many other honors, Carl Barks was one of the three initial inductees into the Will Eisner Comic Book Hall of Fame for comic book creators in 1987. (The other two were Jack Kirby and Will Eisner.) In 1991, Barks became the only Disney comic book artist to be recognized as a "Disney Legend," a special award created by Disney "to acknowledge and honor the many individuals whose imagination, talents, and dreams have created the Disney magic."

As Roy Disney said on Barks's passing in 2000 at age 99, "He challenged our imaginations and took us on some of the greatest adventures we have ever known. His prolific comic book creations entertained many generations of devoted fans and influenced countless artists over the years.... His timeless tales will stand as a legacy to his originality and brilliant artistic vision."

Contributors

Donald Ault is Professor of English at the University of Florida, founder and editor of *ImageTexT: Interdisciplinary Comics Studies*, author of two books on William Blake, editor of *Carl Barks: Conversations*, and executive producer of the video *The Duck Man: An Interview with Carl Barks*.

Alberto Becattini has taught high school English since 1983. He writes for Italian and U.S. publications about comics, specializing in Disney characters and American comics. He is a freelance writer and consultant for The Walt Disney Company-Italy, contributing to *Zio Paperone, Maestri Disney, Tesori Disney*, and others.

J. Michael Catron is the editor of *The Complete Carl Barks Disney Library*.

R. Fiore, he explains, makes his way in life working Square John jobs, not far from Historic Duckburg. This marginal existence has even led onto the grounds of the Walt Disney Company, which is an interesting place. He's been writing about comic strips and animation longer than you've been alive, my child.

Craig Fischer is Associate Professor of English at Appalachian State University. His Monsters Eat Critics column, about comics' multifarious genres, runs at *The Comics Journal* website (tcj.com).

Jared Gardner studies and teaches comics at the Ohio State University, home of the Billy Ireland Cartoon Library & Museum. He is the author of three books, including *Projections: Comics and the History of 21st-Century Storytelling* (Stanford University Press, 2011). He is a contributing writer to *The Comics Journal*.

Leonardo Gori is a comics scholar and collector, especially of syndicated newspaper strips of the 1930s. He has written, with Frank Stajano and others, many books on Italian "fumetti" and American comics in Italy.

Thad Komorowski, an animation historian and digital restoration artist, has a longstanding professional relationship with Disney comics. He is a regular contributor to Fantagraphics's Disney archival collections. He is the author of *Sick Little Monkeys: The Unauthorized Ren & Stimpy Story* and co-author of an upcoming history of New York studio animation.

Rich Kreiner is a longtime writer for *The Comics Journal* and a longtime reader of Carl Barks. He lives with wife and cat in Maine.

Ken Parille is the author of *The Daniel Clowes Reader* (Fantagraphics, 2012). His writing has appeared in *The Nathaniel Hawthorne Review, The Journal of Popular Culture, The Boston Review, The Believer*, and *The Comics Journal*. He teaches literature at East Carolina University.

Stefano Priarone was born in Northwestern Italy about the time Carl Barks was storyboarding his last Junior Woodchucks stories. He was a contributor to the Italian complete Carl Barks collection and wrote his thesis in economics about Uncle Scrooge (for which he blames his aunt, who read him Barks's Scrooge stories when he was 3 years old).

Francesco (Frank) Stajano is a Full Professor at the 800-year-old University of Cambridge, a Fellow of Trinity College, a founding director of two hi-tech start-up companies, and a licensed teacher in the Japanese "Way of the Sword." He has co-authored books on Don Rosa and Floyd Gottfredson.

Matthias Wivel is Curator of Sixteenth-Century Italian Painting at the National Gallery, London. He has written widely about comics for a decade and a half.

Daniel F. Yezbick teaches comics, film studies, and writing at Forest Park College. His essays on Barks and Disney comics have appeared in a variety of anthologies. He is the author of *Perfect Nonsense: The Chaotic Comics and Goofy Games of George Carlson* (Fantagraphics, 2014). He currently lives in South St. Louis with his wife, Rosalie, their two children, and one wise, old hound.

Where did these Duck stories first appear?

The Complete Carl Barks Disney Library collects Donald Duck and Uncle Scrooge stories by Carl Barks that were originally published in the traditional American four-color comic book format. Barks's first Duck story appeared in October 1942. The volumes in this project are numbered chronologically but are being released in a different order. This is Volume 19.

Stories within a volume may or may not follow the publication sequence of the original comic books. We may take the liberty of rearranging the sequence of the stories within a volume for editorial or presentation purposes.

The original comic books were published under the Dell logo and some appeared in the so-called *Four Color* series — a name that appeared nowhere inside the comic book itself, but is generally agreed upon by historians to refer to the series of "one-shot" comic books published by Dell that have sequential numbering. The *Four Color* issues are also sometimes referred to as "One Shots."

Most of the stories in this volume were originally published without a title. Some stories were retroactively assigned a title when they were reprinted in later years. Some stories were given titles by Barks in correspondence or interviews. (Sometimes Barks referred to the same story with different titles.) Some stories were never given an official title but have been informally assigned one by fans and indexers. For the untitled stories in this volume, we have used the title that seems most appropriate. The unofficial titles appear below with an asterisk enclosed in parentheses (*).

The following is the order in which the stories in this volume were originally published.

***Donald Duck* #54 (July-August 1957)**
Forbidden Valley

***Walt Disney's Comics and Stories* #206 (November 1957)**
Cover
Sagmore Springs Hotel (*)

***Walt Disney's Comics and Stories* #207 (December 1957)**
Cover
The Tenderfoot Trap (*)

***Christmas in Disneyland* #1 (December 1957)**
The Black Pearls of Tabu Yama (*)

***Donald Duck* #57 (January-February 1958)**
Cover only

***Walt Disney's Comics and Stories* #209 (February 1958)**
Cover
The Persistent Postman (*)

***Walt Disney's Comics and Stories* #210 (March 1958)**
The Half-Baked Baker (*)

***Walt Disney's Comics and Stories* #211 (April 1958)**
Wishing Stone Island (*)

***Walt Disney's Comics and Stories* #212 (May 1958)**
Cover
Rocket Race Around the World (*)

***Walt Disney's Comics and Stories* #213 (June 1958)**
Cover
Dodging Miss Daisy (*)

***Donald Duck* #60 (July-August 1958)**
Donald Duck and the Titanic Ants!
Water Ski Race

***Walt Disney's Comics and Stories* #215 (August 1958)**
Cover
Battle of the Echoes (*)
[a.k.a. Echoes, a.k.a. Mocking Bird Ridge]

***Walt Disney's Comics and Stories* #216 (September 1958)**
Cover
Old Froggie Catapult (*)

***Donald Duck* #47 (November 22, 1974, The Netherlands; first publication), *Walt Disney's Comics and Stories* #550 (August 1990; first U.S. publication)**
Donald The Milkman (*)
[a.k.a. The Milkman]

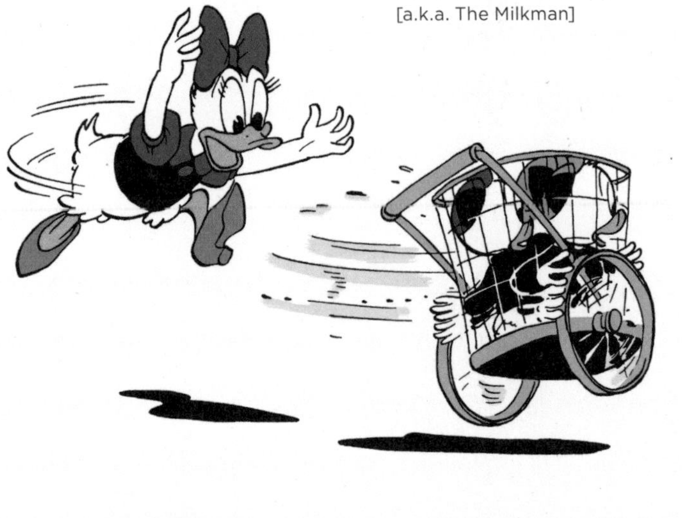